The Blue Rose Regency Romances:

The Culpepper Misses Series 1-5

COLLETTE CAMERON

Blue Rose Romance®
Portland, Oregon

Sweet-to-Spicy Timeless Romance®

Contents

The Earl and the Spinster

Even when most prudently considered, and with the noblest of intentions, one who wagers with chance oft finds oneself empty-handed.
~Wisdom and Advice—The Genteel Lady's Guide to Practical Living

1

Esherton Green,
Near Acton, Cheshire, England
Early April 1822

*W*as I born under an evil star or cursed from my first breath?

Brooke Culpepper suppressed the urge to shake her fist at the heavens and berate The Almighty aloud. The devil boasted better luck than she. *My God, now two* more *cows struggled to regain their strength?*

She slid Richard Mabry, Esherton Green's steward-turned-overseer, a worried glance from beneath her lashes as she chewed her lower lip and paced before the unsatisfactory fire in the study's hearth. The soothing aroma of wood smoke, combined with linseed oil, old leather, and the faintest trace of Papa's pipe tobacco, bathed the room. The scents reminded her of happier times but did little to calm her frayed nerves.

Sensible gray woolen skirts swishing about her ankles, she whirled to make the return trip across the once-bright green and gold Axminster carpet, now so threadbare, the oak floor peeked through in numerous places. Her scuffed half-boots fared little better, and she hid a wince when the scrap of leather she'd used to cover the hole in her left sole this morning slipped loose again.

From his comfortable spot in a worn and faded wingback chair, Freddy, her aged Welsh corgi, observed her progress with soulful brown eyes, his muzzle propped on stubby paws. Two ancient tabbies lay curled so tightly together on the cracked leather sofa that determining where one ended and the other began was difficult.

What was she to do? Brooke clamped her lip harder and winced.

Should she venture to the barn to see the cows herself?

What good would that do? She knew little of doctoring cattle and so left the animals' care in Mr. Mabry's capable hands. Her strength lay in the financial administration of the dairy farm and her ability to stretch a shilling as thin as gossamer.

She cast a glance at the bay window and, despite the fire, rubbed her arms against the chill creeping along her spine. A frenzied wind whipped the lilac branches and scraped the rain-splattered panes. The tempest threatening since dawn had finally unleashed its full fury, and the fierce winds battering the house gave the day a peculiar, eerie feeling—as if portending something ominous.

At least Mabry and the other hands had managed to get the cattle tucked away before the gale hit. The herd of fifty—no, sixty, counting the newborn calves—chewed their cud and weathered the storm inside the old, but sturdy, barns.

As she peered through the blurry pane, a shingle ripped loose from the farthest outbuilding—a retired stone dovecote. After the wind tossed the slat around for a few moments, the wood twirled to the ground, where it flipped end over end before wedging beneath a gangly shrub. Two more shingles hurled to the earth, this time from one of the barns.

Flimflam and goose-butt feathers.

Brooke tamped down a heavy sigh. Each structure on the estate, including the house, needed some sort of repair or replacement: roofs, shutters, stalls, floors, stairs, doors, siding...dozens of items required fixing, and she could seldom muster the funds to go about it properly.

"Another pair of cows struggling, you say, Mr. Mabry?"

Concern etched on his weathered features, Mabry wiped rain droplets from his face as water pooled at his muddy feet.

"Yes, Miss Brooke. The four calves born this mornin' fare well, but two of the cows, one a first-calf heifer, aren't standin' yet. And there's one weak from birthin' her calf yesterday." His troubled gaze strayed to the window. "Two more ladies are in labor. I best return to the barn. They seemed fine when I left, but I'd as soon be nearby."

Brooke nodded once. "Yes, we mustn't take any chances."

The herd had already been reduced to a minimum by disease and sales to make ends meet. She needed every shilling the cows' milk brought. Losing another, let alone two or three good breeders...

No, I won't think of it.

She stopped pacing and forced a cheerful smile. Nonetheless, from the skeptical look Mabry speedily masked, his thoughts ran parallel to hers—one reason she put her trust in the man. Honest and intelligent, he'd worked alongside her to restore the beleaguered herd and farm after Papa died. Their existence, their livelihood, everyone at Esherton's future depended on the estate flourishing once more.

"It's only been a few hours." *Almost nine, truth to tell.* Brooke scratched her temple. "Perhaps the ladies need a little more time to recover." *If they recovered.* "The calves are strong, aren't they?" *Please, God, they must be.* She held her breath, anticipating Mabry's response.

His countenance lightened and the merry sparkle returned to his eyes. "Aye, the mites are fine. Feedin' like they're hollow to their wee hooves."

Tension lessened its ruthless grip, and hope peeked from beneath her vast mound of worries.

Six calves had been guaranteed in trade to her neighbor and fellow dairy farmer, Silas Huffington, for the grain and medicines he'd provided to see Esherton Green's herd through last winter. Brooke didn't have the means to pay him if the calves didn't survive—though the old reprobate had hinted he'd make her a deal of a much less respectable nature if she ran short of cattle with which to barter. Each pence she'd stashed away—groat by miserable groat, these past four years—lay in the hidden drawer of Papa's desk and must go to purchase a bull.

Wisdom had decreed replacing Old Buford two years ago but, short on funds, she'd waited until it was too late. His heart had stopped while he performed the duties expected of a breeding bull. Not the worst way to cock up one's toes...er, hooves, but she'd counted on him siring at least two-score calves this season and wagered everything on the calving this year and next. The poor brute had expired before he'd completed the job.

Her thoughts careened around inside her skull. Without a bull, she would lose everything.

My home, care of my sister and cousins, my reasons for existing.

She squared her shoulders, resolution strengthening her. She still retained the Culpepper sapphire parure set. If all else failed, she would pawn the jewelry. She'd planned on using the money from the gems' sale to bestow small marriage settlements on the girls. Still, pawning the set was a price worth paying to keep her family at Esherton Green, even if it meant that any chance of her sister and three cousins securing a decent match would evaporate faster than a dab of milk on a hot cookstove. Good standing and breeding meant little if one's fortune proved meaner than a churchyard beggar's.

"How's the big bull calf that came breech on Sunday?" Brooke tossed the question over her shoulder as she poked the fire and encouraged the blaze to burn hotter. After setting the tool aside, she faced the overseer.

"Greediest of the lot." Mabry laughed and slapped his thigh. "Quite the appetite he has, and friendly as our Freddy there. Likes his ears scratched too."

Brooke chuckled and ran her hand across Freddy's spine. The dog wiggled in excitement and stuck his rear legs straight out behind him, gazing at her in adoration. In his youth, he'd been an excellent cattle herder. Now he'd gone fat and arthritic, his sweet face gray to his eyebrows. On occasion, he still dashed after the cattle, the instinctive drive to herd deep in the marrow of his bones.

Another shudder shook her. Why was she so blasted cold today? She relented and placed a good-sized log atop the others. The feeble flames hissed and spat before greedily engulfing the new addition. Lord, she prayed she wasn't ailing. She simply couldn't afford to become ill.

A scratching at the door barely preceded the entrance of Duffen bearing a tea service. "Gotten to where a man cannot find a quiet corner to shut his eyes for a blink or two anymore."

Shuffling into the room, he yawned and revealed how few teeth remained in his mouth. One sock sagged around his ankle, his grizzled hair poked every which way, and his shirttail hung askew. Typical Duffen.

"Devil's day, it is." He scowled in the window's direction, his mouth pressed into a grim line. "Mark my words, trouble's afoot."

Not quite a butler, but certainly more than a simple retainer, the man, now hunched from age, had been a fixture at Esherton Green Brooke's entire life. He loved the place as much as, if not more than, she, and she couldn't afford to hire a servant to replace him. A light purse had forced Brooke to let the household staff go when Papa died. The cook, Mrs. Jennings, Duffen, and Flora, a maid-of-all-work, had stayed on. However, they received no salaries—only room and board.

The income from the dairy scarcely permitted Brooke to retain a few milkmaids and stable hands, yet not once had she heard a whispered complaint from anyone.

Everybody, including Brooke, her sister, Brette, and their cousins—Blythe, and the twins, Blaike and Blaire—did their part to keep the farm operating at a profit. A meager profit, particularly as, for the past five years, Esherton Green's legal heir, Sheridan Gainsborough, had received half the proceeds. In return, he permitted Brooke and the girls to reside there. He'd also been appointed their guardian. But, from his silence and failure to visit the farm, he seemed perfectly content to let her carry on as provider and caretaker.

"Ridiculous law. Only the next male in line can inherit," she muttered.

Especially when he proved a disinterested bore. Papa had thought so too, but the choice hadn't been his to make. If only she could keep the funds she sent to Sheridan each quarter, Brooke could make something of Esherton and secure her sister and cousins' futures too.

If wishes were gold pieces, I'd be rich indeed.

Brooke sneezed then sneezed again. Dash it all. A cold?

The fresh log snapped loudly, and Brooke started. The blaze's heat had failed to warm her opinion of her second cousin. She hadn't met him and lacked a personal notion of his character, but Papa had hinted that Sheridan was a scallywag and possessed unsavory habits.

A greedy sot, too.

The one time her quarterly remittance had been late, because Brooke had taken a tumble and broken her arm, he'd written a disagreeable letter demanding his money.

His money, indeed.

Sheridan had threatened to sell Esherton Green's acreage and turn her and the foursome onto the street if she ever delayed payment again.

A ruckus beyond the entrance announced the girls' arrival. Laughing and chatting, the blond quartet billowed into the room. Their gowns, several seasons out of fashion, in no way detracted from their charm, and pride swelled in Brooke's heart. Lovely, both in countenance and disposition, and the dears worked hard too.

"Duffen says we're to have tea in here today." Attired in a Pomona green gown too short for her tall frame, Blaike plopped on to the sofa. Her twin, Blaire, wearing a similar dress in dark rose and equally inadequate in length, flopped beside her.

Each girl scooped a drowsy cat into her lap. The cats' wiry

whiskers twitched, and they blinked their sleepy amber eyes a few times before closing them once more as the low rumble of contented purrs filled the room.

"Yes, I didn't think we needed to light a fire in the drawing room when this one will suffice." As things stood, too little coal and seasoned firewood remained to see them comfortably until summer.

Brette sailed across the study, her slate-blue gingham dress the only one of the quartet's fashionably long enough. Repeated laundering had turned the garment a peculiar greenish color, much like tarnished copper. She looped her arm through Brooke's.

"Look, dearest." Brette pointed to the tray. "I splurged and made a half-batch of shortbread biscuits. It's been so long since we've indulged, and today is your birthday. To celebrate, I insisted on fresh tea leaves as well."

Brooke would have preferred to ignore the day.

Three and twenty.

On the shelf. Past her prime. Long in the tooth. Spinster. *Old maid.*

She'd relinquished her one chance at love. In order to nurse her ailing father and assume the care of her young sister and three orphaned cousins, she'd refused Humphrey Benbridge's proposal. She couldn't have put her happiness before their welfare and deserted them when they needed her most. Who would've cared for them if she hadn't?

No one.

Mr. Benbridge controlled the purse strings, and Humphrey had neither offered nor been in a position to take on their care. Devastated, or so he'd claimed, he'd departed to the continent five years ago.

She'd not seen him since.

Nonetheless, his sister, Josephina, remained a friend and occasionally remarked on Humphrey's travels abroad. Burying the pieces of her broken heart beneath hard work and devotion to her family, Brooke had rolled up her sleeves and plunged into her forced role as breadwinner, determined that sacrificing her love not be in vain.

Yes, it grieved her that she wouldn't experience a man's passion or bear children, but to wallow in doldrums was a waste of energy and emotion. Instead, she focused on building a future for her sister and cousins—so they might have what she never would—and allowed her dreams to fade into obscurity.

"Happy birthday." Brette squeezed her hand.

Brooke offered her sister a rueful half-smile. "Ah, I'd hoped you'd forgotten."

"Don't be silly, Brooke. We couldn't forget your special day." Twenty-year-old Blythe—standing with her hands behind her—grinned and pulled a small, neatly-wrapped gift tied with a cheerful yellow ribbon from behind her. Sweet dear. She'd used the trimming from her gown to adorn the package.

"Hmph. Need seedcake an' champagne to celebrate a birthday properly." The contents of the tray rattled and clanked when Duffen scuffed his way to the table between the sofa and chairs. After depositing the tea service, he lifted a letter from the surface. Tea dripped from one stained corner. "This arrived for you yesterday, Miss Brooke. I forgot where I'd put it until just now."

If I can read it with the ink running to London and back.

He shook the letter, oblivious to the tawny droplets spraying every which way.

Mabry raised a bushy gray eyebrow, and the twins hid giggles by concealing their faces in the cat's striped coats.

Brette set about pouring the tea, although her lips twitched suspiciously.

Freddy sat on his haunches and barked, his button eyes fixed on the paper, evidently mistaking it for a tasty morsel he would've liked to sample. He licked his chops, a testament to his waning eyesight.

"Thank you, Duffen." Brooke took the letter by one soggy corner. Holding it gingerly, she flipped it over. No return address.

"Aren't you going to read it?" Blythe set the gift on the table before settling on the sofa and smoothing her skirt. They didn't get a whole lot of post at Esherton. Truth be known, this was the first letter in months. Blythe's gaze roved to the other girls and the equally eager expressions on their faces. "We're on pins and needles," she quipped, fluttering her hands and winking.

Brooke smiled and cracked the brownish wax seal with her fingernail. Their lives had become rather monotonous, so much so that a simple, *soggy*, correspondence sent the girls into a dither of anticipation.

My Dearest Cousin...

Brooke glanced up. "It's from Sheridan.

As is oft the case when wagering, one party is a fool and
the other a thief, although both may bear the title nincompoop.
~Wisdom and Advice—The Genteel Lady's Guide to Practical Living

2

What maggot in Heath's brain had possessed him to set out on the final leg of his journey to Esherton Green on horseback when foul weather threatened? The same corkbrained notion that had compelled him, the Earl of Ravensdale, one of the most eligible lords on the Marriage Mart, to miss the peak of London's Season in exchange for a saddle-sore arse.

He pulled his hat more firmly onto his head. The bloody wind tried its best to blast every last drop of rain either into his face or down the back of his neck, and he hunched deeper into his saddle. Fat lot of good that did.

The sooner I've finished this ugly business with the tenant, the sooner I can return to London and civilization.

The road from the village—if one deigned to grace the rutted and miry track with such distinction—lay along an open stretch of land, not a single sheltering tree in sight. He hadn't spotted another living thing this past hour. Any creature claiming half a wit laid snuggled in its nest, den, or house, waiting out the foulness. He'd seen two manors in the distance, but to detour to either meant extending his time in this Godforsaken spot.

People actually *chose* to live here?

Hound's teeth, he loathed the lack of niceties, abhorred the quiet which stretched for miles. The boredom and isolation. Give him London's or Paris's crowded and noisy paved streets any day; even if all manner of putridity lined them most of the time.

Despite his greatcoat, the torrential, wind-driven rain soaked him to the skin. Heath patted his pocket where the vowel proving his claim to the farm lay nestled in a leather casing and, with luck, still dry. He'd barely spared the marker a glance at White's and hadn't taken a peek since.

Reading wasn't his strong suit.

His sodden cravat chaffed unmercifully, and water seeped—drip by infernal drip—from his saturated buckskins into his Hessians. He eyed one boot and wiggled his toes. Bloody likely ruined, and he'd just had them made too. Stupid to have worn them and not an older pair. Wanton waste and carelessness—the calling cards of sluggards and degenerates.

Ebénè snorted and bowed his head against the hostile weather. The stallion, unused to such harsh treatment, had been pushed to the end of his endurance, despite his mild temperament. The horse increasingly expressed his displeasure with snorts, groans, and an occasional jerking of his head against the reins.

"I'm sorry, old chap. I thought we'd beat the storm." Heath leaned forward and patted the horse's neck. Black as hell at midnight when dry, now drenched, Ebénè's silky coat glistened like wet ink.

The horse quivered beneath Heath and trudged onward through the sheets of rain.

Indeed, they might have outpaced the tempest if Heath hadn't lingered at breakfast and enjoyed a third cup of Turkish coffee at Tristan, the Marquis of Leventhorpe's, home.

Leventhorpe actually enjoyed spending time at his country house, Bristledale Court. Heath couldn't understand that, but as good friends do, he overlooked the oddity.

Reluctance to part company with Leventhorpe hadn't been Heath's only excuse for dawdling. Leventhorpe had proved a superb host, and Bristledale boasted the latest comforts. The manor house's refinement tempted far more than venturing to a rustic dairy farm with the unpleasant tidings Heath bore.

He'd won the unwanted lands in a wager against Sheridan Gainsborough. The milksop had continued to raise the stakes when he didn't have the blunt to honor his bet. And it wasn't the first time the scapegrace had been light in the pocket at the tables. To teach the reckless sot a lesson, Heath had refused Gainsborough's I.O.U. and demanded he make good on his bet.

When the sluggard offered a piece of property as payment instead, Heath had had little choice but to accept, though it chaffed his sore arse. A tenant farmer and his family would be deprived of their livelihood as a consequence. No one—including this dairyman, months behind in his rents—should be put out of his means of income because a foxed dandy had acted rashly.

Now he owned another confounded piece of English countryside he didn't need nor want. He didn't even visit his country estate, Walcotshire Park. With a half dozen irritable servants for company, he'd spent his childhood there until fifteen years ago when, at thirteen, he'd been sent to boarding school. Instead, Walcotshire's steward tootled to Town quarterly, more often if the need arose, to meet with Heath.

A ripple of unease clawed his nerves. He shifted in the saddle. Discomfort inevitably accompanied thoughts of *The Prison*, as he'd come to regard the austere house, a scant thirty miles from the path Ebénè now plodded.

For a fleeting moment—no more than a blink, truthfully—he contemplated permitting the farmer to continue running the dairy. However, that obligated Heath to trot down to the place on occasion, and nothing short of a God-ordained mandate would compel him to venture to this remote section of green perdition on a regular basis. Not even the prospect of Leventhorpe's company. The marquis would be off to London for the remainder of the Season soon enough, in any event.

Heath had experienced enough of country life as a boy. The family mausoleum perched atop a knoll overlooking the cemetery held more warmth and fonder memories than *The Prison* did. The same could be said of his parents buried there. A colder, more uncaring pair of humans he had yet to meet. He wouldn't have been surprised to learn ice-water, rather than blood, flowed through their veins.

Besides, he didn't know a finger's worth about cattle or dairy farming other than both smelled horrid. He swiped rain from his forehead and wrinkled his nose. How could his favorite cheese be a result of such stench? The reek had carried to him on the wind for miles. How did the locals tolerate it? An irony-born grin curved his lips. Much the same way he tolerated London's, he'd wager. People disregarded flaws when they cared deeply about something or when convenient to do so.

Gainsborough hadn't blinked or appeared to have a second thought when he put up his land as collateral for his bet. He'd laughed and shrugged his thin shoulders before signing the estate over, vowing the neighbors adjacent to Esherton Green would jump at the opportunity to purchase the farm. Then, snatching a bottle of whisky in one hand and snaring a harlot years past her prime around the waist with the other, he had staggered from the gaming hell.

Heath hoped to God the man had spoken the truth, otherwise, what would he do with the property? A gusty sigh escaped him as he slogged along to make the arrangements to sell his winnings. He should've been at White's, a glass of brandy in one hand and cards in the other. Or at the theater watching that new actress, a luscious little temptation he had half a mind to enter into an arrangement with—after his physician examined her for disease, of course.

Heath sought a new mistress after Daphne had taken it into her beautiful, but wool-gathering, head that she wanted marriage. To him. When he refused, she'd eloped with another admirer. That left a bitter taste on his tongue; she'd been cuckolding him while beneath his protection.

Thank God he always wore protection before intimate encounters and insisted she underwent weekly examinations. Laughable, Daphne daring to broach matrimony when she'd already proven herself incapable of fidelity. Not that married women were better. His mother hadn't troubled herself to provide Father a spare heir before lifting her skirts for the first of her myriad of lovers.

Both his parents had died of the French disease, six months apart.

Heath snorted, and the horse jerked his head. Now there was a legacy to be proud of.

If and when he finally decided to become leg-shackled—at forty or fifty—he'd choose a mousy virgin who wouldn't draw the interest of another man. A chit painfully shy or somehow marred, she'd never dare seek a lover. Or perhaps a woman past her prime, on the shelf, whose gratitude for saving her from a life of spinsterhood would assure faithfulness.

Not too long on the shelf, however. He needed to get an heir or two on her.

Didn't matter a whit that half of *le beau monde* shared their beds with multiple partners. His marriage bed would remain pure—well, his wife would, in any event.

A gust of wind slammed into Heath, sending his hat spiraling into the air. The gale lifted it, spinning the cap higher.

"Bloody hell."

Ebéné raised his head and rolled his big eyes at the cavorting cap then grunted, as if to say, *I've had quite enough of this nonsense. Do find me a warm comfortable stable and a bucket of oats at once.*

Two more miserable miles passed, made worse by the absence of Heath's head covering. Water trickled down his face and nape, and, with each step, his temper increased in direct proportion to his dwindling patience. The return trip to Bristledale Court would be more wretched, given his sopped state, and dusk would be upon him before he reached the house.

He should have accepted Leventhorpe's suggestion of a carriage, but that would have meant Heath's comfort at the expense of two drivers and four horses. He shivered and drew his collar higher. He anticipated a hot bath, a hearty meal, and a stiff drink or two upon his return to Bristledale. Leventhorpe boasted the best cognac in England.

Heath glanced skyward. The roiling, blackish clouds gave no indication they had any intention of calming their fury soon. He wiped off a large droplet balancing on the end of his nose. Strange, he hadn't paid much mind to storms while in Town. Then again, he wasn't prone to gadding about in the midst of frightful gales when in the city either.

Perhaps he could bribe a cup of tea and a few moments before the fire from the tenant.

What was his name?

Something or other Culpoppers or Clodhopper or some such unusual surname. The bloke wouldn't likely offer him refreshment or a coze before the hearth once he learned the reason for Heath's visit. Guilt raised its thorny head, but Heath stifled the pricks of unease. A business matter, nothing more. He'd won the land fairly. The tenant was in arrears in rents. Heath didn't want another parcel of countryside to tend to. He knew naught of dairy farming.

The place must be sold.

Simple as that.

Keep spouting that drivel, and you might actually come to believe it.

Although gambling is an inherent tendency in
human nature, a wise woman refrains from partaking,
no matter how seemingly insignificant the wager.
~Wisdom and Advice—The Genteel Lady's Guide to Practical Living

3

Brooke scrunched her forehead and tried to decipher the words. Not only did Sheridan possess atrocious penmanship, the tea had ruined much of the writing.

...writing to inform you I have...

A large smudge obliterated the next few words. She smoothed the wrinkled paper and squinted.

Esherton Green...new owner.

Brooke couldn't suppress her gasp of dismay as she involuntarily clenched one hand around the letter and pressed the other to her chest.

New owner? Esherton Green was entailed. Sheridan couldn't sell it. *Yes. He could.*

Only the house and the surrounding five acres were entailed. Even the outbuildings, though they sat on those lands, hadn't been part of the original entailment. The rest of the estate had been accumulated over the previous four generations and the barns constructed as the need arose. She'd memorized the details, since she and Papa had done their utmost to finagle a way for her to inherit.

He'd conceived the plan to send Sheridan half the proceeds from the dairy and farm, so she and the others could continue to live in the only home any of them remembered and still make a modest income. They'd gambled that Sheridan would be content to pad his pockets with no effort on his part, and wouldn't be interested in moving to their remote estate and assuming the role of gentleman farmer.

And our risk paid off. Until now.

She needed the acreage to farm and graze the cattle. Their milk was sold to make Cheshire's renowned cheese. Without the land, the means to support the girls and staff was lost.

"What does he have to say?" Blaire exchanged a worried glance with her twin.

Blythe pushed a curl behind her ear and slanted her head, her intelligent lavender gaze shifting between the paper and Brooke. "Is something amiss, Brooke?"

"Shh." Brooke waved her hand to silence their questions. The tea had damaged the writing in several places. She deciphered a few disjointed sentences.

Pay rent...reside elsewhere...at your earliest convenience...new owner takes possession...regret the necessity...unfortunate circumstances...commendable job managing my holdings...might be of service

Brooke's head swam dizzily.

"Pay rent? Reside elsewhere?" she murmured beneath her breath.

She raised her gaze, staring at the now-frolicking fire, and swallowed a wave of nausea. Sheridan had magnanimously offered to let them stay on if they paid him rent, the bloody bounder. How could she find funds for rent when he'd sold their source of income? They already supplemented their income every way possible.

Brette took in sewing and embroidery and often stayed up until the wee morning hours stitching with a single candle as light. The twins managed a large vegetable, herb, and flower garden, selling the blooms and any excess produce at the village market each week during the growing season. Blythe put her musical talents to use and gave Vicar Avery's spoiled daughters weekly voice and harpsichord lessons.

The women picked mushrooms and tended the chickens and geese—feeding them, gathering their eggs, and plucking and saving the feathers from the unfortunate birds that stopped laying and found their way into the soup pot.

The faithful staff—more family than servants—contributed beyond Brooke's expectations too. Mabry and the other two stable hands provided fish, game fowl, and the occasional deer to feed them. Duffen spent hours picking berries and fruit from the neglected orchard so Mrs. Jennings could make her famous tarts, pies, and preserves, which also sold at the market. And dear, dim-witted Flora washed the Huffington's and Benbridge's laundry.

Sheridan remained obligated to care for them, save Brooke, who'd come of age since he gained guardianship of the girls. It would serve him right if she showed up on his doorstep, sister, cousins, pets, and servants—even the herd of cows—in tow, and demanded he do right by them.

Brooke didn't know his age or if he was married. Did he have children? Come to think of it, she didn't have an address for him either. She'd directed her correspondences to his man of business in London. Where did Sheridan live? London?

Was he one of those fellows who preferred the hubbub and glamour of city life, rather than the peace and simplicity of country living? Most likely. She'd never lived anywhere but Esherton. However, the tales Papa told of the crowding, stench, and noise of Town made the notion of living there abhorrent.

Heart whooshing in her ears, she dropped her attention to the letter once more.

Expect your response by...as to your intentions.

Her gaze flew to the letter's date. Tea had smudged all but the year. Moisture blurred her vision, and she blinked furiously. The unfairness galled. She'd worked so blasted hard, as had everybody else, and that pompous twit—

"Brooke?" The hint of alarm edging Brette's voice nearly undid her.

Fresh tears welled in Brooke's eyes, and she pivoted toward the windows to hide her distress. After dragging in a steadying breath, she forced her leaden feet to carry her to the unoccupied chair and gratefully sank onto the cushion. However, flattened by years of constant use, it provided little in the way of padding.

She took another ragged breath, holding the air until her lungs burned and willed her pulse to slow to a somewhat normal rhythm. Though her emotions teetered on the cusp of hysteria, she must present a calm facade. The quartet weren't given to histrionics, but something of this magnitude was guaranteed to cause a few waterworks, her own included. Pressing shaking fingers to her forehead, Brooke closed her eyes for a brief moment.

God help me. Us.

"I fear I have disquieting news." She met each of their wary gazes in turn, her heart so full of dismay and disbelief, she could scarcely speak.

God rot you, Sheridan.

"Sheridan..." Her mouth dry from trepidation—*how can I tell them?*—she cleared her throat then licked her lips. "He has sold the lands not attached to the house."

The study echoed with the girls' gasps and a low oath from Mabry.

Outrage contorted his usually jovial face into a fierce scowl. "The devil you say!"

Freddy wedged his sturdy little body between Blaike and Blaire, his soulful eyes wide with worry.

"Told you the day be cursed." Duffen shook his head. Highly superstitious, he fingered the smooth stone tied to his neck by a thin leather strip. A lucky talisman, he claimed. "Started with me putting on my left shoe first and then spilling salt in me porridge this morning."

"Sheridan cannot do that." Blaike looked at Brooke hopefully. "Can he, Brooke?"

"Yes, dear, he can." Brooke scowled at the illegible scribbles. She took her anger out on the letter, crumpling it into a tight wad before tossing it into the fire. "He's offered to let us stay on if we pay him rent."

The last word caught on a sob. She'd failed the girls. And the servants.

She couldn't even sell the furnishings, horseflesh, or carriages. Everything of value had long since been bartered or sold. The parure set would only bring enough to sustain them for a few months—six at the most.

What then? They had no remaining family. No place to go.

She clenched the cushion and curled her toes in her boots against the urge to scream her frustration. She must find a position immediately. A governess. Or perhaps a teacher. Or maybe she and the girls could open a dressmaker's shop. They would need to move. There were no positions for young ladies available nearby and even less need for seamstresses.

London.

A shudder of dread rippled through her. Nothing for it. They would have to move to Town. They'd never traveled anywhere beyond the village.

Did she have the legal right to sell the cattle and keep the proceeds? She twisted a curl beside her ear. She must investigate that posthaste. But who dare she ask? One of her neighbors might have purchased the lands from beneath her, and she couldn't afford to consult a solicitor. Perhaps she should seek Mr. Benbridge's counsel. She couldn't count the times he'd offered his assistance.

Silas Huffington's sagging face sprang to mind. Oh, he'd help her, she had no doubt. *If* she became his mistress. Hell would burn a jot hotter the day that bugger died.

"Did he say who bought the lands, Miss Brooke?" Duffen peered at her, his wizened face crumpled with grief. Moisture glinted in his faded eyes, and she swore his lower lip trembled. "That churl, Huffington?"

Brooke shook her head. "No, Duffen, I'm afraid Sheridan didn't say."

What would become of Duffen? Mrs. Jennings? Poor simple-minded Flora? Queer in the attic some would call the maid, but they loved her and ignored her difficulties.

How could Sheridan sell the lands from beneath them?

The miserable, selfish wretch.

Never had Brooke felt such rage. If only she were a man, this whole bumblebroth would have been avoided.

"Man ought to be horsewhipped, locked up, an' the key thrown away," Duffen muttered while wringing his gnarled hands. "Knew in my aching joints today heralded a disaster besides this hellish weather."

"Perhaps the new owner will allow us to carry on as we have." Everyone's gaze lurched to Blaire. She shrugged and petted Pudding's back. The cat arched in pleasure, purring louder. "We could at least ask, couldn't we?"

A flicker of hope took root.

Could they?

Brooke tapped her fingers on the chair's arm. The howling wind, the fire's crackle, and the cats' throaty purrs, filled the room. Nonetheless, a tense stillness permeated the air.

Why not at least try?

"Why, yes, darling." Brooke smiled and nodded. "What a brilliant miss you are. That might be just the thing."

Blaire beamed, and smiles wreathed the other girls' faces.

Duffen continued to scowl and mumble threats and nonsense about the evil eye beneath his breath.

A speculative gleam in his eyes, Mabry scratched his nearly bald pate. "Aye, if he's a city cove with no interest in country life, we might convince the bloke."

"Yes, we might, at that." Brooke stood and, after shaking her skirts, paced behind the sofa, her head bowed as she worried the flesh of her lower lip.

Could they convince the new owner to let them stay if she shared her plans for the farm? Would he object to a woman managing the place? Many men took exception to a female in that sort of a position— the fairer sex weren't supposed to concern themselves with men's work.

Hands on her hips, she faced Mabry. "Ask around, will you? But be discreet. See if our neighbors or anyone at the village has knowledge of the sale. If the buyer isn't local, we stand a much better chance of continuing as we have."

What if the buyer was indeed one of the people she owed money to?

Not likely.

She would have heard a whisper.

Wouldn't I?

Something of that nature wouldn't stay secret in their shire for long. In Acton, rumors made the rounds faster than the blustering wind, especially if the vicar's wife heard the *on dit*. The woman's tongue flapped fast enough to send a schooner round the world in a week.

Brooke turned to Duffen. Often loose of lips himself, he *had* to keep her confidence. "We want this kept quiet as possible. I cannot afford to have our debts called in by those afraid they'll not get their monies."

Duffen angled his head, a strange glint in his rheumy brown eyes. He toyed with his amulet again. "Won't say a word, Miss Brooke. Count on me to protect you an' the other misses."

She smiled, moisture stinging her eyes. "I know I can, Duffen."

Wringing his hands together, he nodded and mumbled as he stared into the fire. "Promised the master, I did. Gots to keep my word. Protect the young misses."

"Brooke?" Blythe's worried voice drew everybody's attention. "What if the owner wants to reside at Esherton? What will we do then?"

Only ninnyhammers mistake preparation meeting opportunity as luck.
~*Wisdom and Advice—The Genteel Lady's Guide to Practical Living*

ifting his head, Heath squinted into the tumult swirling around him.
At the end of a long, tree-lined drive, a stately two-story home rose
out of the grayish gloom. A welcoming glint in a lower window
promised much-needed warmth.

Deuced rotten day.

The indistinct shapes of several outbuildings, including two
immense barns and an unusual round structure, lay to one side of the
smallish manor. A cow's bawl floated to him, accompanied by a
pungent waft of damp manure.

Ebénè must have seen the house and stables too, for the tired horse
quickened his pace to a trot, ignoring Heath's hands on the reins.

"Fine, get on with you then."

He gave the horse his head. Splattering muck in his haste, the beast
shot down the rough and holey roadway as if a hoard of demons
scratched at his hooves.

The thunderous crack of an oak toppling mere seconds after Heath
passed beneath its gnarled branches launched his heart into his throat
and earned a terrified squeal from Ebénè. The limbs colliding with the
earth launched a shower of mud over them. A thick blob smacked Heath
at the base of his skull then slid, like a giant, slimy slug, into his collar.
The cold clump wedged between his shoulder blades.

Of all the—

Another horrendous, grinding snap rent the air, and he whipped
around to peer behind him. The remainder of the tree plummeted,
ripping the roots from their protective cover and jarring the ground
violently. More miniature dirt cannonballs pelted him and Ebénè.

Could the day possibly get worse?

The horse bucked and kicked his hind legs.

Yes. It could.

Heath lurched forward, just about plummeting headfirst into the muck. Clutching his horse's mane and neck, he held on, dangling from the side of the saddle.

The mud oozed down his spine.

I'm never setting foot outdoors in the rain again.

With considerable effort, he righted himself then turned to look at the mammoth tree blocking the drive. Had the thing landed on him, he'd have been killed.

Another ripple of unease tingled down his spine, and he glanced around warily. Didn't feel right. He couldn't put his finger on what, but disquiet lingered, and he'd always been one to heed his hunches.

He returned his attention to the shattered tree and the ground torn up by the exposed roots. Disease-ravaged. He glanced at the others. Several of them, too. Dangerous that. They ought to come down. He'd best warn the new owners of the hazard.

You are the new owner.

Heath swiped a hand across his face, dislodging several muddy bits. Nothing like arriving saturated and layered in filth to evict a tenant.

He scrutinized the dismembered tree. A man on horseback could traverse the mess, but passage by carriage was impossible. To expedite the sale, it might be worth paying the tenant to remove the downed tree. That meant delaying tours to prospective buyers for at least a day or two. Unless a neighbor familiar with the place was prepared make the purchase at once—a most convenient solution.

Turning his horse to the unremarkable house, he clicked his tongue and kicked his heels.

A few moments later, Heath halted Ebénè before the weathered stone structure. A shutter, the emerald paint chipped and peeling, hung askew on one of the upper windows, and the hedge bordering the circular courtyard hadn't seen a pair of pruning shears in a good while. Jagged cracks marred the front steps and stoop, and a scraggly tendril of silvery smoke spiraled skyward from a chimney missing several bricks. An untidy orchard on the opposite side of the house from the barns also showed signs of neglect.

The manor and grounds had seen better days, a testament either to the tenant's squandering or to having fallen on hard times. No wonder Gainsborough hadn't been reluctant to part with the place. Why, Heath had done the chap a favor by winning. Gainsborough had probably laughed himself sick with relief at having rid himself of the encumbrance.

Ebénè shuddered and shifted beneath Heath.

Poor beast.

Heath scanned the rustic manor then the barns. Should he dismount here or take the miserable horse to the stables? A single ground floor window in the house glowed with light, rather strange given the lateness of the afternoon and the gloom cloaking the day.

The entrance eased open, no more than three inches, and a puckered face surrounded by wild grayish-white hair peeked through the crack. "State your business."

This shabby fellow, the tenant farmer? That explained a lot.

Heath slid from the saddle, his sore bum protesting. The mud in his shirt shifted lower. Shit.

"I'm the Earl of Ravensdale, here to see the master."

A cackle of laughter erupted from the troll-like fellow. The door inched open further, and the man's entire head poked out. He grinned, revealing a missing front tooth.

"Mighty hard to do, stranger, since he's been dead these five years past."

The man snickered again, but then his gaze shifted to Ebénè and widened in admiration. The peculiar chap recognized superior horseflesh.

Ebénè nudged Heath, none too gently.

The remainder of Heath's patience dissolved faster than salt in soup. He jiggled the horse's reins. "My mount needs attention, and I must speak to whoever is in charge. Is that you?"

"Is someone at the door, Duffen? In this weather?"

The door swung open to reveal a striking blonde, wearing a dress as ugly and drab as the dismal day.

Heath's jaw sagged, and he stared mesmerized.

Despite the atrocious grayish gown, the woman's figure stole the air from him. Full breasts strained against the too-small dress, tapering to a waist his hands could span. And from her height, he'd lay odds she possessed long, graceful legs. Legs that could wrap around his waist and...

Though cold to his marrow, his manhood surged with sensual awareness. He shifted his stance, grateful his long overcoat covered him to his ankles. He snapped his mouth shut. Evict this shapely beauty? Surely a monumental mistake had been made. Gainsborough couldn't be so cold-hearted, could he?

Heath snapped his mouth closed and glared at the grinning buffoon peeking around the doorframe. Making a pretense of shaking the mud from his coat, Heath slid a sideways glance to the woman. Probably thought him a half-witted dolt.

She regarded Heath like a curious kitten, interest piqued yet unsure of what to make of him. Her dark blue, almost violet, eyes glowed with humor, and a smile hovered on her plump lips. The wind teased the flaxen curls framing her oval face.

A dog poked its snout from beneath her skirt and issued a muffled warning.

"Hush, Freddy. Go inside. Shoo."

The dog skulked into the house. Just barely. He plopped onto the entrance, his worried brown-eyed gaze fixed on Heath. She neatly stepped over the portly corgi, and the bodice of her gown pulled taught, exposing hardened nipples.

Another surge of desire jolted Heath.

Disturbing. Uncharacteristic, this immediate lust.

Rainwater dribbled from the hair plastered to his forehead and into his eyes. He swiped the strands away to see her better.

"Miss—"

A disturbance sounded behind her. She glanced over her shoulder as four more young women crowded into the entry.

Blister and damn. A bloody throng of goddesses.

Surely God's favor had touched them, for London couldn't claim a single damsel this exquisite, let alone five diamonds of the first water.

Gainsborough had some lengthy explaining to do.

The one attired in gray narrowed her eyes gone midnight blue, all hint of warmth whisked away on the wind buffeting them. She notched her pert chin upward and pointed at him.

"You're him, aren't you? The man who bought Esherton's lands? Are you truly so eager to take possession and ruin us, you ventured out in this weather and risked catching lung fever?"

Bought Esherton's lands? What the hell?

A wise woman refrains from laying odds,
well aware that luck never gives, it only lends,
and will inevitably demand payment, no matter the cost.
~Wisdom and Advice—The Genteel Lady's Guide to Practical Living

5

*H*e's come already.

Brooke's hope, along with her heart, sank to her half-boots at the peeved expression on the man's chiseled face. Much too attractive, even drenched, mud-splattered, and annoyed.

The girls' sharp intakes of breath hadn't gone unnoticed. She hid her own surprise behind a forced half-smile. Her breasts tingled, the nipples pebble hard.

It's the icy wind, nothing more.

She imagined his heavy gaze lingering on her bodice.

Why couldn't he have been ancient and ugly and yellow-toothed and...and balding?

Shock at his arrival had her in a dither. She'd counted on a scrap of luck to allow her time to prepare a convincing argument. To have him here a mere hour after reading Sheridan's letter had her at sixes and sevens. The letter must have been delayed en route, or her cowardly cousin had dawdled in advising her of the change in her circumstances.

She'd lay odds, ten to one, on the latter.

The gentleman still stood in the rain. That would make a positive impression and gain his favor when she broached the possibility of her continuing to operate the dairy and farm.

Come, Brooke. Gather your wits and manners, control yourself, and attempt to undo the damage already done.

"Looks like a half-drowned mongrel, he does." Duffen sniggered, his behavior much ruder than typical.

Brooke quelled his snicker with a sharp look. "See to the horse, please, and tell Mr. Mabry we have a guest. Ask him to join us as soon as he is able."

"Yes, Miss Brooke. I'll get my coat." Duffen bobbed his head and went in search of the garment.

She wanted the overseer present when she explained her proposition to his lordship. After all, although she'd read dozens of books and articles on the subject, Mabry's knowledge of the dairy's day-to-day operation far surpassed hers.

Brooke folded her hands before her. "He'll return momentarily, Mister...?"

The gentleman, with hair as black as the glorious horse standing beside him, crooked a boyish smile and bowed. Yes, too confounded handsome for her comfort. The wind flipped his coat over his bent behind. "Heath, Earl of Ravensdale at your service, Mistress...?"

"Earl?" *He's a confounded earl?*

An earl wouldn't want to run a dairy farm, would he?

She scrutinized him toe to top. Not one dressed like him. His soaked state couldn't disguise the fineness of the garments he wore or the quality of the beautiful stepper he rode. The wind tousled his hair, a trifle longer than fashionable. It gave him a dashing, rakish appearance. She shouldn't have noticed that, nor experienced the odd sparks of pleasure gazing at him caused.

A lock slipped onto his forehead again. The messy style rather suited him. Where was his hat anyway?

She winced as a boney elbow jabbed her side.

"Tell him your name, Brooke."

Ah, Blythe. Always level-headed. And subtle.

"Forgive me, my lord. I am Brooke Culpepper." Brooke gestured to the foursome peering at the earl. "And these are my sister, Miss Brette Culpepper, and our cousins, the Misses Culpeppers, Blythe, Blaire, and Blaike."

His lips bent into an amused smile upon hearing their names, not an uncommon occurrence.

Named Bess, Mama and Aunt Bea had done their daughters an injustice by carrying on the silly B name tradition for Culpepper females. Supposedly, the practice had started so long ago no one could remember the first.

Brooke dipped into a deep curtsy, and the girls followed her lead, each making a pretty show of deference. She wanted to applaud. Not one teetered or stumbled. They'd never had cause to curtsy before, and the dears performed magnificently.

Freddy lowered his shoulders and touched his head to his paws, a trick Brooke had taught him as a puppy.

Lord Ravensdale threw his head back and laughed, a wonderful rumble that echoed deep in his much-too-broad chest. At least, it looked wide beneath his coat. Maybe he wore padding. Silas Huffington did, which, rather than making him look muscular, gave him the appearance of a great, stuffed doll.

A very ugly doll.

"What a splendid trick, Mistress...?" His lordship inquired after her name again.

"It's miss, your lordship." Brette nudged Brooke in the ribs this time. "We're *all* misses, but Brooke's the eldest of the five and—"

Brooke silenced her with a slight shake of her head.

A puzzled expression flitted across the earl's face. He took her measure, examining her just as she'd inspected him, and a predatory glint replaced his bewilderment.

Her gaze held captive by his—titillating and terrifying—the hairs from her forearms to her nape sprang up. Awareness of a man unlike anything she'd ever experienced before, even with Humphrey, gripped her.

A man of the world, and no doubt used to snapping his fingers and getting whatever he desired, including wenches in his bed, Lord Ravensdale now scrutinized her with something other than inquisitiveness. The look couldn't be described as entirely polite either.

He wasn't to be trifled with.

She'd bet the biscuits Brette made today, Brooke had piqued his interest. Why, and whether she should be flattered or alarmed, she hadn't determined. What rot. Of course she was flattered. What woman wouldn't be?

He approached the steps, his attention locked on her. "There's no *Mister* Culpepper?"

Brooke tilted her head, trying to read him. Why didn't she believe the casualness of his tone?

"No, not since Father died five years ago." She pushed a tendril of hair off her cheek, resisting the urge to wrap her arms around her shoulders and step backward. The wind proved wicked for April. Why else did she remain peppered in gooseflesh? "Didn't Cousin Sheridan inform you?"

"Cousin? Gainsborough is your cousin?" Disbelief shattered his lordship's calm mien. His nostrils flared, and his lovely lips pressed into a thin line. His intense gaze flicked to each of the women, one by one. "He is cousin to *all* of you?"

"Yes," Brooke and the others said as one.

The revelation didn't please the earl. He closed his eyes for a long moment, his impossibly thick lashes dark smudges against his swarthy skin. Did he ail? He seemed truly confounded or put upon.

Wearing a floppy hat which almost obliterated his face, Duffen edged by her. He yanked his collar to his ears. "I'll see to your horse, *sir*."

"Duffen, that will do," Brooke warned gently. She wouldn't tolerate impudence, even from a retainer as beloved as him. "Lord Ravensdale is our guest."

Astonishment flitted across Duffen's cragged features before they settled into lines of suspicion once more. Duffen hadn't expected a noble either.

"Beg your pardon, Miss Brooke."

He ducked his head contritely and, after gathering the horse's reins, led the spirited beast toward the stables. Eager to escape the elements, the stallion practically dragged Duffen.

"My lord, please forgive my poor manners. Do come in out of the wretched rain." Brooke stepped over Freddy and turned to Brette. "Will you fetch hot tea and biscuits for his lordship?"

Brooke sent him a sidelong glance. "And a towel so he might dry off?"

"Of course. At once." Brette bobbed a hasty curtsy before hurrying down the shadowy corridor.

Hopefully, she would brew just enough tea for the earl. They were nearly out of tea and sugar, and there would be no replacing the supplies.

Brooke motioned to Blaike. "Please stir the fire in the study and add another log? I don't wish his lordship to become chilled."

Her attention riveted on their visitor, Blaike colored and stuttered, "Ah…yes. Certainly." After another quick peek at him, she pivoted and disappeared into the study a few doorways down.

He'd been here mere minutes and the girls blushed and blathered like nincompoops. Brooke pursed her lips. It wouldn't do, especially not when he might very well be here to put them out of their home. She drew in a tense breath.

Lord Ravensdale stepped across the threshold and hesitated. He wiped his feet on the braided rag rug while his gaze roved the barren entrance. A rivulet of rainwater trailed down his temple. Soaked through. He'd be lucky if he didn't catch his death.

Surely claiming the lands hadn't been so pressing he'd felt the need to endanger his health by venturing into the worst storm in a decade? A greedy sort and anxious to see what he'd purchased, perhaps. Well, he'd have to wait. She wouldn't ask Mr. Mabry or the other hands to show the earl around, not only because the weather was fouler than Mr. Huffington's breath, but Brooke needed the men attending the cows and newborn calves.

Lord Ravensdale exuded power and confidence, and the foyer shrank with his presence. Except for Brette, the Culpepper women were tall, but he towered above Brooke by several inches. He smiled at Brooke, and her stomach gave a queer little somersault at the transformation in his rugged features. Devilishly attractive. A dangerous distraction. He was the enemy. He'd bought Esherton, practically stolen her home, with no regard to how that would affect her family.

Don't be fooled by his wild good looks.

He shoved wet strands off his high forehead again.

Freddy crept closer, his button nose twitching.

Brooke brushed away a few of Freddy's hairs clinging to her skirt, unexpectedly ashamed of her outdated and worn gown. She hid her calloused hands in the folds of her gown. She would wager the Culpepper sapphires that women threw themselves at Lord Ravensdale.

Fashionable ladies dressed in silks and satins, with intricately coiffed hair, and smooth, creamy skin, who smelled perfectly wonderful all the time. Lord Ravensdale's women probably washed with perfumed soap. Expensive, scented bars from France. Pink or yellow, or maybe blue and shaped like flowers.

Brooke couldn't remember the last time she'd worn perfume or used anything other than the harsh gel-like soap that she and Mrs. Jennings made from beef tallow. Their precious candle supply came from the smelly lard too.

Why the notion rankled, Brooke refused to examine. Except, here she stood attired like a country bumpkin covered in dog and cat hair, with her curls tied in a haphazard knot and ink stains on her fingers. She couldn't even provide his lordship a decent repast or light a candle to guide him to the study, let alone produce a dram of whisky or brandy to warm his insides.

Nonetheless, they...*she* must win his favor.

She straightened her spine, determined to act the part of a gracious hostess if it killed her. "Sir, you should take off your coat. It's soaked through."

While his lordship busied himself removing his gloves, she studied him. He had sharp, exotic, almost foreign features. She shouldn't be surprised to learn a Moroccan or an Egyptian ancestor perched in his family tree somewhere. High cheekbones gave way to a molded jaw and a mouth much too perfect to belong to a man. A small scar marred the left side of his square chin. How had he come by it?

She could almost envision him, legs braced and grinning, on the rolling deck of a pirate ship, the furious waves pounding against the vessel as the wind whipped his hair.

Stop it.

Hand on his sword, he would throw his head back and laugh, the corded muscles in his neck bulging; a man in command against nature's wrath.

"The ride here turned most unpleasant."

Lord Ravensdale's melodic baritone sent her cavorting pirate plunging off the side of the fantasy ship and into the churning waves. Brooke clamped her teeth together. What ailed her? She'd never been prone to fanciful imaginations.

After tucking his wet gloves into his pocket, his lordship unbuttoned his tobacco-brown overcoat.

Almost the same color as his eyes.

"A tree fell as I passed by. I'm afraid it left rather a jumble on the drive." He flashed his white teeth again as he advanced farther into the entry.

Retreating, she allowed him room to shrug off the soggy garment. A pleasant, spicy scent wafted past her nose. Naturally, he smelled divine. She peered past him and to the lane. A tree and a tangle of branches lay sprawled on the road to the house. She stifled a groan. How were they to remove that disaster with one horse and a pair of axes?

Releasing a measured breath, she closed the heavy door.

Lord, I don't know how much more I can bear.

"If you'll permit it, my lord, I shall have my cousin take your coat to the kitchen to place beside the stove." She extended her hand. Not that it would dry completely in the few minutes he would be here, but perhaps he would appreciate the gesture.

He passed her the triple-caped greatcoat then removed a wilted handkerchief from his jacket pocket. A slight shudder shook him as he wiped his face. "I'm afraid the elements did rather get the best of me."

As if he'd cued it, a blast of wind crashed into the house, rattling the door and windows. The corridor grew dim as the storm renewed her fury. The pewter sky visible through the windows paralleling the door suggested dusk had already fallen. Brooke furrowed her brow. His lordship didn't dare delay at Esherton. His return journey to—wherever he'd come from—became more perilous by the moment.

And he couldn't stay here.

They hadn't an empty bedchamber to accommodate him other than Papa and Mama's, and a stranger amongst five eligible women might give rise to gossip. Besides, expecting her to house him when he'd arrived to put them from their home was beyond the pale, accommodating hostess or not.

Playacting wasn't her strong suit. Pretending to welcome the earl when she wanted to treat him like a plague-ridden thief strained her good manners and noble intentions. Had she been alive, Mama would've chastised Brooke for her unchristian behavior and thoughts.

"Blaire, please take his lordship's coat to the kitchen and fetch one of Papa's jackets for him."

Papa's coats had been too old to sell, and Brooke refused to make them into rags. It seemed disrespectful, almost disloyal, to treat his possessions with such little regard. She'd allowed Duffen and Mabry their pick. Therefore, the remaining coats were quite shabby. Still, a dry, moth-eaten jacket must be preferable to saturated finery.

"You and the others join us in the study as soon as the tea is ready."

Brooke wanted the quartet present for the discussion. After all, the sale of the lands affected their lives too. Besides, the earl made her edgy. Perhaps because much was at stake, and there'd been no time to prepare an argument to let them continue as they had been.

Her cousin seized the soaked wool, and after a swift backward glance, marched to the rear of the house.

Lord Ravensdale inspected the stark entry once more. Rectangular shadows lined the faded walls where paintings had once hung. He ran his gaze over her, lingering at the noticeable discolored arc at her neckline where a lace collar used to adorn the gown. She hid her reddened hands behind her lest he notice the missing lace cuffs as well. They'd been sold last year for a pittance.

She hadn't been self-conscious of her attire or the blatant sparseness of her home before, but somehow, he made their lack of prosperity glaring. Rather like a purebred Arabian thrust into the midst of donkeys. Pretty donkeys, yes, but compared to a beautiful stepper, wholly lacking.

Freddy crept forward and dared to sniff around his lordship's feet. Then, to Brooke's horror, the dog proceeded to heist his leg on one glossy boot. Yellow pooled around the toe as she and Blythe gaped.

"Freddy, bad boy. Shame on you." Blythe scolded, bending to scoop the cowering dog into her arms. Her cheeks glowed cherry red. "I'll put him in the kitchen, Brooke."

Whispering chastisements, she scurried away, the dog happily wagging his tail as if forgiven.

Mortification burning her face, Brooke raised her gaze to meet Lord Ravensdale's humor-filled eyes.

"Perhaps I might trouble you for *two* towels?" He raised his dripping foot and grinned.

Brooke tried to stifle the giggle that rushed to her throat.

She really did.

A loud peal surged forth anyway. Partially brought on by relief that he wasn't angry, partially because in other circumstances, she might have indulged in a flirtation with him, and partially to release nervous tension.

If she didn't laugh, she would burst into tears.

He smiled while pulling at his cuffs. A bit of dirt fell to the scarred floor. "So what's this nonsense about Gainsborough selling me Esherton? Your cousin lost the place to me in a card game and said you were months behind in rents."

In the event one is unwise enough to venture down
wagering's treacherous pathway, decide beforehand the rules by
which you'll play, the exact stakes, and at which point you intend to quit.
~Wisdom and Advice—The Genteel Lady's Guide to Practical Living

6

Heath clamped his jaw against a curse at the devastation that ravaged Miss Culpepper's. One moment she'd been glowing, mirth shimmering in her gaze and pinkening her face, and the next, her lovely indigo eyes pooled with tears. They seeped over the edges and trailed down her silky cheeks, though she didn't make a sound.

How often had she wept silently so others wouldn't hear? He'd done the same most of his childhood. He brushed his thumb over one damp cheek. What was it about this woman that plucked at his heart after a mere ten minutes acquaintance? He didn't know her at all, yet he felt as if something had connected between them from the onset.

Did she sense it too, or was it only him? Perhaps he'd caught a fever and delusions had set in.

She blinked at him, her eyes round and wounded. And accusing. "We're not behind in the rents. He's been paid on time each month. Except the month I broke my arm."

Shit, another lie. What have I gotten myself into?

Deep pain glimmered in the depths of her eyes, which were too old and wise for someone her age. This woman had clearly borne much in her short life.

And she hadn't known her home had been lost in a wager gone awry.

She'd thought Heath had bought the estate. Though what difference that would have made in her circumstances, he couldn't fathom. Gambled away or purchased, the consequence remained the same for the women. They'd be ousted from their home. At least he held a degree of concern for their wellbeing, unlike their callous cousin.

Surely they must have someone who could be of assistance to them.

What sort of a vile blackguard gave no thought to his kinsmen, especially five females without means? As apparent as the mud on his boots and sticking uncomfortably to his spine, they were poor as church mice. In all likelihood, the holy rodents fared better since they would eagerly accept crumbs. Gut instinct told him the Culpeppers might have little else, but they had their pride and wouldn't accept charity.

Miss Culpepper drew in a shuddering breath and averted her head. She wiped her eyes as her sister entered the corridor bearing a meager tea tray upon which rested a mismatched tea service, a napkin, a single teacup and three small biscuits.

A wave of compassion, liberally weighted with remorse, engulfed him. He'd never experienced poverty such as this, and yet, they offered him what little they had.

Damnation.

He didn't want a blasted dairy farm, even if angels did make it their home.

Composing herself, Miss Culpepper shifted toward a door farther along the hallway and offered her sister a wobbly smile.

Miss Brette—wasn't that her name?—peered between him and her sister, her nose crinkled in puzzlement. Her gaze lingered on her sister's damp cheeks.

Astute woman.

One of the twins trailed Miss Brette.

Heath had no idea what her name was, but she bore a large black jacket and a towel. He strained to distinguish the women's features in the shadowy corridor. Another violent surge of air battered the house, and the women's startled gazes flew to the entrance.

He feared the windows might shatter from the gale's force. A breeze wafted past, sending a chill creeping along his shoulders. The house radiated cold. This drafty old tomb must be impossible to keep heated, but not one of the Culpepper misses wore warm clothing.

"My lord, this way if you please." Miss Culpepper motioned to the doorway the girl dressed in green had disappeared into earlier. "We'll give you a moment of privacy to dry yourself and exchange your coat for Papa's. It's rather worn, I'm afraid, but it should be a mite more comfortable than wearing yours."

The trio filed through the entrance, slender as reeds, each of them.

32

A natural physical tendency or brought on by insufficient food? Mayhap both.

Heath followed, guilt's sharp little teeth nipping at his heels. He glimpsed the tray as Miss Brette arranged it on a table before the fireplace. How they could be charitable, he didn't know, and, had their situations been reversed, honesty compelled him to admit, he mightn't have been as hospitable. Not much better than their snake of a cousin, was he? The notion left a sickening knot in his middle and a rancorous taste on his tongue.

Actually, the foul taste might have been a spot of mud he'd licked from his lip. Pray God the dried crumb was mud and not some other manner of filth.

"Let's give his lordship a moment, shall we?" With a wan smile, Miss Culpepper ushered her wards from the study.

Frenetic whispers sounded the moment they left his sight.

Heath made quick work of exchanging the jackets. The one he donned smelled slightly musty and a hint of tobacco lingered within the coarsely woven threads. Too big around, the garment skimmed his waist. The Culpeppers didn't get their height or svelteness from Mr. Culpepper's branch of the family. Heath tugged at a too-short sleeve, and his third finger sank into a moth hole.

What had brought this family to such destitution?

He'd lacked human companionship and love his entire childhood—and by choice, a great deal of his adulthood also—but never wanted for physical comfort or necessities. Their circumstances appeared the reverse of his. Company and affection they possessed aplenty, but scant little else. Nonetheless, they didn't act deprived or envious, at least not from what he'd observed in his short acquaintance with them.

The truth of that might prove different upon further association. In his experience, the facade women presented at first glance proved difficult to maintain, and before long, they revealed their true character. Rarely had the latter been an improvement upon his initial impression.

Standing before the roaring fire, he relished the heat as he toweled his hair and dried his neck and face again. Heath glanced around the room, taking in the extraordinarily ugly chairs and cracked leather sofa. He'd seen nothing of value or quality in the house. Everything of worth had likely been sold ages ago.

He scraped the cloth inside each ear and came away with a pebble-sized clump of muck from his left ear. Too bad he daren't untuck his shirt and rid himself of the irritating blob resting at the small of his spine like a cold horse turd. He eyed his boots. No, he wouldn't ruin the tattered scrap he held by wiping the filthy footwear. If it weren't wholly unacceptable, he'd have left the Hessians at the door, but padding around in one's stockinged feet wasn't done.

He rolled his eyes toward the ceiling. Much better to soil the floors and carpet instead.

No sooner had he set the cloth aside than a sharp rap sounded beside the open door. Miss Culpepper peeked inside. Her gorgeous violet gazed skimmed him appreciatively. "Better?"

"Much, thank you." Spreading his fingers, he warmed his palms before the blaze. How had he managed to get dirt beneath three nails? He glanced sideways at her. "I don't recall a storm quite this furious."

"Yes, it's the worst I can recollect as well." She glided into the room, perfectly poised. She might have been starched and prim on the exterior, that heinous dress doing nothing for her figure or coloring, but a woman's curiosity and awareness had shone in her eyes when she took his measure a moment ago.

The corgi peeked around the doorframe then made a dash for the sofa. His fat rear wriggling, he clambered onto the couch. Freddy stood gazing up at Heath, panting and wagging his tail, not a jot of remorse on his scruffy face.

So much for banishment to the kitchen.

The four other young women filed in behind Miss Culpepper, their demeanors a combination of anxiety and curiosity.

God above, Heath would relish the expressions on the faces of the *ton's* denizens if these five—properly attired, jeweled and coiffed, of course—ever graced the upper salons and assembly rooms. He had half a mind to take the task on himself, if only to witness *le beau monde's* reaction.

He smiled, intrigued by the notion. Might be damned fun.

There'd be hissing and sneering behind damsels' fans as the milksops, dandies, and peers tripped over one another to be first in line to greet the beauties. One incomparable proved difficult enough competition, but an entire brood of them? What splendid mayhem that would cause. One he could heartily enjoy for weeks...months perhaps.

Heath rubbed his nose to hide a grin.

Yes, the Culpepper misses would provide the best bloody entertainment in a decade.

Course, without dowries or lineage, the girls' respectable prospects ran drier than a fountain in the Sahara.

He firmed his jaw. Not his concern. Making arrangements to sell the farm and return to London posthaste was. And not with five beauties in tow, even if he could persuade them to toddle along.

His gaze riveted on the blondes, Heath perched on the edge of one of the chairs. It tottered, and he gripped the arm as he settled his weight on the uneven legs. What did one call this chair's color anyway? Vomit? He'd seen pond scum the exact shade outside Bristledale Court's boundary. Why in God's name would anyone choose this fabric for furniture?

After sinking gracefully onto the sofa, and nudging aside a sleeping cat in order to make room for two of the young women to sit beside her, Miss Culpepper poured his tea. "Milk or sugar?"

The girl in yellow sat in the other chair while the twin attired in green plopped onto a low stool and, chin resting on her hand, stared at him.

Never had Heath experienced such self-consciousness before. Five pairs of eyes observed his every move. What was their story? His task would've been much easier if they were lazy, contentious spendthrifts sporting warty noses and whiskery chins.

"My lord?" Tongs in hand, Miss Culpepper peered at him, one fair brow arched, almost as if she'd read his thoughts. "Milk or sugar?"

He flashed her his most charming smile—the one that never failed to earn a blush or seductive tilt of lips, depending on the lady's level of sexual experience.

Her eyebrow practically kissing her hair, Miss Culpepper regarded him blandly. The twins salvaged his bruised pride by turning pink and gawking as expected. The older two exchanged guarded glances, and he swore Miss Brette hid a smirk behind her hand.

Heat slithered up his face.

Poorly done, old man.

These weren't primping misses accustomed to dallying or playing the coquette. He doubted they knew how to flirt. Direct and unpretentious, all but the youngest pair had detected his ploy to charm them. Rather mortifying to be set down without a word of reproach by three inexperienced misses.

Miss Culpepper waved the tongs and flashed her sister a sideways glance, clearly indicating she thought him a cod-pated buffoon.

"Just sugar please. Two lumps." He ran his fingers inside his neckcloth. The cloying material itched miserably.

Heath relaxed against the chair, squashing a cat that had crawled in behind him. With a furious hiss, the portly beast wriggled free and tumbled to the floor. Whiskers twitching and citrine eyes glaring, the miffed feline arched her spine, and then, with a dismissive flick of her tail, marched regally to lie before the hearth.

"I'm afraid you've annoyed Pudding." Chuckling, a delicious musical tinkle, Miss Culpepper lifted the lid from the sugar bowl and dropped two lumps into his tea. Four remained on the bottom of the china. "She holds a grudge, so watch your calves. She'll take a swipe at you when you aren't looking."

She passed him the steaming cup then scooted the small chipped plate of biscuits in his direction. Her roughened hands that suggested she performed manual labor. The other cat, its plump cheeks the size of dinner rolls, raised its head and blinked at him sleepily. The animals, at least, didn't go hungry around here. Miss Culpepper's keen gaze remained on him as she settled further into the couch,

The other girls' attention shifted between him and her, as if they anticipated something. They obviously regarded her as their leader. A log shifted, and sparks sprayed the sooty screen.

Heath took a swallow of the tea, savoring its penetrating warmth and pleasant flavor. A most respectable cup of tea, though a dram of brandy tipped into the brew wouldn't have gone amiss.

A branch scraped the window. What he wouldn't give to stay put in this snug study, sipping tea and munching the best, buttery biscuits he'd ever tasted. But Leventhorpe expected him for dinner and had requested his cook prepare chicken fricassee, a particular favorite of Heath's. Still, the return ride, battling the hostile elements after darkness had blanketed the land, didn't appeal in the least.

"My lord, you—"

"Miss Culpepper, could—."

She smiled, and Heath chuckled when they spoke at the same time.

Biscuit in hand, he gestured for her to continue. "Please, go on."

"You said Cousin Sheridan lost Esherton Green's lands to you in a wager?" Smoothing her rough skirt, she crossed and uncrossed her ankles.

Was that a hole in the bottom of her boot? A quick, covert assessment revealed the other women's footwear fared little better.

Heath paused with the teacup to his lips. "Yes."

"Might I ask when?" Her gaze rested on his lips before sliding to the cup. A dash of color appeared on her high cheekbones, made more apparent by the hollows beneath them.

She'd experienced hunger and often.... Still did, given the thinness of her and the others. Compassion swept him. If he were their blasted cousin, they'd never want again. Except, a cousin didn't inspire in him the kind of interest Brooke did.

"You see, I only received his correspondence today and the letter had suffered substantial damage." She shrugged one slender shoulder while running her fingers through the sleeping corgi's stiff fur. "Truthfully, I couldn't decipher half of it, but I had the distinct impression he'd sold the lands, and we'd be permitted to remain in the house if we paid rent. I can prove payment in full through this month."

That's only a few more days.

Her words rang of hope and desperation.

And how would they pay future rent? Open a house of ill-repute?

He skimmed his gaze over the assembled beauties. They'd make a fortune, but a more repugnant notion he'd never entertained. Besides, the house had been wagered as well.

Hadn't it?

Hell, he hadn't read the vowel, but rather made a show of perusing the note. He preferred not to read anything in public, especially not surrounded by *le beau ton.* A hint that he struggled to read the simplest phrase and the elite would titter for months.

But the fact remained that he journeyed here to sell whatever he'd won. Except now, he didn't know precisely what had been wagered. He would have to return on the morrow, after he'd spent the evening studying the slip of paper in—

Blast. The marker lay tucked in his greatcoat.

In the kitchen.

The two women who'd hustled away with his dust coat wouldn't dare go through his pockets. Would they?

Miss Culpepper mistook his silence for encouragement. "You see, Mr. Mabry and I—and the girls as well as the other staff—have run the dairy ourselves for the past five years. Cousin Sheridan received half the proceeds each quarter for allowing us to remain here and operate the farm. We hoped the new owner would permit us the same arrangement."

She raised expectant blue eyes to his. Her hands fisted in her skirt and her toes tapping the floor belied her calm facade.

He swept the other girls another swift glance.

Their thin faces were pale, and worry and fear filled the eyes peering back at him.

A wave of black rage rose from Heath's boots to his chest. When he got his hands on Gainsborough, he'd thrash him soundly. Pretending absorption in chewing the rest of his biscuit, Heath forced his pulse and breathing to slow.

He relaxed into the chair and placed an ankle on one bent knee, smearing his trousers with mud. Hopelessly stained, they'd be sent to the church for the beggars. Drumming his fingers on the chair's threadbare arms, he scrutinized the women again.

Features taut, gazes wary, they held their breath in anticipation of his response.

A litany of vulgar oaths thrummed against his lips. Blast their cousin to hell and back for putting him in this despicable position.

Heath did not want a dairy farm. He did not want to care for or worry about these women more than their own flesh and blood did. He most certainly did not want to *ever* have to venture to this stinking, remote parcel of green hell again. And he didn't have it in him to put these women out of their homes.

"We would work hard, your lordship." The girl in rose—Blaire or Blaike? Maybe he ought to number the lot of them—gifted him a tremulous smile.

Heath rubbed his forehead where the beginnings of a headache pulsed. "I'm sure you would."

God rot you, Gainsborough.

Her twin nodded, a white curl slipping to flop at her nape. "Yes, besides the milk, we also sell vegetables, flowers, and herbs..."

Anything else?

"And eggs, mushrooms, pastries, and jams," Brette finished in a breathless rush.

What no sewing, weaving, or tatting?

She threw her sister a desperate glance. "And I sew and take in embroidery."

Ah, there it is.

"And Blythe..." She pointed to the girl wearing yellow.

Yes, what does Blythe do?

Heath's gaze lingered on the eldest Miss Culpepper.

Or Brooke? Surely she has a skill to sell too.

He uncrossed his leg then leaned forward, not liking the direction the conversation had taken, the distress in the girls' voices, or his cynical musings. "You're to be commended and sound most industrious—"

Blythe squared her shoulders, a challenge in her eyes. "I give music lessons, and Flora takes in laundry."

Who the blazes is Flora?

He straightened and cast an uneasy glance at the doorway.

Good God, please tell me not another sister or cousin?

"Brooke maintains the books and manages the production and sale of the milk and cattle." The first twin spoke again.

Devil it, impossible to tell the two apart except for their clothing. Identical, right down to the mole beside their left eyes.

The other twin piped up. "We all—"

Miss Culpepper raised a hand, silencing her. A long scratch ran from her small finger to her wrist. Her ivory face seemed carved of granite, the angles and lines rigid. She slowly stood, her bearing no less regal than a queen's, and the stony look she leveled him would've done Medusa proud.

God, she was impressive.

He pressed his knee with his chilled fingertips. Yes, warm flesh, not solid rock. *Yet.*

"Enough, girls." Resignation weighted her words. They echoed through the study like a death knell.

The four swung startled gazes to her. A rapid succession of emotions flitted across their lovely faces, each one convicting him and adding more weight to the uncomfortable burden he already bore.

Damn. Damn. Damn.

"You're wasting your breath, dears. His lordship made his decision before he arrived." Miss Culpepper angled her long neck, her harsh gaze stabbing straight to his guilty heart.

"Didn't you, Lord Ravensdale?"

A woman of discernment understands that a deck of playing cards is the devil's prayer book, and a gentleman possessing a pack is Satan's pawn.
~*Wisdom and Advice—The Genteel Lady's Guide to Practical Living*

Brooke waited for Lord Ravensdale to deny her accusation.

He ran his hand through his shiny hair and stared past her shoulder. A muscle jumped in his jaw.

Tic or ire?

She curled her nails into her palms against the anger and despair sluicing through her veins. If she had to look at his handsome face or listen to his half-hearted platitudes one more minute, she wouldn't be able to keep from whacking him atop the head.

Yes, blaming him seemed unfair, but this situation was too, made more so because she'd kept her end of the bargain these many years and that slug...worm...*maggot* of a cousin had gambled away their lives.

How dare Sheridan?

His lordship turned his attention to her. Did concern tinge in his eyes?

She briefly closed hers to hide the rage that must've been sparking within them, and also to block his lordship's troubled expression.

Don't you dare pretend to care, you opportunistic cawker.

Lord Ravensdale heaved a low sigh.

Her eyelids popped open.

Ought to be on stage so someone can appreciate his theatrics.

He rubbed his nape. "Miss Culpepper, ladies, I—"

Duffen shuffled into the study, scraping a hand atop his wild hair in an unsuccessful attempt to tame the unruly bush. "Miss Brooke, Mabry will come up as soon as he can. A calf's turned wrong. Said he couldn't leave just now."

Brooke simply nodded, not trusting herself to speak. Mabry wasn't needed, in any event.

"I rubbed your horse down, my lord, and saw him settled." Duffen rested his bleary gaze on Lord Ravensdale, his dislike tangible.

His lordship curved his perfect lips into a narrow smile before placing his hands on the chair's arms and shoving to his feet. The signet ring on his small finger caught the fire's glow. "Thank you for your trouble, but I'm set on leaving in a moment. I don't wish to travel after dark. I require a few more minutes of your mistress's time, and then I'll be on my way."

His intense stare heated the top of Brooke's head as surely as if he'd placed his fire-warmed palm there. Refusing to raise her attention from the hole in the carpet, she slid her foot atop it. Had he noticed? She drew in a long, controlled breath. Her composure hung by a fine strand of sheer will, and she'd be cursed if she would let him see her cry again. Or let the girls see, for that matter. She didn't cry in public.

Their faces when Brooke had exposed his lordship's purpose...the despair and hopelessness... God, to have been able to spare them that anguish. They didn't lack intelligence and understood perfectly what their circumstances had been reduced to in the course of these past two hours.

So blasted, bloody unfair. Men didn't have these worries, but women without means had few opportunities.

"Miss Culpepper?" Lord Ravensdale prompted.

Persistent isn't he?

Mud-spattered boots appeared in her line of vision. She followed the lean length of his lordship's leg, past muscular buckskin-covered thighs, narrow hips, and his hunter green and black waistcoat to the pathetic excuse of a neckcloth drooping round his neck. An emerald stick pin glinted from within the folds. She'd missed the jewel earlier.

Firming her lips, she stared pointedly at his faintly-stubbled chin. Must be one of those gentlemen who required a shave twice daily. Humphrey hadn't.

What would it feel like to trace her fingers across his jaw?

Brooke Theodora Penelope Culpepper, have you lost your wits? Cease this instant!

He had the audacity to tilt her chin upward, forcing her to meet his chocolaty gaze.

Why must he be the man to awaken her long dormant feelings? Feelings she thought she'd succeeded in burying. Tears flooded her eyes, and she attempted to avert her face.

He would have none of it, however. "I will call at eleven tomorrow, at which time we can continue this discussion."

"Why?" Brooke jerked her chin from his gentle grasp. She angrily swiped at her eyes and retreated a couple of paces. "Why bother returning? Just send a note round, and tell us when you've sold the lands and what your directives are. I won't have you coming here and upsetting my family or staff anymore."

Duffen angled closer, his eyes gone hard as flint. "Did I miss somethin'? I thought, Miss Brooke, you planned on askin' his lordship if we could carry on like afore."

Brette rose and wrapped an arm around Brooke's waist. She gave it a reassuring squeeze. "Unfortunately, the earl has other plans, Duffen."

"I didn't say that." Lord Ravensdale retreated and planted his hands on his hips. His ebony gaze roved each of them, perused the study, lit on Freddy and Dumpling still sleeping soundly on the couch, before finding its way to Brooke once more. He sent a glance heavenward as if asking for divine guidance. "I'm not sure what I shall do. Give me the evening to ponder and see if I can devise something that will benefit us all."

"I assure you, my lord, I'll not concede our home without a fierce fight and before I use every means at my disposal."

And you can wager with the devil on that.

His lips turned up in a wickedly seductive smile, and he caressed her with another leisurely glance. So sure of himself, the pompous twit. Used to taking what he wanted, consequences be hanged.

A wave of scorching rage swept her. The earl needed to leave. Now. Before Brooke lost what little control she held. She wasn't given to violence, but the urge to punch him in his perfect, straight nose overwhelmed her.

She patted Brette's hand. "Please retrieve his lordship's coat, and take the others with you. I wish to have a moment alone with him."

With a curt nod, Brette whisked from the study as their cousins scrambled to stand. After sending Lord Ravensdale glances ranging from accusatory to wounded, they scurried from the room.

Brooke squeezed her hands together to stop their trembling. She'd only eaten a piece of toast today, and hunger, along with the disastrous afternoon, made her head spin. "Duffen, please see to the earl's mount."

"Did that, an' now I have to go into Satan's playground again?" He stuffed his cap onto his head, and with a mutinous glower, buttoned his coat. "Should've waited by the entrance. I'd have been no wetter or colder."

Muttering, he stomped to the door. "Bet my breeches he'll get lost on the way home, he will. Pretentious cove, strutting about in his fine togs, lording it over the poor gels. Haven't they been through enough?"

Brooke made no effort to chastise him, since her sentiments closely echoed his. She followed him to the doorway. Presenting her back to Lord Ravensdale, she spoke softly for Duffen's ears alone. "Please tell Mabry he needn't bother coming to the house."

Duffen gave a sharp nod. "Why'd he bother to come at all? Upset the young misses, he did. Lord or not, the man hasn't the sense of a worm."

He slashed Lord Ravensdale a scowl that would've laid out a lesser man before disappearing into the dark corridor, still grumbling beneath his breath.

"Yes, why bother coming at all? Couldn't your man of business have seen to the sale? For surely that's what you intend." She crossed her arms and glared at Lord Ravensdale, unable to keep the scorn from her tone. "You don't look the sort to worry yourself about the running of an estate. You probably don't venture to your own holdings unless you make a token visit once every now and again. Probably more concerned with the tie of your cravat or the goings on at White's or Almack's."

I've become a harpy.

His lordship appraised her coolly while exchanging Papa's coat for his own.

No, definitely not padded. Those broad shoulders and chest are natural muscles, more's the pity.

It seemed most unfair that he should be gifted with wealth, looks, and a physique to rival a Greek god's. An attractive package on the exterior perhaps, but the trappings hid a blackguard's treacherous heart.

With a great deal of difficulty, he struggled into his coat, the wetness and tight fit presenting a humorous challenge. Swearing beneath his breath, he wriggled and twisted. Had her life not been shattered, she might've chuckled at his antics.

His elbow caught at an awkward angle near his ear, and he curled his lip in irritation. He glanced her way and opened his mouth.

She arched a brow.

Don't you dare ask for my assistance.

Freddy would fart feathers before she offered to help the earl.

He snapped his mouth shut and a closed expression settled on his features. "You know nothing of me, Miss Culpepper, and your blame is sorely misplaced."

"Indeed. And on whom shall I place the blame then?"

"If you must blame someone, blame your confounded cousin for being a self-centered sot. Blame your father for not providing for you." At last, he rammed his arm into the sleeve. He waved a hand in the air. "Blame The Almighty for making you a woman, and not a man capable of providing for himself and his family."

Too far!

Brooke gasped and narrowed her eyes. She fisted her hands and clamped her teeth together so hard, she feared they would crack.

Forget the blasted cane. She longed to run Lord Ravensdale through with the rusty sword hanging askew above the fireplace, the arrogant bastard. She *had* provided for her family, despite the odds against her, and despite being a woman.

God forgive her, but she hoped the earl did catch a nasty chill or get lost on his journey to wherever he stayed. Or, better yet, fall off his magnificent horse and suffocate on a pile of fresh cow manure. She doubted he'd experienced a moment's discomfort in his entire life, and he had the gall to amble into Esherton today—as if strolling Covent Garden or perusing the oddities at Bullock's Museum—and nonchalantly destroy their lives.

She might be able to forgive him for winning the wager. After all, the rich thought nothing of losing a few hundred pounds, a prized piece of horseflesh, or a millstone of an estate. Josephina assured her gambling was the rage in London's upper salons. But the earl's indifference to their dire circumstances? And then having the ballocks to lay the blame for her predicament on her sex?

How callous and coldhearted could he be?

As coldhearted as Sheridan, and he is your cousin, which makes him the greater fiend by far.

Seething, Brooke pointed to the door. "Take your—"

Brette returned with Lord Ravendale's greatcoat. Mouth pursed, she passed it to him then moved to stand and stare into the waning fire. Her slumped shoulders and bowed head spoke of her distress.

He'd done this to her gentle sister.

Brooke clenched her jaw to quiet her quaking and suppress the vulgar suggestion she longed to make regarding where he could shove his opinions. She continued to shake uncontrollably.

Rage? Cold? Fear? Hunger?

Yes, those had her quivering like the leaves on the tormented trees outside.

Hugging her shoulders, she gazed out the blurry window. The rain had ebbed. Dusk wasn't far off, the mantle of night hovered on the horizon though the afternoon hadn't seen its end. She swept the clock a glance. A jot beyond half-past two. He'd been here a mere half an hour? The disastrous change he unleashed upon their lives ought to have taken much longer. Unfair how one man could snuff what little joy had survived at Esherton in less than a blink of an eye.

After securing his jacket, his lordship donned his damp overcoat. He gave his right chest a light pat, and a slight smile skewed his lips.

Done with the niceties, Brooke faced him fully.

"See yourself to the door, and don't bother us with your presence again. The house and surrounding five acres are entailed. Sheridan had no legal right to use them as collateral. Do what you will with the rest of the property, but understand I intend to seek counsel regarding the ownership of the herd and the use of the outbuildings. They sit on entailed properties, and you won't be permitted use of them. I...*we* haven't labored like slaves for five years to have you destroy everything we've worked for."

Would he call her bluff?

She hadn't any right to make those claims. Only Sheridan did.

Would Lord Ravensdale know that? Would he make an arrangement with her cousin regarding occupation of the house? God, then what?

The two devils would deal well together, she had no doubt.

"Believe me when I say, my lord, I'll cause you no small amount of grief for the havoc you've wrought on my family." How, she had no idea, but when an uneasy look flashed across his features, she relished the small victory her false bravado provided.

Brooke presented her back. If she never laid sight on the man again, it would be too soon.

It infuriated her all the more that she had ever entertained the slightest interest in the fiend.

She closed her eyes and drew forth every ounce of faith she possessed. *We've been through hard times before.* God would see them through this too. *Wouldn't He?* He'd met their needs thus far. *Barely.* He wouldn't fail them now.

He already has.

She opened her eyes, blinking away another round of burning tears, further testament to her overwrought state. Since when did she snivel at the least little thing? Why, until today, she hadn't cried since Papa died.

See what the earl had reduced her to? A weeping ninny.

Freddy snorted and rolled onto his back, still sound asleep. His tail twitched and his paws wiggled. A low whimper escaped him. Likely dreaming of his younger days when he drove the cattle. He'd been quite the herder until old age relegated him to snoozing the day away.

Get up, Freddy, and pee—or worse—on his lordship's boot again.

Brette gathered Pudding from the hearth before settling into one of the wingback chairs. She obviously didn't intend to leave Brooke alone with the earl again. Propriety prohibited it, as did Brette's protective nature.

Thank you, Brette.

The cat curled into Brette's lap, her leery gaze on the earl. She'd not soon forgive him for crushing her into the cushions. Pudding was a pout.

After sending Lord Ravensdale an unreadable look, Brette petted the cat and stared into the fire's remaining embers. No sense adding another log when they'd vacate the room as soon as Lord Ravensdale took his leave.

Brooke whirled around at a light touch on her shoulder.

He stood mere inches away, close enough that she smelled his cologne once more. Such forwardness wouldn't be tolerated. She opened her mouth to say as much, but his chestnut eyes held no hostility, only warm empathy.

She swallowed, wanting to glance away, but her dratted eyes refused to obey. What was wrong with her today? Out of character for her to be mawkish over a man, weep like a child, or wallow in self-pity.

"I will go, for now, because this weather forces me to." Brows pulled into a vee, he looked to the window. "But be assured, I will return with a satisfactory solution, and I intend to communicate with your cousin regarding the matter of the house and grounds."

A bitter laugh escaped Brooke. "Unless your solution involves allowing us to run the dairy farm and remain in our home, I strongly doubt you will have any suggestion I would welcome."

"You will agree to what I propose, Brooke." He ran his forefinger along her jaw and smiled. "You haven't a choice, have you?"

Brooke tried to ignore the flash of sensation his touch caused. Why did this man have this power over her? "We'll see about that, my lord, and I haven't given you leave to use my given name."

He glanced at Brette.

Her eyes shut and head resting against the chair, she appeared to have dozed off. No wonder. She'd been up past midnight finishing a lace collar for Josephina.

Lord Ravensdale edged closer to Brooke and bent his neck, his mouth near her ear. "Oh, I intend to use much more than your name, Brooke."

Always remember, gaming wastes two
of man's most precious things: time and treasure.
~*Wisdom and Advice—The Genteel Lady's Guide to Practical Living*

8

Heath grinned as he marched to the entrance.

Brooke smelled incredible. Not of perfume, but her natural scent. Womanly, warm, and sweet.

He'd wanted to gather her in his arms and bury his face in the hollow of her neck. After less than an hour's acquaintance, he already ached for her. Of course, three months of forced celibacy might have something to do with his randy state.

Cheeks glowing, Brooke had stared at him, dazed. However, a spark had glinted in the center of her eyes, and male instinct assured him the glimmer hadn't been entirely shock or ire. He'd piqued her interest and what's more, she'd responded to him physically.

His remark about using her had ruffled her feathers. True, he had been a mite crude, but she didn't seem the sort who'd appreciate flowery speeches or false flattery. She'd been honest and direct with him and deserved the same in return.

Brette, on the other hand, had scowled at him, not a hint of anything but hostility within her narrowed gaze. Tiny she might be, but Brooke's sister remained a force to be reckoned with and one he didn't want to cross. Much better to have the other four as allies in his newly formed quest to win Brooke over.

A notion had taken hold as they'd sat in the study, one that would provide for her and her family, and allow him to dispose of the albatross he'd won. The whole debacle seemed quite providential when he considered the situation, though he didn't believe in that sort of mythical nonsense. The facts remained: he required a new mistress, and Brooke was desperate for a means to provide for her family.

They complicated things a bit, but could work to his favor too, especially if his contract with Brooke included settling a monthly sum on her that would allow her to continue to care for the other four until the quartet married.

Several delightful ways she might express her gratitude crossed his mind, including a bottle of his finest champagne and a bath teeming with fragrant bubbles.

Why not marry her?

Heath faltered mid-step.

Where had that ludicrous thought come from? The bowels of Hades?

He wasn't ready to marry, didn't want to ever, truth to tell. But if he didn't, his reprobate of a cousin, Weston Kitteridge, would inherit and obliterate what scant remnant of honor and respect the Ravensdale legacy retained. Holding a title wasn't all pomp and privilege. The earldom required him to marry. A martyr for his title.

Eventually.

Heath resumed his progress through the hallway, his pace somewhat slower.

Brooke had intrigued him from the moment she appeared in the doorway. No woman had gotten his attention, snared him, so completely in such a short time. That he couldn't ignore. Not only a delectable morsel, she possessed a keen mind, evident in the years she'd operated the dairy. She had a practical head on her lovely shoulders—shoulders he itched to strip naked and trace with his lips—and she'd already proven she would willingly sacrifice herself for the wellbeing of others.

In all likelihood, she remained as chaste as the day she'd been born, but wisdom dictated an examination by his physician before Heath penned his signature to any agreement between them. He would be generous, of course. Provide her with an annual income and a comfortable cottage once he tired of her.

No doubt she'd prefer the farm, but instinct told him he wouldn't grow weary of her soon. He had no intention of nursing the dairy along in order for her to return to it in a few years, and resume the heavy responsibilities of operating the place. Besides, no woman should have to labor so hard to live in poverty.

He could give her that much at least—a comfortable existence for the rest of her days. Perchance she would even decide to marry after their association ended. Many women made respectable, even exceptional, matches, after being a kept woman.

Daphne's features sprang to mind.

And others didn't bother waiting until they'd been given their congé.

What had started as a miserable outing had proved advantageous after all. Not a direction he'd expected the day to take, but such an opportunity shouldn't be squandered. Some—not him, mind you— might call it a blessing in disguise.

Opening the entry door, he released a soft chuckle.

Taken aback, she'd gaped at him like a cod fish, her blue-violet eyes enormous and her pink lips opening and closing soundlessly. Heath had bent halfway to kiss them when her sister's exaggerated throat clearing had brought him up short. He'd forgotten Brette napped in the chair.

Rather touching, how protective the sisters were of one another. He hadn't experienced that sort of bond with another human. Not that it bothered him. One didn't miss what one had never had. Emotional balderdash and sentimental claptrap he could do without, thank you.

The esteem he held for his friends, Alexander Hawksworth and Leventhorpe, was the closest Heath had ever come to an emotional attachment with anyone, including his mistresses. Must be a family curse handed down from his glacial parents, and theirs before them. The Ravensdales weren't hailed for their warmth and geniality, but that didn't stop them from coupling like rabbits with any partner willing.

He had put a stop to that practice...almost.

Grateful the storm had abated somewhat, he ran down the stoop stairs. An occasional blast of cold air accompanied a thick drizzle. Far better than the monsoon that had blown him here, nonetheless.

Hunched within his baggy coat and oversized cap, Duffen waited at the bottom of the stairs.

Ebénè, however, was nowhere in sight.

Heath scanned the drive before casting a glance at the barns. "Where's my horse?"

"Hadn't the heart to make the poor beasty stand in the rain an' cold. I thought..." Staring at the ground, the servant stuffed his hands into his jacket pockets and shuffled his feet. He darted a quick look at Heath before returning his attention to the dirt. "Thought I might take you to your horse an' give him a few more minutes out of the weather."

He scuffed his boot uncertainly.

"Most considerate of you." Heath shook his head, curling his mouth at the corners. "Ebéné is already miffed at me for the journey here. I'm sure he won't welcome the return trip. Thank you for thinking of his comfort."

Duffen rolled his shoulders before angling toward the outbuildings. "Aint the horse's fault you got a hair up your arse an' set out in weather evil enough to bewitch the devil himself."

Heath scratched his upper lip to cover his smile.

Ought to reprimand him for his impudence.

After turning away, the servant lumbered down the path to the barn. Amusement outweighed propriety and Heath dutifully followed the disgruntled little elf of a man. The pathway forked, and instead of continuing on the trail to the stables, Duffen veered to the other branch.

Heath stopped and looked at the barns. "Isn't my mount stabled in one of those?" He pointed to the buildings. Light shone from the south end of the farthest one. The lowing of cattle echoed hollowly from within the two long structures.

Duffen looked over his shoulder and shook his head. He didn't stop plodding along.

"No, the herd's indoors 'cause of the storm. There's no room. Besides, several cows have newborn calves, and more are in labor or expected to birth their babes any day." He jerked his head toward a beehive-shaped stone building. "Puttin' your stallion in the carriage house seemed wiser. There are stalls in there, an' it's quieter."

That's a carriage house?

Heath would bet Ebéné a carriage hadn't graced the inside of the building for a good number of years. Lady Bustinza's monstrous bosoms drooped less, and the dame was six and eighty if she was a day. He shook his head, and with another brief glance at the stables, raised his collar and continued onward. He wouldn't make it to Leventhorpe's before darkness fell. Traveling at night—the only thing he hated worse than riding in the rain.

Other than a dagger in his boot, he bore no arms. Not that he expected trouble, but a wise man prepared for any eventuality. *Should've taken Leventhorpe's carriage.* He allowed himself a rueful smile. He'd grown soft, too used to the comforts of his privileged life.

Duffen faced forward again but waited for Heath to catch up.

Scrunching his eyes and pulling his earlobe, the servant gave him a sideways glance. Duffen opened his mouth then snapped it closed, glaring past Heath. "Don't s'pose you'd help an old man with somethin'."

Heath grinned. Despite himself, he liked the cantankerous fellow. The poor man shouldn't have been working at all at his age. He could spare a minute or two more. "And what might that be?"

"We store the extra feed and grain in the dovecote 'cause it's harder for the vermin to get to it. The only way inside is through them holes on top and the door." He cackled and shoved his hat upward, exposing his wizened face. "The rats sure do try, though, let me tell you. Caught one gnawin' at the door the other day. Clever little beasts, they are."

"I'm sure." Heath took the servant at his word.

A crow perched on the dovecote's upper edge took to the sky, its croaking call stolen by a gust of wind whipping past. Heath shivered and secured the top button of his coat then dug around in his pocket and found his gloves. Damp leather didn't do much to stave off the chill permeating him, but he tugged them on, nonetheless.

Damn, but he'd never been this miserably cold.

"Dark omen that." Duffen pointed to the bird zig-zagging across the sky. "Bad luck to see a lone crow atop a house."

Heath eyed the dour man and swallowed a chuckle. Like anyone could see the moon tonight with clouds thick as porridge. Not the least superstitious, he didn't believe in fate either. "Well, I don't think a pigeon cote qualifies as a house, so there's nothing to worry about, is there?"

"You city coves don't know much, do you?" Disgust puckered Duffen's face. "It's a house for pigeons an' doves, aint it?"

Not in the last century.

Heath surveyed the ancient structure, and the spots of grass sprouting atop the roof.

Or two.

"Mark my words, my lord. You'll wish you never set foot on Esherton Green's lands afore the moon rises."

Almost sounds like a threat.

Where in God's name had Brooke unearthed the man? Was he the best she could find to employ? She probably couldn't afford to pay him much and no one of substance would work for the pittance she offered.

His patience running thin, Heath strode across the grass. "So what is it you need help with?"

"Can't get the door open. Think it's jammed." Duffen planted his hands on his hips and scowled at the barns. "Mabry an' the other hands don't think I pull my weight round here. I'll be damned—beg your pardon, my lord—before I ask 'em for help."

He begs my pardon now?

"Let's be about it then. I truly need to be on my way." The drizzle had turned into rain once more, though the wind hadn't returned in force.

"This way, your lordship."

Duffen trudged round the backside of the building, Heath in his wake.

Heath obligingly turned down the latch and, levering his legs and shoulders, gave the door a hefty shove. It sprang open with surprising ease. He tumbled to his knees on the circular floor, cracking the left one hard. Pain wrenched the joint.

Damnation.

Eyeing the hundreds of dung-encrusted nesting holes lining the sides, he brushed his palms on his coat. "It didn't seem all that stuck—"

Pain exploded at the base of his head.

A prudent woman holds this truth close to her heart:
gambling is the mother of all lies, and good luck, her fickle daughter.
~Wisdom and Advice—The Genteel Lady's Guide to Practical Living

9

After telling Brette she needed a few moments alone and to tell Mrs. Jennings to serve dinner early, Brooke puttered about the study. She banked the fire before closing the drapes and blowing out all but one candle. Brette had taken the cats when she left, and only Freddy remained curled on the couch, dozing. Every now and again, he opened his eyes to make sure she hadn't left him. She'd rescued him as a puppy from an abusive, slick-haired showman at a county fair, and Freddy seldom let Brooke out of his sight.

A flush suffused her for the dozenth time since Lord Ravensdale had left her gaping like a ninnyhammer.

He'd been about to kiss her.

She was positive.

Mesmerized by his beautiful eyes and mouth, she would have let him. *Let him?* Encouraged him.

With her sister sitting right there, watching.

What had come over her?

Brooke had experienced desire before. She'd nearly married Humphrey, though the mild pleasantness he'd stirred in her didn't compare to the wild tempest of sensations his lordship had rioting through her. Thrilling and frightening and certainly not the sensations a practical spinster should've been entertaining.

Must be because he was a practiced man of the world with a swashbuckler's bold good looks and comportment, and Humphrey had been a quiet, mild-mannered man. More of a reserved poet sort than a swaggering, cock-sure, womanizing—*remember that, Brooke...the earl's no doubt a womanizer*—pirate.

Brooke rubbed her fingers against the sofa's roughened backrest as the last embers of the fire faded. Did Lord Ravensdale think her circumstances so desperate, he could take liberties with her? Had she given the rogue cause in the few moments they'd been acquainted to think she'd be receptive to his advances?

Brow knitted, she stilled her fingers, replaying the few minutes he'd been here in her mind. No, she'd behaved with complete propriety, and absolutely nothing about her attire was remotely suggestive or alluring. A nun wore finer, more seductive clothing.

Did the man go about kissing women he'd just met on a regular basis? The notion, much like soured cream, curdled in her belly.

Enough ruminating.

She wanted to inventory the larder before dinner. While they'd waited for the calving to occur, their stores had declined severely. Could she make do for a little longer since she didn't know whether she could sell the calves now?

There's always the bull fund.

Brooke flexed her hands and firmed her lips. No. She wouldn't touch the hoarded reserve. If she did, then she admitted she'd lost Esherton Greens. Her heart wrenched. That she could not do. Not yet. Not until every last avenue had been explored. There must be a way.

Please, God. A miracle would be most welcome.

She pivoted to the door, and her gaze landed on the small package sitting where Blythe had set it earlier.

What a perfectly horrid birthday. Brooke wouldn't celebrate the day ever again. Not that there'd been any real festivities in the house since Mama died. There'd been little time or inclination, and even less money, for such frivolity.

Poverty and grief had denied the girls much.

Brooke lifted the forgotten gift. She turned it over and squeezed gently. Something soft. What had the sweethearts done?

She slid the ribbon from the package. Dangling the yellow strand from a finger, she unfolded the plain cloth—one of the girl's handkerchiefs—and a stocking slid to the floor.

Tears welled again as she bent to retrieve the white length. Where had the dears found the money to buy yarn to knit a pair of stockings? Hers had been repaired so many times, the patched and knobby things scarcely resembled the pair she now held to her face.

A sob escaped her, and she pressed the back of her hand to her mouth to stifle the others scratching up her throat. Tilting on the precipice of hysteria, she drew in a measured breath. Where was the logic Papa boasted of? The common sense Mama instilled in her?

Histrionics solved nothing. Her guide must be calm reason.

And cunning.

She would outmaneuver Ravensdale, the jackanape, one way or another.

Stupid, stupid Sheridan to wager her farm in a miserable card game. For Esherton *was* hers. Perhaps not legally, but in her heart, it had always been hers. She loved the drafty house—crumbling entry and shoddy condition and all—and often daydreamed about restoring the treasure to its former glory. As a child, she'd roamed the meadows and orchard, climbed the gnarled trees, and petted the newborn calves. Every night, the soft moos of the cattle lulled her to sleep, and most mornings a songbird's trill woke her.

Somehow, she must persuade Lord Ravensdale to allow them to stay.

But how?

She fiddled with a loose thread dangling from her cuff.

Stop before you unravel the whole edge.

Could she offer Lord Ravensdale more profit? Use the parure set as collateral? Was there another way to procure funds; anything else they could sell or barter?

She glanced around the office. Not in here, or the rest of the house, for that matter. Oh, to have a treasure buried somewhere on the estate. Alas, her family tree held no buccaneers, addlepated relations ranting of secret stashes of gold, or long-lost kin seeking to bestow a fortune on their surviving family members.

Brooke tapped her chin.

They'd already searched the attic, and hadn't unearthed anything of value. Still, some of her ancestors had traveled broadly, and perhaps an artifact or two that might be pawned or sold remained buried in a corner or trunk. She would send Blythe and Brette above stairs tomorrow to burrow around in the clutter a mite more.

When he'd first inherited, Brooke had asked Sheridan if she might buy the unentailed lands from him, using the parure set as a down payment. The grasping bugger had said no. He'd wanted the regular income and possession of the grounds too.

Would Lord Ravensdale be open to the suggestion?

That only partially solved the problem, though, since Sheridan retained the house and would continue to demand rents. She couldn't afford to make land payments and also send him money monthly. Not on the dismal profit the farm made.

Swiping a hand across her eyes, Brooke sighed, her shoulders slumping.

What a blasted muddle.

She would have to write Sheridan. Discover exactly what he proposed. Bile burned her throat. This helplessness, the lack of control over her fate and the others', nearly had her shrieking in frustration.

Damn the injustice.

She would send a note to Mr. Benbridge, seeking an appointment. He and his wife had been absolute dears after Papa died, despite Brooke breaking their son's heart. They'd assured her they understood her decision to decline Humphrey's proposal. An unpleasant suspicion had always lay tucked in a cranny of Brooke's mind; she hadn't been good enough, of a high enough station for their son. Her refusal had relieved them.

After Humphrey left, Josephina admitted her parents—landed gentry with deep, deep pockets—wanted their children to marry into a higher social class. Mr. Benbridge had refused no less than seven offers for Josephina's hand—none from gentlemen with a title greater than a viscountcy—and now at one and twenty, Josephina feared she'd end up like Brooke.

On the shelf. No offense intended.

However, Brooke hadn't anyone else to ask for advice. Mr. Benbridge would know what direction to point her, and Mrs. Benbridge claimed many connections in London. Her sister, the Viscountess Montclair, was an influential woman, or so Mrs. Benbridge often boasted. Brooke would ask her for a reference and to pen letters on her behalf, should, God forbid, they actually have to leave Esherton.

Brooke dropped the stockings and wrapping onto the desk. Shivering, she sank into Papa's chair. Had she known she would remain in the study longer, she'd not have let the fire die. She placed two pieces of foolscap before her then stared at the paper.

She shoved one aside. Not now. Impossible to write Sheridan today. Too much anger and hurt thrummed through her to pen a civil word to the cull.

She tapped the other piece of foolscap, not certain how to approach Mr. Benbridge about her delicate situation. Best not to say too much.

Just send a missive along, ask if she could call in the next day or two, and also, if he might spare her a few moments to ask his advice.

Wiggling her toes against the chill permeating the room, Brooke wrote the brief note. She put the quill away then sprinkled sand on the ink. If the weather cooperated, she would send the letter round with one of the stable hands in the morning.

A short rap on the door preceded Duffen poking his head inside.

Freddy lifted his ears and thumped his tail once.

"Do you have need of me this evenin', Miss Brooke? My bones have ached somethin' fierce all day. This wicked weather is hard on old joints. Thought I'd ask Cook for her sleepin' tonic an' retire early."

Duffen shuffled so slowly, she expected his stiff joints to creak.

"Certainly," Brooke said and smiled. "Please forgive me for the necessity of sending you into the rain twice today."

Grimacing at the new ink stain on her forefinger, she stood. Why couldn't she manage a quill without getting ink on herself? Rubbing her fingers together, she came round the desk and, after gathering her new stockings in her unstained hand, collected the candlestick with her other.

She gave Duffen another warm tilt of her mouth. "Thank you for seeing our guest on his way. Let's hope he doesn't make an appearance again any time soon."

"Don't like the man." He frowned and rubbed his amulet. "Greedy, no good churl."

At his fierce tone, Brooke gave him a sharp look. "I understand you're angry with him. I am too, but we must get him to cooperate with us."

"I aint grovelin' for the likes of that cheatin' bugger," Duffen muttered. "Mebe he'll take you at your word an' not come back."

They exited the study into the unlit hallway, Freddy pattering behind.

"I think he'll return, but I plan on being better prepared the next go round." She raised the candle to look Duffen in the eye. "I promise you, as I told Lord Ravensdale, I shall do everything within my power to keep our home."

"What about...nicking him off?" Duffen averted his eyes and tugged on his earlobe.

Brooke stopped abruptly and stepped on Freddy's paw. "Pardon?"

The dog yelped and scampered away, giving her a wounded stare.

"I'm sorry, Freddy. Come here, let me see. Duffen, hold the candle please." She bent and examined the dog's paw. After assuring herself he hadn't sustained a serious injury, she straightened.

Arms crossed, she regarded Duffen. He did say the most peculiar things at times. What went on in that head of his? "Don't jest about something so appalling. Lord Ravensdale may be our adversary, but I do not wish the man dead."

"He'd let you and the other misses starve." Duffen jutted his chin out, his eyes suspiciously moist.

"That's harsh, Duffen, and I believe you know it. His lordship doesn't realize how dire our circumstances are."

"Beggin' your pardon, but he'd have to be blind not to see our sorry state." He scratched his scrawny chest, frustration glittering in his toast-brown eyes.

Brooke retrieved the candleholder, her heart aching for the old retainer, and they continued along the barren hallway. "He's only acting to better his interests, and it's a wise business move on his part."

"Why are you defending him?" Duffen snorted and gave her a look suggesting she'd gone daft.

Why am I defending him?

She entered the welcoming kitchen, Duffen at her side.

"You don't need to worry yourself, Miss Brooke. I promised your father I'd take care of his girls. I've done what needs be done."

One who desires peace and contentment, neither lays wagers nor lends.
~Wisdom and Advice—The Genteel Lady's Guide to Practical Living

10

Eyes closed, Heath rolled onto his back, and instantly regretted the movement as agony ricocheted inside his skull. He covered his face with an elbow and swallowed. Nausea toyed with his stomach and throat.

Holy Mother of God.

Not dead then. Death wouldn't be painful, would it? Unless this was hell. No, hell was hot. Dank and cold permeated this place. Where was he?

He forced his eyes open a slit.

Ah, the dovecote.

Duffen had clobbered him, the crusty old goat.

At Brooke's direction? What did she say to the servant before he stomped from the study?

Heath squinted at the faint light filtering into the top of the domed ceiling.

Early morning?

He'd been unconscious the entire night. Slowly, afraid any sudden movement might send his head rolling across the grain-smattered floor, he sought the entrance. Closed and likely locked tighter than a convent of giggling virgins.

He sucked in a long breath and wrinkled his nose at the stench. Pigeon *and* cow manure.

Splendid.

He flexed his stiff shoulders and spine. The stone floor didn't make for the most comfortable sleeping accommodations. In the weak light, he scrutinized the culvery. To his surprise, a flask and a lumpy cloth—perhaps a napkin—lay atop a pair of ratty blankets beside a bucket atop bulging grain sacks.

All the comforts of home.

Groaning, he struggled to a sitting position. He removed his gloves and waited for another dizzying wave to subside before exploring the source of pain. Heath brushed a tender fist-sized lump behind his left ear and, wincing, probed the area gently.

No blood.

His skull hadn't been split open, thank God, but he would boast a cracking good headache for a day or two. He coughed, flinching and holding his head as agony crashed through his brain again. Make that a whopping headache for a bloody week.

What had the puny whoremonger bashed him with? A boulder? No, more likely one of the several bricks scattered near the door.

Heath inhaled then released a holler. "Help, I'm locked in the dovecote."

His brain threatened to leave his head through his nose. Shouting like a madman would have to wait a few hours, until he could be certain the act wouldn't slay him.

Would Leventhorpe start searching for him immediately or assume he'd taken refuge at an inn along the way. In that event, his friend might delay until as late as tomorrow to sound the alarm. But sound it, his friend would.

Had he mentioned Esherton Green by name to Leventhorpe?

Heath couldn't remember, blast it.

He could scarcely string two thoughts together. He closed his eyes and sucked in an uneven breath to lessen the throbbing in his head and ease his churning stomach. Neither helped a whit.

He pressed two fingers to his forehead.

Think. What will Leventhorpe do?

Aware of Heath's reputation for fastidiousness, Leventhorpe would dismiss any notion of a woman waylaying him. Besides, when expected somewhere, Heath didn't cry off unless he sent a note round.

Leventhorpe had probably been in the saddle since before dawn. He possessed a dark temper, far worse than Heath's. Miss Culpepper had no idea the nest of hornets she would disturb if the Marquis of Leventhorpe became involved. The chap couldn't abide any form of lawlessness or breach of conduct.

Heath had underestimated Brooke's desperation. What did she think to accomplish by having her servant knock him in the head and confine him, both severe offenses against a peer?

My God, maybe she'd intended to kill him.

Disappointment like none he'd ever known squeezed his lungs. He didn't want to believe that of her.

He slid two fingers inside his right boot. His knife remained sheathed there. His gaze wandered to the supplies. Why bother with food and water if she planned on disposing of him? Perhaps she thought to blackmail him into giving her the lands. He'd have to rethink that mistress notion. Bedding a bloodthirsty wench didn't appeal.

If he hadn't felt so bloody wretched, he would've given vent to the fury heating his blood. No matter. There'd be plenty of time for anger later—after he'd escaped or been freed, for he hadn't a doubt his stay in this oversized birdhouse wouldn't be an extended one. Either she would come to her senses—because he wouldn't bend to coercion—or Leventhorpe would out her scheme.

She'd better hope it wasn't the latter.

Just you wait, Brooke Culpepper.

A crow's harsh call sounded.

Heath lifted his gaze to the ceiling and met the beady, ebony gaze of an inquisitive bird sitting on one of the upper beams. Hopping sideways, the crow eyed him then the supplies. The storm had passed, and jagged rays of sun formed a crisscross pattern within the structure. Nonetheless, the place held as much hominess and warmth as a tomb.

Terribly thirsty, he half-crawled, half-scooted to the flask. His skull objected by cruelly stabbing him with each lurching motion. After unscrewing the top, he took several satisfying gulps of rather tangy water. Better, but food might help settle his stomach more. He pulled the cloth away and revealed two hard rolls, a chunk of Cheshire cheese, and dried apples.

Not the most sumptuous of meals, but prisoners couldn't be persnickety.

Did the Culpeppers break their fast with this simple fare every morning? Probably, and inexpensive porridge too.

Despite the coolness, sweat beaded his brow and trickled into his temple hair. God, he feared he would cast up his accounts. Except he hadn't eaten since yesterday morning, and his stomach lay empty. He sought his handkerchief. Gainsborough's marker crackled inside his greatcoat. After patting his face and returning the hopelessly wrinkled cloth to his pocket, Heath withdrew the paper.

Time to find out exactly what he'd won in that confounded wager.

Sighing, he relaxed against the grain sacks and bent his knees. He unfolded the I.O.U then smoothed the paper atop his thighs. He stared at the writing. One short, sloppy paragraph with Gainsborough's— *damn his eyes*—and a witness's signature affixed to the bottom. His forehead scrunched in concentration, Heath nibbled a roll and squinted at the black scrawls.

Despite the best tutors and regular beatings meant to encourage him to pay attention to his lessons, he could barely read. Heath was known for his sharp wit and droll humor, and few people knew the truth. Those who did, he paid well, *very well*, to keep their silence on the matter.

He traced his forefinger over the top line. The letters on the page didn't always make sense. They appeared turned around, the words and sentences impossible to read. He long ago decided the issue a deficit in him, and the knowledge mortified him to his core. Toddlers scarcely out of diapers could read better than he.

The page blurred. His eyelids felt weighted with stones, too heavy to lift. He blinked drowsily, jerking his neck abruptly when he nearly dozed off. Pain seared him once more.

"Dammit to hell."

His shout startled the crow. The bird screamed in alarm and streaked to the exit atop the dovecote. An ebony feather spun slowly to the floor.

His movements sluggish, Heath crammed the unfolded paper into his pocket. Reading the marker would have to wait. Mouth dry, he licked his lips. He fumbled for the flask, intent on quenching his thirst before resuming his slumber. The cool liquid slid into his mouth, and bitterness assailed his tongue. He went rigid.

Drugged?

He spewed the water onto the floor and hurled the flask against the opposite wall.

Struggling to keep his eyes open, he tugged a horse blanket from the sack beside him. After draping the threadbare length across his chest and shoulders, he slumped against the bags.

Words slurred and chin resting on his chest, he mumbled, "Brooke Culpepper, you'll regret the day you crossed me."

Sleep claimed him a moment later.

Brooke rose before dawn, having lain awake most of the night. While drinking a cup of tea—more hot water than tea—she had poured over the farm's ledgers, searching for the slightest way to afford rent and make land payments at the same time. Even if Lord Ravensdale agreed to sell her the land, which she doubted, it was painfully clear she hadn't enough money to pay both.

Now, midmorning, she sat at Papa's desk, a throw Mama knitted draped over her shoulders. Freddy slept in his favorite corner of the sofa. No fire burned in the hearth or candles in the holders. Heavy shadows hovered in the corners the light from the windows couldn't penetrate.

Similar darkness haunted the recesses of her heart.

She had concocted every conceivable scenario she could imagine, and each resulted in losing Esherton and leaving the only home she'd ever known. Brooke tapped her fingertips together, pondering the pile of notes before her. The funds for a bull lay upon the scarred desktop. Sufficient to see her and the girls to London and settled in inexpensive lodgings, but scant more to live on and no provision for the servants at all.

The parure sat atop the desk too.

She lifted the blue velvet lid, worn thin on the edges from hundreds of fingertips touching the fragile fabric. The sapphire and diamonds winked at her from their secure nests. She lifted the tiara high and rotated the circlet so the stones glittered in the cheery ribbons of sunlight filtering through the window. This set had adorned Culpepper women for five generations, since her blond-haired blue-eyed Spanish grandmother wore it for her wedding. Tragically, she'd died before reaching her new home, but her legacy lived on through the jewels.

Selling the gems…a betrayal of Brooke's and the quartet's heritage. Who could she entrust the set to who knew how to barter and wouldn't cheat her? She must receive top price for the sapphires, and that would only occur in London.

Perhaps the Benbridges would know of someone.

She'd sent Rogers, a stable hand, round to their house with the missive over an hour ago. The girls had headed above stairs straightway upon her suggestion they search the attic one more time after breaking their fast this morning.

A stuffed pheasant missing an eye as well as part of a wing and foot propped the study door open part way. Its remaining eye reproached her for the indignity. Fingering the knobby wool atop her shoulders, Brooke half-listened for a knock at the house's entrance. If Rogers returned with an invitation for her to visit the Benbridges this afternoon, she'd need to change into her best gown and set out at once in the dog cart.

She also wanted to speak to Duffen this morning. His peculiar declaration last night before he trundled to bed still nagged. He assured her he'd only warned Lord Ravensdale to stay away from Esherton Green—not the servant's place at all, as she sternly reminded him—but doubt niggled, nonetheless. One more thing to compound her stress.

Duffen hadn't been happy at her reprimand, and for the first time, turned surly toward her. He'd stomped away, mumbling beneath his breath. Mayhap the time had finally arrived to relieve him of his duties—he had become more confused and difficult of late—but to set him aside would destroy the dear. Especially since he, too, had nowhere else to go.

She returned the tiara to its place on the once-white satin, now yellowed to ivory. Would Lord Ravensdale put in an appearance today as promised, despite Duffen's threat? If his lordship came round, she prayed she'd be at the Benbridges. Otherwise, she'd not be at home to callers.

Fewer than twenty-four hours didn't allow time enough to hatch a fool-proof plan.

Fool proof?

She didn't have a plan except to sell the jewels. Rather difficult to hatch a scheme when something nullified each idea she dreamed up. Elbows on the desk, Brooke closed her eyes, buried her face in her hands, and let the tears flow.

Papa, I vowed I'd take care of the girls, and I've failed you. And them. I don't know what to do. Our situation is impossible.

Raucous pounding at the entrance followed by raised voices in the hallway snared her attention. Brooke swiftly wiped her cheeks. She yanked the ratty throw from her shoulders, and after glancing around for a place to hide it, settled on stuffing the makeshift shawl into the desk's kneehole.

"Excuse me. What do you think you're doing?"

Blythe? She'd answered the door instead of Duffen? Where was he?

Brooke slid open the desk drawer then pushed the hidden latch to the secret compartment. One eye trained on the doorway, she rapidly gathered the money and jewelry case. After cramming them into the small cubicle, she clicked the latch, shoved the drawer closed, and locked it. She returned the key to its hiding place in a slot beneath the chair's seat.

Blythe, a strange inflection somewhere between irritation and awe in her tone, exclaimed, "You cannot push your way inside, you great looby."

Drat, Lord Ravensdale—more persistent and annoying than an itch one couldn't reach.

Still, Brooke's lip curved at Blythe's pluck. "Probably the first time the earl's been called a looby, eh, Freddy?"

Barking, the dog bounded to his feet and then ran up and down the length of the couch, pouncing and yapping.

"Hush, I cannot hear."

Freddy obediently plopped onto his bottom before snuffling his haunch in search of a flea.

Brooke leaped from the chair, smoothing a few wayward tresses into place. She'd been in rather a hurry when she'd piled the mass into a loose knot, mainly because she couldn't stand to see herself in the gown she wore—one of Josephina's cast-offs from several seasons ago. Brooke swept the front of the saffron muslin a critical glance and grimaced. The heinous color washed out her complexion, making her look sallow and sickly. However, her wardrobe consisted of four gowns, and she couldn't be picky. She pinched her cheeks and bit her lips to add a dab of color to her face.

Thankfully, no pet hair clung to this garment, and the cut and fit were acceptable. She stopped short of scrutinizing her reflection in the window to make sure her appearance met the mark. She'd tired of the thin, pale face staring at her from her dressing table mirror.

Why did she care how she looked anyway? She wasn't trying to impress Lord Ravensdale. The opinion of the flea Freddy scratched away at concerned her more than anything the earl might think.

Rubbish.

"I insist upon seeing your master or mistress," a cultured male voice—clearly irritated and condescending—demanded. "And you would do well to show your betters more respect."

Brooke cocked her head. Assuredly not Lord Ravensdale, but two visitors in the same number of days? Unheard of.

"My betters?" A dangerous inflection entered Blythe's voice. "And who might *you* be?"

A theatrical, masculine sigh carried into the study. "Lord Leventhorpe, if you insist on knowing. You really are the most impudent servant."

"And I believe you're the most pompous ars—donkey's rear I've ever had the misfortune of meeting," Blythe retorted.

This man clearly possessed the common sense of a potato, speaking to Blythe that way. She would verbally filet him—in the most ladylike manner possible, of course. Blessed with a quick wit and sharp tongue, Blythe did have a most…eloquent way with words.

Brooke strained to hear their conversation, more amused than she'd been in a long while.

"Again, I must insist on speaking with the proprietor of this…er…house," Lord Leventhorpe said.

"Well, your high-and-mightiness, you can insist all you want, but I already told you before you rudely shoved your way inside, no one is home to visitors today." Exasperation rang in Blythe's voice. "Leave your card, if you must, then take your odious self off."

"I shall do no such thing. I'll remain until I am received." Heavy footsteps tread along the corridor. "Where might I wait? In one of these rooms?"

Doors swished opened then clicked closed in rapid succession.

Snoopy bugger.

"Oh, for the love of God, are you completely dense? Do feathers occupy your skull, or is it altogether empty?" Slightly breathless, as if she'd had to scurry to keep up, Blythe said, "You cannot go poking about in people's homes."

"Then be a helpful chit, and tell me where I might await your mistress or master. A good friend of mine has gone missing, and Ravensdale intended to call here yesterday."

'Tis a simple truth that life depends on probabilities, and those who wager had best be prepared to pay the penalty for taunting fate.
~Wisdom and Advice—The Genteel Lady's Guide to Practical Living

*L*ord Ravensdale. Missing?

Brooke didn't need to see her reflection to know she'd grown pale as milk. She felt the blood rush to her feet, washing her in a wave of dizziness. She'd never fainted before, but feared she might swoon from alarm. Pressing a hand to her forehead, she tore to the study door.

"Duffen, what have you done?"

Rushing through the opening, she barely stopped short of plowing into a giant of a man with fiery auburn hair and a scowl fierce enough to set demons to trembling. She toed aside the pheasant and pulled the door closed behind her.

Freddy didn't need to anoint another lord's boots.

She craned her neck to meet the man's eyes.

And I thought the earl tall.

"I tried to stop him, Brooke." Blythe hurried to Brooke's side, delivering the gentleman a glower as hostile as the one he leveled at the women. "But the pig-headed oaf wouldn't listen."

So I heard.

"I'm aware. I heard him." Brooke met Lord Leventhorpe's cynical gaze, shadowed beneath thunderous brows. "I beg your pardon. I didn't mean you're a pig-headed oaf."

Though your decorum dictates otherwise.

"Yes, he is, and a boorish buffoon too." Blythe gave an insincerely sweet smile, ire radiating from her.

He quirked those hawkish eyebrows, his gaze swinging between Brooke and Blythe before settling, heavy and disapproving, on Brooke.

Judgmental, uppity prig.

"Am I to assume you are mistress here?"

She angled her head in affirmation.

He turned startling blue eyes to Blythe, and stared for a long, rude moment. The corners of his mouth tilted upward fractionally. "And I've blundered and called you a servant. However, you must admit," he flicked a black-gloved hand up and down, "your attire lends one to leap to that conclusion."

As did the cobwebs and dust clinging to her gown from rummaging about in the attic.

Blythe grunted, and thrust her chin out. "Fools jump to conclusions, *my lord.*"

Brooke dipped into a reluctant curtsy. False deference peeved her, but Mama had drilled proper decorum into her, and rousing this irritated man further was foolishness.

"I am Brooke Culpepper, and this is my cousin, Miss Blythe Culpepper." Brooke canted her head toward Blythe, who grudgingly bobbed a shallow curtsy. "She and I, as well as our sisters, are the mistresses of Esherton Green."

"Tristan, Marquis of Leventhorpe. My estate is several miles east of here." His attention riveted on Blythe, he bent into the merest semblance of a bow—so short as to be almost insulting.

Seemed Lord Ravensdale chose friends as arrogant and pretentious as he, or did the marquis play a game with her cousin? *Tit for tat? Cat and mouse?*

Blythe narrowed her eyes and firmed her lips before averting her gaze. Wise on her part.

They hadn't time for verbal sparring. Duffen must be found at once.

His lordship canted his head in the open door's direction. "Are you aware there's a tree blocking the drive? Rather a mess to traverse."

"Yes, it fell yesterday, and I haven't set the servants to removing it yet." As if she had the manpower for such a task.

"Not bad enough to keep you from intruding." Blythe scratched her cheek, leaving a faint smudge. Attic grime.

His lordship's lips quivered again, and mutinous sparks spewed from Blythe's eyes.

Time to separate them.

"Blythe, we must find Duffen. He was the last to see Lord Ravensdale yesterday. Get the other girls to help you search." Brooke slid a sideways glance to the serious-faced man watching the exchange.

"In fact, ask Mabry to have the stable hands look as well. As long as no cows are in labor, that is."

Lord Leventhorpe made a sharp gesture. "I think my friend's disappearance takes precedence over cattle."

The caustic dryness of his words could have set kindling afire.

Brooke folded her arms and returned his harsh perusal. "Not around here, it doesn't, my lord."

Worry crinkled Blythe's usually smooth forehead. She laid a hand on Brooke's forearm. "Do you think something is truly amiss?"

A grunt-like snort exploded from the marquis.

Brooke met his lordship's gaze square on.

Yes, I do, but I'll swallow snails before I admit it without more evidence.

She'd known Duffen three and twenty years and this irksome man three minutes. Her loyalty lay with the servant. For now.

His lordship coolly returned her scrutiny, his features granite hard. He didn't seem the merciful, forgiving sort. No, more like the eye-for-an-eye type of chap.

"Duffen is dotty and prone to muttering beneath his breath, but to suggest he would have anything to do with anyone's disappearance, most especially a lord's, is pure silliness." Blythe brushed at a cobweb on her skirt. "He's always been protective, almost grandfatherly, toward us girls."

"Rather like a decrepit, old rooster trying to rule young chicks and just as comical, I'd wager." His lordship offered this droll opinion, earning him frowns from the women.

"As you've never met him, I'm quite sure I don't know how you arrived at that assumption, my lord." Renewed ire tinted Blythe's cheeks. "Brooke, what are your thoughts?"

"I honestly don't know." If only she could reassure her cousin. She looked to the entrance, still gaping open. A gargantuan russet horse stood docilely out front, awaiting its owner. The sun streamed into the entry, and tiny dust particles danced in the bright warmth. Such a contrast to yesterday. "He did make a peculiar remark last night, and I haven't seen him today. Have you?"

Where were Duffen and Lord Ravensdale?

"No." Eyes wide, Blythe shook her head, setting the curls framing her face to bobbing. "He might be off napping. He's done that oft of late."

Dread knotted Brooke's stomach. She didn't dare contemplate what Duffen might have done. Perhaps the earl's disappearance was a horrid coincidence. *And the cows pooped green gold.*

"I'll notify the girls. Where do you want us to search first?" Blythe pointedly avoided looking at Lord Leventhorpe. Not intimidated easily, her cousin might have met her match in the daunting behemoth. "His usual haunts in the house and on the grounds?"

"Yes," Brooke said. "I'll be along to help as soon as I can."

As soon as she could escape the marquis's suspicious regard.

Blythe spun about then hurried down the corridor, his lordship's fractious gaze never leaving her.

Before turning the corner, she cast a swift glance over her shoulder. *Please let her find Duffen right away so we can sort this out.*

God willing, Lord Ravensdale had taken shelter somewhere on the way to the marquis's. Or perhaps he'd been thrown from his horse and lay injured on the route. But wouldn't Lord Leventhorpe have come upon the earl then? Not that she truly wished Ravensdale harm, regardless of the mean-spirited thoughts she'd harbored about him yesterday. But after Duffen's menacing remarks last night...better the earl be lying hurt somewhere than the alarming alternative.

She swallowed a lump of revulsion and fear.

"So you admit Ravensdale called?"

His lordship's terse question wrenched Brooke's attention to the present unpleasantness.

"Certainly. I never implied otherwise. He arrived unannounced, soaked to the skin, I might add. After a small respite before the fire in the study, he went on his way. All in all, he didn't remain above three quarters of an hour." Brooke turned to enter the study. She looked behind her as she pressed the latch. "Would you prefer to wait in here or take part in the search?"

Freddy forced his stout body through the opening. He sniffed the air, and after taking one panicked look at Lord Leventhorpe, ducked his head and retreated into the study. He disappeared around the desk to skulk in the knee well.

His reaction to Lord Leventhorpe caused Brooke no small amount of discomfit. Freddy loved everybody...except the marquis, it seemed. Her unease heightened, she made a mental note of Freddy's reaction. Dogs were good judges of characters. A moist, black nose pressed against the small space beneath the desk's middle panel and sniffed loudly through the crack.

Lord Leventhorpe removed his hat and followed her into the room. "I'd like to ask you a few questions, starting with the peculiar remark this Duffen fellow made."

Shouts and clamoring roused Heath from a fitful slumber and an equally disturbing dream. A hobgoblin had knocked him on the noggin and locked him in a giant birdhouse, intending to feed him to an elephant-sized gray-plumed bird with violet-blue eyes and a shock of curly white feathers atop its head.

The commotion grew louder and closer.

"Lord Ravensdale?"

"Ravensdale!"

"Yer lordship, can you hear us?"

Heath bolted upright, pain and memories simultaneously assaulting him. He stumbled to his feet, his head throbbing with a crusader's vengeance.

"In here." A hoarse croak emerged. He swallowed. "I'm in here. Inside the pigeon cote."

More commotion echoed outside the building before the door jerked open.

Heath blinked at the outline of several people illumined in the archway. Unsteady on his feet, he waited until they stopped wavering before speaking. "Someone send for the magistrate. I've been attacked and abducted."

A small figure dashed away. Brette. No doubt to warn her sister she'd been found out. He couldn't wait to hear the elder Miss Culpepper's fabricated explanation for his treatment.

A fellow Heath didn't recognize stepped forward. "Your lordship, I'm Richard Mabry, Esherton's overseer. I'll send one of my lads to fetch the magistrate straightaway. Are you injured?"

Mouth dry as sand, head stuffed with wool and swollen three times its normal size, and tormented by an invisible hand that jabbed a jagged knife into his skull each time he spoke or moved, Heath barely contained a snarl. "If you consider being wacked on the head with a brick and then drugged senseless injured, then yes."

Shock registered on Mabry's craggy features before his gaze sank to the toppled bricks left of the entry. "Do you require a physician? Can you walk to the house, or do you need us to carry you?"

Hell of a lot of dignity in that, carted about like an invalid or a babe. Heath lifted an unsteady hand to his stinging face. A cut lay across his cheekbone. He hadn't noticed the scratch the first time he awoke. "No, yes, and no."

Mabry's beetle brows wiggled. "Sir?"

Heath forced his leaden feet to move forward. At least he thought he moved. A slug in molasses moved faster.

"No, I don't need a physician." *Might be a good idea to have one take a gander.* "Yes, I can walk. And no, I do not need to be carried." *You will if you keel over onto your face.*

Mabry gestured to a short, lanky man. "Run to the house, and let Miss Brooke know his lordship has been found."

As if she doesn't know where I've been all along.

The fellow bobbed his head before trotting away.

"I'd feel much better if you'd allow me the honor of assisting you, my lord. Miss Brooke will have my head if further harm comes to you." Mabry tentatively wrapped a burly arm around Heath's waist.

Heath choked on a scoffing laugh. "I doubt that, Mabry."

Nonetheless, Heath leaned into the man, grateful for the support. Lurching outside, he closed his eyes. The sun's glare proved excruciating and increased the ferocious thrumming inside his skull.

"I'll go on ahead and tell Brooke to prepare a chamber for his lordship. He shouldn't travel in his condition."

Heath turned his head in the direction of the voice and cracked one eye open. Blythe, the feisty oldest cousin.

"I would appreciate it." Pretenses be damned. He needed to sit down, before he toppled like a tap house drunkard. Devil it, how far away was the house?

Another sturdy arm wrapped around his other side.

"I see you've managed to make a muddle of things, Raven. Could have sworn you toddled here to sell the place, not take a snooze in a pigeon coop half-filled with shi—er...dung."

Leventhorpe?

Heath squinted at him, the sun's rays slicing straight to his brain. He'd have smiled but wasn't certain the motion wouldn't have split his skull like walnut. "About damned time you showed up."

"And that's the thanks I get for parting with my mattress before the sun awoke. I even missed breaking my fast and my customary cups of coffee." He gave Heath's ribs a gentle press. "You're welcome."

Several torturous minutes later—minutes which left Heath seriously considering asking someone to knock him unconscious again—Leventhorpe and Mabry hauled him up the steps.

Like blond-haloed angels of mercy, the Culpepper misses hovered at the entrance.

Leventhorpe's stride faltered, and he shot Heath a look of such incredulity, he would've laughed if he hadn't been afraid he'd disgrace himself on his friend's overly shiny boots. His reaction upon meeting the women yesterday had been much the same.

"Five bloody unbelievable beauties," Leventhorpe muttered beneath his breath. "My God, five. And not one a hopper-arsed or corny-faced."

Only one snagged Heath's attention. The one that had captivated him from the start, damn his eyes. *Damn her eyes.*

Her face somewhere between ashen and a sickly yellow, and wearing a dress uglier than the one she'd worn yesterday, Brooke met his gaze for an instant before squaring her shoulders and issuing orders. "Mr. Mabry, he needs a physician. Please ride to the village as soon as you've assisted his lordship upstairs."

"I'll notify the magistrate too, Miss Brooke."

Her eyes rounded, the irises growing enormous, and the slim column of her throat worked. "Yes, yes, quite so."

She blinked then blinked again, regaining her composure, but the unsteady hand she raised to tuck a silky curl behind her ear betrayed her true state.

"Blythe, have Flora bring the tea you brewed upstairs, and the hot water and towels too. Oh, and please have Mrs. Jennings heat the leftover stew from last night." She faced the twins. "Everything is prepared in Mama and Papa's room?"

They intended to put him in the master suite?

As one, the lookalikes nodded, but remained silent and exchanged an anxious glance. They turned reproachful gazes on him.

Their silent chastisement grated against his pride. Confound it, he was the victim here.

Not the only one, as you well know.

"Any sign of Duffen?" Brooke laid a hand on Brette's chill-reddened arm.

Why didn't they wear outer garments? He shivered within his greatcoat. Didn't they possess pelisses, or spencers, at least?

"Not yet, Brooke." Brette stepped aside to allow Mabry and Leventhorpe to guide Heath into the entry. "We wanted to get his lordship to the house as quickly as possible. We'll start looking again."

Heath wavered, and Brooke steadied him with a palm to his chest. The contact burned through his garments. She must have felt something too, because she snatched her hand away and rubbed it against her hip. Brow creased, she stared out the doorway.

He detected no mercy in the gaze Brette directed at him. So much for winning the cousins and sister to his cause. The task would be harder without their support. Did he still want Brooke for his mistress? Despite his suffering and the ghastly gown she wore, he couldn't pry his gaze from her pretty face.

Yes, confound it to hell and back again. He did. Why did he want her when any number of females would eagerly warm his bed? He'd address that particular after he determined her guilt. However, everything about her demeanor this moment screamed innocence.

"Where is the chamber you're putting him in?" Leventhorpe's grip tightened. "He's about to collapse."

Acting his overbearing self, as usual. Bossy as an old tabby.

"I am not." Heath took another swaying step.

Brooke whirled to stare at him. Sincere concern shimmered in her dark-lashed eyes, or else she was the best damned actress he'd seen in a long while. Better than that petite morsel he'd contemplated making his paramour. Compared to Brooke, the other woman seemed a tawdry tart.

"Do you need to be carried, my lord?" She wiggled her forefinger, beckoning the stable hands enter who'd followed them to the house.

"No. I am not going to collapse." Wouldn't do to have Brooke think him a weakling. That he cared an iota about her opinion of him gave testament to how hard he'd been whacked. Dashed the sense out of him.

"Stubble it, Ravensdale." Leventhorpe adjusted his support as he assisted Heath up the risers. "A ninety-year old, one-legged crone leans on her cane less than you're hanging on me."

Mabry grunted his agreement. "Not a light cove either."

"True, Mr. Mabry." Leventhorpe hoisted Heath higher. "You might consider a slimming regimen, Raven."

"Shut up, Trist," Heath all but growled, past caring what anyone thought of him. Flecks darted and danced before his eyes. He needed to lie down. At once.

Upstairs, Mabry took his leave, although Heath insisted he didn't need a physician.

"Nevertheless, my lord, I think it wise to have you examined." Brooke fluffed a pillow on the turned-down bed. Uncertainty clouded her indigo eyes. Her gaze flitted to Leventhorpe before she exchanged a telling glance with Blythe. Leventhorpe unnerved her. Good. She wasn't likely to try another stunt with Trist looming over her.

Her cap askew, a timid maid limped into the chamber. Arms twig thin and her gaze riveted on the floor, she bore a wooden tray laden with a teapot, cup, steaming bowl of something scrumptious smelling, two slices of bread, butter, and a spoon and napkin.

His stomach growled when he inhaled the heady aroma.

Brooke cast him a disconcerted glance then gave the servant a kind smile. "Thank you, Flora. Please set it on the table, there."

She pointed to a three-legged table near the toasty fire in the hearth.

Heath held his breath as Flora shuffled to the table, the tray wobbling with each awkward step. She had one leg shorter than the other. He inspected her shoes. A cobbler could build up the left sole, and she would walk much easier. Not a priority when money at Esherton appeared scarcer than frost in Hades.

"Need anythin' else, Miss Brooke?" Head cocked to the side, Flora peeped upward through stubby eyelashes and played with the stringy strand of hair that had escaped her cap.

Brooke offered another encouraging smile. "No. You may go. Make sure you eat luncheon today. You forgot again yesterday."

"I'll do it now." Flora hobbled out the door, leaving it open behind her.

Heath stared at Brooke's lips. What would they taste like? Sweet or fruity?

Why did she have him obsessing over every part of her anatomy? He could find no fault in her appearance, from her oval face, perfectly sculpted rose-pink lips, dove-white hair, surprisingly dark, winged brows, and thick lashes framing astonishing purple-blue eyes to her creamy skin, breasts he guaranteed would overflow his palms, and a backside that begged to be fondled and ridden.

Must be the injury to his head—had him waxing raunchy poppycock.

Leventhorpe propelled him toward the bed, and after urging Heath to sit, tugged off his boots and tossed them on the floor. Arms folded, Leventhorpe perched a hip on the arm of an overstuffed chair beside the bed.

Clearly exasperated, Blythe faced him, hands on her hips. "My lord, your presence isn't needed. Why don't you wait in the study?"

"Good idea." Brooke nodded her agreement as she dipped a cloth into a basin of water. "I shall come down and answer your questions when Lord Ravensdale's hunger is appeased and he is resting comfortably."

Which hunger?

Heath must've made a noise—*Good God, did I say that aloud?*—for Brooke frowned, and Leventhorpe let loose a hearty guffaw.

"I'm staying." Leventhorpe looked down his superior nose, something he'd perfected over the years to put underlings in their place. One look usually sufficed to send the offender dashing for cover.

Blythe rolled her eyes heavenward, muttering, "Of course you are, obstinate bore."

"I heard that." Leventhorpe removed his gloves then his hat and tossed the lot on the chair's torn cushion.

Blythe offered a syrupy smile. "You were meant to."

He chuckled, and Heath speared him a sharp glance. A roguish grin lingered on Leventhorpe's face. Not a typical reaction from his reticent friend. As Brooke went about removing Heath's greatcoat and jacket, Leventhorpe looked on.

Every innocent brush of her hand or bump of her arm stoked Heath's awareness of her. She bent to her task, and her bodice gapped. He itched to touch the flesh his eyes caressed, but forced his focus away, all too aware they had an audience. Perusing the rather dusty chamber, he caught the sardonic curling of Leventhorpe's mouth.

Brooke tossed the overcoat to the foot of the bed and turned her attention to his jacket. She released the top button. Did her fingers tremble the merest bit?

"I can undress myself," he said, though the way the bedchamber weaved up and down, he wasn't at all certain he could.

Leventhorpe stopped scrutinizing the room—or was it Blythe that he studied?—to quirk a brow at Heath. "Of course you can, but let her fuss over you anyway."

Heath's neckcloth came next. He hated the confounded things. Always felt half-choked, but gentlemen of the *ton* didn't go about with their necks exposed.

"Lie back, my lord." Brooke passed the strip of cloth to her cousin.

At her prompting, Heath reclined against the pillows, and once he'd settled, she drew the bedcoverings to his waist. The pounding in his head lessened to a steady pulsing, and the chamber ceased to dip and sway like a ship on stormy seas.

Her lower lip clamped between her pink lips, she dabbed at the cut on his face.

He inhaled her fresh fragrance. A mole peeked at him from the right side of her neck, and he longed to kiss the small dot then explore the long swan-like column with his lips. The décolletage of her gown hinted at the lush swells of flesh it partially concealed. Would her nipples be pert and rosy or ripe and pink? Unbidden images of him laving her succulent tips with his tongue bombarded him.

His manhood jerked, momentarily stirring the bedcovers.

Busy spreading a pleasant-smelling salve on the scratch, Brooke didn't notice. He hoped. Irritated at his lack of control, and to keep from embarrassing himself, he turned a bland stare on Leventhorpe. The wicked twinkle in his friend's eye said plainly that *he* had noticed. "I don't need you mothering me, Trist. Go below and find someone to pester."

Leventhorpe yawned behind his hand and blinked drowsily. He looked done in. Likely he'd never sought his bed when Heath didn't return last night.

"I've no intention of mothering you, Raven. Removing your boots is the extent of my nurturing skills, I assure you." He inclined his head toward the women. "I'm making sure one of these sirens doesn't slide a knife between your ribs to finish the job."

Harsh gasps escaped the women.

Fury snapped in Blythe's eyes, but censure shimmered in Brooke's.

Bristling with indignation, Blythe whirled to Leventhorpe. Voice quivering, she stabbed a finger at him. "How dare you? We've been nothing but hospitable to Lord Ravensdale, and your ugly insinuations—"

Brooke touched Blythe's arm. "He has the right to worry about his friend."

Blythe pursed her lips and lowered her gaze. "But he doesn't have the right to accuse us of such evilness."

"I agree, but Duffen is in our employ." Brooke's gaze rested on Heath. "If he is responsible—"

Heath gave a derisive snort and paid the price as pain kicked its hind feet against his skull. "He is responsible. He deceived me into helping him then clobbered me with a brick when I turned my back."

"Then we must make things right." Her steady gaze met his. Nonetheless, he swore dread lingered in the depths of her unusual eyes. "It's the honorable thing to do."

My God, so convincing. She even had him believing her theatrics. He observed her through half-closed eyes. Unless this wasn't a performance. Perhaps he'd wronged her, and she hadn't been behind Duffen's actions. Difficult to believe, but perhaps the gnome truly had acted of his own volition.

Some of the tension eased from Heath.

Duffen, on the other hand, was in it up to his eyeballs. Did he understand the consequences of his misplaced bravado? Imprisonment or worse if Heath brought charges against him. And Leventhorpe would insist upon it.

Brette hustled into the chamber, the corgi on her heels.

Upon spotting Leventhorpe, the stout canine skidded to a halt. His nostrils flared and twitched before he crouched and skulked to hide beneath the draperies. Leventhorpe's mouth slanted downward, and he scratched his nose. He regarded the snout visible under the frayed window coverings.

Heath pressed his fingertips to the knot behind his head. Dogs usually adored Leventhorpe, but Freddy had clearly taken an aversion to him.

Breathless and pushing a damp lock off her forehead, Brette made straight for her sister. "We found Duffen. He's in a bad way."

Brooke paled and clutched the cloth she'd been tending Heath's scratch with.

"And, Brooke, Rogers has returned from the Benbridges." Panting, Brette tossed Heath an anxious glance.

Who's Rogers?

Brooke dropped the wet rag into the basin before reaching for a dry towel.

Heath breathed a mite easier, grateful for the reprieve. Her hovering over him, her breasts and lips mere inches away...pure torment.

"Rogers isn't alone," Brette added.

Blythe turned from the teapot, giving Brette a puzzled stare. "He's not? Did Mr. Benbridge accompany him?"

A nonplussed expression swept Brooke's face.

"Did Mrs. Benbridge and Josephina come to call? It isn't like them not to send a note round first." She shook her head and tossed the towel aside. "I cannot possibly receive them at the moment. We haven't any tea left, and with Lord Ravensdale and Duffen—"

"No, Brooke." Brette drew nearer and clasped her sister's hand. "Humphrey's here. In the drawing room."

Man is a gaming animal by nature, which is
why he'll make foolish wagers against impossible
odds and still remain convinced he'll come out ahead.
~Wisdom and Advice—The Genteel Lady's Guide to Practical Living

Grateful for the interruption in her ministrations to Lord Ravensdale,
Brooke would've hugged Brette if her news hadn't been so
horrendous.

Touching and smelling him, gazing into his gold-flecked irises
scant inches away rattled her senses and strained her composure past
endurance. His tense muscles had bunched and twitched while she
undressed him, tantalizing her wickedly. The tautness of his jaw and
erratic breathing suggested she had affected him as much. Yet he'd
uttered not a sound apart from one gravelly groan—quickly silenced—
when she'd brushed his torso while unbuttoning his coat.

A shiver of desire had rippled from her breasts to the juncture of
her thighs at the guttural noise. What kind of woman lusted after an
injured man, and one who sought to deprive her of her home? Perhaps
she'd lost her faculties. Perhaps the strain of running the farm and
caring for her sister and cousins had addled her at long last.

Add that to the tidings that Humphrey had returned from abroad,
and at this moment waited below stairs, and she teetered on the verge of
hysterical laughter or frenzied weeping.

Humphrey? For the love of God. Why now?

Could anything else possibly happen to make this day more
calamitous?

Brooke took a steadying breath. First things first.

"Where did you find Duffen?"

"In the carriage house. The earl's horse is there too. He's fine, my
lord," Brette assured Lord Ravensdale. She spared Lord Leventhorpe a
brief glance. "Oh, and I had your mount taken there as well. The barns

are full of cattle at present."

Both men murmured thank you, and Lord Ravensdale smoothed the bedding over his lap, as if uncomfortable or in pain.

Guilt prodded her.

"Most wise." Brooke searched her sister's pale face and stricken eyes. She wouldn't be this distraught if matters weren't grave. "What's wrong with Duffen? Does he need a physician as well?"

God's bones, how could she afford a physician's fee for two patients? Her remaining finances dwindled faster than ale in a hot tap room full of thirsty sailors.

On the cusp of tears, Brette nodded. "I think he's had an apoplexy. He cannot move or speak."

Voice breaking, she covered her face and wept.

Dear God.

The day just worsened considerably.

"Losing his home has been too much for him." Her back to the men, Brooke shut her eyes and pressed a palm against her forehead where a vicious beating had begun.

It's been too much for me too.

She sensed the lords' contemplative gazes trained on her and lowered her hand. Had they any notion of the havoc their presence wreaked on this household? Drawing on the last dregs of her composure and fortitude, she schooled her face. She mustn't show signs of feminine weakness, for Lord Ravensdale must be convinced of her ability to operate the farm.

Let it go, Brooke. That dream has died a drawn out, excruciating death.

If only she could turn the clock back to yesterday. Relive the past twenty-four horrific hours. Somehow, some way change the course of destiny.

"See to your man and your guest, Miss Culpepper. I'll stay here until the physician arrives." Lord Leventhorpe spoke to Brooke, yet his attention remained focused on Blythe pouring a cup of tea. He yawned again.

Perhaps a thimbleful of humanity warmed the marquis's blood after all.

"I'll even feed him," Leventhorpe offered with a sly twist of his lips.

"You bloody well will not." Lord Ravensdale levered himself more upright, his shirt rumpling at the neck and exposing a delicious expanse of hairy chest. "I can feed myself."

Brooke swallowed and tore her focus from the black, springy curls. What had she done to deserve such unholy torture? Shouldn't an adversary be reviled? Not in her case. She flitted around him like a moth to a flame. Stupid. Fatal.

"Go, stay with Duffen. Keep him calm and comfortable." Brooke gave Brette a swift hug. "Tell him I'll come as soon as I'm able. Doctor Wilton should be here within the hour."

Wiping her eyes and face, Brette gave a sharp inclination of her head and swept from the room.

Brooke gathered the bowl, napkin, and spoon. How could a man's muscled chest be so devilishly tempting? And why did she notice when disaster raged around them? *Stupid question.* He'd mesmerized her, that's why.

Brooke jerked her gaze to Blythe. "Please go with her. Duffen may need your herbal tea too."

"Of course, although if he's had an apoplexy, I don't want to give him anything until the doctor examines him." Blythe carried the teacup to Lord Ravensdale, seemingly oblivious to his lordship's physical charms. "Sip this slowly. It will ease your stomach. I'm sorry, but I cannot give you anything for your headache until you've seen Doctor Wilton. It's unwise if you have a concussion."

"Thank you." Lord Ravensdale sniffed the light brew. "May I ask what kind it is? It smells minty."

"It is. We grow three kinds of mint at Esherton. It's a favorite of the villagers." She flashed Lord Leventhorpe a mocking glance. "Should I taste it first, my lord? Aren't you worried I might try to poison Lord Ravensdale?"

Those two rubbed each other the wrong way—like flint and steel, sparks and all. Their immediate and intense dislike hadn't lessened a jot.

His lordship moved his hat and gloves to the floor then edged onto the chair's seat. Lines of exhaustion creased the corners of his eyes. He crossed his legs at the knee and, elbows resting on the chair's arms, tented his fingers together. "I regret my earlier accusation. I'm sure the brew is perfectly harmless."

Blythe paused at the threshold, her scrutiny shifting between the men. Her features strained, she searched Brooke's face. "Do you want me to stay with you until you've seen our unexpected guest?"

Bless her. Blythe understood how awkward the encounter with Humphrey would likely be. Brooke shook her head, though facing Humphrey alone after these many years had her palms damp and pulse skittering. "No. Duffen is more important."

"If you're certain." Misgiving resonated in Blythe's voice. Nevertheless, she took her leave after another scathing scowl at Lord Leventhorpe.

Brooke passed Lord Ravensdale the soup, deliberately keeping her attention on his forehead. Her traitorous eyeballs kept trying to sneak a peek lower. "Be careful, my lord. It's hot."

"I'm neither an invalid nor a lackwit, Miss Culpepper." He regarded the cup and bowl he held. "Am I to hold and consume the tea and soup at once?"

Heat singed her face. Ungrateful cur. She bit her tongue. *Be gracious.* No sense riling the ornery bear further.

"No, of course not." She accepted the teacup he extended and, after moving a lamp aside, set it upon the bedside table within his reach.

His rancor took Brooke aback and cooled her ardor as effectively as diving naked into a snow drift. He couldn't be too bad off if he was this disagreeable, could he? She fussed with the items on the nightstand. "I'll return as soon as I know Duffen's condition and see my guest on his way."

She rounded the end of the bed, but paused halfway to the door.

Except for his wan face and a pinched look about his mouth, Lord Ravensdale didn't appear too incapacitated. The pulse in his corded neck beat rhythmically as he regarded her, his countenance indecipherable. A healthy brute like him ought to recover quickly, oughtn't he?

"Please believe me, I honestly had no notion of Duffen's actions." She clasped her hands, when Ravensdale only blinked, his face an impassive mask. Didn't he believe her? More disconcertingly, what did he intend to do when the magistrate arrived? "I am horrified you've been harmed. I pray you recover swiftly."

He slanted his dark head but remained stone-faced and silent.

Hope shrank. Not quite ready to forgive and forget. Not that she blamed him, entirely. She'd be hard-pressed to muster a speck of compassion for a bounder who cracked her on the noggin.

"Who's Humphrey?" Lord Ravensdale's quiet question

reverberated as explosive as a cannon in the silent room.

Nearly out the door, she halted and looked over her shoulder. He held her gaze captive as his, accusing and condemning, scraped over her. Leventhorpe appeared to have dozed off, but roused himself to crack an eye open and peer her way.

Busybody.

Her hand on the doorjamb, she whispered, "He's the man I almost married."

Brooke flew down the corridor, Lord Ravensdale's astounded expression etched in her brain. What? Didn't he think her capable of having a beau? Was she too old and unappealing in her cast-off gown that the notion stretched the extremes of his imagination?

The idea hurt more than it ought. Lord Ravensdale's opinion of her shouldn't matter a jot, but confound it all, it did. She sighed. Upstairs lay a man who fascinated her beyond common sense and shouldn't even cause her to bat an eyelash, and below waited a man she should be eager to see, but wasn't.

Humphrey.

Brooke descended the stairway, in no hurry to reach the drawing room. Shouldn't she be more excited at the prospect of seeing him again? She'd loved him beyond reason at one time. Now she felt nothing more than warm sentiment at seeing an old friend. Why had he come, anyway? Could he still harbor a morsel of affection for her?

Her heart fluttered.

Excitement or trepidation? It mattered not. Her circumstances remained much the same, except Papa no longer lived, and paupers claimed deeper pockets than she.

She couldn't wed Humphrey, not unless he could accept the whole bundle that came with her. Why didn't the idea of becoming his wife hold the thrill it once had? Hold up there. Putting the cart before the horse, wasn't she? His visit could be attributed to any number of reasons, and jumping to conclusions generally led to trouble.

What if he had married or was betrothed?

No, his sister would have mentioned it.

Unless either had occurred recently. Possible. Brooke hadn't seen Josephina in weeks. Almost...almost as if she'd been avoiding the Culpeppers.

Nonsense and rot. Goodness. See what fatigue and an overactive imagination wrought.

Unease slowing her steps, Brooke approached the open double doors. She could do this. Taking a bracing breath, she painted a bright smile on her face and silently entered the same room in which she'd told Humphrey she couldn't marry him.

Unaware of her presence, he stared out the window's narrow leaded glass window. Sunlight played across his features, emphasizing his perfect profile. A crimson riding coat strained across his broad shoulders. Cream pantaloons, tucked into boots, hugged muscular thighs. He held his hat in his right hand and, every once in a while, tapped it against his leg.

"Hello, Humphrey."

He spun to face her.

The same, but different.

He'd filled out, become more striking in a mature man-of-the-world sort of way. His tawny blond hair and hazel eyes hadn't changed. Neither had the charming smile that brightened his suntanned face upon seeing her.

His appreciative gaze stroked her, and then he hurried across the room, his boots rapping a sharp staccato on the bare floor. He lifted her fingers to his warm lips and pressed a light kiss to the knuckles. Scandalous to touch his mouth to an unmarried woman's bare hand, but this man had kissed her lips, so pretending shock would be pointless.

The top of her head and his were almost level. She'd never noticed that before. Probably due to the recent acquaintance of the two towering Titans above stairs.

"Brooke. Even lovelier than I remembered." Humphrey clasped her hand, joy shimmering in his eyes. Her insides gave a strange quiver. "I've missed you, more than words can express. Please accept my belated condolences for the loss of your father."

"Thank you. I miss him still." Moisture glazed her eyes for a moment, not only for Papa's early death, but for what she and Humphrey had lost, and what could never be. She forced a cheerful smile. "So, what brings you to Esherton today? I must say, I was quite surprised to hear you had paid a call."

He offered a sheepish grin, reminding her of the shy, young man who'd courted her.

"I was with Father when your note arrived. I begged him to allow me the honor of responding in person. He and Mother request your company—and the others too, of course—for tea tomorrow at three o'clock." He passed her the invitation, a scented piece of fine stationery. "We'll send the carriage round for you."

He chuckled, the familiar melodic rumble warming her troubled heart. "When I left, Josephina had interrupted her preparations for London to make a list of sweets she wanted Cook to prepare."

"London?" Bother it all. The London Season. The Benbridges usually departed after the calving ended. Brooke had contacted Mr. Benbridge just in time.

"Yes. My sister is determined to snare herself a husband this Season. My aunt has suggested that a certain marquis would be a brilliant match, poor chap." Humphrey peered behind her. "Where are the others? Josephina said you're all unmarried, as impossible as that is for me to believe. Given your uncommon beauty, I must wonder at the lack of intelligence of the eligible men in the area."

What men? Your arrival home brings the total to precisely one.

Shouldn't she feel a rush of pleasure at his compliment instead of this slight edginess?

He caressed her palm with his thumb. "I'm delighted you didn't find another to take my place in your heart."

There it is.

Her pulse gave a happy little skip, despite her misgivings. His glowing eyes and appreciative smile provided a much needed salve to her chafed womanly confidence. A pair of seductive, black-lashed eyes, a hint of cynicism flashing in their depths, rudely intruded upon the special occasion. She kicked them aside, much the same way she would a mouse attempting to scurry up her skirts. Lord Ravensdale would not rob her of this moment.

"I'm afraid we've had a pair of unfortunate events since I sent my letter round this morning. I'm awaiting the physician's arrival." Brooke gently withdrew her hand from his and then clasped hers together.

Humphrey frowned, genuine concern creasing his forehead. Such a kind man. "What's happened? Is it your sister, or one of your cousins?"

"No, they are fine, but Duffen—you remember him, don't you?"

"Indeed, I do." Humphrey nodded. "Who could forget that crusty devil?"

Brooke gave a half-smile. "Unfortunately, we think he's had an apoplexy. Brette and Blythe are tending him."

"Most unfortunate." He cupped her elbow. No rush of pleasure accompanied his touch.

"You said a pair of events. What else has happened to distress you?" Humphrey laid a finger on her cheek. "I see the anxiety in your eyes and in the stiff way you hold yourself when you're distraught."

He did know her so very well. Comfortable and safe. He'd always made her feel that way. Not disjointed and tumultuous and confused and...tingly, like the growly beast upstairs did.

"A visitor to Esherton has been injured. He's with his friend above stairs waiting for the doctor to examine him as well."

She couldn't tell Humphrey of Duffen's perfidy. Or that the most alarmingly attractive man she'd ever laid eyes upon now owned the farm, leaving them paupers. Or that two powerful peers occupied her parents' bedroom, and what they might do to her and Duffen turned her spit to dust and stopped the blood in her veins.

"Visitor? A beau?" Humphrey scratched his jaw, appearing a bit uneasy...or jealous?

Ridiculous. He'd been gone five years and hadn't once written to indicate he yet harbored feelings for her. And she wasn't naive enough to think he'd played the part of a monk during that time. Brooke waved her hand and gave a short shake of her head. "No, no, nothing of that nature. He's curious about the dairy operation, that's all."

Ravensdale did have an interest in Esherton's dairy, in a manner of speaking.

Humphrey darted a glance to the window. "You do have some of the finest cattle in the area."

Brooke suppressed a smile. She knew more about distilling whisky than he did about milk cows. He'd never possessed a desire to step into his father's and grandfather's shoes, even if they had become vulgarly wealthy producing the most coveted cheese in all of England.

"What's the nature of his injury?" His regard sank to the expanse of rounded flesh visible above her bodice, and Brooke stifled an urge to tug the neckline higher.

"I'm afraid," Lord Ravensdale said, "I suffered a rather nasty crack to the base of my skull."

Brooke gasped and whirled to face the entrance.

He stood in his stockings, buckskins, and gaping shirt, looking for all the world like the man of the house. Pain darkened his eyes to jet and ringed his mouth in a tense, white line.

The idiot. Brooke feared he'd plop onto his face at any moment. Serve him right, odious man, except he'd probably sustain another injury and blame her. My God, all she needed was for Ravensdale to injure himself further while in her home.

Surely that's what she felt, worry he'd further injure himself, nothing more.

Humphrey's eyes widened as he took in his lordship's dishabille. Gentlemen did not present themselves half-dressed and shoeless. He flashed Brooke a bewildered look. Nonetheless, good breeding and faultless manners prevailing, he bowed.

"Humphrey Benbridge, at your service."

Always the proper, irreproachable, *predictable* gentleman. Where had that unbidden thought sprouted?

Humphrey clasped her hand and raised it to his lips again, almost as if claiming her. Silly man. He needn't worry Lord Ravensdale contended for her affections. A flush heated her cheeks at the absurd notion.

"You must be the visitor Miss Culpepper spoke of. She and I are old, and very dear, friends." Humphrey gave her a jaunty smile and a conspiratorial wink. "And I hope to become much more in the near future."

What? Seriously? He just waltzed in here after five years and wanted to take up where they'd left off? *The gall.*

"Isn't that so, Brooke?" He attempted to draw her to his side, a possessive gleam in his eyes and a challenge firming his jaw. "Our time apart has been quite unbearable."

Yes, and that was why he'd corresponded regularly and hurried home at the first opportunity. Brooke nearly gnashed her teeth at his forwardness and posturing, but instead schooled her features into what she prayed resembled composure. "Mr. Benbridge, may I introduce you to Esherton Green's guest, Heath, Earl of Ravensdale?"

A suitable expression of awe skittered across Humphrey's boyish face. Like his parents, men of rank and prestige easily impressed him. Foolish. A title didn't automatically signify good character. This very moment, Esherton housed two examples attesting to that fact.

Humphrey bent into another fawning bow. "It's an honor, your lordship."

Such shallowness rubbed Brooke the wrong way, and the momentary happiness at seeing her old friend faded.

Lord Ravensdale inclined his head the merest bit, likely afraid further movement would part his head from his shoulders, the fool.

Where was that dimwit Lord Leventhorpe? Why had he let the earl out of bed?

Ravensdale sauntered forward, his movements measured.

To the casual observer, he appeared confident and relaxed. Brooke, however, recognized someone struggling to disguise their pain with self-assured cockiness. The set of his jaw, taut shoulders, closed hands, and straight line of his brows all screeched pain. She wasn't catching him if he plunged to the floor. He deserved to be knocked halfway to senseless. Once again, she withdrew her hand from Humphrey's, her gaze trained on his lordship the whole while.

What was he about? Why torture himself by leaving his bed when he obviously suffered?

Lord Ravensdale folded his arms and rested an entirely-too-muscled shoulder against the fireplace. His ebony gaze slashed between her and Humphrey. The predatory glint smoldering in the depths of his eyes hitched her breath and raised the hair at her nape. The urge to flee the room overwhelmed her. Instead, she dug her toes into her boots and defied him with her gaze.

Lord Ravensdale placed a hand at the back of his head.

He's in pain.

His handsome mouth inched upward. "Well, this is rather awkward."

What was?

"How so?" Puzzlement replaced Humphrey's friendly smile. He shot her a questioning glance.

She raised her eyebrows and inched a shoulder upward then angled her head, scrutinizing the earl. She hadn't a clue what he blathered about.

His lordship's magnetic gaze held Brooke's in silent warning. "Brooke's my mistress. Aren't you, love?"

Wagers gone awry at the gaming table
turn friends into foes and lovers into enemies.
~Wisdom and Advice—The Genteel Lady's Guide to Practical Living

13

Four days later, wrapped once again in the tattered throw and wearing her gray gown, Brooke leaned against the barn and gazed into the far pasture. Blast, but she wished she could call Ravensdale, the rakehell, out for his scurrilous declaration.

Whirring wings and vibrant plumage announced a cock pheasant's taking wing. A refreshing breeze teased the loose curls framing Brooke's face and set the blushing pink cuckoo flowers bordering a marshy patch to swaying. The morning sun's rays caressed her upturned face.

She would freckle.

She didn't care. Let her fair skin turn bread crust-brown and wrinkled as a crone's.

A few minutes ago, Mabry had let the dappled black-and-white newborns into the paddock for the first time. They explored the thick green grass, never straying too far from their mothers' sides. Occasionally, a frisky calf approached another curious baby, and they'd frolic a few minutes, butting heads and kicking up their heels, before a soft, maternal moo had them skipping to the safety of their anxious parents.

Buford had sired fourteen calves, including a set of twins.

Fourteen, four, or forty, it mattered not.

Not anymore.

There would be no more calves bred at Esherton. At least not beneath her watch.

Most of her hard-earned notes lined Doctor Wilton's pocket, and the rest would soon follow as he returned daily to check his patients' progress. Despair unlike Brooke had ever experienced sank its ruthless talons into her fragile heart and her little remaining hope, tearing them into lifeless shreds.

Two evenings ago, after the magistrate had finally arrived and attempted to question him, Duffen suffered another seizure and lapsed into unconsciousness. Doctor Wilton didn't expect him to survive until nightfall, which meant she'd never know why the servant attacked the earl. Perhaps a misguided notion about protecting the women had coiled, serpent-like, around his fragile mind until the pressure meshed reality with delusion.

She shut her eyes against the disturbing image of him lying, frail and frightened, on his narrow cot. People would do all manner of reprehensible things when driven by desperation. To protect those they loved. She'd already forgiven Duffen for the harm he'd caused, but suspected hard-hearted Lord Ravensdale never would.

No, not hard-hearted. Distant and reserved more aptly described him. An impenetrable shell encompassed the earl. Except his keen eyes. Emotions glittered there, most of which stripped her bare, leaving her vulnerable and uncertain. Yet, she yearned to find a way through his hard exterior, to see if, as she suspected, the man within was warm and caring.

He'd suffered a serious concussion and wasn't permitted anything more strenuous than lifting a fork for a week. His alarmingly brief consultation with the magistrate had Brooke fretting about what they'd discussed. The doctor admitted he'd told Lord Ravensdale that, had his injury been any lower, his lordship would likely have died.

God. Brooke opened her eyes, blinking several times to focus in the glaring sun.

However, Doctor Wilton also reassured her that if the earl obeyed his orders, he would make a full recovery. After his preposterous declaration in the drawing room, he'd fainted dead way, and only Humphrey's quick reflexes had prevented the earl from splitting his head on the cracked tile hearth. He and Leventhorpe—who'd stumbled in half-crazed with worry upon awaking and finding Ravensdale missing—carried Ravensdale upstairs, where he still remained.

Humphrey made his escape shortly thereafter, promising to extend another invitation to tea when things returned to normal at Esherton.

That would be never.

He breathed not a word about Lord Ravensdale's ludicrous declaration, but his gaze, hurt and betrayed, accused her just the same.

Had there been a glimmer, an iota of a chance for reconciliation between her and Humphrey, the earl had successfully snuffed that light out and thrust her into bleak darkness once more.

Heaven help her if Humphrey believed the preposterous lie, bandied the falsehood about, told his parents and sister...

He would. Without a doubt.

Social status meant everything to the Benbridges. They'd want no further association with her. Any hope of help or advice from them had gone up in tiny cinders when she burned the unopened tea invitation.

No, when his lordship let loose the colossal lie.

Brooke shuddered and tugged the shawl tighter.

She cared not for her reputation—well, perhaps that wasn't entirely true, but naught could be done for that besmirched travesty at this point—but the quartet's characters could be tarnished by association with her. Rumors that she'd become a kept woman, factual or not, further damaged any hope of them making respectable matches.

Damn the earl. Damn him for winning Esherton and being so eager to sell the farm. Damn him for the wily game he played. And double damn the attraction she felt for him.

Had he given no consideration to the number of lives he ruined with his fabrication? Mistress indeed. As if she'd ever agree to such a sordid arrangement. What in blazes did he hope to gain by sullying her? She sighed and pursed her mouth. Perhaps her ruination had been his sole intent. A perfectly executed revenge for an offense he presumed her responsible for.

Furious beyond civility, she'd left his care to the others, refusing to see him, even when he requested her presence. Then demanded it.

She wasn't a servant he could order about at his whim. Yet, a part of her desperately longed to check on Ravensdale. To brush his hair from his forehead, touch his warm skin, make sure he fared well. Bah, she was hopeless.

When had her emotions become so fickle?

Since she paid his fee, the physician reported the earl's progress to her daily. Seemed his lordship possessed the constitution of a draft horse and the temperament of caged lion, and he'd be up and about—and hopefully, on his bloody way—in no time.

Leventhorpe had forcefully let it be known he had no intention of vacating the premises until his friend could travel. To his credit, the marquis had sent for food and clothing. Likely the sparse meal he dined on the first night, more watery stew, thinly-sliced bread, and a complete absence of spirits of any kind, had alerted him to the desperate condition of Esherton Green's barren larder.

Every able-bodied man had spent the next morning clearing the road to the house. By early afternoon, a path wide enough for a carriage to pass through had been opened and a wagon had arrived, stuffed with food and other supplies, accompanied by not one, but two coaches. A pair of haughty valets, three plump, giggling maids, a monstrous black groomsmen, two footmen—who appeared to be twins and set Blaike and Blaire atwitter—and a French chef, Leroux, had streamed from the conveyances.

For the first time in years, Esherton boasted a full staff and larder. Beside herself with glee, Mrs. Jennings hadn't stopped grinning, despite her missing front teeth.

At least everyone had plenty to fill their stomachs now, except that Brooke possessed no appetite. Worry tended to rob one of the desire to eat, even if the menu boasted the most elaborate meals the household had ever known.

The house overflowed with people, and no room had less than three occupants at any given time. Servants slept in the halls, for pity's sake, hence Brooke's sojourn to the stables for few a moments of much-needed solitude. She'd told no one of her destination, needing a place to grieve in peace.

Fragile as her tattered dignity, her facade of poise and self-control threatened to shatter with her next breath. She rested her head against the barn's splintery wood. In less than a week, her life had crumbled to dust. A fat tear crept down her cheek. Then another. And another.

They poured forth as wrenching sobs worked their way past her constricted throat. Awash in misery, Brooke pressed a length of the shawl to her mouth, shut her eyes, and tucked her chin to her chest, at last giving vent to her desolation.

"Here now, there's no cause for waterworks," Lord Ravensdale's baritone rasped as he enfolded her in his strong arms. He rested his chin upon her crown. "Hush, sweetheart. Things aren't entirely hopeless."

"Yes. They are. Completely and absolutely. You've ruined everything," she whispered against the wall of his chest. She should pull away. Curse him to Hades and hell. Plant him a facer or yank out his splendid hair by the roots.

Instead, she burrowed closer, wrapped her arms around his waist, and wept like an inconsolable infant. Strong and sensible had become wearisome, and she was exhausted from the burden she'd carried for years. So tired of worrying and scraping to make ends meet.

His scent wrapped around her senses, soothing and reassuring as he rubbed her spine and shoulders. Long moments passed, and calm enshrouded her at last. She released a shuddery sigh.

Lord Ravensdale placed a long finger beneath her chin and tilted her face upward. He kissed each tear-stained cheek then her nose, likely red as a pie cherry. Lowering his mouth until it hovered a mere inch above hers, he closed his eyes. He grazed her lips, his warm and firm, at first feather light then more insistent, demanding a response.

Her resistance fled. Moaning, she slanted her head and allowed him the entrance his probing tongue sought. Heaven surged through her, melting her bones, bathing her in a haze of sweet sensation. Humphrey's kisses hadn't been anything more than mildly pleasant, not this mind-wrenching, searing blast of desire.

A cow bawled, and Brooke tore her mouth from Heath's. Head lowered, she stepped from his embrace and dried her damp face on the wrap. She braved flashing him a glance.

Hatless, his black hair gleaming in the sunlight, he wore a sky blue jacket and white pantaloons. Brilliant colors to emphasize his olive skin. He lounged against the barn, ankles crossed and arms folded, looking the perfect picture of health. Perhaps a little wan about his wickedly dark eyes—definitely some foreign blood there somewhere—but otherwise, his handsome self. The scratch on his cheek had faded to a slender brownish ribbon. He observed her every move, those intense eyes of his missing nothing. Like his namesake, the raven.

Why must he be so blasted attractive?

Why did she react the way she did in his presence? To his kisses? She'd never dreamed a kiss could scatter her wits to the stars.

He gave a knowing smile, as if he'd read her thoughts. A man of his caliber and experience probably knew exactly what his kisses did to her.

Adjusting the shawl, Brooke swiveled to gaze at the calves again. Better than making a spectacle of herself. A few strands of hair had worked loose when she'd hugged his chest, and the breeze blew them into her face. She swept the tendrils behind her ear. She should say something, anything, to break the awkward, sensual silence between them.

"What are you doing out of bed? You're not supposed to be up for another three days."

She could have bitten her tongue in half for asking. It was nothing to her if he chose to ignore the physician's orders.

Liar.

"I couldn't stand one minute more confined to that room or Leventhorpe's incessant fussing. My God, who knew the man was such a nervous old biddy?" He chuckled, the low rumble sending delicious tingles along her flesh. "You'd think I'd nearly died."

She glanced over her shoulder then pushed the bothersome strands flitting across her face from her eyes. "You could have. Doctor Wilton said as much."

His lordship grinned, and her stomach lurched peculiarly. Ought to have broken her fast. Needed her wits to banter with the crafty likes of him. Why had he sought her here, anyway? To steal a kiss?

Theirs had been no stolen kiss but given freely.

He tapped his head as his long strides carried him to her side. "No, too stubborn and too hard-headed to cock up my toes. At least that's what my friends tell me."

"Hmph." She wasn't about to dispute his assertion. Add arrogant and indulged to the list too. Oh, and fabricator of enormous taradiddles designed to ruin innocent young women. She compressed her lips, her earlier feelings of magnanimity giving way to irritation.

"So, Brooke, what are we to do?"

"Pardon?" Holding her wayward hair in place, Brooke leveled him an inquisitive look.

Hands clasped behind him, he stared straight ahead. He could do whatever he pleased. She, on the other hand, had as many options as a condemned woman standing on the gallows with a noose tightened round her neck.

He levered away from the barn.

"I'm aware how dire your circumstances are." He flicked her an unreadable expression before boldly tucking a tress behind her ear.

Sensation spiraled outward at his soft touch.

He cupped her head, gently caressing the sensitive area below her ear.

She clenched her jaw against the sigh, or rather the purr, which had the impudence to try to leave her mouth.

He is your foe, Brooke.

She peered at him. "And...?"

"I have a suggestion, a proposition to make that would—"

She released such a loud, unladylike snort, two calves venturing near the fence scampered to their mothers. "Hmph, that mistress nonsense? You don't seriously think I'd consider becoming a kept woman? Especially of a man I met just days ago."

She tilted her head to look directly into his eyes. Damn his beautiful, thick-lashed eyes. They turned her knees to porridge and caused peculiar flickers elsewhere too.

Come now, Brooke. You're made of sterner stuff. Where's your backbone?

"Why would *you* want that, my lord? It makes no sense at all. Is this revenge for what Duffen did to you?" She narrowed her eyes and gestured between them. "Your way of punishing me? I told you, I had nothing to do with his idiotic decision to smack you on your hard head."

Lord Ravensdale bent nearer and trailed his fingers along her jaw. "No, I took a fancy to you immediately."

She gasped. Her legs nearly gave way, and her already frayed nerves burst with longing.

His pupils dilated, nearly covering the iris.

With desire? Had hers done the same? Just in case, she averted her gaze. He already held too much power over her. Had the nature of their acquaintance been different, she might have dared pursue the attraction between them. He stirred her like no other. But the lots had been cast and providence hadn't favored her.

"Immediately?" She rearranged her shawl. "Are you always so impetuous?"

"No, but I made the decision to offer you my protection while sitting in the study the day we met. I decided it was the least I could do to rescue you from your circumstances."

Her attention snapped to him. *He's serious.* Did he think she'd thank him for his chivalry?

"I'm quite fond of you already, though I'm sure you'll find that difficult to believe." He smiled tenderly and brushed his thumb across her lower lip. "You'd be well-cared for, and I'd treat you kindly. I would also provide for your family."

Brooke gawked at him, her befuddlement swiftly turning to blistering outrage.

I'll bet you would, you cawker.

"Just like that?" She snapped her fingers in his face.

Startled, he blinked. Did he think she'd leap at his offer? Throw herself at him and cover his face with grateful kisses? Toss up her skirts and let him have his way with her behind the stables?

"I've taken a fancy to her, so I'll make her my fancy piece?" she mocked in imitation of his deep voice. "How magnanimous of you."

He had the audacity to grin, one hand resting on her shoulder.

Blast his handsomeness.

Ooh, if only she were a man... She'd wipe that smug look off his face.

"Of all the brazen, buffleheaded, conceited things I've ever heard, that tips the scales as the most contemptible. Pray tell me what about me makes you think I'm a loose-moraled strumpet?" Tears stung behind her eyelids. Why did he alone make her cry?

"Quite the opposite, Brooke." His focus sank to her mouth. "It's your innocence and purity I find irresistible."

"If that's meant to be a compliment, I assure you, it fell far short of its mark, my lord." She whirled away from him. Her thoughts rattled around in her head like pebbles in a tin when he touched her. Of all the outlandish—

Her innocence and purity? Not after he finished with her.

What an infuriating, insulting man!

She'd wager he hadn't considered her desires...er, mayhap not her desires, but her wants. Drat, not wants either, her needs. Bother and blast, why did everything she think regarding him sound provocative and lust-filled?

Arms crossed, she spun to face him. She had a proposition for him too. Let's see how willing he was to gamble for what he wanted. She had nothing to lose at this juncture.

She'd risk it all, everything she owned.

Lord Ravensdale regarded her calmly. He possessed the upper hand, and the cur knew it.

She clenched her hands, itching to box his ears. "You won the lands in a wager, so you're obviously a gaming man, my lord. Give me the opportunity to win them back. We have nowhere else to go. This is our home, though I'm sure to you it's rather a hovel. But my sister and cousins, we have each other, and we're content with the little we've been granted."

Not precisely true. The girls wanted more, deserved more, as did the servants, but they'd done the best they were able with the pathetic lot God or providence had handed them. Grumbling and complaining only served to ferment bitterness. Mama had always preached thankfulness and contentment. Easier said than done, however.

"And what do you have to wager?" He arched a dubious brow. "I mean no disrespect, but the house and grounds are bereft of anything valuable."

"I have the Culpepper grand parure set. It's worth a sizable sum." Brooke savored the dash of victory his astounded look provided.

His intense gaze chafed her. "And you would wager the jewels, the only thing you have left?"

"I'd hoped to sell them to provide Brette and our cousins with small marriage settlements, but keeping our home is more important." She notched her chin higher. "Besides, I haven't anything else of worth to wager."

"I disagree."

Brooke frowned. "What? Look around you. You can see we've only cast-offs, worn-out and broken furnishings. I don't know if the cattle are mine to sell, and I own no other jewelry. Trust me when I tell you there are no stores of silver or fine art hidden in the attic."

He slowly swept his heated gaze over her then bent his lips into a lazy smile.

"You mean me?" She released a caustic laugh. "You want me to wager my virtue?"

Beware: wagers are war in the guise of sport,
and there can only be one winner.
~Wisdom and Advice—The Genteel Lady's Guide to Practical Living

14

That's precisely what Heath meant.

Granted, that made him a cur, a blackguard, and a rake of the worst sort. He hadn't come to Esherton Green intending to despoil an innocent, but once the idea formed, he'd pursued it. He'd been an unmitigated ass announcing Brooke was his mistress in front of Benbridge. Jealousy must have loosened his tongue and warped his common sense. He regretted the outburst, even if he couldn't remember a word of it.

He didn't even recall making his way below stairs or anything beyond Brooke leaving the chamber to speak to her former love. Nothing for the next twelve hours either. Leventhorpe took it upon himself to apprise Heath of the sordid details once he'd regained his senses.

Heath would rather have remained oblivious to his stupidity.

It didn't make a whit of sense, his fear of losing her. Still, he offered Brooke the one thing, short of marriage, he had available. From what he'd observed, mistresses generally fared better than wives, anyway. Besides, didn't she realize that tongues already flapped? He and Leventhorpe had been sleeping in her house for days, for God's sake.

Servants talked. Benbridge *had* talked. Tattle had already circulated back by way of Leventhorpe's staff.

Now Heath must see the act done.

Her position was worse than when he'd arrived, and most of the blame lay on his shoulders. If he gave her the money to restore the place, not only was it a horrid business move, people would still assume she'd traded her favors for the funds. The consequences would be the same; she and the girls would be shunned. He'd learned that, if nothing else, in his lifetime. People assumed the worst, almost as if they relished another's misfortune.

Yes, he was selfish. His conscience could raise a breeze and rail at him all it wanted, but he couldn't get Brooke out of his mind, and he intended to have her. And deserting her and her family, leaving them as paupers, her reputation in tatters with no recourse was not an option.

If she wanted a wager, fine by him. Let her believe she held a degree of power. It cost him little enough, and if it helped her salvage a remnant of pride, well, he'd make the concession. He owed her that and much more.

Taking a broken woman to his bed didn't appeal, but introducing this seething temptress to the pleasures of the flesh...that would be worth suffering a scratch or two. Her resourcefulness, her feistiness, even her mutinous violet eyes spewing darts at him this moment fascinated him. He'd enjoy teaching her to channel her spiritedness in the bedchamber. Oh, the wild romps they'd have. His groin contracted in a rush of pleasure.

She'd captured his admiration and his lust.

He had more than enough blunt to set up a house for her and another for her family. He'd allow her servants to tag along if they wanted. However, he had no intention of that brood being underfoot when he introduced Brooke to passion. Therefore, he would mandate separate residences.

Her eyes flashing ire, she pursed her prim little mouth, in all likelihood to keep from telling him to go bugger himself, something he had seriously considered, truth to tell.

Even with his head thrumming severely enough to turn his hair white and grind his teeth to powder, he'd battled arousal for four days straight. She'd consumed his thoughts and dreams. Hour upon hour of lying on the lumpy mattress, constantly thinking of her, imaging all the erotic things he'd like to do to and with her, had him marble hard. If he hadn't shared the chamber with Leventhorpe, Heath would've been tempted to relieve his randy state himself. A perpetual erection ached like the devil.

Why she consumed him, he hadn't the foggiest notion. He'd bedded beautiful women before, many exceedingly intelligent and witty too. But Brooke...something about her, something he couldn't quite name, mesmerized him, bewitched him until he'd become consumed with her.

Her sultry eyes and subtle shudders proved she wasn't immune to him. She'd kissed him freely and, given her heated responses, desire consumed her too. However, she didn't recognize her need for untapped passion, which hinted all the more of her innocence. He'd be glad to teach her to recognize what she felt, and more. Much more.

Warm heaviness weighted his loins. Too bad they didn't have a signed agreement already. Taking her against the barn or over the fence held a provincial sort of appeal. Well, perhaps not with chocolate-eyed calves looking on. He twisted his lip into a droll smile.

Hell, who did he think he fooled? He would take her anywhere, anytime, as many times as he wanted once she'd become his.

Her concern for her reputation was only natural. Women of her character and integrity didn't barter their bodies in exchange for protection on a regular basis. Nevertheless, he recalled a handful who'd been content as pampered Persians with their decision to accept a gentleman's protection.

Besides, Brooke had several people to think of other than herself. Had it been only her welfare at risk, the war Heath intended to wage to win her would've been much more difficult and complex. But instinct told him she'd accept the stakes he demanded for their wager to ensure the others' wellbeing if convinced she would be the victor.

She worried her lower lip and fingered the god-awful cover, which had slipped to her lower spine. Her work-worn hands revealed how hard she'd labored. Never again would she have to do so. He'd see to her comfort for the rest of her days.

He eyed her shabby clothes, the toes of her half-boots worn almost through. First order of business as her protector: hie her to a London modiste and order an entire wardrobe, right down to her unmentionables. Naturally, he'd be present for the fittings.

She heaved a gusty sigh, her full bosom straining against her gown's fabric.

Well, perhaps not the very first order of business. Slaking his desire topped the list.

"Let's be totally candid regarding the stakes, shall we?" She scooted her gaze around the area. Only docile cattle chewing cud peered at her.

Did she worry someone might overhear?

He sent a casual glance to the meadows and the curving path to the house. Alone. No one eavesdropped on their conversation, though a small rotund ball of fur scuttled their way. The corgi had escaped.

"I'll wager my—

Heath raised his hand. "I have one, rather personal question I require an answer to before we proceed."

A confused expression whisked across her face. "And that is...?"

Deucedly awkward this.

He cleared his throat. He had to know if she'd been intimate with Benbridge, damn his jealousy. "I am most selective in the women I take to my bed."

Her fair brows dove together, and a strangled sound, not quite a gasp, escaped her. A rosy glow tinted her cheeks. "I really don't care to hear about the women you've bedded, my lord, since I have no intention of *ever* becoming one of them."

"You've asked for a chance to win your farm. Do you want to hear my terms or not?" Irritation liberally dosed with pain raised its gnarly head. A punishing cadence had begun in one temple a few minutes ago, stealing his patience. Heath rubbed the side of his head in small, circular motions with two fingers.

Brooke glared at him then waved her hand in an arc. "By all means, my lord. Shout it from the rooftops for all I care."

"Are you a virgin?"

The air left her in a long hiss, and her eyes fairly spat indignation. "You mean to tell me you only take innocents as your mistresses? What kind of despot are you?"

"No, if you are, you'll be the first." He nonchalantly straightened a cuff. Damn, but the notion she hadn't slept with Benbridge exhilarated him. Silence reigned, and he lifted his gaze.

Emotions flitted across her features so quickly, he was hard-pressed to identify all of them. Her chest rose as she inhaled a large expanse of air, scorn sparking in her eyes.

"That's it, you cocksure toff. Take your confounded wager and...and stuff it up your stiff arse! I'll find another way to save my home." Brooke hoisted her skirts and spun on her heel toward the house. "Asking about my virginity. My God, who does that?"

She caught site of Freddy scampering their way and frowned.

"I'll take that as a yes." It pleased Heath beyond ridiculous. He would be her first. *And only.*

She whipped around. "You insufferable blackguard. Why, if I were a man—"

"I'm heartily grateful you're not." He winked and gave her an unabashedly wicked grin. "Calm down. I only meant to spare you a degree of embarrassment. I usually have my physician examine my mistresses for disease prior to signing our agreement and regularly thereafter."

She fisted her small hands, an expression of such incredulity on her face, he fought not to laugh aloud. His humor would rile her all the more.

"Please tell me you're not serious? Do you have any idea how utterly degrading and offensive that is?" She patted her thigh, silently calling the wheezing dog to her side.

Heath shrugged. "Nevertheless, I require it, but for you, given your innocence, I'll make an exception."

She rolled her eyes heavenward as she shook her head. "How benevolent of you. What if I'm not? Is our deal off?"

A flicker of jealousy stabbed Heath. Perhaps his earlier joy had been premature.

Freddy plopped to the ground beside her, tongue hanging out and panting as if he'd just competed in the English Triple Crown. How old was the pudgy beast, anyway?

"No, you'll endure an examination before a contract is signed." He didn't doubt she wished him to the devil at the moment. "So, I'll ask you again. Are you a virgin?"

She responded with a terse nod, and another shock of color flooded her cheeks.

He bit the inside of his mouth to keep from smiling.

Brooke folded her arms and cocked her head to the side. "What else?"

"I'll have my solicitor draw up a document which will include provision for you, your family, and the terms of our separation when the time comes. You will relocate to London, and I will sell the lands I won in the wager from your cousin."

Her eyes narrowed to slits, and she pressed her lips together but remained silent. Outrage and frustration oozed from her.

"Our initial contract will be for a year." He'd never kept a mistress longer. Brooke might be the first. "I'll provide a cancellation clause if we don't suit."

"I don't care about your contract poppycock. My word is my oath.

But know this, I will not agree to the sale of Esherton Green. Forfeiture of my body and virtue are worth more than the lands."

She had him there.

Brooke planted her hands on her hips, and Freddy licked his chops and wagged his tail.

"Here are my terms, my lord, and they are not negotiable." She shut her eyes for a second before snapping them open. She launched her battle plan. "Should I lose, I will accompany you to London as your mistress, but you will allow everyone else to remain here, including the servants. You will bestow generous marriage settlements on the four girls, and arrange for sponsors for their come outs. You will also permit Esherton to retain the proceeds from the dairy and farm."

Heath folded his arms. Came up with that too damn quickly for his liking. "Is that all?"

"No." She scowled and pushed her wayward hair behind her ear again. "Mabry will carry on as overseer, and you will permit me to hire a respectable woman of quality to act as a companion to my sister and cousins, both here and when they are in London. An annual allowance to further the estate's recovery wouldn't be amiss either."

She paused, appearing deep in thought, her brows drawn together. "Oh, and I shall be permitted at least two extended visits to Esherton Green annually."

Heath should've suspected Brooke wouldn't acquiesce without a skirmish. He didn't half mind her terms, except the stipulation for keeping the blasted farm. But if he didn't have to manage the place, he would concede the point.

"And if you win?" He braced himself for her demands.

My ballocks fried to a crisp.

"If I win the wager, you sign over to me, free and clear, the lands you won from Sheridan."

That's all she wanted? No bulging purse, new wardrobe, household furnishings...or the hundred other things she and the others lacked?

She extended her hand. "Agreed?"

Heath clasped her roughened palm. It fit neatly within his grasp, as if it had been molded to nestle there. "Yes, the instant you win."

She wouldn't be allowed the victory. They had yet to decide on what game to play, but it mattered not. He might not be able to read worth a damn, but he remembered every playing card dealt and didn't lose at the tables.

Across the expanse of deep green, three figures separated from the house and moved toward the barns. Leventhorpe and two of the other Culpepper misses. At this distance, which two Heath couldn't discern. "What's your pleasure?"

"Excuse me?" Her back to the house, Brooke squinted up at him from where she squatted beside the dog, now lying with his feet in the air, eyes closed, enjoying a tummy rub.

"*My pleasure?*" She almost choked on the words. "Awfully confident you'll be the vanquisher, aren't you? Pride goeth before a fall, my lord."

He chuckled. Never short on pithy remarks, was she? "What game of cards do you prefer?"

Her chagrin transformed to cunningness. A shrewd smile bent her mouth. "I never agreed to a card game."

Alarm dug its sharp little talons on his already pulsing scalp. "Not cards?"

Devil it, what had he agreed to?

A horserace? Did she ride? He examined the barn. Did she own a horse? Surely not a drinking game. Visions of Brooke guzzling brandy or whiskey like a saloon tart churned his stomach. Blister it. What did women wager on besides cards? The color of silk best suited for an embroidered flower?

Men gambled on any number of outlandish things. White's betting book overflowed with one ludicrous wager after another, from what soup might be served at Lady Jersey's to how many pups a hound would birth and everything conceivable in between. Once there'd been a stake on the number of gentlemen a certain courtesan could service in one night.

Heath never participated in that sort of rubbish. Irresponsible and a waste of good coinage, especially when London's streets teemed with orphans and beggars. Even a small portion of money gambled away daily would improve the lives of the less fortunate.

He silently saluted Brooke for outwitting him this round. He ought to have realized she wouldn't choose the obvious. Hadn't he learned anything about her? Predictable she was not.

"Very well, what sort of challenge did you have in mind?" Good God, what if she chose a stitching or baking contest or some other such womanly nonsense? "It must be a competition we're equally capable of."

"Sounds as if you're worried, my lord." Her smile widened, and still crouched beside Freddy, she twisted to look at the milling cattle in the paddock.

Mabry exited the barn and made for the far side of the enclosure where a gate hung. The nervous cattle shifted away from him. Freddy wriggled to his feet then ran to the fence. He trotted up and down, snuffling and whining.

"Hold there, Mr. Mabry." Brooke straightened and waved at the servant.

He pivoted toward them and doffed his hat. "Miss Brooke, your lordship, I didn't know ye were out here."

Was that a Scottish brogue? Heath hadn't noticed it before. But then, he'd barely been able to stand.

"We've only been here a few minutes. I wanted to see the calves." She approached the fence. "They are healthy, it appears."

Heath trailed her, his uneasiness increasing. What was she plotting?

"Hearty lot, these calves be." Mabry gestured in the cattle's direction. "Each one sturdy and healthy. Even the twins there."

He pointed to a pair of spotted calves suckling, while their poor mother straddled them.

Freddy yipped, repeatedly looking at Brooke then the cattle, and then placed his front paws on the lowest fence rail. Mabry bent and scratched behind the dog's ears.

Heath winced as the servant stepped in a pile of warm cow dung.

Unperturbed, Mabry scuffed his boot in the dirt several times and laughed. "He wants to herd the beasties. In his blood, it be."

"And so he shall." Brooke turned triumphant eyes to Heath, her exquisite features alight with joy. "I wager Freddy can separate the calves from their mothers and herd them into the barn in under five minutes. Mabry will stand at the door to prevent the calves from reentering the paddock. You may keep the time." Her gaze slid to his torso, and his muscles bunched as if she'd touched him. "You do have a watch, don't you?"

Heath removed the silver time piece and flicked it open.

"Wager?" Mabry scratched his chest and glanced between them, leeriness scrunching his weathered face. "What sort of wager?"

Brooke inclined her fair head at the dog, caressing him with a doting glance. "Freddy is going to save Esherton for us. His lordship and I have agreed on the stakes. If I win, the lands his lordship won from Sheridan belong to us."

"And if you lose, Miss Brooke?" Mabry's penetrating gaze probed Heath's and disapproval laced his voice. Did he suspect the nature of the rest of their bet?

"Not to worry, Mr. Mabry." She smiled and hugged her wrap tighter. The loose hairs framing her face fluttered in the light breeze. She gave a small shudder. From cold or excitement? "Trust me. I'd never place a bet I wasn't confident I would win. I'm not a fool."

The overseer firmed his mouth and gave a sharp nod. "I do trust ye, lass." His expression sour, he shifted his focus to Heath, "You, sir, I do not."

Brooke laughed and the sound pelted Heath with another round of...what? What did she make him feel? He'd never experienced the taxing sensation before.

Panting, his fluffy tail wagging furiously, the squat corgi pranced before her, all but begging to take after the cattle.

Heath eyed the old dog then counted the calves. Fourteen. Almost three calves a minute, and Freddy had gasped as if dying from his jaunt from the house. Not bloody likely he could get the calves inside in five minutes.

"Are you sure he's up to it? He's not a young pup." Brooke would never forgive him if the dog dropped dead from exertion.

"I'm sure. And he is too." Her eyes sparkling with mirth, she broke into an excited grin before stooping again. She gathered the dog into her arms. "So, my friend, are you ready to have some fun, just like you used to?"

Freddy squirmed and licked her face.

Heath had never seen Brooke this happy, and unbidden warmth washed over him at her delight. If only he were the source of her joy, rather than her consternation.

Yes, women coerced into becoming mistresses are generally elated at the prospect and with the men who compel them, idiot. A wife on the other hand...

No. Wife.

She seemed most confident she'd win. What then? He didn't give a fig if she won the lands. He did care that she might escape his bed, and, even after their short acquaintance, the knowledge that he'd not see her again left him more disquieted than he would have believed possible.

Marry her.

Holy hell, why did the bothersome thought keep bludgeoning him? Marriage didn't loom on his horizon for many years yet to come. And it wasn't as if she'd have him now, in any event.

"You'll not win, your lordship." She smiled, a sad little twist of her plump lips. "You see, I have too much to lose, while you have nothing."

Heath rubbed his chin, and ignored the stab of guilt her words caused. "We shall see."

Brooke handed Freddy to Mabry. The little dog, a quivering bundle of concentration, kept his black-eyed gaze riveted on the uneasy bovines.

Freddy in his arms, Mabry moved to the barn's entrance. His stiff-legged gait and cinched mouth revealed he disliked Brooke's decision, but he respected her enough to allow her to carry on.

The cattle shifted and the cows sidled the humans nervous sideways glances. The calves sensed something afoot and huddled near their mothers. Easier or harder for the dog to work them? Heath knew damn little—all right, nothing—about the four-legged pooping machines except how a thick steak covered in onions and mushrooms tasted on his tongue.

Brooke stood on her toes, arms resting on the top rail. Yes, her shoe had a hole in the bottom. She slid Heath a glance then dropped her attention to his pocket watch. "Are you ready?"

Confidence oozed from her. Rather adorable. He, on the other hand, experienced unfamiliar apprehension. Most troubling.

"Once I say start, the clock doesn't stop for any reason. Agreed? There will be no multiple trials." Freddy didn't have more than one go round in his roly-poly little body in any event.

"Of course." She wrinkled her nose and swatted at a fly buzzing about her head. Hundreds of the pesky insects hovered near the animals and manure littered ground. "Why would we need to stop?"

"Just so, but I won't have you crying foul and demanding another go."

Do you hear yourself? You've already cornered her. Show a modicum of empathy, for God's sake.

Brooke's mouth formed a thin-lipped smile, though her gaze rebelled. "I would have the same assurance from you then, my lord."

"You have it."

"Are ye ready?" Mabry called.

She crooked a winged brow at Heath, and he gave a curt nod, his watch at the ready.

"Yes, Mr. Mabry. You may proceed." She scooted closer to the fence, tension radiating from her.

Mabry placed Freddy on the ground by his feet then dropped to one knee beside the trembling animal. Speaking softly, he stroked Freddy, and the dog lay down, his beady gaze fixed on the cows. The next instant, the overseer gave two shrill whistles.

Chunky body scraping the ground, Freddy tore to the cattle, scattering them every which way. With unbelievable finesse, the small dog worked the livestock, separating a calf from the rest. One, two, three—he swiftly isolated the calves and drove the bawling trio to the barn. Whipping about, the corgi headed into the fray of milling hooves once more.

He showed no signs of fatigue, devil a bit.

Sweat beaded Heath's brow.

Brooke chewed her lower lip, her hands clenched atop the rail.

He glanced at his watch when Freddy maneuvered four more calves through the open doors. Heath had assumed the dog would work the animals one at a time. Ignorance on his part. Brooke might very well have him on the gibbet, a rope about his neck.

Then what? He wouldn't let her go.

You'll have to marry her, old chap.

"Will you shut the bloody hell up?" he muttered beneath his breath. Damnable shrew, his conscience.

Brooke gave him a hurried, quizzical look. The clouds overhead reflected in her clear eyes. "I beg your pardon? Did you say something to me?"

"No, just having a bit of difficulty with the sun glaring on my watch."

She fidgeted with the travesty of a shawl across her bosom, her worry evident. "Did you start timing when Mabry whistled?"

Did she fret Heath would cheat? Well, he hadn't shown himself to be an honorable chap, to this point, now had he?

"Not to worry. I started at the whistle."

"What goes on here?" Waving his arm toward the paddock, Leventhorpe planted a booted foot on the bottom rail. The weathered wood shuddered and groaned.

At Leventhorpe's appearance, Brooke's eyes rounded, the irises shrinking to a miniscule ebony dots. She stiffened before her lips split into a welcoming smile for her sister and cousin.

God above, Heath adored her expressive eyes and ready smile.

Facing the now-dusty enclosure, the Misses Brette and Blythe sandwiched Brooke and spoke in quiet tones. Each sent him a glower of such blue-eyed antagonism, he'd no doubt Brooke had shared the terms of their wager. Thank God they weren't men, or he'd be called out at once. Deserved to be run through by all of them.

Heat slithered from his neck to his face.

Accustomed to women's admiration, he'd never experienced such feminine enmity and found the hostility most disturbing. However, he acknowledged he'd brought their censure upon himself. The oddest urge to check his head for horns and his bum for a twitching, pointed tail gripped him.

Contrition lanced sharp and burrowed deep, where, every now and again, it gave him a vicious jab, reminding him what a cur he'd become. He'd proved no better than the men who'd held his title before him. Self-seeking, arrogant bastards, the entire lot.

The stink from a fish lingered long, especially rotten ones. He, too, bore the familial stench prevalent in his lineage. He'd prided himself on being superior to his forefathers, yet today proved he'd become the worst sod of the bunch. Though his ethics, conscience, integrity— whatever the blasted thing was that kept hounding him to do right by Brooke—nagged worse than a fishwife, he couldn't let her go.

"What's the little terror doing to the cattle?" Leventhorpe peered at Heath before scanning the chaos on the other side of the fence.

Heath cleared his throat. "If Freddy manages to get the rest of the calves—" *Damn, only five left.* "—into the barn in the next," he checked his watch, "three minutes, Miss Culpepper takes ownership of the Esherton's lands I won in the wager."

Leventhorpe chuckled and slapped Heath on the shoulder. "You're letting that fat, ancient dog decide something of such importance?"

"So it seems." Heath kept his attention glued to the puffball darting about the pen, yipping and snapping at the bovines' feet.

Leaning over the top rail, Leventhorpe studied the dog's progress. He canted his head toward Freddy. "And if he doesn't get them all inside, what then?"

Heath angled his back to Brooke and murmured, "She becomes my mistress."

Leventhorpe's jaw slackened for an instant. He jerked upright, condemnation blistering in his gaze. "You are an absolute, reprehensible arse, Raven."

"I'm aware."

"I do believe I'm ashamed to call you friend. I should call you out." Shaking his head, Leventhorpe directed his attention to the paddock. "Ho, there, Freddy. Good boy."

Freddy almost had another pair of calves to the barn.

Leventhorpe hollered and clapped his hands. "There's a smart chap."

Scooting around a stubborn cow bent on protecting her calf, the dog stiffened. He skidded to a halt, his nose in the air then spun and faced the fence. One glimpse of Leventhorpe, and Freddy tucked his tail between his legs and bolted for the barn.

A sensible woman realizes that to achieve the
greatest advantage in gambling, one doesn't wager at all.
~*Wisdom and Advice—The Genteel Lady's Guide to Practical Living*

15

"Freddy, no." Brooke's distressed cry was echoed by her sister and cousin.

His craggy face mirroring the devastation that must surely ravage hers, Mabry trotted into the barn after the dog.

I lost. Oh my God, no. I lost.

Pressing close to her sides, Brette and Blythe each wrapped an arm about her shoulders and glared murderously at both men. Brooke was half convinced that, had her sister and cousin possessed a blade, they would have run the lords through. She might very well have cheered them on and helped dig the graves afterward.

Ruined.

Her head swam with dread and disappointment so pungent, she could taste it, bitter and metallic on her tongue.

"Brooke, your lip is bleeding." Brette plucked a handkerchief from her bodice.

Brooke hadn't noticed she'd bitten her lip. She dabbed at the cut as wave upon wave of panic surged ever higher, rising from her stomach, to her chest, and thrumming against her throat.

His mistress. I am...will be...a fallen woman.

She clutched her shawl and swung to glare at Lord Leventhorpe. "You did that on purpose."

His eyes darkened to cobalt. "Miss Culpepper, I had no notion of what went on here when I asked these ladies to point me in the direction my senseless friend had wandered."

The calves Freddy had directed to the barn trotted out and, amid much mooing and lowing, found their anxious mamas. Several set to nursing at once.

"You didn't have to call out to Freddy." Tears clogged her throat, but she refused to cry in front of these scapegraces or her family. "You know he's terrified of you."

"I but encouraged the dog. I assure you, there was no deliberate intent or subterfuge to cause you to lose."

"He did so do it deliberately." Blythe's voice dripped venom. "He and Ravensdale whispered back and forth when we arrived."

The marquis shook his burnished head. "Such a suspicious mind, Miss Blythe. Does it ever become wearisome?"

"Not where you're concerned." Blythe planted her free hand on her hip. "What did you say to him then?"

"I told him he was an absolute a—" Lord Leventhorpe cupped his nape. "Um, that is, a disreputable fellow, and promptly fell to cheering the dog along."

"Hmph. I'll just bet you did." Brette didn't believe his excuses either.

It didn't matter. What was done was done.

Brooke had given her word, and integrity compelled her to keep it. Ironic that. She would lose her virtue because of her honor. The devil must be dancing a jig in hell at her quandary. Had the situation been reversed, and she'd won by means less than laudable, would she have given the earl another chance to best her?

No. Too much depended on winning.

Lord Leventhorpe crossed his arms and addressed Lord Ravensdale. "You should be in bed instead of making silly wagers to ruin young innocents."

Blythe and Brette inhaled sharply.

Did the man have no filter on his mouth? Did every thought gush forth like a muddy river breeching its banks during a flood? However did these two featherheads manage in London amongst the *haut ton*?

Leventhorpe frowned, his keen gaze vacillating between Ravensdale and Brooke. "I, for one, cannot condone this ill-conceived wager."

"Leave off, Trist." Lord Ravensdale raised a hesitant gaze to Brooke. Instead of triumph and gloating, his eyes teemed with compassion and an unfamiliar glint. He snapped the watch closed then returned it to his waistcoat pocket.

Leventhorpe sent a vexed glance skyward. "Why the confounded theatrics? It's a simple enough fix. I'll leave and you can retrieve the mongrel—

"Freddy is not a mongrel, you red-headed baboon," Blythe snapped.

Blythe acted a constant shrew with Lord Leventhorpe. Why? Dear God, surely not for the same reason Lord Ravensdale flustered Brooke out of her polite decorum.

Brette jutted her chin upward a notch and nodded her head. "To us, he's family."

Leventhorpe sighed, a put upon expression on his face. Did he understand what had just transpired? Had Ravensdale explained the whole of it?

"You can start the affair again, and I give my word, I shall stay in the house, out of sight the entire time." Leventhorpe jerked his thumb in the manor's direction.

Brooke shook her head as she stepped away from her sister and cousin's protective embraces. "No, your lordship, we cannot start over. Lord Ravensdale and I agreed to a single challenge, one time only. That, too, was part of our bargain."

Mabry exited the barn, Freddy in his arms. He approached the fence, his gaze seething. "Cheap shot, that was. I've a mind to call ye out, uppity lord or not."

"You'll do no such thing." Brooke took Freddy from him. "I need you to carry on for me until this conundrum is fixed."

How could she sound composed? Inside, she tilted on the precipice of histrionics. Quaking, Freddy buried his head in her shoulder. Why did Lord Leventhorpe frighten him so? Freddy would've won her the wager if Lord Leventhorpe hadn't intruded. The knowledge she'd set this trap and snared herself...well, it grated her raw.

Ravensdale taking her to his bed didn't scare her. Or repulse her. Quite the opposite, truthfully. He'd unearthed feelings in her she hadn't realized existed. She would've been lying if she denied that his dark good looks and well-defined muscles enticed her.

Before his outlandish proposal, she'd given up on knowing a man intimately—although if mating proved anything like what she'd witnessed between Buford and the cows, the act seemed rather violent and favored the male of the species. The only benefit to the females, as near as she could discern, was the babes they'd soon bear.

Good God!

What if a child resulted from her union with his lordship? No, she'd insist measures be taken to prevent a pregnancy. Such things existed, didn't they? She'd ask Doctor Wilton on his next visit and pray he didn't expire from shock at such a scandalous question from an unmarried woman.

"Miss Culpepper, I would speak with you privately."

Brooke jerked her attention to Lord Ravensdale. Serious and somber, he gazed at her intently. Why the Friday face? He'd trounced her. Shouldn't he be grinning and celebrating? Instead, his eyes, the planes of his face, even his sculpted mouth suggested poignant reserve.

"We've serious matters to discuss." His expression grew grimmer.

Eager to get on with it, the boor. If he thought to bed her at Esherton, butterflies flitted about in his head. She wouldn't bring shame to the family home by lifting her skirts beneath Esherton's roof.

The morning breeze had ceased, and the chorus of innumerable flies within the paddock, in addition to the bees zipping from clover to flower in the fields, carried to her. The faint scent of sandalwood wafted by.

Which of the lords did it belong to?

Leventhorpe.

Raven's...Ravensdale's scent had been burned into her memory, and he didn't smell of sandalwood. Realization blindsided her. Freddie's first owner, the abusive charlatan, had reeked of the scent. No wonder the dog hied for the nearest hiding spot when he whiffed Lord Leventhorpe. If only she'd made the connection sooner. She nearly strangled, stifling her scream of frustration.

Odd that this perfect spring day should portend the onset of her tainted future. Yet, in the innermost recesses of her being, in a miniscule cleft she'd allow no one access to, a bud of relief formed. She'd secured the girls' futures, and the knowledge lifted a tremendous burden from her mind and heart.

A year wasn't so terribly long. And, in fact, she rather suspected she might enjoy her time as his lordship's kept woman. So be it. She'd make the best of this. Mama always said when the bread went stale, add some spices, egg, and cream, and make bread pudding.

"Please take him to the house and give him a treat, poor thing." Brooke passed Freddy to Blythe then kissed his snout. "You did your best, didn't you, my sweet boy?"

He thumped his tail once, his brown eyes apologetic.

Blythe hugged the quivering dog to her chest and murmured into his fur. He crawled up to snuggle against her neck.

Leventhorpe approached and, after a slight hesitation, scratched behind Freddy's ears.

Brooke held her breath as Freddy went rigid, his small eyes leery.

"No need to be afraid. I won't hurt you," his lordship said while petting the dog. At least Freddy hadn't bitten him.

A song thrush swooped to perch atop a post several lengths farther along the fence. The bird cocked its head before flitting to the ground and poking about for insects. Oh, to live the simple life of a bird.

"Brette, go with Blythe, please, and ask Cook to prepare two tea trays. Have one served in the parlor for Lord Leventhorpe and yourselves. Have the other delivered to the study." Brooke tucked her hand in the crook of Brette's elbow and guided her away from the paddock to where Blythe waited.

Brette patted Freddy when Lord Ravensdale moved aside. "Certainly. I believe we've fresh ginger biscuits, Shrewsbury cakes, and tarts baked just this morning."

How long it had been since they'd indulged in such lavishness? The quartet wouldn't go without again. The notion brought Brooke a measure of consolation.

Half-turned in Lord Ravensdale's direction, Brooke said, "I shall meet you in the study in twenty minutes, my lord. I must speak with my overseer. If you will excuse me, please?"

"Brooke. Blythe. Brette!"

Everyone turned to the frantic shouts coming from the house.

Blaire, skirts hoisted to her knees, hurtled through the grass, her white stockings flashing as she dashed to them. Her ragged sobs rent the air. "Duffen's gone. He's dead."

Esherton Green's Cemetery
Two Mornings Later

"Amen." Reverend Avery closed his Bible, the slight thump jarring Brooke to the disagreeable present.

Over already?

She'd been woolgathering, remembering happier times at Esherton with Duffen. Dry grittiness scraped her eyes when she blinked.

Hiring the reverend to preside over the funeral had consumed the last of her money. He'd been most reluctant to perform the ritual. Duffen had once called him an ignorant hypocrite more interested in lining his pockets than saving souls. Brooke rather agreed with Duffen's assessment, but as no other clerics resided within a day's ride, Reverend Avery it must be.

Would Duffen approve? Brooke didn't know, but she couldn't bury him without a ceremony, no matter how brief or coldly delivered by the officiator.

Shouldn't she be crying? Why couldn't she weep? Her heart ached, but no tears would come.

She scanned the huddled foursome's red-rimmed eyelids before shifting her attention to Mrs. Jennings and Flora, also sporting ruddy noses and cheeks. Not a one wore a coat, but instead had a blanket wrapped around their shoulders against the deceptively mild day's chilliness. Mabry's bloodshot gaze gave testament to his sorrow at the loss of his long-time comrade.

Was she alone incapable of grieving? No, she mourned Duffen's loss deeply, but she'd no more tears to shed, and she had the futures of many people to organize in a short amount of time. A niggling headache pinched behind her eyes from the constant strain. His lordship hadn't said when they would depart for London, but she doubted he'd twiddle his thumbs for a couple of weeks.

Perhaps later, when duty and responsibility didn't demand her attention, she could find a private spot to vent her heartache. At present, the manor overflowed with bodies. Why, just this morning, she'd made her way to the kitchen before first light, bent on a cup of the delicious new tea Leroux had brought. In the near dark, she'd stumbled upon a footman sprawled on a pallet and mashed his hand beneath her foot.

The starchy clergyman gestured to the rich mound of soil piled beside the yawning hole in the earth. Steam rose, a silvery-white mist, where the sun warmed the ground. "Miss Culpepper?"

Brooke drew in a fortifying breath. Since Duffen had no relatives, and as the senior woman of the house, the task of sprinkling Duffen's coffin with the same dirt he'd toiled in most of his life fell to her. She'd discarded protocol and allowed the girls to attend the graveside eulogy. Duffen deserved more than a pair of stable hands, Mabry, and herself to bid him farewell.

Lords Ravensdale and Leventhorpe—*would the man never leave?*—paid their respects as well. It rather astounded her and warmed her heart, despite her misgivings about the taciturn pair. Leventhorpe, however, repeatedly checked his watch and glanced to the drive, as if anxious to have the matter done with. Boorish of him, given he attended of his own volition.

Brooke loosened the glove from her hand, one finger at a time, reluctant to bring the simple service to an end and leave the dear little man who'd guarded her and the others fiercely for years. He'd been the grandfather they'd never had. A peculiar little bird of a grandfather, but loving all the same.

Lord Ravensdale waited a discreet distance away, determined to have their postponed conversation today. What did he seek anyway? She harbored no secrets. They had their agreement. Did he fear she'd renege on the bargain? Quite the couple they made, neither trusting the other, but they would share a bed and the most intimate of relationships. She firmed her lips against irony's cutting reproach.

The man had followed her about, much like a nervous puppy, the past pair of days. All solicitousness, almost as if he cared for her, he said little, but watched her every move with his unnerving gaze. His concern and attention warmed her, wooed her, further eroding the crumbling barrier she'd erected to keep him at bay.

Why of all men, flying in the face of everything logical and wise, had her disloyal heart picked him? A shuddery sigh escaped her. She couldn't deny the truth any longer; not even to herself.

She didn't like how vulnerable that made her.

"I'll take your glove, Brooke." Blaire held out her hand.

"Thank you."

Brooke passed the glove and unused handkerchief to her cousin. She crouched and stared at the humble casket. Sighing again, she scooped a handful of damp earth. A day past a week since Lord Ravensdale disrupted their lives.

And Sheridan, don't forget his dastardly part in this misfortune.

She swept the graveyard with her gaze, lingering a moment on the house and barns in the distance. The cattle, like giant dollops of cream, blotted the emerald meadows.

So much had changed in such a short amount of time.

"Kingdoms rise and kingdoms fall in a day," she whispered to herself.

"What was that, Miss Culpepper?" Reverend Avery peered down his nose at her.

"Nothing." After standing upright once more, she opened her fingers and allowed the dirt to drop. The clump hit the coffin, the sound harsh and final. Tears finally welled. Muffled weeping from the others filled the air as the small crowd turned and trekked down the lengthy, wending path to the house.

"Reverend, please join us for our midday meal." Lord Ravensdale extended the invitation. "I would beg a moment of your time afterward to discuss procuring a grave marker for Duffen."

"Yes, yes, of course. Shall I meet you at the house? I'm recovering from a bout of poor health and don't wish to linger outdoors any longer than I must." Prayer book tucked beneath his arm, the long-faced cleric eyed the house in the distance, a hungry glint in his eye. He swallowed, and his over-sized Adam's apple fought to escape the folds of turkey-like flesh drooping his collar.

"Certainly." Brooke brushed her hands together. "We'll be along in a moment or two, after I say my final farewells to Duffen. Have a drop of brandy in your tea. That should help stave off any ill effects of the out of doors."

She had forgotten the sumptuous spread Leroux had promised to have prepared for them after the funeral, at Leventhorpe's request. The marquis's attempts to get into the women's good graces were endearing, if somewhat audacious.

The same couldn't be said of Reverend Avery. She didn't want to suffer the stodgy cleric's depressing presence for a moment longer, but for Duffen, she would. She hadn't the funds for a headstone, and when pride attempted to rear its horned head and object to his lordship's generosity, she slapped the emotion aside like a fly atop a pastry. Duffen's loyalty warranted the honor. Besides, as her protector, Ravensdale was within his rights to make the decision and pay the fee.

Protector.

Despite her acceptance of her new station, and the startling realization she loved him, her stomach quavered. He'd made no demands on her, nor presented a contract either, as yet.

Brooke bent her forefinger and wiped beneath her lower eyelashes, touched by Heath's...Raven's—drat it all—Ravensdale's kindheartedness. How *did* mistresses address their protectors?

My lord? Master?

Not exactly something taught in the schoolroom.

"Here, allow me." His gaze tender, he patted the moisture from the edge of her lashes with the edge of his handkerchief. He did have the most mesmerizing eyes she'd ever seen in a man. After drying her face, he rubbed the dirt from her palm and then each finger in turn.

Such a simple act, but sensual too. Her irregular breathing and cavorting pulse gave testament to her awareness of him as a desirable man. She searched for similar discomfit in him but found unruffled composure.

"How am I to address you?" Heavens, she sounded wanton as a wagtail. Dry mouth, that was why. Brooke swallowed before running the tip of her tongue across her bottom lip. "Do you prefer Ravensdale, my lord... Raven... Heath?" *Good God, babies babble less.* "Please understand, I have no notion of how this mistress business works."

Except for the amorous congress part. One didn't breed cattle and not have a firm grasp of what coupling entailed. Rather undignified to be approached from behind, but under the cover of dark and with one's eyes—*and ears*—firmly squeezed shut, she ought to be able to manage well enough. She pursed her lips when he still didn't answer her.

"What *do* I call you?"

He kissed her forehead, his lips soft, yet firm, at the same time.

"How about husband?"

Understand this: once the die is cast, everything you've gained can be lost.
~Wisdom and Advice—The Genteel Lady's Guide to Practical Living

16

The quandary ricocheting in Heath's mind burst forth like a cannonball scuttling a ship, blasting his defenses wide open and setting him adrift. Yet subjecting Brooke to the degradation he'd proposed gnawed and chafed him until his conscience and soul lay raw and bloody. Seemed he wasn't cut from the same stuff as bounders and scapegraces after all.

He would marry her, though every fiber of his being cringed in trepidation. Cold, unfeeling, heartless—the negative traits of his sire, and the Earls of Ravensdale before his father, haunted Heath, reproachful and condemning. Could he summon the modicum of deep regard or warm sentiment that created satisfied wives and contented children?

Would he endure contention and strife the remainder of his wedded life as his parents had? Their battles had been legendary. Or, God forbid, do to his offspring what they'd done to him?

No, Brooke possessed a loving nature and generous spirit, unlike his mother. The knowledge was a balm to his wounded soul. A soul he'd not recognized needed healing until Brooke forced him to tear open the protective cover, rip off the scars and scabs, and see the festered wound deep within. She would help heal the putrid mess, restore wholeness to him.

Her character and birth alone made Brooke entitled to more than the degrading position he'd offered her. Brooke was nothing like the wife he'd determined would suit him. He feared one day Brooke would break his once impenetrable heart. Exposed and vulnerable, he possessed no protection from the winsome witch. She'd charmed and enchanted, bewitched and beguiled, cast her spell to where he no longer governed his thoughts.

But to lose her…let her go…

No, his noble intentions didn't extend that far. He would give her a choice. The parson's mousetrap, or revert to their original agreement. He must have her one way or another.

What woman wouldn't choose countess before courtesan?

He wouldn't let himself examine his fascination with Brooke past his physical fascination. Too dangerous… terrifying. What did *he* know of love? Nothing. No, better not to scrutinize his feelings too closely.

A week's acquaintance made a feeble foundation for marital bliss, but a few brilliant matches had started with less. Peculiar how seven days ago, marriage constituted nothing more than a business arrangement, a mutually beneficial union of convenience the earldom required of him. Today, he had selected Brooke, for no other reason than he couldn't bear to leave her or face another day without her.

His life prior to this was shrouded in an ash-gray cloud; seeing, hearing, tasting, living life in part, unaware of how much more vibrant and intense each sense—everything, for that matter—might be experienced. Brooke had awoken him to this new brilliance, and he'd lay odds, he'd only had a glimpse of what was possible.

Hell, she'd practically emasculated him. And worse? He didn't mind. Besotted by a violet-eyed, fair-haired Aphrodite with a heart bigger than England's tax coffers.

"What say you, Brooke?" Heath cupped her jaw, and rubbed his thumb across her soft cheek.

"Beg pardon?"

Her pale face, incredulous gaze, and mouth rounded into a perfect O of surprise, suggested she believed him insane, or perhaps he'd sprouted another nose or two upon his face.

Heath glanced around. Alone. The others had trekked halfway to the house already. Good. No one needed to witness Brooke's bafflement or his ineptitude at proposing. Should have done it properly, with flowers or a piece of jewelry. Perhaps a sonnet or a poem.

Women liked that sort of thing.

"Husband? You?" Her strangled squeak echoed with the same finality as the rat he'd seen seized in the jaws of a wharf cat one day at the docks.

"Yes." He grinned when her eyes widened further. "I thought you might prefer becoming my wife rather than my mistress."

High-minded of you, ruddy bounder.

Brooke shook her head. "Wife. Me?"

Had he so dazed her she couldn't string more than two words together? He'd shocked himself, so her stupefied expression didn't surprise him.

She spun away and stomped a few feet before halting to peek over her shoulder as she spoke to herself. "Why would he marry me? I'm a nobody, and he's an earl. We don't know each other, let alone like one another."

He flinched inwardly. Thorny prick, that. Couldn't fault her for her bluntness or the truth as she perceived it. She'd no reason to think he felt anything other than lust. Worse than a stag in the rut, he'd been.

Like, lust, love, luck...all different sides of the same die.

"Perhaps his head injury has addled him?" Hand on her chin, she squinted at Heath for an extended moment. "How does one know, I wonder? Surely there are other signs."

"Am I supposed to respond?"

Emotions vacillated upon her face. She stared, scrunched her eyebrows, and twisted her lips one way then the other. She rubbed the side of her face, blinking several times, and then pressed her mouth into a single, hard line.

He could almost hear the pinging of the thoughts careening about in her head. He cocked his. Not the reaction he'd expected, but Brooke had yet to do anything predictable. Heath strode to her. Best lay it out bare as a baby's arse. He gathered her into his arms, pressing a kiss into the soft hair atop her crown.

She didn't resist, although she trembled like a newborn kitten.

"These past days I've realized there's no woman more worthy of the title of countess than you, Brooke. You are more generous, noble, and self-sacrificing than any female of my acquaintance." He shrugged a shoulder and tweaked her pert nose. "I have to marry, in any event."

"How gallant of you." Mockery dripped thick enough to scoop with a shovel.

"Brooke, are you coming?" The Culpeppers hesitated at the bottom of the sloping hill. They exchanged wary glances before grasping their skirts and clomping up the rutted track. Four damsels to the rescue. A flock of yellowhammers pelted to the sky, yellow smudges against the blue, when the women tramped by.

Deep in conversation, Mabry and the man of God continued on their way. Mrs. Jennings and Flora had made the drive already, anxious to get inside and see to the rest of the meal preparation.

Leventhorpe faced them and planted his fists on his hips. He sent a peeved glance heavenward and lifted his hands. In supplication? Irritation?

Heath chuckled, enjoying his friend's aggravation. The Culpeppers had Leventhorpe at sixes and sevens, and a mouse in a maze fared better than the poor sot.

"I must be mad." Brooke twisted her glove in her hands and darted the oncoming quartet a guarded look. "They'll think me dicked in the nob—my head in the wool pile."

Heath's heart skidded sideways. Would Brooke say yes? He hadn't been altogether sure. Still wasn't.

She wobbled her glove at the others, who'd paused in ascending the hill. "Go on. I'll be inside shortly."

"Are you sure?" Brette's intelligent gaze flicked to Heath then to her sister. "We can stay. It's no bother."

Plucky for someone so tiny.

"Yes, I'm sure. His lordship and I have some, um, business details to discuss."

Business?

Is that how she saw his proposal? Well, why wouldn't she? There hadn't been a hint of anything remotely romantic in the way he asked her. He'd not wooed her, offered any trinkets, or pretty speeches.

Become my wife or mistress? Which will it be?

She presented her sister a tight-lipped smile and gestured at the house. "Go along, and check if everything is in order for our meal. And see that the reverend has a warm toddy."

They turned and obediently trundled in the direction they'd come. Several times one of the blondes either glanced over her shoulder or turned halfway round to observe Brooke. The scowls they hurled at Heath condemned him to a fiery afterlife and eternal damnation. No easy task winning their favor. Or Brooke's, though only her approval mattered.

The women met Leventhorpe on his way up the hill, and he circled one hand above his head. "Oh, for God's sake, are we performing some heathen burial ritual designed to ruin my boots?"

"Yes, your lordship." Her face serious as a parson's, Blythe pointed to the cemetery. "March around each headstone two times, skip through the center of the graveyard, perform a somersault while reciting The

125

Lord's Prayer, and kick your heels together before taking a hearty swig of pickle juice."

She winked. "That will assure Duffen turns over in his grave."

A chorus of giggles erupted, Blythe's the loudest.

Leventhorpe emitted a rude noise, somewhere between a snort and a growl.

Heath laughed outright.

Brooke couldn't prevent the smile twitching the corner of her mouth. "He's not been around women much, I'd guess. Has he sisters?"

"No, and his mother died when he was a toddler. The marchioness was a dotty dame. Ten years older than her husband, she didn't permit a single female house servant." Heath winked then waggled his brows. "The old marquis had a wandering eye and roving hands."

"Have *you* any sisters? If we marry, you're essentially inheriting four." She set her jaw, and a stubborn glint entered her eyes. "And the dairy farm too. I won't give it up."

Infernal farm and confounded cows. After the week he'd just spent, his favorite cheese could go to the devil with his blessings. He'd never be able to eat the stuff without remembering the dairy's stench.

"No, I haven't any sisters, but I rather like the chaos a gaggle of spirited women stirs up. I've been imaging the response the five of you would garner in London."

"Have you? Why?"

"Let's just say the *ton* has never experienced anything like the Culpeppers."

"Hmm, I suppose not."

They wandered to the cart track used to haul coffins to the graveyard. "I expected you would insist on the farm in your settlement negotiations. I'll make it a wedding gift to you."

Brooke stopped abruptly and stumbled over a root.

Heath grasped her arm to steady her. His fingers completely encircled her upper arm. Too thin. He'd see to it she'd not experience hunger again, darling girl.

"You will? Truly? To do with as I wish?" She clutched his arm, her eyes sparkling with excitement. "Would you allow me to build a simple house on the acreage so there's never an eviction worry again?"

A calf bawled, and a cow answered with a series of lowing grunts. Several more entered the fray, calling and mooing, their cries disturbing the peaceful morning.

Who would want a house nearer that racket?

Heath edged closer until his thigh brushed her skirts. He placed his hands on her shoulders, drawing her further into his embrace.

"Build a mansion, if you like. Anything to make you happy and keep a smile on your face." He touched her lips with his thumb. "Do you know, you rarely smile? Your lot in life hasn't been easy, has it?"

Brooke shook her head, the fair curls framing her face dancing. "I'm not complaining. It's been worth it." She contemplated the retreating women. If she retained regrets, she masked them behind the pride and love shining in her eyes. Her gaze brushed him, hovering an instant on his lips before flitting to a hawk circling overhead. She rolled a slender shoulder. "They needed me."

Simple as that. No excuses, pouting, or compunctions. She'd done what needed doing and did the job a far cry better than most men of his acquaintance would have. Any idiot decreeing women the weaker sex ought to be rapped upon the head with a cane.

"What of that Benbridge fellow? Do you love him?" Heath could have bitten his tongue off for blurting the question. He sounded like a jealous beau. What if she loved the young scamp? Jagged pain stabbed his middle.

Brooke's eyes rounded for a moment before she shook her head. "No, Humphrey is an old friend, but his parents would never permit a match between us. Besides, as I told you, we're a package deal. He had no interest in taking on such a large encumbrance." A forced smile bent her mouth the merest bit. "Truthfully, I cannot say I blame him. They've been a challenge."

"I promise, things will be better from now on. I'll do everything in my power to make your life easier and to make you happy." And by God, he meant it. Could Brooke hear the sincerity in his voice? He'd become a moon-eyed milksop. And liked it. A great deal, truth to tell. He, the reticent earl, known for his restraint and reason, issuing whimsical promises like a love-struck swain.

He almost touched his jaw to make sure it didn't hang slack at the epiphany that jostled his carefully structured life. In one week's time, Brooke had come to mean more to him than anything else: his title, his fortune, his friendships—few though they were—even Ebéné.

Nonsensical fairytales consisted of such fluff.

Stuff and nonsense.

Wonderful stuff and nonsense.

"I..." Her eyes misted, and she blinked as she stared at him, a mixture of awe and wonder on her face. She laughed and threw her arms around his neck in a fierce hug. "Thank you. Thank you. I feel like the weight of the world has been lifted from my shoulders."

He angled away to see her face. "May I take that as a yes?"

Gaze averted and pink tinging her cheeks, she nodded. "Yes, I'll marry you."

"Immediately?"

"Yes, as soon as the banns are read and arrangements can be made." Her flush deepened to rose and her gold-tipped lashes fanned her cheekbones. "But I still don't know how to address you."

"My friends call me Raven, but I like Heath best." He opened his hand, splaying his fingers over her smooth cheek and jaw.

Her focus slipped to his lips, and her voice acquired a husky edge. "When we first met, I would have said Raven suited you better."

"Coming from your lips, the name takes on an entirely different significance." He could almost imagine she'd whispered an endearment. Sap. Captivated, enamored sap. "By all means, call me Raven."

"No." Her eyes had grown sultry. "While it's true they are intelligent birds, they're also associated with dark omens."

"Then call me darling, or my love."

Her mouth formed another startled O, and she tucked her chin to her chest as color flooded her face.

He tipped her chin upward until their gazes met. A quick glance behind him assured Heath the others had almost made the orchard. "A kiss to seal our agreement?"

"All right." She shut her eyes and parted her lips in invitation.

No hesitation.

His soul leaped. How quickly could he secure a special license? Soon his week-long erection would finally be appeased.

The devil it will.

Not with Brooke as his wife. He'd have a perpetual rod jabbing his leg for the next fifty years. Long after his legs became too feeble to support his weight, his eyes too weak to see her delicate features, or his ears too dim to hear her delightful laugh, his penis would jump to attention whenever her scent teased his nostrils.

Her essence...addictive. An aphrodisiac of innocence and womanliness.

He feathered kisses atop her cheeks and chin, until at last he tasted her honeyed lips.

She sighed and opened her mouth, melting against him like wax above a flame.

Passion laced with a sweetness he couldn't identify engulfed him. A little moan escaped her when he cupped her buttocks and urged her against his hardness. She stood on her tiptoes, nestling her womanhood against the evidence of his arousal.

The jangle of harnesses followed by the creaking of coach springs, clomping of hooves, and snorts of winded horses yanked him from the ambrosia he'd been sampling.

One arm encircling Brooke at her waist—he doubted she could stand on her own, she leaned so heavily on him—he examined the road to the house. Two carriages drew up before the structure, one quite unpretentious and the other a crimson and black monstrosity he didn't recognize.

As Leventhorpe and the Culpepper misses approached the conveyances, the girls' heads dipped together and bobbed a bit. Probably pondering who the passengers were. Leventhorpe increased his pace and, in a few steps, led the small troupe.

"Who in the world?" Brooke shaded her eyes. She gasped and clutched Heath's arm too tightly, her nails biting into the flesh through his coat and shirt. "No, it cannot be."

He covered her hand with his. "What is it? Who is that?"

Pale as the fine blackthorn blossoms amidst the overgrown hedgerow surrounding the graveyard, Brooke turned her alarmed gaze to him. "I cannot be sure because I've never met him, but I think he," she pointed at the man peering from the carriage doorway, "might be our Cousin Sheridan."

Marrying without love is like gaming with an
empty purse; alas you have lost before you begin.
~*Wisdom and Advice—The Genteel Lady's Guide to Practical Living*

"You've met him." Brooke gripped her skirts, raised them ankle high, and matched Heath's stride as they hurried along the path. She sidestepped a muddy patch. Laden with bulging pink blossoms, wild cherry tree branches overhung the roadway, which was littered with the damp remnants of last evening's rain shower. Brooke neatly stepped over a dinner plate-sized puddle. "Is that my cousin?"

Please say no.

"Indeed." Tension firmed the contours of Heath's face into taut lines. "I'm curious why he's here on the heels of losing the wager to me and threatening you with eviction. You say you've never met him?"

He maneuvered around a deep puddle.

"No." What business had Sheridan here?

"Watch your footing. This path is a travesty of ruts and hollows." Heath dipped her a swift glance before regarding the new arrivals. "Gainsborough hasn't visited prior to this?"

Brooke shook her head. "Never. He left the farm's operation and the girls' care to me."

Sheridan yawned then frowned as he examined the house and courtyard. Displeasure contorted his features and curled his upper lip into a sneer. What did he expect? An opulent mansion with manicured grounds on the pittance he allowed them? Upon spotting the girls, he stopped scowling, and a disturbing smile skewed his mouth.

She leaped over a larger puddle. No man should regard his cousins with such speculation, like a commodity to market and sell to the highest bidder. Hound's teeth, she'd been afraid of this. Why did men regard her sister and cousins like delectable fruit, free for the picking and sampling?

"Heath, I don't trust Sheridan. Do you see the way he's leering at the girls?" She hitched her skirts in order to quicken her pace. "He's guardian to them. I cannot help but think his presence here doesn't bode well."

Heath gave a curt nod and quickened his stride. She possessed long legs but had to trot to keep up. They were practically upon the group, although no one appeared to have noticed them.

"That's deucedly unfortunate. How old are they? How old are you?" He regarded Brooke, running his gaze from the worn toes of her half boots, to the dated bonnet atop her head. "Ought to know if I'm leg-shackling myself to a chit long on the shelf."

Brooke's heart skipped an uncomfortable beat. Did he tease, or did he think her too old?

His strong mouth edged upward on one side, and he winked.

Brooke chuckled. "I'm afraid I'm ancient. Three and twenty."

"Tsk, tsk. You'll need a cane and spectacles before the year ends, as will I. I'm eight and twenty. What are the ages of the others?"

Brooke hastily told him.

"Immediately upon reaching London, I'll petition for guardianship." He gave her hand a light squeeze. "My connections reach much farther and higher than Gainsborough's. Your cousin's reputation isn't, shall we say, pristine. Leventhorpe's distantly related to the Lord Chief Justice, and I won't hesitate to request his help. I have little doubt my request will be granted."

"But what happens in the meanwhile?" She sucked in an unsteady breath. "He...he cannot take my sister and cousins, can he?"

Heath slipped an arm around her waist and gave her side a quick caress. "Over my dead body."

Relief flooded her. It had been so long since anyone else had helped bear the burden of the quartet's wellbeing. They reached level ground at the same time the foursome and Lord Leventhorpe gained the horseshoe-shaped courtyard.

Sheridan waited for them, appraising her sister and cousins much the same way a perspective buyer for one of the cows or calves did. She wouldn't have been surprised if he lined the quartet up on the auction block, peered in their mouths, and took a gander at their legs to see if they would bring a high enough price.

Another man, attired entirely in black, climbed from the second carriage.

Four visitors in a week? All male? Had Esherton Green become a favorite destination for men who wished to wreak havoc on the quiet, respectable lives of the Misses Culpepper? They had better not plan on staying in the house. Unless she crammed one on a larder shelf and stuffed the other in the drawing room window seat, no sleeping quarters remained.

The sun glinted on the newcomer's honey-colored head as he too peered around before stretching. Her sister and cousins resumed their covert whispers, taking his measure as assuredly as Sheridan took theirs. The golden man broke into a wide grin and lifted a hand in greeting as Leventhorpe marched to him. They knew each other?

"Blast me, what's Hawksworth doing here?" Heath's question harnessed Brooke's musings.

Winded from her near run—surely that caused her breathless voice and not his lordship's hand curled at her waist—she regarded the Adonis. Josephina had shown her a book portraying Greek gods and goddesses. This man with his curling hair and hewn features very well might have stepped from the pages of the volume. "You're acquainted with him?"

"Yes, he's Alexander Hawksworth. A good friend of Leventhorpe's and mine. He's the rector of a large parish outside London."

A man resembling a mythical god preached about the Christian deity? She'd wager his church's pews didn't sit empty Sunday mornings.

"Perhaps he should marry us." Heath grinned, amusement crinkling the corners of his eyes, but then the humor slipped from his face faster than a hot iron erased wrinkles. "No, never mind. I wouldn't hear the end of it from either of those buffleheads."

At the precise moment Sheridan and Reverend Hawksworth swiveled in her direction, Brooke lost her footing on a slick spot. She clutched Heath's coat and scrambled to regain her balance. One moment she skidded along, legs spread wide, the next, she lay on her back, Heath half atop her. She opened her eyes, and ceased to breath. From knee to shoulder, his sinewy form mashed into her, and she welcomed his weight. The blistering heat in his eyes sent a pang burning from her breast to her nether regions before suffusing her entire body in prickly warmth.

The sensation wasn't unpleasant. Not at all.

"I say, remove yourself from my cousin's person at once." Sheridan charged in their direction, his mouth puckered tighter than an old maid expecting her first kiss. "Get off her, this instant."

Heath whispered in her ear. "Let me handle this, please."

Oh, I don't think so.

She hadn't time to respond before Sheridan descended upon them. He glared at Heath then turned a vapid gaze on her as she sprawled beneath him. "Which one are you?"

Heath rolled off her, and after standing, extended his hand to Brooke.

"I'll assist her, Ravensdale." Sheridan thrust his square hand at her. "She's my ward, after all."

"Hardly, since I'm of age. Besides, I've never set eyes on you before in my life." Brooke ignored Sheridan's assistance and accepted Heath's. Her cousin would get no quarter from her. If he thought he could troop into Esherton and take over now, he was in for a most unpleasant surprise.

When Heath didn't promptly release her hand, Sheridan's crafty gaze narrowed, but he bent at the waist, nonetheless. "Sheridan Gainsborough, your cousin, come to survey my estate before taking you and your sisters to—"

"Three are my cousins, which you ought to know since my father appointed you their guardian five years ago." God's bones, fury whipped her temper. Who did the lickspittle think he was, showing up unannounced and having the ballocks to dictate to her? "And you only own the house and five acres. Or did you forget you wagered away the rest to Lord Ravensdale here?"

She jabbed her thumb at Heath's chest.

Brooke extracted her hand from his loose hold and glanced behind her at her skirt. Mud-streaked from hem to bum. She skimmed Heath's tight buttocks and long legs. Him too. Nevertheless, she quirked an eyebrow at Sheridan.

Well, she silently challenged him. *Deny it, you cur.*

"Er, yes, quite right." He puffed out his chest and attempted to look down his bulbous nose at her, reminding her of an outraged bantam rooster. All bluster and no might.

Considering she boasted four inches on him, his pretense proved ridiculous.

Heath's lips quivered, and amusement glinted in his eyes. Or mayhap approval lit his gaze.

"Brooke, are you all right?" Brette, wide-eyed with worry, reached her first. The twins and Blythe came next with Leventhorpe and Hawksworth bringing up the rear.

"I'm perfectly fine." Aside from wanting to lay Sheridan out.

Blaike edged around Sheridan, her eyes averted. Astute girl. She perceived a lecher when she encountered one. She examined Brooke's gown. "I'm afraid the material might be permanently stained. Best we get you into the house and have it laundered at once."

"That rag is hardly worth salvaging." Sheridan scrutinized her sister and cousins. "Every one of you looks like you stepped from the poorhouse. What have you been doing? Gallivanting in the woods? It's a good thing I arrived, cousin. From what I've observed, you have no notion whatsoever of how to run a profitable estate or supervise young ladies of quality."

The hawk screeched. At least Brooke thought the bird had made the harsh cry. It may have been one of the girl's irate shrieks. Or hers.

Jackanape.

Brooke's breath left her on a drawn-out hiss as slurs romped about in her head, begging to be hurled at the oaf. She clenched her teeth and fists to keep from spewing the vulgar filth—a proper lady didn't know such foul oaths—in front of those assembled and to keep from popping Sheridan in his globular nose. Her betrothed didn't need to see or hear her acting the part of a termagant.

"I'd watch my tongue if I were you, Gainsborough. You haven't a pickle's knowledge about the commendable efforts these women," Heath swept his hand in an arc to include all the Culpeppers, "have made to keep this farm operating, no thanks to you."

"And I suppose you do?" Sheridan speared Heath a dark look. "By the by, why are you here?"

"I might ask you the same thing." The devil inhabited the stare Heath stabbed at Sheridan.

Sheridan's bravado wilted. "If you insist on knowing—

"Oh, I do." Silky, but dangerous.

A flush further reddened Sheridan's blotchy cheeks. "I decided to take a break from the London scene and acquaint myself with my cousins."

"Chased out of town by debt collectors or threatened with debtor's prison, I'd bet." Leventhorpe took a position beside Heath. "Have I the right of it?"

A ruddy hue turned Sheridan's ears purple. He shuffled his feet and pulled at his neckcloth. "Um, nothing of the sort."

Ah, the marquis had hit the target, spot on.

The reverend made a leg. "Lovely ladies, please allow me to introduce myself, as neither of my ill-mannered friends has done so. Reverend Alexander Hawksworth, but please call me Hawksworth. I look round for my esteemed uncle when I hear anyone say reverend outside my parish."

Brooke and the foursome curtsied, but Sheridan smirked and made no move of deference.

Heath made the necessary introductions.

"Didn't your uncle skip off with the baker's daughter?" Leventhorpe scratched the back of his neck. "Or was it the tailor's? I cannot quite remember, but the gossip columns buzzed for weeks."

"Neither, you dolt." Hawksworth smiled, a flash of white teeth, and his green eyes crinkled. "Aunt Elspeth was a nun. Terrible scandal. Anglican priest hieing off to Gretna Green with a Catholic nun. But He," he pointed heavenward, "had other plans for her. She had six children at last count. Happy as grigs, they are."

"*Reverend*?" Blaike wiggled her brows at Blaire. "I must say, I didn't see that coming. I thought he commanded the stage or opera. Something much more...colorful, with those looks."

Blaire nudged Brette. "Told you he wasn't Sheridan's valet."

Hawksworth pressed his hands to his chest in mock offense. "Valet, dear me. Really?" He glanced at his somber garb. "It's the togs, isn't it? But the church frowns on me wearing anything flamboyant or ornate. I really rather adore bright colors, particularly blue."

He looked pointedly at her blue gown.

"Enough of this drivel. Might we make our way into the house?" Sheridan swept the structure a disdainful glance while fussing with his waistcoat.

Brooke bristled. He had no right to criticize the staid old manor. Through prosperity and poverty, the building had been a pleasant home and for generations had witnessed the births, lives, and deaths of Culpeppers.

The breeze shifted direction, filling the air with the barn's aroma. Sheridan's bug-eyes bulged and, frantic, he groped around in his jacket. Gasping, he yanked a handkerchief free. He slapped the cloth over his nose. "My God, what is that unholy stench?"

"I said the same thing when I first arrived." Heath gave a hearty laugh. "You'll get used to it."

"Not as long as I draw a breath." Sheridan shook his head. His face pressed into the fabric muffled his words. "Gentlemen, I really must discuss my plans with my cousins."

He notched his nose higher, daring to put on a superior facade. Didn't he realize he ranked the lowest of the men present? Pretentious toady, and with his face mashed into the handkerchief, Brooke found it impossible to take him seriously.

He drew the cloth away and took a tentative sniff, scrunching his nose at once. Considering the size of the appendage, it rather resembled a pleated dinner roll. Not an attractive sight. "I am famished, and I must change from these travel-soiled clothes."

"Not too terribly road-stained as London is less than an hour's coach ride away," Leventhorpe muttered.

Touché.

Sheridan curled his lip but kept silent.

Leventhorpe might not be such a bad sort, after all, once you got past his prickly exterior.

"Indulge me a moment, Gainsborough." Reverend Hawksworth flicked his hand as if Sheridan were a bothersome insect before turning a brilliant smile on Brooke. Each service, his church probably burst with parishioners, and mostly of the female persuasion, or she wasn't a Culpepper.

Sheridan rolled his eyes skyward and huffed his displeasure. Crossing his arms, he tapped one foot impatiently and scowled like a lad denied a bonbon.

Worse than a petulant child.

Reverend Hawksworth lifted her hand, although his mouth remained a respectable distance above it. Good thing, too, since she hadn't donned her glove again. "May I tell you how honored I am to meet the future Countess of Ravensdale?"

How in the world did he know about Heath's proposal?

"Countess?" A chorus of voices echoed, including Sheridan's, which ended on a hoarse squeak. Fury radiated from his rodent gaze.

The quartet swung their confused gazes between Brooke and Heath, before, one by one, they rested their attention on her. Their expressions fairly screamed the questions they didn't voice.

Better his wife than his mistress, righto?

She flashed Heath a sideways glance, distrust and betrayal squeezing her ribs between their vice-like claws. Had he feigned ignorance regarding the timing of Hawkworth's arrival? Possibly. Yet to this point, Heath hadn't been dishonest. That she knew of, in any event.

She scrunched her toes in her boots. Face it. Theirs hadn't been the sunniest of acquaintances from the onset. And she did say yes to his proposal despite that. Had her good sense flown in the face of desperation?

Lovely way to start a marriage.

Forced marriage, Brooke.

No, not forced. Convenient.

Everything about the union smacked of convenience on both their parts. Except, her heart had become engaged somewhere over the course. When, she couldn't quite say. When he'd fallen in the drawing room? Kissed her outside the stables? Followed her around like a trusting puppy after Duffen's death?

Fear kept her from acknowledging in her mind what her heart had insisted for days. Laughable if the situation weren't so pathetic and clichéd. The whole matter screamed of a Drury Lane drama.

The reverend released her hand. "I hope you'll permit me the honor of performing the ceremony."

The claws dug deeper, drawing her soul's blood.

"You knew of Lord Ravensdale's plans to marry me?" How? She'd only learned of them a few minutes ago.

"Indeed." Hawksworth patted his chest. "I have the special license right here."

Brooke whipped round and confronted Heath.

"You pretended to know nothing about his arrival, yet he has a license?" Brooke poked him in the chest. Hard. "You deceiving bounder. What else have you lied about?"

He who mistakenly believes gambling a
harmless amusement has never looked into the ravaged
faces of those made victims by another's wasteful pastime.
~Wisdom and Advice—The Genteel Lady's Guide to Practical Living

Heath rubbed the back of his head as Brooke and her angel-haired entourage flounced inside the manor. Brilliant. An infuriated, distrustful bride.

Sheridan trailed them like an unwelcome stray, his mangy tail tucked between his legs.

"Am I mistaken, or is all not as it should be between you and your lady, Raven?" A deep furrow creased the bridge of Hawkworth's nose. When the last woman disappeared through the entrance, he turned an expectant gaze on him.

Heath brushed mud from his elbow as he made his way to the house. "How the blazes did you know we'd become betrothed?"

Falling in step beside him, Hawksworth pointed at Leventhorpe. "He sent a message two days ago. Said to get a special license and be here today, ready to perform your nuptials."

Hawksworth cast a practiced gaze to the graveyard. "And a funeral? The same day? Not precisely tasteful. I ran a bit behind schedule in London obtaining the license, hence my tardiness. I did wonder why Leventhorpe, and not you, made the request though, Raven."

"Because he's a bloody, interfering arse." Heath marched to the house, just short of a run. He needed to talk to Brooke, explain the situation to her, convince her he'd known nothing of Hawksworth's arrival until the moment he exited the carriage in all his celestial glory.

What if she changed her mind?

No, with Sheridan's unexpected arrival, she had more reason than ever to marry him.

He hoped.

He'd seen the fear she'd tried to hide. Her cousin frightened her, or perhaps the power he'd been granted over her sister and cousins caused her trepidation. But that didn't mean she wasn't livid with Heath.

"Explain yourself, Trist, and be quick about it." Heath gave Leventhorpe a sideways glare.

Leventhorpe shrugged as the trio climbed the steps, their boots clinking on the stones. "You talk in your sleep, Raven."

Heath snorted. "I do not."

"Trust me, you do, and you snore like a bloody lion in the process of choking on haunch of water buffalo. Your bride has my condolences in that regard. I really ought to warn her, but she might change her mind, and you'd be an even more unbearable sot." Leventhorpe gave a theatric yawn behind his hand. "It's a wonder I'm able to function at all, I've become so deprived of sleep."

Hawksworth chuckled and gestured between Heath and Leventhorpe. "The two of you share a room? That ought to be interesting."

"Yes, and he's been muttering on in his sleep about marrying Miss Culpepper for days now...or, rather, for nights."

"I have not." Had he? Damn.

"Yes, you have. Incessantly. Enough to force me to bury my head beneath my pillow to muffle your nattering and become desperate enough to send for Hawk."

They handed their hats and gloves to the waiting footman. He promptly trotted down the hallway, no doubt to assist in serving the meal.

"I thought I'd give you a nudge, Raven, since your conscience had already made the decision for you. And until last evening, we didn't know if Avery would officiate at the funeral." Leventhorpe inhaled deeply, peering in the dining room's direction. "Hmm, something smells delicious."

"Damned presumptuous of you." Heath scraped his hand through his hair. "Now she's furious with me. Thinks I manipulated her again."

"Again?" Hawksworth peered at him, his gaze teeming with amusement and curiosity.

"Yes, that respectable miss lost a wager to Raven and agreed to become his mistress." Leventhorpe gave Heath a brusque nod. "His terms, by the way."

Shit.

The comment pealed loud and reproachful in the entry.

"You intended to make that young woman your paramour?" Disapproval sharpened Hawksworth voice and features. "Far below par, and you well know it."

"Yes, I bloody well know it, which is why, after the funeral, I asked her to marry me."

Hawksworth grunted and folded his arms, looking very much an avenging angel. "Is there a single romantic bone in your body? Anywhere? I realize you're not a sentimental chap, but proposing on the heels of a funeral service... Damned crass, that."

"Exceedingly gauche." Leventhorpe nodded his agreement, his attention straying down the corridor again. "But when one is desperate..."

"Why marry someone you've only known..." Hawksworth glanced to Leventhorpe for help.

"A week."

"Eight days." Heath promptly regretted the correction when his friends exchanged mocking glances.

"Yes, the extra day makes *all* the difference." Leventhorpe drawled the word, earning him another murderous scowl from Heath.

"I should think a longer acquaintance would be beneficial to both of you." Hawksworth narrowed his eyes, his astute gaze probing. "Intelligent people do not decide to marry after a week unless they fall in love at first sight. Which I find beyond belief in your case. No offense intended."

I'm not supposed to be offended when one of my closest chums insults the hell out of me?

Leventhorpe's shout of laughter muffled Heath's rude noise.

"Raven? Love at first sight? Oh, that's rich." Leventhorpe's shoulders continued to shake. "Lust, yes. But love? Not him. Never him."

He hooted again.

Fine friend, boorish knave.

"Well, I cannot stay here, and I won't leave without her."

Where was Brooke? Heath craned his neck, gawking first along the passageway and then up the stairway. Had she retreated to her chamber to avoid him?

"Neither will I take her with me unless she's my wife. It would spell her ruination."

He peeked in the study. Nope, not there.

"I promised her and her family a better life than they've had, and I mean to keep my word."

Maybe she'd escaped to the barn again.

"And that rat bastard of a cousin will dance naked in court, scrawny ballocks bared for the royals, before a single Culpepper accompanies the sod anywhere."

"Sounds like love to me." Hawksworth lifted a hand and raised his fingers one at a time. "Putting her needs before yours. Unwilling to be apart from her. Wanting to provide and care for her...and her family."

He wiggled his four fingers and waggled his eyebrows like an inebriated court jester.

"Oh, and the desire to protect her." Up sprang his thumb.

"Don't preach to me, Hawk, when you know nothing of love." Was she in the kitchen?

Leventhorpe regarded Heath, a speculative spark in his eye. "Hmm, as impossible as it is for me to believe, Hawk's made some valid points. And you did mumble something that sounded like love in your sleep, though your speech was so garbled—rather like a drunk chewing a mouthful of marbles—I might have been mistaken."

"Don't be an imbecile, Trist." As much as Heath wanted to deny everything Hawk had said, a measure of truth resonated in his friend's words. He'd be hung if he'd admit it to his two smirking cohorts.

Do I love Brooke?

The theory explained much.

Hawksworth shook his head so hard, a shock of hair tumbled onto his brow. "It's either love, or the knock on your head Leventhorpe wrote me about has deprived you of your reason, in which case, I cannot in good conscience perform the ceremony."

"My thoughts exactly." Thumping echoed above, much like a toddler kicking their heels during a fit of temper. Leventhorpe raised his gaze to the vibrating ceiling. "What's going on up there?"

Heath rolled a shoulder and raked his hand through his hair again.

A calculating gleam entered Leventhorpe's gaze. "Did she say yes when you proposed?"

"I did." Brooke stood just inside the drawing room.

A small sigh of relief escaped Heath. He detected no trace of anger. Wasn't she still upset? He ran an appreciative gaze over her. She'd changed into a simple cream gown, with puff sleeves and a wide emerald ribbon below the bust. Pink and green embroidered flowers edged the hemline. An odd combination of vulnerability and determination shadowed her hollow cheeks and wary eyes.

His heart welled with emotion. *Love.* He loved her. Damn, but this pleasure-pain wasn't what he'd expected. It was more, so much more, and it scared the hell out of him.

Had she heard their entire exchange? Her gaze skimmed Leventhorpe and Hawksworth before landing on Heath. Her soul stretched across the room and touched his.

Yes. She had.

A loud crash reverberated overhead, followed by hollering and violent banging. She flinched, her face draining of color.

"What the devil is happening above stairs?" Heath pointed upward.

Anxiousness replaced Brooke's composure. She clasped her hands before her.

"It's Sheridan." After a hurried glance behind her into the drawing room, she glided farther into the entry and lowered her voice. "I'd like us to exchange vows at once."

"You're not still upset that Leventhorpe arranged for Hawksworth to be here? That he has a license?" Heath extended a hand in entreaty. "Please believe me, I didn't know until the moment you did."

Her shoulders slumped, and she sighed. "It's of no consequence. You'd already asked me to marry you, and I agreed. I've explained the situation to my sister and cousins. Although they are not happy with the circumstances, we are in agreement that the urgency of the situation requires an immediate wedding."

The caterwauling and crashing overhead increased in fervor.

Her gaze searched his. "If you are willing, my lord."

"Of course, I am. Nothing would please me more." He spoke the truth. Marrying her had become his greatest desire, more so than bedding her. Heath glanced at his dirty pantaloons. "You don't want me to change first?"

"No." She cast a troubled glance toward the stairs. "Sheridan's determined to keep me from marrying you and forcing us all to return to London with him. He's threatened to raise an objection during the ceremony on the preposterous, and untrue, grounds that I'm betrothed to another. He thinks to delay the wedding long enough to take custody of my sister and cousins, and I haven't a doubt in the world that his intentions aren't honorable."

"Rotten bounder." Murder glittered in Leventhorpe's eyes. "I'd like to see him try."

She thrust her adorable chin upward and squared her thin shoulders. "We've locked him in the twin's bedroom. That's what the commotion above stairs is."

"Well done, Miss Culpepper. A little isolation usually calms the soul." The reverend raised a speculative glance to the ceiling as bits of dust and plaster sifted down. "However, in this case, given the ruckus above, I'm inclined to believe demonic forces might have been released instead."

He stepped forward. "May I ask how old you are? I cannot legally marry you in England unless you are of age."

"I'm three and twenty. I have proof in the study."

"Good by me." He gestured to the drawing room entrance. "Shall we?"

"Um, what of the vicar?" Had everyone but Heath forgotten about the other man of the cloth?

Brooke's lips curved into a closed-mouth smile.

"He's feasting in the dining room. I explained a dear friend of the groom's had arrived and desired to perform the nuptials. I don't know which peeved him more: missing the promised meal or the ceremony fee." She fidgeted with her skirt, her gaze cast to the floor. "I'm afraid I assured him he'd be paid anyway, and I...I don't have the funds."

A ferocious hammering and several unsavory curses sounded from above.

"I'll pay the fee, but I think it's best we get on with the vows, posthaste." Heath took her elbow and guided her into the drawing room. Petal soft skin met his fingertips. Was the rest of her as silky? He would know tonight.

And he'd worship her with his heart and body.

Her family sat primly on the sofa and ugly chairs, Freddy perched on Miss Blythe's lap. Wariness cloaking them, they stood when Brooke and the men filed into the room. The dog eyed Leventhorpe but remained on the sofa where Blythe had placed him. He wagged his tail once.

Progress.

"Hawk, is there an expedited ritual?" Heath gave Brooke's arm a reassuring squeeze.

The sound of wood cracking and more cursing rent the air.

Everyone's attention raised to the ceiling. To the Culpepper misses' credit, all remained composed aside from disconcerted expressions.

"Sheridan's destroying the house," Brooke whispered. "He's a madman."

"Hawk?" Urgency prodding him, Heath bit out the name harsher than he'd intended. "The ceremony?"

"Short and sweet it is." Hawksworth glanced round to everyone assembled. "I'll assume no one here objects to the union?"

Leventhorpe and the Culpepper misses gave negative shakes of their heads.

"Excellent. Ravensdale and Miss Culpepper, join hands."

Heath clasped Brooke's hands.

She raised her gaze to his, her eyes bright and clear, before she flushed and her lashes swept her cheeks. He almost convinced himself something more powerful than desperation and fear warmed her eyes.

Hawksworth faced Heath and Brooke. "Miss Culpepper...what's your full name?"

"Brooke Theodora Penelope Culpepper." Did her voice tremble the merest bit?

Hawksworth cleared his throat. "Why, Ravensdale, I don't know your full name. Three and ten years acquainted and I just now realized that."

"Oh, for the love of God." Leventhorpe stomped to lean against the closed doors. "Do get on with it before that lunatic," he jabbed his forefinger straight up, "interrupts."

"It's Heath Adrian Lionel Sylvester Kitteridge, Earl of Ravensdale." Heath clasped Brooke's cold, damp hands tighter. Yes, she quivered like a newborn lamb.

Hawksworth scratched his chin. "Hmm, five names? Most impressive."

One of the twins tittered, but a stern glance from Brooke hushed her.

"Wise to leave off the preliminary parts, I think." Hawksworth pointed above them. "Wilt thou have this woman to be thy wedded wife, to live together after God's ordinance in the—"

"I will. I take Brooke to be my wedded wife, for richer, for poorer, in sickness and in health, to love and to cherish, till death us do part." Heath bent his head toward Brooke. "Her turn. Hurry."

"Wilt you have this man to be thy wedded husband—"

Footsteps pounded above along the corridor leading to the stairway. *Bloody maggoty hell.*

Heath shook his head. "Skip that part."

Hawksworth shot a knowing glance overhead. "Yes, quite. Forget the formal mumbo jumbo too. Brooke, will you take Heath to be your husband?"

She tilted her head and met Heath's gaze head on. "I will."

Thumping on the stairs caused the quartet to gasp and clutch one another's hands, except for Blythe, who bolted to the desk.

Heath slid his signet ring off his little finger. "I'm sorry, it's much too big. I'll purchase you a wedding ring when we reach London. Maybe amethyst to match your eyes."

Leventhorpe snickered but turned the laugh into a hearty cough at Heath's scowl.

Heath slipped the heavy gold onto Brooke's slender finger.

She covered the band with her other hand before shooting the doors a distressed look.

Hawksworth inhaled in a huge lungful of air and raced through the last few lines. "Forasmuch as Heath and Brooke have consented together in holy wedlock, and have witnessed the same before God and this company, and thereto have given and pledged their troth either to other, and have declared the same by the giving and receiving of a ring, and the joining of hands; I pronounce that they be man and wife together. In the Name of the Father, and of the Son, and of the Holy Ghost. Amen."

Hawksworth grinned and wiped his perspiring forehead. "Just barely legal in God's eyes. You may kiss your bride."

"No. Later." Blythe held a quill at the ready. "Hurry, you must sign the license."

Footsteps thundered in the entry.

Hawksworth, Heath, and Brooke dashed to the desk.

Heath snatched the quill as Hawksworth spread the license atop the desk.

He couldn't read the damn thing. No time for pride. "Where do I sign?"

"Just there." Hawk pointed.

Heath scribbled his signature then passed the quill to Brooke.

"And Lady Ravensdale, you sign here." Hawksworth indicated

another place on the parchment.

She neatly affixed her signature.

"Let me in. I forbid Brooke to marry that cur." The drawing room door handles rattled violently before the panels shuddered as Gainsborough smashed something against them.

"I don't believe I care for our cousin, Brooke." Brette frowned at the door.

The others murmured their assent.

"Dammit, I say. Let me in."

"If you insist." Leventhorpe yanked the door open then dodged aside.

Red-faced and sweating, a blob of spittle hanging from the corner of his mouth, Gainsborough plowed into the room. He skidded to a stop and tottered when the carpet wrinkled underfoot.

Growling deep in his throat and hackles raised, Freddy leaped to his feet.

Gainsborough swung his furious gaze from Brooke, to Heath, to Hawksworth then fixed his attention on Brooke. A jeer contorted his features. "I'll never permit the marriage to be consummated. I'll have it annulled."

A small gasp escaped Brooke. She grasped Heath's hand. "I'm of age. He cannot do that, can he?"

"No, he cannot..." Leventhorpe followed Gainsborough into the room's center.

Gainsborough spun to face the other man. "I most certainly—"

"...if he's incapacitated and locked up." Leventhorpe planted Gainsborough a solid facer.

Bone crunched, and Blaire buried her face in her twin's shoulder. Gainsborough teetered, his eyes rolling back into his head, before he crashed to the floor, blood seeping from his nose.

Blythe grinned and clapped. "Well done, my lord."

He swept her a courtly bow.

"I believe this gentleman, and I do use the term with extreme disdain, has a reservation in a dovecote for the next, oh, say three days?" He flexed his fingers then rubbed his knuckles. "Is that sufficient time, Raven?"

"Indeed." He lifted Brooke's hand and kissed the back of her hand. "This time tomorrow, we'll be in London, and I'll be seeking guardianship."

She gifted him with a brilliant smile.

Hawksworth leaned forward and examined Gainsborough's prone figure. "I believe you broke his nose, Leventhorpe."

"Which can only improve the hideous appendage," Brooke said. "Looked rather like a bull elephant seal I saw in a book once."

After moment of astounded silence, laughter filled the room.

"Ladies, would you care to show me to the dining room?" Hawksworth extended both elbows. "The wonderful smells have tempted me beyond resistance this half hour past."

Blaire and Blaike swooped in like bees to a flower.

Typical reaction to Hawksworth—women making a cake of themselves. Surely The Almighty had a delightful sense of humor, permitting a man with Hawk's extreme good looks to be a man of God. Not that the vocation had been Hawk's first choice, but a parish proved a more desirable workplace if one must earn one's living than the battlefield or the deck of a rolling ship.

"By the by, Raven, I'm grateful you and your lovely bride came to an accord on your own. I asked Hawk to bring a license because I wouldn't have permitted you to besmirch her by making her your mistress. I fully intended to see you marry her, even if it meant I held a gun to you during the ceremony." After winking at Brooke and giving Heath a mocking salute, Leventhorpe offered his bent elbows to Blythe and Brette. Wearing bemused expressions, they, too, departed the room.

A grin etched on his face—Leventhorpe had flummoxed him, by God—Heath directed the footmen to remove Gainsborough to the dovecote and see him secured there.

Brooke stared out the window, her profile illumed by the filtered rays bathing the window. She appeared almost ethereal, her hair a shiny halo in the golden light. Twisting the ring on her finger, she turned soulful violet eyes to him. "Could we wait until we get to London to consummate the marriage?"

Some claim fortune favors the bold. However,
believing such rationality applies to love and happiness
is as ridiculous as wagering against the sun rising each morn.
~*Wisdom and Advice—The Genteel Lady's Guide to Practical Living*

19

Brooke ran the brush through her hair, the long strokes soothing her rattled nerves. She'd passed the remainder of the day in a haze except for Heath's response to her question. That she remembered clear as crystal.

"No. We cannot."

His scorching gaze had threatened to singe the ends of her hair and turned her insides quivery and warm. Disturbing, yet tantalizing too. What that man did to her with a simple look...

She trembled head to toe.

"Of course he wouldn't want to wait."

She didn't really want to either, but fear of the unknown made her hesitant.

Brooke glanced at her bed covered in a handmade quilt Mama had sewed many years ago. The small bed had suited her well all these years. With Freddy tucked at her side, dozens of books had been read snuggled beneath the comforting bedclothes. And buckets of tears had dampened the pillows too.

Her gaze swept the tiny chamber meant for use as servants' quarters and scarcely bigger than the kitchen larder. Its ceiling sloped to the eaves on one side. Heath had better watch his head, or he'd be cracking his noggin on a beam. The girls shared the other two larger bedchambers, the twins' now affixed with a temporary door thanks to Sheridan's earlier violence. Brooke didn't mind. She liked her private sanctuary, the one place she could go and be alone. No expectations or demands in this cranny of the house.

Until Heath came to claim his husbandly rights tonight. Thank goodness her chamber was situated on the uppermost floor and the opposite side of the house from the quartet's. Nonetheless, everyone beneath the roof would know what she and Heath were about. Heat consumed her, and she lifted the heavy mass of hair from her neck, allowing the air to cool her nape.

Brooke pondered the bed again. Would his feet stick over the end? "Hardly big enough for me, let alone two people."

An image of them toppling onto the floor amidst the marriage act leaped to mind.

Good God. Every thump and bump would be heard below. She pressed cool hands to her hot cheeks.

Someone, likely Brette or Blythe, had put fresh sheets on the bed and set a vase of flowers on her dressing table. Extra candles had also been placed throughout the room. A wine bottle and two glasses sat upon a tray. Leventhorpe's doing, likely. Brooke jumped to her feet, her nerves threatening to erupt from her skin. She rubbed her hands up and down her bare arms, not to warm her flesh, but to lessen her tension.

Poor Freddy had been banished to the twins' room for the night. He'd slept with her every night of his life. Would Heath forbid it in the future? Maybe he would be one of those husbands who only entered her chamber to conduct his conjugal visits and then returned to his room to sleep. The notion didn't cheer her. Mama and Papa had always shared a bedroom.

Brooke sighed, hugging her arms snugger around her shoulders.

Married to a practical stranger. Yet far preferable to becoming Heath's mistress. She wouldn't lie to herself and pretend she didn't find him deucedly attractive—his raven hair, intelligent eyes, sharp-hewn face, and sinewy muscles... She secretly thrilled that he'd chosen to wed her. And bed her.

Brooke smoothed a wrinkle from the bottom sheet before fluffing the pillows. No palatial chamber here. She straightened the primrose and sage coverlet. Fingering the silky border, she smiled.

How could she love Heath? Ridiculous. Impractical. Unwise.

Affection took time to develop. Didn't one need to know everything about someone to become enamored and fall in love?

No. She'd known Humphrey for years and had intimate knowledge of his likes, dislikes, preferences, and habits. The mild, comfortable affection she'd harbored for him resembled a skiff ride on a calm lake. Only an occasional fish jumping to catch an insect interrupted the serenity.

Heath, on the other hand...what she felt for him: wild, intense, unpredictable sentiments that left her muddled and excited and...yearning. A journey on rolling waves to an undetermined destination, but one she'd gladly travel with him by her side.

A soft *click* as the door closed announced his arrival.

Brooke whirled to face her husband. Her breath left her in a whoosh.

Attired in a black banyan, he held a pink rose. Where had he gotten a rose? The black hairs exposed by the vee of his robe tantalized. Were all women so obsessed with chest hair?

She wiped damp palms on her nightdress. White, unadorned, and nearly sheer from frequent laundering, the garment wasn't in the least alluring, yet his eyes darkened and the lines of his face tautened as he examined her leisurely.

A seductive grin skewed his lips, and he extended the rose, advancing farther into the room. "For you."

"Thank you." Brooke reached for the blossom.

Rather than releasing his hold, he wrapped his other palm around her hand and drew her near. Heath trailed the silky petals over her cheek then lower to her neck and finally brushed the flower across the flesh exposed above her modest neckline.

Brooke parted her lips on a silent gasp, her nipples going rigid. How could such a simple gesture make her want to crawl atop him and kiss him until she couldn't breathe? He couldn't breathe?

"When I touched your arm today, I wondered if the rest of your skin would feel as petal soft." He ran two fingers over her collar bone before dipping one into the valley between her breasts. "It does."

Brooke shivered and closed her eyes lest he see the lust he stirred in her. She'd never considered herself a sensual woman, but Heath wrought cravings and sensations impossible to ignore.

A moment later, his firm lips replaced his exploring fingers. He feathered little kisses and nips behind her ear, the length of her jaw and neck, and then nuzzled the juncture of her throat. A pleasant, aching heaviness weighted her breasts and filled her abdomen and between her legs.

She shifted, restless for something. Drawing away, Brooke smiled at him and laid her palm in the crisp mat on his chest. She rubbed her hand back and forth, enjoying the friction of the curls and the ecstasy on his face. Wanton power sluiced her. She had caused his response.

He groaned and gripped her buttocks, lifting her against his turgid length.

Brooke kissed his chest, pushing aside the silk covering his molded shoulders. She couldn't get close enough to him, couldn't taste enough of his salty-sweet skin. She darted her tongue out, tracing it over one of the chocolate-colored circles on his chest. His nipples were much darker than her pink-tinted ones, though hers were larger by far.

Another gravelly moan escaped him, and Heath tossed aside the rose before scooping her into his arms.

"I feared you'd be reluctant tonight." He traced his tongue across her parted lips. "I see I needn't have been worried." His fingers clenching her ribs and thigh, he sucked her lower lip into his mouth. "Tell me you want me too, Brooke."

He swept his tongue into her mouth, sparring with hers for a moment.

Heady dizziness encompassed her. If his kisses did this to her, what would making love with him do? She would never be the same. Didn't want to be. Heath brought an awareness she hadn't known existed. Hadn't known she'd lacked.

"I want to feel you against me. Your legs entwined with mine." Brooke wrapped her arms around his neck, pressing her breasts against his chest. "I want you inside me—"

He pulled his head back, his expression gone stern. "And just how do you know about that, pray tell me?"

Laying her fingertips across his mouth, she grinned. "I raise cattle. Did you forget?"

"Hmph." His disgruntled expression softened as he carried her to the bed. "Not the same at all."

"At all?" Brooke smiled, twirling her fingers in the long hair at his nape. "How is it different?"

"Animals mate out of instinct, a primitive drive to reproduce and appease lust-born urges. Some humans—most, actually—are little better." Heath's knees bumped the mattress, yet he didn't lower her. His gaze unfathomable, he stared at her, an intensity she'd never seen in his eyes before. "But humans, the few fortunate ones, find love. The act is an expression of their adoration."

His embrace tightened when he said the last words.

Brooke went completely still. Falling in love in a week's time was improbable and irrational. Could Heath—this proud, enigmatic, wonderful man—feel the same for her as she felt for him?

"Brooke... I..."

She laid her hand on his cheek and summoned every ounce of bravado she possessed. "Are you saying you love me?"

What if he says no?

"Yes, although I don't understand how or why it came to be." Happiness sparked in his eyes, and he turned his head to place a kiss in her palm. "I only know I couldn't leave you and return to London alone. Ripping my heart from my chest would be less painful."

His eyes grew misty and his voice hoarse. "And I was such an unmitigated, unforgiveable arse, suggesting you..." His gaze caressed her face before he bent and kissed her mouth reverently. "Suggesting you become my mistress."

He rested his forehead against hers. "Dare I hope, in time, you might come to forgive me and perhaps feel tenderness for me?"

Brooke blinked away the tears pooling in her eyes.

"I already have, and I already do." Unaccustomed bashfulness seized her, and she nestled her face in the crook of his neck. His pulse beat—strong and steady, like him—beneath her cheek.

"Oh, God, I love you." A shudder rippled through Heath, and he crushed her closer. "I didn't believe in love, dismissed it as foolish nonsense, didn't believe it ever possible for the likes of me."

She nodded against his chest. "I know. I'm as stunned as you."

He laid her on the bed then fanned her hair over the pillow.

"You have the most beautiful hair I've ever seen." His hands at his waist, he paused in untying the belt. "I know I said we couldn't wait to consummate the marriage because of the risk your cousin poses, but if you're afraid, we could delay a day or two."

Heath loved her. She had wanted him for days. Brooke lifted her arms to him. "I don't want to wait."

"Thank God." A wicked smile curved his mouth as he bent and tugged her night-rail over her head. He inhaled sharply, and his nostrils flared as his ravenous gaze feasted on her breasts in the muted candlelight.

She yanked the covers over her chest, not ready to wantonly display her womanly assets to him. Perhaps in time.

He shrugged from the ebony silk and the garment slid to the floor. As if he sensed her need to become acquainted with his body, he stood like a Greek statue, allowing her to look her fill. She couldn't detect an ounce of fat on his powerful form. A well-muscled chest and torso, covered in curly raven hair, tapered into a narrow waist and hips. The dense thatch at his groin arrested her attention. From the patch sprang an impressive phallus.

Bloody gorgeous and arousing beyond belief.

His member twitched, bobbing up and down, and grew even larger.

Her mouth went dry. Just how enormous did the thing get, and more on point, could she accommodate something that size?

Heath edged onto the bed and slid beneath the covers. He gathered her into his arms, tucking her to his side and laying one muscled thigh across her legs. His penis, greedy beast, flexed against her hip.

"Aren't you going to snuff the candles first?" Brooke cast an anxious glance at the flickering tapers. They bathed the room in a soft light a more experienced woman might consider romantic.

"No, love. I want to see and worship every inch of you. I want to cherish the expression on your face when I enter you and bring you to completion." He splayed his fingers atop her abdomen. "And I want you to see what you do to me. The power you hold over me."

He reached between them and laid his manhood on her thigh.

"You do this to me." Pressing her hand atop the velvety length, he spread hot, fervent kisses over her breasts. He traced one nipple with his tongue before pulling the tip into his mouth and sucking.

Brooke gasped. Sparks streaked from her breasts to her toes, igniting every pore along the way. "Dear God..."

She arched into his mouth and let her legs fall open to his exploring hand. Heat spiraled higher and hotter, threatening to consume her with each lave of his tongue and flick of his experienced fingers. The warm stiffness of his penis pulsed against her palm. She grasped the flesh and squeezed gently. "It's so soft, yet hard too."

Heath moaned against her neck. "You're killing me."

Brooke stopped fondling him instantly, biting her lip as he slipped his long fingers into her. She instinctively clamped her muscles around him, squeezing tighter as aching pleasure surged to her womb. A throaty cry tore from her.

"No, don't stop." He groaned and ground his pelvis against her hand.

The urge to rotate her hips overtook her with such ferocity, Brooke had no resistance. She bucked and pumped, aware of the hungry, whimpering noises she made, but not caring.

"That's it, sweetheart. You're nice and wet, almost ready for me."

Wet? That was a good thing?

He moved his fingers faster, deeper.

Oh God, yes, wet is good. Very good.

She spread her legs wider.

"Good girl," Heath breathed in her ear.

He positioned himself over her, the tip of his penis bidding entrance. Cupping her face between both palms, he kissed her with such tender reverence, if he hadn't already told her of his love, his kiss would have exposed the secret.

"Look at me, Brooke."

She forced her eyes open, drowning in overwhelming sensation and need.

"Heath? I need..." A throaty groan escaped her. "I want..."

He smiled, the corners of his eyes crinkling. "I know."

Slowly, he entered her, refusing to relinquish her gaze.

Brooke sighed at the rightness of it. *This* was what she wanted. Needed. Yet, it wasn't enough. More. There must be something more. Clutching his back, she wriggled her hips. Almost frantic with yearning, she rubbed her breasts against his chest.

He stopped his gentle invasion into her womanhood and wrapped one strong arm around her shoulders and one beneath her hips. "Now, love. Now."

Brooke surged upward as Heath plunged. A gasp tore from her as stinging pain seared her center. She trained her gaze on him, trusting him as the most marvelous of feelings radiated from where he joined with her.

"It feels wonderful," she whispered, testing the sensations by rocking her hips.

"It gets better, darling." He arched his spine, his corded neck muscles rigid. "Let me take you to heaven, where angels like you belong."

His breathing harsh and heavy, he began a rhythmic thrusting.

Brooke caught his tempo as he ground into her. She wrapped her legs round his waist and let him carry her heavenward. The world ceased to exist around her. Only she and Heath and this moment of incredible bliss mattered. And just when she thought she could bear no more, when her soft whimpers become small cries of desperation, she fractured and screamed his name, convulsing over and over as indescribable ecstasy ravaged her.

A moment later, he roared his fulfillment.

She welcomed each pounding thrust, knowing he enjoyed the same rush of pleasure she just had. Breathing heavily, he flopped onto his back, pulling Brooke atop his sweat-slicked chest. Several moments passed before her ragged breathing and thrumming heartbeat returned to normal. Delicious drowsiness surrounded her. No wonder Buford had rutted until the moment he'd keeled over. Not a bad way to die at all.

"Never, in all my days, have I ever experienced anything that...that incredible." Heath hugged her fiercely, his lips pressed to the top of her head.

Brooke snuggled into his side and yawned. Head on his shoulder, she ran her fingers through his chest hair. "Can we do it again? I should like to try making love the way the cows do, with you from behind."

Heath grinned and tweaked her nose. "In a bit. I need awhile to recover."

The candles had burned to nubs when Brooke finally roused enough to pull the coverlet atop her and Heath. She gazed at his sleeping form. Her husband. She smiled and shook her head then lay down, her head nestled on his shoulder again.

"What are you smiling about?"

She tilted her head to look at him. Exotic eyes regarded her. She really did need to ask him about his heritage. "I thought you were asleep."

"Hardly, with a tantalizing siren beside me. I shall be in a constant state of arousal until the day I die." The bedding shifted above his pelvis.

She peeked beneath the blankets and giggled. "Poor man. That has to be uncomfortable."

He caressed her shoulder and arm. "Why were you smiling when you thought I was asleep?"

"I imagined what I'd tell our children when they asked how we met." She scratched her nose where his hair tickled her. "I'm not sure I want them to know a wager brought us together and we wed after a mere week. Not a very good example, I shouldn't think."

"Ah, but imagine what a romantic tale we've created. It will serve as an inspiration for our children, to believe true love really does exist." Heath chuckled and palmed her breast, gently pinching the peak.

A jolt of pleasure speared her. "It does, doesn't it?"

The wisest of gamblers have this in common:
They quit while they are ahead.
~*Wisdom and Advice—The Genteel Lady's Guide to Practical Living*

London, England
Late May 1822

Brooke drew in a steadying breath and smoothed the satin of her lavender ball gown for the umpteenth time as the carriage lurched to a stop before an ostentatious manor. Nervous didn't begin to describe her state, not only for herself, but her sister and cousins. A horde of insects rioted inside her stomach, making complete nuisances of themselves, horrid little pests.

Beside her, Brette fidgeted with the silk tassels of her reticule, and on the opposite seat, Blythe, Blaire, and Blaike's features suggested they were about to be offered up as human sacrifices. Not too far off the mark, truth to tell.

In their evening finery, hair intricately coiffed, and jeweled to the hilt, thanks to Heath's generosity, the Culpepper misses and her, the new Lady Ravensdale—blast, but it was proving difficult to remember to answer to her new title—were about to attend their first formal ball. Brooke would rather have stood on her head naked in Hyde Park. But as soon as the Season ended, they would return to Culpepper Park, the name they'd dubbed the lands Brooke now owned, to check on the new house's progress.

Sheridan had signed an agreement and greedily accepted a sizable sum to disappear from their lives forever. Hopefully, they were rid of him for good.

Heath squeezed the fingers of her gloved hand and grinned like a Captain Sharp with a winning hand at cards. "Trust me, dear. None of you has anything to fear."

"Easy for you to say. You're accustomed to the predators and vipers in there." She pointed at the house, every window ablaze with light. A good dozen people paused to stare at their coach.

The carriage door swung open, and a black liveried footman placed a low step beside the carriage. His eyes widened to the size of moons when he glanced inside. A delighted smile stretched across his handsome face. He turned and motioned to another footman.

The second footman hurried to their conveyance. Upon spotting the women, he tripped, nearly planting his face on the coach floor.

Heath slid Brooke a smug glance that said, *See, I told you.*

Yes, but gullible footmen were a far cry from the denizens of High Society, who were wont to devour young ladies with the swiftness of piranhas.

As they assembled on the pavement, Brooke took the girls' measure. Heath had suggested the jeweled tones for their gowns. Amethyst for her, light blue sapphire for Brette, jonquil beryl for Blythe, emerald green for Blaike, and pink ruby for Blaire. Superb choices, and with the matching gemstones each wore, truly regal.

A hush settled upon the guests lined up like docile cattle on the pavement and steps to enter the manor. Every eye turned to look at the new arrivals, and the crowd parted to allow them entrance. Heath and Brooke led, Brette and Blythe followed, and the twins brought up the rear.

Brooke's jaw almost bounced off the floor upon entering the glittering mansion. Never had she seen such opulence. Two eight-foot chandeliers blinded her with at least one hundred candles each. She couldn't decide which offended worse: the garish rose marble floor or the abundant gold gilding plastered on practically everything not moving. Even the hostess wore copious layers of gold.

Brooke sent a reassuring smile over her shoulder. The quartet's stunned faces no doubt mirrored her own.

"Steady on, ladies. Chins up and eyes forward. Incomparable, every last one of you." Heath led them to a gaping butler, his jaw sagging so widely, a pigeon might've nested in the cavity.

"Pretty much the reaction I had, too, upon seeing them for the first time, Withers."

Withers drew himself up, his prickly black eyebrows wiggling like caterpillars in the throes of mating...or dying. "Indeed, my lord. A most astounding collection of young ladies, if I may say so."

The majordomo bowed so low, his nose threatened to scrape the floor. Several dandies also made exaggerated bows, while the *haut ton* ladies' fans snapped to attention and waved furiously. Their tongues probably flapped just as fast.

Heath murmured their names into the butler's ear.

"Ah, may I offer my most sincere solicitations, my lord?"

Heath inclined his head. "Thank you."

Withers cast a languid gaze over the crowd then notched his nose skyward. "Lord and Lady Ravensdale, and the Misses Culpepper."

A low buzz built in volume as more people pushed and shoved their way into the entry and peeked from the ballroom, including the flummoxed Benbridges.

Blythe waved her fingers at their neighbors who continued to gawk.

A tall, auburn-haired man elbowed his way through the gawkers. A blond god followed, a merry twinkle in his eyes. Thank goodness. Brooke had never thought the day would come that she'd welcome Lord Leventhorpe's intimidating presence.

"We thought you might need a hand." Leventhorpe grinned and winked.

Reverend Hawksworth chuckled. "I do believe a near insurrection is at hand."

The gentlemen extended their elbows and, with a Culpepper on each arm, led the way into the ballroom. Elbowing and shoving one another in a most ungallant fashion, a score of gentlemen trotted after them. Miffed ladies did too, but for entirely different reasons—to snatch wayward beaus and husbands back to their sides.

Heath placed Brooke's hand on his arm and whispered in her ear. "My love, the Culpepper misses have tumbled the stuffy *ton* tits over arse."

Brooke burst out laughing. "Come, husband. I've a feeling we'll have our hands full with those four. I did warn you before we married and you became their guardian, however."

"I wouldn't have it any other way." He tilted her chin up, and in full view of the scandalized onlookers, kissed Brooke full on the mouth.

The Marquis and the Vixen

A woman of noble character will at all times remember,
calm composure flummoxes the schemes of evil-intended people.
~Dignity and Decorum—The Genteel Lady's Guide to Practical Living

1

London, England, Late May, 1822

Flimflam and goose-butt feathers!
One hand hiding her mouth, Blythe Culpepper gaped as she trailed her cousin, Brooke, and Brooke's husband, Heath, the Earl of Ravensdale, into the mansion.

Surely that wasn't authentic gold gilding the ornate cornices? Squinting to see better, she surveyed the grand entrance. *Yes. It is.*

And not just the sculpted cornices either. The plasterwork and practically every other surface, excluding the coffered ceiling's elaborate paintings and the rose-tinted marble floor, boasted the shiny adornment.

Everything pink and gold and glittery. And costly.

"What a despicable waste of money." Flinging Heath a hasty glance, Blythe checked her muttering. It wouldn't do to offend him or their hostess within a minute of arrival.

The peeress, swathed in gold satin and dripping in diamonds— *three diamond bracelets? On each wrist?*—stood beside an enormous urn. Blythe fought the scowl tugging at her mouth and brows. Disgusting, this brazen flaunting of wealth.

Clamping her slack mouth closed, she reluctantly passed a waiting footman her silk wrap. A chill shook her, puckering her flesh from forearms to shoulders. Maddening nerves. She hadn't expected the pomp, or the mob's crush, to affect her.

A simple teardrop-shaped beryl pendant nestled at the juncture of her breasts, and Blythe pressed a hand to the expanse of flesh exposed above her wide, square neckline. Did she dare tug the bodice higher?

After dressing, she'd attempted to, but the fabric had remained stubbornly form-fitting, the slopes of her bosoms pushed skyward for the world to ogle at their leisure.

Repressing a scornful grunt, she tipped her mouth a fraction. In twenty years, the smallish, twin pillows had never garnered much ogling. Probably little need to fret in that regard.

Tripping over her gown remained an entirely different matter.

Her secondhand garments had always been too short for her tall frame. Since exiting the carriage, this ball gown—its sheer silk overdress atop the yellow jonquil swirling about her feet—had become snared thrice upon her slippers' decorated tops.

She would have to endure these outings for the remainder of the Season, and she didn't relish sprawling, bum upward, before the *ton's* denizens. Tapping her fan against her thigh, she estimated how many public jaunts the Season might entail and hid an unladylike groan behind an indelicate cough.

God spare her.

The instant the final dance note faded, she planned on trotting back to the country's quiet civility—to the humble, familiar way of life she preferred. Or perhaps she'd contrive a minor scandal. Nothing too ruinous, merely shameful enough to see her banished in moderate disgrace.

Yes, that might do.

This gaudy, glistening parade quite shred her normally robust nerves. A calculated, hasty departure might be just the thing. After all, she hadn't come to London to marry. Acquiring a husband ranked below cleaning the chamber pots and mucking the stalls on her to-do list. Unless, of course, she found a man who adored her the way Heath cherished Brooke.

Fanciful imagining, that. Stuff and nonsense. Fairy-tales. At least for Blythe.

According to Mama, even as a toddler, Blythe had possessed a determined—some might say daunting—personality. Now, as an adult, the unfeminine characteristic chaffed men's arses and patience raw. No one who knew her had ever used acquiescent and her name in the same sentence, and she wouldn't scheme to snare a husband with false biddableness.

Humbly accepting the dowry Heath had bestowed upon her hadn't made the prospect of wedding more tempting, and though grateful for his generosity, she couldn't expect him to provide for her indefinitely. In a month, she'd be of age and free to make her own decisions, which included returning to Culpepper Park and the new house Brooke had commissioned.

Somehow, Blythe would eke out an existence there. A slight shudder rippled the length of her spine. No more giving music lessons though. At least not to spoilt brattlings like the vicar's daughters. For five interminable years, she'd endured that trial.

With a determined tilt of her head, she sucked in a calming breath and returned Heath's encouraging smile.

He and Brooke preceded Blythe and her cousin, Brette, into the immense entry. Blythe's twin sisters, Blaire and Blaike, slowly wandered in wearing identical wide-eyed, stunned expressions.

Taking in the ostentatious manor, and the more flamboyant assemblage, Blythe craned her neck, catching her toe on Brooke's slipper. "Excuse me."

Perchance as boggled by the crass display of wealth, Brooke didn't respond, just slowly swung head this way and that.

Beneath the glaring candlelight of two eight-foot chandeliers, Blythe blinked again, as did her sisters and cousins—five flaxen-haired, gawping country bumpkins brought to Town.

Who could blame them?

They'd been accustomed to starkness, want, and poverty, and the grandiose entry sparkled like the Pharaoh's tomb she'd once seen in a drawing.

The urge to hike her gown to her knees and bolt to the carriage's safe and anonymous confines—like the fairytale character Cendrillon— had Blythe grasping her frothy skirt with both hands, one white-satin-slippered foot half-raised.

Whose beef-witted idea had it been to introduce the Culpeppers to society?

Heath's. Their proxy fairy godmother. He believed it might prove amusing.

To whom?

Her fan clutched in one hand—too bad it wasn't a magical wand with mythical powers—Blythe surreptitiously lifted her gown a fraction and disentangled her slipper's beaded toe from her hem again. At this rate, she'd make a spectacle of herself before she'd stepped onto the dance floor, the singular thing she hadn't dreaded. Musically inclined her whole life, the prospect of dancing didn't worry her. *Much.*

Their ensemble had drawn considerable attention already, some speculation less than affable from the barbed stares and pouting moues slung their way, and tonight's introduction to *la beau monde* was important to Brooke's and the other girls' success.

None of the Culpeppers had relished visiting London, but these past weeks had changed everyone's minds, excluding Blythe's. The streets boasted refuse and manure, and the city stank worse than the dairy barns during summer's peak temperatures. Beggars and orphans abounded, as did women of loose virtue. The stark contrast between the opulent display currently surrounding her and the hollow-eyed, rag-garbed street urchins she'd seen on the drive here grated.

Grossly unfair, the patent disparity.

Perhaps enduring years of hunger and lack had embittered her toward the affluent more than she'd realized.

"Look at the cherubs and nymphs." Her voice low and lilting with amused embarrassment, Brette elbowed Blythe. "They're everywhere and completely naked."

They were indeed.

As the majordomo announced their troupe in an onerous monotone, Blythe answered the smile of a striking man, who dipped his curly, sun-kissed head at her. Broad-shouldered, with a sculpted face, and attired in the height of fashion, he was quite the handsomest man she'd ever seen.

Merriment lit his features, and his smile blossomed into a satisfied grin. His fawn-colored gaze lazily traveled from her insignificant bosoms to her toes then made the reverse journey to once again hover on her breasts before boldly meeting her eyes. His pleated at the corners again, a testament to a man accustomed to smiling habitually.

Her stomach reacted most peculiarly, all floppy and churning.

And her breasts?

Why, under his appreciative regard, the dratted insignificant things swelled and pebbled proudly. Quite forward of them, given their unimpressive size. Warmth skidded up the angles of her cheeks, and she averted her gaze.

Hound's teeth.

First time she'd ever blushed or had her bosoms betray her. Next thing she knew, the perky pair would scramble from her bodice's lace edge and wave a jaunty hello.

Her cousin edged nearer and splayed her fan, concealing their lower faces. She bobbed her fair head to indicate the ballroom entrance where a crowd spilled forth, perusing and prattling about the newcomers. "Look, Blythe. The statues on either side of those double doors are too."

"Are what?" What was Brette yammering about? Oh. Naked. The statues of Greek gods were naked as a needle. "Must be why those silly girls are giggling and pointing."

Raised on a farm, Blaike smirked and Blaire grinned, their pansy-blue eyes twinkling. The male anatomy didn't intrigue them quite as singularly as it obviously did the sheltered society misses. Nonetheless, the statues' manly endowments left nothing to the imagination.

Well, one remained endowed.

The other's male bits had snapped off in a debutante's hand, causing another round of frenetic tittering. From the way their scolding hostess descended upon the women, Blythe would have bet her pendant the god had lost his penis to curious groping before.

"Thought you might need a hand, Ravensdale." A mocking male addressed Heath from over Blythe's right shoulder.

Good God.

Blythe stiffened, refusing to look behind her.

The rumbling baritone could belong to only one man. The insufferable Marquis of Leventhorpe.

Perfectly horrid.

Her first foray into High Society, and he attended the same gathering, his presence as welcome as a crotchety, old tabby cat. He'd rubbed her wrong, and they'd crossed words, ever since meeting at Esherton Green, her childhood home. A more arrogant, difficult ... humorless ... stubborn person than Lord Leventhorpe didn't strut the Earth.

His scent, crisp linen mixed with sandalwood, enveloped her, warning her he'd drawn nearer. Too near. His breath tickled her ear as he mumbled almost inaudibly, "Your mouth was hanging open like a pelican's. Again."

She pressed her lips together and steadfastly disregarded the distracting jolt his closeness and warm breath caused. He'd startled her. Nothing else.

What's a blasted pelican?

Something with a vast mouth, no doubt, but dancing naked atop hot coals was preferable to asking the behemoth to explain.

"What a rag-mannered boor you are to mention it, my lord." Speaking under her breath and from the side of her mouth, she commanded her lips to curve congenially while examining her family and mentally cursing him to Hades.

For once, no one noticed their verbal sparring.

Looming several inches above her, Lord Leventhorpe's chest—a thick, wide wall of virile maleness—blocked her view. Tempted to shift away, she forced her feet to stay planted. He was the largest man she'd ever met, and as one of Heath's closest friends, she must learn to tolerate Lord Leventhorpe's intimidating presence. Surely sainthood and a seat at the Lord's Table awaited her if she managed the Herculean task.

The auburn-haired devil enjoyed provoking her, and like a nincompoop, she regularly succumbed to his goading. She normally possessed a level head, and that he should be the person to have her at sixes and sevens, exasperated her.

A growl of frustration formed in her throat, and she clenched her teeth and hands.

"Ravensdale, you have your hands full." Leventhorpe skirted her, giving a cynical twist of his shapely lips as he passed. "I would deem it the ultimate privilege to assist you with these exquisite ladies."

She didn't believe his sycophantic posturing for an instant. At Esherton, when he'd accused the Culpeppers of abducting Heath, she'd seen the real Lord Leventhorpe, and this fawning deference concealed a stone-hearted, grim-tempered cawker.

His penetrating gaze—as heated and blue as a cloudless noonday sky in August—probed hers as if he strove to read her mind and emotions. Most disconcerting, and none of his blasted business. Maddening how he scrambled her thoughts and agitated feelings she couldn't decipher.

A spurt of amusement lit his eyes, and she narrowed hers.

Stop staring, you oversized, handsome baboon.

Immediately, Lord Leventhorpe's expression became shuttered and inscrutable. He rubbed the side of his nose and canvassed the entry before offering an enigmatic half-smile. "If you need help escorting the ladies, Hawksworth and I would be honored to assist."

"Reverend Hawksworth is here too?" Blythe peered over her shoulder.

Yes, indeed. Grinning, Reverend Hawksworth wended his way through the throng.

Charming, witty, and the perfect gentleman, he rivaled the fair god who'd smiled at her earlier. She slanted Lord Leventhorpe a contemplative glance. How could such two startlingly dissimilar men—one angelic and one demonic—be Heath's closest friends?

Brette perked up, her cheeks pinkening and eyes sparkling when the cleric joined them. At Esherton Green, Blythe had suspected her cousin's interest in Reverend Hawksworth, and Brette's reaction tonight confirmed it.

Chuckling, he cut his jungle-eyed gaze to the gawkers surging from the ballroom. "I do believe a near insurrection is at hand. Arriving with five incomparables is hardly fair play, Raven. I expect histrionics, swooning, and apoplexy in record numbers this evening. Perchance a bit of fervent, and not altogether hallowed, petitioning of the Almighty as well."

Nodding at something the butler said, Heath grinned. "Ah, I never intended fair play. I would wager from the reaction I'm seeing, the *ton* will never be the same. What say you, Withers?"

"Indeed not, my lord." Something on the room's far side gripped the butler's attention, and his mouth tipped lower as his brows scaled the distance to his receding hairline.

A giggling young lady held the statue's appendage in the air, swinging it back and forth. Their ruddy-faced hostess, Lady Kattenby, tried to extricate herself from the oblivious dame grasping her arm.

Blaire and Blaike giggled until Brooke hushed them with a severe look. "Girls, unseemly behavior isn't humorous, and dangling *that* most certainly is not funny."

Actually, it rather was.

As were the guests' faces, especially the women, most of whom made no effort to avert their rapt gazes from the display.

"I beg your pardon, my lord." Withers gave Heath a brief bow. "I must see to Apollo's ill-used ... er ... limb at once."

Blythe hid a grin behind her fan.

Lord Leventhorpe, Heath, and Reverend Hawksworth burst out laughing.

"A limb's an exaggeration in my estimation." Heath's shoulders shook again.

Brooke tapped his arm with her fan. "Hush, darling. Remember the girls."

Withers marched to the ballroom's entrance and, after retrieving the length of marble, rather than discreetly concealing it in his fist or tucking it into his tailcoat pocket, reverently laid the member atop his flattened palm and strode to an abashed footman.

Gingerly taking the stone between his gloved forefinger and thumb, the mortified servant hustled from the entry, his ears tinged scarlet at the sniggering in his wake.

To stifle the laugh burbling behind her teeth, Blythe bit her lip.

"That's not something you see every day." A grin flashing in his eyes, the reverend extended his elbows to her and Brette.

A most unconventional man of God, to be sure. If Blythe recalled correctly, the vocation hadn't been his choosing. Something to do with the previous vicar, an uncle, eloping with a nun. Quite a scandal ensued.

"Shall we?" Reverend Hawksworth canted his head. "There mightn't be seats left. The benches and chairs tend to fill rather quickly, and there is quite a crush this evening."

Blythe released a relieved huff. Lord Leventhorpe wouldn't be her escort into the ballroom. She'd spent a lifetime wrangling her temper and unruly tongue into submission. Yet, thirty seconds with that abominable wretch shriveled her self-control to a puff of dust, and she became a razor-tongued shrew.

Lord Leventhorpe's impressive brows dove together and twitched before he resumed his normal austere mien and politely bent his arms for Blaire and Blaike.

What went on in that head of his?

Never mind. Blythe truly didn't want to know.

"Ladies, allow me to claim the first two sets, please." Reverend Hawksworth chatted amiably as he guided them to the only remaining seats, a partially occupied bench. He dashed Blythe a contrite smile. "And, Miss Brette, may I request the supper dance, as well?"

Ah, he returned Brette's regard. Her cousin would search far for a man as worthy as the handsome rector.

When Brette didn't immediately respond, Blythe slid her a questioning glance.

"Reverend, to be honest, I'm not sure what's acceptable. Perhaps we should wait until we are seated so that Heath or Brooke may advise me?" Brette procured a hesitant smile. "If they agree, I would enjoy a dance with you."

Strange. Why the reticence? True, Brette fretted about stirring a dust up, but Reverend Hawksworth obviously intrigued her.

Reverend Hawksworth's brows elevated several inches as he peered at the others trailing them through the horde. "I don't recall the last time I saw dancers missing steps to gawk at new arrivals." He gave a bemused shake of his head. "But then, I don't attend many gatherings. I only did tonight because Raven asked Leventhorpe and me to be on hand. Truthfully, I'm surprised Leventhorpe agreed. He loathes large gatherings and comes to Town during the Season for Parliament, not for the socializing."

Perhaps Blythe would be spared Lord Leventhorpe's company more than she had anticipated, if he didn't care for crowds.

Reverend Hawksworth gave Brette a conspiratorial half-wink. "I do believe your brother-in-law finally realized the furor introducing five diamonds of the first water would cause. Never been done before, that I'm aware."

The Adonis from the entry fell into step beside Blythe, and her stomach did that weird, quivery thing again. He was even more appealing than she'd first believed, and his eyes weren't brown at all, rather an unusual topaz with dark green flecks. A deep earthy tone circled his irises, explaining why his eyes appeared brown from a distance.

He flashed a rakish smile, revealing well-tended teeth.

Splendid. She couldn't abide poor hygiene.

"Hawksworth, I beg you. Introduce me to these charming ladies, so I might claim a dance with each." Though the Adonis included Brette in his appeal, his gaze never left Blythe, and the curving of his lips caused another unfamiliar jolt.

The reverend shook his head. "Too late, Burlington. I've already requested sets and the supper dance with Miss Brette." He slightly raised the arm her fingers lay upon. "And Ravensdale ought to make the introductions, not me."

Burlington—was he a mister? A Lord? Something else?—wrinkled his forehead in mock horror. "Troublesome etiquette rules." His brandy-tinted gaze sought Blythe's. "If Ravensdale agrees, would you favor me with the supper dance?"

A trifle forward, but ...

"I would like that." No feigning diffidence. He was an attractive man, and he'd captured her interest in the entry, something unanticipated, truth to tell. "I must confess, I don't claim a substantial appetite."

For years, the Culpeppers had survived on insufficient food, and although they had plenty to eat now, she couldn't manage generous portions. Given her height, she doubted she'd ever possess an enticingly rounded figure like the young ladies occupying the bench farther along. The figures of the older women with them had evolved into rotundness—not something Blythe worried about.

Once the rest of their group made it to the bench—Leventhorpe, a dark, menacing deity dwarfing everyone, his keen, raptor gaze combing the ballroom—Heath made quick work of the introductions.

Blythe's admirer was Mr. Courtland Burlington, the second son of the Earl of Lauderdale. No title, therefore no worries about a lowly gentlewoman aiming her sights too high.

Not that she'd set her cap for Mr. Burlington. Much too soon for that. This was her first assembly, after all. Nonetheless, he presented quite a dashing figure and, given the envious looks regularly flitting in his direction, much sought after by females.

"I'm delighted to make your acquaintance, Miss Culpepper." Mr. Burlington lifted her hand as he bowed, kissing the air above her fingers. A stickler for propriety or affecting courtly conduct? Would he mind awfully that she found decorum about as useful as a well-gnawed chicken bone?

Blythe half-anticipated a frisson or tremor to skitter along her spine as had occurred at Leventhorpe's touch, but Mr. Burlington's fingers pressing hers elicited nothing more thrilling than a mild, pleasant warmth.

Hmm. Disappointing.

Must have been nerves or repugnance that had induced her strong reaction to the cold marquis.

The plainer young lady of the nearby quartet grinned and waved, and Lord Leventhorpe responded with a cordial nod and a warm upturn of his mouth, earning him satisfied smiles from her companions before he angled away.

"My cousin, Francine Simmons, and her friends," he said to no one in particular, though his attention remained upon Blythe as she extricated her hand from Mr. Burlington's.

Miss Simmons leaned close, speaking to the sable-haired beauty beside her. The pretty girl's expression hardened, and she and the older dames—relatives, judging by the strong familial resemblance—pelted the Culpeppers with reproachful, gray-eyed glares.

Why?

As Blythe and the others conversed, the foursome brazenly eavesdropped, frequently dipping their heads together and whispering. A gentleman claimed the lovely girl for the next dance, and Miss Simmons, her shoulders slumped and countenance dejected, plucked the bench's braid edging, wistfully contemplating the dancers.

Prodding Blaike's side, Blaire whispered, "Look there."

"Good heavens." Blaike stared pointedly at two men striding their way.

"Hush," Brooke gently chastised behind her fan. "Whispering is vulgar and unkind. You are neither."

"Ravensdale." Hand extended, a man wearing army crimson, and bearing a fresh pinkish scar along his left cheek, approached their group accompanied by a—for lack of a better description—buccaneer.

Sporting a neat beard, and his ebony, shoulder-length hair tied with a black ribbon, the man appeared to have stepped straight off the deck of a privateer. Blythe expected to see a parade of barefoot, cutlass-bearing pirates behind him.

Heath, Lord Leventhorpe, and Reverend Hawksworth broke into exuberant grins. After much hearty handshaking, shoulder slapping, and laughing, Heath introduced the newcomers. The officer was Lieutenant Julian Drake, and the sharp-eyed, swarthy fellow, Oliver Whitehouse, captain of the *Sea Gypsy*.

Ah, a sea captain. And he appeared part gypsy too.

"Looks more like a pirate to me," Blaike murmured to her entranced twin.

Captain Whitehouse leveled her an indecipherable look. He'd heard her. Nonetheless, bold interest shone in his obsidian eyes.

"How fare you, my friend?" He touched Leventhorpe's arm and jutted his strong chin to indicate the other men. "It's been a good while since we gathered in one place."

Another attractive gentleman approached, his nose flattened peculiarly. He reeked of rosewater, and from his togs and elevated chin, Blythe would eat gravel if he wasn't a peer.

Every man's visage grew guarded, except Mr. Burlington's, and Lord Leventhorpe and Captain Whitehouse exchanged a speaking glance.

The newcomer's oily gaze slid over Blythe then her sisters and cousins, before lighting upon Lord Leventhorpe and turning antagonistic. "Yes. We haven't all been together since Leventhorpe shattered my nose in an unfair fight."

Fate cares not about schemes or plans, and oft' Fortune, not men,
deserves credit for good and bad circumstances.
~ *Dignity and Decorum—The Genteel Lady's Guide to Practical Living*

Unfair fight, my arse.
"Phillips." Tristan managed not to snarl Seymour Phillips's name,
though contempt riddled his tone, earning him a cocked brow from
Blythe—*that is, Miss Culpepper*—her sooty-lashed eyes brimming with
curiosity and a dab of laughter too.

She mocked him.

"You broke his nose? Like you broke Cousin Sheridan's? Do you
make a habit of mashing faces, my lord?" At Phillips's brazen regard,
her gaze wavered between him and Tristan, wariness replacing her
inquisitiveness and spurt of amusement.

Not short on intelligence, by George. Miss Culpepper recognized a
poltroon when she met one. Or possibly, it was Tristan who aroused her
suspicion. Given their instant, mutual animosity, the latter seemed more
likely, especially since he had broken Sheridan Gainsborough's nose
when Gainsborough interfered with Ravensdale's wedding.

"Yes, I did. And no. I don't." Tristan refused to be baited, and her
slightly rouged lips thinned a fraction, a mysterious glint shadowing her
eyes. At least he assumed her mouth rouged. Too dewy and rosy to be
natural, surely, unless she'd dined upon berries recently.

What kind?

A taste of her delicious mouth, made for hungry kisses and sensual
smiles, would answer the question. A blast of sensation straight to his
groin strangled his carnal musings.

*What the hell is wrong with me, lusting after a woman who clearly
loathes me?*

Fiddling with her fan, she took Phillips's measure, toe to top before
scooting Tristan a covert peek. Good manners prohibited her asking the

how and why of his corking Phillips. Nonetheless, her expressive eyes fairly shouted for an answer.

How would she respond if he told her?

Well, you see, Miss Culpepper, it started with a pox-ridden whore, and Hawksworth, the reluctant vicar.

"Phillips, when did you return to England?" Ravensdale's question broke the weighty silence and wrenched Tristan abruptly back to the bustling ballroom.

Flouting propriety and drumming his fingertips along the bench, Ravensdale made no effort to introduce Phillips to the ladies. Brilliant strategy upon Raven's part. Without an introduction, Phillips couldn't address the women directly. When he'd married Brooke, Ravensdale had vowed to protect the Culpepper ladies, and his decorum breach proved his seriousness.

Phillips hauled his appreciative gaze from the women, pique sharpening his angular face. "A month ago. And I'm glad I did, else I would have missed this," he gestured to the exquisite blondes, his hint as brazen as a skirtless harlot, "delightful spectacle."

Still not getting an introduction, you bugger.

Phillips offered his usual suave smile.

No Culpepper responded with anything more enthusiastic than a placid gaze. Not even the twins—the youngest, most impressionable of the lot.

Uncanny how two people could look exactly alike. Dressed in identical gowns except for the color, he had no idea who was Blaire and who was Blaike. How old were they again? Scratching his eyebrow, he wracked his brain. Had anyone ever told him? How old was Blythe, for that matter?

She observed Phillips, a marginal pucker between her winged brows.

As if sensing Tristan's scrutiny, Blythe swiftly schooled her features into blandness once more while unfurling her fan. However, she couldn't conceal the spark glinting in her iris eyes. A sapphire-violet fire, waiting to be fanned into flames, smoldered below her composed surface. He'd seen the firestorm more than once—truthfully, he'd caused a conflagration or two—and found her temper invigorating.

How perverse.

A knowing glance passed between Lady Ravensdale and Brette before their nonchalant gazes returned to Phillips as well.

Yes, by God. All five were on to old Phillips and his reptilian wiles. Good thing too.

He'd fathered more than one by-blow, and suggestions had circulated for years that the serving wenches hadn't willingly engaged in the dalliances. No doubt his female servants lamented his return to London. *Le beau monde* had been blessed with his absence for two—or was it three?—years while the cull toured the continent before journeying to India. At least that was the drivel his sire, the viscount, spread about Town.

Tristan didn't believe a syllable, especially after a highborn young woman became scarce and later hastily married an elderly sot before giving birth to a daughter a mere four months after the nuptials. Tattle had it, Phillips had ravished her.

The woman's father, the Duke of Coventry, had threated to call Phillips out, hence the cur's abrupt departure from England. Awfully convenient, Coventry's dying recently, paving the way for Phillips to scuttle home and muck about in the dank dens he favored. Rumors had circulated that Phillips's father, the doting and blind-to-his-son's-faults Viscount Rotherton, had greased more than one fist to assure his son escaped justice.

Phillips resembled an enormous cockroach—Tristan's nostrils quivered—right down to the sour smell that copious quantities of cologne failed to completely conceal.

"Memories are peculiar things, aren't they, Whitehouse? They're quite dependent upon the perceptions of the person recollecting." Reverend Hawksworth lifted a short, blond hair from his forearm, inclining his head toward Phillips.

Perturbed, Phillips pressed his lips into a pout, his regard of the Culpeppers bordering upon lascivious.

"I seem to recall that after insulting Leventhorpe, Phillips took the first swing." Hand straddling his hip, Hawk regarded Whitehouse.

"Aye, that's my memory as well. What say you, Drake?" Dislike deepened the lines framing the captain's mouth and feathering the corners of his eyes. He flexed his fingers near his waist as if instinctively reaching for a cutlass.

Hands clasped behind his back, Drake nodded, his eyes flinty. "Indeed. That's exactly how I remember it too."

"You were ape-drunk that night, Hawksworth. How could *you* remember anything?" Phillips's mouth slid into a sideways sneer as he bared his craven talons. "Isn't drunkenness one of the sins you preach against?"

Miss Brette's eyes rounded, and her mouth parted as she and the Culpeppers, plus Lady Ravensdale, swung their attention to Hawksworth's flushed face.

Had Phillips forgotten Hawk's pugilist skills? Even a man of God possessed limited patience. From his sharply drawn brows and balled fists, Hawksworth might be near his snapping point.

How would Phillips like his nose shattered again? Or mayhap his jaw this go round? Hawk could easily do either.

"Stubble it, Phillips." Tristan's warning met with an unrepentant, cocky grin.

The one time Hawk had gotten pished, and for a bloody good reason too, and Phillips, the colossal arse, had to humiliate him for it. Typical.

Blythe speared Phillips a scorching glower, muttering something inaudible beneath her breath and behind her fan which sounded suspiciously like cod's head or codpiece.

Knowing her, probably the latter. Tristan rather appreciated the comparison.

"Gentlemen, this discussion is wholly inappropriate, especially with young ladies present." Lady Ravensdale stood and motioned to the younger women, succinctly ending the unpleasantness. "I'll thank you to cease or continue it elsewhere. Besides, I should like to dance with my husband since I haven't had the opportunity. Blythe, would you please act as chaperone until I return?"

"Of course." Blythe offered Mr. Burlington a penitent smile, and annoyance poked Tristan's ribs. Hard. She'd never been half as accommodating or agreeable to him.

What did he care?

A more provoking, outspoken virago he'd never had the ill-fortune to meet. His embittered mother notwithstanding, God rest her tormented soul.

Truthfully, being the primary beneficiary of Blythe's dislike grated.

In response to Burlington's proprietary smile, she curved her lips, her cheeks acquiring the same flushed glow as her mouth.

Perhaps she wasn't that perceptive after all. True, Burlington was a pleasant enough fellow, but as many young blades were wont to do, he generally treated women as passing amusements, something to trifle with and conquer until another caught his fancy. Nevertheless, women had tamed rakehells far worse than him.

Tristan gave a mental shrug. No concern of his.

He'd been asked to help a friend, and that was the only reason he'd accepted the Kattenbys' invitation tonight. Suppressing a yawn, he perused the ballroom, still humming about the Culpeppers.

Bloody insane. That's what Raven is.

One or two beauties might have been manageable, but five? Humor jerked the corners of Tristan's mouth. His friend would rue the day he'd ever entertained this hair-brained notion. Wouldn't surprise him if Raven wound up bald as a billiard by Season's end, and he had nice hair too.

Set the *le beau monde* upon its arse, indeed.

"I shall save the next set for you, Mr. Burlington." The beatific smile Blythe bestowed upon Burlington squeezed Tristan's lungs.

Damnation. And double damn that he'd noticed.

"That won't be necessary, Blythe. You may dance this set." Though Ravensdale's lips slanted, no humor glinted in the astute gaze he raked over Phillips. "Whitehouse and Drake, I would appreciate you escorting a twin onto the dance floor, and I've already given Hawk permission to dance with Miss Brette."

Well done. Tristan indulged in a gloating grin.

Ravensdale had snuffed Phillips's intent to beg an introduction and a dance with one of the sisters or cousins faster than a pinched candlewick. He wouldn't be adding one of their number to his list of conquests.

"I would beg you save me the supper dance then, Miss Culpepper, since I won't have the pleasure of a dancing this set." Tristan couldn't resist goading Phillips, knowing full well Ravensdale would accept Tristan's request as speedily as he'd spurned Phillips's.

Ravensdale's stunned expression was reflected in the other astounded gazes whipping to Tristan.

Hell.

Ignoring the impulse would have been wiser except he'd agreed to dance with each Culpepper. Damn awkward, this doing the pretty balderdash. No more favors for friends. Tristan suspected Ravensdale intended to utilize him, and perhaps poor Hawk, as surrogates to help chaperone and manage the goddesses the entire season.

Not bloody well likely. Tristan truly couldn't abide crowds for extended periods. An hour at most, and he made for the exit.

A disgusting memory assailed him, rendering him mute and immobile for a moment. Swallowing a surge of nausea, he shook his head to dispel the buzzing in his ears and the sudden onslaught of dizziness.

What had they been discussing?

The supper dance.

Had Blythe responded? "Miss Culpepper?"

What else could he say? He hadn't a clue whether she had answered.

Her lively gaze assessing, Blythe slanted her head the merest bit, the amber gems entwined in her curls winking under the chandelier's radiance. "I'm sorry, Lord Leventhorpe, I already promised the supper dance to Mr. Burlington."

"Perhaps a waltz later, then." Tristan flexed his fingers against the desire to wipe the delighted smile from Burlington's face.

Give over, Trist. You'd have the same smirk on your face if she'd said yes to you.

He would've?

The awareness gave him pause.

He would.

Only because it withered his ballocks to have coxcombs like Burlington best him.

"Blythe." Subtle censure tinted Lady Ravensdale's tone. "You've other unclaimed dances."

Tristan almost stuck a finger in his ear and wiggled it to make sure he'd heard correctly. Had she encouraged her cousin to dance with him? Some turnabout there.

"I shall save you the last waltz, Lord Leventhorpe." A corpse displayed more genuine enthusiasm upon being laid in a coffin. Blythe looped her hand through Burlington's elbow and glided away, laughing at something he murmured to her. She'd never appeared more vivacious or beautiful.

Giving Phillips a contemptuous glare—and hopefully a parson's curse damning him to purgatory—Hawksworth offered Miss Brette his arm, and they set out after the others.

A bevy of whispers behind fans and gloved hands trailed the Culpeppers' progress. Gentlemen peered with brazen interest through their quizzing glasses, while ill-disguised envy pinched many ladies' features. A goodly number of friendly smiles greeted them too.

Yes, Raven had stirred a beehive, and when bees are riled, someone is sure to get stung.

Tristan searched for a servant. After that exchange he welcomed a glass of punch. No. He really wanted a finger or two of whisky, but he was a quarter way to bosky already.

"Seems like you and I have been found wanting, Leventhorpe." Phillips glared after the departing couples.

First sting went to Phillips. That bounder could expect many more sharp pricks from Raven and the Culpeppers.

"Don't include me in your company. I spent several days as a guest of the Culpeppers at their country estate." Vast exaggeration there. He'd arrived at Esherton Green looking for Ravensdale and had refused to leave without his friend. And calling their malodorous dairy farm and ramshackle house an estate was equivalent to calling the Prince Regent a Devil's Acre beggar.

"Awful uppity for country wenches." Phillips scratched his prominent chin. "Though I wouldn't mind sampling their charms. I admit a penchant for blondes. That one in yellow is a prime article and seems the most spirited. I've found that trait commonly carries into bedding the gel."

A fury-induced haze momentarily stole Tristan's tongue.

"Makes for a delicious shagging." His voice deepened by lust, Phillips licked his lips. "Especially if they resist."

Would the House of Lords bring charges against Tristan if he disposed of Phillips once and for all? Probably. Even if they celebrated the cur's demise with fireworks and Champagne afterward. Subduing his wrath, he drew his spine upright, fully aware his immense size daunted shorter men.

He scowled down at Phillips. "Unless you want me to break your nose again, I suggest you take your leave. *Now.* And stay away from the Culpeppers—"

"Tristan, dearest." His cousin's singsong voice beset him.

He speared a gaze heavenward, begging God for patience as she, no doubt prompted by her domineering companion, Rosemary Sanford, glided his way. He'd exhausted his reserves of forbearance by not pummeling Phillips and had scant left to cushion his terse response to Francine.

"You were saying, Leventhorpe?" His lips skewed mockingly,

Phillips folded his arms.

Francine seized Tristan's forearm. "Tristan, I told Rosemary you would dance with her this evening since you rudely left the last ball without doing as you'd promised."

He hadn't promised.

Francine had pleaded with him to dance with her friend, and he'd said he'd consider it. He'd done so, contemplating the notion for a lengthy two seconds before deciding he'd prefer to go home and cut his already groomed toenails.

Why Francine kowtowed to the likes of Rosemary Sanford, he couldn't imagine. Though irrefutably beautiful, Miss Sanford was an inconsiderate friend, and he'd bet Bristledale Court and his mother's many glittery baubles that she had manipulated Francine to get to him.

That woman hunted for a title this Season, or he was a twiddle poop.

At eight and twenty, his poor, spinster cousin desperately strove for acceptance and regularly made a cake of herself to please her scheming friend.

That nettled more than Miss Sanford's designs on the marquisate.

"Since Leventhorpe is escorting Miss Sanford, may I request the next set, Miss Simmons?" Phillips extended his arm, challenging Tristan to say no.

Phillips clearly baited Tristan, and as tempted as he was to tell Francine not to, she probably hadn't enjoyed more than a dance or two this evening. Most assemblies, she didn't dance except with Tristan. She'd gaze longingly at laughing couples while huddled with the other plain wallflowers.

If she could abide Phillips's sweet and sour odor for the dance's duration, Tristan wouldn't begrudge her a few moments of happiness.

Francine colored, her cheeks two candy-apple red blotches, and grasped Phillips's elbow a mite too exuberantly. "I'd be delighted, Mr. Phillips."

Smiling coquettishly, Miss Sanford blinked her big, brown calf-eyes at him. "You wouldn't snub me in full view of the Kattenbys' guests, would you, my lord?

The wise woman recognizes and
disdains the schemes of pretentious social climbers.
~Dignity and Decorum—The Genteel Lady's Guide to Practical Living

3

After wandering down a corridor, Blythe slowly ambled to a stop. This wasn't right. Nothing seemed the least familiar.

Botheration.

She searched the passageway behind her. After leaving the lady's retiring room, she'd apparently taken a wrong corridor. Or two. She had best retrace her steps before she found herself completely turned round.

She possessed a dismal sense of direction. If she ever found herself in the heart of London without an escort, she would wander about in circles for a month. Then again, it might take them that long to find her in this astonishingly vast and complex house.

The next dance belonged to Lord Leventhorpe. She smiled, a trifle impishly. Perhaps her conscience had deliberately misguided her to avoid what was sure to be a trying half an hour. She'd be obligated to bear his touch and converse with him the whole while.

Considering their longest prior communication hadn't been above five minutes, they might scratch one another's eyes out before the music ended. Lifting her skirt to enable her to walk quicker, she grinned. Mayhap she ought to remove her gloves. Her nails were longer. He, on the other hand, was much taller.

Truthfully, her preoccupation leading to her becoming lost could be blamed on pleasurable musings about Mr. Burlington.

Her cotillion with him had been lovely. An excellent dancer, he possessed a ready wit and a readier smile. More importantly, he made her comfortable. They'd conversed and laughed easily, and when their dance ended, Blythe admitted she'd been startled and not a little disappointed. She'd never expected to meet a gentleman of his caliber this early on, and he'd quite assailed her logic and senses.

Usually a pragmatic woman, her woolgathering was as foreign and distasteful as those strange fishy-smelling black beads their hostess had served at a dinner party three nights ago.

Blythe had taken a spin around the ballroom with several distinguished gentlemen. And she'd refused an equal number of disappointed beaux's requests, because she'd already promised the remainder to others. Mr. Burlington's had been the most enjoyable by far.

In his company, she forgot the crowd and hubbub, and she happily anticipated the supper dance and dining with him. Her next partner didn't rouse the same cheery expectation.

Whatever had possessed Lord Leventhorpe to ask for a dance? And a waltz, no less.

More importantly, whyever had she agreed?

He'd stirred her sympathy, she grudgingly admitted. That knowledge practically sent her into an apoplexy. A shiver raised her flesh, and she briskly rubbed her arms above her elbow-length gloves. Gads, just thinking about Lord Leventhorpe agitated her.

Two corridors intersected, and she paused to collect her bearings.

Right or left?

Ah, the marble-topped mahogany table with the heinous vase she'd seen before.

Now I remember.

Whisking along, her slippers silent upon the burgundy Aubusson runner, Blythe passed the table. Another two turns, and she'd be at the landing. She held her breath, straining to hear the music as she marched along.

A quadrille. Not too late after all, devil it.

Lord Leventhorpe would have his troublesome waltz. If she found her way downstairs again.

When she'd refused him the supper dance, she'd glimpsed something startling in the depths of his eyes. So staggering, in truth, that she'd almost gone onto tiptoe and pulled his head down to examine their blue depths closer.

Vulnerability was the last emotion she'd ever expected to see. *Ever.* He hid it well, which piqued her curiosity. What caused a man as outwardly frosty as a winter gale to disguise shyness?

Blythe loved a riddle, and Leventhorpe, it seemed, was more than he presented. "Now to uncover why." His discomfiture shadowed eyes floated before her, and she quirked her lips. "He's an enigma, to be sure."

Head bowed, she toyed with her pendant, deep in reverie as she approached a black-velvet-curtained alcove. At the corner, she bumped into a man. Smelling of rosewater and something else, a peculiar tangy scent—stale sweat, perchance?—he steadied her with surprisingly strong arms, given their wiriness.

Drat.

Mr. Phillips, another inscrutable man. In a crafty, scheming fashion rather than a mysterious, intriguing one. "Do you usually wander corridors talking to yourself?" His languid gaze slithered over her. "An unwise habit for a beauty such as yourself."

"Talking to myself is unwise?" Blythe raised a dubious brow. His lewd implication hadn't escaped her, but she wouldn't give him the satisfaction of acknowledging his crassness.

"No, I meant—" Mr. Phillips smiled and loosened his grip, though he didn't release her. "It's of no import. I believe you may have crushed my quizzing glass."

"I beg your pardon." Barely subduing the urge to recoil and hurry to the retiring room to scrub her arms where his cold, damp fingers touched her, Blythe disengaged herself and stepped backward. She hadn't hit him hard enough to break anything. "I'll replace the piece if it's damaged."

He would have to prove it first. Doubtful he owned a quizzing glass, and if he had one in his possession tonight, he'd tucked it safely away.

The lovely woman she'd seen on the other bench earlier emerged from the alcove, a syrupy smile bending her mouth as the curtain fell into place.

Hmm, interesting. Had he come from there too? Why the need for the lowered curtain?

A *tête-à-tête*?

Swathed in haughtiness, the woman swept to Mr. Phillips's side. "How clumsy of you, though to be expected from a clodpoll newly introduced to Polite Society."

Mayhap she'd like to see what else clodpolls were capable of. How much did she value her hair? Blythe could sheer a sheep in fifteen minutes. She would have those gorgeous coffee-colored locks off in ten seconds.

Much as she would've liked to give the chit a verbal set down, the music below had ceased.

She must hurry, or she would miss the waltz with his lordship. A minute ago, she'd been half-wishing that very thing, and now she was quite desperate to make sure she didn't. Mimicking the woman's lofty mien, Blythe lifted her chin and examined the passage beyond them. "As we've not been introduced, I find it presumptuous to assume you know anything about me."

"Everyone here tonight knows *who* the Culpepper interlopers are." The brunette's retort rang harsh and venom-laced.

They did? How peculiar. Had Society nothing better to occupy their consideration? That was what came of being idle and wealthy. And bitchy.

"Miss Sanford, please allow me the honor of making the introductions." Mr. Phillips offered a ghost of a bow. "Rosemary Sanford, may I present...?" He peered expectantly at Blythe, his lips edging upward into what he, no doubt, considered a charming smile. He resembled an overly sleek, grinning Cheshire cat. "I'm afraid I don't know your given name, Miss Culpepper."

And it's going to stay that way. I'm not completely ignorant of social graces.

"I believe it's proper to wait to be introduced, is it not? And that same decorum prohibits me from speaking further to you." She inclined her head. "If you'll excuse me, I've promised Lord Leventhorpe the next dance."

The rude, inarticulate sound Miss Sanford released could only be described as a hiss of displeasure. Eyes narrowed to wrathful slits, she stared down her nose at Blythe, or tried to. Rather awkward and comical when Blythe stood several inches taller.

"*You're* dancing a waltz with the marquis?" Miss Sanford's mouth curled into a full sneer.

"Yes. He's a *very close* family friend." Not quite the truth, but the jealous chit needn't know that. Besides, Miss Sanford had stood up with his lordship already. Blythe had seen her pressing into him, a seductress's smile slanting her flawless mouth. "I believe I spotted you dancing with him earlier? Why, did he not request a waltz with you also? How utterly disappointed you must be."

Truly wicked of Blythe to taunt, but Miss Sanford rose to the bait readily.

Another disgruntled sound echoed in her throat, and Miss Sanford lifted her fan threateningly.

Did she think to dictate who Lord Leventhorpe danced with? If they were more than mere acquaintances, her vexation might have merit, but on her first night amongst the upper crust, Blythe had no idea if Miss Sanford was a particular favorite of Lord Leventhorpe's. The chit certainly showed possessive tendencies and a dismal temper too.

Lord Leventhorpe hadn't seemed particularly enthralled with her company, but given his skill at concealing his emotions, his lack of exuberance didn't reveal much.

Francine Simmons emerged from the retiring room, a confused sulk marring her forehead. "There you are, Rosemary. I thought you were still inside. You left without telling me? I was waiting in the adjoining chamber as you asked me to. Did I misunderstand?"

"I needed to speak with Mr. Phillips, and I don't have to tell you my every movement, Francine. I declare, you are positively suffocating at times. I don't know how I abide you." With that snide comment, Miss Sanford gripped Mr. Phillips's arm and sallied forth, hauling him toward the stairs.

Toss pots.

He glanced behind him, giving Blythe another disturbing smile. Something queer about that man. Something uncanny—almost eerie or treacherous—in his eyes. She'd hate to bump into him alone in a secluded spot. Why, even now, with other women present, her skin tried to scamper off her bones and cower in the alcove's dark corner.

A sniffle drew her attention to the dejected woman hunched beside her.

"I don't know why I tolerate her." Miss Simmons rubbed her red-rimmed eyes, worsening their appearance. "On a charitable day she's selfish and inconsiderate ... and entirely thoughtless."

"I'm sorry." Oh, to be able to shave that snotty-nosed miss's head bare as a hog's bristly behind. "Is there anything I can do to help?"

"No. I'm just overwrought. I shall be fine in a moment or two." Miss Simmons shook her head and produced a despairing little laugh. "I have fragile nerves, Rosemary says."

Hmm, with that creature for a friend, the Lord himself would require a calming draught. An immense one.

"I'm Blythe Culpepper." Offering a sunny smile, Blythe touched Miss Simmons's elbow. So much for propriety. Blythe fished her

185

handkerchief from her bodice. "Here. Dry your eyes, and I shall walk to the ballroom with you. Who are you here with?"

Miss Simmons wiped her face then blew her nose. "I came with Rosemary, her mother, and grandmother. I live alone, you see. Well, I have a small staff. My parents are dead, and Tristan, that is, Lord Leventhorpe, is my only living relation. We're second cousins." Melancholy tinged her voice. "Rosemary permits me to accompany her to social gatherings as long as I do as she bids."

I'll bet she does.

She patted another tear leaking from the corner of her eye.

"You live alone? Why don't you live with Lord Leventhorpe?" How could he permit this obviously lonely woman to reside by herself?'

"Oh, Tristan has offered, many times, but I want my independence. Mama and Papa left me enough to be comfortable if I economize, and if I lived in the country with him— Oh, dear. I oughtn't to have shared that. Utterly gauche." Her face blooming with color, she hunched a shoulder. "I hold a trifling hope that I might meet a gentleman who would take me to wife. Silly, I know."

Pained rejection reduced her voice to a whisper with her last words, and Blythe's heart wrenched. Mere weeks ago, her circumstances had been desperate and seemingly impossible, until Heath had rescued them. Who would rescue Francine?

Lord Leventhorpe?

Perhaps a word in his ear was in order, though he didn't seem the sort to readily take suggestions. If intervening helped this pitiable woman, the effort was worth annoying his lordship.

"A lovely woman such as yourself, Miss Simmons, should continue to harbor that wonderful dream."

"Thank you. You are most kind." At Blythe's compliment, Miss Simmons's mouth formed a surprised O and color dashed her face again. "Rosemary said beautiful women like you ..." Cheeks deepening to crimson, she cast her gaze to the floor. "Never mind. I'm sure she is mistaken."

Blythe had a pretty fair notion what Miss Sanford had told Miss Simmons.

Miss Simmons's possessed a good complexion, her gray-blue eyes held keen intelligence, and her hair shimmered with the same umber shades as Lord Leventhorpe's. If she wore the right colors and styles—

not like the drab oatmeal-colored sack she had on—arranged her striking hair differently, and added the faintest touch of cosmetics, she would be quite attractive. Her self-confidence was an entirely other matter.

Perhaps Blythe and the other Culpeppers might assist in that regard. And keeping Miss Simmons away from that self-serving Sanford banshee seemed the obvious place to start.

The prelude's first few notes drifted up from below, and Blythe quickened her pace. During the dance would be the perfect time to broach the subject of his lordship's cousin.

"Lord Leventhorpe doesn't stay with you when he comes to town?" Probably had a house. Bachelors didn't like the restrictions of living with female relatives. At least her nefarious cousin Sheridan never had. Thank God the Chancery Court had appointed Heath their guardian, ridding the Culpeppers of ever having to deal with Sheridan again.

"No, Tristan has lodgings at White's. He quite loathes London and never stays at his house on Mayfair. I'm not sure he even maintains staff there. He only ventures to Town for important Parliamentary matters." Brushing a tendril away from her eye, Miss Simmons gave a sad smile. "You needn't pity me. I don't mind being alone. I have my charitable meetings and Church. And every now and again, I receive an invitation to call."

When was the last time anyone had listened to the poor dear? Blythe smiled tolerantly as Miss Simmons prattled on, oblivious to the pair of ladies approaching from the other direction. Stepping to the side, Blythe waited for them to pass and answered their friendly smiles with her own.

"And I enjoy reading. Have you been to The Temple of the Muses, Miss Culpepper? Such a wonderful bookshop. Oh, and I quite adore riding. Tristan takes me two or three times a week when he's here. He is a dear underneath his aloof manner. His mother was dotty, you see, and his father ..." Cutting Blythe a hesitant, sidelong glance, she chewed her lower lip indecisively.

"His father?"

Miss Simmons was a store of useful information. It gushed from her like milk from a cow's full teat. There was much more to the reserved marquis then Blythe had imagined. Not that she'd imagined anything about him, of course, other than uncharitable thoughts at Esherton Green when she'd pondered if he'd docked his devil's tail, how often he filed the horns his hair concealed, and how he managed to shove his cloven hooves into boots.

Miss Simmons exhaled a hefty breath and scooted closer. "The former Lord Leventhorpe was a lecherous, depraved scoundrel." Her voice soft and low, she nervously peered around. "Or so I've heard whispered. No one tells a lady anything directly, for fear of our tender sensibilities—most irritating and utterly ridiculous—but for years I've overheard snatches about his deplorable behavior."

Splendid. Miss Simmons had a fiery streak buried in her. Though how could she not when she shared Leventhorpe's blood?

Blythe looped her hand through Miss Simmons's crooked elbow. "I have two sisters, and we have lived with our two cousins since I was eight. The five of us get along famously, but sometimes I crave time alone."

"Miss Culpepper, would you ...?" Miss Simmons screwed up her courage and blurted, "Would you come for tea? Your sisters and cousins, too?"

Evidently accustomed to rejection, her eyes round and anxious, she fiddled with the folds of her fan.

Blythe grinned and nodded. "If you agree to call me Blythe."

"And you must call me Francine." They reached the staircase's bottom. "I was named after Tristan's mother."

Arm in arm, they entered the ballroom, and coppery hair, a head taller than the rest of the guests, snagged her attention. Arms crossed and his countenance one of polite boredom, Lord Leventhorpe leaned a shoulder against an arched windowsill and perused the room. From the black of his cutaway coat and breeches, to the gold and burgundy of his waistcoat, he blended with the decor.

His languid gaze roved the entrance, and he straightened upon spying her.

An amiable smile brightened his face, his attention dipping to Francine before swooping back to Blythe. His lips bent more as he strode in their direction, moving with the lithe, natural grace of an athlete, his long legs rapidly covering the distance.

Had he watched for her?

Upon reaching them, he executed an exaggerated courtier's bow, and Francine giggled.

Even Blythe's lips curved at his silliness. She'd not have believed him capable of the overplayed gallantry.

"Trist, you're uncommonly chipper." Francine touched his arm, peering at him hopefully "Did you enjoy your dance with Rosemary, then?"

Blythe quashed her irritation. It would take time to wean Francine from her dependency upon Miss Sanford's self-serving approval.

"It was unremarkable." Though he answered Francine, his attention remained upon Blythe.

Francine's face fell, her earlier buoyancy evaporating. "Oh. I'd hoped ... Never mind."

He chucked her chin. "But, my dear, I saved the supper dance for you. Now tell me. What have you two ladies been up to?"

"You did? The supper dance, truly?" Francine beamed once more. "Blythe ... I mean Miss Culpepper, has been most kind and graciously consented to come for tea."

Goodness. Miss Simmons's emotions vacillated hot and cold.

Lord Leventhorpe's chestnut brows shot skyward. "Indeed. Might I join you?"

Francine's jaw slackened, and she blinked, rather like a confused owl. "Of course. Why, I believe I shall ask the Culpeppers to call. And Reverend Hawksworth. He's always kind. Oh, and the Wimpletons, of course." She glanced around. "I must find something to write on. Please excuse me." She hustled off, a plump brown wren, decidedly cheerier than she had been upstairs.

"What have you done to my cousin?" Extending his elbow, Lord Leventhorpe stared after her retreating form. "I don't recall when I've seen her that animated." His intrigued gaze dipped to Blythe's, and a sensation much like warm silk caressed her. "Thank you. She needs kind friends."

"She's sweet. I'm going to speak with Brooke about taking her under our wing." Blythe regarded him candidly. "If you're amenable to the suggestion."

"Miss Culpepper, I would be immensely grateful."

To her surprise, they'd reached the dance floor. Why, if they continued to speak of Francine, the waltz might be bearable after all.

"I bumped into Mr. Phillips upstairs. I believe he'd been sequestered in an alcove with Miss Sanford. She left Francine in the ladies retiring room, and spoke rather unkindly to her."

"No surprise there. Miss Sanford's friendship with my cousin is prompted by ulterior motives." An elusive emotion shadowed his lordship's eyes, deepening the blue to cerulean. "Phillips wasn't forward with you, was he? He's ..." He bent his head as they took their place upon the floor. "He's a disreputable sort."

His concern surprised and touched her. Perhaps Brooke was right, and Lord Leventhorpe possessed a heart after all. "I gathered as much. He attempted to extract my given name. I refused."

The waltz began, and Blythe dipped into a curtsy as his lordship bowed, his unusual lion's head stickpin in the folds of his cravat catching her eye. Its ruby eyes and diamond mouth twinkled in the incandescent light. A family heirloom?

Stepping into his embrace wasn't what Blythe had anticipated either. Though not as light on his feet as Mr. Burlington, Lord Leventhorpe proved a superb dancer, especially for such a towering man. She frequently stood taller than men and quite liked having to look upward to meet his eyes.

Mr. Burlington had been on eye level with her.

So?

Like the muscular statues in the entry, his lordship's shoulder was thick and rounded, the sinewy flesh flexing beneath her fingertips. What other parts of his anatomy might be as generous? Heat stole up her cheeks, and her breathing sputtered for a moment.

Oh, for the love of God, Blythe. Stop.

Of a slimmer build, Mr. Burlington had been solid, but didn't boast the marquis's bulging physique.

Nothing wrong with that. He wasn't scrawny or twitchy like Mr. Phillips, repulsive man.

She and Lord Leventhorpe danced well together, their forms nicely proportioned. As they rose and fell to the orchestra's strains, his lordship's subtle scent wafted to her. Swaying in his arms, she took a deep breath. In addition to his usual sandalwood, Blythe detected cloves and fresh linen. And perhaps a hint of brandy?

Mr. Burlington's cologne had been musky.

Both smelled pleasant, yet distinctly different, like the men themselves.

Stop comparing them, for pity's sake.

Lord Leventhorpe fell silent once their dance began, and the delight of being held in his strong embrace was unexpected and disconcerting. A month ago, she'd have believed herself dicked in the nob for entertaining such an absurd notion as enjoying a waltz with him.

Did his thoughts run parallel to hers, confusion meshed with pleasure? She entertained no misconceptions about his prior sentiments toward her.

Blythe slanted her head, and her gaze collided with his half-open sapphire eyes, the tips of his lashes feathered auburn. She stumbled, mashing his toes.

Had he observed her while they circled the floor?

The gentle upward sweep of his mouth sent a frisson to the tips of her toes, and she missed another step. So much for confidence in her dance skills.

He drew her infinitesimally closer, though surely only because of her momentary clumsiness.

She ought to object, but her tongue seemed content to stay silent.

Say something.

"Francine says you take her riding."

His attention dropped to Blythe's mouth before he nodded. "Yes. When I'm able. Because we prefer the park to ourselves, I collect her at seven o'clock."

The music ended, and after a hesitant moment, he released her and gave a short bow.

Well, that hadn't been unpleasant at all.

Blythe curtsied then accepted his arm as she searched amongst the crush for her family. Encountering several hastily averted, speculative gazes, she fought a smile.

Quite a number of busybodies in attendance.

His lordship escorted her to their bench, albeit by a circuitous route. "If you would like to join us, I'm sure Francine would be delighted."

At the nearness of his mouth to her ear, Blythe gave a start. He seemed particularly fond of doing that.

"Alas, I fear I don't ride sidesaddle. I never learned how. There wasn't a need at Esherton Green, nor much opportunity with an old nag fit only for our dogcart." She pulled a face and gestured with her fan. "But I think we must learn now. It's expected, isn't it?"

"Usually, not always. I don't think anyone should be forced to do something they find objectionable." A peculiar inflection entered his voice, and a flash of pain glinted in his eyes for an instant.

With considerable effort, she dragged her gaze from his and located her family.

Mr. Burlington waited with Brooke and Heath. The girls' escorts must have already claimed them for the supper dance. Unaccustomed to dancing all evening, Blythe's feet had grown sore, and she welcomed the opportunity to sit for a while.

As if reluctant to relinquish her, Lord Leventhorpe slowed his pace. "Miss Culpepper, I would be happy to teach you to ride sidesaddle. If you would like to learn."

The man was full of surprises tonight. What next?

A warbling love sonnet for a shy wallflower?

A race through The Green Park in his underthings?

No, he was too taciturn for either, but his unexpected offer touched her.

"You have a sweet-tempered mare and a sidesaddle tucked in your London mews, my lord?" She wasn't going to learn to stay balanced atop that ridiculous contraption while seated astride a giant of a horse. Men should be made to ride on the stupid thing since they insisted ladies do so. No, a sedate pony or donkey would do perfectly until she mastered the skill. "I cannot conceive of you seated upon either. I've seen that immense, russet brute you ride. That beast looks to be descended from a mythological creature."

She grinned at his flummoxed expression. He didn't know she jested. Lord Leventhorpe was too serious by far.

"I raised Bucephalus from a foal." He summoned a grin and scratched his nose. "Buce is named after Alexander the Great's gargantuan steed, said to have had an immense head."

"A most fitting name." They had nearly reached the others. "You've other horseflesh in London too?"

"I have several horses and carriages at a local livery. Raven asked me to let him know if I spotted horseflesh appropriate for women at Tattersalls, and last week, a brilliant mare caught my eye. Perhaps you'd care to accompany me to the auction tomorrow to view the mare?"

And now an offer of an outing? Blythe rather liked this Lord Leventhorpe.

"I'd like to, and the others may want to attend also. That way we can see if the mare suits before Heath purchases her. Is it permissible? I didn't think women were allowed."

"If you are in my and Ravensdale's company, it's acceptable." Lord

Leventhorpe lifted a shoulder. "If he doesn't purchase the mare, I shall. She's a rare beauty sporting a champagne coat with a creamy white mane and tail."

"Oh, she sounds gorgeous. Heath has suggested we wait until we return to the country to learn to ride, but, I confess, I crave the outdoors and would adore early morning jaunts. I used to take a lengthy walk with Freddy at dawn each day."

He slanted his brow. "Never had a beast detest me more than that aged, gone-to-fat corgi."

"Brooke thinks your cologne set the dog against you at Esherton. A man wearing a similar fragrance abused him. At the end, Freddy warmed to you." She dropped her hand as they reached the bench. She'd like the feel of his solid forearm flexing beneath her fingertips. "Brooke, Lord Leventhorpe has generously offered to teach us to ride sidesaddle."

An exuberant grin lit Mr. Burlington's face. "One of my greatest pleasures is riding, and I would enjoy sharing the experience with you. That is, if Leventhorpe doesn't object."

The look in his eyes warmed Blythe to her mistreated toes. A handsome man's admiration did bolster one's confidence, yet the intensity in Lord Leventhorpe's gaze while they danced meant more.

Probably because he didn't loathe her any longer. No one relished being disliked.

Mr. Burlington turned his affable gaze to his lordship. "Leventhorpe, would I be imposing? I helped teach my three younger sisters, and would be happy to volunteer my time and services."

"Not at all, Burlington. Unless Ravensdale prefers the ladies wait." Lord Leventhorpe's tone belied his words. Over her head, he regarded Heath, and as certain as Freddy had peed on Heath's boot at Esherton, a silent message passed between them.

She'd done that very thing with her sister and cousins myriad times.

Enough doubt niggled to steal her earlier enthusiasm about the lessons. She cast Lord Leventhorpe a glance, and her heart flipped when she caught him regarding her. What she wouldn't give to read his thoughts.

Was he considering reneging because Mr. Burlington offered to help? That made no sense. She would think he'd welcome another hand. None of the Culpeppers had ever sat a sidesaddle. Though the task might prove considerable, they might as well learn here as at home. And she would be assured of time with Mr. Burlington, affording her the opportunity to become better acquainted. More importantly, riding lessons meant escaping the house and spending time in the outdoors, and after her stay in London, both appealed more than either man.

Liar.

Enough. She refused to examine her musings further.

"I think Lord Leventhorpe may have taken on more than he wagered, and I'm sure he would appreciate any assistance he can gather, Mr. Burlington. I'm quite looking forward to learning, aren't you, Brooke?" Clasping her hands, and painting a bright smile upon her face, Blythe turned to Lord Leventhorpe. "Is the day after tomorrow too soon to begin lessons?"

Though circumstances appear to confirm schemes laid in advance,
when motives are selfish, expect unforeseen and unpleasant results.
~Dignity and Decorum—The Genteel Lady's Guide to Practical Living

4

"*T*here he is." Tristan pointed to Hawksworth slumped atop a lopsided table in a fusty corner. "Looks practically pickled."

"What's he doing in The Ship & Whistle?" Ravensdale surveyed the unsavory establishment through the grungy window.

"Probably assumed we wouldn't look here. It's a favorite of sailors and servicemen. Cheap prostitutes and cheaper spirits." Tristan dipped his head as they entered the tavern, the stench of unwashed bodies, sweat, vomit, and spilled ale causing a reflexive surge of bile.

"Ho there, Ravensdale. Leventhorpe." Phillips and a handful of his cronies, all foxed to the gills, stumbled into the establishment. "Come to hire a wench for the evening too?"

Never fastidious or selective, Phillips had retained a flaxen-haired running-to-fat tavern harlot. He pinched her full buttocks. "We can share her, can't we, darlin'?"

She leaned into him. "Sure, guv.'"

"No. We cannot." Tristan glowered at Phillips.

Ravensdale shook his head. "I'll pass."

Tristan and Ravensdale each, for entirely different reasons, never entertained light skirts.

"What about Hawksworth? That Friday face looks like he could use a bit of cheering." Phillips's jibe earned him a blank, glassy-eyed stare from Hawk.

"M' lifesh ended now anyway." Hawksworth's slurred speech testified to his drunk-as-a-wheelbarrow condition. "Might ashh well 'urry i' along." Grinning sloppily, he squinted and tried to focus. "Where ish she?"

Ape drunk, Hawksworth wasn't capable of a cockstand.

He wasn't capable of standing at all.

"At least one of you three has a working set of ballocks." *Slapping his chest, Phillips chortled and grabbed Hawksworth's arm.* "Come on, man. Let's get you upstairs, unless you want to take her here." *He slid Tristan a sly look.* "Some men enjoy an audience."

Tristan clamped his jaw and balled his hands, sweat beading his upper lip and soaking his armpits. Had Phillips learned of his humiliation? Zounds. How?

Phillips turned to the harlot. "You don't mind, do you, Shelly, sweetheart?"

She grinned, revealing a mouth of yellowed teeth, and drew her grungy, stained blouse low on her sagging breasts. "Naw, makes i' more fun. I charges extra fer peepers, though."

"Up with you, Hawksworth." *Phillips tugged Hawk's arm again, attempting to rouse him from his chair and stupor.* "Shelly knows her trade and several unique tricks too. You'll not be disappointed."

Bloody eager to watch, pervert.

"Leave him be. Unlike you, he isn't keen on acquiring the pox." *Ravensdale glowered at Seymour and his comrades, who'd formed a taunting semicircle around them.*

Seven to three. Not the best odds.

Hawksworth slouched with his eyes closed and chin slack against his chest. Make that two. Rather dismal chances, actually. Couldn't be helped.

Shoving Phillips's hand away from Hawk, Tristan sliced Ravensdale a silent message. "We want no part of your doxy."

"Wot's wrong wif ye, luv?" *The strumpet sidled up to Tristan, her foul odor revolting. From her stench, she'd already been busy this evening. She rubbed against him, releasing another unpleasant whiff of her unwashed body.*

Queasiness twisted his stomach tighter.

"Ya prefer tuppin' gents?"

Doubled up with glee, Phillips choked on his laughter, his drunken entourage also guffawing.

"You haven't always felt that way, Leventhorpe." *Phillips grinned nastily and scratched his groin.* "I seem to recall something my father let slip. Something your father shared at Brooks's while deep in his cups one day."

Father was usually in his cups.

"Stubble it, Phillips." Ravensdale dragged his hand through his hair, compassion tinting the gaze he sent Tristan.

He and Hawksworth, alone, were privy to the event that haunted Tristan, and they didn't know the whole of it. He had never been able to speak of the horrific humiliation.

"Wasn't there an instance when you had quite a public display of lust, Leventhorpe?" Phillips held up two fingers. "One that involved two prostitutes?"

Tristan's well-placed facer broke Phillips's nose.

Tristan bolted upright, cursing and disoriented. Darkness enveloped him, and for an instant, he didn't know where he was.

God.

He rubbed his face before lying down once more.

A nightmare. Not his usual, though.

Pure fate, Whitehouse and Drake had happened along that evening, in time to prevent Ravensdale and Tristan from getting completely thrashed. They had jumped into the ensuing fray, balancing the odds nicely. The five had been the greatest of chums ever since.

Nothing quite like fighting side-by-side against a common foe to forge unbreakable bonds of friendship. A week later, they'd shared mutual misgivings too, when the same diseased slattern, tortured and beaten to death, washed ashore on the River Thames's beach.

Tristan closed his eyes against his musing and the accompanying disquiet. He kicked off his bedcovers, and after punching his pillow into an acceptable shape, flopped onto his stomach.

Slumber didn't embrace him.

The rhythmic *tick-tocking* of his bedside table clock usually lulled him to sleep. He cracked an eye open and glared at the indiscernible oval face in the pre-dawn half-light.

What time was it?

Too early to rise, by half.

He hadn't heard a peep from Peasley, and the valet took particular pleasure in slinging open the window coverings the moment the first ray of sun brazened the horizon.

In the distance, a dog barked, and a moment later, an answering woof sounded.

Yawning, Tristan stretched his legs, encountering several furry paws despite his mammoth mattress. Clio and Thalia sprawled at the foot of his bed, softly snoring and twitching every now and again.

He ought to make them get off the bed.

Despite regular brushing, the dogs shed terribly, and White's chambermaid fretted when she had to clean the collies' hair from the coverlet and furniture. The extra vails Tristan offered for her inconvenience lessened her vexation a jot. More than once, he'd endured his valet's wrath as Peasley tutted and fussed while ridding Tristan's togs of hair before permitting him to present himself in public.

For the first time, Tristan had stayed until a ball's confounded end—very nearly a miracle thanks to the humiliating experience his despot of a father had foisted upon him at thirteen.

Wide awake and agitated after last night's ball, he hadn't found his bed until after half past two. Yet each time he shut his eyelids, a halo of silvery hair, violet-blue eyes below delicate honey-blond brows, a pert nose, and stubborn chin taunted him. He'd been hard-put not to stare at the firm teacup-sized bosoms teasing her bodice's neckline during their waltz. He'd fallen into an agitated slumber only to have Phillips encroach upon his dreams.

He didn't trust Phillip's, and Burlington's interest in Blythe chaffed worse than a week bare-arsed in a new saddle, though why it should confounded Tristan.

Worry and concern.

That was what this unease centered in his gut was. None of his blasted business, by God. The Culpeppers weren't—Blythe most assuredly wasn't—his concern.

Stop thinking about her, and go to sleep.

His rebellious musings ignored him.

Tristan had told Ravensdale about Blythe's unnerving upstairs encounter with Phillips, and evidently, Raven had conveyed their mutual disquiet to his wife.

For the evening's remainder, Lady Ravensdale had insisted the Culpeppers visit the retiring room *en masse*. Until they became familiar with *haut ton* protocol, and accumulated a set of trustworthy friends, Tristan applauded her decision.

Years of experience guiding the tightknit quartet would serve her, and them, well in London. Tristan admired the Culpeppers' unity.

Genuinely kind and friendly, they'd soon have a circle of supporters.

Surely Ravensdale's melon had gone soft for descending upon London with his new family in tow. With that lot churning High Society's staid waters, Tristan might have enjoyed this Season. However, his abhorrence of crowds prevented any such thing. His habit of imbibing a couple of stiff drinks before venturing to a gathering sufficed when he did so once a fortnight at most.

But, *damn my eyes,* Ravensdale had asked for his help, which meant multiple forays weekly.

Mayhap Tristan would purchase a barrel of whisky. He shook his face in his crisp pillowcase's folds. No. He'd not end up a fuddled drunkard like his father.

Then you need to find another way to deal with your dread.

Grunting, Tristan turned onto his back and stared at the inky canopy. He scratched his bare chest before tucking his hands underneath his head.

Promising to teach the Culpeppers to ride.

Had *his* melon gone soft?

Now he'd have to bear Burlington's insufferable presence too. He wanted to hate the man, but couldn't. Not for being a favorite with the ladies and taking advantage of what many offered freely. Tristan, Heath, and Hawksworth were anomalies in that regard, though they weren't monks, just exceedingly selective.

Well ... Heath had been prior to marriage. Now, tits over arse in love, Raven would never betray Lady Ravensdale.

The epitome of discretion when it came to his dalliances, much like Drake and Whitehouse, Burlington didn't possess despicable habits. He came from a long line of respectable peers, and the Earl of Lauderdale was an upright chap, if a bit thin in the pockets. Other than a weak constitution, Burlington's older brother boasted an exemplary character too.

Damme.

Burlington had to have one unsavory practice. He was too bloody perfect by far. Only his lack of title made him less desirable to some women. Others mightn't care.

Did Blythe?

She wasn't the sort, which made Burlington more of a threat.

Clio twitched and whined in her sleep. Probably dreamed of running the fields and herding the cattle at Bristledale. Tristan should have left the dogs there, but truthfully, he missed them and found London lonely.

The blame for that, too, could be plopped at his doorstep.

A stack of unopened invitations lay piled atop the corner secretary where he'd tossed them.

He didn't relish returning to his empty rooms at White's, and since he stayed in most evenings—at least he had until this confounded Season—he found the dogs welcome company. True, he'd rented these quarters for a decade, and they bore his personal touch and preferences, but the pleasant rooms weren't home.

Only at Bristledale Court, away from Town's observant eyes, attending ears, and flapping tongues, did he find a degree of respite.

As for the house bearing witness to his disgrace as a youth, he'd have sold the place and its furnishings for a pittance without an iota of regret within a week of inheriting the marquisate if the damned thing weren't entailed. He couldn't bear to pass the residence and went out of his way to avoid the street altogether.

No matter how many times he told himself what had happened those many years ago wasn't his fault, he couldn't rid himself of the dirty, used feeling. And with Phillips's return, more people might soon know of his degradation.

A thirteen-year-old, even one the size of a grown man, should never be forced to have his first sexual encounter with jaded prostitutes reeking of cheap perfume, and witnessed by debauched lechers. He'd tried to resist, but against the women's well-honed skills, he'd battled in vain. Even as his mind screeched no, and he'd pleaded and screamed for them to stop, his healthy, young body on the cusp of manhood had responded.

Growling deep in his chest, Tristan flopped a bent arm across his face, as if to hide the scene replaying behind his eyes for the thousandth time. The whores' appreciative coos and laughter mixed with the men's vile remarks regarding his immediate and impressive erection echoed in his dreams.

In his waking hours too.

His stomach roiled, and his nostrils twitched. He'd never forget the putrid smells either.

When a sodomite had asked to have him, and his sire drunkenly agreed, Tristan fought loose of the men restraining him. After he broke the bugger's groping hand, he'd fled the house and stayed either at school or as a guest of chums until he acquired his own lodgings at eighteen.

He never saw his father again.

Not even upon his deathbed, when Father repented of his lifetime of depravity and sent word, begging Tristan to visit him in order to make amends before he died. Better that his sire had changed his ways and sought reconciliation and forgiveness when he had time to make restitution. Precisely like the selfish, old marquis to lay the burden of forgiveness on Tristan.

Why should he grant Father forgiveness?

So he could enter eternal slumber with a contented heart and pure conscience? Hawksworth had argued, many times, that forgiving Father would bring healing and peace.

Tristan's loud snort rent the heavy silence, and Thalia raised her head, giving a weak woof.

He would never have peace. Not while he drew breath.

Every day for the past fifteen years, he'd striven for that elusive state. Just when he thought he'd made progress, that he'd finally put the taunting shadows to rest, something stirred them again. Like Phillips last night. And to know Father had spoken of the incident ... How many of the others present had as well?

Tristan gave a savage groan. Devil and damn. The lot, no doubt. His distance from *ton* activities had protected him from the bitter knowledge.

Thomas Gray had it right. *"Where ignorance is bliss, 'tis folly to be wise."*

Thalia lifted her head when Tristan made another inarticulate sound of revulsion.

By God, when he had children—*if* he had children—he'd be a decent father, far superior to his sire. A deuced better husband too.

Clio crawled up his side then laid her pointed muzzle atop his chest.

The dogs sensed his distress.

Tristan ran a hand down her spine. "I suppose you think I should walk you?" She thumped her tail once. "You do realize I'll have to tie my cravat myself?" Two more thumps and a whine confirmed the dog's need.

Thirty minutes later—Peasley would have apoplexy when he discovered Tristan's rudimentarily tied neckcloth—Tristan slipped his arms into his greatcoat. A serving boy had taken the dogs out while he had eaten a hasty breakfast. For expediency, Tristan had stuffed bacon between the croissants flaky folds before gulping two strong cups of Turkish coffee. After a sleepless night, he'd need the restorative beverage to keep him alert today.

After snapping leads onto the dogs' collars, he collected his cane and made his way outside to his waiting landau.

"Good morning, my lord. Your paper." Jones passed the news sheet to Tristan then stepped to hold the carriage door open. The morning proved brisk, though the first rays of sunshine glinting off the vehicle's azure paint, promised a temperate day later. "The ladies are energetic early, I see."

"Good morning, Jones." Tristan wedged the paper beneath his arm and passed the leads to the driver before stepping into the landau. "They were most insistent we have an early constitutional today."

At his whistle, the dogs bounded into the conveyance. Hopping onto the opposite, blanket-covered seat, they raised their pointed snouts and sniffed. London's air seldom lacked for odors.

"The Green Park as usual, your lordship?" Jones asked as he snapped the reins and, with a slight lurch, the vehicle rolled forward.

"Yes." Crossing his legs, Tristan pulled the folded news sheet free. He skimmed the first pages. Nothing original or fresh. Just the same drudgery rewritten from a different perspective than yesterday's. And the day before's. He'd grown weary of the rhetoric already, and Parliament wouldn't recess soon. *More's the pity.*

Squinting as the conveyance turned in the sun, he scratched his nose. Hiring someone to vote in proxy didn't appeal. Granted, many peers condoned the practice, but until he had reason—other than loathing London—to avoid Parliamentary proceedings, he'd not abdicate his responsibilities.

Clio jumped onto the seat beside Tristan, sending his cane

clattering to the floor. Her claws digging into his thigh to stay balanced, she shoved her wet nose underneath the paper, knocking several sheets loose to join his cane. Tail happily wagging, she licked his cheek.

"No. Clio." He pointed to her sister. "You belong there. Off with you."

Head lowered, Clio did as bidden. Lying across the opposite seat, her muzzle resting upon her paws, she watched him soulfully.

"Don't look at me like that. Peasley will have my head if he finds a single strand of dog hair upon my clothing, and I have several calls to make before I can return to my lodgings. Would you have me disparaged?"

She licked her chops, her tail twitching.

As he bent to retrieve his cane and the scattered news sheets, his attention fell upon the natter column. Such claptrap was good for the rubbish bin, a fireplace, or picking up after the dogs' occasional accidents.

He scanned the neat print.

London's first formal glimpse of Ldy R and the four Ms Cs caused a considerable stir last evening. ... Mr. B showed a distinct penchant for the elder Ms C, much to the disappointment of many a fair maid.

He was one gentleman amongst many to pay marked attention to the five diamonds of the first water. Even the reclusive Ld L put in an unexpected, coveted appearance.

No matter how well-intended or magnificent the scheme,
one should occasionally consider the consequences.
~Dignity and Decorum—The Genteel Lady's Guide to Practical Living

5

Tristan snatched the paper from the floor.

*One has to wonder if Ld L has finally decided to pursue matrimony
with one of the newly arrived blond beauties.*

No. He most emphatically had not.

*This columnist means to watch Society's reaction and predicts the
thwarting of many a well-laid scheme ...*

Tristan checked an annoyed grunt and seized his cane. The silver
lion's head grip hid a sword handle. He never ventured anywhere on
foot without the weapon.

Once he gathered the news sheets into an untidy pile, he laid them
beside his leg.

A rather tame assessment and not altogether contrived, discounting
the nonsensical twaddle about Tristan pursuing matrimony. Relaxing
into the seat, he tapped his fingers on the landau's side as they neared
the park.

How long did Raven expect him to help with his newly acquired
family?

Tristan could cry off. Except ... he reluctantly admitted to a
perverse fascination. He might be almost as eager to see what High
Society made of the ladies as Ravensdale.

Le beau monde could be as fickle as a Friday night whore, and her
favors bought as easily. All the more reason to be nearby, in case this
ill-hatched scheme unraveled.

Tristan would arrange the riding lesson details after calling and collecting whichever of the young ladies wanted to venture to Tattersalls. The landau rolled to a stop and, after alighting and untangling the dogs' leashes, Tristan grabbed his cane. Taking a refreshing breath, he set a brisk pace toward Constitution Hill, waving for Jones to collect him on the other side, as he did each morning.

Whistling softly, Tristan mentally catalogued the day's priorities.

He should call upon Francine and, again, advise her about her choice of companions. Blythe, her sisters, and her cousins were exactly the type of friends Francine needed—kind, decent women—not the string of ambitious chits who continually used Francine for their gain.

Farther along the lane, a short-legged bundle of fur-covered fat pelted between two gnarled trees chasing a cow in desperate need of milking.

A cacophony of shouting, barking, and mooing echoed throughout the park. Ears perked in excited interest, Clio and Thalia tugged at their leashes, tails wagging furiously.

"Freddy. Stop."

"Come back, ya ruddy beasty."

"Stop, Clover. I needs t' milk ye."

Tristan faced the racket's direction.

Blythe, a pink and white confection, her bonnet's ribbons trailing behind her, tore across the green followed by a milkmaid, her skirts yanked to her knees, and a lad clenching a rope in one hand and holding his cap atop his head with the other.

Ah, a bovine escapee from adjacent St. James Park's milk lines, and the Culpeppers' corgi loved to herd cattle. Tristan wagered the little devil hadn't been able to resist the runaway cow.

A teenage groom sprinted past Blythe, slicing a diagonal path, intent on cutting the panicked cow off. Another man, noticing the ruckus, gave chase as well, and beyond him, another chap moved toward the animal, though at a more sedate pace.

Pulling his hat lower, the latter abruptly turned in the opposite direction and proceeded to briskly walk away.

With the sun shining in his eyes, Tristan couldn't make him out. Perhaps he'd decided his help wasn't needed to capture the panicked beast. A wonder she didn't knock her hind hooves from beneath her with her bulging udders wildly careening like kettle-sized, milk-filled clappers.

Tristan whistled an imitation of one he'd heard the overseer at Esherton Green use with Freddy. He immediately whirled and trotted Tristan's way, his tongue nearly dragging the pavement along with his leash. Failing eyesight and the distance contributed to the dog's inability to recognize Tristan.

Wait until you realize it's me. You'll be off the other direction faster than angels fleeing hell.

The cow continued to dash along, her enormous udders making Tristan wince with each swing.

Thank God he wasn't a milk cow.

Sunshine, golden and bright, filtered through the tree-lined lane, casting interwoven shadows along the path. He bent and, after unclipping Clio's and Thalia's leashes, pointed at the cow. "Fetch."

Panting, her hair flopping onto one shoulder and her bonnet askew, Blythe dashed onto the pavement. Freddy, a doggy grin splitting his gray face, waddled to her. "Naughty boy. Chasing poor Clover."

Tristan approached cautiously. He didn't need the dog tearing off in a panic too. Squatting, he extended a hand. "Hello, Freddy. There's a good chap."

Freddy skulked closer, his haunches practically hugging the ground and sniffed timidly. He licked Tristan's fingertips then peered at Blythe for approval.

Swiping at a tendril tickling her cheek, Blythe crouched, the graceful curve of her mouth sweeping into a pleased grin. "Well done, Freddy." Patting the dog, she seized his lead and turned a brilliant smile upon Tristan. "He doesn't fear you any longer."

"The wayward cow has been caught." Tristan steered his gaze behind her.

Looking over her shoulder, she stood. "I was about to enjoy a cup of fresh milk when a rail-thin urchin startled Clover." Melancholy riddled her voice. "I felt a jot homesick, and the cows reminded me of Esherton Green. I milked cows almost daily at home." She shook her head, causing a few more curls to tumble loose, and gave a little self-deprecating laugh. "I don't suppose that's altogether ladylike."

"I quite enjoy a cup of fresh milk." Not exactly the fact. He did claim a particular fondness for clotted cream and milk in his coffee. Fresh from the cow's teat, and drunk from a communal cup? No. He managed to conceal his miniscule repugnance-born tremor.

The lad led the docile beast, the rope now circling Clover's thick neck, while the milkmaid, obviously his sister given the smattering of freckles also covering her broad face, guided the cow with a hand to her black and white dappled neck.

Thalia and Clio trotted behind, a safe distance from the cow's hind legs, and the groom and other gentleman brought up the rear.

"Miss, I'm afeared I left the cup yonder. To thank ye fer yer help, I'd be pleased to give ye a drink fer no cost ifn ye want to walk back." The girl repeatedly glanced in the vicinity of connecting St. James Park. "It were kind of ye to give the beggar child yer blunt."

Did a father, or perhaps an employer, expect the milkmaid? Would the children be chastised for the loss of a sale? Tristan passed the lad a shilling and the lass two. "You each keep a coin. The other is to pay for the sales you've lost."

The boy's face lit like fireworks above Vauxhall Gardens. He bobbed his moppy head. "Thank ye, m'lord."

"Thank ye, again, fer yer help, m'lord. Miss. Gents." After pocketing her coins and attempting a clumsy curtsy, the milkmaid headed for St. James Park, her brother chatting and gesturing excitedly about what he intended to buy with his money.

"That was kind of you, my lord." With a soft sigh, Blythe turned to her groom as Freddy and the collies sniffed one another in greeting. "Bennett, would you please fetch the carriage?"

Endeavoring to remedy the havoc her adventure had caused to her hair, she shoved a clump below her bonnet. Holding the hat in place, she tucked a few more strands underneath the brim. After tying the ribbons, she brushed ineffectually at her dress. "I fear I must repair my appearance before anyone else comes upon me this disheveled."

Charmingly tousled, she'd never looked lovelier to Tristan.

Stains marred the palms of her gloves, and grass smeared her gown's front near her knees. One long green streak emphasized the delicious mounds of her plump buttocks, testifying to a tumble or two as she chased the cow.

Uneasiness snuffed his appreciation.

God's toenails. Had anyone else seen her?

Tristan stretched to his full height and canvassed the vista. No one in sight. Not even the fellow who'd decided against helping earlier.

Thank the ungodly hour for the park's solitude. Why had Blythe ventured out this early with only a young stable hand for a chaperone? Most imprudent. Doubtless, besotted by her beauty, the whelp hadn't been able to deny her request, despite possibly risking discharge.

She wouldn't want word spread about that she'd been seen with grass-stained skirts. Foul minds might speculate that someone had given her a green gown, and she certainly didn't want the tattlemongers whispering she'd been tumbled in the park.

Likely as not, Raven wasn't aware Blythe had ventured out. A conversation with him seemed judicious. Not altogether safe for her if the man who'd abruptly departed was who Tristan suspected.

"Leventhorpe, is that you?" Wiping perspiration from his brow with his handkerchief, the fellow who'd succeeded in stopping the cow grinned at Tristan.

"Clancy Maddox?" Tristan extended his hand. "By George. It's been a long time. What, ten years or more? Not since university."

"Eleven." He sent Blythe a curious glance. "I was two years ahead of you."

"Allow me to present you." Tristan made the introductions before leashing his dogs.

"Thank you for your assistance, Mr. Maddox." Blythe picked up Freddy. The panting dog sagged against her, tuckered from his jaunt.

Women of refined breeding didn't tote portly corgis about, or run pell-mell through The Green Park. Another thing he needed to address with Lady Ravensdale and Raven. What Blythe might have been free to do in the country would be frowned upon in Town and could lead to wagging tongues. Something they didn't want if they wished successful come-outs.

Sure as fish guts stank, Blythe didn't care.

Kissing the top of Freddy's head, she shifted the dog, and her reticule slid to her wrist. "He thinks he's young, and though he tried to help with the runaway cow, I fear he did more harm than good."

"Where are you staying, Maddox? Are you here for a while?" Tristan jammed his cane between his side and arm then took the dog from her. Freddy eyed him warily, yet after a moment, laid his head upon Tristan's shoulder and released a long, throaty sigh.

So much for not wearing dog hair today.

"I've let rooms on St. James Street." Maddox placed his hat tighter upon his head. "I'm considering staying and opening an office here. A decade in the colonies was long enough for me. The provincials lack England's refinement and culture."

They reached the lane's end as Ravensdale's carriage drew to a stop behind Tristan's landau. A third conveyance leisurely eased past, the team clopping at a sedate pace. The collies loped to Tristan's vehicle, and in a moment, tongues lolling, sat perched atop the seat peering expectantly at him.

Maddox tipped his hat. "It was a pleasure to meet you, Miss Culpepper. I bid you good day."

"Likewise." She fished a card from her reticule. "Please come for tea tomorrow. I wish to thank you properly. This is my cousin-in-law's card. Mine are at the printers."

His brows dipped together as he read the card. "Ravensdale? I wasn't aware he'd wed recently."

"Yes." Cinching her reticule's handle, she turned somewhat away from another slow-passing carriage. "He married my cousin a short time ago."

"Thank you for the invitation to tea." He bowed to Blythe. "I look forward to seeing Ravensdale and meeting his bride."

She nodded a farewell as she made for her carriage.

Awkwardly balancing Freddy and worriedly watching Blythe's retreating form, Tristan shook Maddox's hand. "I lodge at White's. Be sure to look me up."

"I shall." Maddox's gaze gravitated to Blythe. "Will I see you at tea as well, Leventhorpe?"

"I expect so." Tristan canted his head in Blythe's direction. "There are five of them, and Raven's asked me to make myself available to assist with that tribe of beauties."

"Five? *Five?*" Maddox chuckled and shook his head. "Egads, that ought to be something. Glad I'm back in time to see it, I am."

"A common consensus, my friend." Tristan gave a conspiratorial wink.

"Till tomorrow then." With a carefree wave, Maddox, swinging his cane, headed in the direction he'd come.

Careful to keep his staff secured underneath his arm, Tristan adjusted a now-drowsy Freddy.

How much did the little piglet weigh?

A pair of carriages rumbled past, their occupants craning their necks, no doubt curious who else dared the common at this unchristian hour. The park appeared to be a favorite destination for those enjoying an early morning constitutional today.

He deposited the leashes in his landau and gave instructions to

Jones before meeting Blythe at her carriage.

Arms akimbo and one toe tapping, she considered Maddox's retreating form. She turned her puckish regard upon Tristan, pinning him with her direct gaze. "You made it sound like Heath's taken on a Herculean task." Pique sharpened her features and voice. "We're not that difficult."

"I didn't imply *you* were. It's the rest of the upper ten-thousand—London actually—that will be difficult to manage. They've never encountered anything like the Culpeppers." He chuckled, and answering humor sparked in her eyes.

"I can well imagine." She scratched behind Freddy's ears, and he opened an eye. "I think you've found a friend."

"He's a good sort." Tristan patted Freddy's haunch and bent his head toward the groom standing ready to hand her into the carriage. "That was well done of you back there."

"Thank you, m'lord." He grinned at Blythe. "I thought Miss Culpepper would outpace me. Never seen a lady run that fast."

"See what I mean?" Tristan whispered in her ear, delighting in the blush infusing her cheeks as she entered the carriage

She extended her arms for Freddy. He groaned and scrambled onto the seat, where he promptly curled into a ball.

Tristan signaled Jones, and with an understanding slant of his head, the driver clicked his tongue and flexed the reins.

"I'll accompany you. I need to speak with Ravensdale." Before she could object with a single syllable, Tristan stepped in right behind her and shut the door with a portentous thunk. He stretched his legs before him. "Pray tell, what were you doing gamboling around London before an acceptable hour with a stable lad as chaperone?"

Scheming seldom results in anything extraordinary or eternal,
for anything worth having is freely given.
~*Dignity and Decorum—The Genteel Lady's Guide to Practical Living*

6

"My lord, I assure you, you needn't accompany me, and I wasn't 'gamboling' around London. I merely sought to walk Freddy in the park, as it appeared, you also intended with your collies." Blythe ground her teeth in vexation as she settled against the toast-gold, velvet squabs. That she managed to speak and not snipe or shout brought her a modicum of satisfaction. "And Bennet is perfectly acceptable for a chaperone."

Wasn't he? Should she have brought her maid too? She hadn't bothered with that sort of propriety in the country, where the only things that might set upon her were a stray cat or disgruntled crow.

"A peer walking his large dogs, a short sword concealed within his walking stick," Lord Leventhorpe indicated the elaborate staff tucked into the corner by his seat, "is deuced sure safer than a maiden with a fuzzy, waddling walrus and a smitten stable hand, scarcely more than a wet-behind-the-ears lad, for protection."

His cutting wit drew blood, and that he spoke the truth rankled. Nearly blind and missing several teeth, Freddy, the epitome of decrepitude, offered as much protection as the one-eyed stuffed pheasant in Esherton's study.

Picking dog hair from her spencer, she surreptitiously studied Lord Leventhorpe. Alternating sunbeams and shadows filtered through the windows as the carriage rolled past the row of impressive trees. The light played over his rugged features, making it impossible to read his expression.

Austere or staid? Mayhap somber? Taciturn? Grave?

Definitely not giddy. *Never* giddy.

Despite her frustration, a smile tickled her mouth.

Had he deduced she'd left without notifying anyone and decided to take it upon himself to tell them?

Quite possibly.

That fit the self-righteous, overbearing lord she'd met at Esherton. The amiable, enjoyable man of last night had vanished with the moon and stars' disappearance, and the sanctimonious lord, the one who believed it his duty to inform others of their shortcomings, had returned. Weren't demons supposed to prowl about at night and slink into their dank and gloomy hidey-holes at first light, not the reverse?

Did he think her a wholly inconsiderate bacon wit? She'd left a note with Jenkin, their butler, saying she'd gone for a walk, for pity's sake. Suppressing an urge to kick Lord Leventhorpe, she pressed her half-boot's heel against the seat and petted Freddy instead.

Despite her late night, she'd awoken at dawn, a habit she'd not overcome from years of rising early at Esherton. Desperate to escape the house's confines and London's cramped busyness, she'd sought refuge in the singular place remotely resembling Esherton Green. Her sisters—everyone, barring Cook—had been abed when she'd slipped to the mews. Bennet, alone, prowled the stables, and she'd bade him ready a conveyance and accompany her to the park.

He'd eagerly agreed, much preferring that task to mucking the stalls. Biting the inside of her mouth, she pressed her fingers into Freddy's pudgy back. Would her impulsiveness result in Bennet's chastisement?

Bother. Before asking him, she should've considered the possibility.

Cocking a lofty auburn brow at her, Lord Leventhorpe folded his ridiculously muscled arms across his Spanish-brown-encased chest. Slight disapproval gleamed in his blue eyes, more of deep slate at the moment. His mild, clean scent permeated the carriage's confines, which shrank with his hulking presence.

"Miss Culpepper, appearing in public before seven in the morning is not done. Especially with a lad younger than you— Oomph."

A particularly sharp turn sent him sliding his seat's length, and a giggle escaped her as she braced herself and Freddy to prevent the same.

Scooting to his corner, he anchored his shoulders firmly and stabbed a forefinger in the direction of the driver's seat. "Who, from the careening and uneven pace of this vehicle, has likely not driven a carriage. Ever. Not only is it unsafe, your behavior gives rise to gossip."

Bennet's inexperience explained the rocky ride to St. James Park and why she'd anticipated that last jostling corner. She'd blamed poor roads and worn springs. Warning Lord Leventhorpe would have been charitable, but his flailing about trying to retain his seat proved too amusing to forego. On the other hand, Heath would not be pleased that someone inexperienced had handled the matched team and risked damaging an extremely costly conveyance.

"It's well beyond seven, my lord. Much closer to eight, I'd estimate." She didn't own a watch. "I cannot think it too terribly unfashionable, though somewhat unpopular, with sluggish souls reluctant to part with their mattresses before noon."

London's elite were a lazy lot.

Lord Leventhorpe's regard dropped to her grass-stained gown, disapproval fairly oozing from him.

Running in the garment hadn't been the wisest of decisions. She'd done enough laundry to know the delicate fabric was ruined. Regret chastised her at the shameful waste. Next time, she'd wear one of her well-worn gowns and pretend to be a servant. A borrowed maid's cap and cloak could be donned for good measure too. That shouldn't raise eyebrows or give rise to censure.

Grasping the seat as the carriage careened again, she caught a glimpse of her muddy half-boots. Her shoes had been sensible, though, and after a thorough cleaning would be no worse for wear.

"Blythe." His lordship's voice was low and affable, not condescending or judgmental. Something akin to concern tempered his deep baritone.

Chagrin pricked her. Perhaps she'd been off the mark, and he meant to be helpful.

He gestured at her gown. "I won't be specific as to why, but if the wrong person had seen your gown thus ... Well, they may have concluded you immoral or fast, and your reputation would have suffered greatly."

She gaped at him, something she'd done a great deal since arriving in London. "Because of grass stains? What in the world could be construed as immoral or fast about that?"

"Er, yes. Well ... it leads to speculation as to … uh, that is, how they might have been acquired." He peered out the window and clawed at his lumpy neckcloth.

Oh. *Oh!*

Rot and bother. She sought the dirt-streaked floor, certain her cheeks had turned the same shade as her spencer and gown.

He'd used her given name. On purpose? Or had it been a slip of the tongue?

"I need to speak with Ravensdale about arranging riding lessons, in any event, and to inquire if your sisters or cousins wanted to venture to Tattersalls with us today." His mouth curved rakishly, and she caught a glimpse of the charismatic man of last evening.

Hmm. Perhaps he meant to take advantage of their opportune encounter. Last evening he had said he'd call today. "My lord, forgive me if I overstep the bounds. Is it customary to call before breakfast?"

Lord Leventhorpe's wide grin creased the corners of his eyes. "Not at all. Raven's cook makes the most delicious crepes, and I crave them today. They aren't nearly as tasty at White's."

"She does, indeed. I've not eaten and confess I'm hungry myself." Blythe had been so intent upon conversing with Mr. Burlington last night, her food had gone almost untouched.

The carriage pitched, and she and Lord Leventhorpe clutched the sides. Good thing minimal traffic lined the streets. A blind hobgoblin possessed better driving skills than Bennet.

Righting his cane, Lord Leventhorpe settled into his corner once more. "Did you enjoy your first ball? The dancing? Your dinner with Burlington?"

His questions took her aback. Small talk, or was he genuinely interested?

"Yes, more than I expected to, truth to tell." Freddy laid his head in her lap and sighed. Activity outside the window suggested London had awakened fully in the past hour. "What do you know of Mr. Burlington?"

She couldn't ask Heath because he'd tell Brooke, and then there'd be a bevy of questions launched Blythe's way. Why a man she'd newly met fascinated her, she wasn't ready to explain. Perhaps because he was the first to show genuine interest and not suggest an illicit relationship as had been the case when the Culpeppers had been pauper poor.

If Mr. Burlington's temperament mimicked his lordship's, stern and unapproachable, she wouldn't have been intrigued the least. Except she'd caught a glimpse of an entirely different man last evening, one Lord Leventhorpe seemed at pains to conceal.

Why? What tumult went on in that fiery head of his?

Drawing her attention from the street, she tucked another tendril of hair beneath her bonnet.

Lord Leventhorpe regarded her impassively.

Didn't he intend to answer? She'd probably broken a rule asking him about Mr. Burlington. Someone ought to write a book listing the ridiculous social expectations and decrees. They could call it the *Lady's Guide to Proper Comportment*, or some other such drivel.

He sliced a look outside before setting that disturbing azure-eyed gaze onto her. "He's a decent chap. Comes from good stock. No bad habits that I'm aware of." Lifting a shoulder slightly, he adjusted his glove. "Enjoys himself. Not a serious fellow, by any means."

He'd succinctly answered her question but hadn't told her anything, and his last words held a cautionary inflection. Perchance they weren't friends, or he didn't think it his place to discuss Mr. Burlington.

"You've a dab of dirt smearing your cheek, just there." Lord Leventhorpe indicated her cheek with a long finger.

Covered in dog hair, mud, and grass. Perfectly lovely.

Blythe wiped her face. "Did I get it?"

"No. You smeared the blob more." He chuckled and moved his fingers over his cheek, in imitation of where her smudge was. "You look rather like an adorable ragamuffin who's been making mud pies."

Blythe rubbed the spot again then examined her gloves. Earth marred the fingertips. Whether from wiping her face or from her tumbles in the park, she didn't know. Probably ruined her gloves too. "Better?"

"No. Allow me." He swiftly removed his black leather glove. "Lean my way a mite."

Blythe complied, and he bent and brushed his thumb along her cheek a couple of times.

Sensation darted outward, raising the flesh along her shoulders and arms.

The shards of silver in his gaze glittered as he stared into her eyes, and his touch lingered a fraction longer than entirely necessary. "You have the loveliest eyes and the most perfect mouth I've ever seen."

Such was the wonder in his voice, he almost seemed to speak to himself.

Blythe wet her lips, gone abruptly dry as autumn leaves.

His gaze riveted upon her mouth, tension tightened his lips.

He had the most beautifully sculpted mouth she'd ever noticed, and that included the Greek gods from last night's ball. Were Lord Leventhorpe's as warm and firm and tasty as they appeared?

What the blazes did Mr. Burlington's lips look like?

Did he have lips?

He must, of course.

A wheel sank into a hole with bone-jarring force, abruptly interrupting Blythe's mental rambling and pitching her and Lord Leventhorpe headfirst. His hat flew from his head as he tumbled from his seat onto his knees and reflexively wrapped his arms around her to keep her from plunging to the floor.

With a yelp of outraged surprise, Freddy bumped into Blythe's back, somehow managing to scramble onto the seat.

Their faces mere inches apart, Blythe couldn't haul her gaze from the glinting specks in Lord Leventhorpe's eyes. His focus sank to her lips, and his enlarged pupils revealed his arousal.

Would he kiss her?

Did she want him to?

Illogically, yes.

Breath suspended, she remained perfectly motionless. Waiting.

Lowering his head, he tightened his embrace an instant before his lips whispered across hers.

A brilliant light burst behind her eyes, and every bone in her body turned molten. She clutched his lapels, certain if she let go, she'd slither to the floor.

He ran his tongue along the seam of her lips, and, sighing, she readily capitulated and parted her mouth, eager to taste more of him.

They taste even better than they look.

The carriage jerked to an abrupt halt, and his head banged hers as they toppled to the floor, Lord Leventhorpe—Tristan—sprawled atop her and Freddy landing upon him.

The door sprang open almost immediately. "Where have you—"

Blythe craned her neck to peer beyond Tristan's immense shoulder.

"Devil and damn." He swore beneath his breath before lifting his head and twisting to look behind him.

The entire household had awoken, and they'd trooped outdoors upon sighting the carriage.

"Good morning, Heath. Brooke. Girls." Stifling an absurd urge to laugh at their dumbfounded expressions, Blythe wiggled the fingers of her free hand in greeting. The other remained lodged between her and his lordship, trapped against his rigid abdomen. "We had a bumpy ride."

Blaire and Blaike burst into giggles.

Blythe didn't recall ever tittering that much at seventeen. She'd been the serious, sensible one. Except ... she'd giggled at Tristan mere moments ago.

"It must have been an extremely bumpy ride."

One of them snickered, but buried underneath his broad, delicious-smelling, *hard* body, Blythe wasn't sure which one. "Bennet hasn't much practice driving."

"Clearly." A glacier held more warmth than Heath's voice. "Do get off her, Leventhorpe. Your arse splayed upward atop my ward before I've even broken my fast rather annoys me and puts me off my food."

"I rather like it," Tristan whispered, his lips turned up devilishly as he waggled his eyebrows.

I do too.

Blythe gave him a playful shove. "Off before you cause a scandal."

He brushed her breast and hip as he untangled himself—surely unintentionally—yet hot, tiny pulses lingered where he'd touched her. After clambering from the carriage, Tristan righted his clothing, his expression gone unapproachable again.

Hmm, in public he was one man, in private another. Intriguing.

Heath assisted Blythe to the pavement. His brows swooped together upon noticing her soiled attire. The look he shot Tristan demanded an explanation. "We shall discuss this inside."

Replacing his hat, Tristan dipped his chestnut head in acknowledgement.

Heavens. Heath didn't think they ...? Heat suffused her. Utter hogwash.

"Wise, I think." Brooke cut her dark blue gaze to the sidewalk.

Nurses pushing prams and early morning-goers dotted the strip.

Curiosity glimmered in the twin's eyes as they grinned in unison.

They'd barrage Blythe with questions the instant they cornered her alone.

"Blythe, you should mend your appearance before anyone sees you." Heath looked to Bennet. "After you've seen to the horses and carriage, I wish to speak with you in my study."

Hat in his hands, Bennet shifted from foot to foot, apprehension furrowing his brow. "Yes, sir."

"Heath, please do not blame Bennet. I asked him to drive me." Blythe gave Bennet an encouraging smile. He mustn't lose his position because of her. "If anyone's at fault, it's me. I should have waited for the driver."

"You shouldn't have gone out alone at all, Blythe. This isn't Cheshire." Brooke stepped closer and lowering her voice, touched Blythe's arm. "You'll have to curb your impetuousness while in London. I know you're not happy here, and I'm sorry. Be that as it may, you cannot take off pell-mell whenever you've the urge. It isn't safe, and there are others to consider."

Blythe tamped her instinctive sharp retort. Brooke was right. Instead, she offered a falsely bright smile. "Of course, Brooke." Shoving her bonnet in place, Blythe searched for Freddy. There he was, already disappearing into the house. She angled toward the steps, eager to get off the street before passersby took notice of anything untoward. "I do hope breakfast is ready. I'm famished."

Thirty minutes later, everyone sat round the dining table. Blythe had changed her gown and repaired her appearance, the whole while inundated by questions from Brooke and the others. Most likely, Tristan had endured the same interrogation from Heath.

Startling how a petal soft wisp of a kiss had her thinking of him as Tristan rather than Lord Leventhorpe. And she hadn't had a single thought of Mr. Burlington in the past hour.

Surely she hadn't already become as fickle and flighty as half of the women she'd met last night.

His plate heaped with crepes, Tristan took a drink of coffee. "Since I promised to call today to discuss riding lessons and our excursion to Tattersalls, I invited myself to join Miss Culpepper in her carriage." A boyish smile curved his mouth as he forked a piece of crepe. "And, I hoped to sample these."

Teacup halfway to his lips, Heath paused. "And you didn't give consideration to the impropriety of sharing a carriage alone with her?"

"We weren't alone. Freddy was there." Tristan popped the bite into his mouth and winked at the twins, who'd erupted into more giggles.

Blythe almost dropped the knife she'd been using to spread strawberry preserves. He'd made a jest. Who was this jovial stranger?

"All right, not my wisest decision. In my defense, I think I spied Phillips at the park, and quite frankly, I had concerns about Blythe returning home alone." Tristan tapped his forefinger atop the lace tablecloth. "I suppose I might have followed in my landau. But I didn't, which I'll admit, may have provided the rumormongers fodder."

He'd done it again, used her first name, and no one as much as blinked. Perhaps because Tristan was such a close friend of Heath's, it was permissible. Or ... after the kiss, did he now think of her in more personal terms, as she did him?

"Heath, no one saw us. No harm's been done." She bit into her toast.

No one barring Mr. Maddox. And the drivers and passengers in the three—four?—carriages at the park. And anyone who'd glimpsed the inside of Heath's carriage as they passed. And those walking the street when they arrived home.

Botheration. A paper-thin line distinguished boldness from folly, and she may have inadvertently crossed it.

Two footmen and Jenkin entered, carrying enormous bouquets of flowers. "Ma'am, the drawing room can hold no more." Jenkin raised a spray of peach roses. "Where would you like these arrangements placed?"

Brooke's mouth curved. "Full? Already? I suppose the green salon then, Jenkin. Heath, have you room in the study? It's barely nine o'clock. I cannot imagine what the house will look like by noon."

"A confounded hothouse." Relaxing in his chair, he gave his head an amused shake. "I don't want to consider how many callers we'll have today." His lips twitching, he perused the dining room. "I may need to purchase a bigger house." Focusing upon each woman in turn, he rubbed his temple. "A *much* bigger house."

Tristan laughed, a melodious deep-throated rumble that teased her ears. The transformation from dour lord to amused rapscallion caused

Blythe's heart to stutter oddly. Who was the real man? The affable chap who laughed easily or the caustic fellow? What had caused his prickly façade?

"Didn't you give that consideration before you launched this farce?" Undeterred by Heath's reproving scowl, Tristan indicated the women with a sweep of his hand. "What time will be convenient to take the ladies to Tattersalls?"

"Oh, I adore horses." Excitement lit Brette's eyes, and she leaned forward. "We're allowed to go, aren't we, Heath? I'm quite looking forward to our riding lessons too."

"As am I."

Blythe's fork clattered to her plate as she swung to the dining room's double doors.

Bearing an enormous variety of yellow flowers, Mr. Burlington—looking entirely too virile in a cinnamon-colored coat and beige pantaloons tucked into glossy Hessians, and wearing a confident smile—stood beside a disapproving Jenkin.

Mr. Burlington's God-like good looks drew the women's attention, aside from Brooke. She only ever had eyes for Heath.

They, like her and Tristan, had disliked each other upon first meeting.

Entirely different circumstances though.

"Sir. Madam. Mr. Burlington was most insistent he had urgent news to impart that could not wait until after breakfast, despite my urging that he wait in the drawing room, or better yet, return at a Christian hour."

Offering an apologetic quirk of his mouth—*his lips aren't as full as Tristan's*—Mr. Burlington patted Jenkin's shoulder. "I own, I exaggerated a mite about the importance of my visit. Surely desiring the company of these lovely ladies begs a degree of forgiveness?"

The majordomo's features puckered in further censure.

"Excuse me for calling unfashionably early." Holding the flowers, he approached the table, apparently intending to join them. "I wanted to make sure I was available to assist with the ladies, and Miss Culpepper assured me last night I'd be welcome, despite my forwardness."

His tawny gaze found Blythe and hovered upon her lips before skimming her bosoms.

The pair didn't offer as much as a tiny twitch this morning, and more incredibly, she detected not a jot of remorse for his brazen taradiddle.

He gave a flourishing bow. "These are for you, Miss Culpepper."

"Thank you. Yellow is my favorite color." Her gaze swerved to Tristan.

He regarded Mr. Burlington aloofly, though a hint of mockery tugged one umber brow upward. His gaze gravitated to hers, a question lurking in the ocean depths. Did he suspect Mr. Burlington lied?

"Won't you join us, Mr. Burlington?" Brooke indicated the chair beside Blythe as she bestowed a soothing smile on Jenkin. "Would you please see to a place for our unexpected guest?"

"At once, my lady."

"Oh, Jenkin, put these in water too, will you?" Mr. Burlington thrust the bouquet into Jenkin's arms. A lily brushed Jenkin's aquiline nose, depositing fine orange pollen over the tip, giving him the appearance of a giant duck. "I sincerely appreciate your gracious tolerance of my poor manners."

Jenkin's features softened the minutest amount. "I'll return with them in a few moments, sir."

If putting in an unacceptably early appearance was Mr. Burlington's singular fault, Blythe could forgive the *faux pas*, since she quite loathed tardiness. However, he'd fabricated that tidbit about her, which pricked rather sharply. She couldn't abide liars or contemptable treatment of servants.

After scooting his chair in, Mr. Burlington gazed round the table. "What time are we off to Tattersalls?"

A week later, as the sun hovered between Hyde Park's horizon and the bright cloudless sky directly overhead, Tristan sat astride Buce, with Ravensdale and Burlington on either side atop their horses. No hint of a breeze teased the trees' lush foliage, and already the temperature promised to be quite warm.

A line of lissome blondes wearing stylish riding habits, each a different rainbow hue, and regally seated aside, negotiated a wide turn about Rotten Row and trotted to Francine.

She laughed, and after reining her horse round, clapped. "Splendid, ladies. You've quite got the knack of it. Well done."

"They're coming along nicely, aren't they? Francine has been a Godsend." Tristan shook his head. "I wouldn't have guessed she'd be such an apt teacher."

"They are enjoying themselves, which is what matters to me." Ravensdale rested an elbow atop his saddle. "They quite abhorred the notion of coming to London, if you recall. Blythe most particularly."

"Truly? I cannot imagine why. London is the epitome of culture, other than Paris, of course. I'd say Miss Culpepper is thriving here." Burlington's appreciative gaze remained fixed upon her.

Shows what you know.

Burlington moved forward a few paces. A newborn, blind kitten sucking a teat was less attached. Wholly besotted, he apparently didn't care who knew. He'd been impossible to deter, and not a day had passed without his company. A bit pompous and prone to embellishing the truth, he was still an amiable sort.

Tristan would have rather he concealed a vile, scandal-worthy secret, since it was difficult not to like the chap, and he'd been a dab hand at assisting with the lessons, even if he was barely short of a popinjay.

The men needn't have tagged along any longer, but none suggested they cease.

Tristan didn't want to stop, nor did he wish to examine the reason why, though a befuddling suspicion jostled about in his mind.

"There are those who prefer the country's calm to London's chaos." *Including me.* "The Culpeppers were accustomed to a much quieter way of life on their dairy farm."

Why Tristan felt the need to explain, to defend Blythe, he didn't examine.

"Dairy farm?" That caught Burlington's attention. He tossed Ravensdale a surprised look. "They possess an estate? Most unusual for women. Do they own equal shares?"

"No." Raven spared Burlington a perfunctory glance. "Their cousin owns the farm. At least part of it. I won the rest from him and deeded it to my wife as a wedding gift."

Disappointment flooded Burlington's features. As a second son, it was no secret he needed to marry a woman with a heavy purse. Ravensdale had generously dowered Blythe, but still, given Burlington's lavish taste, that wouldn't last long—a year or two at best.

Which mattered more to the fop? Blythe or deep coffers?

Adjusting his position in the saddle, Tristan slapped his reins against his palm.

Blythe must be aware of Burlington's infatuation. Did she return his regard? She wasn't a woman to display her emotions, willy-nilly, but kept them secreted. Her eyes hinted at her sentiments, but even an astute person would have to peer closely to see what lurked in their fascinating, periwinkle midst.

Since their kiss in the carriage—rather, since Tristan had stolen a taste of her utterly delicious lips, a kiss he could feel if he closed his eyes and pressed his lips together—she'd acted differently toward him. Her earlier hostility had been replaced by a watchful wariness and tentative cordiality, which seemed to increase as they saw each other daily, often more than once.

She'd granted him a waltz at each ball, something he looked forward to more than these morning rides. The pleasure of holding her tempting, svelte form made attending the nightly circuses almost bearable. He limited himself to a single dance, reluctant to have his thoughts coiled in her silvery tresses, or unable to rid her from his mind or dreams.

At least he no longer feared casting up his kippers or sweating through his shirt at public assemblies. More importantly, for the past three routes, he'd foregone his customary pre-appearance brandies.

What mystic power did she hold over him, that in a matter of weeks, he anticipated the future with renewed enthusiasm? He wanted to spend time with her, conversing, or strolling in serene silence. She wasn't one of those females who needed to fill the tranquility with senseless chatter.

When in her presence, his spirit found a peace wholly foreign to him; a vast contrast to the frequent and disturbing libidinous urges she also roused. Urges which accelerated to an uncomfortable level, sometimes requiring the discreet rearranging or concealment of his nether regions, easier done when not uncomfortably swollen like a Cumberland sausage.

"My lady will soon have to put aside her daily excursions." Ravensdale inched his horse near Tristan, saying in a low tone, "I'm going to be a father, Trist."

Tristan grinned, at once overjoyed for his friend and also experiencing a bewildering, envious pang. "Congratulations." He cut his gaze to Burlington, raptly gawping at Blythe. "I assume you're not making the joyous news public."

"Not yet." Ravensdale gave a short shake of his head then firmed his mouth, a shadow replacing the earlier joy in his eyes. "I heard you had an unfortunate encounter with Phillips yesterday afternoon."

"That's a marked understatement. I threatened to call the bastard out if he mentions the *incident* again." The churl had cornered Tristan as he left his lodgings, almost as if he'd been lying in wait. Retaliation for Tristan mangling his pretty face likely spurred Phillips's obsession. Or else he was an unconscionable bully who delighted in taunting others.

"Why such rubbish should matter to him after all these years, I cannot imagine. I think he finds perverse enjoyment in goading you." Raven waited until two young bucks rode by, animatedly discussing the bevvy of blondes they'd passed. Craning their necks for another glimpse, they collided and almost unseated the other, much to their snorting and prancing horses' displeasure.

Shaking his head, Raven grinned at their retreating forms. He dragged his focus to Tristan. "Because Phillips knows you still suffer the humiliation."

"Well, I refuse to hide my head or be ashamed any longer. I'm not proud of what happened, but I have come to accept I wasn't to blame. Hawksworth will be pleased. He's preached that particular, as well as forgiveness, countless times." Lifting a shoulder, Tristan twisted his mouth into a sardonic smile. "I suppose most adolescents would have been proud. You know that's not my way."

Raven quirked an eyebrow. "True. Monks boast more of their sexual exploits, and England doesn't harbor many monastics."

An exuberant, musical laugh floated across the green.

Blythe.

Wearing a robin's-egg-blue habit, she cantered her mare in a wide circle.

Like a bird to air, she'd taken to riding, and Tristan found himself awaking with renewed expectancy each morning, eagerly anticipating the lessons. No nightmares had plagued him either, despite running into Phillips at several functions and enduring his spiteful taunts. Only Rosemary Sanford annoyed him as much.

She continued to be a pushy, painful carbuncle. Now that Francine enjoyed the Culpeppers' company, Miss Sanford found her less malleable and less available. Unfortunately, that meant Miss Sanford had become tediously forward. Tristan feared she'd set her cap for him, and she had proven as tenacious as a hound tracking a scent. He could scarcely use the privy for fear she'd pop from the shrubberies or be waiting outside when he exited.

A pair of riders joined the women, and in a moment, the group headed to the waiting men.

Squinting, Tristan released a disgusted puff.

Phillips and Miss Sanford. Again.

Raven had finally conceded and introduced his newly acquired family. Perhaps tomorrow's lesson would take place elsewhere since that pair had invited themselves three mornings in a row now, and after yesterday's ordeal, Tristan was done up with Phillips. His continued pursuit of Blythe proved worrisome too, particularly since Tristan had spied him in the park the day the cow wreaked havoc.

Miss Sanford, her seat excellent, galloped her horse ahead, clearly showing off.

Phillips remained with the others, but Lady Ravensdale

maneuvered her docile mare, forcing him to the outside, away from her wards.

Undeniably ravishing in a black and plum habit, a breathless Miss Sanford ambled to a stop beside Tristan. "I bid you good day, my lords. Mr. Burlington. Isn't it a glorious morning? Why, I think we may have a delightfully warm summer this year."

In London, that meant stifling and putrid. All the more reason to return to Bristledale Court's fragrant meadows and fresh air.

"Good day, Miss Sanford." Scarcely glancing her way, Burlington bid her a distracted hello as Ravensdale and Tristan exchanged a brief look. Perhaps a proclamation would be forthcoming from him soon.

She wrinkled her nose peevishly at Burlington's lackadaisical greeting.

"Pleasant day to you, Miss Sanford. Excuse me." Touching his hat, Ravensdale kicked his horse's sides and trotted to meet Lady Ravensdale. Likely to watch Phillips too.

"I'd hoped to see you at the Lockwood's soirée last evening." An invitation in her gaze and her lips bent coyly, Miss Sanford took the opportunity to sidle her horse near enough that their legs touched.

Buce dipped his massive head and snorted.

I agree, my friend.

Her cloying perfume assailed Tristan's nose, and he sneezed. "Beg your pardon."

Had she doused herself in the potion hoping to bewitch him? Or render him unconscious so she could have her way with him? Wouldn't do to gag and cough. Turning his head away, he gulped in a fresh breath. What he wouldn't give for a brisk breeze at the moment.

"I confess, I missed your company, my lord." A seductress's smile curved Miss Sanford's mouth, and the tip of her tongue darted out.

"I was otherwise engaged." And would be until naked cherubim, smoking cheroots, danced at Almack's. Her brazenness left him cold, and not a little worried for *his* virtue. He didn't trust her scheming wiles.

"Ho, Leventhorpe. Look who I ran into." Whitehouse and Maddox bore down on them, and Whitehouse half-saluted, half-waved. "Maddox has purchased a building near the docks, and I came upon him on my way here."

"Excellent to see you again, Maddox." Tristan took the opportunity to edge Buce away from Miss Sanford. "I'm glad you've decided to stay in England."

The other riders joined them. Introductions were made and greetings exchanged.

Scowling at Phillips, Burlington made for Blythe like a hawk swooping to claim its prey.

She nodded, a sweet smile stretching her kissable lips. The white feathers affixed to her hat's brim bounced as she responded to Burlington's comment.

Something he'd taken pains to make sure no one else heard.

The desire to push Burlington off his saddle onto his tight arse nipped at Tristan.

Lifting her head, the graceful arch of her swanlike neck stretched high to see above the crowd, she gifted Tristan with a stunning smile before veering her gaze to Francine.

He didn't doubt his huge grin made him look a lack-wit. She couldn't be that enamored with Burlington if she smiled at him that way. Could she?

Burlington noticed the exchange, and a frown briefly tightened his features. He touched Blythe's arm, regaining her attention.

Well, perhaps he'd permit Burlington to stay in his seat. Poor love-sick swain.

You're not far off yourself, old chum.

Twaddle. Tristan wasn't the type to let feckless emotions run rampant.

Cheeks rosy, Francine fiddled with her reins and sent several covert peeks Maddox's way. She'd seemed quite taken with him when they'd met at tea last week.

Tristan heartily approved. Mayhap he could enlist Blythe's help in that regard. What a perfect excuse to call upon her. They could play matchmakers.

Maddox extracted his watch from his waistcoat, and after glimpsing the face, sighed. "I'm afraid I have an important appointment. I'm quite looking forward to dinner tonight, Lady Ravensdale."

"We have special entertainment planned." Lady Ravensdale slanted her head.

"Not special, I'm afraid." Blythe rubbed her mare's sleek neck. "I've been coerced into singing and playing the pianoforte."

"*Adequate* entertainment for a simple evening at home, I'm sure."

Miss Sanford's tone and falsely sweet smile indicated anything but.

"You haven't heard Blythe sing, Miss Sanford." Brette lifted her pert nose, a challenge in her tart response. "She's gifted."

"I'm rather anticipating her performance." Burlington turned to Blythe. "Perhaps you'd honor me with a duet?"

Burlington's puppy-like adoration caused Tristan's stomach to toss. Of course he sang. Probably had a ruddy brilliant voice too. Tristan's could be described as ordinary.

"Miss Simmons, dare I hope you will be in attendance?" Maddox's ears glinted scarlet in the early morning sun.

Blythe's gaze flew to Tristan's and, lips trembling, she wiggled her winged brows. Amusement frolicked in her eyes as she overtly slashed her gaze between Maddox and Francine.

Tristan swallowed a snort of laughter as Francine turned radish red.

"Francine, I assumed you planned to join me this evening." Miss Sanford's mouth formed an unflattering pout. "We're attending the theater tonight. Might you also be, Lord Leventhorpe?"

"No, I've been extended an invitation to dine with the Ravensdales, as has my cousin, and I'm sure I'll enjoy Miss Culpepper's musical performance far more than Othello." He smiled at Blythe. He loathed Shakespeare, an unpopular sentiment among the tragedy-loving upper ten thousand.

"How ... gallant of you." Miss Sanford jutted her chin, scraping her caustic gaze over Blythe and the other ladies. She formed her lips into such a brittle smile, her face threatened to shatter with the slightest bump. "Another time then, my lord." She swung her horse in the opposite direction. "Mr. Phillips, I must return home. Mama and I have a fitting this morning."

"An appointment you've suddenly recalled, I dare say." Phillips smirked at her stormy glare.

"I shall accompany you, if you don't mind. I needed a word with you, Phillips." With a flash of his white teeth, Burlington lifted Blythe's hand. "Until tonight. The hours apart will be unbearable."

To prevent his guffaw, Tristan set his jaw and studied the array of leaves overhead. Why, there must be a dozen different verdant shades.

"I bid you good day." Phillips lifted his hat, and after a final, lecherous ogling of the ladies, and stabbing Tristan a darkling glare, he followed Miss Sanford.

Mrs. Sanford ought to rein her daughter in. Keeping company with gentlemen of Phillips's ilk, even if he was in line for a viscountcy, wasn't to Miss Sanford's benefit.

An almost indecipherable frown furrowed Blythe's forehead when Burlington left. Because she didn't want him to go, or because of whom he'd departed with?

Smoothing her features, she gave Tristan a saucy smile. "You promised me a Gunter's ice when I mastered trotting, and given this warmer weather, I would relish the treat."

"You did promise, Tristan. And she's quite accomplished already." Francine shared a smile with Blythe.

Tristan couldn't have been more pleased at the friendship developing between them.

"Gunter's will have to wait. We have fittings too. Gentlemen, if you'll excuse us." With a regal nod, Lady Ravensdale indicated the women should follow her. Everyone, including Ravensdale and Francine trailed behind her.

"We can discuss a time for your reward tonight, Blythe," Tristan said as she passed him.

"Excellent, my lord. By-the-by, I told Brooke I would sing if you joined me." Laughing naughtily, she tore after her family.

"I'll be damned." Whitehouse chuckled. "You're smitten, Leventhorpe."

"I'm no such thing. I've come to enjoy the company of Raven's new family, and I've found I can tolerate public gatherings far better when they are," *she is,* "nearby."

When he was a child, Mother had forbidden any female house servants due to Father's wandering eye and groping hands. Tristan had believed the lack, in addition to the traumatic loss of his virginity, had predisposed him against females.

The Culpeppers had infiltrated the barrier he'd erected, and while the wall remained, he didn't feel quite the need to protect himself or be constantly on guard. He rose in his saddle to turn and peer behind him. Blythe's splendidly rounded derrière tucked into her sidesaddle bounced softly, earning an appreciative smile from him. The soft mounds would fit nicely in his hands.

Hell. Whitehouse *might* be right.

Was right.

How, in such a confounded short time, had that happened? How had he made room in his bruised heart for her?

Fingering his glass of port, Tristan crossed his legs and relaxed into the gold and navy brocade settee. Blythe sat before the pianoforte, her long, slim fingers dancing atop the keyboard as she sang a lively duet with Burlington. To Tristan's sheer delight, Esherton's bawling calves carried a tune better than the chap.

Burlington hit a particularly discordant note—*make that the sheep and crows too*—and Tristan flinched, though he studiously controlled his features and stared at his glass lest he laugh aloud. No one appreciated being laughed at, but, by God, couldn't Burlington hear himself?

Did Lady Ravensdale fear the cut-crystal mantel lamps might shatter? Or perhaps the diamond-paned leaded glass windows? Daring to shift his attention from his tumbler's scarlet contents for a moment, Tristan inadvertently snagged Ravensdale's eye and the trembling of his friend's lips nearly undid him.

Raven struggled as mightily as Tristan to curb his ill-timed humor. God help them if anyone dared snicker.

Blythe's beau wasn't perfect after all, and Tristan indulged in perverse, child-like satisfaction at the knowledge. Lifting his glass to take a sip, he hid his grin at the swiftly pained and masked expressions, determined and politely set mouths, and the occasional widened or startled eyes Burlington's inept performance produced.

God's toenails. Tone deaf as a flowerpot.

No. The comparison was unfair to the modest vessel.

Francine, more animated and prettier than Tristan had ever seen her, thanks to an extraordinary makeover by the Culpeppers, chatted quietly with an attentive Maddox. A union between the two would be a welcome blessing. Perchance the time had come to have a pointed discussion with Maddox and probe his intentions.

She deserved a decent man, and Tristan hadn't a qualm about Maddox. However, if he didn't have a serious interest in Francine, better to end things at once rather than break her fragile heart. Regardless, it was impossible to deny their absorption in one another. Both seemed oblivious of the camel caterwauling across the room.

Tristan scratched his nose, checking another troublesome sideways tug of his mouth.

Did camels caterwaul?

A silent petition to The Almighty followed lest he lose control of his tenuous grasp.

Despite his unfortunate lack of talent, Burlington sang with gusto. Tristan had to give him credit for exuberance if naught else. Thankfully, Blythe's lovely voice penetrated Burlington's off-key, baritone warbling.

Brette hadn't exaggerated. Blythe was profoundly talented. Rather unfortunate that respectable ladies of station couldn't take to the stage or sing opera. Tristan didn't doubt she'd be tremendously successful— with a bloody mile-long line of suitors waiting to become her protector.

His earlier joviality fleeing, he pinched the bridge of his nose to ease the tension his scowl created. He'd cherished the unexpected truce that had sprung up between them. He deemed few women his friend, yet that description best fit the easy companionship they'd forged.

What you feel for her is markedly more than friendship.

A woman as striking as Blythe wouldn't remain long on the marriage mart, and the way Burlington diligently pursued her, Tristan had expected an offer by now. Why he hadn't made one perplexed more than a little.

Why Tristan minded confounded a great deal.

You know why.

He ought to forbid himself to ponder it. After all, *he* wasn't shopping for a marchioness. Yet. Still, he couldn't toss aside his disquiet like last month's gazette, which aggravated all the more.

Do shut up.

Blythe ended the piece with a flurry of notes, and everyone broke into applause and polite words of appreciation. Oblivious that the praise wasn't for him, Burlington beamed and nodded as if he'd made a stellar debut presentation and didn't budge from her side.

Blasted cheery ... tenacious ... grinning barnacle.

"Leventhorpe, I distinctly heard Miss Culpepper say she agreed to perform if you joined her." Whitehouse leaned a shoulder against the fireplace's Italian Bardiglio marble mantel, his mouth pulled into a slight smirk. "I don't believe I've had the pleasure of hearing you sing."

Pausing in her perusal of the sheet music, Blythe lifted her head, a silent plea in her gaze. "Yes, your lordship. I'd quite appreciate it."

Freddy's howling would've been preferred if it spared her

Burlington's grating bellow in her ear as she'd endured the past three songs.

"I'm afraid I don't sing." Tristan took a hefty swallow of wine. Not precisely true. He rather enjoyed singing and played the piano and violin too. Just not in front of an audience. True, the dinner had been intimate, and only a dozen people occupied the cozy, tastefully decorated drawing room, but he couldn't bear spectators.

Not since ...

"I understand." She bit her lower lip's outer corner, her shoulder slumping the tiniest bit. She flipped a couple more pages, hesitating briefly every now and again, before riffling through a few more. Probably trying to anticipate precisely how awful Burlington's contribution would be. "I'll find something suitable in a moment."

Suitable for a croaking bullfrog?

Blythe had graciously borne the evening's entertainment burden and had to have tired. Earlier, the women had harmonized to *The Joys of the Country*, and Drake, an accomplished pianist in his own right, had expertly played a Pleyel sonatina. Nevertheless, she'd played diligently for nearly an hour now.

"Heath tells me you have talent yourself, my lord." Lady Ravensdale looked up from the ... whatever it was she stitched— probably something for the babe given the tiny shape—and smiled at Tristan.

Bending his lips guiltily, Raven scratched his jaw. "I might have mentioned it in passing."

Miss Blaike—or was it Miss Blaire?—clapped her hands. "Do humor us, my lord."

The pained look her twin slid Burlington said what no one dared.

For the sake of everyone's hearing and sanity, Tristan's resolve wavered.

"Please, Tristan," Francine implored sweetly. Desperately.

Ah, so she had been aware of the yowling.

"Oh, very well, if you agree to a game of loo afterward, Miss Culpepper." That relieved Blythe of further entertainment duties. Someone else would have to step in, or those present would have to find another activity to pass the time.

Please God, anything but charades.

"Bravo, Leventhorpe." Drake raised his glass in a mock salutation.

Tristan finished his wine and after setting the glass upon the marble-topped end table, blew out an extended, silent breath. *Get on with it, old m*an. He swung his foot to the floor. "I'm not accomplished by any means. Feel free to chat throughout, or cover your ears with your hands or pillows. I shan't be offended."

Could he ask them to look in the other direction too? Or remove themselves to another room?

"You're humility is admirable, my lord." A trifle reticent this evening, likely due to Hawksworth's surprising absence, Miss Brette rubbed Freddy's belly. "I'm sure your performance will be most pleasurable."

He gave her a gallant bow. "I shall endeavor not to disappoint."

Or break out into a cold sweat.

A grateful smile wreathed Blythe's face, and his stomach, or heart, or something in his torso, flopped uncomfortably.

He was almost certain the cause wasn't indigestion, nerves, or a fatal illness, though he didn't rule out poisoning. Phillips had been at the adjacent table at Brooks's when Tristan met Drake and Whitehouse there this afternoon. Fortunately, for once the cull had kept his mouth shut.

Through hooded eyes, Tristan indulged in a lingering appraisal.

God, Blythe was beautiful.

More than beautiful—exquisite—with her eyes glinting brightly in the candlelight, a slight flush of pleasure pinkening her cheeks, and her mouth berry red from nibbling her lips. A mouth formed for bewitching smiles and honeyed kisses.

Blythe had blossomed in recent weeks, and glowed from plenty to eat, enough rest, and happiness. Her gown, a soft white with fine embroidered vines and purple flowers, the same vibrant shade as her eyes, hugged her ribs and emphasized the tempting flesh peeking above the neckline. Her skin couldn't possibly be as silky and soft as it appeared.

He'd never explore those rounded bits of loveliness.

Listen to him. Even his thoughts waxed poetic, and he didn't like poetry. Ridiculous, confusing, emotional drivel and rhyming poppycock written by infatuated, corkbrained ninnies.

"The vanquisher claims the plunder," Drake murmured, giving Tristan a devilish wink as he strode past *accidentally* kicking Drake's foot and earning him a wicked chuckle.

He was one to talk. That conversation wasn't fit for mixed company.

At the pianoforte, Tristan stood to the side, making it clear Burlington should move. "If you wouldn't mind? I need to stand there to read the music. My seat on the settee is available ..."

Burlington reluctantly conceded, but not before seizing Blythe's *ungloved* hand and ardently pressing his lips to the knuckles.

Bold, indeed, and outside the bounds. Tristan rather envied his audacity.

"Thank you for the duet." Her gaze narrowed almost imperceptibly as she extricated her hand and then smiled round the room before meeting Tristan's eyes. "Do you know *The Last Rose of Summer*?"

"I've heard it often enough, and I can read music." On the pretext of studying the music, he bent nearer. In truth, he wanted to sniff her perfume. She wore something different tonight, a light, musky scent with a hint of mint and vanilla? The glimpse of the lush valley between her breasts came as an unexpected treat. "You're wearing different perfume?"

She started, a half-smile bending her mouth. "Why, yes. It was an early birthday present from my sisters and cousins. They had a custom scent created for me. I'd been using a scent Heath gave Brooke since I had no perfume of my own."

"Might I sit rather than stand?" Giving in to impulse, he flipped his tails out of the way and eased onto the dainty bench's edge. Much less intimidating than standing and being the object of everyone's focused attention. Besides, Blythe sat closer to the others, and created a sort of human barrier.

Hiding behind a woman. How ungallant. He sneered inwardly. *Poltroon. Coward. Nidgit.*

"Of course." She scooted over, yet his rear hung halfway off the rectangular stool.

Claiming all but an inch, scarcely enough to be considered a respectable distance between them, he cleared his throat, now dry as parchment. This mightn't' have been a clever notion after all. A glass of anything cool would have been advisable given the more delectable view of her breasts as she bent forward to arrange the pages. His fingers twitched, yearning to explore the gentle slopes. The thin material of her gown did little to hide her long, slender legs, and the knowledge her bum rested so close to his caused an embarrassing rise in his trousers.

Think of something else.

"Your birthday is coming soon?"

"In ten days' time." Satisfied the pages were placed to read easily, she set her slender fingers to the keys. Veering him a sidelong look, she began the introduction. "The Wimpletons' have graciously agreed to host my birthday ball since Heath's house doesn't have a ballroom. You were sent an invitation."

Probably in the stack with his other unopened correspondences. He must hire a secretary. Or lease a house in Town and retain a butler. Dammit. He'd never entertained that idea before. What had beset him?

A whiff of perfume teased his nostrils and assaulted his senses.

Blythe had.

Dangerous entertaining such whimsical notions. No good could come of it. It was almost better when they'd been at constant odds. "And I most assuredly will be attending. Someone has to protect you ladies from the ne'er-do-wells."

"I'm sure Heath's counting on it. He's looking a trifle haggard these days." She chuckled, that throaty purr unique to her. "Miss Sanford too."

Tristan turned to her so swiftly, he almost lost his seat and grabbed the pianoforte's mahogany edge to keep his balance. He could use a nip of something. Anything. Tepid tea would do. He swallowed then gave a small cough. "Why do you say that?"

"I overheard her speaking, or venting, rather, to her mother at the modiste the other day. Quite by accident, I assure you." Coyness filled Blythe's indirect gaze, and a peculiar inflection shaded her tone. "I got the distinct impression she intends to be the next Marchioness of Leventhorpe. By Season's end."

With that unnerving disclosure, Blythe lifted her voice in song.

Tristan fell off the bench.

Of this one can be certain: there is always someone
with a mind more devious and a scheme more sly than yours.
~Dignity and Decorum—The Genteel Lady's Guide to Practical Living

8

A week later, sitting in Tristan's barouche, Blythe took in the bustle outside Gunter's Tea Shop. Given the number of carriages parked below the maples, many others had craved a cool ice on the warm day.

"What flavor do you recommend, my lord?" Patrons in the curricles beside Tristan's enjoyed an assortment of extravagant confections including a frozen berry-tinted treat and one that surely must be chocolate ice cream.

Though they'd operated a dairy farm, she hadn't tasted ice cream. None of the Culpeppers had ever indulged in anything extravagant or decadent. How did one choose from such an array of heavenly treats?

Tristan glanced up from his position beside his burgundy barouche's wheel. A few auburn curls dared to caress his beaver hat's rear brim. Attired in a cornflower blue jacket—an exact match to his eyes—black pantaloons emphasizing his long, muscular legs, tucked into slightly dusty Wellingtons, and a black and royal blue striped waistcoat encircling his torso, he cut a dashing figure.

Much too dashing for her to remain immune.

"I'm quite partial to the bergamot myself. It's a citrus similar to an orange. The barberry is also tasty." Tristan removed his gloves, and after acknowledging the greeting of a gentleman leaning against Berkeley Square's railing with a slight tilt of his head, laid the buff-toned leather on his equipage's edge. "I suggest you do the same, even if it's not the thing. When the ices melt, they can become quite messy. Your gloves are sure to become sticky and soiled."

"I'd like a barberry, please." Blythe drew off one glove. Wearing new cream kid-leather half boots, a soft green, almost white chintz overlaid with ivory lace and embellished with scalloped edges, and a brushed velvet eggshell-toned spencer, she resembled a giant gardenia. "Do you know what flavor you'd like, Blaike and Blaire?"

"Vanilla," they said in unison before bursting into giggles.

Of course they'd want the same flavor.

"Two vanillas, one barberry, and one bergamot." Tristan passed the young waiter a few coins.

"Yes, my lord." After another lingering look at the striking twins, the servant trotted across the square, dodging conveyances on his circumventive route.

Blythe might have accompanied Tristan to Gunter's alone without fear for her reputation—propriety allowed the excursion—but Brooke had deemed it wise to have the twins join them.

He hadn't objected to the extra company when he'd come to collect her and make good on Blythe's promised reward.

She had chaffed a mite at the forced chaperonage. After all, she'd been anticipating a precious hour or two alone with Tristan, and with the twins in tow, she'd be acting the part of governess. Though sweet, and not difficult of temperament, they possessed typical seventeen-year-old flightiness.

Mayhap not typical.

Blythe had never been featherbrained.

"Blythe, our friend Lady Claire is waving for us to join her and her grandmother. Might we?" Blaire indicated a cheerful redhead seated in a barouche farther along the square.

An elderly matron wearing a ghastly contraption teeming with ribbons and feathers atop her gray-peppered head smiled indulgently as Lady Claire, bouncing in her seat, waved and gesticulated enthusiastically at the twins.

"We can see you and his lordship. No one can suggest anything untoward." Blaike gathered her reticule and parasol, her gaze straying hopefully to her bubbly friend.

"I have no objection, but—" Blythe shook her finger as the twins leaped to their feet before she finished. "Mind your deportment."

Cause no scandal had been drilled into her these past weeks until she mumbled the phrase in her dreams.

Tristan assisted them to the pavement and chuckled as the grinning girls linked arms and hurried to their waiting friend.

"How do you tell them apart? They even have the same mole beside their left eyes." A slight crease lined Tristan's high forehead as he stared after them. "I have to memorize what they're wearing each time I see them, and that's after someone else addresses each, and I've deduced who is who."

Blythe laughed and shook her head. "If you spent more time with them, you'd notice they have distinct features and characteristics. Blaire also has a mole below her right nostril. Blaike is more gregarious."

"Ah, good to know." He rested his elbows atop the barouche's side. "You seem to be enjoying London now."

A more youthful, relaxed man had replaced the stern one she'd met at Esherton. Removing her other glove, she slanted her head in contemplation. "I suppose so. More than I'd expected, honestly, and I've met a few charming people. I do loathe the constraints imposed on women here. I crave the outdoors, and I cannot even go for a walk by myself. The riding lessons have made my stay bearable."

As had his company. Once he'd stopped being a cross-as-a-bear boor. He and Heath were two of a few men who enjoyed and participated in intelligent conversations with her.

Tristan's expression grew pensive, and he cut her an indirect gaze.

Ah, the intriguing bashfulness again. What a paradox.

Almost as puzzling as why she went all soft and warm inside whenever he gazed at her like that.

"I have ..." He scratched his ear and cast his focus to the pavement.

A breeze caressed the maple leaves overhead, sending them cavorting and dancing to a soundless melody, their gentle rustling nature's harmony.

"This is the first Season I recall that I haven't been ready to depart for Bristledale Court upon a week of arriving in London."

Squinting, Blythe wiggled her toes in vexation. Guineas to goiters that was not what he'd been going to say at all.

Almost as if nervous, he drummed his square fingertips along the barouche's gleaming edge, his focus flitting here and there ... everywhere except on her.

"Oh? And why is that?" She'd pry the truth from his lips by one means or another. Blinking coyly and forming a moue in the same fashion she'd seen other wide-eyed misses gaze at their beaux, she almost choked on an inward snort.

Tristan stared at her as if she'd sprouted a disagreeable growth on her chin.

Her attempt at flirtation had fallen flatter than an oatcake. Seems neither she nor Tristan was adept at the art.

Now what?

Laying her gloves beside her atop the cherry-toned leather seat, she swept him a casual glance. And almost swallowed her tongue at the heat simmering in his azure eyes. Blue eyes ought to be cold, icy, yet molten lava tinged his irises.

Good heavens. Did he imply ...?

Surely he hadn't meant *she* was the reason. Had he?

Pleasant tremors tickled her spine and arms. What a stupendous, utterly wonderful notion. One that might alter her perception of London and her future dramatically.

His lips tilted almost shyly, and he clasped the carriage door in a white-knuckled grip. "I—"

"Here you are, sir. Miss." The servant passed Blythe a dainty cup brimming with pinkish deliciousness. He handed Tristan his then looked about in bewildered disappointment for a moment. "Where are the other misses?"

Another conquest for her sisters.

"They've joined Lady Claire." Blythe indicated the black and gold carriage. She wanted to dump her barberry ice atop his neatly parted hair for interrupting Tristan. Now she mightn't ever know what he'd intended to say.

"Yes, I see them." Tendrils of sweet vanilla dribbled down the glass's sides as the waiter scurried to the twins.

Blaike and Blaire had taken to London much better than she. Their enjoyment was genuine, hers a practiced pretense, made more bearable by Tristan's regular company. The girls seldom spoke of returning to Esherton ...well, the newly constructed house there. It wasn't quite finished. Brooke wanted to make the final decisions regarding the interior.

Did Blythe alone long to escape the city?

"Might I ask why you all have names that begin with a B?" Tristan winked and gave her a crooked grin. "It's rather unusual and a bit confusing."

Relaxing against the squab, Blythe raised a brow good-naturedly. "My mother and aunt wanted to continue a long family tradition. Every woman has been bestowed with a name beginning with the letter B. As you've no doubt discerned, Mother and Aunt Bess had to resort to some, ah, creativity. Poor Brette and Blaike have feminized male names. I don't think I'll bother with the custom when I marry. I already stutter and stumble saying our names half the time"

"Oh, I don't know. I'm partial to Brenna, Brownen, Brianna, and Byrony." He took a bite, and Blythe couldn't haul her gaze from his pursed lips.

How delicious a kiss would be from his slightly reddened mouth at this moment.

Tristan took another bite, closing his eyes and making a contented sound.

God help her.

She scarcely checked the urge to lean forward and brush his lips with hers. Instead, she swallowed and attempted to gather her scattered thoughts. Spooning a taste of her ice, she savored the sweet coldness tingling on her tongue and cooling her overheated senses.

Grinning, he lifted his spoon. "You could expand the tradition to your sons. I rather like Bradford and Beauregard."

"Those are nice, I agree, and thus far, we've been spared a surname beginning with B. But gads. Can you imagine the confusion then?" Chuckling, she shook her head while enjoying another taste of her ice. "This is splendid, Tristan. Thank you."

"Blythe, I ..." A shadow darkened his face, and he shrugged. "I made you a promise, and I always keep my word."

Polite coolness had replaced the earlier velvety warmth of his tone, and she glanced at him sharply. In the past few seconds, something had changed drastically. His countenance grew aloof once more with the exception of a few stray sparks lingering in his gaze that he hadn't yet extinguished.

What the devil?

Taking another mouthful, she scoured her mind for a reason for his abrupt transformation. How had talking about names beginning with B caused him to retreat behind his staunch comportment again?

Might as well see what he'd been about to say, even if it made her a forward hussy. She preferred candid speech to polite ambiguity or subtle intimations. "You were about to say something, my lord?"

His expression bland, he finally met her gaze straight on. Every hint of anything other than formal civility had vanished. "It was of no importance."

Dash it to Hades.

"If you're through, I have another appointment."

The nugget of hope that had had the audacity to raise its pathetic head shriveled in her chest and retreated to a safe cranny to bashfully hide once more.

Stupid heart.

Stupid him.

"That's the longest set, and possibly the most energetic cotillion, I've ever danced." Laughing and breathless, Blythe sank into a curtsy on the Wimpletons' ballroom floor. Her birthday ball was well-attended, a crush, truth to tell, and she'd been dancing nonstop for the better part of an hour.

Mr. Burlington, a fine sheen of sweat on his upper lip, bent above her hand. "Quite the most enjoyable one I've ever been privileged to share with someone as beautiful as yourself. Would you do me the honor of another set?"

A third? That wasn't done unless ... Did he intend to propose?

She pressed a hand firmly to her middle to ease her sudden collywobbles.

Anticipation or dread?

A month ago, she'd have predicted anticipation. Now ... Trepidation better described the peculiar sensation assaulting her middle.

Yes, wouldn't readily pass her lips. As clichéd as the phrase was, she needed more time. To get to know him better. Get to know Tristan better, especially after their outing to Gunter's Tea House. To decide whether she could abide Town life for more than this Season.

"I'm afraid the rest of my dances are already promised." She shouldn't have been relieved, and guilt kicked its petulant heels hard against her ribs. Wouldn't a woman desperately in love hurl convention aside to be with their sweetheart?

She would. But Blythe didn't love him.

"Ah, I should have anticipated that." Winking devilishly, he straightened and fished his kerchief from a pocket. "Next time I shall claim them all."

Acceptable if they were betrothed.

He dabbed his forehead, and after finishing, tucked the cloth away.

Placing her hand into his crooked elbow, he guided her toward the terrace. "Would you walk with me outdoors for a spell? It's rather overwarm inside."

"A splendid idea." Unless he had another purpose for the suggestion.

Nonsense.

Even if he intended to propose, he wouldn't publicly. He'd been the embodiment of politesse these weeks past. She'd no reason to expect he would be otherwise tonight.

Besides, she feared her underarms were damp, such was the crowd, and her ball gown was an original. Hopefully, her perspiration wouldn't stain the fabric.

The Wimpletons, in collaboration with her dear cousins and sisters, had hosted an elaborate birthday ball in her honor. The house overran with yellow, peach, and white flower garlands and bouquets, as well as people wishing her well. She'd never had a grand birthday celebration, certainly nothing of this magnitude, and found herself overwhelmed and uncharacteristically emotional at the generosity and kindness.

A month ago, London and Society had rather appalled her, and now, the Season held more appeal than she'd ever foreseen. That didn't mean permanent residence in the malodorous city enticed. Visiting with the knowledge she'd be leaving and not returning was one thing. Staying on, enduring the continual scrutiny and rigid structures set by Society ... She shuddered slightly. And to think, some people thrived in this environ.

As Heath had predicted, the Culpeppers had niggled their way into *le beau monde's* good graces, after first rendering the *ton* off balance. Now they'd become wildly popular—as if she cared a beggar's purse about that sort of approval—and choosing what assemblies to attend had become a daily ordeal. A quiet evening at home had become a coveted thing of the past.

Such an abundance of flowers and sweetmeats arrived each morning, they'd started sending the previous day's tributes to local hospitals and orphanages.

The situation proved more amusing than flattering. Several gentlemen had called upon her, yet only two had captured her interest. Between Mr. Burlington's marked attention and having developed an unusual, yet comfortable, friendship with Tristan, deciding which gentlemen's company she preferred flummoxed her more than a little.

No. That was a fribble's nonsense.

Mr. Burlington affections were as transparent as new glass. He constantly complimented her, and in recent days had hinted strongly of a future together, yet Lord Leventhorpe—the deucedly complicated enigma—continued to rouse her curiosity, and she feared, had engaged her heart.

One man was pleasant and predictable, like summer weather. The other, a discordant winter tempest. Given the choice between an easy-going, cheerful, good-natured god and a reticent, sometimes surly, impossible-to-figure-out man, the choice was obvious to a blind crone.

Only it wasn't. And that vexed her all the more.

Logic and reason clearly weighed in Mr. Burlington's favor, so other than patent foolhardiness, why did she prefer Tristan?

Yes, he had a splendid physique, and reliving their world-tilting kiss had kept her awake many nights, but muscles and a well-formed mouth weren't criteria for selecting a husband.

They could be. If he was the man.

Mr. Burlington hadn't approached Heath to ask for her hand—not that he had a say now that she'd reached her first and twentieth birthday—but, as surely as burning wood snapped and popped, a proposal would be forthcoming. She was as positive as Friday following Thursday it would be soon, too. Very soon. Perhaps tonight even.

She could be happy with Mr. Burlington, perhaps not blissful, but more than comfortable. Couldn't she? Everyone expected her to accept his proposal. Catching her lower lip between her teeth, she peeked at him through her lashes. He doted on her, rather in a smothering fashion at times, and seemed anxious to please. And he was gallant and strikingly handsome.

Why then, did something unidentifiable niggle at the recesses of her mind, enough to keep her from admitting to herself that her response to him was anything more than physical attraction? Maybe her lack of experience with men was to blame, although in recent weeks, she'd been exposed to all manner of males. Charming, witty, shy, awkward, arrogant, even a few who'd tried to steal a kiss and whose toes she'd tromped in response, or whose acquaintance she'd preferred to have been spared.

Mr. Phillips's taunting smile encroached upon her contemplations.

The last two balls, he'd attempted to maneuver her into isolated niches. No surprise that he'd identified each nook and cranny, every hidey-hole and dark corner in the grand homes they'd been invited into. Pests and vermin always found the best places to lurk.

Mr. Burlington patted her gloved hand as they approached the terrace. "I'll find you a seat, and then I'll fetch us something to drink. We can take our walk after we've had our beverages."

Ever the considerate gentleman.

A bead of sweat trickled between her breasts, and she unfurled her fan. Enthusiastically waving her fan, she welcomed the cooling breeze, insufficient as it was. "That sounds lovely. I'm fair parched."

"As am I." He smiled down at her, a sensual glint in his russet gaze.

After exiting the French windows, they paused for a moment beyond the threshold, and she inhaled the mild, blossom-scented air. Framed by flowering shrubs, roses, and an assortment of other blooms, the terrace would be stunning in the daylight. Lanterns, scattered here and there, lit the lawn and illuminated a quaint, fairy-like footpath. She yearned to explore the wending, moonlit trail through the manicured shrubberies.

They rounded the house's side, and Blythe smiled in delight. A carved stone bench beckoned. It sat nestled between another pair of French windows and a pillar topped with a Grecian pot overflowing with flowers and greens. A faint light gleaming behind the partially drawn drapes revealed an unoccupied paneled library. No one milled this darker side, suiting Blythe fine. She relished a few moments of solitude, one of the things she'd craved most since leaving Esherton. "Perfect. I shall wait here."

Mr. Burlington lifted her hand, and after bestowing a fervent kiss upon the back, gently embraced her. His eyes darkened to jet-black shards, and his breath quickened.

He was going to kiss her.

She ought to object, yet her curiosity demanded satisfaction. Would his kiss be as devastating as Tristan's?

"Blythe." Mr. Burlington's mouth grazed hers, tentatively then more forcefully. He made a satisfied sound in his throat and sidled nearer, trailing his lips to her ear. "So beautiful."

Pleasant, though not world-tilting.

Blythe should've been disappointed, and yet she couldn't summon the false emotion.

"Please stop." She lightly shoved his shoulders. "Someone might come upon us."

A kiss in the garden wasn't likely to get her bundled off to the country, was it?

Breathing harshly, he released her. "I'm sorry. I've no excuse except that I was overcome by your beauty and the romantic setting. I've wanted to kiss you since the first moment I saw you." He flashed a boyish smile. "Please forgive my forwardness. I've been desperate to ask you—"

A laughing couple ran off the corner steps, likely seeking privacy as well. From what she'd glimpsed, the elegant garden provided several ideal locations for clandestine trysts.

"I should have stopped you sooner, but I confess to being curious." No sense pretending maidenly shyness. She'd wanted to know, and now she did.

His tawny brows peaked, and his lips curved into a gratified smile. "You were? And ...?"

Jiggling her closed fan at him, she laughed and sank onto the bench. "A lady never kisses and tells." Particularly if the kiss had merely been adequate.

Unlike Tristan's pulse-skipping, thought-scrambling assault on her senses.

"Please fetch our beverages, and then we can take a pleasant stroll." Perusing the tidy yard and neat flower beds, she pointed her fan at the flagstone walkway. "I'd like to explore that charming path. Do you know where it leads?"

"No, I've not had the occasion to wander it." His gaze skimmed the garden, the corners of his mouth tilting downward. "Are you certain you wish to remain here alone?"

Blythe relaxed against the seat's granite back. "I'm not alone. More than a score of people are a few feet away. I need simply call for assistance should I require it."

She could wrestle a calf or a sheep to the ground, so escaping a beau's unwanted attentions, should the need arrive, didn't concern her overly much.

"True. I'll return shortly." Mr. Burlington nodded slowly, before his face brightened, and he strode away, a perfect combination of male grace and refined breeding.

You could do far, far worse, Blythe.

She closed her eyes, and breathed in the perfumed air. Somewhere in the garden, honeysuckle bloomed.

The air escaped her in a frustrated puff.

Marrying into the upper crust hadn't been part of her plans when Heath towed them to London. She'd assumed she'd marry a simple man with simple ways and simple wants. Mr. Burlington, though not titled, came from a distinguished family and was accustomed to a privileged life. More on point, he adored living in London, relished the hubbub, the assemblies, the noise.

How would he support a family? Her dowry would only go so far, and she'd eat her slippers before she'd accept another groat from Heath. Perhaps Mr. Burlington possessed his own wealth or had an income or allowance from another source.

She couldn't ask him though, now could she?

No, but she could ask Heath.

Blythe didn't mind hard work, and economizing was second nature. They could live modestly ... Well, she could. Could Courtland?—Mr. Burlington? She wasn't ready to call him by his given name yet which revealed much.

What about love?

Her eyes shut, she waved her hand before her nose, chasing away a persistent insect.

Perhaps her pleasant feelings toward Mr. Burlington would grow into something more. It was feasible. Why, a few short weeks ago, she couldn't abide Tristan.

He hadn't indicated interest beyond friendship, and he still kept a part of himself reserved ... almost as if he concealed a great secret or objectionable characteristic.

For a few moments that day at Gunter's she'd ventured to think he held her in esteem, until he'd donned his impenetrable mask again. She'd love to get beyond his exterior and have a glimpse of the real man. For the umpteenth time, Blythe tried to analyze her fascination.

"What is it about you, Tristan?"

"I cannot imagine why you whisper of one man when you've scandalously kissed another." Miss Sanford's haughty sneer nearly sent Blythe toppling off the bench in much the same way Tristan had tumbled onto his bum the other night.

Blythe bolted upright, her eyes popping open. "I cannot imagine why *you* think it your concern."

The chit had seen the kiss and wouldn't keep her painted lips sealed. Blythe peered beyond Miss Sanford's rigid posture. Had anyone else seen?

A dark figure, arms crossed, rested his shoulder against the house's corner.

Phillips.

Double Hades and purgatory.

Those two spent far too much time skulking about together for a couple not engaged romantically. Most peculiar given Miss Sanford's determination to leg-shackle poor Tristan.

Miss Sanford tromped to the bench's end, all pretense of civility gone. She placed her fists against her ivory and turquoise silk-clad hips and glowered. "Did Mr. Burlington propose?"

Of all the unadulterated gall.

Blythe made a pretense of smoothing her already wrinkle-free satin skirt embroidered with gold spangles before half-spreading her French painted brisé fan. The impulse to verbally flay Rosemary Sanford overwhelmed her, and she had to lock her teeth and take a pair of deep, calming breaths. Apparently, Mr. Phillips and Miss Sanford had been close enough to see the kiss, but not hear her conversation with Courtland.

"Well. Did he?" Miss Sanford stamped her foot.

Petulant child.

Blythe could have sworn no one had been nearby when she'd arrived on this side of the terrace. What had Phillips and Miss Sanford been doing? Lurking in the greenery? Something was off with those two.

Blythe offered a noncommittal smile and ran her fingertips along the fan's lace edge. "I can't imagine why you think it your affair."

Her face contorted with loathing, Miss Sanford bent near Blythe. "It is my business if you intend to continue to throw yourself at Lord Leventhorpe. He's mine, you ... you country ... *neep*."

"Neep? Calling me a turnip's the best you can do?" Blythe stood five feet, ten inches tall. Did the diminutive nit think she intimidated her? She shoved Miss Sanford aside as she rose

Phillips stiffened and slowly eased upright, yet made no move to intervene.

Weasel.

Blythe elevated her chin, drawing her spine to its full extension.

God, how she wanted to slap the termagant's hoity-toity face. "I have a word of advice for you, and if you've an ounce of common sense in your spiteful, conceited, prettily-styled head, you'll listen."

"I'm sure you've no advice I'd ever consider taking." Miss Sanford swallowed audibly and flung Phillips a hasty glance. "Why don't you and your hick sisters take yourselves back to the country where hobgoblin scarecrows like you belong?"

"Two of those *scarecrows* are my cousins, including *Lady* Ravensdale." Blythe unfolded her fan fully and made a pretense of drawing a finger down the delicate ribs to the handle. "We used to kill our own chickens. Do you know how?" She spared Miss Sanford a fleeting glance. Blythe hadn't killed a fowl, but she'd seen it done many times. Farm girls didn't have time for squeamish stomachs.

Miss Sanford clasped her throat, her eyes round as twin British crowns. "I'm sure I don't—"

"Like this." With a twist and a jerk, Blythe snapped her fan's handle, the crack echoing eerily loudly in the terrace's isolated corner.

Miss Sanford's jaw dropped as she took a stumbling step backward with a strangled shriek. "Mr. Phillips!"

Phillips remained alert, yet disregarded her plea.

What did she think? He'd suddenly become gallant? What exactly was their relationship?

"You'd better disabuse yourself of notions where Lord Leventhorpe is concerned. A few days ago, he told me succinctly that, 'cows will produce whisky before I'd ever marry Rosemary Sanford.'" Blythe's jubilant smile held no warmth. "His words, not mine, dear."

"That's a foul lie!" Miss Sanford released an infuriated gasp and swung her arm.

Blythe seized her palm in mid-air.

"I *shall* hit you back, and I promise you, your nose won't be the same." Blythe jerked her head toward Phillips. "Do you wish to look like him? Or worse?"

"You ... you trollop. Why am I not surprised you'd resort to such violent measures?" Miss Sanford yanked her hand free. "I'm going to tell Mama."

Tattling toddler.

"Please do. And be sure to explain why you are prowling around unchaperoned with Mr. Phillips and how you tried to strike me first." Blythe tossed her broken fan onto the bench. "Consider carefully who my cousin-in-law is and who's in Lord Ravensdale's inner circle before you make an enemy of him. You mightn't find a single peer or respectable man willing to court you."

"Ooh. Ooh!" Miss Sanford fisted her hands and growled—*really growled*: a frustrated, infuriated suppressed roar—before turning on her heel and stomping across the terrace. She pushed Phillips hard in passing, and he laughed.

"Miss Sanford, I told you not to cross that vixen." Lust laced his sinister chuckle.

Where was Mr. Burlington? Shouldn't he have returned with her ratafia by now?

Well, Blythe wasn't dimwitted enough to loiter here with Mr. Phillips nearby. She might have the scandal she had wished for weeks ago, and now she wasn't quite ready to quit London.

She gathered her ruined fan—more wanton waste. When would she learn to control her temper?

"Miss Sanford is accustomed to having her way." Phillips meandered toward her, his bearing alert and predatory.

Botheration. Blythe had rid herself of one menace, merely to be confronted by another.

She rounded the bench, intent on gaining the stairs leading to the yard. Unfortunately, that meant moving farther away from those assembled along the veranda and circumnavigating the shrubberies, which completely concealed her from view until she made the patio's other side.

"No need to scurry away. I simply want to ask you a question." He angled across the stones to the other set of stairs.

Blast.

He would cut her off, and finding herself cornered by that cawker spelled ruination. Heath had candidly warned them of Phillips's propensity to deflower innocents.

Waiting until he reached the top riser, she whirled and bolted toward the French doors.

"Dammit." Phillips sprinted after her. "Wait."

Blythe's hem tripped her, but she managed to regain her balance. The ruffled border ripped when she tore it loose. The gown could be repaired. Her reputation couldn't. She must make the library.

The slight hesitation gave Phillips the fraction he needed to reach her. He snaked an arm around her waist, and before she could twist free, crushed her to his chest. Chuckling lecherously, he panted against her neck.

"Let go, you oaf." Blythe reared away as she brought her knee up, jabbing his groin and shoving his chest with all her strength. The instant his grip loosened, she sprang free.

Cursing, he grabbed his crotch and doubled over. He tottered away a couple of steps, hunched like a hundred-year-old crone. "You'll pay for that, bitch."

She seized her skirts, and after hauling them to her knees, kicked him in the arse, sending him into the bushes below. "Touch me again, and I'll see you castrated faster than snipping a baby bull."

Shaking, more from fury than fear, she sprinted to the French doors.

Empty, thank God.

Panting, she eased the door open and slipping inside, took care to slide the lock home, even though Phillips wouldn't follow her any time soon. She needed a few moments to compose herself, and then she'd go in search of Heath and tell him what Phillips had attempted.

Dash it all. She couldn't.

As certain as sheep grow wool, he'd challenge Phillips. She pressed a hand to her forehead. The annoying ache that she'd attributed to nerves and excitement thrummed full on now.

Truthfully, she wanted to find Tristan and fall into his arms and ask him to break Phillips's nose again. Break a lot more than his nose. She summoned a wry grin. She'd become bloodthirsty of late.

She drew one side of the drapes closed and had grasped the second panel to do the same, when upset voices penetrated the door.

Blythe froze mid-movement.

"She tried to hit me, Mama. If I hadn't dodged her, she'd have broken my nose as she threatened to do."

Lying virago.

"Shh, Rosemary, hush. Here, step inside, and I'll tell you what must be done. That Culpepper chit will not hinder our well-laid plans. You *will* be Lady Leventhorpe."

The devil she will.

The door handle dipped.

Blythe dove behind the drawn drape. Drat, her toes stuck out, and she could be seen from outside. Under cover of the velvet and obscured by an oriental screen, she dashed to the corner beside the window.

Cowardice didn't compel her concealment. Quite frankly, she wanted to know what those conniving women planned.

Tristan must be warned of their scheming.

Ears straining, she held her breath as the door swished open followed by the soft clacking of two pairs of heels.

"Rosemary, we must up our strategy immediately." The door clicked shut. "The Season is almost at an end. We'll arrange for you to be found in a compromising situation with Lord Leventhorpe. Tonight."

One who acts with integrity and love will always be
victorious over another's calculating and conniving schemes.
~Dignity and Decorum—The Genteel Lady's Guide to Practical Living

9

W here was Blythe?
   Ridiculous, this need to know her whereabouts. Or how much
pleasure he drew from simply watching her ... listening to her.

Sipping champagne, Tristan stretched his neck and perused the
colorful crowd swirling about the floor. The mirrored walls made the
teeming room appear more crowded. Resting a shoulder against a
Grecian column, he examined the ballroom and what he could see of
the veranda, card room, and entrance from his strategic position.

Nothing.

She hadn't returned after exiting with Burlington, though he'd re-
entered several minutes ago and chatted with that American heiress,
Margaret Hemple.

Why had he left Blythe outside?

Perhaps he hadn't, and she'd come inside by way of another door.
The house did boast three other entrances from the garden.

Should he go in search of her?

He flexed his jaw.

She might not appreciate his interference or the knowledge that he
supervised her whereabouts.

Mrs. Hemple laughed and stepped closer to Burlington, placing her
hand on his arm and fluttering her eyelashes.

He murmured something while delivering one of his charming
smiles, and her upturned face pinkened. Bending nearer, he covered her
hand in a proprietary manner as he whispered in her ear.

Brows faintly scrunched, she flung a fleeting glance at the doors
and slowly nodded.

After another brilliant smile, and pressing an indecently long kiss to her hand, he finally made his way outdoors once more.

Frowning a touch, Tristan took another sip of the sparkling wine and combed the room. *Again.* Fourth time in as many minutes. *Hopeless sot.*

He'd seen Burlington and Mrs. Hemple driving together in Hyde Park two days ago, and three days prior to that, he'd come upon them at Gunter's. Thank God it hadn't been the same day he'd treated the Culpeppers to ices.

Did Blythe know her beau's devotion had strayed or at the least was divided?

Should Tristan tell her? More on point, would she care? Would Burlington's perfidy devastate her?

He derived no satisfaction from having at last discovered Burlington's flaw.

Blythe seemed quite entranced with him, and if the cur meant to toss her over for a wealthy widow, better it happened now. Damnation. Too blasted bad he couldn't blacken Burlington's eye if he did. Pursuing her and engaging her affections if he didn't mean to act honorably was outside the bounds.

To be fair, Mrs. Hemple had only arrived in London a fortnight ago, and Tristan's subtle questioning of Ravensdale and the Culpepper misses revealed that Burlington still sent Blythe bouquets daily and called as frequently. In recent days, he'd accompanied the Culpeppers to several gatherings as well. He couldn't have progressed to anything more than a flirtation with Mrs. Hemple, could he?

Did he mean to court two women simultaneously?

Blythe needed to know about Burlington's duplicity, yet Tristan didn't want to be the one to crush her heart. He cherished their amiable truce, and hurting her would be twisting a jagged, rusty knife in his chest too.

If Burlington wasn't trustworthy during courtship, would he stray after marriage?

Undoubtedly. Men of that ilk inevitably did.

Tristan stifled a yawn, rubbing the bridge of his nose with two fingers.

He hadn't been sleeping well again lately, except nightmares weren't the cause. Each time he dozed off, a vivacious, silver-haired, lilac-eyed, laughing nymph cavorted across his drowsy mind, jarring him awake. He couldn't quiet his mind or musings *or primal urges* when it came to Blythe.

Now he had a fresh concern regarding her.

She was going to get hurt. It couldn't be helped. Either she was told now or, far worse, she'd learn of Burlington's treachery later.

It wasn't his business, Tristan reminded himself for the umpteenth time. Fat good that did. His conscience and desire guffawed in unison.

If it hadn't been for his promise to Raven, and how seriously Tristan took his position in the House of Lords, he would've been tempted to make for Bristledale Court straightaway. He had no right entertaining fanciful musings about his closest friend's ward when Tristan wasn't looking to wed yet. That was why, other than a single snatched kiss, Tristan had steadfastly kept his acquaintance with Blythe a casual friendship, nothing more.

Except, the bond was much more. At least to him. Fate recklessly trod a path of destruction over his well-laid plans and laid siege to his heart.

He canvassed the room again.

No sign of her, or Phillips and Miss Sanford, blister it. They'd disappeared outside also, after exchanging a brief word with Burlington when he'd returned without Blythe.

Pathetic, Tristan knowing those trivialities. Everything regarding Blythe interested—*fascinated*—him. Attending these deuced functions didn't intimidate nearly as much with her present. Even if he wouldn't claim more than one dance, and his gut churned constantly with disquiet wondering if Burlington would propose, and she'd accept.

Particularly since Burlington's eye had strayed in recent days.

Perhaps his excursions with Mrs. Hemple meant nothing, and he intended to offer for Blythe, which made him an unconscionable knave for encouraging Mrs. Hemple's hopes.

A betrothal would put an end to Tristan's friendship with Blythe. No man approved of his wife keeping company with bachelors. He'd miss their witty conversations and her delightful, throaty laugh. No other woman compared to her.

If Burlington made her happy and content, Tristan wished them well. Who was he to reveal Burlington's perfidy? Perhaps Blythe didn't want to know. She wouldn't be the first woman to turn a blind eye to her husband's indiscretions.

Tristan couldn't offer her anything until he'd abolished his demons, and a sweetmeat tossed amongst starving urchins would last longer than

Blythe on the marriage mart. She sensibly preferred Burlington's amiable personality, and Tristan knew full well others regarded him as unapproachable fellow.

He *had* been reserved prior to meeting Blythe. He hadn't smiled or laughed as much before becoming acquainted with the charming, strong-willed, vexing, sharp-tongued, wholly enchanting vixen.

Whitehouse had the right of it.

Tristan was smitten, and there wasn't a hell-fired thing he could do about it.

Still, caring for Blythe's wellbeing at assemblies was the least he could do for her and Ravensdale. Raven could scarcely watch all the moon-eyed swains and cocksure-blades swarming the other Culpeppers. One less woman to fret about would ease his mind and Tristan's.

He snorted softly.

God, listening to his vacillating, mental claptrap made him want to slap himself. With a cudgel.

Phillips's persistent interest in Blythe proved disconcerting.

Hence at social functions, Tristan spent half his time following the unsavory cull, and the other half evading Miss Sanford's dogged pursuit. Why didn't the two leave off when the objects of their attentions didn't return their regard? Hadn't she or Phillips a morsel of pride? Or could they be so self-absorbed that they disregarded the other party's feelings? Not a healthy mindset and one that would certainly result in disappointment.

If it hadn't meant he would've had to enter into the parson's mousetrap, he would've claimed a secret betrothal to rid himself of Miss Sanford.

"Looking your usual pensive self tonight, I see Leventhorpe. Must be really enjoying *this* ball. I think it one of the better assemblies this Season, personally." Hawksworth's lopsided grin belied his sarcastic comment. Squinting, he scrutinized the ballroom's far side. "What the deuce have you been glaring at by the French windows the past fifteen minutes or more?"

"I see you finally escaped your parish." Tristan spared him a sideways glance. "How'd you manage that?"

Hawksworth chuckled, pulling his earlobe. "My official duties brought me to this side of Town, and Drake cordially invited me to accompany him." He cocked his head, quirking a brow. "And don't think you can avoid answering the question by distracting me. You've downed two flutes of champagne, danced not at all, and the darkling scowls you've directed at Burlington and the benign beveled panes there," he jerked his head indicating the room's other end, "have more than one tongue wagging."

Tristan wasn't about to tell Hawksworth. "I'm contemplating whether I can make my escape."

Outside, to find Blythe.

Hawksworth shrugged and looked over his shoulder. "With this throng, I don't think our hosts would notice. There's hardly room to mill about. Smashing success." His keen gaze bored into Tristan. "How are you managing? You look all-in."

"Fine, as long as I keep my senses dulled." He paused in raising his empty glass when Phillips stomped past, a leaf poking from the hair above his ear, a smudge, suspiciously resembling dirt, along his knee, and ire smoldering in his eyes.

Blythe. If Phillips touched her...

Phillips made straight for Miss Sanford as she whispered to her mother and grandmother, all three staring pointedly in Tristan's direction.

That trio of Medusas couldn't be conspiring anything good.

Thrusting his glass at Hawksworth, Tristan swiveled toward the French windows. "See if you can discover what Phillips has been up to. He looks like he's been frolicking in the shrubberies. Be discreet."

Jaw set and gut knotted, Tristan strode to the exit, dodging dancers and earning more than one vexed pout and scowl of displeasure.

Phillips's rumpled appearance, and his reputation for forcing women, as well as Blythe's continued absence, wreaked havoc upon Tristan's usually stoic conduct.

A glowing Francine and beaming Maddox intercepted him at the threshold.

Bloody he—

Tristan barely prevented the oath tapping irately at his teeth.

"Just the person we've been searching for." Francine fairly bubbled, her eyes sparkling and her cheeks rosy. "I ..." She gave Maddox an adoring gaze and nestled nearer him. "We wanted you to be the first to know."

"Am I to assume felicitations are in order?" Nothing of interest on the terrace beyond them caught Tristan's attention; therefore, he momentarily put aside his worry and offered a congratulatory smile.

Maddox's mouth lifted at one side as he slipped Francine's hand into his elbow's crook. "I hope you aren't offended I didn't approach you first, Leventhorpe. We were strolling the gardens, and I couldn't wait another moment to ask Miss Simmons, Francine, to become my wife."

"Not offended at all. I'm delighted." Tristan shook Maddox's hand and then pressed a quick kiss to Francine's forehead while surreptitiously scouring what he could see of the veranda and lawn. "My sincerest happy wishes to you both."

Dammit, where is Blythe?

"We want to marry straightaway, as soon as the banns have been read." Francine laid her hand on Tristan's forearm. "Tristan, would you give me away?"

A surge of emotion rendered him speechless. He swallowed and cleared his throat. "I would consider it a tremendous honor."

"Splendid. Come, darling, let's share our joyous news." Maddox led her away, and a crowd of well-wishers promptly gathered about them, though Miss Sanford wasn't amongst them.

Francine and Maddox made a brilliant couple and they were smitten with one another. Tristan found their devotion charming and truly touching. Perhaps his pessimistic nature had softened.

A trifle more light-hearted than he had been mere minutes before, he turned onto the veranda. A quick sweep of its length confirmed Blythe's absence. Hands braced at his hips and jaw tense, he turned one way then the other.

Which should he search first?

The garden, the pathway, or the veranda's other side? What about the lane to the mews beyond the fence?

He scratched his nape. Come to think of it, he hadn't seen a single Culpepper, or Raven, for that matter, for a good while. Not that he'd have noticed, intent as he'd been on seeking Blythe.

Besotted. Thoroughly and entirely. And doomed to disappointment.

"There you are, my lord. I worried you meant to stand me up for my dance." Lady Ravensdale glided his way, a vision in cream and lavender, a mischievous smile brightening her lovely face. "Although, I suspect you'd prefer my cousin to partner you."

She knows?

Tristan managed to keep his jaw from unhinging and crashing into his chest.

Winking, she swept nearer. "Your secret is safe with me, Lord Leventhorpe."

"I wouldn't be so inconsiderate as to miss our dance, my lady." Actually, he'd completely forgotten the commitment. He wasn't about to address her second statement. If the day ever came that he admitted to what she insinuated, it wouldn't be in public.

"I'd offer to let Blythe dance in my stead, but I don't believe I've seen her since her set with Mr. Burlington. She's quite in demand tonight. It is her birthday celebration, after all."

Had the inflection in her voice altered the merest bit when she said Burlington's name?

Placing her hand upon his extended arm, Lady Ravensdale accompanied him inside. The blast of heat and body odors of a hundred people crowded into the insufficient space assailed him.

"Perhaps she's in the retiring room having a lie down." Lady Ravensdale smiled at a group of matrons chatting in hushed tones to one side of the windows. "She was feeling peaked earlier."

"She's unwell?" Had something happened with Phillips or Burlington to cause her malaise? Tristan could barely restrain himself from bolting upstairs and asking.

"No, nothing of that nature. She claimed a slight headache from the excitement. I advised her to take a powder and lie down with a cold cloth upon her forehead." Giving him a sympathetic smile, she curtsied prettily as the strains of a waltz filled the air. "I've sent her sisters to check on her and expect her to join us shortly."

"I'm relieved to hear it. I grew concerned when she didn't return after venturing outdoors with Burlington." Why didn't he blather a little more—go ahead and confess his infatuation?

"My lord, it's not my place to tell you, and I abhor gossip ..." Lady Ravensdale bit her bottom lip, and cast a guarded look about as he guided her past other swaying couples. "I overheard Mrs. Hemple a short while ago, quite inadvertently, I assure you." Her lavender-blue eyes so like Blythe's, Lady Ravensdale raised her pained gaze to his.

"What has you distressed, my lady?"

"Mr. Burlington has asked to pay his address to Mrs. Hemple, which must mean he has decided she would make a suitable bride. I'm afraid Blythe will be made a laughingstock."

Tristan missed a step, but quickly recovered and swung his head to the gaping French windows. Then why the hell had Burlington gone outdoors? To deliver the unpleasant news to Blythe? "Please forgive me, Lady Ravensdale. Are you certain? Burlington seems most devoted to Miss Culpepper."

She nodded, the curls framing her face pirouetting at her exuberance. "Oh, yes. I was in the retiring room suffering from a bout of nausea. They weren't aware I was behind the screen, and I was too discomfited and disturbed by Mrs. Hemple's announcement to make my presence known afterward." A blush tinted her face. "Mrs. Hemple confided her 'joyous news' to Lady Wimpleton. I think they are distant cousins, but I may have that wrong. I have no reason to believe she lied. I do want Heath to speak with Mr. Burlington before I tell Blythe in case I heard incorrectly."

Tristan would bet Buce she hadn't.

God rot Burlington, the unscrupulous knave. Tristan maneuvered Lady Ravensdale round Mrs. Sanford and her portly partner.

Miss Sanford's mother summoned a brittle smile and tilted her head before dragging her partner, huffing and puffing and sweating like a lathered horse, off the dance floor.

Had she overheard?

She'd practically followed Lady Ravensdale and Tristan as they'd danced at the expense of Mrs. Sanford's rotund partner who appeared about to expire from exertion. A naked doxy delivering a sermon from Hawksworth's pulpit claimed more subtlety than the eavesdropping Mrs. Sanford.

Damn. Tristan needed to find Blythe and tell her before that she-cat or her gloating daughter did. "Raven told me your wonderful news, my lady. Congratulations."

"We are very happy." A glorious smiled wreathed Lady Ravensdale's delicate features.

Their dance ended, and they went through the perfunctory bow and curtsy. Her eyes clouded when she gazed past him.

"Botheration. Heath has heard as well, I'll wager." Lady Ravensdale waved shortly at Miss Brette standing beside Ravensdale, a troubled expression tugging his black brows together. "My lord, I know it's not my place, nor yours, and I don't wish to impose or make you uncomfortable. But if you care for Blythe as much as I suspect you do, perhaps you can help ease her mortification and salvage her pride a degree?"

Given the wry twist of her lips, Tristan's astonishment must have reflected upon his face. "How so? We've established a truce of sorts, but Miss Culpepper is not exactly fond of me."

His heart twinged as he spoke, and she laid her hand on his forearm.

"You're wrong in that regard, my lord. Very wrong."

A man consumed with love or lust schemes more than countless criminals, and a diligent woman guards herself against his ploys.
~*Dignity and Decorum—The Genteel Lady's Guide to Practical Living*

10

Blythe waited several interminable seconds after the library door clacked shut before daring to move. Tristan must be warned of Miss Sanford's intent to entrap him. Blythe ought to have exploded from behind the curtains and stopped the ill-hatched plotting, and had she not been utterly flabbergasted, she'd have corralled her wits sooner and done so.

Now she understood her instinctive dislike of Miss Sanford from almost the first moment she'd met her. The pert hussy possessed a warped soul.

She'd not sink her sorceress's talons into Tristan if Blythe could help it.

Edging along the drapery, she finally reached the door. She fumbled with the blasted lock until it slid loose then whipped the door open. After a quick glance about the room and veranda, she slipped outside. No sooner had she shut the door then Mr. Burlington strode across the veranda, his eyes crinkled at the corners in excitement.

"Please forgive my tardiness." He drew his golden brows together a degree and sliced a swift glance behind her into the library. "I was detained. I hope you didn't become impatient, darling."

Darling?

Surely that meant he intended to propose.

Not now.

She didn't have the time to gently turn him down, for refuse his offer she must. He didn't stir anywhere near the kind of intense emotions or turmoil Tristan did, and those few minutes in the library overhearing Miss Sanford's wicked intentions had compelled Blythe to face what she'd denied for weeks now.

Stupidly, and against her better judgment, she'd gone and fallen in love with crotchety, obstinate, impossible Tristan. Her perverse heart had chosen the one man she could never have.

Love had an irregular sense of humor.

Casting about for a reason to stall the inescapable, she waved at Mr. Burlington's empty hands. "Where are our drinks?"

His cheerful expression faltered momentarily, and he gave a contrite laugh. "Eager to return to you, I forgot them."

What had he been doing then? He'd been gone upward of fifteen minutes.

He took her hands and gave her a sensual smile, calculated to soothe her ruffled feathers, she'd wager.

"You know I adore you, don't you, Blythe?" Advancing a pace, he cupped her upper arms, and brushed his thumbs back and forth, his eyes darkening to mahogany. "You captured my heart from the first moment I saw you. I knew you were refreshingly different from the coy misses. You're singularly unique. Special."

A bit overdone, there.

"Mr. Burlington ... Courtland ..."

"I want to marry you, dearest heart, I do—"

"I know you do, and I am honored—"

"But," he dipped his golden head as if intending to kiss her again, "I'm sure you also understand why I cannot ask you to be my wife."

Blythe leaned away and squinted at him. "You cannot?"

He continued to give her that roguish smile, the one that had set her heart aflutter and her bosoms puckering the first night she'd met him.

Nothing fluttered or puckered or gave the tiniest twitch.

"Cannot?" she croaked again. A dim-witted parrot sounded more intelligent. Blythe almost stuck a finger in her ear or shook her head to make sure she'd heard him correctly.

He had said, *cannot*, hadn't he?

And he expected her to understand why?

He seemed nonplussed for a flash.

Kicking her tangled emotions to next year, she narrowed her eyes further and examined every plane and angle of his handsome face, scrutinizing his countenance objectively for the first time.

How had she missed the slightly petulant turn to his mouth or the shrewd glint in his arresting eyes these past weeks? Those characteristics had been there, surely? Naiveté couldn't be blamed entirely. Truth to tell, she'd not wanted to see past his attractiveness and his apparent devotion. He *had* been courting her. She was neither slow-witted or given to fanciful imaginations.

Icy tendrils slithered round her shoulders and arms as she eased from his embrace. Shivering, she hugged herself. No honorable man called a woman darling when announcing he couldn't offer her marriage. What was his game?

"Please humor me and explain why we cannot marry." This should prove highly enlightening.

Courtland recovered his composure, or rather summoned his most engaging air, and closed the distance between them. Touching her cheek with his forefinger, he trailed it to her ear. "Surely you understand these things. My brother is not well. I'll likely inherit the title, and though I'm sure your dowry is quite adequate for a commoner ..."

Blythe slapped his hand away. What she yearned to do was plant him a facer. Right in his too-perfectly-straight, noble cork.

"Are you saying I'm not rich enough for you to marry, Courtland, or is it my lack of position that's objectionable? Or perchance both? I'm not wealthy *or* highborn?"

He blinked stupidly, as if surprised by her reaction. "Sweeting, don't take on so. No need to kick up a dust. I didn't expect to love the woman I take to wife."

How forward thinking of you. Dolt.

Tapping her chin, he delivered another of his disarming smiles.

Instead of his touch sending giddy ripples along her nerves, she fought the urge to cast up her accounts upon his gleaming shoes. She wrapped her arms tighter about her shoulders and drew her chin away.

He cradled her cheek in his palm. "You hold my affection, darling. I do love you, more than I believed I'd ever love a woman, and I am determined for us to be together. And I know you love me too. I've seen it in your eyes and the way you smile at me. You haven't been the least coy or reserved. Why, it's apparent, even to others. Several have congratulated me on my good fortune."

Had she been that humiliatingly obvious?

Stupid, stupid, *stupid* green girl.

"Although we cannot wed, Blythe, I have contrived a way for us to be together."

Did he not see the visual daggers she was hurling at him or the tense line of her mouth as she battled to subdue the curses she'd overheard in Esherton's barns?

His arrogant confidence raised her ire another notch. Fine then. Sent it hurtling heavenward, screeching in livid umbrage. "Do tell, Courtland. You've clearly thought this through. I'm most anxious to hear what you have *contrived.*"

He nodded a mite too eagerly, and she curled her toes and fingers tightly to maintain her composure. How would he like a nose like Phillips's? With precisely the right angle and enough force, she was certain she could manage something similar ...

"Such arrangements are not uncommon, and with a rich wife, I can indulge your every want." He brushed her cheekbone with his thumb.

"How ... generous of you."

"I know you were dreadfully impoverished in your prior life, and must covet the fineries you've been denied." He cast a hasty glance around and dared sidle a pair of paces closer. Indecently close, truth to tell. "I'll treat you far better than my wife, I assure you. I merely want her money, nothing else. She's simply an inconvenience I must endure." He skewed his mouth to the side. "Well, I'd have to beget an heir. Perhaps a spare as well to assure the title continues."

Why stop at two? Try for a half dozen.

Blythe went rigid and dropped her clenched hands to her sides as her stomach pitched to her shoes. Pasting a falsely sweet smile upon her face, and carefully modulating her tone, she unfurled her fingers. Better to scratch his deceiving, conniving, treacherous ... blackguard eyes out. Good God. What had she ever seen in this conceited, self-centered lout?

"Are you suggesting..." She sucked in a slow, steadying breath.

Lord, help me not to attack him.

Cocking her head, she forced the foul words past her tongue. "Are you offering me carte-blanche? You're suggesting I become your mistress?"

She pressed a hand to her roiling middle. Pity women couldn't fight in affairs of honor. She'd call the ruddy cur out, except she neither knew how to brandish a sword nor fire a pistol. Heath did, and would challenge Burlington in a blink if she told him about the affront. With a babe on the way, that bloody well wasn't going to happen.

"Yes." Courtland grinned excitedly, moving forward and compelling her to retreat until she bumped into the pillar beside the doorway. "It's the flawless solution—"

Flawless? No.

"—don't you agree?"

Agree? When cows poop gold.

"Phillips suggested the brilliant remedy. We can be together, sweeting, and I can do my duty to my title and family." He reached for her again, but she evaded him, fervently looking about for something to clobber him with in lieu of a club.

How could a man be so dense? Thick as oak and ignorant as a rock. Did he think she'd grasp the chance? That the honor of becoming his paramour held such appeal she'd toss her reputation and her family's into the gossips' cesspool?

Courtland winked conspiratorially and waggled his eyebrows. "I've already selected an heiress."

Poor woman, whoever she was.

"Oh. Is she someone I know?" The pillar shuddered, and the pot atop it rattled when Blythe—intent upon dodging Courtland's grasping hands—bumped into it.

Uneasiness creased the edge of his mouth, and he slowly shook his head. "I don't believe so. She's an American widow, and tonight, she agreed to allow me to court her."

Hence his tardy return. Did he expect Blythe to wish him joy?

He tipped his mouth into a boyish, almost bashful smile. "That's what delayed me. I'm sorry I wasn't forthright from the beginning. I worried you might take offense and react peevishly, but you're such a sensible woman—"

"How considerate of you." Tarring and feathering was too good for the likes of him. Nipping his ballocks off might be appropriate.

She dropped her broken fan, and he promptly bent to retrieve it.

Ever the gentleman.

She seized the potted plant, staggering from its surprising weight. She lowered her voice seductively. "Courtland?"

"Yes, darling?" He glanced up, his brandy-colored eyes widening in shocked comprehension.

"I wouldn't be your *whore* if the king decreed it." She released the plant atop his head, smiling in satisfaction when he toppled like a foxed-to-the-gills tippler.

Happy birthday to me.

Two laughing couples swept up the steps, stumbling to a stop and bumping pell-mell into one another upon spying him. A startled yelp escaped a woman as she clutched her companion's arm.

With the exaggeration of someone who'd practiced the art repeatedly, the other lady pressed her hand to her bosom, shut her eyes, and swayed dramatically. "Is he ... dead?"

One could hope, but if so, the gibbet awaited Blythe. She'd likely only concussed Mr. Burlington though. A few more curious passersby peeked above the bushes before breaking into frenetic whispering.

One fellow raised his quizzing glass and peered through the lens, as if he needed help distinguishing a man's prone form splayed upon the pavers, dirt sprinkled upon his face, and a red geranium upright upon his forehead. "I say, what happened to Burlington?"

"I declined his proposal." He had made a proposition, all right. Just not an honorable one. "As you can see, he didn't take the refusal well. Keeled over straightaway."

With her assistance.

He moaned and moved his head slightly, earning him sympathetic murmurs from the quartet.

Blythe neatly stepped around him. She couldn't dredge up an ounce of remorse. "You might want to summon a physician."

Or don't. Let the bugger rot.

She'd ruined her chances of making a suitable match. Whether Burlington was a cur or not, plopping pottery atop aristocratic heads, especially gorgeous, eligible ones, didn't fly well with the upper ten thousand.

Just as well.

She'd allowed the pomp and flattering male attention to woo her, fool her into thinking Society wasn't horrid after all. People did, indeed, see what they wanted to see. Well, no more. Succumbing once to foolhardiness might be excused. Doing so again made her fair game and she deserved everything slung her way.

She inhaled deeply. Enough self-castigations for now.

No one knew better than she how gullible and susceptible she'd been. There would be plenty of time to dwell upon her foolishness and chide herself to purgatory and back. Right now, she must alert Tristan. It might be too late already.

Fearing what she'd eaten today was about to make a reappearance, Blythe lifted her skirts and bolted into the library. Stumbling over the threshold, she yelped in alarm when a hand clamped onto her arm.

Phillips.

And he wasn't alone. Miss Sanford also occupied the room.

Vengeance glittered in their hardened gazes.

Why in blazes did Blythe keep encountering these miscreants? Did Fate simply have a rancorous streak?

"Unhand me!" She wrenched free of his grasp and spun to flee whence she'd come, except Phillips sprinted to the door ahead of her.

He smiled—equally gloating, arrogant, and merciless—and shoved it shut with an ominous thud. The lock slid home disconcertingly loudly, but the rasp of him dragging the curtains closed caused the hairs along her nape to lift.

Hopefully, Phillips slamming the door alerted the foursome outside. Would they notify anyone? They might think Blythe was simply having a fit of temper. Or were they too focused on Mr. Burlington to have noticed?

"Precisely the person we sought." Miss Sanford's expression settled into crafty lines, and half-seated upon the divan's gold and taupe damask rolled arm with her arms crossed, she slanted Mr. Phillips a sly glance. "So, Mr. Burlington threw you over, did he? Cannot say I blame him. Personally, I found it astonishing he'd deemed to wallow in muck."

"Tsk, tsk." Mr. Phillips stood with his arms akimbo, eyeing Blythe toe to top. "Serves you right, putting on airs. He's picked another mark, has he? Someone with a much flusher purse. His family might possess an old title, but they're pauper-poor, and he has to marry for money. Some of us have been blessedly spared that obligation."

Had Mr. Phillips and Miss Sanford been listening at the door? How else would they have known what had transpired between her and Mr. Burlington?

"I'll allow, I did rather admire his other clever notion." Leering at Blythe's bosoms, Phillips ran his tongue over his protruding bottom lip. "Wait. I suggested the idea."

Every part of Blythe tried to shrivel to escape his lewd appraisal. If only she had her shawl to shield her cringing flesh. She thrust her chin upward and marched to the interior door. They could bugger themselves before she rose to their bait. Miss Sanford's presence in the library gave Blythe hope she hadn't yet succeeded in cornering Tristan.

With an unladylike snarl, Miss Sanford leaped to her feet. Blocking Blythe's path, she jabbed a forefinger at her. "You're not going anywhere. I'm tired of you interfering. It's taken me the better part of two Seasons for Lord Leventhorpe to pay me any note."

Blythe released a snort worthy of a bull's admiration. "Vain imaginations from a chit too dull-witted to see the truth."

"You're not going to destroy what I've striven for. I won't be forced to marry that ancient, smelly, doddering fool my uncle has selected for me because he insists I gain a title." Flapping her hand, Miss Sanford sneered, her face contorted like a child in the midst of a tantrum. "Especially since Mr. Burlington has tossed you aside."

Her exultant smirk proved she relished Blythe's situation.

Find Tristan.

As Blythe sidestepped to go past, Phillips seized her from behind, trapping her with an arm below her breasts and his other pressed across her chest in a crushing embrace. "You're staying here with me, in order for Miss Sanford to snare herself a lord."

Not if Blythe wanted to keep her virtue, she wasn't.

From the satisfaction shining in their evil gazes, it didn't take a scholar to discern that was precisely what Phillips and Miss Sanford intended.

My total ruination.

He licked her ear, pressing his forearm into her breasts until she feared they'd breach her bodice.

Revulsion sluiced through her and sent her scalp puckering.

Stomping upon his foot with her heel—blast, what she wouldn't have given for her sturdy half-boots—she gulped in a huge breath, prepared to let loose with a banshee's screech meant to peel the paper from the walls, warp the coffee-and-emerald-toned marble encasing the fireplace, and bend the brass tools propped to one side.

Phillips anticipated her scream and slapped his sweaty, dirt-streaked palm over her mouth.

Writhing against him, she gagged and choked.

Chuckling, the sound gravelly and deranged, he dragged her, struggling and attempting to bite his hand, away from doorway. His sour odor sent another surge of burning bile to her throat. Blythe's lighter weight and his iron grip prevented her from wriggling free.

The key clasped in her gloved fingertips, Miss Sanford glided from the library with a triumphant smile and mocking wave.

Now how would Blythe warn Tristan?

An instant later, the lock turned.

The witch had locked Blythe in the library with Phillips. How could anyone be that calculatingly evil?

Miss Sanford had arranged for Phillips to despoil her because she mistakenly believed Blythe competed for Tristan's affections?

Nipping her neck hard, Phillips seized her embroidered muslin gown at the nape. His breath coming in ragged gasps, he ripped the fabric down her back, accidentally giving her the small amount of slack she needed to slip free.

His debauched laugh as she sprinted away toppled her stomach. Her neck throbbed where he'd bitten it though she didn't think he'd broken the skin. She didn't dare touch it to find out. She needed both hands to preserve her modesty.

"I hoped you'd be a fighter. They're the best to bed. Not the chits who whimper and beg for mercy. They concede too easily." The crazed glint in his eyes intensified. "I'll wager you'll fight until the end."

He's utterly mad.

She darted behind the settee, trying to keep her breasts somewhat covered while searching for a weapon with one eye and keeping her other trained on Phillips.

Grinning evilly, he stalked forward. "No one knows you're in here except Rosemary, and I'm certain, for once, her lips are tightly sealed. Both doors are locked. You cannot escape me, Blythe."

God, please.

Blythe crept along the settee. She had one chance, and it meant baring her bosoms to Phillips's lascivious scrutiny. Scooting another few inches, she bit her bottom lip and deliberately let her bodice dip lower, revealing her insignificant *décolletage*.

He paused midstride, his gaze flicking to hers before gravitating to her breasts again. He licked his lips, his face gone taut with lust. "If I didn't know better, I'd think you were teasing me with your tits."

Disgusting, crude pig.

"You won't get away with this. Heath will kill you." Her gown slid to her elbow, the golden embroidery threads shimmering where the lamps atop the fireplace mantel cast their glow. She left the torn material where it gathered at her crook, the entire side of her breast visible.

His gaze remained riveted to her exposed flesh. Just the distraction she needed.

A few more inches.

Phillips was almost upon her.

She released her dress, and the lace-encrusted cloth bunched at her waist.

Jaw sagging, he gaped.

She seized the poker.

Understanding dawned, and head down, like an infuriated, thwarted bull, he lurched forward, blaring profanities.

Shrieking, she thrust the poker with all her might as he collided with her, slamming her head into the marble at the same instant the French window shattered and a madman's bellow filled the room.

Dropping the poker, she slumped to the floor, Phillips's weight crushing her, as something warm and sticky gushed down her face. She struggled, trying to call for help.

"Tris ... tan."

"Blythe, sweetheart." A moment before she slipped into the frothy black fog wreathing her head and senses, torment-filled ocean-blue eyes hovered above her.

God can't stand schemers; therefore,
the poor and rich alike fall into the pit they dig for others.
~Dignity and Decorum—The Genteel Lady's Guide to Practical Living

"Blythe, darling? Can you hear me?" Disregarding the crowd merging into the study from both entrances, Tristan roughly shoved Phillips off Blythe.

Phillips moaned, but didn't move.

Tristan didn't spare him a second glance as he stripped off his coat then gently laid the cutaway upon her chest and torso, providing her a modicum of modesty.

Pulverizing an unconscious man was outside the bounds, but, God help him, he ached to render Phillips a beating he wouldn't recover from. Tristan gritted his teeth against his rage. "Hell."

Blood oozed from a gash on the side of her head.

When he'd heard her scream and broke the door ... He would kill Phillips if she hadn't already.

Pressing his handkerchief to the wound, he attempted to staunch the blood's flow and shield her from the curious onlookers. "Sweeting, wake up."

"Tristan? Miss Sanford ... don't trust ..." Moaning, she opened her eyes briefly, her gaze black and panicked, before they fluttered closed again, and she fell insensate once more.

The library continued to fill with snoops and gossips, and perhaps, a few truly concerned people. Their voices rose and fell in undulating waves of speculation, distress, and censure.

Without fail, the busybodies would take it upon themselves to jump to conclusions and render a judgment then eagerly pass the falsehoods along before knowing what had actually happened.

The intruders' comments melded together in a grating mélange.

"What happened?"

"Is she dishabille under his lordship's coat?

"Why is Phillips lying there?"

"Is he bleeding?"

A woman gasped. "He looks ... *dead.*"

"Stuff and nonsense. His chest is rising and falling," a man calmly advised.

"Oh dear, you don't suppose he ...?"

"Compromised her?"

"She does rather look set upon."

"What's Lord Leventhorpe about?"

"Whatever was Miss Culpepper doing alone with Phillips? Surely she knew better."

"Perhaps it was an arranged *tête-à-tête* that went too far."

Nothing of the sort. A coddled, scheming wench and a black-hearted whoremonger merely conspired to ruin an innocent.

The prattle droned on as guests tossed conjecture about like confetti at a wedding until Tristan bit the inside of his cheek to keep from shouting for the lot to bugger off.

Drake crouched beside Tristan and swore softly. He touched Tristan's shoulder, speaking low. "Whitehouse went to fetch her family and the Wimpletons. Hawksworth and I shall deal with Phillips."

"No. Leave him." Tristan met Drake's acutely troubled gaze, but refused to grant Phillips a glance. If the bloody arse weren't already dead, Tristan wasn't sure he wouldn't strangle him on the spot. He meant to reserve that pleasure for the field of honor.

A fireplace poker, the tip bloodied a good four inches, lay beside Blythe. Her blow hadn't been a missish swat. She'd meant to impale Phillips, and had done a hell-fired job.

"Is he still alive?" Tristan ground the question out between clenched teeth. Maybe Phillips's earlier groan had been his last.

Drake gave a terse nod. "Regretfully."

"Will you act as my second?" Tristan took Blythe's cold hand in his. He was a useless nurse. His luncheon tried again to reappear, and he swallowed the burning scraping his throat. "Can't see Hawksworth in the role. Man of God and all, and I won't put Raven in that position."

"Aye. You mean to call Phillips out then." It wasn't a question.

"Better me than Ravensdale. He has a passel of women he's responsible for and a child on the way."

"Really? I'd not heard. Still, Miss Culpepper's not your responsibility." Drake shifted, glaring over his shoulder and gesturing away inquisitive guests venturing too near. He turned to Tristan. "Some will question your purpose."

Tristan sat on his heels, chin tucked to his chest and palms pressed to his thighs. He spoke discreetly. "She'll have to be married at once. You know that. The scandal will be monumental. Who better than me to wed her? I've spent a great deal of time with the family since their arrival in Town. If Raven can be convinced to claim Blythe has agreed to wed me, that gives me the right to demand satisfaction. Announcing our betrothal will validate her refusing Burlington, and we can spread it about that's why he set his sights on another."

Burlington wouldn't refute the falsehood. It might ruin his chances with his fresh conquest.

"Dear God, what has happened?" Lady Ravensdale and the Culpepper misses descended on Blythe like avenging angels, crowding around her and forcing Tristan to move aside. Face wan, Lady Ravensdale motioned to Ravensdale, thunderous rage sparking in his eyes and hardening the angles of his face. "Heath, please have Lord Wimpleton send for a physician at once. And someone, hand me that knitted throw on the armchair there."

Hawksworth swiftly complied, and in moment the blanket protected Blythe from prying eyes.

Damn, Tristan would have liked to call for the magistrate too. A waste of time, though. A peer would never see the inside of Newgate much less have his aristocratic neck draped with a noose. Phillips stood a better chance of mysteriously disappearing, something Tristan wasn't averse to. All the more reason to meet Phillips upon the dueling field. Theirs would not be a match to first blood match. Someone should have dispatched Phillips long ago.

Tristan would meet with his solicitor in the morning and change his will. Better to err on wisdom's side and be prepared.

Would Phillips choose pistols or swords?

Pistols.

He was too cowardly to risk a test of blades.

Clasping his nape with one hand, and resting the other upon his hip, Tristan stood above the women surrounding Blythe, their pretty faces ravaged by angst and apprehension. He wasn't family, and he had no right to remain, excepting his impulsive intent to claim Blythe as his newly betrothed. But his feet, as if weighted with loadstones, refused to move.

Blythe remained motionless, her face ashen and her glorious hair, red-tinged on one side, spilling about her head.

If Whitehouse hadn't overheard the commotion between Blythe and Burlington and promptly sought Tristan ...

He'd almost been too late.

Scorching fury nearly choked him, the blazing heat setting his blood afire. He made an inarticulate sound, half growl and half oath, causing Miss Blaike—or was she Miss Blaire?—to flick him a confused look. He hadn't experienced hatred this intense since ... No. Not even when he'd been victimized and publicly shamed.

His need to protect Blythe, now more than ever, diminished everything else.

"We need handkerchiefs." Brette thrust her dainty chin upward and extended her hand. "Now, if you please."

Several ladies and gentlemen obliged, including Hawksworth.

"Let's allow Miss Culpepper and her family some privacy, shall we?" Lady Wimpleton took charge and ushered the curious gawkers from the library. "We've supper to eat, and the musicians continue to play. Go along now. I shall keep you apprised of the situation, but Cook will have my skin if her preparations have been in vain. A footman will watch for the physician and deliver him here straightaway." Her gaze scooted to Phillips, and scorn twitched her lips. "I shall send a servant with linens, though I'm sure the carpet is beyond redemption."

With a sharp-eyed, telling glance at her husband, she followed their guests from the room.

Lord Leventhorpe looked askance at Phillips, making no effort to assist him. "Ravensdale, have you any idea what has transpired?"

Ravensdale nodded curtly as he veered his attention to the women. "I've a suspicion, but would prefer not to discuss it now."

"Just so. My thoughts as well. My support is yours, of course, in whatever manner you should need it." Wimpleton's attention fell upon the pillar lying beside a bookshelf. "I see you made good use of that wretched thing at last."

Tristan didn't dare look at where Hawksworth and Drake had dragged Phillips. If Blythe's blow hadn't knocked the bastard off his feet, Tristan would have leveled him.

He closed his eyes and clamped his teeth until they ached.

Rustling behind him drew his attention. Prodding with one foot, Whitehouse nudged Phillips in the side, none too gently. "Wake up, you piece of ..." He slung a shielded glance at the women hunkered around Blythe. "Odious lump of horse excrement."

Blaike raked Phillips with an infuriated glare. "That's much too polite a description for the likes of him. A barnful of ripe, maggoty cow manure is less offensive."

"Is there water to be had? Or spirits? I imagine a splash or two ought to revive this rabble." Whitehouse examined the room before poking Phillips harder. "What about smelling salts or a vinaigrette?"

The Culpeppers shook their blonde heads, and Brette said, "We don't faint, and I don't recall a single instance where we've needed salts.

How badly had Blythe speared Phillips? Brilliant on her part. She had to have been terrified. Another rush of wrath heated his blood. The dastard would use his injury as an excuse to avoid the duel, and Tristan had no intention of allowing Phillips to escape the repercussions of his actions this time.

Phillips cracked an eye open and weakly shoved at the tormenting shoe. "Leave off trying to crack my ribs, you bloo—"

"Stubble it." Whitehouse jabbed Phillips's side once more. "There are ladies present."

"Not all present are worthy of the title, I can assure you." Groaning, Phillips crawled to his knees, one had clasping his crimson-stained lower abdomen. Curling his lower lip, he glowered and jerked his chin in Blythe's direction. "That one's a teasing wh—"

Whitehouse planted his foot on Phillips's chest, sending him flying onto his back.

"Damn you, Whitehouse." Phillips struggled into a sitting position, white-lipped and shaking.

Tristan was upon him in three strides. He hauled Phillips to his feet, and tugged him within an inch of his nose, snarling into the sod's frightened face. "That's my betrothed you're maligning."

Phillips blanched and sputtered, his frantic gaze circling the room. "I ... I ... didn't know."

"What's he talking about, Heath?" Confusion riddled Lady Ravensdale's harried whisper.

A cunning edge replaced Phillips's unease. "It seems no one did. How very peculiar."

"You accosted and compromised the woman I've pledged to marry." Tristan had to swiftly establish his right to demand satisfaction, even if he lied like Zeus in the process. He'd worry about Blythe's reaction later. If she found marriage to him abhorrent, he would at least have protected her from dishonor by giving her his name and a marchioness title. He'd allow her to live where she chose and provide for her the rest of her days. Hell, he'd grant her a divorce, though they were harder to come by than King Solomon's treasures.

"Blythe's to marry Lord Leventhorpe?" one of the twins said. Impossible to tell which with his back to the women. "When did that occur? Why didn't anyone tell us?"

"I thought Mr. Burlington held her affections." The other twin?

Bad enough they looked exactly alike, but identical voices too?

"A ruse, perhaps?" Brette hit the mark closer than Tristan liked.

Did she suspect he spoke out of turn?

"Or perhaps, there's no betrothal at all. I hadn't heard a word of it. Why would an affianced woman agree to meet me privately?" Phillips stood a mite straighter, confident in his smug arrogance.

Perchance Blythe had merely nicked him, more's the pity.

Tristan shook him, and Phillips winced, pressing his other hand to his groin.

"Surely she understood what such a clandestine arrangement with me entailed, and she chose ruin regardless."

The men's outraged exclamations mixed with the women's shocked gasps.

"Considering I have you in my grasp, you're an utter beef-wit to continue to besmirch her honor." Giving Phillips a mocking slap, Tristan permitted himself a gratified smirk and stepped away. "I demand satisfaction. Name your second."

"Leventhorpe, no. That's my place." Ravensdale's vehement protest was muffled by a ruckus in the corridor and Lady Ravensdale's quickly stifled cry of protest.

The door exploded open, banging into the shelving beside it and sending several volumes tumbling to the floor. Everyone's attention hurtled to entrance.

Miss Sanford plowed into the library, followed closely by her thin, stern-faced elderly uncle, the Earl of Marfontaine. She rapidly scanned the room, her focus alighting upon Blythe. "I told you, Uncle Rupert, she was in here with Mr. Phillips." Miss Sanford pointed a shaking finger at Blythe. "After rejecting his proposal, she clobbered poor Mr. Burlington and, wanting to be alone with Mr. Phillips, demanded I leave."

What was she about? Dragging her uncle in to witness Blythe's disgrace? Was this another attempt to discredit Blythe? Pathetic and contemptible.

"As I explained earlier, and as Miss Sanford has this instant confirmed, Miss Culpepper was more than willing to accept my advances." Keeping his distance from Tristan, and clutching his stomach, Phillips, pale and sweating, edged toward the door. "I tried to warn Burlington of her duplicity, but the man wouldn't listen."

"Stay right where you are, Phillips." Ravensdale shut the door in the face of goggle-eyed, eavesdroppers, preventing Phillips's escape.

No doubt several guests also stood beyond the drawn drapes listening at the shattered French window. The pillar's convenient location had enabled Tristan to hastily break in. Otherwise ...

Sure enough, glass crunched and someone hurriedly shushed another lurker. Whitehouse tramped to the drapes and, notorious for his devilish glowers, stuck his dark head between the folds. The noise of scurrying footsteps and muted voices filtered through the heavy fabric.

"And stay away." Whitehouse took a position at the mangled window, acting as a deterrent if others dared to venture near enough to listen.

It didn't matter. The gossipmongers wouldn't stop talking about tonight for a decade.

A partially disrobed woman, bleeding from her temple, found alone in a library with a man skewered in the gut, and both lying upon the floor unconscious provided tattle simply too delicious not to bandy about. And Phillips's reputation as despoiler of innocents was the Devonshire cream atop the gossip's cocoa.

Triston shut his mind against the names people would be calling Blythe else he would finish Phillips now.

"I'll be going then." Phillips unsteadily sidled closer to the door.

"You've been challenged to an affair of honor. And if my ward had been 'more than' willing, as you vulgarly claim, pray tell me why she's unconscious and you've been stuck with a poker? I don't believe you for an instant." Ravensdale crossed his arms and slid Tristan a sideways glance. "You will name your second before leaving, or I shall demand satisfaction as well."

"I tell you, no duel is necessary." Phillips waved a hand in an exaggerated gesture. "I pardon Leventhorpe for striking me. I understand he's in a dudgeon. There's no need for such extremes over a woman. She's not even highborn."

Every Culpepper's gaze pelted him with blue-violet darts.

Maybe Tristan would save them a great deal of trouble and run Phillips through with the poker now. He searched the room. Where had the tool gotten to?

Hawksworth, ankles crossed and one hip resting against the black walnut, leather-topped desk, rested one hand upon the brass length, a knowing gleam in his eye.

Knows me too hell-fired well.

"Did you hear me? I pardon you for striking me." Perspiration beaded Phillips's forehead and upper lip.

Caused by pain from his injury? More likely a coward's fear of looking down a pistol barrel.

"How magnanimous of you. I assuredly don't pardon you, especially since I can think of nothing more worthy of defending than the virtue of the woman who shall soon be my wife."

By God. I mean it too. I shall willingly forfeit my life for Blythe's honor.

Tristan must marry her before the duel, to assure she was provided for if Phillips proved lucky.

A rivulet of sweat trickled from Phillips's temple to his jaw. Fear, most assuredly. "Well, as for Miss Culpepper's injury, we became too rough in our play. I shall make my apologies when she is recovered."

"That's outside enough! I shan't permit another lascivious word spoken in the presence of my sister and cousins." Lady Ravensdale angled her chin proudly and decapitated Phillips with her affronted gaze. "Gentlemen do not discuss such uncouth matters in the presence of innocent young ladies."

"But Miss Sanford just proved I spoke the truth." Phillips sounded quite desperate. Men that preyed upon women and those weaker than themselves frequently revealed themselves limp-spined cravens when faced with equals or someone stronger.

Phillips cowered before Tristan's more formidable figure.

"Balderdash and poppycock. My lying niece didn't validate your sorry tale, and she is not without fault in this." Marfontaine gave her a severe look. "Rosemary, I heard you conspiring with your mother."

He seized her elbow when she shook her head and opened her mouth to protest.

"Be quiet, chit. It took me threatening to cut your Mother off to finally pry the truth from her. As it is, she'll not get a groat for the next month." He sketched a brief bow to the Culpepper misses, his wiry fingers clamped Miss Sanford's arm. "Permit me to introduce myself. The Earl of Marfontaine. I humbly apologize for my niece's involvement in this bumblebroth. Rest assured, she will be dealt with severely."

"Uncle ..." She twisted her arm, trying to break free. "You don't understand."

"Enough." He gave her a slight shake. "I've already spoken to Lord Bexley. You will be married by special license the day after tomorrow."

"No. No! I'm sorry." Weeping noisily, she clawed at his hand. "Please, Uncle Rupert. Mr. Phillips forced me to help him. He threatened me, said he'd beat and despoil me or worse as he had dozens of other women if I didn't. If I helped him, and kept quiet about my involvement, he promised he'd make sure Lord Leventhorpe was made to marry me. He gave me his word."

The word of a scheming cur—worthless.

Miss Sanford had outed Phillips, made him an enemy, and Tristan almost felt a jot of sympathy for her. Good thing he intended to meet Phillips in two days' time, or he feared what might happen to her. Phillips possessed a violent, vengeful streak.

"Tell them, Mr. Phillips," she wailed. "You bragged about your conquests. Said you had at least a dozen by-blows."

More offended gasps and ire-laden noises escaped those present.

The wintry stare Phillips skewered Miss Sanford with caused Tristan's heart to trip. There was the ruthless villain Phillips took such pains to conceal. Evil shadowed his eyes before he veiled his hatred.

"That's utterly despicable." Lady Ravensdale presented her back, giving him the cut as Blythe stirred and put a hand to the side of her head.

Swinging to Tristan, Miss Sanford extended her free hand, fat tears leaving dual paths down her pale cheeks. "Please. I love you. I'll do anything. Don't let him make me marry that odious old man. He farts and belches constantly." She hiccupped and swiped at her wet face. "And he smells of cabbage and tobacco."

"You'll marry him, or I'll ship you off to a convent in France or Spain." Marfontaine's mouth bent a fraction, and he chuckled, the rasping drier than straw in August. "You like your luxuries far too much

279

for that stark way of life, my dear."

"Miss Sanford, as I've tried to explain to you numerous times, I have never entertained any notion of courting or marrying you." Tristan cut Blythe a rapid glance.

She appeared to be rousing. Eyes open, she blinked in confusion.

"It's because of her, isn't it?" Thrusting her arm at Blythe, Miss Sanford laughed, a high-pitched cackle tinged with desperation or madness. "She's completely compromised. No one will have her now."

"I shall." Tristan's attention remained on Blythe.

Her unfocused eyes widened slightly, and her lips parted.

Marfontaine propelled Miss Sanford to the door. "Gel, if you don't leave off, I'll commit you to Bedlam instead of foisting you on poor Bexley. Might be better for him in any event. He'll likely cock up his toes within a year to escape your shrewish tongue."

Phillips waited until Marfontaine opened the door. "By-the-by, Miss Sanford ..."

She flung him a belligerent scowl, snapping, "What?"

A purely evil smile arced his mouth. "Leventhorpe claims he and Miss Culpepper are trothed."

Phillips's gleeful announcement had the desired effect.

Miss Sanford collapsed into Marfontaine's arms, sobbing.

"But why would Lord Leventhorpe say he and Blythe are to be married if they aren't?" Brette addressed the question to no one in particular.

"We are."

The faint response had every eye in the room ricocheting to Blythe propped against Lady Ravensdale.

It can be plainly confessed of the old and
young, he wise and the ignorant,and the rich and the
poor, that despite their best schemes, circumstances far
more often govern mankind, than man controls circumstances.
~*Dignity and Decorum—The Genteel Lady's Guide to Practical Living*

"Lord Leventhorpe waits in the drawing room." Brooke tentatively touched Blythe's arm as she gazed out her upper story bedroom window. "You must see him. There's much to discuss and put to right about last night."

"Yes. I know." Blythe let the lace panel fall into place as she swiveled and smiled at Brooke. "Don't look pensive. Everything will work out." *How, I have no idea.* "The situation isn't a complete catastrophe." *Pretty dashed close, however.*

Groggy and muddled, Blythe had believed the scene in the Wimpletons' library part of a wretched dream when she'd agreed to the betrothal. His desperation, or perhaps the emotion in the depths of his vivid blue gaze had been pleading. Nevertheless, it had silently called to her across the distance, drawing the response from her before she'd considered the consequences.

Once she'd regained her wits, there'd been plenty of time to consider the magnitude, and her foolish impulse, though propelled by compassion and a befuddled state of mind, had further complicated the impossible situation.

Uttering those two little, yet significant words, "We are," had been immensely satisfying. Miss Sanford's reaction to Blythe's verbal blow, even more so. Shame pricked her conscience. Deliberate unkindness wasn't a trait she normally exhibited.

What had possessed Tristan to declare they were betrothed?

Compassion? Pity?

She dared not hope he felt something more.

"I won't have you miserable or forced into a marriage." Brooke wrapped an arm around Blythe's waist. "Heath has spoken to Leventhorpe. He's sincere about his offer, and I suspect he cares for you. Leventhorpe isn't the scoundrel I'd first judged him to be." Her mouth hitched to one side. "Though he is quite the most aloof and unreadable man I've met."

"Not at all. That's a well-rehearsed protective front. Tristan is sensitive beneath his stern mask." Blythe scrunched her brow while fingering the silky turquoise tassel dangling from the curtain tie-back and observing a pair of mourning doves that had swooped onto an elder's branch, the lone tree in the tiny side garden. "I think he's been wounded, terribly hurt, somehow."

What had happened to create such a lasting scar and the hardened barrier he kept securely around himself?

An extended silence met her oral musing. She pried her attention away from the cuddling grayish-brown birds to find Brooke staring at her, head canted to the side and a speculative spark in her dark-lashed eyes.

"What's that look for?" After running her fingers through the silky strands one last time, Blythe dropped the tassel.

"You defended him and called him Tristan." A grin threatening, Brooke adopted a maternal mien instead. She twirled a curl near her ear. "Might I ask how long that has been going on?"

"An inadvertent slip of the tongue, I assure you. But if he's to be my husband, I suppose I'd better become accustomed to it." Unless Blythe could convince him to cry off. Not likely, any more than he'd forgo that preposterous duel. The scandal wouldn't just tarnish her. The disgrace would affect the rest of the family, too, and possibly ruin Brette and the twins' chances of a decent match.

Plain ludicrous how Society believed a marriage license and murmured vows—often insincere and broken within days of their utterance—remedied the slightest hint of ruin.

"Blythe ...?" Uncertainty colored Brooke's voice. She released a hefty breath. "Mr. Burlington ...? Deuced awkward, this," she muttered beneath her breath. "What are your feelings regarding him?"

"I plopped a Grecian urn upon his conceited head last night. What's that tell you?" Twisting her mouth into a droll semblance of a smile, Blythe patted Brooke's shoulder. "Never fear. Any iota of girlish attraction I naively harbored for him vanished the instant he suggested I become his mistress."

Brooke's mouth hung slack. "He didn't."

Blythe raised a brow. "He did. After politely explaining why he couldn't marry a poor commoner."

Brooke cradled her stomach. "Oh, I'm quite furious, and that cannot be good for the babe. I hope you cracked his skull, the devious churl."

"I'm sure he's sporting a nasty, well-deserved headache." Blythe gathered a frilly pillow from the floor, and after tossing it onto the bed piled with several others, she rubbed an eyebrow. "And his heiress is welcome to him, although I feel sorry for the woman."

"As do I." Sighing, Brooke examined Blythe's gash. "How's your head today? Doctor Barclay said you weren't concussed, thank goodness."

"It's fine. Just a mite tender." Tristan meant to see this farce through, did he? A tiny part of her—truth to tell, a huge, soft, womanly chunk deep inside—thrilled that he'd defended her honor and risked censure by fabricating their betrothal. Still, he mustn't risk his life in an affair of honor.

Besides, not for an instant did she believe Phillips would fight fairly. If something happened to Tristan, she'd never be able to forgive herself. Surely gentlemen had a proviso for calling a duel off?

"How badly did I wound *him*?" Speaking Phillips's name was akin to gobbling fresh cow dung. She pressed two fingers to her temple where her head ached worse than she'd let on. The small cut, barely an inch long, was centered upon the walnut-sized, purplish lump near her temple.

"I'm not sure. Last night I didn't think his injury serious, though I may have misjudged." Straightening the pillows upon Blythe's four-poster bed, Brooke frowned then lifted a shoulder. "Lieutenant Drake paid him a call this morning to inquire who Mr. Phillips had named as his second. The Lieutenant met the physician leaving, and he claimed Mr. Phillips's wound was quite severe, that damage had been done internally. The gash has become putrid, and he battles a fever."

"I don't suppose the poker was altogether clean." God forgive her for the satisfaction that brought her.

"God willing, he'll die and the world will be spared his odious presence. And Lord Leventhorpe will be released from the duel." Brooke punched a lace-edged satin pillow. In anger or to fluff it? "I know that's horrid of me, but at this moment, I don't have a charitable thought in me."

"I might be responsible for his death then. I didn't intend to stab him." Blythe shuddered and tucked her chin to her chest. "But he deserved it, and yet I feel guilty. All I could think of was protecting myself. He meant to ravish me."

Brooke arranged the last pillow atop the cheerful green and turquoise counterpane before flying to embrace Blythe. "Stuff and nonsense. He is an evil man. Heath has told me of his reputation and that he's suspected of killing a ... a woman of ill-repute."

"My God. He is vile." Blythe may have done London and women a service if Phillips expired.

Tears glistened in Brooke's eyes, and she took Blythe's face between both hands. "You did what you had to. He isn't worthy of your sympathy. He meant to force you, and during a ball, at that. On your birthday. The man's daft as a Bedlam patient if he truly believed he'd succeed without severe consequences."

"Do you think he coerced Miss Sanford?" The iota of pity Blythe mustered was for gouty Lord Bexley. He'd seemed pleasant enough on the one occasion she'd met him, reeking of food and another other odd, medicinal odor.

"Perhaps, but she jumped at the opportunity to compromise you. A decent woman, frightened or not, would have promptly reported Phillips's suggestion. Remember, young women of quality are constantly chaperoned. Therefore, the likelihood of him carrying out his threat was minimal, as she knew that full well. I'm convinced that's why she helped him get you alone. I'd not waste your compassion on her."

"Miss Sanford spent a great deal of time with him unchaperoned. Perhaps her mother hoped to snare Phillips if Tristan avoided Miss Sanford's tentacles." Blythe pressed two fingers to her forehead. "Likely her mother's where she learned her despicable behavior."

A gentle rap upon the door preceded Brette's entrance.

"Yes, dearest?" Brooke clasped Blythe's hand.

"I've been sent to fetch you. The men grow restless. They're driving me near to shrieking with their pacing and babbling about the need for a special license in between making rather vile suggestions regarding Mr. Phillips. Each of which I agree with wholeheartedly." She raised her pert nose skyward. "I may have made a few fairly creative notions myself, one of which entailed him galloping Rotten Row atop a nail-laden saddle. Without pantaloons."

Blythe offered a wobbly smile and squared her shoulders. "Let's be about it then. From one blaze into another."

A few short minutes later, *too short*, she stood outside the study door. "Am I to speak with Lord Leventhorpe alone?"

Brooke grasped the handle. "I think that best, don't you?"

"Yes. This conversation will be awkward enough without an audience." She preceded Brooke into the comfortable study decorated in beige and sage green. Unlike the Wimpleton's darkly paneled room, Heath preferred an airier atmosphere. Yesterday, she'd trimmed the ladder ferns in their wicker stand placed before the simple linen window panels.

Freddy and the men rose at their entrance, and Heath indicated a striped armchair in verdant shades adjacent to Tristan's.

Blythe met Tristan's unreadable gaze for a fleeting moment as she made her way to the armchair, and her stomach flopped.

The planes of his face taut, he resumed his seat. Not precisely an exuberant groom.

"Do either of you require anything?" Brooke turned from the door, Heath at her side. She patted her hip. "Freddy. Come."

The corgi dutifully waddled to her, his tongue lolling and stubby tail wagging.

Given the empty brandy glass near Tristan, and the haggard lines bracketing his mouth and pleating the corners of his eyes, he could use a strong cup of coffee.

"I would dearly love a cup of my herbal tea. You know the mixture I use for soothing headaches? Would you mind terribly brewing a pot for me? The herbs are in a marked tin in the larder." Blythe managed a smile for Tristan. "Would you like coffee? We have a lovely Turkish blend."

"Yes. That would be most welcome." His reply wasn't exactly terse, yet neither was it warm. Grayish-purple half-moon shadows ringing his eyes attested to a sleep-deprived night.

"I shall give you fifteen minutes alone before I have the tea and coffee brought in." After giving Blythe an encouraging smile that didn't diminish the apprehension shining in Brooke's eyes, she swept from the room.

"I'll return within a half hour to discuss the settlement terms with you both." Heath delivered a genuinely warm smile. "I confess to being delighted that you are to marry, though, I would have bet high odds against anything of the sort when you first met."

He closed the door softly behind him, and for several interminable moments, the room remained silent.

What was Tristan thinking? Did he regret his impulsive gesture?

"You are well, Blythe?" The gentleness of his inquiry propelled her gaze to his. Compassion and something more intense emanated from his beautiful eyes.

"Yes. Other than a slight headache, I haven't suffered ill effects." Except a restless night and a reputation tainted beyond redemption. A room full of the *ton's* denizens had seen her partially clothed. It mattered not that Phillips hadn't been successful in despoiling her.

Tristan folded his hands in his lap then promptly unclasped them and laid his palms upon his black clad thighs. "You recall what happened, then?"

"If that's your way of asking if I remember agreeing that we are to be married, yes. I remember." Dragging in a great breath, Blythe jumped to her feet. She clasped her hands before her. "I feel I must tell you that I won't hold you to your offer. I know you said it to protect me in a perfectly ghastly situation."

Tristan stood as well, forcing her to crane her neck to meet his eyes. "Why were you in the library alone with him?"

"I ..." She spun away, not wanting to think about what had happened, how close she'd come to being ravished. Her knees grew shaky and her chest tightened with remembered fear as a shiver wracked her. She rubbed the raised flesh along her bare arms. "I was trying to find you."

"In the library? Why would you think to search for me there and not the ballroom or card room?"

The sunny rays filtering through the window enticed her, and she sought their tepid warmth. "I overheard Miss Sanford and her mother scheming last night and wanted to warn you of their intent to entrap you. When I entered the library, Phillips restrained me while Miss Sanford locked the door."

A robin swooped to the ground below the elder, and after giving her an inquisitive look, took to searching for insects.

"You meant to protect me? What did they plot?"

She nodded, shortly. "That you'd be found in a compromising

situation with Miss Sanford at the ball and thus be forced to marry her."

He laughed, a warm, soothing rumble, filling the room and surprising her with his genuine amusement.

"You aren't angry?" She frowned, canting her head. "I should think you'd be furious."

With measured steps, he approached her, a mysterious bend to his mouth.

She dropped her gaze to the floor, afraid he'd see her love for him shining in her eyes.

"Ah, Fate had another plan, and Miss Sanford's duplicitous actions compelled me to claim you as mine." He cupped her shoulders, his large hands heavy, yet comforting. "Something I've yearned to do for weeks, though I doubted I would ever have the right."

Blythe jerked her head up and squinted. Had she mistaken his meaning? "What exactly are you saying?"

"I'm saying that I want to marry you and no other." Tristan drew her, unresisting, into his embrace. He chuckled again as she gaped, unblinking, at him. He ran his thumb along her lower lip and slanted his head at the window. "You had better close your mouth before yonder bird thinks to perch upon its lusciousness."

Her focus slid to his lips, and she pursed hers. Did she do that intentionally, to torment him?

"You've not given any indication you considered me anything other than a casual friend." Leaning into his arms, Blythe searched his face, emotions dancing across hers. "At one time, you couldn't abide me."

He firmed his embrace, edging closer until his thighs brushed her skirt, and he could feel her trembling legs. Resting his cheek against her unmarred temple, he whispered into the sweet fragrance of her hair, "You vexed the hellfire out of me, causing more intense feelings than I'd ever had for a woman. I didn't understand them for what they were."

Her expression softened, drawing him into the depths of her sapphire eyes, trapping him in their guileless, mysterious spheres. "You are the most complex man. After you kissed me, I believed you'd decided you weren't romantically inclined toward me."

"Utter gibberish." He kissed her hairline before feathering kisses down her cheek and the length of her jaw, lingering at the provocative corner of her mouth. "I never had to battle attraction so hard in my life."

Her sooty-tipped lashes fluttered closed, and she breathed out a sigh.

Needing no further invitation, he claimed her mouth, urging her lips apart with the tip of his tongue, delving into the sweetness of her mouth.

Blythe stood on her toes and entwined her arms about his neck. Catching onto the art of kissing with alacrity, she mimicked his actions. Their tongues jousted in a timeless melody of passion, until his groin swelled uncomfortably, and they both panted for breath.

Tristan drew away first.

Tupping his closest friend's ward in the study wasn't done. Well, not before exchanging vows, in any event. Afterward ... He eyed the armchair, and an unexpected, most unwelcome flash of discomfort assailed him. Did he tell Blythe of his childhood humiliation?

No. Not now.

After they consummated their marriage, and he'd introduced her to the blissful aspects of physical joining, he might be ready to share the tale with her.

Or perhaps he never would.

That ugliness was in the past. She was his future.

Tucking her to him, he murmured into her hair. "I suppose I ought to go down upon a knee and propose formally, only I'm reluctant to release you."

Blythe chuckled against his chest, her slender arms encircling his waist. "I rather think a proposal while being held in your arms is much more satisfying and romantic."

"Blythe Culpepper, will you honor me by consenting to become my wife?" He kissed her ear, and she giggled.

"What?" She nudged his ribs. "No dramatic protestations of undying love or how I've made you the happiest man on earth?"

He drew away a fraction, drinking in her flushed features. "If that makes you happy and is what you want, I shall be delighted to do both."

"Oh. Pooh. I don't need pretty speeches. A man's actions show his affection and character much more clearly than mere words, and last night you risked everything to protect me." The look she gave him sent his pulse sprinting, and his manhood gave an eager twitch.

Whoa, boy. Patience.

"Am I to assume your answer is yes?" Tristan framed her jaw with his forefinger and thumb, caressing the silky flesh of her jaw. "I am ecstatic."

"Yes. I'll marry you." She shook her head, the silvery curls glinting halo-like in the sunlight. "I certainly never dreamed I'd be eagerly anticipating wedding the stern, rigid man I met at Esherton Green."

"Eagerly?" He waggled his eyebrows wickedly.

She gave him a coy wink. "Indeed. Most eagerly."

"Excellent. I've already purchased the special license. The ceremony will need to take place tomorrow. I know that's rushing things a jot—"

Her fair brows furrowed, and she stepped from his embrace, giving him a tight, closed-lipped smile. "I'd hoped for more time. I realize the scandal of last night prohibits a lengthy betrothal, but a week or two to prepare for a wedding—"

"I'm afraid that's impossible." He rubbed his nape. Blast, he hadn't wanted to discuss the duel on the fringes of what *was* possibly the happiest moment of his life. "The duel takes place the day after tomorrow, and we must wed first, because if I'm injured or killed—"

Blythe gasped, and balled her fists. "You mean to go through with the challenge? The day after we wed?"

He hadn't expected Blythe to be thrilled about the notion. Given the furious glint in her eye, she wouldn't concede easily. In fact, he hadn't intended to tell her about the duel until after the deed was done. That had seemed bloody brilliant when he'd first contemplated it. If Phillips bested him, she'd be married and widowed in under twenty-four hours, and she needed to know that Tristan had legally provided for her.

"You cannot meet that swine." Her chest rose and fell rapidly with her agitation. "He's a cur and a cheat. He'll not fight nobly, and you must know that to be true."

"It's a matter of my honor, Blythe." Mere moments ago, happiness and something akin to adoration had shone in her eyes. Betrayal shadowed her exquisite features now. He touched her arm. "A man is nothing if he does not keep his word. My honor is paramount to me."

Pursing her pretty mouth, she brushed a curl from her forehead.

"According to Brooke, Phillips is gravely ill from the wound I inflicted. He won't be able to meet you. I'm surprised you didn't know that."

He did, yet didn't believe a word. Phillips was a bloody coward and would use any excuse to waylay the inevitable confrontation. In fact, at Tristan's behest, Drake and Whitehouse watched Phillips's residence, lest he try to sneak away. Again.

"I shall wait until he is recovered then. However, meet him I shall." Phillips couldn't be permitted to live and despoil more innocents. And if Miss Sanford had the right of it, he might be guilty of more appalling crimes. "He's escaped justice far too many times. He must be held accountable."

She closed her eyes, her lips trembling. Her lashes slowly lifted, and his heart turned to stone at the resignation and defeat in her eyes. "Then I regret, my lord, that I must decline your offer of marriage. I'll not be married and widowed within a day's time."

"Be sensible. Your reputation is in tatters. I offer you my name and security." He reached for her, and she fled behind the desk.

Shrugging, she placed the porcelain inkwell upon its matching tray. "I hadn't intended to marry well. I'll retire to the country."

"Blythe ..."

Three sharp raps echoed outside the door before it swung open. Lady Ravensdale, Raven, and a footman bearing a laden tray stood there smiling expectantly.

The moment they cleared the entrance, Blythe bolted for the exit.

"Blythe, wait, please." Tristan's long strides ate the distance across the leaf-patterned Axminster carpet.

Lady Ravensdale swung her confused gaze between them. "Is something amiss?"

Blythe reached her, and neck bent, shook her head. "No. I simply have no desire to be widowed the day after I marry. So, I've refused Lord Leventhorpe's offer of marriage."

"You have? Truly?" Ravensdale's confounded expression would have earned a chuckle and likely a taunt or two had the circumstances been different.

"Oh, Blythe." Lady Ravensdale crestfallen countenance revealed her devastation.

Without marriage, Blythe was utterly ruined.

"I'm sorry. Please forgive me. I know what this means." She offered a tremulous smile. "I shall pack at once.

Folly whispers marriage is a scheme for contentment,
but in truth, marriage is strenuous work.
~Dignity and Decorum—The Genteel Lady's Guide to Practical Living

13

"There, that's the last of them. I feel quite wicked owning this much clothing." Early the next morning, Blythe placed the last of her unmentionables in her trunk.

Brooke promised to send the chest along later. For the journey home, Blythe would make do with a valise. Wisdom decreed she take a satchel in the event of unforeseen circumstances, although the trip to Culpepper Park could be achieved in a day.

The new house was habitable according to Brooke, though not fit for entertaining. That suited Blythe perfectly. Months might pass before she'd be in the mood for company.

Meg, Blythe's abigail since arriving in London, agreed to journey with her, though Meg had no desire to remain in the countryside and would promptly return to London. No matter. Blythe had seen to her toilette for years. She didn't require a maid.

"Are you positive you won't reconsider?" Blaike sniffled into her handkerchief.

This separation would be the first for the sisters.

Blaire tortured her square scrap of cloth, twisting and tormenting its damp length repeatedly. "This whole affair is wretchedly unjust. I don't believe I care for London after all. Such supercilious people. Why, you are the victim. How dare they judge you?"

"You should at least stay at Heath's estate. There's no staff or furnishings at Culpepper Park." Brette passed Blythe a pair of slippers. "I'll allow, I'm quite miffed that you are to go alone."

Stay in a mausoleum of a manor—Heath's unflattering description—and with strangers for staff? Dreadful, by any measure. Returning to the dairy's familiar security and comfort held far more appeal.

"I understand, Brette, but we've discussed this already." A dozen times or more. "It's what I want, and besides, our old furniture was moved to the new house." Considerable effort went into her forced, cheerful smile. "I shall be fine."

"Hmph." A vulgar noise escaped Brette.

Blythe carefully tucked the embroidered slippers underneath a gown. She'd likely never wear either at Culpepper Park. The trunk overflowed with beautiful clothing and fallals, most unsuitable for a country gentlewoman. Heath insisted she take her new wardrobe, however.

"Why shouldn't everyone leave then?" Legs dangling over her chair's arm, Blaike gesticulated into the air.

"I'm the one unacceptable to Society. If I leave immediately, we hope to lessen the shadow cast over the rest of you. If everyone departs hastily, that implies you are guilty as well, and you are not. I won't have you disparaged on my account. For respectability's sake, I shall retain one or two servants from the village, so put that fear aside."

"I thought, perhaps, you weren't averse to Lord Leventhorpe. You'd spent a considerable amount of time in his company these past weeks, and that day at Gunter's, he looked like a man besotted." Blaike sent Blaire a silent message and threw her kerchief atop the night table.

Ah, the twins had noticed the tense exchange between Blythe and Tristan that day.

"He did indeed." Scarcely pausing, Blaike launched another protest. "Won't you reconsider? Heath says his lordship is a dab hand at pistols. You should trust him."

Trust Heath or Tristan?

She did trust them both. Phillips, however, garnered the same confidence as Lucifer.

"Girls, I'm to depart within the hour. What's done is done. I've refused Lord Leventhorpe, and that is the end of it. He was most gallant to claim a false betrothal and offer to wed me to preserve my status. I do harbor a fanciful hope that since I cried off, he won't feel the need to follow through with that ridiculous duel." After all, he couldn't claim her as his affianced, and consequently the reason for his challenge no longer existed. Then again, men were so blasted difficult and prideful, he might pursue the idiocy.

Blythe had seen one way to offer Tristan a reprieve from the duel and save face as well as preserve his honor. If only he would put aside his confounded stubbornness and seize the opportunity.

God, please, let him.

If he didn't, she would pray Phillips wouldn't recover, and what manner of foulness did that make her? Wishing for a man's death?

A pout upon her lips, Brette wandered to the window. Parting the lace, she eyed the sky. "The weather has taken a sour turn. Perchance you should delay your departure. Those clouds look as ugly as the ones that brought that fierce storm the day Heath arrived at Esherton Green."

"Looking like a bedraggled puppy." Blaire grinned for the first time today.

Blaike snickered. "A cross mutt too."

"He could have caught a nasty chill." Glancing behind her, Brette frowned, her worried gaze shifting from the full trunk to Blythe. "I wish you'd wait until this bluster passes. It makes me uneasy to have you traveling in foul weather."

"In England, a cloudy sky is hardly unusual, and neither are summer rains. The road is quite passable, even after a good shower. I'm not concerned." Bless Brette's heart, she simply sought a means to persuade Blythe to stay.

For the girls' sake, she couldn't. The sooner she put distance between herself and them, the better. *Le beau monde* considered her soiled goods, and much like a spoiled piece of fruit spread rot to others nearby, her presence tainted the rest of her family. Besides, she possessed no desire to endure the speculation regarding her pathetically short-lived betrothal.

Oddly, Burlington's treachery bothered her little. She was more peeved at herself for being a ninny and judging a man by his outward appearance. It chaffed to admit she'd been shallow as a puddle.

After she'd agreed to wed Tristan, crying off pierced like a double-edged blade—deep, and lethal. Her heart had nearly fragmented when she'd told Tristan she wouldn't marry him. But if it meant his life might be spared ... She shrugged mentally and offered a conciliatory smile to the distraught girls. "Sometimes we must make sacrifices so those we love won't suffer."

"Hmph." Flopping against her chair and kicking her feet in the air, Blaike shook her head. "And sometimes, those who love you don't give a cow's stinky behind what others think."

"I must go." London held no appeal for Blythe any longer, and the sooner she departed, the sooner she could nurse her mangled heart.

Six hours later, swathed in her sensible wool traveling cloak, Blythe warmed her gloved hands before a sooty stone fireplace in The Coach and Arms common room. Damp to her marrow, she flexed her jaw to still her chattering teeth. God's bones, she was half frozen. The sputtering fire valiantly sent a plume of orange sparks skyward, failing to thaw her stiff fingers and toes.

With its bare-beamed ceiling and darkish interior, the modest inn smelled of stale ale and fresh bread. More importantly, it provided a haven from the unremitting torrents.

London's earlier blanket of pewter clouds had transformed into a churning, black tempest complete with lashing rain, bursts of lightning, and deafening thunder. They'd barely traveled ten torturous miles the last three hours; the roads had become impossibly mucky and impassable. The tenacious driver and team had pressed onward as far as they could. With the wrathful charcoal sky showing no signs of easing its tantrum, and dusk flirting across the horizon, Blythe bid him stop at the next lodgings.

Since leaving London's outskirts, Meg had sighed and complained incessantly, and by the time the carriage squished and slid to a halt in the inn's muddy courtyard, Blythe couldn't wait to send the pampered maid to the kitchen to make tea and inquire about a hot meal.

Evidently, the weather had caught several other travelers unawares as well. Besides Blythe, a young couple, who appeared to be newlywed, a kind-faced cleric, a trio of motley soldiers, and a couple of burly, tartan-clad Scots occupied the humble taproom. A formidable matron attired in crackling black bombazine, and who loudly ordered her mousy companion about, had also been present when Blythe arrived.

Every chamber was taken, excluding a miniscule, fireplace-less attic room, more closet than bedchamber, with scarcely enough space for a narrow cot, an uneven nightstand, and rickety chair.

From the dust-covered cobwebs gracing two corners, spiders had been the lone inhabitants for a long while. Grateful for a bed, Blythe didn't quibble at the exorbitant price the flustered innkeeper demanded. She hadn't slept last night, and today, the pounding winds hammering the carriage, as well as Meg's grumbling mile after miserable mile, had prevented any rest in the carriage.

What else was Blythe to do?

Sleep near the hearth or in a corner of the common room as the soldiers and Scots intended, or curl onto the carriage seat as her driver had volunteered to do?

Her head, bum, and back ached, and tears threatened constantly. Better the inadequate cupboard where she could cry in privacy then a public room where her virtue might be jeopardized.

Turning her profile to the soldiers' intent scrutiny, Blythe prayed her chamber boasted a sturdy lock or a strong bolt. Propping the chair beneath the handle might provide added protection. She bent her lips a fraction. Knitting needles were stronger than the chair's spindly legs.

Meg had fussed about having to sleep upon a pallet in the kitchen. Blythe ignored her carping and pointedly didn't invite the servant to share her tiny room. After an eternity in the carriage with the peckish servant, Blythe's head ached nearly as fiercely as her heart, and she needed the quiet and solitude the chamber promised. Accustomed as she was to years of hardship and want, the humble room reminded her of her bedchamber at Esherton Green. Besides, a pallet for the maid wouldn't fit in the chamber.

The innkeeper's red-faced wife, carrying a tray laden with heavenly smelling soup, bread, and cheese, bustled past.

"Miss, ifn' ye mean to sup, ye'll have to eat in here. The private rooms be taken, and two hirelin's, blast their lazy, ungrateful hides, didn't come to work. I can't be waitin' on ye upstairs. Yer maid will have to see to yer needs." She jerked her chins in the kitchen's direction, sending her crepey neck jostling. "Pompous chit, that one."

"In here is perfectly fine." Eyeing the occupied tables, Blythe leisurely removed her gloves. Three had chairs available, or she could take a seat upon the wooden bench below the filmy window, which rattled in protest every now and then from a gust of contentious wind.

Holding hands and murmuring softly, the couple sank onto the bench, their heads close together.

Blythe wouldn't—couldn't bear to—perch on the end of their

bench and listen to their enamored chatter. To save Tristan's life, she'd relinquished her opportunity for love, but that didn't mean she couldn't yearn for the intimacy the couple shared.

Which table would it be then?

The cantankerous elderly dame? The scruffy soldiers? The fuddled Scots, already gulping their third pint since arriving? Or the pleasant-faced Man of God?

With a friendly nod, he waved her to his corner table, set slightly apart from the rest in a partial nook beside the fireplace. "Please, lass. I'd be pleased to have your company."

Giving him a grateful smile, she untied her bonnet as she sank onto a well-worn chair. "Thank you, Reverend ...?"

"Reverend Heaven." He chuckled softly, a merry twinkle in his warm gaze.

Disbelief must have shown in her eyes.

As if praying, he pressed his hands together. "Honestly. The name's of Welsh origins."

Returning his easy smile, Blythe laid her gloves and rain-splattered bonnet atop the gouged and dented tabletop. "I imagine, given your profession, it's been the subject of many conversations."

"Indeed. Mrs. Heaven's first name causes a bigger stir." He leaned forward and winked. "It's Angel. Not Angela or Angelina. Just Angel. We named our sons Gabriel and Michael."

Blythe chuckled. "Brilliant. You've no daughter?"

"Alas, no." He pulled his earlobe while casually scrutinizing the other occupants. "But we considered Mary or Martha."

Meg tromped into the taproom, her mouth bent into a belligerent scowl. She crossly plopped Blythe's and Reverend Heaven's food atop the table, sloshing stew over the bowls' edges in her frustration. "I'm being made to help in the kitchen."

Blythe checked her sharp retort. "It's kind of you to lend a hand. They are short staffed, and the inn is full."

"I care not. I am not a scullery wench. I didn't agree to this." She flipped a hand scornfully at their food. "First thing in the morning, I'm returning to London. You cannot stop me."

Meg lifted her nose as haughtily as an Almack's patroness and stamped past the soldiers.

How did she propose to do that? By post chase? Without funds?

Blythe would pay for her return to the city, but Meg would have to seek other employment. A servant with airs proved intolerable, and Brooke would be advised of Meg's unacceptable attitude.

One scarlet-clad chap tilted his chair onto two legs and grasped Meg's arm in passing. "Interested in some company, sweetheart?"

"No, you foul oaf." Meg pushed him over then, amidst the hoots and guffaws of his compatriots, stormed into the kitchen, declaring, "I'm never leaving London again."

"That one's carrying a cartload of bitterness." Reverend Heaven buttered a piece of bread.

"She's unaccustomed to discomfort." Lifting her spoon, Blythe sniffed the stew appreciatively. "Had I known, I wouldn't have asked her to accompany me."

He tilted his head, his keen gaze assessing and nodded sagely. "You, I would venture, are familiar with hardship. I see pain and suffering in your eyes, but you haven't become bitter."

Yet.

She didn't want to become a lonely, cynical harpy.

Battling the harsh sting of tears behind her eyelids, Blythe lowered her gaze and took a bite of the savory stew rather than answer.

"I've been told I'm a good listener, Miss ...?"

Startled, she blinked away her tears, her watery gaze springing to his.

Compassion emanated from his kindly face. "And I'm sworn to confidence."

"Forgive me. I'm Blythe Culpepper, and I'm returning to my family home near Cheshire after an ... unpleasant sojourn in London."

The outer door flung open, and a gust of frigid, wet air billowed in. Blythe shivered, still not warmed. She'd likely sleep in her clothes and cloak given she'd only seen one quilt atop the thin mattress in her teeny closet of a room.

At first light, she'd be on her way. Now that home loomed near, eagerness overtook her. She'd sorely missed the country. If she had her way, she'd never venture to Town again.

"That fellow arrived upon a huge horse, just now. No luggage either." Reverend Heaven chewed his bread thoughtfully, his elbow resting atop the table. "Must be in a great hurry, or he was caught unawares. I don't envy him. He's soaked through. Must be utterly miserable. Do you mind if he joins us as well? Looks like he could use something hot in his belly and our table is nearest the fireplace."

Casting a disinterested glance over her shoulder, Blythe faltered, and her breath refused to leave her lungs.

A man, an immense man, stamped his booted feet and shook off his sodden greatcoat. Water sprayed in all directions and puddled at his feet. He pulled his hat from his head, revealing dark auburn hair.

Tristan.

A tiny gasp escaped her, and she dropped her spoon. It bounced off the table and onto the floor, clanging loudly each time the metal careened off a surface.

"Do take care, miss." The irritable ebony swathed tabby narrowed her eyes and clasped her chest above her ample bosom. "You startled me so, I may swoon. My heart is not strong. Miss Timmons, my vinaigrette at once."

Miss Timmons cast a pained glance ceilingward before dutifully rummaging in a traveling case and momentarily procuring an engraved silver vial.

"Please forgive my clumsiness." What was Tristan doing here? Blythe determinedly forced down the swell of anticipation seeing him caused.

There might've been a number of reasons he'd stopped at this inn. He didn't live far from Esherton Green. Mayhap there'd been an urgent need for him to return to his estate, and the vile weather had forced him to stop here as it had her.

Or perhaps Phillips had died—her heart pitched, bum over head—and Tristan decided to quit London rather than face the *ton* as a jilted man. She'd discerned quite some time ago that he endured assemblies and routes. He didn't enjoy them.

"Do you know him?" Reverend Heaven's question caught her off guard.

How should she answer? Yes. She knew him, and leave it at that? Yes. We were betrothed for two wonderful minutes? Yes, he was a pompous, aggravating boor, and she adored him with her entire being, enough to save his life by refusing to wed him?

Intent upon retrieving her spoon and regaining her composure before answering, Blythe bent and had clasped the handle. A pair of muddy boots appeared beside the table.

Bother and blast. And ... and damnation!

Her scrutiny slowly traveled from his mud-caked toes, past his muscled calves tucked into the dirt-pelted Hessians, skimmed his narrow waist, and followed his torso's vee to his wide, russet-covered shoulders. His size never failed to impress her.

Or others.

Every person stared their way, and Miss Timmons's mouth hung slack in awe.

I know the feeling, dear.

He'd removed his greatcoat and must have deposited the garment and his hat and gloves with the innkeeper.

She almost smiled.

Likely he didn't recognize the preferential treatment he received. He took it for granted, as did most gentry and peers.

It didn't take a scholar to recognize a nobleman flush in the pockets. No doubt the fawning hostler offered Tristan a room too, at the expense of another unfortunate guest who would have to find other accommodations or sleep before the cinder-covered hearth.

"Miss Culpepper." Tristan inclined his head the merest bit before his attention swerved to Reverend Heaven, now standing. "Tristan, the Marquis of Leventhorpe, sir. Thank you for entertaining my betrothed until I could join her."

"Betrothed, you say?" The Reverend's brows vaulted to the top of his forehead as he shook Tristan's extended hand. "I'm Reverend Heaven, my lord."

Tristan's expression didn't alter a jot at the cleric's unusual name.

"Formerly betrothed." Blythe leveled Tristan with what she hoped was an impassive stare. "What are you doing here?"

After the men took their seats, Tristan gestured for the innkeeper then summoned a crooked smile. "I called at Ravensdale's and was told you'd left for Esherton. I followed."

"You followed." She snapped her fingers. "Just like that? Had you no care for the dismal weather or your health?"

"Just like that." He grinned mischievously. "I did think to borrow Raven's greatcoat."

Reverend Heaven chuckled, his keen gaze sparking with interest.

"Reverend, I might have need of your services." Tristan patted his pocket and winked. "I have a special license. I've rather muddled things, and I hope to put that to rights."

Impossible.

Blythe kicked him beneath the table. "We've had this discussion."

Wedding him meant he would face Phillips. She could never live with herself if Tristan lost his life defending her. Far better to be alone and desolate, and know he lived, than alone and desolate if he died. Yet, refusing the thing she most wanted took her absolute resolve.

The innkeeper hurried to their table, bearing a frothy tankard. He placed the mug before Tristan and foam trailed down the pewter side. "My lord?"

"Miss Culpepper dropped her spoon. Please bring another when you serve my meal. Have you a private dining room available?"

Tristan passed the man a coin, earning a gap-toothed grin that rapidly transformed into a fretful frown. "No private dinin' room, Sir. I might be able to arrange for ye to use a chamber for a short spell. This weather has us overflowin'. I'll need a few minutes to work somethin' out."

"If we could have use of a chamber, for half an hour even, I would certainly show my appreciation." Another coin changed hands.

Blythe leaned back in her chair. "Do you do that often? Bribe your way to achieve what you want?"

"I prefer to call it compensation for extra effort. He's overworked, and from the looks of this place, he could use the coin." Tristan combed the room from end to end and gave a half jerk of his head "He'll not receive a groat more than he's earned from them, despite the hardship having this many patrons at once has caused."

"I believe you require privacy." Reverend Heaven stood. "I shall be warming myself before the fire if you should need me. Please excuse me, Miss Culpepper, my lord."

He took his chair with him, preventing anyone else from sitting at their table. Clever man. In a moment, he sat before the now roaring fire, legs extended, hands crossed atop his rounded abdomen, and eyes shut. Resting or praying?

"I have a chamber. We can talk there with the door ajar. I'll allow you ten minutes." Blythe gathered her belongings. Despite his nonchalance, blue tinged Tristan's lips, and he'd shuddered more than once. Probably soaked to the skin, and without a warm bed to sleep in, he might catch lung fever.

"That's all the time I require." Tristan nodded and stood. "Let me tell the hostler to hold my meal."

A few minutes later, and slightly out of breath from climbing three flights, she entered her miniscule chamber and immediately set about lighting the candle atop the nightstand.

Tristan leaned against the doorjamb, his arms crossed, grinning like a baboon. "I've seen carriages and biscuit tins with bigger interiors."

"You jest, but I either accepted this room or slept below." Surprised by the room's pleasant temperature, she released her cloak's frogs, before shrugging its weight from her shoulders.

Tristan moved to assist her.

He hung the cloak over a wooden peg beside the rock chimney then tentatively skimmed the gray stones nested together. Leaning against their heat, he smiled in satisfaction. "This is why this chamber is warm." He patted the rocks behind him. "The heat from the fire below radiates off them."

"That's all well and good, and I'm grateful I won't freeze in my sleep." Casting a wary glance at the open door, Blythe sat upon the mattress, its meager depth harder than frozen ground. Wiggling her bum, she attempted to find a comfortable position. A night sleeping upon this mattress and she'd ache from toe to nose. "Why did you follow me? I gave you my answer yesterday."

"You did, and at first I had determined to accept your rejection, and allow you to disappear from my life. Though, I must tell you, I've experienced gut punches that hurt less." He crossed his ankles, closed his eyes, and pressed into the rocks. "This is rather splendid. I can finally feel my fingers again."

"Tristan. Will you please make your point?" Exhausted, she had no more reserves, and the tears she'd held at bay for the past twenty-four hours stung her eyes again. "You've used five of your minutes blathering about nonsensical rubbish."

He opened his gorgeous, black-lashed eyes, his gaze slicing straight to her soul.

"I love you."

A sob escaped her, and she pressed her fist to her mouth, struggling for control.

In an instant, he was beside her then pulling her into his strong embrace. He smelled of horse and rain and sandalwood, and she'd never inhaled anything sweeter.

"I know why you refused me." He kissed the top of her head while running his huge hands over her back and shoulders.

"You do?" The great slab of his chest muscle muffled her words.

"Of course you do. I told you. It's because you insist upon dueling Phillips."

"Liar." He squeezed her ribs.

Prepared to give him a set down, she stiffened her spine. "I am not—"

Tristan settled his strong mouth atop hers, his hot, voracious kiss stifling her protest and launching it to the Earth's remotest corner. "You will let me speak my piece, or I shall silence you with a kiss each time you open your delicious mouth." He dropped another breath-hitching kiss on her lips. "Understand?"

She nodded, a half-smile bending her lips. "I rather like your kisses—"

In a flash, she lay upon her back, his mouth and tongue searing her senses. The cot shuddered, groaning and squeaking, underneath his substantial weight. She wound her arms around his back. Hardly the actions of a woman refusing a suitor.

But he loved her.

"I suspected the real reason behind your rejection. When I spoke with Miss Brette today, she confirmed it." Using his forefinger, he traced her jaw, sending spirals of sensation skittering everywhere. "If we didn't marry, I wasn't honor bound to see the challenge through."

"Wait until I see her—"

By the time he finished kissing her again, Blythe seriously considered closing the door, stripping him naked, and having her way with him. Where had he learned to kiss like that? To render her incapable of coherent thought as tantalizing currents sluiced through her? Punishment via kisses that turned her bones to jelly wasn't disagreeable at all.

"Is it true? Is that why you won't marry me, Blythe? Did you recant your acceptance in order to nullify my reason for challenging Phillips?" The anguish in his azure gaze lacerated her resolve.

"Yes." A tear leaked from her eye, and then another. She cupped his stubbly jaw. "I love you. I'd die if you were injured or killed meeting Phillips. I know men, especially peers, have a code you live by, and I know how important your honor is to you. I'd rather live in disgrace for the remainder of my days then risk harm coming to you."

"If you are willing to forego respectability, and face rejection, gossip, and scandal to spare me, then I am willing to live with the dishonor of repudiating my challenge." He kissed her nose. "I don't know whether Phillips will survive his festered wound, but if he does, I won't face him on the field of honor."

"Truly, Tristan?" She searched his eyes for a sign of regret and found none. "Some might call you a coward or ridicule you."

He elevated a brow. "I find honor without a cause is worthless. You are my cause. Naught else matters."

Some men might be given to flowery and romantic speeches. The sincerity of Tristan's simple heartfelt words surpassed them all.

Pressing a tender kiss against her lips, he whispered, "Will you marry me? Here? Tonight?"

Tristan waited, his breath suspended and constricting his lungs, for Blythe's answer.

Each mile he'd ridden, rain dripping into his collar and wind blasting his face with ice-cold pellets, he'd kept one goal at the forefront of his mind: to convince her that the greatest honor he would ever know would be to make her his marchioness and begin his life anew with her.

The wonder of her had crept into the recesses, the very core, of his being, and entrenched her spirit into his innermost places. Nothing that had ever come before, nothing he would face in the future, compared to the need to make her his life's partner.

He'd finally healed of his past humiliation, and though he'd never deem large gatherings his favorite pastime, the fear haunting him for almost two decades had vanished. She'd vanquished it.

Love had healed and restored him, a man filled with self-loathing.

Lips parted, plump and reddened from his kisses, Blythe peered into his soul. "I shall gladly marry you, but you need to know something about me, Tristan."

He propped his head upon his hand as he caressed the creamy column of her throat. Her breasts' perky tips taunted him below the bodice of her simple poplin traveling gown.

"And what is that?" He brushed her hair from her forehead, enjoying the excuse to touch her.

"I'm an ordinary woman of simple origins. Yes, I've endured poverty. I've also been blessed with a loving, supportive family." She entwined her fingers with his. "I haven't been scarred by tragedy, nor are there dark secrets in my past which torment or cause me angst. Perhaps couples who overcome great odds and conflict are grateful when they finally admit their love as we have, but, honestly I cannot regret the peaceful, quiet, normal life I've lived."

"Ahem. Perhaps we should commence with a ceremony?"

Tristan whipped his attention to the gaping doorway framing Reverend Heaven then chuckled as he levered off the bed. "Yes, Reverend. We'll meet you below in five minutes."

"Miss Culpepper? You are in agreement?" Reverend Heaven scratched his left eyebrow. "Are you of age?"

"I am, to both." She scooted to a sitting position. "I celebrated my first and twentieth birthday two days ago."

Reverend Heaven rubbed his hands together. "Well then, I'd say the Almighty has been working overtime arranging this storm. By-the-by, I insist you take my chamber, and I shall occupy this one." His wink wasn't the least chaste or holy. "Mine has a bigger bed."

An hour later, after having been congratulated soundly by the hostler, his wife, and the inn's occupants, who'd assembled to witness the simple ceremony, and after finally eating, Tristan guided Blythe into the reverend's former chamber.

The bed was indeed bigger. By a good six inches.

"Are you nervous?" Normally a female family member explained what a bride could expect on her wedding night. "Do you have questions about tonight?"

Blythe's smile wasn't that of a timid virgin as she stood before a cracked oval mirror and unpinned her hair. "I was raised on a farm, Tristan. I know the ways of males and females."

"Yes, well, there are differences." He swept his hand down his front. "No fur or feathers."

"Or tail." Looking pointedly at his coat, she laughed, the deep, musical chuckle that he adored. "I believe we need to be naked to do the job properly."

"Have I married a vixen?" He made short work of divesting his clothing until only his pantaloons remained. She might have been familiar with farm animal anatomy, but the engorged penis of a highly aroused man might be a mite much. Particularly a man of his stature and build.

She stepped from her dress, a bold goddess, and draped the garment over the chamber's single chair. Her stays and stockings followed, and in a few tantalizing moments, she untied one shoulder ribbon of her chemise. No false blushes or pretense of demureness.

That was his Blythe.

"Let me." He brushed her hand away while kissing her collarbone.

She shuddered and sagged against him, her breath coming in short pants. "I've wondered what it would be like to have you possess me."

The fabric slipped to her waist as he cupped her breasts from behind and continued to nibble the sensitive flesh of her nape and neck. "You've imagined bedding me?"

"Uh hum. But I believed you loathed me." Her head fell forward, and she clasped his forearms as he slowly explored her abdomen. Then lower.

A sound, half-gasp, half-moan, escaped her open mouth, as she pressed her plump buttocks against his rigid length, demanding to be freed of its constraint.

He nipped her shoulder and gave her a little shove. "Lie down."

She complied, scampering underneath the coarse sheets, her curious gaze riveted to the bulge at his groin.

He unbuttoned the falls and tugged his pantaloons off.

She chuckled throatily when his member sprang free. "I'm quite looking forward to experiencing that."

He pounced upon her. "What, no maidenly shyness?"

"None whatsoever." She lifted her arms in invitation, a saucy smile teasing one corner of her mouth. "Now, husband, why don't you introduce me to passion?"

"With pleasure, my love."

Her eyes grew sultry. "Oh, I don't doubt it will be immensely pleasurable."

And it was. Both times.

Schemes and goals motivated by love and honor are the most noble of all.
~Dignity and Decorum—The Genteel Lady's Guide to Practical Living

Epilogue

Bristledale Court, Late August, 1822

"Look, darling." Sitting at a tea table centered upon the veranda, Blythe pointed to a pair of fawns. They followed their mottled mother from the woods bordering Bristledale Court's expansive greens where Blaire and Blaike strolled, arm in arm, beneath matching white lace parasols.

The day, vibrant with sunshine and a cloudless cerulean sky, promised a sweltering afternoon.

"This year, the mallow deer herd is greater than usual." Tristan folded his news sheet, and after setting it aside, extended his hand. "Walk with me, please. I have something I'd like to discuss with you."

Blythe patted her mouth with her serviette before taking his hand and collecting her parasol. "Of course."

"You are enjoying your sisters' visit?" Tristan led her off the covered promenade and into an elaborate parterre featuring topiaries, hedges, and a circular koi pond teeming with silvery and orange koi as well as pink water lilies.

"Very much. I essentially grew up with four sisters. I miss them, and I never thought to admit it, but I miss the chaos too." A subtle fragrance perfumed the air, and Blythe bent to sniff the heather-toned lavender. Nearly time to harvest it for linen sachets.

He nodded, a contemplative expression creasing his handsome face. "I know we decided against me applying for guardianship of the twins, since Ravensdale is wholly honorable and will do what is best for them. This past fortnight, having had an opportunity to become acquainted with Blaire and Blaike, I've come to a conclusion."

Blythe sloped her parasol against the sun. "A good one, I hope."

He chucked her chin. "Never fear. I quite like your sisters. And that's why I think they need an education beyond the schooling you've told me about."

Blythe stopped short. "Are you serious? Gentlewomen don't attend higher education."

"Blythe, they are quite brilliant, and they've a hunger for knowledge I'm loath to leave unsated. I don't think I've ever encountered two keener female minds."

"Well, I don't know whether to be miffed or pleased. Are you implying I'm a dimwit?"

"Nothing of the sort. You simply aren't leaving my side. Ever."

Blythe followed the twins' progress as they occasionally pointed to a bird or plant. "They are unique, aren't they?"

"They are. Do you think they'd be receptive to the notion, or would they feel like we were trying to rid ourselves of them?" He shaded his eyes from the glaring sun and stared after the oyster-and-Pomona-green clad pair. "It's an opportunity few women have. On the other hand, I fear it may set them up for disappointment later in life by giving them a taste of freedom they may not want to relinquish for marriage."

"Hmm, I suppose it might. We'll never know unless we put the suggestion to them." She tucked her hand into his elbow, deliberately pressing her breast into his arm. "Besides, sometimes relinquishing one's freedom is quite divine."

His wicked chuckle sent a jolt of desire straight to her woman's center. Tristan had introduced her to an extremely creative and most satisfying bed sport this morning, which had restricted her liberty for several delicious moments.

"Ho, Leventhorpe." Drake waved as he, Whitehouse, and Brette, accompanied by several others, including Francine and Maddox, stepped onto the veranda.

Tristan returned his greeting. "Ah, the rest of our houseguests finally stir."

"Not everyone rises with the roosters, darling." Blythe sent him a teasing smile. "I do rather prefer sunrise myself."

"I know why you favor mornings." Tristan swung her into his arms. "You like a rousing romp first thing, Lady Leventhorpe."

"Indeed, I do." She laid her head against his chest, and he rested his chin atop her head. "Did Lieutenant Drake's news of Phillips's partial recovery cause you regret or angst?"

"Not a wit. I spent far too long fretting about Society's opinion of me, and I am enjoying the liberation immensely." He kissed her crown, giving her a little squeeze. "I'm thoroughly delighted you rendered him incapable of performing as a man. Who knew an infection could cause such damage?"

"I can't bring myself to feel the slightest regret." Fingering the button of his jacket, Blythe pursed her lips. Phillips's wouldn't be ruining anymore women, though the knowledge he'd not be punished for the viler acts he was suspected of rankled. "Surely the House of Lords has the power to hold him accountable."

"Not for despoiling a willing woman, and there's no proof of aught else." He patted her shoulder, lingering to caress the sensitive spot at the juncture of her neck that turned her knees to custard. "What think you of the other news Whitehouse divulged?

"You mean Miss Sanford ... er, Lady Bexley?" In truth, the crafty jealousy she'd meant for evil had worked for good, and Blythe owed her a debt of gratitude. Not that a formal thank you would be forthcoming. "I pity her. Widowed within weeks, and banished by the heir to the dower house with a pittance of an allowance. Once her mourning period is over, she'll be prowling about for a new husband, or cats don't meow."

"That's true, although I referred to the tattle regarding Burlington."

Cocking her head, she permitted herself an impish grin. "Mrs. Hemple is to be congratulated on her good fortune for escaping the parson's mousetrap. Wise woman, having Mr. Burlington shadowed. Three indiscretions in as many weeks. Tsk, tsk. She's well rid of him."

"I quite agree. I'd like to break his perfect nose for suggesting you become his mistress." Turning them toward their waiting guests, Tristan used the opportunity to wrap his arm about her trim waist and cup her ribs. "You've filled out a bit since we married."

"Are you suggesting I'm running to fat?" Contriving a playful pout, she swatted his arm. "Fine way to speak to your wife when she's increasing."

"You mistake my meaning, darling." Casting a deliberate glance at her swollen breasts, he waggled his eyebrows and bent his sculpted lips, perfect for blood-heating kisses. "I simply worried for the babe's and your health. I'm not complaining in the least."

"Devilish knave." Her contented smile betrayed her joy.

"And that's exactly why you love me." He dropped a kiss onto her crown. "Happy, my love?"

Blythe tilted her chin, cupped his angular cheek. "Beyond my grandest schemes."

The Lord and the Wallflower

An insightful woman acknowledges that every
person receives their due according to what they've intended.
~Appearances and Attitude—The Genteel Lady's Guide to Practical Living

Bristledale Court
The English Countryside
Late August 1822

Brette Culpepper peeked around the carved door case, her stomach flipping in excitement.

Yes.

Engrossed in the objects before him, Lord Danfield hadn't a clue he'd played straight into her and Ophelia Thurston's plans.

Absolutely perfect.

Jolly good fun, this.

Bent at the waist, his expression one of awed concentration, the viscount closely examined the carved jadeite and white nephrite collection displayed beneath the glass covering.

Just as Brette had intended.

Well, more aptly, she'd hoped he couldn't resist the temptation. After she'd learned of his fascination with the foreign trinkets during supper last night, she'd broadly hinted at the vast assortment housed in Bristledale's library.

A library conveniently situated on the opposite side of the manor from where dignified footmen roamed scorching rooms, offering cooled champagne to overheated guests.

Brows furrowed, Lord Danfield lifted his head and stared outside through the open French windows, murmuring something while grazing his fingers along his jawline. Moonlight lit the veranda beyond, and a scant summer breeze carried a fountain's lyrical burbling into the house.

Even from her position by the door, Brette caught a faint whiff of jasmine.

No surprise the rather bashful lord had escaped this evening's noisy throng and made his way to the figurines. Wise move on his part. He'd been spared Major Wilkerson's exuberant vocal rendition. Lowing cattle claimed more musical aptitude than the jovial officer.

More than one disconcerted guest had emptied their champagne flute in a single swift pull before eagerly seizing another, as if hoping to mute the effects of the next amateur performer. If those presentations were anything like Major Wilkerson's, several more glasses of champagne might be in order before the entertainment recommenced.

"Utterly fascinating." Lord Danfield leaned nearer the case, paying particular attention to the more risqué carvings arranged along the back row. His red-tinged ears glowed noticeably; a close match for the shot of fiery hair topping his head.

To smother an undignified laugh, Brette clamped her teeth together. She, too, had blushed scarlet the first time she'd gazed upon the more scandalous statuettes. Tristin, the Marquis of Leventhorpe, their host and her cousin-in-law, possessed several such sculptures, which Lord Danfield seemed determined to commit to memory.

Down to every last naughty detail.

Danfield glanced toward the entrance for an instant, and Brette ducked behind the doorframe.

Had he heard her? Seen her?

She turned and, waving her hand, beckoned Ophelia.

The sable-haired beauty hovered near a curtained window, darting anxious glances up and down the corridor's length. As arranged earlier, they'd left the others on the pretense of needing to visit the ladies' retiring room during the musical intermission. After seeking Mrs. Thurston's permission, of course.

Ophelia's mama had nodded distractedly, a pinched look upon her lightly powdered face.

Apparently, after sitting through the major's vigorous performance, she'd needed a few moments' reprieve to collect herself. Next time, she might consider stuffing a scrap of cloth in her ears as Brette intended to.

Ophelia, her frilly ivory and rose pink skirts swishing in her haste, whisked to Brette's side.

She fiddled with her fan's lacy edge. "Danfield's inside? Alone?"

"He is, indeed." Brette's tummy gave another giddy quiver.

She adored this part—bringing star-crossed sweethearts together.

So romantic and daring.

Like a story from a gothic novel except without all the drama and gloom.

Her fifth matchmaking jaunt since entering society, and so far, three rousing successes. The fourth—

She grimaced, the spasm in her middle caused by sick remorse rather than glee.

That had been a colossal disaster. So much so, she'd briefly considered forfeiting her newly self-appointed profession as Cupid's assistant. And she'd been having so much fun, too. Plus, the meddling—*no, no, I'm helping people*—gave her a purpose.

By Jove. This time would be different. She'd made sure of it.

Unlike her last unpleasant matchmaking escapade, Brette had investigated this moon-eyed pair thoroughly, and nary a scolding wife or piqued betrothed would caper along to interrupt her plan.

It honestly hadn't occurred to her that either person mightn't have been honorable in asking her to arrange a tryst. The ways of the upper ten thousand continued to baffle and frequently appall her. Fairly new to elite circles, she wasn't familiar with many *haut ton* members' connections, and she'd blundered by arranging for an affianced widower to meet with a humble, but sweet, newly-come-into-her-vulgarly-large-inheritance debutante.

If it hadn't been for Rector Alexander Hawksworth—Alex in her most private of thoughts— happening upon Brette as she'd opened the conservatory's door to permit Miss Marshall her rendezvous... A slight shudder rippled across Brette's shoulders, raising the hairs at her nape to rigid attention. *Gads.* She swallowed and pressed her palm to her stomach. The notion didn't bear pondering for long, or the dainties she'd nibbled earlier might sour in her stomach.

The rector had averted a monumental disaster when, less than a minute later, the widower's betrothed—the influential Lady Covington—famous for her swift temper, cutting tongue, and unforgiving nature had sailed their way.

"Given your humble origins, Miss Culpepper, you'd do well to apply your energies to acquiring a measure of decorum and social acceptance." Superior nose elevated and tone condescending, Lady Covington had flounced away. Stern disapproval had lined her lovely, but haughty, face as she towed her philandering, a-decade-her-junior intended to the ballroom, giving him an earful as they went.

The incident haunted Brette still.

Not only would Miss Marshall have been ruined, so, too, would Brette's family. Lady Covington, on intimate terms with a number of Almack's peeresses, would've seen them yanked from Society's loftiest perch and tossed into London's festering gutters. Never mind that Brette claimed a marquis and an earl as kin now. A featherless duck would've gained entrance to an assembly before the Culpeppers ever set a foot inside an elite parlor or drawing room again.

And unlike her sister and cousins, Brette adored the social whirlwind, though she diligently kept that secret to herself. Preferring the country's serenity to Town's chaos, her family would have been nonplussed, at the least, and disapproving, at worst, if they'd known of her fascination with metropolitan life. They probably wouldn't have objected an iota if Lady Covington succeeded in having them blackballed.

According to Alex, Lady Covington was most unforgiving, and her betrothed, Phillip Lapley, a notorious womanizer. In order to get his hands on Miss Marshal's fortune, he'd have compromised the girl to force her into marriage.

Swine.

Shaken to her core, for two weeks afterward, Brette diligently refrained from all forms of plotting whatsoever. Except in her mind, of course. No harm in fantasizing and matchmaking there. Oh, she'd merrily united several woebegone wretches in the private alcoves of her imagination. But there the lovesick couples stayed, forever doomed to worshipping from afar, no one the wiser, save she.

Until, at another house party, she'd spotted Ophelia lurking within a curtained nook, peering dreamily at Lord Danfield as he spoke to Mr. Waters, a kindly merchant. Earlier that same day, Brette had stumbled upon the viscount loitering behind the shrubbery in the gardens near a secluded gazebo. An expression of moon-eyed adoration had wreathed his face as Ophelia and her brothers passed by.

If ever two people were destined to make a smashing match, Ophelia Thurston and Patrick, Viscount Danfield were. A shame if they should miss their chance at happiness, especially since Brette possessed the means to bring them together.

How could she have said no when Ophelia, wringing her hands, her doe-like eyes glimmering with tears, confessed her undying love for Lord Danfield? She'd begged Brette to arrange an assignation. Nothing too scandalous, of course. Simply a short, respectable few moments to speak together without Mrs. Thurston's eagle eye watching her daughter's every move.

However had Ophelia learned of Brette's hush-hush hobby? Surprised, but pleased, Brette had nudged Alex's warning into a remote corner of her mind, hidden it beneath a blanket of good intentions, and eagerly agreed to help.

"He's inside, waiting," Brette whispered with another harried glance along the corridor's length.

Not waiting, precisely, but he'd welcome Ophelia's unexpected appearance. No doubt about that.

Brette would allow them five minutes, discreetly hovering outside the open door for propriety's sake. Afterward, she'd escort the enraptured young woman to her protective mother's side. Mrs. Thurston seldom permitted Ophelia out of her sight unless in the company of her trio of brothers. The moment must be seized. Another mightn't come along anytime soon.

A lilting whistle carried to them, and Brette and Ophelia exchanged troubled glances before peering into the passageway.

Botheration. Someone approached.

Probably Alex Hawksworth. Worse than a songbird with his perpetual, cheerful warbling, but my, could he sing. Even better than he whistled, which said something.

Why hadn't he been impressed upon to entertain this evening?

Now *that* Brette would've enjoyed. He possessed a lovely baritone, and many a lady, from aged dowagers to knobby-kneed girls fresh from the schoolroom, sighed rapturously when he sang. Or spoke. Or walked into the room—all masculine grace, power, and beauty.

And when he smiled— Lord help the woman he directed that devastating flash of teeth toward. Including her. Come to think of it, she responded in the most peculiar fashion whenever he drew near. Most disconcerting.

His appearance right now, however, was a major inconvenience. He'd disapprove of her interfering. The last time, he'd scolded her, kindly but soundly.

"No matter how well-intended you might've been, Miss Culpepper," he'd insisted with a look not quite patronizing but not benevolent either, "when it comes to matters of the heart, people should let Nature take her course."

Showed how little he knew of love. Obviously, he'd never experienced the emotion.

She hadn't either, but she'd read several novels on the subject. Besides, it didn't take someone with extensive practice to realize that people, afraid of making a mistake or looking an unrequited fool, needed a slight prod in the right direction. Particularly if they'd each confessed their tendre to a mutual third party. Say, a well-meaning miss, fresh from the country with too much time on her hands and too little to do.

"Hurry, Ophelia." Brette gripped Ophelia's elbow, tossing a frantic glance toward the muted chatter and laughter filtering to them from the other guests. They'd be missed soon, if they hadn't been already. "You've only a minute or two now before we must return."

In the midst of a fancy trill, the whistling ended abruptly.

Blast me.

Alex had spotted them.

Brette dug her nails into the woodwork. He'd ruin everything she'd worked so hard to organize. Did he think it easy to arrange these stolen moments for others?

She wrinkled her nose. For pity's sake. Unmarried women were guarded more closely than the king's treasury.

What could possibly happen in five little minutes?

Naturally, his position required his disapproval of romantic ventures, but surely even he, pledged to uphold morality and abstinence from fleshly corruption, possessed an amorous speck beneath his stark and entirely proper clothing. *Poise and prim all the time.* For a handsome man, he was positively stuffy.

Unfair.

Her conscience gave her a disappointed jab. Not true. Not at all, actually. Mayhap she merely wished it, to make him less appealing.

He possessed a delightful sense of humor, and she'd never have guessed he was a man of the cloth when they'd first met. In fact, he'd been so charming and grand, his looks so arresting and charismatic, her cousin, Blaire, had assumed him an actor or opera singer, despite his somber togs.

Brette mistook him for a valet.

Until he spoke, and the notion dissolved as rapidly as finely ground spice in stew. With his angular cheeks, full lips, and strong jaw, he would've been brilliant on the stage and amassed a following in short order.

As it was, his parish pews overflowed with enamored ladies, from dewy-eyed misses to dames long past their prime. Given the impossibly scanty bodices Brette observed on Sundays, a sermon on modesty wouldn't have gone amiss. Last week, if Miss Lacewell had sung any more exuberantly, Brette had truly feared that her bosoms would escape the straining fabric's confines, and the reverend would've had to preach with his eyes pinched closed.

"Too bad *he* cannot claim position or wealth." Attention glued to the golden-haired man strolling in their direction, Ophelia whispered in Brette's ear, her voice annoyingly breathy. "Mr. Hawksworth by far the handsomest man I've ever laid eyes upon. Godlike even, but pauper poor." She sighed theatrically. "Mama says I must marry a man with a title. She's determined it should be so. And I do favor Lord Danfield more than other lords."

And his wealth, too, I'll be bound.

"Money and station aren't everything." Brette sneaked the rector a sideway look. Alex was one of the most decent men she'd met since her sister, Brooke, married Heath, the Earl of Ravensdale.

Nonetheless, in the immoral and pretentious upper circles, wealth and position ranked near the top. Pitiful, really. To place such importance on two criteria having nothing to do with a person's character and which could in no way guarantee happiness or contentment.

"Rather too bad, isn't it? An infinite waste of superb manhood." Ophelia sighed wistfully again. "He'll probably marry a mousy, plain-faced, flat-as-a-washboard-chested dowd who's memorized an annoying amount of scripture."

For someone madly in love with the viscount, she sounded most inappropriately enraptured.

Her pink tongue trailed her lower lip as her gaze trailed to Alex's groin.

Hmm. And not as innocent as her big, rich caramel eyes and virginal gown suggested.

"Ah, Miss Culpepper. Miss Thurston." Alex strode toward them, his fair brow cocked meaningfully and a barely restrained smile twitching his mouth's corners. "Your mother inquires after you, Miss Thurston. I told her I thought I'd last seen you in the corridor outside the peach parlor. I'm sure that's where you're away to now, isn't it? No one lurked about when I passed moments ago. You should escape notice if you hurry along."

Ophelia formed her rosy bowed mouth into a moue, and after an extended, regretful glance at the cracked doorway, tossed her glossy chestnut curls and flounced off in the direction she'd come.

Brette pressed her forefinger to her upper lip and shook her head once. Had she misjudged Ophelia's interest in Lord Danfield? Did his title and wealth enchant her, rather than any true affection? Surely not.

Alex joined Brette at the door and toed it open another inch.

Danfield had gravitated to the case's other side and now faced the door, though his attention remained riveted on the knickknacks.

My, he certainly seemed intent on satisfying his curiosity.

Alex drew her away and bent near her ear—a considerable distance since her head barely reached his shoulder. Of the five Culpepper misses—well, two were married now—she alone possessed a petite stature and greenish tinted eyes. She assumed she resembled a forgotten ancestor.

"Danfield's rather a lackluster sort," Alex whispered as if an authority on the chap. "Always has his nose in a fusty tome and would rather study ancient specimens than flirt with young, empty-headed misses."

Brette glanced upward, almost returning his infectious grin. Almost. She mightn't be terribly miffed, but he wouldn't be forgiven just like that either.

He boasted the most mesmerizing eyes, a spectacular green, like newly sprouted spring grass. Bright, cheery, and framed by honey-tipped lashes so lush, they appeared coffee-brown from a distance. He smelled wonderful too. Sandalwood, starch, and a woodsy, soapy smell. Clean and fresh. Quite irresistible. If she were the type to be taken with such, which, being a practical sort, she was not.

His gaze, oddly mesmerizing, held hers and for an instant, she quite forgot her purpose for being in the passage.

"Particularly flighty, title-hunting ninnies," Alex said.

What? Oh, he meant Ophelia.

True, Ophelia was flighty, and she did seek a titled husband, but if she were enamored with the gentleman, surely that made all the difference.

Careful to keep her voice subdued, Brette murmured, "Shows what you know, Al—Mr. Hawksworth." *Blast me twice.* Did he notice her blunder?

"I've asked you, repeatedly, to call me Alex or Hawk."

Yes, he had. Heat crept from her neck to her hairline, and she snapped her fan open, welcoming the faint breeze.

His smile widened, crinkling the corner of his eyes in a merry manner. He sniffed lightly. "I like your perfume. Is it new?" He bent near her again and boldly smelled her hair.

Such an intimate, improper thing to dare.

Brette's jaw hung slack momentarily before she collected herself. Hadn't she just been thinking how pleasant he smelled? It rather disconcerted her to have his mind marching along the same path as hers.

He flashed another disarming smile, and her stomach's renewed flopping had nothing to do with her matchmaking exploits. She fanned herself faster.

Did Alex's smile expand the merest iota more? As if he knew caterpillars, and butterflies, and all sort of ill-mannered insects cavorted about in her middle?

"Gentleman do not sniff ladies' heads, Mr. Hawksworth." What she'd intended as a sternly whispered reprimand came out as an amused observation. Nevertheless, reminding him of his position should put him in his place nicely.

"They do when they smell as lovely as you, and since you've forgotten again, I'll remind you that I've asked you to address me as Hawk or Alex." His melodic whisper held not a jot of repentance.

He most assuredly wasn't cut from the typical clerical cloth.

She'd never noticed the citrine flecks rimming his pupils before. When he was amused, they danced, and he definitely found something funny right now. Her.

Folding her fan, she considered him. Should she be flattered or annoyed?

"That's too familiar, even if you are one of my brother-in-law's dearest friends."

She canted her head toward Lord Danfield, still absorbed in the treasure trove. "Besides, he and Miss Thurston have a tendre for each other. They may not seem well-suited, but that doesn't mean they couldn't be happy together. Who has the right to decide except them?"

Cupping her elbow, his hands surprisingly strong for a cleric, Alex guided her away from the library. An accomplished pugilist, he practiced at least twice weekly, Heath had mentioned once in passing. That probably accounted for Alex's robust grip on her arm. With his parish responsibilities, when did he find the time to spar?

Come to think of it, how had he managed to escape his duties for this house party?

Of much more importance, could she possibly arrange another tryst for Danfield and Ophelia? Brette pivoted halfway around to consider Danfield.

He'd disappeared.

Poor decisions are still poor decisions,
no matter how grand, kind, or gallant the intention.
~Appearances and Attitude—The Genteel Lady's Guide to Practical Living

2

B rette breathed a relieved sigh.

Thank goodness, Danfield chose to exit through the French windows and not the door. Awkward, having to explain why she and Alex skulked outside the library, whispering like impish schoolgirls.

"I thought, given that disastrous incident with Lady Covington, you'd ceased your matchmaking antics, Brette. I'm not persuaded she's forgiven you yet." Alex peered at her, humor and genuine concern brimming in his eyes.

"Oh, pooh. That was ages ago." She shook her closed fan at him. "And I did her a favor, revealing Lapley's libertine character." Though Brette didn't have the impression Lady Covington simmered with gratitude or had been ignorant of her sweetheart's flaws.

Alex propelled Brette along as if demons nipped at their heels. "Want to know what I think?"

"No, not particularly." Brette slanted a brow as she lifted her skirt higher to keep pace with his lengthy strides. Why didn't he mind his own business and stop interfering with hers?

His lips twitched. "I'll tell you anyway. I think you're bored and need a project."

Spot on, there.

"Something worthwhile to satisfy your need to feel useful." He nodded once and directed his attention to the detailed crown molding. "You're accustomed to busyness, and if I may be candid?" He didn't wait for her to agree. "These house parties can be dull as cheap paper at times."

"*You* think so too?" Grinning, she stopped in her tracks. Delighted, she forgave him his boldness in addressing her by her given name and his presumptuousness for interfering too.

Though many deemed the country life of the social elite quaint, Brette found it tediously turtle-paced and eye-crossingly boring. Quite impolite to harbor those uncharitable views, but how many card games, strolls across the green, or sipping of cups and *cups* of tea could one endure?

Or caterwauling passing as singing?

So help her God, if she played one more game of croquet, charades, or shuttlecock, she'd scream.

"Indeed. I dozed off during tea today with no one the wiser." Alex chuckled, that contagious rumble that made her laugh too. "That is, until I released a minute—I'm positive it was quite inconspicuous—snore."

"You snored? During tea?" Shaking her head, she giggled while picturing him dozing, chin slack, over his delicate china cup and biscuits.

"So Lady Ravensdale informed me, after none-too-gently elbowing me awake."

"I should've liked to have seen that." Brette had missed tea today. Intentionally. If forced to tolerate another discussion about the weather, flora, or whom had just become betrothed to whom, she'd begin nipping Leventhorpe's excellent sherry.

Her hand resting on Alex's arm, they entered the ballroom turned recital area. Instead of steering Brette to the neat rows of chairs again filling with guests for the musicale's second half, he directed her toward the makeshift stage.

Mrs. Thurston and her stern-faced husband stood beside the second row, craning their necks this way and that, no doubt looking for Ophelia. She must have made use of the ladies' retiring room after all. Ophelia qualified as a first-rate flibbertigibbet, but she was kind and, occasionally, even thoughtful.

While subtly trying to extract her arm from Alex's grasp, Brette smiled at her cousin, Blythe, the new Lady Leventhorpe. Blythe chatted with her sisters, Blaire and Blaike.

More than one confused houseguest had commented on the oddity of the sisters and cousins having names beginning with B. Even Brette had to admit how perplexing it must be to those newly acquainted with the Culpeppers. The girls had determined amongst themselves that the tradition of females receiving names beginning with B would end with their generation.

Alex canted his head in response to Captain Whitehouse's and Lieutenant Drake's brief greetings as he and Brette made their way past the blond trio. "Come along, Brette."

Obstinate man. He must leave off addressing her so familiarly. People might get the wrong impression about them.

"What are you doing?" Whispering from the side of her mouth, Brette scanned the room and subtly tried maneuvering her arm free.

Alex urged her forward, but no one seemed to pay them much mind. "I don't sing, Alex. Really, I don't. I can barely carry a tune."

Panic welled. She wasn't exaggerating.

She neither sang nor played an instrument for public spectacle, and for good reason. 'Twas a cruel crime against humankind. Compared to her, Major Wilkerson was a gifted vocalist. Her talents lay in baking, sewing, crocheting, and painting. And dancing.

She loved to dance. Especially the notorious waltz. Such grace and flowing movement, and the music...? Utterly entrancing.

Alex's mouth twisted into his ever-ready and oh-so-charming grin. "Weren't you aware?

I'm scheduled to entertain next. I rather like the stage. Wanted to be an actor or a dance master in my youth, truth to tell. Naturally, the misplaced notion was quashed. Not respectable, you know."

Brette easily imagined him upon the stage. Perhaps his experience behind the pulpit lent him the confidence to perform in front of others. An aptitude she didn't share.

"And what does that have to do with me?" Suspicion danced along the column of her spine, and not a delicate, graceful step. More of a heavy-footed stamping. He must be made to understand. They couldn't sing a duet.

Brette was tone deaf. Utterly. Profoundly.

"But, I must have a Heloise to direct my prose too." He gave a flourishing half-bow, enjoying this far more than he ought. "Abelard at your service."

Who the devil are they?

Alex waggled his dark, honey-blond eyebrows and sighed melodramatically. "Such a poignant tale of star-crossed lovers."

She started. Faith, he'd read her mind.

Shaking her head, Brette resisted his gentle onward tug. Unobtrusively, of course. Wouldn't do to draw attention. "I haven't a clue who Heloise or Abelard are, but I'm not going to play her. Unlike you, I'm not accustomed to the masses staring at me."

Blaire fluttered her fingertips in their direction, and Brette summoned a sunny smile and waved in return.

Besides, wouldn't people read something into his selecting her to stand opposite him? *Le beau monde* needed no help contriving juicy *on dit* to bandy about, even if those present tonight were mostly Lord Leventhorpe's intimates. The exception being the Thurstons, his nearest neighbors.

Alex had managed to maneuver Brette to the stage's edge, the sly devil. Unless she made a scene, her fate seemed sealed. Did he think she wouldn't kick up a dust? Not the kind he'd expect. She raised a hand to her forehead, prepared to crumple into a swoon.

Never mind that she hadn't succumbed to the vapors in her life. She'd make the sacrifice to spare the guests a far worse fate than a little concerned *tsking* and tutting.

"Romantic that you are, Brette, you'll like their slightly gothic story. Though I fear their tale ends rather sadly."

She lowered her hand. Perhaps she needn't throw herself on the floor after all.

"They do marry and have a child— unfortunately, not in that order. Which is why her uncle, a diabolical chap, separates them and has Abelard castrated. Poor Albelard becomes a monk, and his beloved Heloise, a nun. They never see each other again."

"That's awful, Alex. Why would you want to share that heartrending account? In love and forced apart? Tragic, if you ask me." She gave her arm another tug, and he released her this time, his attention focused above her head.

His eyebrows shrugged together before his troubled gaze sank to hers. "Brette?"

Apprehension contracted her muscles from hip to shoulder.

Confound it. Now what?

"Miss Culpepper?" Worry permeated Mrs. Thurston's voice high-pitched voice. "Where's my dear Ophelia?"

Brette twisted as Mrs. Thurston descended on her like a general taking to the battlefield, while Mr. Thurston, his countenance grave, spoke to a footman by the ballroom entrance.

His wife's anxious gaze flitted about the room before coming to rest accusingly on Brette.

"I'm sure she'll be along shortly, Mrs. Thurston." No wonder Ophelia escaped her mother's domineering presence whenever possible.

"Don't tell me you left her unattended?" Mrs. Thurston's voice rose even higher, to a disbelieving squeak.

Egad. Such overreaction.

Brette hadn't left Ophelia alone in a brothel surrounded by drunken, pillaging pirates, for pity's sake.

"She was headed to the peach parlor the last time I saw her, not more than ten minutes ago, but I suspect she made use of the retiring room as well." *And I hardly think she needed my assistance there.* Brette veered Alex a puzzled glance before giving Mrs. Thurston an encouraging, if somewhat forced, smile. "I've no doubt she'll be along momentarily."

She had better be.

"Eloped!" Mr. Thurston thundered, waving a piece of paper in the air as he stalked toward his wife. "My daughter's eloped with that twiddepoop Danfield."

"Devil take it," Alex muttered as the room grew tomb silent for a heart-stopping instant before a symphony of whispers started slowly and grew into an ever-increasing frenzy.

Bully for Danfield, though. Didn't think the chap had it in him.

Alex couldn't help but admire the viscount for acquiring mettle at last and daring to cock a snook at propriety. He didn't dare voice his admiration, though. Rectors mustn't condone brash behavior, even if they secretly admired the gumption. But in this case, Alex feared Danfield had made a major misjudgment in choosing the capricious Miss Thurston as his bride.

"Oh, how could she do this to me?" One eye cracked a slit, Mrs. Thurston flung a hand to her chest, her actions suspiciously rehearsed. Her face a mask of motherly anguish, her other arm extended palm upward, she swayed.

Definitely rehearsed.

"Foolish girl. If she'd waited, he'd have offered for her. I'm sure of it." Pale, but composed, Brette steadied Mrs. Thurston. Casting a hurried glance 'round the captivated onlookers, she bit her lower lip.

Anger skewed Thurston's already gloomy countenance. "They're probably halfway to Gretna Green by now. No thanks to you, gel."

"Not in ten minutes, they aren't," Brette countered. "I'll be bound they haven't left Bristledale Court's lands yet."

She made a valid point.

By George, Thurston should've used discretion. Now the chance to salvage his daughter's reputation was slimmer than Satan waltzing in heaven. Surely the codshead realized broadcasting the elopement sealed Miss Thurston's fate. And if Alex wasn't mistaken, the gleam in Mrs. Thurston's eyes resembled cat-like satisfaction rather than genuine motherly distress.

He narrowed his gaze, studying first her calculated distress before scrutinizing her husband's blustering.

Something didn't ring true here.

Mayhap the Thurstons weren't as dismayed as they appeared at this disastrous turn of events.

"I lay the blame directly at your feet, Miss Culpepper. You should've stayed with Ophelia," Mrs. Thurston accused, her faced pinched into bitter lines.

What, and hold her hand as she attended to her personal needs?

"Let's gather the facts before jumping to conclusions." Leventhorpe wound through the guests, murmuring reassurances.

Astute chap. He'd immediately assessed the situation.

"Let's retire to my study where we can discuss this privately." He beckoned to Lady Leventhorpe. "My dear, would you please sing for our guests in Hawk's stead? And perhaps you can play the piano and our company might also enjoy impromptu dancing?"

Anything to keep the houseguests occupied. Her ladyship possessed extraordinary talent, and the sooner the visitors were distracted, the better.

Lady Leventhorpe bowed her neck. "Of course."

Ravensdale and his lady, Brooke, joined Brette.

"I'll accompany you to the study," Raven offered. "But, we'll need riders to intercept Danfield as soon as possible. Drake and Whitehouse, will you attend to readying the horses?"

"At once," Drake agreed, and after an abbreviated bow, he and Whitehouse departed.

Likely they, along with Raven and Leventhorpe, would give chase, while Alex, as usual, would be obliged to stay behind and comfort Miss

Thurston's fretting parents. He would've much preferred to tear across the country, neck or nothing, with the others.

Minutes later, Brette perched serenely on the toast-colored leather sofa's crackling edge.

However, her clenched hands and the occasional flexing of her delicate jaw revealed her agitation. Her determined chin inched upward as she blew out a breath, causing the wispy flaxen strands framing her face to poof upward.

She was an extraordinarily beautiful woman, and the candles' glow caught the platinum riches of her glorious hair and emphasized her smooth, honeyed skin. In the flattering light, everything about her gleamed feminine and petal-soft.

Was her skin truly so smooth? He longed to find out, to explore the satiny contours. Impossible.

Her beauty never failed to impact him thus. He could stare at her, a true and rare incomparable, for hours. Like a perfectly painted portrait. Yet, she couldn't become aware of his fascination.

He'd deduced her love of Town excitement, and his position didn't pay enough to maintain the opulent lifestyle she'd been introduced to. He attended the various soirées and routs as his chums' guest. Their hospitality also provided him with rooms and meals when he visited, else he'd not have been able to rub elbows with the *ton*'s denizens at all.

At times, he rather resembled a parasite, taking advantage of his hosts and those he held dearest. No matter how many times Raven and Leventhorpe assured him such wasn't the case, guilt niggled, poking at Alex's conscience.

He was a man of God now.

He shouldn't crave the opera or theater. Shouldn't anticipate the balls and musicals, the hectic pace of the social set during the Season. Nevertheless, he did, and sacrificing his favorite activities when he'd been obliged to accept his appointment as rector had him tippled for a week.

Ruminating won't change things. Control your thoughts and attend to the matter at hand.

The Marquis of Leventhorpe rubbed his chin, his calm regard shifting from the overwrought Thurstons to Brette. "Remind us again when you last saw Miss Thurston."

"As I explained, we parted in the corridor outside the library. Ophelia indicated she intended to stop in the parlor." Normally, Brette was unflappable, but her turned-up nose and the saucy glint in her eye bespoke her annoyance at being blamed for Miss Thurston's rashness.

Miss Thurston had led many a man on a merry chase before this. Nonetheless, if Brette hadn't been matchmaking again—

Leventhorpe's brows knitted. "Why were you outside the library?"

"Precisely what I'd like to know." Hands clasped behind his back, Thurston paced behind the sofa, exchanging telling looks with his wife every few moments.

Alex may not have wanted to be St. Peter's rector, but he possessed an uncanny ability to read people and persuade them to tell the truth. And, by Jove, the Thurstons lied through their less-than-well-cared-for teeth.

Brette's clear gaze met each of the room's occupants in turn. She angled her elegant chin again, and Alex's admiration grew. She wasn't cowed. Why should she be? She'd acted out of the misplaced goodness of her heart.

He passed his hand over his mouth to hide a budding smile before someone detected his fascination with her.

"I'm waiting for an explanation as to why my daughter didn't go directly to the retiring room." Thurston puffed out his chest and cheeks, his side whiskers dancing beside his fleshy face like giant, writhing caterpillars.

Brette folded her hands in her lap. "I arranged for Ophelia to encounter his lordship in the library, which I realize now was imprudent."

"I should say it was." Mrs. Thurston waved her fan before her flushed face, condemnation shooting from her eyes.

"Please allow her to finish, Mrs. Thurston." Leventhorpe flicked his forefinger. "Go on, Brette."

"I assumed if I acted as their chaperone, a few moments together would be harmless."

Brette's attention swept to Alex for the briefest instant, the faintest whisper of a glance, and he gave her an encouraging partial wink. "Mr. Hawksworth came upon us, and Ophelia left without speaking to Lord Danfield or him being aware we waited outside the library."

Except Danfield had known.

Alex had made eye contact with him and received a rather cheeky grin in response.

"You overstepped the bounds, Miss Culpepper. We entrusted our daughter to your care, and you betrayed our trust." Thurston shook his finger at her before facing Ravensdale. "Your ward is responsible for my daughter's ruination. What do you mean to do about it? You should permanently banish her to the countryside. That should put an end to her meddling. And be aware, I may seek damages in court."

His rampage lacked real conviction. Wouldn't a frantic father rush after his wayward child rather than linger in the study spouting accusations? A parent truly distraught would've done so immediately, and that he didn't roused misgivings.

"Don't fault Lord Ravensdale, Mr. Thurston. I presumed too much and am solely responsible for what's occurred." Brette met his infuriated glare unflinchingly. "I realize my folly in having trusted Ophelia. Pure foolishness on my part."

Mrs. Thurston huffed and spluttered. "You... you dare to blame my precious daughter?"

"Your precious daughter intentionally deceived Miss Culpepper and me, Mrs. Thurston."

Alex had warned Brette this might happen, yet he couldn't blame her entirely. She possessed a servant's heart and wanted people happy. Plus, if he wasn't sorely mistaken, she was more than a bit bored. Accustomed to hard work, few luxuries, and even less time for idleness, she needed something to occupy her and her time.

His parish sponsored a foundling home, and if he could acquire the funds, he wanted to establish a ragged school to offer London's street children a basic education. Surely she could find something to occupy her time at the home. Lord knew the pitiable children would benefit from the attention and love, and given the stern lines wrinkling Raven's forehead, she wouldn't escape this escapade without repercussions.

Alex would do his best to persuade Raven to allow Brette to work off her penance by volunteering at the foundling home or his church, though how he'd tolerate her regular presence without declaring himself, he didn't know.

Raven cupped his nape, giving Brette an assessing sidelong look. Lines of frustration framed his mouth and eyes. "Nonetheless, Brette, as your guardian, I am also responsible. We'll discuss this later, and I shall decide on the best course of action. At present, our main concern is setting out at once. Miss Thurston and Danfield have the advantage of a head start, but they cannot travel far at night by carriage, even with a full moon."

Raven brought this on himself when he married Brooke and assumed guardianship of her sister and cousins. Five diamonds of the first water had him running ragged.

Poor chap. Raven would be bald as a billiard ball and wrinkled as a crone by the time the last Culpepper married.

Alex almost laughed aloud.

Lady Ravensdale sat beside her sister and took her hand. "I know you meant well, Brette, but you acted recklessly. And truthfully, I'm surprised. It's not like you at all. You're sensible and steady." She angled her elegant head, contemplating the Thurstons. "We'll have ourselves a coze tomorrow and get to the bottom of what's really going on."

"I'll tell you what's going on." Thurston stopped his agitated stomping and gripped the sofa's back. "An upstart bumpkin has breached society's boundaries, and my daughter must pay the price."

His jowls shook with his agitation as he resumed his tramping back and forth. The carpet wouldn't be the same, given his tendency to scuff his feet as if lifting them proved too much of an effort. Considering the condition of his estate and person, his laziness wasn't altogether surprising.

Drawing back the weighty cerulean brocade draperies, Alex searched the drive. Several carriages stood at the ready, their coachmen clustered in a circle, chatting. These conveyances belonged to neighbors living close enough to make the moonlight trip to and from home. Had Miss Thurston's bags been hidden within their vehicle?

Her romantic flight had been planned; he hadn't a single doubt.

For parents whose daughter, at this very instant, gallivanted to Gretna Green, the Thurstons seemed remarkably unruffled. And Mrs. Thurston's uncharacteristic lack of tears throughout this ordeal had Alex narrowing his eyes in suspicion. Especially, since he'd seen evidence of her waterworks at the slightest provocation previously. Say, a tear in her hem, an undesirable seating arrangement at dinner, a perceived snub, or being denied the last seed cake slice when another guest selected the dainty first.

Alex dropped the drapery and, after straightening its folds, crossed his arms. "What's done is done. Lieutenant Drake and Captain

Whitehouse rode out just now. If anyone can catch Danfield and Miss Thurston, they can."

"They rode out? Already? Without waiting for my direction?" Rather than appearing grateful, Thurston rapidly blinked his buggy eyes and clawed at his cravat.

"You don't approve, Thurston? I should think you'd be greatly relieved. Drake's a fine tracker. The best, truthfully." Alex fingered the thick, silk cord restraining the draperies.

A knock rattled the study door an instant before Chambers stepped into the room, leaving the door partially open behind him. Lady Leventhorpe's lovely singing voice carried into the study. *She* should have taken to the stage. Truly rare, a talent such as hers.

"I beg your pardon, my lord, but Miss Thurston is outside," Chambers announced. "I assumed you'd wish to see her at once."

Miss Thurston?

Another shock this evening. God spare them any more. Chambers pressed his lips together. "She's in a … froth."

She must be hysterical for Chambers to comment on her state.

"I must speak with my parents at once, Chambers. A most wretched mistake has been averted."

A well-bred woman keeps this truth in the forefront of her mind:
Intentions are irrelevant if perceived the wrong way.
~Appearances and Attitude—The Genteel Lady's Guide to Practical Living

3

Alex couldn't help the smug satisfaction sweeping him. Something about this whole deuced thing had been off from the start, and his qualms led him straight to the Thurstons.

Pushing Chambers aside, Miss Thurston stormed into the room, the Culpeppers' decrepit and poor-sighted Welsh corgi, Freddy, toddling in behind her.

"Ophelia? Whatever are you doing *here*?" Making an odd choking noise, Mrs. Thurston fluttered her hands near her chest and, blinking like a startled owl, veered her husband a stricken glance.

Brette's eyes narrowed until only her blue-green irises showed, an almost humorous contrast to her lips' sweet upward tilt. "You don't exactly appear overjoyed. I wonder why?"

Freddy snuffled his way to Brette and Lady Ravensdale. After giving their slippers a thorough sniffing, he tried to drag his portly self onto the sofa. His stubby legs worked frantically as he hopped and wriggled in vain.

Brette took pity on him and hoisted the pudgy dog onto a cushion, where he promptly collapsed, tail thumping and tongue lolling.

As a child, Alex had wanted a dog, but Mother refused, claiming his frail health wouldn't permit such a *filthy* beast. Later, without a place to call his own, he hadn't succumbed to the urge.

Freddy, his charcoal eyes shining, gazed up at Brette adoringly as she absently scratched behind his ears.

Mayhap Alex would find himself a stray pup and give it a home at the parish. He could certainly use the company. People wrongly assumed he either capered about nightly with his high-born chums or sought the entertainment ladies freely offered.

Far from the truth, that.

Most evenings found him preparing his sermon or dining with a parishioner, usually one with a marriageable daughter. He'd become skilled at maintaining a cordial smile while deflecting the girl's wayward hands groping his thighs beneath the tablecloth.

He *should* have been an actor.

Other nights, a book in hand and drowsy from boredom, he lounged before his smallish coal grate. Those times, loneliness gripped him the worst, and he'd welcome a furry friend's company.

"I couldn't do as you bid," Miss Thurston whined. *Spoilt, pampered child.* "I tried, Mama and Papa, I truly did."

Aha. I knew it.

A man of God oughtn't to be overjoyed at the revelation, but now Brette would be vindicated, and proving her innocence outweighed Alex's failings as a rector.

"But once in the coach," Miss Thurston rattled on, "when Danfield started blathering about our wedding trip. How he wanted to visit moldy Egyptian tombs and hot, dusty ruins. And then—if you can believe it, for I simply cannot—he dragged a musty volume on hiero ... hieroglumps or something as awful sounding and impossible to pronounce from his satchel."

"Hieroglyphs, perhaps?" Lady Ravensdale's shoulders trembled suspiciously as she allowed Freddy into her lap.

"I suppose so." Miss Thurston plopped into a chair, a mutinous pout upon her pretty face. "Well, I tell you, I couldn't go through with the elopement. I couldn't bear a lifetime of that—of *him*. Not even for fifteen thousand annually."

Would she never cease?

Miss Thurston shuddered delicately. "He had the nerve to ask if I knew what a scarab was. He laughed when I suggested it might be a sort of gem. I don't think it too much to anticipate he'd have a trinket for me. Something to show his devotion."

Now Brette's shoulders shook too, and she coughed into her hand.

Her pert nose wrinkling in disgust, Miss Thurston pursed her lips. "But did he have a bauble for me? No, indeed." She stretched the word out, emphasizing her disgust. "He wanted to talk about nasty beetles, munching ... *pooh*. Pooh, of all the ridiculous twaddle. A mere ten minutes, and I wanted to toss Danfield from the carriage."

A distinct snort of laughter echoed from Leventhorpe's direction.

"But, my darling, your reputation's tarnished. You've no choice except to wed him." Mrs. Thurston, her face a peculiar shade between pea-green and ash, forced a brittle smile, the flinty glint in her eyes belying her loving words.

Thurston's perpetual scowl deepened until his eyes became two puffy slices. He pounded the sofa's back. "I shall demand Danfield marry you. You've been compromised."

"Bah, what fribble. He didn't even kiss my fingers." Miss Thurston flapped her gloved hand back and forth. "I don't think the man has an interest in women, truth be known. Unless they've been dead a century or two. Then he's agog over their fusty bones."

Raven elbowing Leventhorpe in the ribs cut short the latter's guffaw.

Her father puffed out his strawberry red cheeks. "You will do as I say, young lady or—"

"I shan't do it." Miss Thurston crossed her arms, thrust her stubborn jaw upward, and glared at her parents. "*You* wanted Danfield's money and position. Would have me sacrifice myself for your benefit and comfort." Her focus slid to the windows, and her features softened. "Besides, I love another, and if he'll still have me, I intend to wed him."

Beneath his breath, Raven muttered to Leventhorpe. "Wonder who might *that* lucky chap be?"

Leventhorpe grinned, hunching a shoulder. "I cannot believe Danfield tried to discuss insects—*poop*-eating insects—while eloping. Only he would find such drivel romantic."

Brette's lips twitched and laughter danced in her expressive eyes before she lowered her glossy head.

Alex yearned to run his fingers through those silky tresses.

"I'm of age, and I shan't be stopped." Miss Thurston speared her parents a mutinous look. "Mr. Waters is a decent man with an adequate income."

At her admission, Brette's head shot up, her mouth forming an O of surprise.

Hers wasn't the only jaw sagging. A pelican might have built a nest in Thurston's gaping mouth.

"Wat ... ters?" he stuttered, yanking at his cravat again and sounding like he'd chewed hot bricks. "The ... the *merchant*, Waters?"

Mrs. Thurston's mouth snapped shut with a loud pop as she collapsed against the sofa, eyes closed, agitatedly fanning her face.

"Dear Lord," she moaned. "Our daughter shall smell of the shop. What will people say?"

Miss Thurston prattled on. "You can choose to support me in this. Or you can oppose me. Regardless, I shall marry Jerome, and you'll see neither me nor a single shilling from him either."

"But, darling," her mother objected.

She gave each of her shocked parents a flinty stare. "I mean it."

Alex feared Ophelia's parents would suffer an apoplexy. Their faces mottled into the most astounding reddish-brown hue, and their mouths worked silently, rather like gasping bass on the shore.

Miss Thurston almost deserved applause.

He'd underestimated the chit. Misjudged her too. He understood her dismay at being forced into a position she didn't want because others deemed it suitable. Blasphemous for a cleric to think those thoughts. Shouldn't his conscience jab or poke or chastise a little? Or a lot?

True, he thought of himself as a Godly man and had enjoyed attending church even before becoming a rector. He didn't have horrendous vices, but he certainly wasn't a saint either. And most assuredly, he had no desire to shepherd a flock of clucking or grumbling ninnies for decades.

He'd rather teach dance or voice, truth to tell.

"You mean to tell me the three of you plotted this conundrum?" Brette stood, and her cobalt satin gown swished softly as she planted her hands on her slim hips. Outrage resonated in each clipped syllable as she pointed her finger at the Thurstons, one by one. It may as well have been a sword, for with every thrust of her finger, they flinched as if impaled. "And you would've let me take the blame? How utterly despicable."

Miss Thurston blushed and fiddled with her gloves. "Unforgivable, I vow."

"I should think so." Lady Ravensdale set Freddy aside and delivered the Thurstons a hair-singeing look.

Brette faced her sister and Raven. "Rest assured, I have learned my lesson well, and shall never again do anything more daring than wear blue stockings. Nonetheless, my heart's at peace because my intentions were pure."

She marched to the door, but before leaving, leveled each person present a stony look. "I made a mistake, and I own my part in this bumblebroth. But each of you was ready to convict me, when in fact, they," she swept her hand toward the unrepentant Thurstons, "should be reproved for their fiendish plot."

From Alex's position beside the window, the woundedness in Brette's lovely sea-green eyes stabbed him. They'd misjudged her, though the circumstances did make her look guilty as sin.

She angled her head regally, and the candles' reflected off the bright tresses. "Danfield is well rid of you, Ophelia."

Mrs. Thurston huffed, "Well, I never..." Ophelia's face crumpled, and she sniffled. *She* dared to cry?

"You might find him dull, but at least he's a man of character and not a lying, deceptive charlatan." Brette's angled jaw revealed her injured pride.

Tiny imp she might be, but her feistiness more than compensated for her lack of stature. As the smallest Culpepper, how challenging it must have been when the others towered above her, their height giving the impression of power and authority.

But the petite spitfire before them? Alex would lay a wager that in a battle of wits, she'd verbally slay them all. Including him.

"I am retiring to my room to pack, and tomorrow I'll be away to— I suppose that's for you to decide, Lord Ravensdale. No doubt a place far from Town." She met Alex's gaze for an instant. *Because she knows I share her view?* "Where, I'll likely perish from inactivity and boredom."

Such exaggerated cynicism shaded her words, he barely refrained from laughing. How well he understood her reluctance. Raven did too, for until he married Brooke, he'd abhorred the country. For a week or two, provincial life might be tolerated, but months on end? No, thank you. One cow looked much the same as the other, and the abundance of rodents and insects, not to mention the early hours...

Again. No. Thank. You.

"Good riddance, I say," Thurston snapped, yanking Alex to the present unpleasant situation. Freddy raised his graying muzzle and growled.

Exactly so.

"I'll remind you, Thurston," Raven intoned, his irritation tangible, "you're speaking of my ward, and had you, your wife, or your daughter possessed better characters, none of this would've happened."

Leventhorpe indicated the door with a sweep of his arm. "I'll thank you to leave my house and not return."

Muttering their indignation, the Thurstons filed past Brette.

She spared them no measure, meeting each of their sulky gazes with accusation and condemnation in hers.

"Please forgive me, Brette. I used your kindness woefully. That was unpardonable." Miss Thurston's apology earned her a tight, closed-mouth ribbon of a smile, but no more.

"If you'll excuse me, I must pack." Brette bobbed a shallow curtsy.

"Brette, darling, don't be hasty." Lady Ravensdale extended her hand. "There's no need to make an impulsive decision. Is there, Raven?"

Raven fairly melted beneath his wife's entreating eyes. He raked his hand through his hair. "Brette?"

Tucking her head to her chest, Brette glided from the room. No music filtered into the study this time. Had Lady Leventhorpe sent her guests to bed early?

Tears had glistened in Brette's eyes as she left. Alex would swear to it, and the desire to protect her seared him, hot and fierce. He'd like to plant Thurston a facer. Might make his protruding nose look better afterward, but rectors didn't keep their positions if they popped men's corks, no matter how justified.

Lady Ravensdale made to follow her sister.

"Let her go, my dear." Raven tucked his wife's hand into the crook of his arm. "She's humiliated and frustrated. Give her until tomorrow to calm and collect herself."

Brette would need more than a night to accomplish that.

Alex plucked a piece of lint from his arm. "My parish sponsors a foundling home, and I am seeking additional patronage for a ragged school I wish to start. Both are in need of directors, as well as volunteers."

He summoned his most beguiling smile. The one that sickened him and made him feel like a fawning toady. Or a coquette after a new gewgaw from her protector. Another thing he loathed about his position: the groveling to gain support for charities.

He'd little pride left, but what he did stung sharply.

Not that he didn't think the causes worthwhile. He did, of course.

If he possessed the means, he would've established a school for the performing arts too. Though when he'd shared the notion at White's a couple of years ago, the incredulous chortles rang in his ears for months afterward.

Ironic. The Season couldn't officially start until the Royal Academy of Art's annual Exhibition, but should a fellow suggest a school for actors, vocalists, dancers, and musicians...

Ah, well. Nothing but a fanciful dream.

On the whole, the rich didn't like parting with their coin unless it benefited them, and performers, no matter their degree of talent or pedigree, were relegated to Society's lowest ranks. "Perhaps an arrangement can be made, and Miss Culpepper can put her skills to use helping others, rather than being banished to the countryside."

"Oh, yes. That's a marvelous idea." Lady Ravensdale seized the notion like a drowning sailor tossed a flotation. "Please say you'll consider it, Heath. Brette's not like the rest of us. She'd waste away in the provinces. She hasn't voiced it, but she much prefers the city. I've never seen her as animated and happy as when we came to Town."

"I suppose, Hawk, you'd like Leventhorpe and me to fund this school of yours? And make a generous donation to the foundling home as well?" Raven's wry smile told Alex all he needed to know.

He'd get his school. Eventually. More vitally, Brette would be spared temporary exile.

"If you feel convicted to do so." Alex bowed his head.

Another religious ploy. Use guilt, and spread it thickly. He'd become quite adept at the practice but loathed himself as a consequence. He longed to be his true self once more. Not a puppet directed by obligation and expectation.

He scratched his eyebrow, suddenly weary to his bones. "I must return to London Monday next, in any event. If it's convenient, Miss Culpepper and her abigail may travel with me. I do have to stop in at High Wycombe on the way, however. I promised my sisters and cousin I would the next time I traveled nearby."

He'd made that promise three visits to the countryside ago, and his conscience chafed him for his reluctance.

Truthfully, he'd rather not call at High Wycombe at all. The youngest of four, Alex had been the only son and a sickly child, as well as his mother's favorite. His sisters still called him Little Alex,

Mother's pet name for him. They and his second cousin, Arthur, the Earl of Wycombe, had pestered him for two years now to find a wife. He couldn't fathom why they deemed his marrying any of their business.

Wycombe had his heir, Lawrence. Alex needn't produce one also. And their scolding and nagging wasn't because they'd found marital bliss. Alex gave a soft snort. No, indeed.

Of his sisters' unions, two had been arranged matches, the other a marriage of convenience.

Wycombe had surrendered to the parson's mousetrap for money; a gross amount, truth to tell. Each seemed as content as one might, given their situations. None of them had ever aspired to marry for affection and viewed leg-shackling as beneficial business arrangement.

Rather cold-hearted and mercenary.

Alex might have relinquished his former life, conceded to family expectations, and become a reverend—after all, what other prospects did he have? Living off his friends' charity indefinitely?—but hounds' teeth, he wouldn't settle when he selected a wife.

Not true. He'd settle, because she wouldn't be Brette.

Picturing her as a cleric's wife, he choked on a suppressed laugh. Lord, wouldn't that be something?

Might alleviate the tediousness of his profession, but she'd be miserable. He'd nothing to offer her anyway, except a charming smile and ready laugh.

Chambers cleared his throat. Why hadn't he promptly left after Miss Thurston's abrupt arrival? As trained to do, he'd disappeared into the room's shadows, temporarily forgotten until he might interrupt.

Leventhorpe pressed two fingers to his forehead, tension tightening his face. This house party wouldn't soon be forgotten, and he despised being gossip fodder. "Was there something else, Chambers?"

Chambers stepped forward and extended a missive to Raven. "Yes, sir. Please forgive the informality and lack of salver, but the messenger claims the matter is most urgent. You're to read it at once, my lord. He's ridden straight from London and awaits your reply below stairs."

Raven accepted the dirty, crumpled letter. A slight frown veed his brows as he inspected the folded paper. "It's from a solicitor. A Mr. Horace Shipwreck, and it's also addressed to Brette."

Lady Ravensdale arched a fine blond brow. "Really? How peculiar. I'm positive we aren't acquainted with him."

"Never heard of him either," Alex agreed.

Raven broke the seal with his thumb and quickly perused the contents. His flexing jaw and whoosh of suddenly released breath didn't bode well.

"What is it?" Lady Ravensdale laid her hand on his arm, and Freddy sat up, head cocked and ears twitching. "Bad news?"

"Shall I give the messenger a reply?" Chambers asked, his features an indecipherable mask.

His composure hadn't cracked the tiniest amount this entire party.

Raven glanced at Brooke then shook his head. "Not presently, Chambers. See that he's fed." He faced Leventhorpe. "Trist, can I impose upon you to allow the chap to sleep in the servant's quarters tonight?"

"Of course." Leventhorpe nodded, though curiosity and concern glimmered in his eyes. "Chambers, please oversee the arrangements. Oh, and send a rider after Drake and Whitehouse, unless they've returned already."

"At once, my lord." The servant closed the door behind him, and Alex took it upon himself to pour a finger's worth of brandy for all present.

Intuition or perhaps a holy prompting told him they'd need the bracing spirit.

After the butler left, Raven lifted the paper. "What I'm about to reveal stays in our inner circle. It's imperative this information is kept confidential."

Alex handed Raven and Lady Ravensdale their tumblers.

"Thank you, no." Her ladyship set hers aside.

Blast. Alex had forgotten that she was increasing.

"I'll take hers." Raven quaffed his before gulping hers too. Something had him thoroughly disjointed. A rare occurrence.

Alex took a measured sip. "May I presume the contents aren't welcome news?"

The taut lines outlining Raven's mouth answered before he did. "No."

"Well, are you going to tell us, or do we have to play charades to find out?" Leventhorpe tossed back his brandy then banged his tumbler onto his desk, causing Brooke to start. He grinned sheepishly. "Sorry 'bout that."

Generally, Raven wasn't shy on words. Whatever the letter's contents, they'd flustered him. "Raven?" Alex calmly coached. "We're waiting."

Raven blew out a heavy breath and waved the dingy paper. It rattled in protest at his rude treatment. "This notifies us Brette's father has died, and she's inherited a decent sum."

Lady Ravensdale's eyebrows leaped in surprise, and she swiped a tendril from her forehead. "Father died more than five years ago, and I assure you, there were no funds left. This must be a perverse joke, or Mr. Shipwreck has the wrong person."

"No, I believe he has the correct person, my dear."

"He can't possibly," she objected. "It makes no sense."

"According to this letter," frowning at the creased rectangle, Raven took his wife's hand, "Brette isn't your sister, after all, but rather another cousin..."

Every bit of color drained from Lady Ravensdale's face.

"...and her father was," he rubbed his thumb atop the back of her hand in a comforting gesture, "an actor of some renown."

A lady of quality is aware that while we judge ourselves by our intentions, others judge us by our behavior. The latter proves the more detrimental.
~*Appearances and Attitude—The Genteel Lady's Guide to Practical Living*

E arly the next morning, her trunks neatly packed and stacked beside her bedchamber door, Brette marched downstairs. Straightening the lace cuff of one of her favorite traveling gowns, a simple jonquil and ivory ensemble, she quirked her mouth. She'd taken extra pains with her appearance this morning. Who couldn't use a mite extra confidence in a situation like hers?

Resolution stiffened her spine.

Silly, punishing her when the Thurstons had manipulated the entire situation.

She'd meant what she'd promised about foregoing her matchmaking jaunts, however. No more. Two disasters were plenty.

Now how would she occupy her time? Embroider a ship's cargo hold of unmentionables?

With luck, Heath would send her to Culpepper Park. At least she knew people in the area and could anticipate a few invitations until her banishment ended.

This morning, she fancied a hearty breakfast before she trundled off to wherever Heath decided she ought to go. As she approached the dining room, laughter filtered from the open doors, and her steps faltered. She hadn't expected anyone to be about yet. Or at least not that many people. The room fairly buzzed with chatter, rustling paper, clinking and clanking china, and an occasional laugh.

At the threshold, she mustered a smile for—

Good heavens. Truly?

Brooke, Brette's three cousins, Heath, Alex, Lieutenant Drake, Captain Whitehouse, and Lord Leventhorpe sat at the table, chatting amiably.

The entire family, as well as the rogues, awake and dressed at half past seven? Most unusual. An eyebrow crept high onto her forehead. And highly—*exceedingly*—suspicious. She supposed she ought to be grateful that the other guests had more sense than to rise so early, else they'd witness her chastisement too.

Nothing for it. She put on a cheerful countenance and entered.

"Happy morning to you. I'm surprised everyone's awake this early." She slid onto the chair the butler held for her. "Thank you, Chambers."

"Tea or hot chocolate, Miss Culpepper?" He held a gold-edged, sapphire blue cup in his white-gloved hand. Did he give her a slight wink?

"Tea, please." Brette arranged her serviette on her lap and raised her head. "I take it you've risen early to give me a grand send off? Most considerate. Where am I away to?"

Please let it be Culpepper Park and not Heath's estate.

She had the distinct impression the staff at Walcotshire Park, though pleasant enough, found the Culpeppers short of the mark.

Chambers placed her teacup and a full plate before her; ham and waffles, her favorite breakfast. A rare treat indeed. His doing, no doubt, the dear.

"Do you require anything else, miss?"

Though his formal demeanor didn't give the slightest hint, he was a soft old bear beneath his perfect suit. She'd taken to sharing tea with him and Cook on the days she ventured into the kitchen to bake one treat or other. No one at Bristledale court knew she made half the biscuits, tartlets, and other sweetmeats they nibbled daily.

She fancied owning her own chocolate shop and serving dainties and other delicacies. But gently-born women didn't labor for their living. She might have if Brooke and Blythe hadn't married well, but now that she boasted an earl for a brother-in-law and a marquis for a cousin, a quaint storefront was out of the question.

Ridiculous social rules.

"This is perfect. Thank you." What better way to be bundled off in disgrace then after indulging in her favorite breakfast?

"Chambers? We require a few moments' privacy."

Lord Leventhorpe's casual request didn't fool Brette, though taking her to task with an audience seemed a speck beyond necessary.

Besides, it wasn't his place, unless he'd decided, as Bristledale's lord, that he should have his say as well. Beyond the pale, nevertheless, for the captain and lieutenant to be privy to her humiliation. After all, they weren't family.

At least not yet.

Given the gentlemen's attentiveness to the twins, she suspected they strove to remedy that situation.

She would not help them.

No, she absolutely would not.

After Chambers ushered the footmen from the dining room, he carefully closed the door. He probably stood guard outside, giving a gimlet eye to anyone who dared venture near.

Taking a sip of tea, she braced herself for the worst.

Maybe they'd decided to send her elsewhere besides the countryside. Like the university in Switzerland Blaire and Blaike were off to in a few weeks. *God help me.* No desire, whatsoever, nudged Brette to traipse across the continent and freeze her backside off in the Swiss Alps. The cold caused her nose to turn rosy and drip most embarrassingly.

She far preferred dancing at Almack's or another assembly room. Not that she minded further instruction. Just not thousands of miles from England. In fact, if she'd owned the resources, she'd start a woman's college in here. Absurd that only men were permitted the privilege of continuing their education.

She dared study Alex from beneath her lashes and caught her breath when she found him regarding her from beneath his lowered lids. A wry smile tugged his handsome mouth upward at the corners, and she couldn't help but smile in return when he gave her a conspiratorial wink.

Quite the pair they were. Neither fit where they'd been thrust, though each did their best to make their circumstances work. A sense of humor and a positive attitude helped.

Raven put down his fork and knife, the clanking drawing her attention to him and Brooke.

Her sister's encouraging smile sent a jot of hope through Brette. Perhaps she wasn't to be cloistered after all.

Patting her mouth with her serviette, she surveyed those assembled. Why rally the troops then? A mite much, particularly since she barely knew the captain or lieutenant. Well, the sooner she heard what her sentence was, the sooner she could accept her fate and be on her way.

"I presume you want to tell me what you've decided. I'll admit I'm astonished you choose to do so while breaking our fast, Heath." She speared a small piece of ham.

Blaire grinned as she raised her chocolate cup. "No more surprised than we were when Brooke dragged Blaike and me from bed before the sun rose."

"I don't remember the last time I awoke this early." Blaike hid a dainty yawn behind her hand. "But the sunrise was spectacular."

"You should view it from a ship's deck." Captain Whitehouse's grin creased his tanned face. "Truly magnificent."

"Well, I suppose I shall when Blaire and I are off to school." Her cheeks pinkening, she took a dainty bite of toast. Her features sobered as she chewed, and she set the toast on her plate. "I heard your latest matchmaking antics went slightly awry, Brette."

"My dear cousin, slightly doesn't begin to describe the disaster. But the calamity ended much better than it might have." Nonetheless, Brette was quite done with ventures of that nature. "Now I must face the consequences, which, I presume, is why you're all here."

A slightly guarded expression on his features, Alex relaxed into his chair, one hand resting on the tablecloth. Now and again, he drummed his fingertips—the right forefinger ink-stained— as if troubled.

Brette scrutinized those seated again. Call it intuition, instinct, or fey, but her skin prickled ominously as something leaden and gloppy, like congealed day old porridge, settled in her stomach. Something else was wrong besides last night's escapade. She put her fork down, her appetite having flown.

"What's going on?"

Heath stood and straightened his already tidy coat. "I've changed my mind. I think it best to have this conversation in private."

"As I advised you." Alex sent Raven a stern look before his gaze drifted to Brette.

Compassion simmered there.

Botheration. Was her fate truly so bad he felt compelled to protect her?

"Why tell me in seclusion? I'm sure everyone is already aware. I promise you, I shan't dissolve into tears." She might later, but never, ever in public.

Brooke leaned forward and clasped Brette's hand. "Brette, dearest. It seems..." She paused but, after drawing a ragged breath, plowed onward. "A letter from a solicitor arrived last night. He claims you're the daughter of an actor named Reginald Wiley."

"Pardon?" Her mouth gone dry as desert sand, Brette swallowed then licked her lips. "Pardon?" she squeaked again, despite her constricting throat.

I sound like a blasted parrot.

Her sleepless night must've had her hearing things. "That's impossible. We've the same parents, Brooke."

Brooke nodded, the ringlets framing her face bouncing with the gesture. "Yes, I believed so too, but the letter mentions a Belinda. It states she was your mother and died giving birth to you."

"Do you believe that's true?" Brette laced her fingers together, squeezing them to maintain her composure. She darted everyone a brief glance before meeting Brooke's eyes once more.

After casting Heath a desperate look, Brooke bit her lower lip and gave a single affirmative nod. "I heard Mama mention someone named Belinda to Papa one time. I was young, not more than five or six, I think. When I entered the room, Mama swiftly changed the subject. But not before she referred to Belinda as her sister."

"Dear God. Are you saying you're not my sister?"

The vice squeezing Brette's chest—merciless in its fierceness and intensity—hampered her breathing. Being trundled off to the country was a horrid enough fate, but this?

The daughter of an actor, not a gentleman farmer. Utterly scandalous by *le beau monde* standards.

If true, it explained the age difference between her and Brooke and why Brette's build was different than her cousins'. Judging by her petite frame, her father must have been a shrimpy thing.

All cousins. No sister.

"Oh, Brette, it doesn't make any difference." Blaike rushed to kneel beside Brette's chair.

She clasped Brette's hand, her lovely sapphire eyes pooling, though she bravely tried to blink the tears away. "We're still cousins, dear one."

In an instant, Blaire, too, kneeled beside Brette's chair. "We've been like sisters. I scarcely remember our parents. What I do remember is how the five of us," she took in each of the girls in turn, "always had each other."

"And that won't ever, ever change." Blythe shook her head vehemently as a single tear leaked from her eye and trickled down her cheek.

Leventhorpe rose to stand behind her chair, placing a comforting hand on his wife's shoulder, his adoration clear.

The men, rather than looking uncomfortable and awkward, gazed at Brette with sincere sympathy and kindness, and she trapped her lower lip to stifle a sob. She did not cry in public. But the compassion, surely that was all it was, radiating from Alex nearly caused her to lose her tenuous grip on her control.

If she hadn't known otherwise, she would've thought he ached for her. Felt her pain.

"Why would our parents—your parents—keep something so significant from us?" Brette could barely get the words out. A peculiar ringing in her ears, combined with the inability to draw a decent breath and the grayish-black flecks dancing before her eyes, had her truly concerned she might swoon—face-first, into her waffle.

You do not swoon, faint, or have fits of the vapors, Brette Anastasia Wiliminia Culpepper.

Stop wallowing in self-pity this instant.

The room fell silent and everyone except Brette exchanged concerned or hesitant glances.

Don't tell me there's more? How could there possibly be more awfulness?

Heath cleared his throat. "We don't know for certain, Brette, and that's why we'll journey to London straightaway to speak with the solicitor who sent the missive."

"But?" Brette dug her nails into her palms. Given the consternation on his face, she wasn't going to like what he had to say.

"Brette, darling." Brooke clasped Brette's hand atop the lace tablecloth. "Mr. Shipwreck gave no indication your parents ever married."

A bastard?

Heath patted Brooke's shoulder as she dissolved into tears.

"Holy Chr—" Lieutenant Drake swore, but cut the vulgarity short at Heath's severe glare.

Captain Whitehouse released a low whistle and shook his head, his long hair brushing his collar.

So, Drake and Whitehouse hadn't been aware after all.

Heath and Leventhorpe, Alex too, must have placed a great deal of trust in the pair to make them privy to this damaging information. God help her if they possessed loose tongues or a penchant for *on dit*. They didn't seem the sort, but...

Hauling her focus upward, Brette met Alex's troubled jade eyes over the dahlia and lily centerpiece. Steam rose in lazy, silvery tendrils from his ignored cup of tea. Did the same torment reflect in her eyes that shone in his? He appeared utterly devastated, in a composed, manly sort of way.

Interesting how much a person's eyes revealed.

A hysterical laugh bubbled up the back of her throat, and Brette flexed her jaw and balled her hands to subdue it.

That rattlepate Miss Thurston's self-caused ruination paled in comparison to this.

When word of Brette's low birth leaked out, she'd be shunned. Shamed. Refused admittance to homes she'd cordially been invited into before. Unless she married a wealthy, titled peer, she'd never set foot in polite society again. She'd be an albatross around her family's necks. The embarrassing relation to be avoided, sent away, lest she bring disgrace on them too.

From where she mustered the strength to stand, she didn't know. "If you'll excuse me, please. I find I need a few moments to myself."

The rest of the men stood, somber-faced all.

"We'll depart as soon as we're packed, Brette." Heath came round to her side of the table, and like an older, caring brother, wrapped her in his embrace. "You needn't fear. We can keep this secret contained."

About as contained as a spark in a haystack.

Soon, the ember would ignite a blaze no amount of water could extinguish. Word would get out. No force on earth could prevent it.

Mayhap Alex's prayers were her only chance for deliverance.

"Everyone in this room would die to protect you." Heath leaned back and his lips bent before he angled his head, indicating the entrance. "And a concerned butler, too."

The French windows clearly outlined Chambers's distinct profile. He didn't worry her. He'd bite off his tongue before saying a word against her. However, the round-eyed maid turning tail and rushing for the servants' entrance, her apron strings flapping in her haste, couldn't be trusted.

Brette allowed herself a bitter smile as Heath followed her gaze and swore.

"Fiend seize it."

"Within the hour, everyone at Bristledale Court will know of my circumstances, and it won't take a week for word to reach London." She did laugh, a sad, haunting rasp. "Don't you think it rather ironic, that I, who fancied myself a matchmaker, am illegitimate and won't ever marry now?"

"Don't say that, Brette." Brooke rushed to her side and cupped her cheek. "There are plenty of men who'd be honored to call you wife."

Brette blinked against scorching tears. "Name one."

Alex met her gaze square on, a gentle smile teasing his firm mouth. "I would."

A wise woman knows life and love do not obey our expectations
but they do obey our intentions, though in ways never anticipated.
~Appearances and Attitude—The Genteel Lady's Guide to Practical Living

5

Alex drummed his fingertips on the plush crimson seat he sat upon. More of Leventhorpe's generosity.

Alex's gig was fine for tooling around London, but he relied upon his friends' benevolence for lengthier trips. He'd depended on them for a whole lot more over the years. One reason why, without other prospects, he'd grudgingly filled his maternal uncle's position as St. Peter's rector. If he hadn't assumed the role, for the first time in over one hundred years, no member of his mother's family would head the parish; as he'd been admonished repeatedly by his manipulative, perhaps even well-intended, family. Guilt proved a powerful motivator.

With each jolt of the equipage, Alex's insides cramped a fraction more.

He anticipated visits to High Wycombe with the same enthusiasm as being bled or leeched. Childhood memories of the ghastly procedures made him wince and his stomach knot. Damned lucky he'd lived to adulthood with all the quackery practiced on him because of Mother's constant fretting.

He'd intentionally timed this trip to avoid Wycombe. The glorious twelfth of August found his cousin gadding to his hunting lodge for a few weeks of grouse hunting. According to family gossip, he spent more time stalking and fishing than attending to his earldom, likely the reason behind Alex's summons to High Wycombe.

Alex hadn't committed to a particular day, rather having promised he'd visit in the late summer or early autumn, when his parish could more readily spare him. With an assistant curate eager to prove his capabilities, Alex needn't fear St. Peter's would suffer from his absences.

He may have also neglected to tell the curate where he'd be. Another deliberate oversight, and one which had prompted the bishop to write him on more than one occasion, suggesting Alex devote more time to his parish and less to his pre-ministry cohorts. And yet here he was, dutifully, if somewhat tardily, attending to his familial summons while disregarding his clerical responsibilities.

And for what?

Other than spending an enjoyable day or two with his numerous nieces and nephews, his trips to High Wycombe usually proved a colossal waste of time. Robust and arrogantly confident, Wycombe ignored Alex's suggestions. Consequently, he'd stopped offering advice years ago. He'd agreed to this visit to pacify his sisters and Mary, the Countess of Wycombe, who fussed about her son's future.

At the rate Wycombe blew through blunt, Lawrence might inherit an impoverished estate, which, no doubt, infuriated the countess. She'd brought a fortune to the union, but once she'd murmured, "I do," she'd retained no control beyond a quid or two. The earl's neglect of the estate and tenants had taken a harsh toll, and the countess had confided in Alex's sisters that she feared they neared financial ruin.

How could Wycombe possibly have exhausted his fortune—his wife's fortune—so swiftly?

Had he mortgaged the estate too?

Then again, when he stabled nearly one hundred horses and half as many hunting hounds, not to mention his obsession with whores, guns, and brandy, it shouldn't have come as a surprise.

The trees parted overhead, allowing Alex a peek of bright, cloudless sky. In the meadow visible through the trunks, he glimpsed a red stag, head raised nobly, horns gleaming underneath the late afternoon sun. A lake, surrounded on three sides by towering pines, glistened blue-green.

The same color as Brette's eyes.

He closed his to block the astonished expressions on everyone's faces at breakfast this morning—her utter incredulity the absolute worst. She hadn't believed his marriage offer—had in fact thought he jested or felt sorry for her. He'd never be so cruel or insensitive. He'd been desperate to smooth the devastation ravaging her lovely face, and the words had spilled from his mouth without conscious thought. Nevertheless, though impromptu, he'd meant them.

He loved her.

Ever since she'd grinned and cheekily suggested he was a valet, his stupid heart willingly lay prostrate at her feet. Of course, having just met her, he couldn't declare himself, and now she believed he but pitied her.

At his declaration this morning, she'd laughed, a husky, watery combination of pain and skepticism.

"Oh, Alex, I wouldn't ever let you make such a sacrifice. Can you imagine what the Church would say? How your parish would react to you marrying a by-blow?" She'd shaken her glossy blond head, her pearl earrings bobbing. "I do thank you for your kind offer. It means more than you can know."

His first proposal, perhaps his only, politely turned down.

To their credit, not one of his friends, not even Leventhorpe, famous for his sarcasm and biting wit, had ribbed Alex about his pronouncement. They knew him too bloody well. Knew he'd been serious.

Their pity galled.

He didn't care in the least whether Brette was legitimate. He did care about *her*, however, and she'd been delivered a devastating blow. She knew the censure she'd endure when the *ton* learned of her birth.

If Raven were wise, he'd quickly find her a husband and send them on an extended wedding trip.

Alex's gut quivered, and he smirked. It wouldn't be him.

Her rejection didn't come as a surprise. She had no interest in a cleric's wife's dull, placid life. She'd probably shock the parishioners with something outrageous. Say, waltzing on Sundays. What a wonderful life. Dancing with her after services until they became too aged and decrepit to stand upright.

As he whistled a favorite, soothing hymn, the carriage turned onto High Wycombe's meandering drive. How many times had he taken this same journey, never with any real enthusiasm?

Majestic oaks, more than a century old, lined the half-mile path. Their dying leaves, in glorious hues ranging from scarlet to apricot, fluttered high above. A brownish-gray hare hopped beneath a bush and raised onto its hind legs, nose twitching and paws poised as it stared at the rumbling giant passing by.

Alex closed his eyes and spoke a very real prayer. God help him get through the next two days, especially if Grandmama was in residence.

His sisters fussed and fretted over him almost as badly as his mother had. And he could expect extra rich delicacies and likely tonics and tinctures sneaked into his food. Last visit, they'd given him a purging concoction, and he'd sprinted to the necessary every half an hour the first day.

By Jove, this time, he'd put his foot down.

He wasn't a sickly lad, and they needed to stop treating him like he'd cock up his toes if he sneezed. At least Wycombe treated him like a man, in his condescending, superior, everyone-is-beneath-me sort of way.

Alex could already hear Grandmama clamoring on about his duty to the earldom. *Just in case, God forbid,* something happened to Wycombe. She'd probably compiled a list of misses she considered eligible, too. No doubt empty-headed chits the difficult old tabby considered malleable.

No wonder the current countess had banished the dowager to her dower house and rarely permitted her to set foot within the manor. Maybe he'd be spared and Grandmama wouldn't be in residence. A small, but most welcome reprieve, if that were the case.

Alex would've been hard-pressed to determine whether class snobbery more afflicted Wycombe, his countess, or Grandmama. In Wycombe's case, the superiority was sadly misplaced.

Time had treated Alex far kinder than his cousin. A decade his senior, bald, round as an apple, and given to indigestion, Wycombe had aged much faster. A life of dissipation and idleness did that to a fellow.

A bird's trill echoed from the treetops, and Alex mimicked it. Lowering the window, he began whistling. Often confined to bed as a boy, he'd taught himself the skill and had learned to imitate several birds quite well.

The coach drew to a stop before his ancestors' stately home, more castle than manor. Tall turrets graced the northern and southern corners, and Roman god statues topped the stone pillars on either side of the grand stairs leading to an imposing entrance. Row upon row of mullioned windows, many set with glorious colored glass images, covered the house's front.

After descending from the coach, he permitted himself a rather uncouth yawn and stretched his arms wide. Two Dalmatians loped to his side, their tails wagging in welcome. "Hallo, boys. Jasper, you've gotten fatter than the last time I saw you." He rubbed behind the dog's ears. "And Clyde, you're sporting more silver on your muzzle. Very distinguished, I must say."

Clyde also received a few pets upon his head.

A moment later, another Dalmatian, smaller and finer-boned, cautiously approached. Five pudgy, clumsy puppies trailed her. Smitten at once, Alex crouched low and cooed softly. "Come here. It's all right. I shan't hurt you." He cocked a brow at the two males. "And which of you chaps is the father of this fine family?"

Jasper bumped the female's nose before sniffing the pups' wee rumps. Clyde plopped his rear on the drive and proceeded to cleanse himself with a great deal of loud slurping and snuffling.

Well, that answered that question.

One bold pup waddled over to Alex and cautiously smelled his boot. Alex wiggled his toes, and, growling, the puppy pounced on his foot. Alex laughed and lifted the sturdy fellow. "Hello there. Aren't you a fine lad?"

The pup licked his face, and Alex chuckled again. He kissed the dog's nose. "I wonder if I can persuade the countess to part with you. Would you like that?"

The pup answered by biting Alex's ear. "Ouch, you tiny terror. That hurt."

"Sir, I am pleased you have finally arrived."

Holding the pup to his shoulder, Alex pivoted.

Stokes, the butler, stood at the entrance, his expression drawn, though not critical. He'd aged since Alex last visited.

"Her ladyship will receive you in the ivory drawing room. She's been awaiting your arrival for days."

She had?

As Alex placed the pup on the ground, guilt kicked her knobby toes into his ribs.

His deliberate vagueness as to his arrival reflected poorly on him. Already prone to nervousness, poor Lady Wycombe had likely demanded her footmen keep a constant vigil for him. A beautiful woman, vain in the extreme, the countess wasn't one typically caught unawares. She took great pains with her appearance and never, *ever* breached decorum.

In short, few met her impossible standards.

After plucking several stiff dog hairs from his jacket, Alex ran up the steps. "It's nice to see you too, Stokes."

Stokes took Alex's measure from toe to top, lingering on the white hairs stubbornly attached to his functional black coat. The countess would not be pleased.

"Looks like I rolled in a kennel." Alex chuckled, brushing at his jacket. "How fare you?" One didn't generally inquire of the servants, but as a cleric, he felt obliged to ask, and

Stokes... Poor chap, it appeared he'd been trampled by the hounds cavorting in the drive.

"As well as can be expected under the circumstances, sir." He bowed his silvery head and indicated Alex should precede him. "If you please."

Alex drew his brows together. "Stokes, is everything all right? You seem ... troubled." Stokes stopped abruptly, and Alex plowed into him on the threshold. "Beg your pardon."

Thoroughly nonplussed for an instant, the normally imperturbable butler drew in a bracing breath and squared his shoulders. "May I presume you did not receive the correspondence her ladyship sent?"

Did disapproval color his voice?

Alex offered an apologetic smile, hoping to breach the stuffy old boy's defenses. "I'm afraid not. I've been away from London for nearly three weeks."

Stokes's nose inched upward. "I see."

See what?

Alex stepped onto the glossy parquet floor. As they had for his entire life, his grandparents' serious countenances stared at him from their ornately framed portraits above the double arched stairways. "Is there something I ought to know before I meet with the countess?"

"Stokes? Is that Alexander?" Lady Wycombe's refined, yet slightly cold voice inquired from a room farther along the corridor. "Do stop dawdling and show him in."

Rather than tactlessly shout down the passageway in response, Stokes instead calmly extended his hand. "Your hat and gloves, sir?"

After Stokes laid them on the marble-topped table, he again gestured for Alex to precede him. "I believe it best for the countess to apprise you."

Such secretiveness.

Likely, Wycombe had finally exhausted her wealth or fathered another by-blow. At last count, he boasted three daughters by three different mistresses. Lady Wycombe had provided him his heir, thirteen year-old Lawrence, and except for his mother's auburn hair, he was an exact replica of his papa, right down to his chubby, red cheeks.

Alex strode into the drawing room, and the countess gracefully rose, pale as milk in an ebony gown. Odd her rising, and odder still her choice of gown. Probably a new trend he wasn't aware of. Always dressed in the first stare of fashion, she enjoyed playing queen of the parlor, and usually when gentlemen called, lifted her hand to be fawned over.

He bent into a courtier's gallant bow.

She liked groveling too and remained obtuse to his mockery.

A wonder The Almighty hadn't smote him long before this for his sins. Was there ever a less rector-like man to declare himself God's servant? Actually, yes. Lancelot Blackburn, a notorious pirate, became an archbishop, proving redemption and transformation were possible even for the worst of wretches. So why didn't that tidbit ease Alex's self-castigation?

"Really, Alexander. I anticipated you days and days ago. It's been ever so difficult, and you were needed. I've already sent a footman to your sisters with word of your belated arrival. They're expected here shortly."

She drew a filmy handkerchief sort of thing from her sleeve and dabbed her eyes, mindful not to smudge her carefully applied cosmetics. Truly a stunning creature, but frigid as the River Thames in winter.

She sniffled, and he squinted.

Were those *real* tears?

He hadn't believed her capable. And why had the troublesome trio been summoned?

He'd intended to call briefly, *very briefly*, at each of his three sisters' houses before continuing to London tomorrow. Though his curator was an excellent cleric, better than Alex could ever hope to be, Alex couldn't remain absent any longer. The bishop only claimed so much patience. Truly, Dalton deserved the position more than Alex did. He enjoyed the work, loved the parish and her people.

He'd actually chosen the profession. Imagine that.

Alex offered Lady Wycombe his brightest clergyman's smile. The one declaring, *Fear not, I'm at your disposal and shall make everything right.* "Tell me what troubles you. Perhaps I can help."

She froze, handkerchief at her ever so lightly rouged cheek and her

China doll eyes widened. "Did you not receive my letter?" She huffed indignantly. "I posted it three weeks ago."

"I've been attending various house parties, most recently as a guest of the Marquis of Leventhorpe." Must she be so miffed? He wasn't accountable to her. "No doubt the letter's stacked neatly atop my desk, awaiting my arrival home."

The countess flopped—actually flopped so firmly her perfect cylinder curls pirouetted—onto the settee upholstered in fuchsia brocade and trimmed in cream braid. She wadded her handkerchief into a ball, unwadded it then wrung the tortured cloth between her hands.

"Oh, dear me, dear me."

"I take it something's amiss?" Alex slowly sank into a chair opposite her.

Typically, she never showed her agitation, but rather kept her emotions hidden behind icy disdain.

"Amiss? I should say so. Wycombe and Lawrence..." Clamping her eyes shut, she drew in a shuddery breath, her lower lip quivering. Her lids crept upward, and such anguish glimmered in the moist depths that Alex sucked in a swift gulp of air.

"What has happened? Have they taken ill? Been injured?" He racked his brain. Who was the best physician in London? "I'm acquainted with several excellent doctors—"

"It's much too late for that, Alexander." She swallowed, touching the wrinkled cloth to the corner of her eye once more. "Charlbury burned nearly to the ground." Anguish shook her wispy voice. "Only a footman and a maid escaped."

"Oh, my God, Mary."

Her sorrowful gaze wandered to her son's portrait above the fireplace's elaborate mahogany mantel.

"You are the Earl of Wycombe now."

Even the greatest of intentions become
tragic actions when delivered without careful thought.
~Appearances and Attitude—The Genteel Lady's Guide to Practical Living

6

Two Months Later
St. Peter's Foundling Home, London

Brette laid the drowsy toddler beside another child already fast asleep on the thin pallet. After brushing a lock of hair from the girl's face, she straightened and searched the sterile room.

Alex's ... Lord Wycombe's former parishioners either rocked infants or sorted clothing and other donations. Six-and-twenty children—the eldest not yet four years of age and the youngest barely two weeks—called this stark space home. And these counted as the fortunate ones. Older ragamuffins either lived on the streets, in orphanages, or in workhouses, the conditions beyond deplorable.

Three more sleeping quarters—equally as full as this one—a kitchen, a director's office, a laundry, and a shabbily furnished sitting room completed the facility.

Silly to have hoped Alex might put in an appearance these past eight weeks she'd volunteered at St. Peter's. He wasn't rector any longer, after all. *Of course*, that wasn't why the carriage dropped her here promptly at ten and collected her at one o'clock three afternoons a week.

Well, perhaps it might be *one* of the reasons. The main motive. The other being atonement for her last matchmaking jaunt, which, in the end, had worked out remarkably well for everyone except her. Ophelia had married her Mr. Waters, and last week, Lord Danfield's banns had been read. Seems he'd found himself a bluestocking as entranced with stuffy tombs, musty mummies, and pooh-eating bugs as he. Even Phillip Lapley had managed to snare himself an American heiress.

Brette sighed and brushed her fingers over her brow.

Since the morning Alex had blurted he would marry her, she'd heard nothing from him. *Nothing.* Surely he regretted his outburst more than ever now that he'd unexpectedly inherited the earldom.

His news had reached their ears within days, coinciding with her reduced circumstances traveling the social circles. He'd attained the Society's highest elevation as she'd been relegated to the *le bon ton's* cellar.

Her worn, but comfortable half-boots clacking on the cold, cement floor as she made her way to the kitchen, Brette curved her mouth into a self-deprecating smile and scratched her neck.

Hopefully, she hadn't acquired a flea or two.

What in the world would Alex have done if she had accepted and afterward he'd come into his title? What a bumblebroth that would have been.

A by-blow countess.

Gossip fodder for a Season or two, at the very least.

True, many people were born on the wrong side of the blanket; London teemed with them, as a matter of fact. They filled the beds in this establishment, poor, wretched darlings. But few, *very few*, rose to lofty or respectable heights.

Alex had simply been acting his usual kind self, and a warm sensation enveloped her each time she contemplated the noble, gallant gesture. She refused to closely examine the peculiar flickering behind her heart. No good could come of it. Not now, in any event.

Alex may not have believed he was destined for the Church, but his innate decency, humility, and compassion made him well-suited for the occupation, despite his misgivings. He hadn't anticipated coming into a title either, but she was sure, he'd do well by it.

How could he not? He cared more for others than himself.

Marching along the narrow passageway, desperately in need of a fresh coat of paint, she puckered her mouth at the lone piece of artwork in the entire place. A rather poor depiction of *The Last Supper*, hanging askew from a bent wire.

She stopped and straightened the lopsided painting. Disrespectful not to. Could she have made a go as a parson's wife?

She'd never know now, but rather thought the answer must be no. She too much enjoyed London's whirlwind of festivities to settle into a sedate, poised lifestyle. Just as well circumstances had taken this unexpected turn before her foolish heart completely succumbed to the golden-haired, green-eyed rogue's charm.

Too late.

Untying her apron, she winked at a big, brown-eyed toddler sucking her thumb and twirling her chestnut hair between thumb and forefinger.

Brette put a finger to her lips and mouthed, "Shh. Go to sleep."

The child grinned around her thumb and promptly clamped her eyes shut.

Adorable cherub.

Brette arched her back and drew in a long, calming breath. After discovering her parentage, an ongoing restlessness had plagued her. Though grateful to have something to occupy her time—she did truly enjoy working with the unfortunate waifs—the discontentment still churned. More like simmered beneath her outwardly composed demeanor, and she half-expected the dissatisfaction to abruptly rise, bubbling and frothing, before spilling over and creating a mess far more intolerable than a thwarted elopement.

She and Heath had yet another appointment with Mr. Shipwreck this afternoon; a weekly occurrence since he'd sent his first disturbing missive. In fact, Heath should be here shortly to collect her, but Brooke, expecting their first child and suffering from morning sickness, had pleaded her excuses and wouldn't accompany them.

Thank God, Heath had taken Brette and her cousins under his wing. Hard to imagine she'd thought him the worst sort of ogre when they'd first met. Yes, indeed, he'd come around nicely.

A half smile teasing the edges of her mouth, she shook her head and removed her white crocheted cap. Wouldn't do to arrive at the solicitor's looking like a servant, but neither had she any desire to contract the louse plaguing the newly arrived children, hence the maid-like head covering. Releasing a breathy sigh, she draped the apron across a bent hook then hung the cap there too.

Her edginess might have been due to the reductions in invitations she'd received in recent weeks, although there weren't too terribly many routs, dinners, and assemblies in October ever.

Whether the trickling off of invites could be attributed to the time of year or the steady spread of her questionable parentage, she couldn't have said. She didn't really want to know, truth to tell.

Naturally, her family wouldn't say if they suspected the latter.

Stumbling across *Fanny Hill: Memoirs of a Woman of Pleasure* in Raven's library—most assuredly he hadn't a notion his shelves contained the scandalous volume—had provided her with several rather erotic hours of entertainment in the evenings.

My, the *interesting* facts one could learn from a book. Positively wicked, but utterly fascinating, too.

Since she'd likely end up a stuffy old tabby, she might as well educate herself on the mysteries that occurred between men and women. Unless she threw her morals to the wind, she would never experience intimacy herself.

Or bear children.

That knowledge hurt. Horribly.

Grossly unfair how in a blink of an eye, her life had been tossed hoof over tail, through no fault of her own. No wonder Mama had guarded the secret so closely. She hadn't expected the truth to come out, which must've meant she'd believed Brette's father had died or wanted no part of her life. Or—Brette feared this might be the real crux of the matter—Mama dreaded the scandal associated with raising a bastard niece.

Honestly, after learning of her pedigree, Brette had expected Raven to promptly remove the family, or at least her, to Walcotshire Park. He'd surprised her by insisting they remain in London, even after Blaire and Blaike, along with their lady's maids and a hired chaperone, sailed to the continent on Captain Whitehouse's ship. Lieutenant Drake had gallantly volunteered to go along to protect them. Or so he'd professed. His interest in Blaike hadn't gone unnoticed by Brette. However, her matchmaking days were truly over.

She missed the twins something awful. They'd been so excited at the prospect of attending college in Switzerland. Brette didn't share their enthusiasm, for her ambitions were much simpler: a quaint establishment on Finsbury Square that would make an excellent chocolate and pastry shop. She would learn this afternoon how much money she'd inherited from Reginald Wiley and, possibly, whether Mr. Shipwreck had determined if her parents ever married.

After donning her bonnet and pelisse in the home's shabby entrance, Brette gathered her gloves and reticule.

"Ah, yer off, are ye?" Mrs. Tuttle, the housekeeper, huffed along the passage. "The bairns favor ye, they do." She winked, her plump face folding like a giant fan. "Ye need yer own bairns. A whole passel.

Some women are meant for motherhood. Ye be one of them."

A tiny ached thrummed in Brette's throat.

Impossible now. Unless she scampered to the country or a village and found a simple man who didn't care a whit about propriety or pedigree. With a family to love, she might not shrivel like grapes left in the sun.

"Yes, I'm afraid I must leave early today. I've an appointment and expect Lord Ravensdale directly." After wrapping her reticule's corded strap around her wrist, she slipped on a glove, taking care to modulate her voice. "Have you had word from Lord Wycombe?"

Breathing heavily, Mrs. Tuttle seized a chair and situated her ample girth atop it. She rubbed her chins and scrunched her eyes, deep in thought. "I think I did hear he'd sent a letter a day or two ago. Ye'd best ask Miss Yeatman. She be the one who opens and reads the post."

An hour later, Brette sliced Heath an astounded glance. She couldn't believe what she'd heard. "Are you saying I'm a wealthy woman, and I own two houses?"

Mr. Shipwreck squinted at her above his spectacles and inclined his head.

"Well, not Croesus or Midas rich, and I have no idea what the houses' conditions or worths are, but yes, you've received a respectable sum. Mr. Wiley invested wisely, and his will names you his sole survivor." He shuffled through a few papers, their brittle pages crackling and crunching. "It says here," he tapped a browned and raggedy-edged parchment, "your birth was chronicled at St. James, outside London."

Raven leaned forward. "Have you investigated her birth registration? Perhaps her parents' marriage was recorded there as well?"

How dear of him to continue to hope.

"It's possible. However, Wiley never mentioned marriage in his letters. Only his daughter, Miss—" He stopped fussing with the documents and, after pushing his spectacles up his nose for the twelfth or thirteenth time, gave her a kindly, closed-mouth smile. "I suppose I should ask what you prefer I call you."

"Please, call me Miss Culpepper. I cannot think of myself as anything else." How could she? "And to avoid further gossip, I think it's wisest."

"Very well. As I was saying, your father never mentioned marriage, just your mother's and aunt's names, your birth date, and where he registered your birth." He flipped over a few papers. "Ah, yes, and it seems he was the disowned and disgraced middle son of the Duke of Bellinghamshire." He glanced up. "Too bad, that. If I recall correctly, the estate passed to his grace's other surviving grandchild. A granddaughter, several years your junior, Miss Culpepper. Not the entailment, of course. But everything else."

Brette arched a brow and inclined her head. "Well, I suppose I should be suitably impressed."

She wasn't.

She would much prefer to continue as the daughter of Thomas and Bess Culpepper.

Raven gave her a teasing grin. "I am impressed. Granddaughter to old Fusty Boots himself. Well, well."

Brette chuckled, something she hadn't done much of lately. "Fusty Boots?"

"Let's say your grandfather wasn't a jovial sort, and his feet, er ... smelled." Heath's eyes twinkled.

"*Hmm.* Glad I don't take after him then. My mother ... Bess Culpepper knew of my father?" Bess would forever be the mother of her heart.

"That isn't clear." Mr. Shipwreck pointed at the file. "I have a letter from her stating she'd gladly take her sister's child and raise you as her own. She doesn't refer to your father." He sank into his chair's back and folded his hands across his abdomen. "If I may speak plainly?"

"By all means." Brette stopped twirling her reticule's silk tassel. All this dancing around politesse seemed a waste of time. What did Mr. Shipwreck fear she'd do? Become hysterical? Swoon? Break the absolutely hideous dog-dressed-as-sailor-in-a-tub inkwell atop his desk?

Honestly, destroying the ugly thing would be an act of mercy to one and all.

"In all probability, Miss Culpepper, your parents weren't married, and if they were, I'll wager the crown, they did so in secret. Even a disgraced duke's son doesn't marry an actress."

"I assumed as much." She couldn't prevent her disappointed sigh. She'd hoped differently, of course. For pity's sake, who wouldn't?

"Your father was a renowned rake and womanizer. From what I've been able to uncover, your mother ran off and became an actress. That's how they met. When she died giving birth, he couldn't be burdened with a child, let alone a newborn, and contacted me to locate Belinda's next of kin. He knew she was related to the Culpeppers."

Perfect. She'd been sired by a rapscallion, and he'd abandoned her.

Mr. Shipwreck scratched his rather prominent nose and gave her what he probably supposed was a reassuring smile. "You've come into an unexpected inheritance, and although I have no doubt it doesn't compensate for your ... unfortunate birth circumstance..."

Well, Brette had asked him for forthrightness.

At least he didn't call me a bastard or by-blow to my face.

"No, it doesn't." She'd not pretend it did, either.

Heath patted her hand. "You, unlike many in your situation, have a supportive family and the means to make something of yourself. If I were you, I'd think long and hard on what's truly most important to you."

She gave a reluctant nod.

"If you've wanted to travel, here's your chance, Brette. Perhaps you have a hobby you've wanted to pursue. Well, now you can." Gaze kind, he shook his head. "Don't make any decisions yet. Give yourself time to absorb all of this."

"Indeed, I shall take your advice to heart." And she would, but as wise and kind as Heath was, he couldn't possibly comprehend her internal battle. Brette stood, and the men did too. "I'd like you to continue to investigate whether my parents ever married. If you'd prefer not to, perhaps you can recommend someone who's capable of the task."

Mr. Shipwreck's mouth tipped slightly as he removed his spectacles. "I assure you, it's no problem to have one of my junior clerks do a mite more probing. Honestly, I hope he's able to find a marriage record buried somewhere."

Brette hoped so too, but given her father's reputation, it wasn't blasted likely. Her emotions swung between anger—he'd abandoned her, made no effort to meet her—and gratitude for his neglect, else she wouldn't have known her cousins.

Mr. Shipwreck bade them farewell and retreated to his cluttered desk as she and Heath exited into the chilly outer office. Three clerks scritched away behind high desks, their thin faces creased in concentration. One, sporting a shock of untamed red hair, raised his head, offering a quick smile, and another leveled her a bland glance before they dutifully returned to their work.

The secretary, Mr. Loomis, jumped to his feet and bobbed his head. "Good day to you, sir. Miss."

"Thank you." Heath canted his head. "We can see ourselves out."

What she would do with the money and houses Wiley had settled on her, she'd decide later. "My lord?"

Heath shook his dark head. "We're family now, Brette. When we are alone, it's perfectly acceptable to call me Heath or Raven."

She withdrew the paper Mr. Shipwreck had given her, listing the houses' addresses. "One house is in Kent, but the other is here in London." Perusing the paper again, she wrinkled her brow. "In Belgrave Square." She glanced at him. "Is that a respectable area?"

Were there shops nearby?

"Indeed." Opening the front door, Heath nodded.

London's dankness and pungent smells assailed her, as did the never-ceasing noise.

He closed the door behind them. "It's not an exclusive area, to be sure, Brette, or even high fashion, but certainly genteel. You couldn't live there alone, naturally. That wouldn't be acceptable."

"Of course not." Absorbed in her ruminations, she permitted him to take her elbow and lead her outside. Descending the stairs, she tucked the paper into her reticule, and not attending to where she was going, bumped into a whistling passerby.

"I beg your pardon—" Startled and embarrassed, she met the gentleman's amused emerald eyes. "Alex!"

My, my. So devilishly handsome in his dark blue Garrick coat, a green and gold striped waistcoat peeking from the folds. Evidently tired of black, he'd chosen not to wear mourning attire, and his colorful togs suited him. *My goodness, suits him well, indeed.* She raked her gaze over him, mindful of her pulse's disturbing cavorting.

And here she stood, wearing one of her plainest, most unflattering gowns. At least her pelisse was first rate. The unusual shade, somewhere between sky blue and jade green, flattered her coloring. Or so Brooke had exclaimed when she'd insisted Brette have a pelisse made from the fabric.

Brette returned Alex's infectious grin. She'd not pretend she wasn't thrilled to see him.

"I say, Hawk ... er, Wycombe, it's glad I am to see you looking hale and hearty." Heath and Alex shook hands. "Are you in Town for a few days? Do say you'll come to dinner tonight. I'm sure my lady won't mind."

Alex hesitated, his keen gaze swinging between her and Heath.

"I wish you'd say yes." Brazen as a dockside whore. But Brette did wish it. She'd missed him awfully. He'd been a constant presence since Heath married Brooke and bundled them off to London.

True, a few days might have gone by without seeing him, but not weeks.

He stepped aside to allow a nurse pushing a pram to bustle past. One eye on the ominous sky, she pulled the blanket higher over her charge. When his gaze encountered Brette's again, a distinct tenderness cradled the corner of his eyes. With what appeared reluctance, he switched his attention to Heath.

A delicious, lovely warmth blossomed in her middle.

"If you're certain it wouldn't be an imposition, and if you'll call me Hawk. Not sure I'll ever get used to the title. I only arrived this afternoon and haven't opened the Berkeley Square house." He shook his head, a half-smile tilting one side of his mouth. "I don't feel I have the right."

"It wouldn't be an inconvenience. Surely you know that." Heath clasped Alex's upper arm. "Why open the house at all? Your rooms at Highfield Place House are untouched, and you're more than welcome to stay with us while you're here."

Brette's stomach fluttered excitedly, and a shiver skittered along her spine. An audacious one she couldn't blame on the brisk, damp wind whipping along the street, scattering the crispy leaves. The sky had taken on a sullen, chain mall hue, guaranteeing rain soon. "Are you walking, Lord Wycombe?"

For a moment, Alex stared at her blankly, a faint flush tinging his angular cheeks. "Forgive me. I didn't realize you were addressing me, Miss Culpepper. But yes, I'm on foot. I needed a spot of air to clear my head."

"Heath, might he ride with us?" She flicked her gloved fingers upward. "I do believe it means to rain."

Another gust blasted into them, and Alex's cologne wafted past. Best dashed smelling man.

A woman could get addicted to his pleasant scent. She eyed him appreciatively. Could get addicted to everything about him, truthfully.

"Of course you must join us. Can we drop you somewhere or will you ride with us to Mayfield?" Heath moved to the carriage where the driver, Peters, stood with the door at the ready.

"No. My business can wait." Alex glanced at the shingle hanging outside the establishment she and Heath had left before following her to the coach. Several other solicitors advertised their vocation along the tidy lane as well.

Their shoulders hunched, the few remaining pedestrians, casting anxious peeks skyward, rushed along, and a man with a brightly colored scarf wound round his neck, his chin tucked to his chest, and his hat drawn low on his head, trotted past on a fine roan.

A landau slowly rolled by, and a young woman's pretty face appeared in the window. One of the Gambwell sisters? Margaret. Catching Brette watching her, she ducked into the vehicle's interior and, a moment later, the shade descended.

First one, then another, fat raindrop splattered onto Brette's bonnet. It would be ruined if she stayed outside, and even though she possessed her own funds now, she disliked wanton waste. "Let's climb into the coach before we're soaked, shall we?"

A few moments later, the pregnant clouds opened up, releasing a deluge. Alex gestured at the onslaught. "Thank you. You saved me from that."

"I ... *We* didn't expect you in the city this soon." Brette dared hope, of course, but he was in mourning and proprieties must be observed.

He and Heath took the opposite seat and relaxed against the pheasant brown squabs. Alex gazed at the passing scenery, unusually subdued and distracted.

"My lord—" Brette ventured.

His mouth quirked again. Most unfair, his being so striking. She couldn't take her gaze from him.

She darted Heath a swift glance. Had he noticed? No, his attention still centered on Alex.

A gentle smile tipped Alex's mouth. "I'd much prefer you call me Hawk or Alex, as I've asked you before. I don't think Raven will object."

"Yes, but you weren't an earl at that time. It would be most inappropriate, and a woman of my questionable station must behave properly at all times." Rather than chuckle at her quip or respond with a witty remark, he searched her face for a protracted moment.

"You've nothing to be ashamed of. Remember that." Alex returned his focus to the rainy outdoors and his thoughts to whatever had him so thoroughly preoccupied.

Yes, something most definitely wasn't right. Heaviness or despair shrouded the lighthearted man she'd come to know these past months.

Brette cast Heath a questioning look.

He'd detected it too. "Hawk, we've been friends for two decades, and I recognize that glum expression. What's wrong?"

Alex lifted a shoulder slightly, his gaze yet riveted on the bleak scenery. "I'm afraid there's ugly speculation that Wycombe's and his son's deaths weren't an accident. That the fire was set deliberately."

Brette gasped and clapped her hand to her mouth.

"By God, never say so." Heath pounded his thigh. "Do the authorities suspect someone?" Alex ceased perusing the deserted street, and his tormented gaze meshed with hers.

Oh, my God.

Disquiet haunting his beautiful green eyes, his voice the merest shred, he murmured, "Me."

Carefully consider others' spoken words and whether
honest intentions are behind them. If not, they are meaningless.
~Appearances and Attitude—The Genteel Lady's Guide to Practical Living

Brette kicked at the leaves dusting the Hyde Park walking path. Yesterday afternoon's rainstorm had shaken myriads loose, and a colorful, soggy quilt covered the ground. Puddles pooled here and there, despite the brightly shining sun. The golden rays failed to warm the air, however, and a nippy breeze chilled her face.

She'd forgotten her handkerchief, and the cold made her nose run. She sniffed loudly, kicking another bunch of leaves.

Unfair. So blasted unfair.

How could anyone suspect Alex of such grotesque crimes as arson and murder? He'd assured her and Heath he had an alibi, but strain, nevertheless, marked his features. How could it not until he'd been vindicated?

A few feet away, a scolding squirrel scampered up a tree and Brooke, strolling with Heath behind Brette, laughed. A trifle wan, Brooke had dared a short walk today. The fresh air would benefit her. The babe too.

Brette couldn't decide if she wanted a niece or a nephew. She planned on spoiling the darling no matter the infant's sex. Spinster aunts were permitted the luxury. Her musings turned to last night. Dinner had passed pleasantly enough, but the undercurrent of Alex's disconcerting revelation had kept the mood somber. He'd departed the house early this morning, leaving word with Jenkin he'd be gone the entire day.

Drat it all.

Brette shouldn't have been disappointed. They were merely friends, and couldn't be anything more. That truth shouldn't have bothered so much. But it did, nonetheless.

An unkind giggle drew her from her musings.

The three Gambwell sisters and their severe mother approached from the opposite direction. The fair weather had lured many outdoors this morning, including unpleasant creatures normally hiding beneath rocks or staying abed until noon.

Margaret Gambwell pointed at Brette and whispered, sotto voce, in Charlotte's ear. "Isn't Bret a man's name?"

Both erupted into gales of laughter while the third and youngest sister, Harriot, coldly stared at Brette.

Third time this week.

She could expect more of the same. Mayhap tomorrow, she'd take her constitutional in The Green Park.

Brette refused to slow her stride or shirk away. Head held high, she continued on, but as she passed the tittering misses, the dame lifted her nose as if she smelled something foul, pointed her haughty gaze skyward, and yanked her skirts aside. The younger women immediately followed suit.

The cut sublime.

An anger-borne flush heated Brette's cheeks, but she braced her shoulders and slanted her head politely. She'd not degrade herself and respond in kind, though she itched to give the pompous quartet a piece of her mind.

"There you are, Miss Culpepper," Alex called, waving his hand and looking exceedingly dashing in a Spanish brown greatcoat. He held a puppy clasped in his other arm. "Please forgive me for my tardiness. I'm afraid Domino here escaped me, and I was forced to chase the rascally whelp."

Impeccable timing. Brette couldn't prevent her overjoyed smile. "Lord Wycombe."

At the envious pouts turning down the sisters' mouths, and the peeved scowl twitching Lady Gambwell's unnaturally dark eyebrows, Brette's smile may have taken on a gloating mien. But only the merest touch. Never anything as vulgar as outright jubilation.

As Brooke and Heath reached her, ready to do battle—she guessed from the displeased expressions tightening their faces—Alex strode to her side and graced her with a rakish smile.

Good Lord.

When he smiled so roguishly, her muddled thoughts refused to order themselves.

The Gambwells seemed similarly afflicted. They stood, gaping like besotted or inebriated nincompoops. Even the married elder.

"Good day to you, Lady Gambwell." He politely doffed his hat while trying to subdue the wriggling mass of black and white he held with a tongue determined to sample Alex's chin and cheeks. "Miss Gambwell. Miss Charlotte. Miss Margar—"

The pup's pink tongue slipped between his lips, and Alex laughed as he attempted to rearrange the excited dog. "Behave, Domino."

"My dear Lord Wycombe," simpered Lady Gambwell, her husband-hunting teeth bared in what she no doubt presumed a smile. A hyena's evil grin right before it attacked its prey. She flapped her purple-gloved hand at her ogling offspring. "You remember my daughters, of course. Girls, curtsy."

Brette raised a skeptical brow.

Is she daft? Of course he remembers. He just greeted them by name.

Like puppets, the trio bobbed their bonneted heads and batted their suspiciously dark eyelashes. A little bee's wax and soot perhaps? Lip rouge too, or Brette hadn't eaten kippers for breakfast.

Careful to keep Domino pointed away from his face, Alex flashed his white teeth again and played the gallant. "How could I possibly forget? You faithfully attended St. Peter's."

Every. Last. Sunday. Sitting in the front pew.

Bosoms displayed like a baker's quarter loafs.

Brette eyeballed their chests. Well, maybe more like dinner rolls. *That failed to rise sufficiently.* Her gaze slid to sixteen-year-old Harriot's flat-as-an-oatcake bosom. *Or at all.*

The Gambwell sisters brazenly simpered and posed, each seemingly determined to draw his attention to them with their wanton antics.

What a ridiculous display. Brette barely kept from rolling her eyes, and instead rubbed behind the pup's one white and one black ear. Alex hadn't been prestigious enough for them as a rector, but as an earl, he'd become the title-hungry cabbage-heads' quarry.

"Who do you have here?" Brette stroked the puppy's spine. She giggled when he flopped backward in Alex's arms, his fat puppy paws in the air, in an attempt to slather her with slobbery canine kisses.

"This would be Domino." Alex bent and placed the rambunctious dog on the pathway.

Domino immediately lunged for the squirrel gathering acorns beneath a nearby oak. His lead brought him up short, but the inconvenience didn't stop the spirited dog from yapping and straining against the leash.

"Lord and Lady Ravensdale." Lady Gambwell finally acknowledged Brooke and Heath. And pointedly ignored Brette.

Last spring, Brette had sat in several drawing rooms, enjoying tea with one or more of the Gambwells, and today, they treated her as if she were fresh horse droppings.

Neither Brooke nor Heath returned her ladyship's forced greeting, just coolly inclined their heads. Pity they possessed too much decency to cut Lady Gambwell and her tittering daughters dead.

"Come along, Brette. I grow fatigued and chilled." Brooke clasped her arm and bestowed a benevolent smile on Alex. "Your tardiness is forgiven, Lord Wycombe, since I cannot remain miffed at my husband's *dearest* friend and our *honored* houseguest."

Oh, bravo, Brooke. Well done, you.

Lady Gambwell made an inarticulate sound, and her face turned an unbecoming puce shade, as if she'd been served a long dead reptile at tea instead of dainties and sweets.

Brette arced a brow and graced him with what she hoped was her sweetest, most flirtatious smile. She normally didn't stoop to low behavior, but for the Gambwells, she'd gladly make the descent this once. "I too forgive you, Alex." Yes, she dared use his given name. Scandalous. "But only if you promise we might venture to Egyptian Hall to view the Laplander exhibition that I've heard everyone singing the praises of."

How's that for bold? Was the exhibition even open in October?

The answering gleam in his eyes told her he knew her game. "It would be my utmost pleasure, Miss Culpepper. I believe they offer sleigh or sled rides too. And of course, I insist that you permit me to take you for a chocolate afterward." He touched his hat's brim. "Ladies."

He effectively dismissed the Gambwells, and they'd no choice but to step aside and allow Brette and the others to continue on their way.

After they'd put distance between themselves and the disgruntled foursome, Brette tapped his arm and chuckled naughtily. "Did you catch their expressions when they learned you stay at Highfield Place House with us, my lord? Or when I used your given name?"

"Indeed. Looked like they'd taken a swig of unsweetened lemonade." His chuckle was every bit as mischievous as hers. "I was able to conclude my business earlier than anticipated, so I collected Domino from the stables where I'd left him yesterday."

Hearing his name, the puppy reared onto his haunches while scratching at Alex's leg. "Down, Domino," Alex admonished firmly but gently.

Alex fell in step beside Heath.

"I hope you don't mind if the puppy stays at the house." Alex struggled to contain the excited dog, weaving between their legs. "If he'll be an inconvenience, I can take him to the stables, though the stable master was in a sour mood after this chap chewed a harness and a grooming brush."

"Freddy will enjoy his company, I think." Brooke gave the high-spirited pup a tolerant smile. "It would do Freddy good to play. He needs the exercise. He's far too fat."

"Yes, but that would require him to move." Brette's droll observation earned her smiles all around.

"Keep him away from my boots is all I ask." Heath chuckled and scooped to scratch Domino's ears. The pup tried to snatch his fingers. Heath straightened, his features serious. "How went your meeting?"

So he knew where Alex had gamboled off to before breakfast.

"Well enough, I suppose. I gave my solicitor the names of the family I dined with the evening Charlbury burned, and they'll be contacted to verify I was with them. Also, given I was in London, and Charlbury Lodge is four hours' hard ride from here, I didn't have enough time to ride there and preside over the Holy Eucharist Sunday morning at eight o'clock. My housekeeper can testify that I arose at half past five that morning, as well."

Hardly an extended arm's length separated Brette and Brooke from the Alex and Heath following them. The men spoke softly, though not secretly, but Alex didn't sound completely convinced to Brette. She slowed her steps, and when the men came abreast, Brooke took Heath's arm.

Brette cut Alex a sidelong glance.

He wouldn't admit it, not to them, but his cheerful demeanor didn't completely hide the disquiet in his eyes.

"Until the matter is completely settled, and until I have the name of who dared accuse me of the foulness, I cannot relax." Alex extended his free elbow to Brette. "I can, however, try to escort you, though with this unruly fellow, I cannot guarantee we won't be tripped."

"I'll take my chances." Any chance to touch him at all. She slipped her hand into the crook.

He tucked his arm close to his side, the movement so natural, she couldn't object. Even if keeping his balance and controlling the dog cavorting at the end of the leash motivated him, rather than an intention to be nearer her.

Walking with him, their arms entwined, and the pup pulling at his leash seemed almost domesticated. Her heart gave its own disjointed tug.

Dangerous, entertaining, fanciful notions.

A leaf tumbled past, and the pup pounced on it.

Alex's forearm flexed, and he instinctively hugged her hand nearer his side.

She couldn't detect an ounce of fat on either his solid arm or firm ribs. Brette laughed as Domino seized the leaf in his mouth, shaking his head and growling. "I think you're going to have your hands full with him."

"Most assuredly. But I've always wanted my own dog. The countess was none too pleased when I brought Domino into High Wycombe, I can tell you. But she'll be leaving shortly and couldn't kick up too much fuss."

"So what happens now? Once your name is cleared, what will you do first?" They'd fallen several paces behind Brooke and Heath.

"I haven't decided. Wycombe neglected the estate, and her finances are in a deplorable state. I suppose I'll start there, and worry about the rest as it arises." He contracted his arm. "How are you? I've been concerned. Has anyone treated you poorly? I'll give them an earful on the pitfalls of a judgmental spirit."

Such earnestness. Brette couldn't deny she enjoyed his protectiveness. "It's expected. Silly though it might be, I'm hopeful a marriage record for my parents might be found. Are you familiar with Fusty Boots, the Duke of Bellinghamshire?"

"I never met the fellow, but I've heard of him. A cantankerous curmudgeon, famous for his foul-smelling feet, so malodorous even his boots couldn't contain the stink. I believe he died a few years past. Why?" Alex twisted his other hand, wrapping the leather lead a few times around it. Domino wasn't pleased by his shortened leash and renewed his efforts to chase anything that moved.

"Supposedly, he was my grandfather, and from your description, I'm not altogether certain that's a good thing. Do you suppose his feet truly smelled so dreadful?"

Heath threw a knowing glance over his shoulder and gave a crisp nod. "Worse. I sat near him once at dinner. Could barely get my food down, and when the fish was served ... God's toenails."

At his unintended joke, they burst into laughter.

A swaggering grin tipping his lips, Alex eyed her square-toed half boots.

Brette poked his shoulder. "Don't you dare suggest anything so ungentlemanly."

They arrived at Highland Park House, and a few minutes later the four assembled in the drawing room, less one sleepy, dappled pup. After depositing a fresh tea tray on the oval table between the burgundy and gold striped silk settees, Jenkin had bidden a footman take the spotted tornado to the kitchen for a snack and a nap.

Brooke, a trifle pale, delicate lines of weariness etching her forehead, sank into the chair nearest the toasty fire. "Brette, dear, would you pour. I'm afraid I feel a trifle unwell."

At once all solicitousness, Heath drew another chair beside hers and took her hand. "Perhaps you should have a rest."

"We'll see, darling. I'm fine for the present." Ah, because dear Brooke didn't want to leave Alex and Brette alone? Did she worry about more tattle?

Brette prepared each cup—two lumps, no cream for Alex—and expertly poured the fragrant tea. After handing everyone their teacup, she motioned to the plate of sweets. "I tried my hand at a new delicacy. It's Scottish black bun, a pastry-covered fruit cake."

"No, thank you. Just tea for me." Did Brooke's tummy trouble her again? This pregnancy business wasn't all the crack.

Alex and Heath each added several treats to their plates. You'd have assumed they'd walked for miles from the way they dug into the pastries and cakes.

A grin wreathed Alex's face as he forked a piece of the black bun. "One of my favorites." He sank his teeth into the flakiness, his brows vaulting to his hairline. "You made this? It's excellent."

"Thank you." His earnest compliment sent heat skittering across Brette's cheeks. "And, yes, I made it a couple of weeks ago. It has to age to reach its full potential. I do like baking though. I might use my inheritance to open a pastry shop."

There. She'd said it.

Three startled gazes snapped to her, yet not one of them objected. *Hmm*, they'd already concluded her prospects were that dismal that she'd need an occupation? Rather disheartening.

The future she'd intended had taken an abrupt turn, and at twenty, Brette couldn't decide which of the limited pathways before her she should take. So much for being the author of her own destiny.

Lips thinned, Brooke pressed her hand to her waist. She truly must not be feeling well.

However, after a deep breath, which she held for a moment before slowly releasing, she perked up. "Oh, I almost forgot. The Goodinghams have invited us for dinner three nights hence. Nothing too terribly large or formal, I don't believe. A dozen guests in all with dancing afterward. Mrs. Goodingham mentioned they're one male short. Shall I tell her you will join us, Hawk?"

Brette's stomach sank to her damp boots. Who else had received a dinner invitation? She hadn't cared before, but the line was slowing emerging between those who intended to shun her and those who would continue to acknowledge and welcome her.

Utter drivel.

She had no control over her birth. It didn't affect her character or worthiness.

As much as she'd enjoyed London and the Season's frenzy, the more staid, less formal country life offered something too. Specifically, the welcome lack of pompous busybodies determining who met the mark and who they deemed beneath their touch.

Brooke chuckled. "I'm still not accustomed to your title, Wycombe."

"I'd be honored to attend, and you can still call me Hawk, if you wish." Alex replaced the snuff box he'd been admiring. "This is new, Raven. How many do you have now?" Alex's mouth moved as he silently counted the boxes displayed on a corner shelf. "Seven-and-twenty. And you've never used snuff."

"I can appreciate beauty, no matter its form." Heath's regard rested on Brooke.

"I'll send a note round this afternoon and tell Mrs. Goodhingham you've agreed to join us, Wycombe." Brooke straightened, her face distressed, and her eyes darkened to midnight blue. "Please excuse me. I'm not feeling well." She clasped Heath's arm. "Would you please assist me to our chamber? I need to lie down."

At once, Brette, Heath, and Alex jumped to their feet.

Heath helped Brooke stand, but instead of wrapping an arm about her thickening waist, he scooped her into his arms.

"This isn't necessary. I can walk." She laid her head against his chest despite her mild protest.

"It most certainly is, and you cannot. I'll not have you risking a tumble." Heath jerked his head toward the entrance. "Hawk, the door please."

Alex hurried to do his bidding, and after they'd stepped into the corridor, he stood sideway in the doorway, hands on his hips, his face taut with concern.

Brette had found him attractive in his staid black, but today, wearing a charcoal-collared hunter green cutaway which emphasized his broad shoulders—how could she not have noticed their breadth before?—buff pantaloons that did his muscled thighs credit, and a daring navy and jade, silver-threaded waistcoat... Well, dragging her gaze from him took colossal effort.

She admired him from beneath her lashes, taking in his patrician profile.

Better find something to do, lest he catch her ogling him. An undesirable shouldn't daydream about an earl. She lifted the brass poker. Ladies didn't attend to their own fire, but having lived a life of poverty at Esherton Green, none of the Culpepper misses put on airs.

Crouching, she prodded the logs then glanced over her shoulder when he continued to remain silent.

He finally swiveled to face her. "How could something as wonderful as carrying a child cause such discomfort?" Sighing, he cupped his nape, disturbing the curls scraping his collar. "Another reason I wasn't equipped for the Church."

Alex's decency far surpassed every man's she knew, Heath and Leventhorpe included. She adored them both now—the big, over-protective gollumpuses—but initially, they'd kept their positive qualities hidden beneath spikey exteriors.

Alex, on the other hand, couldn't have been more transparent.

She canted her head. "Oh? Why do you think you weren't meant for the Church? I disagree. I think you proved yourself an admirable rector."

He lifted a small, framed portrait and examined the likeness. "I questioned—still question—God's design and my purpose. Regularly."

"But, don't we all, at times?" Returning her attention to the fire, she gave the logs an exuberant poke, sending sparks exploding up the chimney.

At the swish behind her, she cast him a startled glance. He'd silently crossed the room and stood a mere foot away.

Leisurely and most enjoyably, she permitted her gaze to climb his thighs, past his trim hips and slender waist, over his chest's broad swell and his cleverly knotted cravat, to his chiseled jaw, and, lastly, his molded mouth.

He extended a hand, but the simple gesture meant much more.

Silently, he beckoned her, and she couldn't refuse his summons any more than a bird voluntarily stopped flying. Their nature compelled them to take wing just as her heart—her gullible, imprudent heart— urged her to answer his winsome command.

She placed her palm in his, welcoming the warm, firm grip, and the delicious tremor shaking her. Slowly uncurling from her squat, she raised her eyes, and the tenderness gleaming in his warmed her blood and her bones to their marrow.

As he cupped her shoulders, drawing her near, the poker slid from her fingers, clanking noisily onto the marble hearth.

"Brette...?"

One syllable, a sensual, throaty, verbal caress. An irresistible snare she'd gladly walk into.

He framed her jaw with his forefinger and thumb, rubbing the bone gently. "I want to kiss you."

"I know." She wanted to kiss him too.

Brette raised onto her toes. How else could their lips possibly meet? Him so tall and she not the least? She must make him understand she welcomed his kiss; he'd never take advantage otherwise. And she did so want his mouth on hers.

So very much. Right or wrong.

Stretching, she arched into him, deliciously, gratifyingly, from hip to breast. Arms looped around his strong neck, she slanted her head and offered him her mouth.

He encircled her, wrapping his arms around her back, his fingers splayed against her sides, and brought his mouth to hers.

A blissful sigh escaped her, followed by a gasp of pleasure when Alex teased her lips apart with his tongue. Her senses came alive, melding into one riotous sensation as his raspy breaths joined with hers. His unique scent, his taste upon her tongue, his hard, rippling muscles beneath her fingertips, and his firm yet velvety mouth moving upon hers engulfed her in the headiest of sensations, as if she floated.

"Ahem."

A prudent woman knows 'tis better to have no
money but a pure heart than to be rich with bad intentions.
~Appearances and Attitude—The Genteel Lady's Guide to Practical Living

Alex plummeted to earth as a clearly exasperated male cleared his throat again.

"*Aa-hemm!*" Raven's irritated voice cooled Alex's ardor faster than a February dip in the Thames.

He and Brette looked—*were*—guilty as hell.

And yet, he didn't want to release her, to let the enchantment they'd shared go. Her tantalizing perfume still teased his senses, and as he'd kissed her, several strands of her silky hair had escaped their pins, one coiling around the wrist of the hand cradling her head.

He locked his legs as she wobbled, and only his arms encircling her kept her from toppling.

Want sluiced through him again. Best change his musings before Raven called him out.

"Dear me," Brette whispered, huskily into Alex's shoulder, as she clutched his lapels.

Panting softly, her gently sloping cheeks nearly the same hue as her soft pink gown, she leaned heavily against him, as unbalanced as he.

She'd tilted his senses, his carefully ordered world right off its axis.

He hadn't a great deal of carnal practice, despite women boldly offering themselves on a regular basis, including former parishioners. But what he'd just experienced with Brette... Mere words couldn't do it justice.

The doorway framed Raven, his legs braced and arms folded. The stance of an outraged guardian. The darkling look he speared Alex made his scalp tingle. Alex had breached an unspoken rule between the five rogues, and Raven wouldn't pardon him readily.

"Why do I continually find my wards in compromising situations with my closest friends? First Trist with Blythe and now you with Brette. It's enough to make me want to trot the girls off to a convent in France." Raven rolled his eyes, but an instant later froze, horror-struck, his arms falling to his sides. He took a couple of uncertain steps. "Blister and damn. Drake and Whitehouse hadn't better look at the twins with anything more than decrepit, grandfatherly attention or I'll—"

Alex released a short laugh and stepped away from Brette, though he kept his hand at her elbow to steady her. "My dear chap. That ship has sailed. Quite literally. How, pray tell, will *you* do anything? Did you seriously not consider the possibility?"

Given the green tinge about Raven's mouth, Alex almost regretted gibing him. Almost.

Alex had detected the covert, and not so covert, looks Drake and Whitehouse gave Blaire and Blaike. And neither of the chaps claimed the degree of gentlemanliness Raven, Leventhorpe, or he did. He'd not voice *those* disconcerting musings, though. Raven couldn't leave his *enceinte* wife to trundle after his wards.

Besides, the damage might already have been done. The twins and their chaperone had sailed weeks ago. Probably no need to worry in any event. Drake and Whitehouse weren't complete and utter scoundrels. *Usually.*

Brette drew in a weighty breath and, her color high, scooted away from Alex. "The girls aren't without common sense. I'd not worry yourself overly much on their account, Heath. And Mrs. Hobbs is a dragon, a true paragon of virtue. Anyone who as much as looks at either twin without proper respect will be whacked soundly upon his nog."

True. The first time Alex laid eyes on the granite-faced dame, he'd winced at her formidable countenance and half expected her to breathe fire when she opened her mouth to speak.

Scowling, Raven stalked to them, his gaze swinging between Brette and Alex the whole while as if trying to read their minds.

He took his guardianship seriously, and Alex respected him for it. Nonetheless, he didn't relish losing one of his dearest chums over a stolen kiss.

Far more than that, and you know it. It can't be. Not yet.

He'd offer for Brette in an instant, but not *this* precise instant.

Not until he'd settled the suspicious fire business, and he could guarantee her safety. And not until he knew the financial status of his estate. He must be able to offer her more than a mere title, a manor in dire need of renovation, and a few scrawny sheep.

A mere title?

How virtuous he sounded. Alex smothered his snort of laughter.

"Be that as it may, explain yourself, Hawk. I'd have expected unacceptable behavior from any of the others, but not from you."

"Why? Because, until a few weeks ago, I called myself a man of God and practiced a wholly different profession? You, of all people, know I didn't seek the position, any more than I sought a title, though I gave the Church my best. I've never professed to be a saint." Alex straightened his rumpled waistcoat, keeping one eye on Brette as she tidied the tea tray.

He'd be bound chagrin prompted her actions more than a desire to help the efficient staff. Did she regret their kiss?

She lifted a plate of dainties and smiling, offered Heath one. "Sweet, Heath?" A diversion?

"What I want to know is what do you intend to do about it?" Raven absently selected the nearest sweetmeat, his unrelenting gaze demanding an answer from Alex.

Raven popped the bonbon into his mouth and immediately grimaced. He managed to chew and swallow the confection before seizing a cup of cold tea and gulping it down. "What in God's name *was* that?"

Alex bit back another laugh, grateful Brette's tactic had worked.

Picking up a serviette, her expression the epitome of innocence, Brette glanced at the plate. "I think it was an almond liqueur filled bonbon."

Clever minx.

Raven might be annoyed that Alex had overstepped the bounds, but he'd approve the match despite his obligatory fussing. A respectable guardian must bluster a mite, and Raven couldn't appear too pleased at the turn of events. He'd feel guilty if he did, as if he hadn't done his duty by Brette.

"I expect you've already proposed. I must say it's high-handed of you, Hawk, not speaking with me first to ask for Brette's hand." Raven wiped his sticky fingers on a serviette.

Devil take it.

Naturally, he would jump to that unfortunate and inaccurate conclusion.

Brette dropped a cup, the shattering china clanging loudly in the silent room as fragments and biscuits scattered across the table and onto the floor. Fetching eyes wide in her perfect oval face, her gaze whipped to Raven then to Alex then back to Raven. "You think—?"

Freddy tottered into the drawing room and, sniffing loudly, made straight for the tea table.

"No, Freddy, you'll cut yourself." Brette rushed to intercept the dog. Gathering him in her arms, she shook her hair from her face and shoulder.

The loose tendrils caressed her cheek, and Alex half-lifted his hand to smooth the moonstruck tresses behind her ear before he caught himself.

"I'm afraid you're mistaken, Heath. There will be no match between Lord Wycombe and myself." She nuzzled Freddy's fat neck. To hide her face?

"Why not?" It did rather smart Alex's pride. Refused before he'd proposed. He was an earl, after all. And he loved her.

Stow it.

A moment ago, he'd been listing the reasons he couldn't marry her

Yet.

Raven blinked, his face a comical mixture of disbelief and astonishment. "Yes, do tell, why not?"

Another time, Alex might have snickered at his friend's bafflement, but not when he reeled from her response himself.

Back half-turned to him, Brette kissed Freddy's tawny head. "Until my circumstances—"

A rather flustered Jenkin loomed in the doorway. "Sir, the Dowager Countess of Wycombe has called. I've asked her to wait in the entry while I inquire if anyone is at home to receive her."

His mien very much suggested he hoped Raven would say no.

Alex sorely wished he would. Grandmother or not, the cagey old bat, couldn't be up to any good.

"Of course they are, you numbskull. I can hear them babbling nonsensical balderdash about my grandson marrying an unsuitable chit." A cane rapped Jenkin's calf. "Move aside, man."

Brette's mouth parted, and she slung Alex an appalled glance.

Wearing an oversized purple bonnet, weighted with enough

plumage to cover an ostrich's arse, Grandmama sailed into the drawing room. She banged her cane raucously with each uneven step.

"Lady Gambwell mentioned you were in Town, Wycombe." Her critical gaze disdainfully swept the room and its occupants. "Though why you've chosen to stay *here* rather than at your residence or with me, I cannot begin to fathom."

For the first time in all the years Alex had known him, Jenkin gaped, speechless. He could hardly haul the dowager from the room, though given his slightly narrowed eyes and elevated brows, the notion had crossed the majordomo's mind.

"Give me a kiss, boy." Grandmama presented her crepey cheek.

A kiss? She wanted a kiss? From Alex? First time for everything.

He dropped a peck on her cool skin. Well, at least he hadn't turned to stone. Or ice. "To what do I owe this unexpected *pleasure?*"

"*Hmph.* You don't fool me, insolent pup. I know you aren't happy I called." She thumped her cane for emphasis, and Freddy buried his head in Brette's shoulder.

Visions of leeches, bloodletting cups, and medieval torture devices popped into Alex's mind. He would've welcomed every single one more than Grandmama.

She hadn't ever a kind or gentle word for him. Not when he'd been a child, and she called him a weak, mewling milksop, and certainly not after he reached adulthood. All her devotion and attention she'd directed to the heir, Arthur, and when poor Lawrence came along, she'd dug her talons into him.

Squinting, her gaze raking him from toe to top, her mouth swept down impossibly further. "Why aren't you wearing black? Have you no respect for your cousins? Is this what's become of associating with riffraff and scallywags?"

"As a rector, I hardly associated with undesirables." The downcast and unfortunate, certainly. Such compassion proved beyond her scope of understanding, however.

She hadn't expected an answer, and from her thinned mouth, didn't like his. She never did. Just criticized and complained and made everyone within hearing distance wish to be somewhere else. Anywhere else.

Alex angled his head and extended his arm. "Please allow me to introduce Heath, the Earl of Ravensdale and his ward, Miss Brette Culpepper."

"Bah, don't waste my time with trivialities." Grandmama turned her critical regard on Brette, a slight sneer on her thin lips, before her arctic gaze gravitated to Alex. Using both hands, she rammed her cane into the unfortunate floor once more. "Do you honestly think to tarnish the earldom or our family name by marrying a common bastard?"

Alex stiffened. "That's outside of enough!"

"I." *Wham.* "Won't." *Wham.* "Allow." *Wham.* "It." *Wham.* The china on the tea tray rattled with each angry blow of her cane.

Her blood thrumming with ire, Brette shifted a cowering Freddy higher in her arms. Convenient she held the nervous dog or, for the first time in her life, she might have slapped another woman's face. Elderly or not.

If Freddy had possessed more than a half dozen teeth, and Brette hadn't been afraid he'd promptly die from the toxins, she would've set him on the hateful dame.

"You have no say in what I do, Grandmama, and if you think I'll permit you to disparage Miss Culpepper, you are gravely mistaken. Apologize."

His grandmother angled her head loftily, the feathers adorning her hat, jerking with the sudden movement. "I shall not. She is beneath me."

Brette had never seen Alex this furious—his square chin set determinedly and his gaze inflexible—and though a prudent woman would've ignored the dowager's rudeness, Brette hurled common sense aside. After all, what did she have to lose?

"Better to claim humble origins and demonstrate kindness and integrity than be highborn without a shred of decency or compassion." She arched a brow and lifted her chin in a challenge. "Or have an elevated sense of one's worth."

Heath's mouth twitched before he brought the quivering flesh under control.

The dowager shook her cane at Brette, coming perilously close to striking her. "Precisely the kind of impudent hogwash I'd expect from a wench of your ilk. That's what comes of being raised with bovines. No breeding or refinement. Common riffraff."

Freddy growled a warning low in his throat.

"You go too far." Alex stepped forward, and his grandmother whopped his leg with her cane. He grabbed the offended calf. "Ouch."

"Wycombe, collect your effects. We're leaving at once. I won't spend another moment in the presence of this ... this undesirable." She brandished the walking stick again, and the urge to yank the menace from the grand dame's arthritis twisted fingers tempted Brette unmercifully.

"Madam, in my home, you will not speak with such disrespect, particularly to my ward." Heath stepped beside Brette in an obvious protective gesture.

Alex limped to her other side.

Two champions. Three, if you counted Freddy's sporadic rumbles. Her heart swelled with appreciation and something much more powerful.

"I am not leaving, Grandmama, and you *will* apologize for your reprehensible rudeness to Miss Culpepper. She is the granddaughter of the Duke of Bellinghamshire, and claims both Spanish and Scandinavian royalty in her lineage. She possesses more blue-blood than you or I. Or have you conveniently forgotten *your* origins?"

The dowager opened her mouth, no doubt ready to deliver a spicy retort, but Alex's stern look muted her. Her savage tongue at least. Her eyes continued a reproachful monologue.

He flicked a forefinger at his grandmother's inflexible expression. "If I recall, we've a commoner or two," he raised another finger, "a traitor, a horse thief, oh, and a ... *courtesan* dangling from various branches of our family's tree."

He wiggled his splayed fingers, and Brette caught the inside of her cheek between her teeth to keep from giggling as the dowager's eyes narrowed further with each unacceptable person he mentioned.

"I'm sure I have no idea to what you're mistakenly referring." The dowager managed to scornfully peer down her nose at her grandson, though he stood a full foot taller. "A courtesan, indeed. Balderdash. Nonsensical twaddle." She sniffed, disdain oozing from her.

"We both know the term is most benevolent, but I strove for discretion, regarding my two times Great Aunt Ruby. Your mother's sister, wasn't she, Grandmama?"

Brette swung her startled gaze to Alex. "A courtesan? Truly? I must hear the tale. And however did you learn about my pedigree?"

His mouth kicked up on one side. "For months, I've listened to Raven and Leventhorpe extol the virtues of two other Culpepper misses."

"So, you intend to defy me?" The dowager completely ignored his references to her dubious relative.

Alex's features softened. "I intend to do what's right and honorable."

"You're a pudding soft fool, Wycombe." Scathing disapproval pinching her features, she shook her head, sending her bonnet's feathers to bouncing one more. "I'm not giving up the field just yet. You wait and see."

Big surprise there.

Heath canted his head, just this side of civil. "Jenkin, please escort the Dowager Countess out."

"With utmost pleasure, sir." Hand on the door, Jenkin stared down the length of his considerable nose. "Madame, if you please?"

And even if she doesn't.

Giving Brette a final haughty glare, the dowager stalked from the room, her cane hammering the floor with each vexed step.

Brette released her pent-up breath. More than a mite disconcerting, being thoroughly disliked by someone she'd just met. "I've the beginnings of a headache." Worsened by the continued pounding of the Dowager Countess Wycombe's sorely abused cane. "And I wish to look in on Brooke as well. If you'll excuse me?"

"In a moment." Heath's raised hand detained her.

Oh, bother.

"We haven't finished our earlier discussion."

Yes. We have.

Usually stoic, he rubbed his knitted brow above his left eye. Likely a drum echoed within his skull too. "Are you or are you not betrothed?"

His question included Alex.

"We are not." If only it were possible. It galled her to admit it, but the dowager was right.

Brette couldn't ask Alex to disgrace the earldom by joining with a by-blow. No evidence existed that proved otherwise, and until it did—*if* it ever did—she'd have to endure the shame. She couldn't ask him to do the same.

Alex dared to finger a wayward curl before looping it behind her ear, staring straight into her soul, his expression so tender, she wanted to weep.

I can't, Alex. Please don't ask me.

"We could be, Brette. In time. After I've put my affairs in order and cleared my name. I'd be honored above all else, if you'd have me."

Even with prudence and discernment, it's
often difficult to determine who causes the most mischief:
Enemies with the worst intentions or friends claiming the best.
~*Appearances and Attitude—The Genteel Lady's Guide to Practical Living*

9

From beneath hooded eyes, primal appreciation warming his blood, Alex regarded Brette as the carriage gently swayed. She and Lady Ravensdale spoke quietly about a blanket Brette was crocheting for the babe.

He'd tried to cry off attending the Goodinghams' dinner party, but Brooke had gently reminded him she'd already sent an acceptance on his behalf. If he wasn't prostrate in bed, *dying,* his absence would reflect poorly on them. Something they tried to avoid presently.

The exaggeration hadn't been lost on him, but he'd taken her point.

They couldn't risk offending those still welcoming Brette into their exclusive parlors. The others were a bunch of pompous windbags, most with a secret or two *or twenty* they wouldn't appreciate bandied about publically. As rector, he'd been privy to more than one guilty confession which made their treatment of Brette harder to stomach.

No oath prevented him from sharing those tidbits now, but his conscience did, blister it.

He covered his mouth with a forefinger, curbing his burgeoning smile. Permitted uncharitable opinions without immediate self-recrimination. How refreshing.

A smile lit Brette's face as she laughed at something her sister, er, cousin said, her unreserved joy adding to her already staggering exquisiteness.

His breath had left him in a gut-punching whoosh when she'd descended the stairs tonight, absolutely ravishing in a sapphire and white gown embellished with silver threads and lace, her glorious halo of moon spun hair twisted into a new and most becoming style, complete with a jeweled circlet sparkling between the shiny tendrils.

Up to now, he'd attributed such sentimental fribble to enamored—or drunken—corkbrains, but when he'd tried to draw in a meager breath and his blasted lungs refused to cooperate, he could no longer deny the phenomenon existed.

How could she possibly have grown more beautiful since yesterday? How could he have become more besotted?

The carriage sank into a bone-jarring rut, nearly vaulting him from his seat. His foot accidently brushed her skirt before he retreated into the coach's shadows once more.

Bestowing him a forgiving smile, her gaze genial, yet slightly hesitant around the edges, she searched his face. When he didn't respond with an upward sweep of his lips, she dropped her gaze and captured her plump lower lip between her teeth.

He'd nibbled that tasty spot of wonderfulness only yesterday. Was she recalling their kiss as well?

Or his botched declaration?

Two proposals and two refusals. Rather bruised his pride, it did.

Why had she rejected him again?

Rubbing his gloved fingers together, he pulled his eyebrows tight. Perhaps she fancied another, unbeknownst to him. Why hadn't that occurred to him before? If so, who was the chap?

Did it matter?

A third proposal wouldn't be forthcoming. The iota of pride he hadn't surrendered while rector demanded he not make himself an idiot over her again.

He'd actually believed she might accept his spontaneous offer this time, if he assured her they'd wait to marry. After all, he wasn't in a position to wed yet, but he'd wanted to claim her as his own, declare to the world she was his. More fool he. Bad enough if they'd been alone, but he'd plunged common sense into the ocean's depths and asked with an audience. Again.

Raven hadn't broached the subject since. Good friend there. Responsible guardian, too.

Would he ask Alex to leave Highfield now? To spare Brette the awkwardness his presence caused?

Alex had half-expected a summons today, requesting he remove himself to his townhouse.

Instead, Raven had invited Alex to join him at White's and

studiously avoided mention of yesterday's farce, directing their conversation to Tattersall's next auction instead.

Ten minutes later, the foursome mingled in the Goodninghams' gold salon, awaiting the final guests' arrival. The dinner party, nineteen thus far, might have been bearable if Lord and Lady Gambwell and their eldest daughters, Margaret and Charlotte, weren't also in attendance. Their eyes brightened like Vauxhall Garden fireworks when they'd spotted him.

He'd almost pivoted and marched to the coach, but Brette's tiny, startled, despairing gasp had set his feet advancing instead. Her adorable chin inched upward, and she pasted a pleasant look upon her face. He'd be bound she'd gnaw her beaded slippers before she let those chits grasp how they affected her.

He would too, by George.

Miss Gambwell, arching her neck to display the length to her best advantage, ran her fingers across the harpsichord's ivory keyboard, all the while giving him a coy look. "I do hope we'll have the opportunity to sing and ... *play* together after dinner."

Well, that's as subtle as an orange pig.

Standing to Alex's left, near a large potted ficus, Brette wrinkled her nose. "God spare us," she muttered to the leaf she fingered.

She seemed edgy tonight, less confident and gregarious than he'd ever observed her. Did she fear someone would be crass enough to mention her questionable birth? Or did she worry she'd be called upon to sing? Perhaps she'd experienced the elder Miss Gambwell's vocal talents before and didn't relish a repeat performance?

"What was that, Miss Culpepper? Can't you sing?" Miss Gambwell's shrewd gaze and sly smile suggested she already knew the answer. Today the she-cat deemed Brette worthy to speak to when in Hyde Park she'd acted as if Brette were beneath her touch?

The Gambwells fell far short of Brette in his estimation. All women did.

"Certainly, I *can* sing. I do possess vocal cords, after all. But so do cows, cats, and crocodiles. Because someone *can* do something doesn't mean they should."

Touché, ma petite.

Alex chuckled and raised his glass in silent salute. His Brette had pluck. He'd give her that.

She grinned in return, but her smile faded quickly when Phillip

Lapley slithered near. "I hoped I might have the privilege of hearing you perform, Miss Culpepper."

Why so attentive now?

Had he learned of her change in circumstances? His kind sniffed out new heiresses with the finesse and accuracy of well-trained bloodhounds.

"Trust me, Mr. Lapley, you wouldn't say so afterward. I hopelessly lack talent." She peered beyond him and stopped tormenting the bush. "Lady Covington isn't in attendance with you this evening?"

"Er ... alas no." He gave her what he probably believed a charming smile. Looked more like a grinning porpoise.

Unfair to the porpoise.

Shoulders slumped and eyes cast down, Lapley affected a sorrowful mien. "I'm saddened to say, Lady Covington has set aside her affection for me."

Probably caught him in a compromising position. For the umpteenth time.

Why would the Goodinghams have invited such a vulgar character to dine? Were they truly that desperate to even their dinner number? Lapley might've been the grandson of a viscount, but his reputation as a womanizing rake didn't make him appropriate company for innocents like their cow-eyed daughter.

The timid mouse fidgeting with her fan couldn't have been more than sixteen. Had they taken leave of their senses?

"I believe after-dinner entertainment includes dancing." And if it didn't, Alex had deliberately dropped a robust hint in his hosts' ears. Since he and Raven outranked the other guests, they'd be obliged to accommodate him. Bold as brass of him, and beyond the pale. He'd possibly put his hostess in a quandary, but she'd oblige.

Particularly since her daughter was of marriageable age, though barely, and he was available. An earl but a few short weeks and already a string of eligible misses had been paraded before him. God help him when the Marriage Mart was once again in full swing, and he took his obligatory seat in the House of Lords.

Beggars eyed a crust of bread with less longing than the bevy of lustful glances he'd received of late.

"Right you are, Wycombe," Mr. Goodingham boomed. "My daughter's eager to practice her steps and her playing. I've paid her music and dance instructors a fortune."

Goodingham's investments in India cotton and silk filled his pockets to bursting. A fat purse opened many doors otherwise closed to men of his ilk. If Brette possessed a grand inheritance, her birth mightn't be of importance to the *ton* either.

Alex positively didn't give a fig which side of the blanket she'd been born on. However, he'd certainly like to share a bed with her, and discover if the rest of her skin was anywhere near as creamy as the tempting mounds mere inches away.

Another notion he wouldn't have dared a few weeks ago, and he aimed a glance ceilingward. Swifter than a rock tossed in the ocean's depths, he'd descended into carnal sinfulness.

Would the Almighty smite him? *For putting off false piety?* For having thoughts he didn't act upon? He couldn't help but think God favored an honest heart above outward pretense.

At least Alex would live and die a happier man.

Goodingham beamed with fatherly pride and affection as he brushed his side whiskers. "Millie floats like an angel upon the dance floor, if I do say so myself."

"Float?" Margaret Gambwell whispered to Alex. "Not hardly with those dimply feet and chubby thighs" After her spiteful remark, she drifted away, and Lapley skittered after her, making straight for Miss Millie Goodingham.

His next unfortunate victim? Hopefully, her parents grew wise to his guiles.

At last, the tardy guests arrived, and moments later, the dinner gong pealed. Everyone swung their attention to their American hostess.

"Please, we won't stand on formality tonight. We've enough of politesse when the Season is full on, don't we?" Mrs. Goodingham tittered and fluttered her fingertips. "Do find yourself a partner to walk through with."

"Well," huffed Lady Gambwell, caustic disapproval drawing the word out. "How ... provincial. I suppose one should expect bumpkin behavior from a colonial." Her lip curling the merest bit, her superior gaze veered to Brette. "And others as ill-bred."

Brette flipped open her fan, mischief twinkling in her eyes. A man could lose himself in those glimmering pools of green-ringed blue. She fanned herself lightly. "Ah, indeed. Especially those hiding their lack of breeding and refinement beneath pretty outward trappings and pretentiousness." Lips tilted, she blinked innocently, as she nonchalantly fluttered her lace-edged fan. "Don't you agree, your ladyship?"

Alex hadn't witnessed a viper bite, but given Lady Gambwell's slit eyes and bared teeth, a lethal attack loomed. Instead, she presented her ramrod stiff spine and all but stomped away.

He cupped Brette's shoulder, whispering, "Please let me take you through. I refuse to escort one of those Gambwell terrors."

"All right. Should we warn her parents, do you think?" Brette jutted her chin toward Lapley fawning over the blushing Miss Goodingham's hand.

Even before Brette had finished her sentence, Mrs. Goodingham rescued the violated appendage and tucked her daughter's palm neatly into the crook of her arm. After offering a cordial, if forced, smile, she murmured a few words to Lapley and towed her smitten daughter away.

"No, her mother's well aware he's a fortune hunter." Alex cupped Brette's elbow as he rotated them toward the dining room. He deliberately held back, waiting for the others to precede them. "I beg you, please save me a dance after supper. If, that is, you can forgive me for my idiocy yesterday."

A waltz. A legitimate excuse to hold her in his arms. More fool he for willingly enduring the torture. He hadn't danced with her since her first foray into the Social World, a few months ago.

A waste of time this, persisting in a fantasy doomed to an unhappy ending. Pure foolishness.

Yet he must ask her.

Brette's incredible eyes filled with gentleness. "I was about to ask you the same thing. I regret hurting you, Alex, but my situation is... Well, you know my circumstances. You must be wise and not act impulsively. A union between us would not serve you at all well."

He lifted a shoulder. "There's nothing to forgive. I must beg your pardon for putting you in an awkward position. We've not ever discussed a match between us, but I shan't regret asking you."

Hand on Raven's arm, Lady Ravensdale glanced behind her as she exited. Her expression clearly said, *Stop chatting and come along.*

"My sister bids us, but I should be delighted to save you a set. I adore dancing, and you're keen on your feet." A glint lit Brette's eyes. "Almost as keen as I am."

Alex arched a brow wickedly. "Ah, we shall see. I don't suppose you'd care to wager on that?"

"And how would we determine the winner of such a bet?" Brette's swift retort bordered on flirtatious.

Hmm, perhaps he should consider a third proposal and do it right this time. Flowers, a few poetic phrases, on one knee. All that sort of thing. And a ring, of course. Something unusual, but enchanting, exactly like her. Perhaps a turquoise tourmaline or an aquamarine.

Don't get ahead of yourself, old chap. Half an hour ago, you'd sworn off ever considering making another offer. Because she smiles and flirts doesn't mean she'll say yes. Bide your time. Determine which way the wind blows before making an utter arse of yourself again.

What seemed like endless boring hours later, the men having finished their port and cigars, and the women their after-dinner tea, everyone reassembled in the parlor. Even with the furniture pushed to the perimeters, only three or four couples could take to the floor at one time.

As for privacy? None, whatsoever.

Unless he maneuvered his partner to the terrace beyond the slightly parted French windows. Given the crisp chill that had crept into his overcoat and beneath his top hat during the carriage ride, Brette wouldn't welcome a stroll outdoors, more was the pity.

Brette excused herself, and the Gambwell misses followed suit

Pleading urgency caused by her delicate condition, Brooke promptly set out after her sister

... cousin.

And when Lady Gambwell also slipped from the room, like a snake after an unsuspecting rabbit, Raven shook his head. "Do you think we'll need to send in reinforcements?"

A lively discourse would no doubt take place. Alex would've liked to be an insect in the retiring room when it did.

"You leave it to me," volunteered Mrs. Goodingham. "I'll not have those uppity harpies harassing my guests." She leaned in and whispered conspiratorially, her American twang both endearing and annoying. "They're here tonight because Millie fancies Harriet Gambwell her dearest friend. And you'll notice, the chit didn't bother to come."

"Perhaps she's indisposed." Alex doubted it.

"No. She was invited to the Fosters' ducal residence for the weekend, *after* her mother accepted our invitation." With that starchy disclosure, she marched from the overwarm room.

Alex took a position near the terrace doors, welcoming the cold air, as much to cool his ardor as his person. He'd been in a constant state of arousal since encountering Brette outside her solicitor's office and a series of cold baths kept him—*it*—subdued. It seemed when he'd cast off his clerical strappings, all the worldliness he'd managed to hold at bay had crashed into him in one huge wave.

More likely, his carnal inclinations had lain dormant until he met Brette, and now, much like his playful pup, they cavorted about, unrestrained. Netting the wind was easier than subduing them. And yet he must resist temptation, no matter how enchanting he found her. He'd not risk a two-decade-old friendship for another delicious kiss, for next time Raven would surely call him out. Or demand Brette marry him.

And Alex wouldn't have her forced into a union she obviously objected to.

The women returned en masse, none appearing the worse for wear, though a decidedly strained smile arched Lady Gambwell's lips and a storm brewed in Lady Ravensdale's eyes.

At her mother's urging, and most reluctantly from the petulant pout she sported, Miss Goodingham settled onto the needlepoint-covered stool before the harpsichord. She gazed longingly at Mr. Lapley, but after her mother's firmly whispered admonition in her ear, Miss Goodingham complied, opening the sheet music. Sulking, she played the waltz's opening stanzas.

Alex promptly found his way to Brette's side and angled his back to the others, intent on claiming a dance. He'd seize every opportunity to hold her in his arms. "May I be so bold as to request this dance? I noticed Lapley eyeing you. I'd spare you that trial. He can't boast the agility of a whale, and he'll mash your toes."

Brette darted Lapley a reserved glance. "I would enjoy a dance, but I must tell you, after what occurred in the retiring room, I expect Brooke to plead a headache and depart soon."

After an indecipherable glance toward Lady Ravensdale, Brette accepted his arm, and he swung her dainty form into his embrace.

A perfect fit.

Like a custom-made glove, his right palm cradled her ribs, his other a faultless nest for her delicate hand. He rubbed his thumb over her rib, noting, with no small amount of manly pride, her sudden intake of breath. Bending his neck the merest bit, he inhaled her intoxicating perfume. Wherever they touched or brushed together with the dance's flowing movement, awareness, powerful and invigorating, sprang to life.

Sweet torture he never wanted to end.

For an instant, he lost track of where he was, until the crowded impromptu dance floor caused him to nearly twirl Brette into another couple. To prevent the collision, Alex drew her scandalously close, their torsos bumping from chest to hip.

Molten desire engulfed him.

His mouth went dry as parchment, his tongue sticking to the roof. *God, think of something else.* He swallowed. "What happened to upset Brooke?"

"Lady Gambwell gleefully informed us your grandmother is so set against me and a possible union between us, that she'll stop at nothing to ruin me. Including fabricating and spreading tales to *le beau monde.*" Brette glanced up, amusement wrestling with disquiet in her gaze. She wasn't as unaffected as she pretended.

Grandmother could expect a terse visit on the morrow. He'd bloody damned well tolerated enough of people dictating to him and trying to control his life. "Tales? What sort of tales?"

Brette's gaze sought his for an instant before flitting away. "She claims my mother was a prostitute."

The bumpy road to hell is paved with good intentions
corrupted by prejudices, misunderstandings, ignorance, and fears.
~*Appearances and Attitude—The Genteel Lady's Guide to Practical Living*

10

S houldn't Brette be more outraged and disgusted by the Dowager
Countess Wycombe? Gloating Lady Gambwell? And her positively
vile daughters? Perhaps if she cared a whit what they thought, she
might've been, but as Mother had sagely advised, only the opinions of
those you love mattered.

Toss the others in the rubbish bin.

Except for going rigid as a poker, Alex hadn't responded to her
crude revelation.

Brette peeked at him, mindful not to seem overly interested. She
wanted to stare boldly, but with so many eyes watching, daren't.

She hadn't meant to burden him with the tattle, but as much as she
tried to ignore the nastiness and pretend she didn't give a fig what those
venom-tongued harpies believed, their malice bruised a mite.

His regard sank to hers, and the outrage simmering in his eyes did
her heart good. "A vicious lie, I'll vow."

He wouldn't believe the scurrilous accusation, even if she couldn't
be as certain. If Mr. Shipwreck could locate a marriage record, or if
someone who'd known her mother would come forward. But why
would they after all this time?

"I cannot be absolutely positive Lady Gambwell's prattle is
fictitious, though I fervently hope she's mistaken." Bastardry was horrid
enough, but the offspring of a strumpet too? How could anyone
disregard so shameful a yoke?

Alex made a gruff, sympathetic noise in his throat, pressing his
strong hand lightly into her side, and a shiver of desire danced across
her shoulders, rippled down her spine, and came to rest heavily in her
hips.

"How distressing this must be for you, Brette."

Others bullying me because of my birth? Or you holding me wonderfully close, yet I know I'm unsuitable for your regard?

She gave herself a mental shake. *Don't be a nincompoop.* He referred to the condemnation, of course.

Earnestness tightened the planes of his face. "I wish I could do something other than tell my grandmother to stubble it and retract her claws where you're concerned. You will tell me if there's anything, won't you?"

Sincerely wish to marry her.

Stop your foolishness. He cannot.

Twice he'd spontaneously—*half-heartedly*—proposed. Was he opposed to genuine, affectionate declarations?

Certainly her station made it impossible to accept him, but a part of her, the romantic who adored bringing other couples together, wanted a fairytale proposal. A declaration of love. Not merely a by-the-by, if you haven't anything else to do with your life, I suppose we might marry.

Or had pity motivated Alex and prompted his asking? He'd shown his compassionate, sacrificing nature many times, so the notion wasn't altogether impossible.

Wholly humiliating, however.

"I presume your solicitor has everything well in hand?" He glanced downward for a moment, kindness and something warmer evident in his eyes.

Brette nodded once and edged nearer. "He's trying to discover whether my parents ever married. I can better plan for my future once I know one way or the other."

Opening an establishment wasn't as far-fetched an idea as it had been a week ago. A respectable woman didn't dare, but a by-blow might. Especially since she possessed her own funds now. But would patrons frequent such a shoppe if owned by someone of questionable pedigree?

"It matters naught to me, and I sincerely apologize on my grandmother's behalf. I shall speak with her tomorrow. She'll cease her futile quest, or, so help me God, I'll cut her funding off." He skillfully steered them away from the Gambwells, lined up like discontented, ready-to-pounce watchdogs beside the hearth.

Brette kept perfect time with him, anticipating his steps, unlike her partners she'd had before. She and Alex danced as one, their movements perfectly coordinated, their souls united for this brief time.

Fanciful imagining on her part, but wonderfully so.

"Oddly enough, Alex, I rather admire her determination to protect you and the title." And Brette did. Everyone ought to have a loyal champion. "Not the dowager's methods, of course, but her caring passionately for you and your future."

Alex's short, harsh laugh drew several curious glances, and the anger in his eyes deepened them to hunter green, the silvery specks in his irises glinting bright against the deeper hue. "Trust me, her interference has nothing to do with great affection for me, and everything to do with the earldom and *her* position. She'd sacrifice her own child if she believed it would improve her social standing one jot."

He spun her in a slow circle, and, to raise the Gambwell chits' hackles, Brette graced him with her most winsome smile.

A slow grin creased his face.

Sliding the merest bit closer, she whispered, "I know it's indecorous, and I should eschew childish behavior, but I do enjoy making the Gambwells jealous. I believe Charlotte's gnashing her teeth." Brette darted a swift glance her nemesis's way. "Yes, yes, she is. And Margaret looks like she's considering hurling that shepherdess figurine at my head."

Alex leveled the chit a direct, don't-you-dare look, and she jerked her hostile attention away, pointedly studying the fireplace's hand-painted tiles.

This time, his melodious chuckle made them the target of several inquisitive looks. He canted his head at the Gambwells. "Let's give them something to be jealous of, shall we? Nothing too unseemly, but enough to stick in their craws for a day or two. If you're up to it."

Was he challenging her?

She examined his face, and only warm regard registered there. But yes, deep within his eyes, a spark of rebellion glowed. Amazing he'd managed to keep this part of his nature subdued as Reverend Hawksworth.

No doubt an answering glint reflected in her eyes, for as much as she adored the hubbub and commotion of the *haut ton*, their loftier airs rankled. As long as she didn't engage in anything too scandalous. She couldn't resist. "What did you have in mind?"

He expertly steered her toward the French doors. "A stroll along the terrace should suffice. It'll be cold."

Probably freezing.

"Well, as I'm quite warm—" Roasting. Her dampened underarms testified to that truth.

Though whether the dancing in the hot parlor or her sensual awareness of him should be blamed, she couldn't determine. "I'd be grateful for a few moments of refreshing air."

And the Gambwells *would* have a conniption fit. A reddened nose and chicken-skin arms were worth it. A ghost of a smile tickled her mouth. My, she'd become something of a rebel.

Across the room, she met Brooke's questioning gaze, and mouthed, "Outside."

Brooke gave a brief nod then directed her attention to the mantel clock before subtly raising her hand, fingers splayed. Five minutes. And Brooke would watch the time. They'd no doubt leave afterward.

In one fluid motion, Alex released Brette's hand and toed the door open so he could exit before her. He deftly swept her through the opening and onto the terrace.

The frigid air hit her with a bone-chilling blast, and she sucked in a small, startled gasp. It was positively freezing. Silvery frost iced the grass and shrubberies already. However, the stars, bright in the ebony sky, twinkled and winked cheerfully, and the half-moon lazily hanging on the horizon appeared to blink as a wispy cloud drifted by.

She leaned her hips against the balustrade and rubbed her arms. "*Brrr.*" Alex stepped beside her, mere inches shy of touching her.

Brette longed to lean into his sturdy heat, enjoy his arms about her as he held her close and warmed her. She yearned to run her fingers through his curls and discover their texture. Most of all, she wanted him to gaze at her with the same unreserved adoration Heath and Tristan looked at their wives.

Silly, selfish dreams, but if one didn't dream, didn't have hope, have something to anticipate and look forward to, what was left?

Work? Drudgery? Despair?

Hope deferred makes the heart sick.

Alex had preached on the topic the last time she'd attended his church. Yes, better to cling to optimism, no matter how slight.

She shivered and clenched her teeth to hush their chattering. Her exposed flesh raised, nubby and rough. Chicken skin? More like a plucked goose.

Alex shifted closer until they touched from calf to shoulder. Utterly glorious, and perhaps a mite *risqué.*

She sneaked a peek into the parlor behind her. As she'd expected.

Brooke, chatting with Mr. Goodingham, stood guard near the French window. Beyond them Margaret, Charlotte, and Miss Goodingham danced. Mrs. Goodingham must have taken to playing.

"Have you news from your alibis?" Brette didn't doubt he'd eventually clear his name, but in the interim, the mud-slinging could be damaging.

Alex glanced down, slanting his mouth into a slight smile. "Yes, and they've corroborated my story. Whoever suggested that I may have been involved in the tragedy will have to go elsewhere to stir their mischief."

Arms crossed, she hunched into herself, wishing she could burrow into his embrace. "Do you have a notion who might have done so?"

He shook his head, the moonlight glinting off the top. "Not for certain, but it could've been a number of distant relatives hoping to inherit if I hanged. Of greater concern to me is whether the fire was an accident. Once the footman is located, I'm sure we'll have the whole of it."

Alex stated it casually, without rancor, as if it were the most natural thing in the world to have people want him dead. He possessed a far more forgiving nature than she.

"I understood that the footman was questioned already." Lord, but the cold numbed her toes.

Yet this time with Alex was too precious to forego. Oh, all right, and the longer they lingered outdoors, the more peeved the Gambwells grew.

He grazed his jaw with his fingertips and gave an affirmative nod. "I believe he was. The maid too. But when the accusation arose against me, the footman disappeared. Slightly suspicious, I'd say, and it sickens me to think someone intended to kill my cousin and his son. Lawrence was only thirteen, poor chap."

"Yes, it's utterly dreadful." She clasped his forearm, fear for him congealing her blood. "Alex, do be careful. People are wont to take desperate measures for power and position, and it seems to me, someone means you harm."

He laid his warm palm on her arm, and she wanted to melt into his body's heat. "Don't distress yourself. I've taken precautions, and I've hired Bow Street runners to look into finding the wayward servant and to determine the fire's cause. Can't help to have my own people investigating as well, I should think."

Someone evil enough to try to convince the authorities he was guilty of murdering his cousins. A malicious person wouldn't stop after one attempt. He must know that too, yet he appeared composed.

Should something happen to him— She hugged her shoulders as a fear induced shudder shook her. *Stop.* She refused to contemplate the horror.

Alex tucked her a mite closer to his side—close enough, in fact, that she smelled his cologne.

So manly, yet clean. Not heavy or cloying.

"I'd offer you my coat, but I fear I cannot put it on again without assistance. I've been imposing on footmen until I hire a valet." He chuckled and bunched his shoulders to demonstrate. "See, the dashed thing allows me little room for movement. The fashion might be all the crack, but I've wondered the entire week what I'll do if I have to move suddenly. Perhaps rescue a damsel in distress or stop a runaway steed. I fear the seams will rip completely apart."

"I rather like how it looks on you."

Assessing him from the corner of her eye, Brette fingered her lovely gown's overskirt. His coat hugged his shoulders and chest and outlined his arm muscles nicely. His simple cleric clothing, though serviceable and clean, hadn't been tailored and hid his impressive physique.

Hand to his chest, Alex bent into a shallow bow, his proximity to her and the balustrade preventing anything more gallant. "Then for you, I shall make the sacrifice."

She shivered again.

"You're cold. Let's return to the drawing room." He took her elbow, and as one, they faced the door as Brooke stepped outside.

"Brette, we're leaving now." Brooke's smile turned radiant when Heath joined her and tucked her into his side. "You'll both catch your death out here. Come away at once."

Alex placed his hand on Brette's arm. "Ride with me tomorrow, before breaking our fast."

She searched his face, the surprisingly dark eyebrows, high cheekbones, and strong, squarish jaw. The lips he'd pressed to hers once. And his mesmerizing eyes, the moonlight reflecting in their depths. Alex's gaze sank to her mouth, and she bit the inside of her cheek to keep from running her tongue over her lower lip.

Not wise. Not wise at all. Say no.

Her traitorous tongue refused to obey logic. "All right." She'd allow herself one more memory.

"At half past—"

"Heath?" Brooke clutched her belly, panic and pain riddling her voice.

One should always base your actions on
good intentions, so your soul won't suffer regret.
~*Appearances and Attitude—The Genteel Lady's Guide to Practical Living*

Coatless, his cravat tossed across the sofa's back, Alex nursed a brandy before the library's dying fire. The gilt bronze mantle clock chimed the quarter hour.

Nearly two.

Tomorrow, he'd pay for the late hour with gritty eyes and a wooly head, but at present, he was too damned comfortable to move. Not even anticipation of his and Brette's early morning jaunt to Hyde Park stirred him.

She'd call it off, in any event, so why seek his mattress's comfort?

Shoeless, his legs stretched before him and his ankles crossed, he rested his head against the chair's high back. Shutting his eyes, he released a long, rumbling sigh. He'd never prayed as fervently, pleading and petitioning the Almighty to spare Raven and Brooke's child, as he had this night.

Shifting, Alex grimaced and rubbed his leg.

It ached from kneeling before the chair he now sat in, but he'd do so again in a blink.

Brooke must stay abed for a spell to recover from a vicious bout of food poisoning, not premature labor after all. The babe would bear no long-lasting ill effects.

Thank God.

How had Brette fared through the ordeal?

He hadn't seen her since the coach had skidded to a stop in front of the house. Before a footman opened the vehicle's door, she'd pressed the latch, jumped to the ground, and calmly and firmly began issuing orders.

From the first instant she'd detected Brooke's distress, Brette had taken the situation in hand, and with a general's boldness and efficiency too. She'd told Lady Gambwell to stubble it and move her rotund self aside as Brette cleared the way for Heath, carrying Brooke, to rush past and out into the night.

And God forgive Alex, he'd chuckled at the offended expression on the woman's face as he'd passed and saluted her.

Utterly priceless.

Unwise to underestimate his petite spitfire. Yes, indeed.

Grinning in remembrance, Alex sipped the superb brandy and exhaled a long breath again. Raven kept the finest spirits on hand, and tonight, Alex had indulged in two—or was it three?—full tumblers' worth; something he rarely did.

He ought to drag his sore self to bed, but the liquor and snug fire had succeeded in lulling him into a drowsy, half-conscious state, and it took rather too much effort to stir himself to the point of rising.

Should he look in on Domino before he retired? Not this late.

Alex needed a few hours rest without the playful terror frolicking about in his bed, nibbling toes, fingers, and ears with needle-sharp teeth, and besides, Cook had fallen in love with the rascally pup and had made him a nice box in the larder.

Not bothering to cover his mouth, Alex yawned widely. The room tilted and slowly spun 'round and 'round

Blast me. Might be half-foxed.

He chuckled and took another swig. He hadn't been soused since learning his uncle had abandoned his parish and run off with a nun, leaving Alex to step in as the new rector.

The fire gave a pair of valiant, yet weak, crackles, even as the coals faded more. Shortly, darkness would claim the already cooling chamber. No help for it. He'd have to drag his tipsy self upstairs.

He reluctantly cracked an eye open.

Or the couch would suffice for the night, but the single crocheted throw wouldn't provide much warmth. However, it might be worth the discomfort to send the unflappable Jenkin into a dither upon discovering Alex snoring away tomorrow—ah, this morning.

The study door whooshed open, and Brette glided in, her cloud of fairy pale hair floating around her shoulders and back, the ends teasing her rounded buttocks. Wearing a pale green robe and matching slippers, she pushed her hair behind one shoulder as she hurried to a bookshelf.

What was she about this time of the morning?

Holding the candle high, she scoured the volumes, her mouth moving silently as she read the titles, touching their spines with her forefinger.

"Aha." She made a satisfied sound in the back of her throat and bent to examine a rather formidable-looking book on a lower shelf.

Alex inhaled sharply, his breath suspended as the outline of her perfectly formed bottom, tipped upward at a most delicious and provocative angle. A gentleman would've averted his attention. He would've mere weeks ago, but tonight, he made no effort to do so, but instead slanted his head for a slightly better view.

I've become a complete lecher.

Brette gasped and straightened, swinging to face the chairs. "Who's there?"

Devil it. He'd frightened her and would have to reveal himself.

He bent forward, allowing her to see him clearly, and wiggled the fingers of his free hand. "I am. Didn't mean to alarm you." Excellent. He didn't sound as foxed as his spinning head suggested. He waved at the hefty book she held. "That looks impossibly droll. Having trouble sleeping and came in search of the most boring tome the library boasts?"

She visibly relaxed and summoned a forgiving smile. "No, I thought to dabble in a little reading about business and enterprise."

Why? Alex examined the ominous book again. "Most assuredly you'll be asleep within minutes of cracking it open if that's truly what you've selected."

Three fine rows creased her forehead, and she glanced at the book. She set the volume and the candle aside before crossing to him. Her gown floated about her hips and legs, swishing softly with her movements, and her hair swayed, silky curls entwining about her shoulders and arms.

"A nymph," he muttered, before taking another swallow, savoring the mellow heat trickling to his belly.

"A nymph, am I?" She arched a fine eyebrow as she bent over him, slouched in his chair.

She sniffed, her adorable nose crinkling. "Alex? Have you been drinking?"

Nodding and grinning like an imbecile, he raised his glass. "I prayed first though."

He couldn't tear his attention from the luscious display inches from his eyes. Her gown gaped enough to give him a glimpse of the creamy globes within, and his groin reacted predictably.

Impure imaginings clanged around in his head. Hell, he wasn't a saint. Far from it, truth to tell. But this was his Brette, his sweet, innocent Brette, and he wouldn't ogle her like a drunken sailor. He dragged his reluctant focus upward to her soft mouth and higher yet to her sympathetic eyes.

Instead of harping or scolding, she brushed his hair from his forehead with her cook fingertips. "I was utterly terrified for Brooke and the baby. I confess, I'm still tense. I suppose it will take a while to recover." She caught her lip between her teeth, and eyed his glass. "Might I have a taste?"

Silently, Alex extended the tumbler.

Giving him a half-smile, she tossed off the last speck of amber liquid and promptly coughed and gasped. "Good heavens," she managed between wheezes. "You might've warned me. It's burning clear to my belly."

His regard locked on her hands pressed to her middle, flattening the planes of her gown tight against her stomach and sloping hips.

Her expression dreamy, she closed her eyes. "It feels rather nice, sort of like when you wake from a nap. Cozy and warm and drowsy."

Opening her sultry eyes, Brette's lips slowly bent upward. An innocent, she couldn't know the siren's invitation in her gaze or that, with her flushed cheeks, half-closed lids, and parted lips, she resembled a woman thoroughly made love to.

Blister it.

Alex dragged her onto his lap, and except for inhaling a brief, startled breath, she appeared unperturbed by his action. He buried his face in her neck, relishing the dove-soft skin, her sweet, clean fragrance, and the weight of her rounded bottom on his lap.

Desire—immediate, electric, and consuming—shot through him.

You're in deep trouble, old chap. Stop this nonsense before you regret it.

If Brette had objected, pulled away, or voiced her displeasure, he might have been able to heed his conscience's chiding. Instead, she sagged into him, draping one slender arm around his neck, and splayed her other hand against his chest as she angled her neck, allowing him greater access.

He trailed fiery kisses along the ivory length, lingering at the sensitive spot behind her ear. A half-moan, half-sigh whispered from her when he licked the tender flesh. Smiling, he dotted her face and jaw with more heated kisses before working his way to her slack mouth.

Scarcely an inch between their lips, Alex waited. He'd give her the choice, let her decide to continue or not.

Brette cupped his face with both hands and brought his mouth to hers, moving the plump pillows across his as he'd taught her the first time. She tentatively searched his mouth with her tongue, her exploration becoming bolder as her hunger grew She tasted of brandy and tea and a trifle minty too.

Desire exploded, shattering the last remnants of his self-control. He'd loathe himself afterward, but right now, nothing mattered but Brette. He wanted to tell her he loved her, adored her, but her earlier rejections made him leery. Afraid she'd flee, he kept silent, instead worshipping her with his mouth and hands.

"Alex,' she moaned, arching into him.

A groan started low in his belly and worked its way to his throat. Alex shifted Brette, laying her across his knees, an arm cradling her back. With his free hand, he explored the loveliness her gown shielded.

The enchantress in his lap tangled her tongue with his, as if she too couldn't control the fiery desire urging her onward. On the verge of completely losing control, he cupped her derrière, kneading the firm flesh, and suckled her lower lip.

His penis, hot, heavy, and demanding, pulsed beneath her thigh.

What are you doing?

Brette wasn't a lightskirt or fast chit. She was the ward of one of his dearest friends. The woman Alex loved. His morals chafed stridently at his behavior, at taking advantage of her inexperience and attraction to him, and the spirits he'd consumed couldn't be blamed either.

He wanted her. Plain and simple. But as his wife, not a frenzied tupping when drink dulled his senses and the day's events caused both of their emotions to run high.

Gently pulling away, he captured her exploring hands, and rested his forehead against hers. "Brette, love, we must stop."

She gave a shaky nod, her lips glowing rosy from his kisses. "I know."

No insurmountable obstacles prevented them from marrying. Her background mattered naught, his grandmother's and family's acceptance of her even less. And as for the *ton*'s approval...? Indeed, perhaps the time had come to drop well-placed hints about those without sin casting stones.

Numerous lofty peers and peeresses would tumble from their self-appointed pedestals if their indiscretions became public. He wouldn't stoop to blackmail, but a preventive whisper here and there couldn't go amiss if it protected Brette from their hypocritical censure.

No, nothing major hindered their joining, except Charlbury's fire. Until he knew the cause, he wouldn't risk Brette's safety. They had plenty of time, in any event. After all, mourning restricted his marrying any time soon, but he could still court her.

Fully aware of how his dazzling looks affected women, he refused to play the carefree charmer for Brette. Their relationship must be built on sincerity and trust. A woman of her character didn't kiss a man, didn't respond as she had unless her emotions were engaged. Of that, he hadn't a single doubt.

"I ... I don't know what came over me." She blushed, an adorable rosy pink tinging her cheeks.

He did, for the same firestorm consumed him, and the knowledge made him more determined to make her his.

Biting her lip, her color still high, Brette modestly pushed her robe lower. For someone short of stature, she possessed the most exquisite legs. Long, elegant thighs—the skin pearly white—that curved into graceful calves before tapering into the daintiest of ankles.

He clenched his jaw to stubble the involuntary protest springing to his tongue as the gauzy fabric covered the tempting lengths.

"Here, let's sit you up." He helped her to an upright position, gritting his teeth when her rounded bottom pressed into his rigid groin. "I must beg your pardon and forgiveness."

"Why?" Brette swept her hair over one shoulder then twisted the glorious flaxen tendrils into a thick rope. The end curled around her breast, the nipple pressing pebble-hard against her robe's delicate fabric.

He swallowed and directed his gaze to the two or three remaining coals glowing in the hearth. "I shouldn't have kissed you. You're overwrought, and I took advantage."

"I kissed you first, and if anyone took advantage, it was me." She pointed at the empty tumbler on the side table, her slightly swollen mouth bending into a winning smile. "I shan't insult either of us by pretending I didn't thoroughly enjoy it."

No feminine qualms, no pretense at affront, Brette's directness was equally refreshing and disconcerting.

"You seemed practiced at the art." She scooted off his lap, her gown settling around her trim ankles.

Alex nearly choked on his surprise.

Good God, was she asking how experienced he was?

She'd be surprised to learn, not so much. Once or twice at university when the other young bucks had sown their oats.

He possessed neither the temperament nor coin to indulge in pleasures of the flesh, and the whole concept of paying women for sexual favors rather disgusted him. Those unfortunates were also someone's daughters. And casual trysts, simply to enjoy a woman's soft curves for an hour or two, hadn't appealed.

"A gentleman doesn't discuss matters of that nature." Curving his mouth, he too rose.

She cocked her head. "Even with a woman he's proposed to twice?"

The muted light made it impossible to read her face, but surely her voice held a wistful note, and his hope burgeoned.

"Especially to such a woman." He winked, rakishly. "He wouldn't want her opinion of him to diminish."

"It couldn't." She gathered her book and candlestick, shyness and yearning playing upon her features. "Shall we walk up together?"

Definitely an invitation. One he was honor-bound to refuse.

"Not yet. I need to look in on Domino." Bloody poor excuse, but he seized it.

He helped himself to the two-pronged candelabra on Raven's desk then used an ember to

light one taper. Raven wouldn't mind, and Alex would return the stand first thing in the morning. He couldn't stumble to the kitchen or his room in the dark, could he?

Brette continued to stand there, hesitant and uncertain, as if striving to summon the nerve to say something. He feared he knew what she wanted to ask, and his answer must be no. Time to distract her and send her on her way.

"I presume our outing to Hyde Park must be postponed?"

She dipped her head. "Yes, but—"

"Just as well," he rushed on, arranging the fire screen snug against the tiles. She mustn't voice what he suspected she wanted to ask. He

413

mightn't have the strength to refuse, and he'd hate himself afterward. If and when he bedded her, it would be honorably, as his wife. Not a rushed dalliance with her sister and brother-in-law but a few doors away.

"I wish—"

"I'll likely not rouse before noon. I indulged too freely, I'm afraid." He forced a chuckle, the sound insincere even to his ears.

"Alex?"

He sighed, and she wrinkled her forehead, obviously confused.

How could she not be? He'd sent her mixed signals, and in her inexperience, she couldn't understand that his eagerness to have her gone had nothing to do with her and everything to do with his tenuous grip on his self-control.

No help for it. He'd have to force her to go.

He covered the distance between them and, after kissing her forehead, turned her toward the door and gave a little shove. "Go to bed, Brette. You cannot be found here, with me, this time of night. Your reputation is already perilously fragile."

"Yes, of course. You're right. Goodnight, Alex." She gave him a final, probing look.

What did she seek? Apparently, she didn't find whatever it was. Shoulders slumping and appearing utterly lost, she glided from the study as silently as she'd arrived.

"Won't be tempted more than you can endure?" he muttered after she'd gone. "Honestly, Lord. That wasn't more than I could endure?" Because he'd nearly reached the point of no resistance, and he didn't much like himself at the moment. The part of him still aching for release gave an angry twitch.

Yes, but if you take her to bed, she'd have to wed you.

Was the notion so horrid?

Not for him, but Brette must come to the match willingly. Because she wanted it—wanted him—as much as he wanted her. Any other start to their marriage would be perpetual sand in their sheets, a constant niggling reminder.

After collecting his things, he waited five minutes before following Brette. Plenty of time for her to make her way upstairs. He quickly peeked in on Domino. As expected, the pup lay sound asleep, nose tucked beneath his spotted tail upon a distinctly unmanly lavender ruffled pillow, a bone nearly as big as the pup's leg beside him.

Alex sniffed then sniffed again. Roses? An eyebrow shot skyward.

Cook had bathed the dog in rose water?

Poor chap; his dignity would be sorely frayed if he knew.

Tiptoeing from the kitchen, Alex headed to the stairway. The smell of an extinguished candle wafted past, and he turned in a slow, cautious circle, seeking the source. There, in the drawing room, tucked onto the bay window seat, her arms folded around her knees and her face buried in them, huddled Brette.

Weeping.

Be aware of the difference between people with
good intentions and those with good character: The former
easily make promises. The latter actually strive to keep them.
~Appearances and Attitude—The Genteel Lady's Guide to Practical Living

12

Indulging in a second cup of chocolate, liberally topped with Devonshire cream, Brette rested her head against the windowpane.

Snoring lightly, Freddy lay curled at her feet, a gray-spattered forepaw covering his equally silvery nose. He was getting old, though he'd perked up a bit with Domino to keep him company.

Outside, everything glistened from the sun's rays reflecting upon the icy crystals clinging to most surfaces. A frosty lace-like pattern edged several windows, a testament to the mid-morning's frigid temperature. Coldness radiated through the beveled glass; a startling contrast to the warm cup she held.

Rather like her fickle emotions, first cold then hot then cold again.

Bah. She'd become a feckless, indecisive beef-wit.

A few brave souls garbed in thick layers of warm clothing dotted the sidewalk and streets, and a horseman, his multi-colored knitted scarf covering his lower face to guard against the nippiness, leisurely ambled past the house. He boldly stared in the ground floor windows and brazenly touched his hat's rim when he spied Brette tucked snuggly in the bay window.

His cheekiness earned him a tiny, closed-mouth smile, but no wave in return. Definitely outside the bounds, that. The horse's single white fetlock jarred her memory. She'd seen the gelding before. Probably in Hyde Park on one of her many walks or rides.

Less than eight hours ago, she'd sat in this same spot, softly weeping, afraid she'd be overheard in her chamber. She waited behind the drawing room's open door until Alex had left the study before seeking the cozy refuge and giving vent to her tears.

When they'd kissed last night, she'd come face-to-face with the undeniable truth. Finally admitted what she suspected, what her heart knew and had hinted at for months.

She loved him. Irrevocably and desperately.

Last night, she'd tried to tell him, and also explain her wanton behavior.

Though the words hadn't come easily—embarrassment had thickened her tongue—she'd wanted him to know she wouldn't have behaved brazenly unless she loved him. She couldn't give him her body without first giving him her heart.

More than anything, she wanted to tell him that she *did* want to marry him. Had since he'd stolen her breath that day at Esherton Green when he'd descended from his coach, his face wreathed in smiles and the sun had glinted off his golden head. It had taken her a while to identify the unaccustomed comfortable feeling.

Maybe someday a man and woman would be permitted to marry simply because they loved each other, and the ridiculousness of class and station and birth wouldn't matter.

Those trivialities *shouldn't* have mattered.

Two souls merging—only that was essential, not the rest of the folderol.

Summoning every speck of courage she possessed, she'd determinedly shoved her heritage and reservations aside, and if Alex asked her again, she'd brave the repercussions, seize love with both hands, and say yes.

Yes, she would gladly marry him. Yes, she wanted him in the ways a woman wants a man.

Yes, she'd face the censure; take the risks loving someone beyond reason entailed. Yes, she would be his for all time.

Except he'd rushed to dismiss her, curtailing her bumbling pronouncement, almost as if he'd feared what she might say. As if he hadn't wanted to hear it.

Doubt, sinister and accusing then raised its troll-like head, and she'd feared Alex's rejection.

Uncertainty plagued her yet this morning, and she hated her misgivings.

She tongued a dab of sweet cream from the cup's rim then licked her sticky lips.

Alex's disquiet wasn't because he hadn't been as aroused as she or hadn't enjoyed their encounter. Raised around livestock, she knew what the insistent bump nudging her bum was. True, genuine concern about being discovered might have prompted him to dismiss her, but something in his demeanor, a leeriness, fairly shouted that something else had brought on his reluctance.

So now, mortified to her soles, she contemplated her next step. Staying underneath the same roof as Alex?

No, too unthinkably awkward.

She couldn't ask Heath to boot him to the pavement without raising suspicion either.

Besides, she didn't want Alex and Heath's friendship jeopardized. Nonetheless, living in the same house as Alex, was impossible. Imprudent too. God knew what mortifying thing she might do next.

Propose to him? Climb into his bed?

The latter rather appealed. Tremendously.

However, until she came of age, Heath and Brooke wouldn't hear of her assuming her own residence. But, would they permit her to winter in the country perhaps? Hadn't she been dreading that very thing mere weeks ago? What a reversal.

She snorted, startling Freddy.

He blinked sleepily before lowering his head and resuming his nap. Time to think logically and sensibly.

If she hired a companion, say someone older, respectable—mayhap a widow—might she pursue relocating to her house on Belgrave Square? Yes, a companion. The idea possessed real merit. But the woman couldn't be stuffy, pompous, or mousy.

Brette tapped her fingernails against the bone china, the soft clicking revealing her restlessness and resounding louder than it ought to have in the quiet room.

Had Mr. Shipwreck unearthed anything more about her parents? Nearly a week had passed since she'd met with him, and he might have news.

She'd send a note round and ask him straight out.

No more demurring, graciously holding her tongue, or pretending hesitancy rather than being straightforward. From this point onward, she'd speak her mind, directly ask what she wanted to know, and worry less about offending others or what they might think.

Uncrossing and then recrossing her ankles with the other leg on top, she perused the too silent drawing room. In fact, the entire house was far too quiet to suit her.

Shortly after breaking his fast, Heath had reluctantly left Brooke to attend to urgent business. Brooke rested in her chamber, and if Alex stayed true to his word, he was yet abed sleeping off his excess drink.

Even in his cups, he'd been a dashed attractive rogue.

The servants scuttled about, whispering and tiptoeing, probably on Jenkin's orders. The poor butler had gone chalk white when Heath had carried Brooke into the manor, and as certain as Freddy was a gaseous bundle of fur, Jenkin would personally ensure Brooke's convalescence remained undisturbed. No hint of anything remotely unsettling would reach her ears.

Bored to her black-slippered toes, Brette yawned. Mayhap she should ask a footman or maid to accompany her on a brisk walk. Anything to occupy her mind and exercise always helped lessen any tension.

She sneezed then sneezed again. Blowing her nose, she eyed the crisp outdoors. A walk mightn't be the best idea after all. She suspected she'd caught a slight cold—nothing much more than a sniffly nose and few sneezes. Not wishing to expose the children, she'd sent word she wouldn't visit the foundling home until she recovered. Likely her escapade on the freezing terrace last night hadn't helped her health either.

A humorless smile tipped her mouth.

After kissing Alex, she'd probably given the illness to him too.

How could they explain that awkwardness? The only two in the household with colds?

As she swallowed the last sip of savory cocoa, she perused the lane once more. A familiar young man—one of Mr. Shipwreck's clerks? Possibly the carroty-headed chap—bundled to his red-tipped ears trotted up the front steps, his breaths forming tiny, frozen clouds before him.

A few moments later, Jenkin entered the drawing room, bearing a salver. "A note has arrived for you, Miss."

Wonderful. The messenger had been Mr. Shipwreck's clerk. Hopefully he brought the news she coveted.

"Thank you, Jenkin." She accepted the missive before placing her empty cup on the chocolate service.

Jenkin tucked the small silver tray beneath an arm. "Shall I remove the chocolate now, Miss?"

"Yes, please." Examining the letter—indeed from the solicitor's office—she inclined her head distractedly. She cracked the seal and swiftly scanned the contents.

Too polite to ask what the missive contained, Jenkin lifted the hot chocolate tray. "Do you require anything else?"

"Yes, a carriage brought round immediately. My solicitor has asked me to visit his office at my earliest convenience." She refolded the note. "And when Brooke awakens, or if Lord Ravensdale returns, will you please tell them I've gone to Mr. Shipwreck's, but I'll return before luncheon?"

"Very good, Miss. Which maid will you take with you?"

"Flora. Tell her we're to leave in the next five minutes." Flora, a trifle slow in the attic, wasn't as essential to the running of the house as the other servants. She'd been with the Culpeppers for the past decade, and when Brooke married Heath, she'd insisted the maid join his household. Inordinately kind, Jenkin assigned Flora simple tasks that kept her busy but didn't overly challenge her.

A few minutes later, Brette hurried along the corridor. As she reached Alex's room, she slowed to a stop. Lifting her hand, she bit her lip. No. She mustn't. Unmarried women didn't knock upon unmarried gentlemen's bedchamber doors. Besides, what would she say?

I enjoyed our passionate encounter last night, and I'd like to repeat it. Now. Tonight. For the rest of my life.

She continued to her room, and after swiftly exchanging her slippers for half-boots and collecting a warm wrap, bonnet, and muff, retraced her steps.

Still no sign of Alex. He truly wasn't accustomed to strong drink.

Twenty minutes later, wearing a fur-lined midnight blue mantle over her pelisse, Brette accepted the coachman's hand as he assisted her from the coach. Frigid air smacked her in the face, and she sucked in an involuntary breath. Hounds' teeth but it was cold. She eyed the leaden November sky. Snow before afternoon or she wasn't blond. Terribly unusual for this time of year.

"Thank you, Peters."

She stuck her head into the vehicle's interior, where Flora sat bundled in several lap robes, her feet resting on a hot brick.

Flora sneezed into her handkerchief three times. A cold too?

Well, at least if Alex did become ill, no one would find it unusual now.

"Flora, why don't you stay in here? I expect I'll be done in less than thirty minutes. Peters can pick up the items I need while I'm with the solicitor, and you can assist him by remaining with the packages."

"Oh, yes, Miss. Thank you, Miss." Her face flushed and eyes watery, Flora sniffed loudly and burrowed deeper into the robe's folds. Yes, most definitely not feeling up to snuff.

Neither could Brette ask the maid to stop at the alchemist and glover when Flora already felt sickly and should seek her bed as soon as possible.

His hand resting on one of the horse's broad rump, Peters scrutinized the barren lane.

In the distance, a pair of riders clopped along as a single vehicle rattled over the cobblestones. Quiet for a weekday morning, but the bitingly frigid temperature and the promise of rare snow doubtless accounted for the lack of activity.

An indistinguishable breed of quaking ducks flew overhead, their ebony bodies' mere shadows against the pewter sky. In a typical vee formation, their wings beating frantically, they veered toward the river. Probably wintering on the Thames. If Brette could manage the housing situation to her benefit, she'd be wintering in London too.

She eyed a smart black coach as it leisurely trundled by Heath's. She'd need a conveyance if her plans came to fruition; a phaeton or curricle would do. In a bold and daring color. Maybe the same brilliant shade of blue as her mantle. Wouldn't that be something? So regal. She'd need horseflesh, too. A matched pair—gray or white—and a mount for riding. A small, gentle mare ought to suffice.

Brette handed the driver her short list. "Here are the items I need, Peters."

"Are you certain, Miss Culpepper? His lordship won't like me leaving you." Most endearing, Peter's consternation and loyalty.

"I shall be fine. You'll be back before I'm finished or soon thereafter. The businesses I need you to frequent are a mere block or two away. Do ask the alchemist for extra elderberry and yarrow." They'd be needed if more of the household took ill with the cold. She veered Flora a glance. "And I don't want Flora to have to sit in Mr. Shipwreck's outer office. The chairs look terribly uncomfortable, and it's rather chilly."

Peters shuffled his feet and fiddled with the list, his indecision apparent.

"I'll take full responsibility, Peters." What could possibly happen?

"Wait until I'm in the establishment before you leave." Surely, no one could object to her visiting her solicitor in broad daylight. She wasn't likely to have arranged a lovers' tryst in his drab office, for pity's sake.

Brette shoved her other hand into her muff. The unseasonably cold weather made her anxious for the lined gloves Peters was to pick up on her behalf. Though the muff kept her hands warm, she couldn't do anything while using it, and when she didn't, her fingers grew red from cold.

"Very well, but promise you'll stay inside until I return." He shut the coach's door. "Sometimes the traffic's difficult, and I might be a few minutes later than expected to collect you."

"I promise." Raising her muff in farewell, she hurried up the steps. Once within the brick building, she stood on her toes and peeked out the square, dusty window beside the door. Peters settled himself in the driver's seat. With a sharp whistle and a practiced snap of his whip, the team surged onward.

Best get to it. Brette didn't want him returning before she'd completed her business. Her stomach constricted as she walked the short corridor's distance. She wasn't altogether certain she wanted to know what was so urgent the solicitor couldn't tell her in the note.

After last night's disappointing incident with Alex, as well as the scare with Brooke, she didn't relish another upset. Taking a bracing breath, she forced her mouth upward and stepped into the office.

"Miss Culpepper." Mr. Loomis leaped to his feet, bumping his desk in his haste and jolting his inkwell and candle holder. The candle tipped precariously, and he grabbed the taper, steadying it. He hastily ran one hand across his wiry hair and tugged at his rumpled coat with the other.

"To what do we owe this unexpected pleasure?"

Hold this truth close to your heart and
remember its perils: We leniently judge ourselves by
our intentions, while harshly judging others by their behaviors.
~Appearances and Attitude—The Genteel Lady's Guide to Practical Living

13

Alex flipped his pocket watch open and grinned. Not even half past seven. Excellent.

He'd enjoyed the invigorating walk here, despite the brisk cold, his lack of sleep, and a head which felt swollen twice its normal size. He'd made excellent time too. Never mind he could scarcely feel his fingers and toes.

Sliding his timepiece into his pocket, he chuckled.

Grandmama didn't rise before ten. The old bird would have a conniption fit upon hearing he'd called this early. And the fuss she'd kick up when she learned why he'd put in an early appearance—

He grinned in anticipation.

'Twould serve his meddlesome grandmother right. Hopefully, the early hour would have her a mite more compliant and her tongue less caustic. He rapped the door knocker three times then, for good measure, banged it twice more, wincing as an answering peal jolted within his skull.

Served *him* right for over-indulging last night.

Last night. Brette. His beautiful, desirable Brette.

His behavior had confused her, but he'd set everything aright today.

Determination to put his grandmother straight had him dressed and shaved by six. He intended to inform her in no uncertain terms precisely what unpleasantness she could expect if she defied him or spread any more slanderous rumors regarding Brette.

After last night, nothing could persuade him his sweet Brette didn't share his feelings. He must somehow convince her to admit it, and to realize that neither of them would ever be happy without the other.

Nothing and no one else mattered.

He pounded the entry with his fist then clapped the knocker several more times. *Answer the door!* His head threatened to burst, and his hollow stomach objected by turning flips. He swallowed. Mayhap he should have delayed long enough to drink a cup—or pot—of coffee and eaten a small repast.

Norris, Grandmama's butler, still shoving an arm in his cutaway, opened the door. A whole two inches.

From his elevated bushy eyebrows to his mouth cinched tighter than purse strings, he radiated displeasure. "My lord," he droned, annoyance accenting each word, "the dowager countess is yet abed. Please return at a more civilized hour."

Norris made to shut the door, but Alex wasn't having it. He shoved his boot into the crack, grimacing as his toes suffered a nasty pinch.

Norris's incredulous eyebrows scampered higher on his forehead.

"*Tsk*, is that any way to welcome a guest?" Smiling reproachfully, Alex shouldered his way inside. "You do know, don't you, Norris, who now pays your wages?"

Didn't hurt to remind the sour-faced servant that Alex expected civility. Particularly to the chap Norris owed his position to.

"Indeed, sir," Norris replied, stiffer than the flooring they stood upon and about as amiable as an angry scorpion. His head barely reached Alex's shoulder yet Norris managed to look down his nose disdainfully while extending his hand.

"I thought so." Alex passed the butler his hat, cane, and gloves before removing his greatcoat and scarf and handing them over. "Good man."

Not wishing to give Grandmama anything else to quibble about, he'd donned mourning togs for his visit. Straightening his coat's rumpled cuff, Alex perused the entry. Each stick of furniture, the paintings, the decorations—everything right down to the crocheted and tatted doilies—were in precisely the same location they had been for at least two decades.

If nothing else, Grandmama remained consistent and predictable. Rigidly immovable in attitudes and habits too. She probably still slept with those damnable cats. Temperamental, pampered beasts.

The last time he'd called, Ambrosia had jumped onto his shoulder and tried to steal his biscuit, right from his mouth. The determined, portly feline had batted his face, her claws extended, when he'd not shared a nibble. The other, younger one, Emerald—named for her eye color—had hissed and given him an open-mouthed sneer each time he moved.

He much preferred dogs. They knew who their master was.

After hanging up Alex's coat, Norris, his posture taut with indignation, preceded him up the stairs. "If you will please make yourself comfortable in the parlor, my lord, I shall inform Madame you are here."

He said it with as much enthusiasm as at the prospect of waking an ill-tempered dragon. Not too far off, by God.

Alex didn't miss the butler failing to offer him refreshments. Or, perhaps, fretting about Grandmama's reaction to an early morning caller, the courtesy had slipped his mind.

"That's all right. I'll surprise her." Too much to hope Norris might have a battle shield tucked away somewhere. A sword and helmet? Perchance a garlic clove?

No, no, that deters vampires. Not crotchety, intrusive grandmothers.

Slack-jawed and gaping, Norris spread his arms wide and flapped them in an attempt to block the corridor.

Giant, agitated penguin.

God help me keep a straight face. Please.

Alex sidestepped the flummoxed butler.

"But, sir, you mustn't. Her ladyship—"

"First door on the right, isn't it?" Alex patted Norris's extended arm as he passed. Norris scampered to catch up. "Yes, but, you cannot simply—"

"I thought so." Alex lengthened his stride.

"M'lord. I must insist. She's nae at her best first thin'." In his desperation, Norris had forgotten his polished speech and reverted to Scots.

Truly overwrought, poor chap. He'd shrink in mortification should he become aware of the slip. Was Grandmama so formidable her staff lived in dread of displeasing her?

Yes.

Alex cast the butler a compassionate glance, but didn't slow his pace. "Break your fast, Norris. I'd hate to think you went hungry on my account. And trust me, you would rather be elsewhere when my grandmother hears what I have to say."

The faithful servant paused.

He wavered, one troubled eye on the closed door, behind which the distinct echo of Grandmama's snoring resounded. Or else a cantankerous walrus with a vigorous head cold resided in her bedchamber. With a regal tilt of his head, Norris consented. "Very good, my lord. Please ring should you or her ladyship need anything."

Wise chap. Undoubtedly far wiser than Alex. "Norris?"

Several feet along the passage already, as if terrified of Grandmama waking and finding him outside her chamber, he swung to face Alex. "Yes, sir?"

"I commend you for your diligence and loyalty." Alex grasped the door handle. With a slight dip of his head, Norris accepted the compliment then made his escape.

Alex waited until the butler descended the stairs before knocking loudly as he threw open the door. "Happy morning to you, Grandmama!"

Whistling a cheerful, uncouth sailor's tune, certain to peeve her, he yanked the thick curtains wide, revealing the rotund tabbies sleeping on either side of her legs. Frost covered the window panes, but no coal burned in her hearth.

Positively freezing in here.

"Alexander?" she mumbled sleepily, her mountain of bedcovers rustling as she sat up, her lacy night cap askew.

He'd truly surprised her if she'd slipped and called him by his given name.

She blinked drowsily while covering a less than delicate yawn. "Whatever are you doing here?" Alarm flitted across her aged face, and she pressed her hands to her lavender, ruffle-clad chest. "Has something happened? It has. I can see it in your eyes. Don't spare me, Wycombe. Tell me all."

Much too early for such theatrics.

"No, Grandmama, nothing has happened except I learned last evening that you're propagating rumors that Miss Culpepper's mother was a whore." Alex bent and attended to the grate. Couldn't have her taking a chill.

Instantly defensive, his grandmother *harrumphed* and relaxed against her buttercup-yellow silk pillows. "*I* didn't start the rumors, my boy."

"Perhaps, but you will cease spreading them and encourage others to do so as well." Once he'd started the fire, he straightened and replaced the poker. He brushed his hands together, but traces of coal dust remained on his fingertips.

"Did Norris let you in? I'll sack him today, the wretch." One gnarled, blue-veined hand petting Ambrosia, Grandmama glared at Alex.

He'd inherited her vivid green eyes, but now looking into the squinted and hostile gaze, he didn't much treasure the gift. His patience near at an end, Alex shook his head, warning her with his gaze. "No, you won't. I but reminded him who pays his wages."

"How utterly common and vulgar."

Yes, better to pretend the staff's wages magically appear from another realm, delivered by a Scottish faerie each month.

She sniffed and curled her lip. "As is calling at this ungodly hour and barging into my private chamber."

"Prepare yourself for even worse crassness. Shall I get your salts in case you faint?" He made a pretense of searching her dressing table for the vial.

"*Pshaw.* Don't be ridiculous. I do not swoon, and I doubt what you say will shock me overly much." Her bravado didn't reach her eyes. Wariness tinged the wrinkled edges. "Out with it."

Arms folded, he relaxed against a gold and purple satin-festooned bedpost. "If you don't cease persecuting Miss Culpepper, I shall cut off your funds and refuse to pay your bills henceforth."

Her jaw sagged for an instant, but she recovered almost as quickly. "You—"

He sharply raised his palm, halting her protest. "Don't say something you'll regret later, Grandmama, for I do not threaten idly."

Hurling him a mutinous glower, she snapped her mouth shut, her teeth clacking with her ire.

She folded her arms, peevishly tapping one arm with her bony fingers.

She's fairly frothing to lay into me.

"I'm sure in recent weeks you've considered your situation. Once I marry, the countess is entitled to the dowager house, and I doubt, given the enmity between you, she'll invite you to remain." He fingered the bed curtain's gold tassel, letting the truth of his words sink in.

She made a rough noise in the back of her throat, but kept her lips firmly pinched together. "Without funds, you'll be reduced to living with one of my sisters." Resolute, Alex didn't spare her. "Most likely rotated between their three households since you make yourself so disagreeable to everyone. I'd much rather you continued in comfort, able to travel and visit as you are inclined to, instead of living at the mercy of others' generosity and whims."

Grandmama averted her gaze, the first traces of vulnerability he'd observed softening her wrinkled face. Dropping her focus to the bedsheet, she plucked at the frayed lace edge. "You've mulled this through, I see."

He sank onto the bed and clasped her cool hand. "I don't want to do this to you, Grandmama. Though you can be difficult and petty, and you seldom have a kind thing to say, I do love you."

Her wide green eyes sought his, and a trace of warmth glimmered in their depths. "You do?"

The two shaky words held such disbelief and hope, his heart softened. "I do. You're the matriarch of our family, and I think if you'd put aside your prickly exterior, you'd find my sisters want to love you too." He kissed her knobby knuckles.

She blinked back tears, and her voice cracked. "I'd ... like that. I've been lonely."

"I know you have, and I want to remedy that. But I adore Brette. I shall do everything I can to win her heart. She's beautiful, kind, and intelligent, and she has the most delightful laugh." *And a delectable bottom and bosoms*. "Her background and pedigree don't matter an iota to me, and I'd much prefer your blessing than a rift between us. However, the choice is yours, Grandmama. I'll not be dissuaded."

Grandmama's lower lip trembled, and she withdrew her hand to collect a handkerchief from her nightstand. A frail, uncertain old woman had replaced the grand, imposing dame. She dabbed the corners of her eyes.

"I understand." She gave him a wobbly half-smile. "A lifetime of habits is difficult to break, and I may need a little time to adjust, but I intend to try. Truly. You will have to bear with me. Please."

"That's all I ask." Emerald crawled onto his lap, and Alex eyed her warily. He held his breath lest she remember her dislike of him. Instead of arching her spine and hissing, she closed her eyes and started purring.

"I think she likes you." Grandmama gave him a tremulous smile, though moisture still glinted in her eyes.

"She detested me the last time I was here. Wanted to use me as a human claw-sharpener." He arched a brow and whispered, "I'm entirely too terrified to move."

"Emerald's accepted you now. You needn't fear.'" She exhaled loudly as she wiped her nose. "Wycombe, how goes the investigation into the fire? Unbearably tragic, and someone dares hint you might have been responsible? Reprehensible."

Back to Wycombe, are we?

"Heard about that, did you?" Alex ran a hand along the cat's spine.

Grandmama's lips turned up the merest bit, her familiar confidence once more in place.

"I have my sources. Actually, Wilma Wobsley mentioned it at supper last evening whilst we dined at Lady Honeycutt's. You think *I'm* difficult. At times, Martha Honeycutt makes Satan look like an inexperienced schoolboy. And Mrs. Wobsley is incapable of keeping the smallest, most trivial of secrets. A woman with a looser tongue or less common sense doesn't exist."

"Perhaps you ought to consider new friends? We are known by the company we keep, aren't we?" He braved scratching Emerald's shoulders, relaxing when she made no attempt to impale his fingers with her teeth or claws.

"Yes, after last evening, I'm of the same mind." She placed her damp handkerchief on the nightstand and prompted, "The fire?"

"Fret not. I have an irrefutable alibi, and I've hired runners to look into the matter for me. In fact, The Bow Street Agency is my next stop this morning. They've already uncovered my accuser. As I suspected, a disgruntled relative. A third cousin who thought nothing of falsely blaming me so he could inherit." Alex scratched behind the cat's ears, and her rumblings grew louder. "Also, a footman's gone missing, and I think that's cause for suspicion."

"Let me guess which ratty cousin. Maximillian?" she suggested, her tone dryer than charred parchment. "Envious churl. Always has been. That's one thing I always appreciated about you. You were never jealous of Arthur."

"True. I didn't envy him at all. I don't think he was altogether happy."

The fire's heat slowly spread, easing the worst of the room's nippiness. His grandmother shouldn't be sleeping in this cold environment. On his way out, he'd speak to Norris and increase the household budget to accommodate more fuel.

Come to think of it, perhaps what Alex had assumed was her preference for sameness wasn't brought about by inflexibility or habit, but rather financial necessity.

He examined her chamber with a more critical regard.

Though her room was tidy and elegantly decorated, the furnishing—everything, truth to tell—was far past its prime. Even her night cap and gown showed signs of wear. Precisely how much had Wycombe allotted her monthly?

Had Alex misjudged her circumstances?

He hadn't yet examined High Wycombe's books. Hertford, his new steward, had found the estate records a confounded muddle. Best contact him and at the very least determine Grandmama's current allowance.

"Alexander?" Her unease tangible, she brushed a silvery lock off her pale forehead. "Yes?"

She hesitated, as if torn.

He patted her hand. "You can tell me. It can't be as bad as all that."

Grandmama scooted back, dragging Ambrosia onto her lap. "I heard something else last night I think you ought to know, though I'm not sure what you can do about it."

Progress already. An hour ago, she'd not have taken him into her confidence.

Setting the cat aside, he stood. He must run multiple errands before returning to Highfield and seeking Brette. He brushed cat hair from his trousers and coat. Times like this, he wished a valet awaited him to attend to the task later. Perhaps after he settled the estate's finances.

Looks like I rolled in the stuff.

He continued to pick long, gray cat hairs from his person. "It concerns your Miss Culpepper."

"How so?" His unease spiraled upward, and he left off ridding his garments of feline fur. Emerald rolled onto her back, presenting her plump belly for petting. Grandmama obliged, scraping her fingers across the cat's round tummy. "I don't know if you are aware, but Wilma Wobsley is the newest Duchess of Bellinghamshire's mother. She claims Bellinghamshire petitioned for Miss Culpepper's guardianship."

Alex froze. "Pardon?"

Conniving blackguard. This changes everything.

"According to Wilma, the Bellinghamshires are desperate for the funds they presumed their Genevia would inherit, and have borrowed heavily against her inheritance. The duke plans on marrying Miss Culpepper off immediately upon being granted the guardianship. There's something about an agreement with her intended allowing them to keep half her inheritance. I'm not positive the arrangement's even legal."

Hounds' teeth!

The prospect hadn't occurred to him. Or Raven, he'd wager. And it surely wouldn't have to Brette. "Her inheritance can't be substantial enough that they'd stoop to those means. Didn't the duke inherit the bulk when he came into the title?"

"I'm not altogether sure. I seem to recall the eldest son had a falling out with Fusty Boots. In any event, his grace has already arranged a match with—" Grandmama shuddered delicately. "God help me, I can hardly bear to say it."

Blood boiling, Alex gritted his teeth. How dare the Bellinghamshires treat Brette like an expendable pawn to gain her piddly inheritance? Undulating waves of unaccustomed rage knotted his gut and thrummed through him. "Who's she promised to?"

Grandmama wrinkled her nose and puckered her lips as if forced to eat wriggling maggots. "The Marquis Duplesse."

No!

"That sod? He's ailing too, isn't he? He's also an unconscionable reprobate, and he's ancient. Seventy, if he's a day." Too much drink and whoring. He'd gone through three wives already. By God, the blackguard would likely infect Brette with the clap or worse.

Grandmama arched him a starchy glance. "I beg your pardon?"

"Don't get your feathers ruffled, Grandmama. You remain inarguably exquisite, but he's a debauched blackguard, fifty years Brette's senior." Alex yanked the bell. He needed to be away, and he wanted a word with Norris first.

"He's nearer eighty, and I think the Bellinghamshires hope he'll die soon, so they can barter your Miss Culpepper again." She shook her head, and her cap slipped lower onto her forehead. "I wouldn't wish that fate on the girl, no matter her background." She shot him a repentant glance. "I didn't mean to sound judgmental."

Alex managed a distracted half-smile.

Musings banged louder than a tinker's wagon in his already

sensitive skull. He wasn't ever downing more than a finger's worth of spirits again.

He raked a hand through his hair. What to do first?

Speak to Raven? Acquire a special license? Meet with the Bow Street investigators? Inquire if Brette's solicitor would speak with him? Trot by the Chancery Court and poke around to determine how far the guardianship request had progressed? Hightail it to Highfield Place House and propose?

Again?

He'd have to borrow Grandmama's coach. Besides the sullen weather discouraging further foot travel, he had no time to spare. On second thought, he'd better collect a special license first. He wouldn't put anything past Bellinghamshire, and Alex wasn't chancing Brette falling into the duke's clutches.

"Alexander. I think I understand how much you care for the girl, but the matter's out of your hands." True remorse made her voice husky. Or his grandmother was an accomplished actress.

No, her concern rang sincere. She hadn't had to share this news with him and in doing so, she'd revealed a change of heart.

"There's no help for it. I'll have to wed Brette by special license as soon as possible." He bent and kissed her cheek. "I would be honored if you'd attend."

"But ... but you're in mourning," she stammered, sitting up and setting the cat aside in her astonishment. "You cannot marry right now. Proprieties must be observed, Wycombe. What will people say?"

Ah, a tinge of censure there.

"If I wait, Brette may be forced to marry Dupresse, and that's far worse than temporarily miffing the *ton* sensibilities. I'm an earl. They'll forgive me. Marrying during a mourning period is neither illegal nor immoral, merely frowned upon."

"You've been spared the *haut ton*'s censure. I assure you, it's most unpleasant." Issuing a resigned sigh, she sagged into her pillows once more. "But, I shall support you. I think Miss Culpepper is a charming girl, and I hope she'll forgive me for my earlier churlishness. Nonetheless, you ought to warn her that at times I can be a trifle obstinate and opinionated."

At times?

"I'm sure you will get on famously. At least I hope so, for I would love for you to live with us, if you are inclined to." Though Grandmama had sworn she'd try, he didn't expect an overnight transformation. Luckily, Brette possessed a forgiving nature.

Tears seeped from his Grandmother's eyes, trailing onto her crepey cheeks. "Truly, Alexander? After I've been so difficult?"

"Truly. But you will be kind to Brette. Promise me."

"I shall, dear, I promise."

A soft rap echoed at the door.

"Come." Grandmama looked expectantly at the entrance.

Her abigail, wearing a severe brown gown and bearing a tray, scooted into the bedchamber. "I took the liberty of bringing your breakfast early, my lady." She sent Alex a nervous, sideways glance. "Since someone rang the bell."

"Very well done of you, Kingstone." Grandmama shoved another pillow behind her back. "I am anticipating my tea this morning. Rising early does invigorate one's appetite." She eagerly lifted the silver dome. "Kippers and ham. Splendid."

"I'll be on my way." Alex strode to the door, determined to apprise Brette of the situation first and worry about the rest of his pressing concerns once she'd agreed to marry him. "Would you mind terribly if I borrowed your coach. I walked here."

Grandmama fluttered her fingers at him. "Indeed. Just inform Norris. I haven't anywhere to go before two o'clock today. Oh, I nearly forgot, dear boy."

Dear boy, am I now? Such miraculous progress already.

Teacup poised at her mouth, she paused. "Bellinghamshire has a man watching the young lady. Following her. Wilma was particularly giddy about the fact. He means to..." She cast a practiced eye at her rapt abigail, who promptly applied herself to selecting Grandmama's clothing for the day. "...remove her from her family's care. Says he has the legal right."

Noble intentions alone are not enough: Commitment, sacrifice,
and even the smallest of actions are more powerful and longer lasting.
~Appearances and Attitude—The Genteel Lady's Guide to Practical Living

*U*nexpected?

The coppery-haired clerk gave Brette a shy smile, and, tucking her fur muff beneath one arm, she answered with a friendly smile.

"I received a note from Mr. Shipwreck asking me to attend him at my earliest convenience."

In the corner, a smallish, pot-bellied stove beckoned, and she crossed the floor's worn planks to warm her hands. She might have saved the effort. The pathetic amount of heat radiating from the under-stoked iron wouldn't have cooked an egg much less boil the water in the dented kettle sitting on a side table with the makings for tea.

Mr. Shipwreck didn't seem miserly, but his help suffered from the cold. Wise leaving Flora in the carriage. She'd have been miserable.

"A note? From this office?" Completely baffled, hands on his hips, the secretary cocked his head before pointing an accusatory stare at each clerk in turn.

Angling her shoulders to the humble stove, Brette dipped her head, indicating the redheaded chap. "Yes. I believe your young man there delivered it."

"I did, along with the other correspondences, as Pauly and I do each morning." A troubled frown crinkled the youth's forehead.

Which of the other clerks was Pauly?

Ah, the expressionless fellow. He slowly blinked at her before applying his quill to whatever he'd diligently been working on before she interrupted.

"And a letter for Miss Culpepper was included in the missives?" Mr. Loomis demanded, peevishly sucking in his cheeks,

The redhead dared a reluctant nod.

"Well, obviously, or I wouldn't be here." Brette conjured her most reassuring smile and attempted levity.

Her efforts fell flat.

Throwing his hands up, the secretary made no effort to conceal his flustered state. "Goodness me. How am I to properly perform my duties if I'm not apprised of the goings-on in this office? Notes being delivered hither and yon, and not as much as a by your leave to me. Unacceptable, I tell you."

"If it's an inconvenient time, I can return later—" Which meant she'd have to wait longer to learn what Mr. Shipwreck had discovered. Drat it all. Besides, no coach waited outside, and she'd have to sit here until it returned.

The inner door swung open, and Mr. Shipwreck, papers in hand and spectacles barely clinging to the end of his nose, poked his head out. "Loomis, I shall need—"

He caught sight of Brette beside the stove, appearing only slightly less astonished than Mr. Loomis at her seeing her in his office. He, however, recovered much more adroitly.

This is very peculiar.

"Ah, Miss Culpepper. I'm glad you've stopped in."

You sent for me.

"I have important news for you."

Hence your summons.

Shoving his eyeglasses up his nose, he perused the room, his bafflement almost comedic. "You're alone?"

"My maid remained in the coach. She's not feeling well." No need to tell him the conveyance wasn't parked before his establishment.

"Come in, please." He stepped aside and indicated she should enter his office. "Loomis, I'll need Miss Culpepper's file, and for heaven's sake, add coal to the stove. How can the staff possibly work if they're half frozen? Prepare the chaps a spot of tea too. Their cheeks and noses are almost as red as Mr. Jacobson's hair."

An exaggeration there. The chamber wasn't *that* cold.

"Yes, sir. Right away, sir. I saw the file this morning. It's here somewhere." Mr. Loomis immediately started riffling through the folders neatly stacked atop his desk, muttering the whole while. "Might've informed me. Can't expect me to read minds. How's a body to perform their job? Perfectly warm enough for me. Can't be pampering the help."

As Brette entered the cozier room, she pressed her lips together to

435

check her smile.

Mr. Shipwreck rolled his eyes ceilingward as he shut the door behind them. "He's as fussy as an old tabby, but meticulously organized, if a mite miserly. And frankly, I couldn't function without him."

After seeing her to a chair, he settled himself behind his desk, folded his hands, and gave her a rather jovial smile. Ink stained the fingertips of his right hand, and his coat appeared as if he'd slept in it. "I finished my notes on your situation last night and intended to send a letter 'round to Lord Ravensdale this morning asking him to bring you by. You saved me the trouble."

"But, Mr. Shipwreck, I received a missive from you this morning." She rummaged in her reticule and, after finding the crisply folded square, passed it to him.

His eyebrows jumped to his receding hairline and hung there suspended as he unfolded the letter. Shaking his head, he thrust the foolscap her way. "I assure you, I didn't write this."

Unease, like a cold, clammy snake, slithered down the length of Brette's spine. The obvious question, *"Who had then?"* pealed loudly in her head.

A sharp rap preceded Mr. Loomis's entrance. He bore the file, holding it reverently as if he carried the crown jewels. "Would you care for a cup of tea, Miss Culpepper? The kettle's already on. I concede, it's a brisk one outside today. Think it will snow? I don't ever recall snow in November before."

Though rattled by Mr. Shipwreck's disclosure, Brette managed to muster a smile for the eager-to-please man. "That's kind of you, but no tea for me, thank you. And, yes, I do believe we should prepare for at least a smattering of snow."

As soon as Mr. Loomis exited, she bent across the desk and collected the letter. "This was delivered by your clerk. The red-haired fellow—"

"Elias Jacobson," the solicitor offered, his countenance as baffled as hers must've been. "He's a trustworthy chap, too." He rubbed his jaw, eyes partially closed in contemplation. "I cannot imagine where it came from. Most disturbing, and I assure you, I shall have an answer from my staff. Entirely unacceptable—slipping correspondences into my posts." He pointed to the letter. "It's going to cost someone their position, I can tell you."

Had Alex's grandmother bribed a clerk to lure Brette from the house? The dowager countess didn't know Heath wouldn't accompany her.

Unless his urgent summons this morning had been part of the ploy too. To make sure he wasn't at home when Brette received the writ.

Bother and rot.

Either Brette's imagination was running amok, or she'd played right into the manipulating woman's hands. What could the old crow hope to accomplish? Blessedly dedicated, Peters couldn't be bribed. There'd be no forgetting to collect her or delivering her to the wrong address. Nevertheless, prudence demanded she send a note to Highfield and inquire if Raven or Alex, or even a footman or two, could convey her home. No sense taking undue chances.

If the dowager was responsible, she had some nerve, and Brette fully intended to inform Alex. Surely, she'd listen to her grandson. As the earl, he headed the family now.

Do you remember her behavior the other day? Does she seem like a dutiful woman?

Pasting a deliberately cheery smile on her face, Brette placed her beaded reticule beside her ermine muff on Mr. Shipwreck's desk. "I'd like to send a note to Highfield, requesting an escort home. Could I trouble you for a piece of foolscap and a quill? While I wait, we can discuss whatever news you have for me."

"I'm in agreement. I think an escort is wise." He pushed an inkwell and quill across the once shiny desktop.

"My driver is running errands for me, otherwise I'd have him deliver the request." In short order, Brette wrote the note and Mr. Shipwreck entrusted it to Mr. Loomis for delivery. "Please deliver this straightaway, and await a response."

"Very good, miss." In a rush, the secretary bustled from the office, and in his haste, overlooked closing the door snugly behind him. "Pauly, quickly man," Mr. Loomis ordered, his reedy voice carrying into the inner office. "This letter needs delivering to Highfield Place House promptly. You're to wait for a response. No dawdling to and from, either, if you value your position. You've pages of documents to copy today."

"Yes, Mr. Loomis." A stool scraped across the floor, followed a few moments later by a door thudding closed.

"Now, then." The solicitor opened her file, his businesslike demeanor in place once more. "I think you'll be well-pleased at what we've managed to uncover on your behalf."

Brette's stomach tumbled giddily. "Please tell me my parents were married after all." Why did it matter so much?

"Indeed." He raised an affirmative brow and smiled broadly.

"And the ceremony was witnessed by several associates of theirs as well as a visiting cleric." He perused the papers. "A Vicar Wonderly, who's a bishop in Lincoln now."

Brette wanted to jump up, shout her joy, and dance around the room. Instead, she settled for happily wiggling her toes in her boots. "So there can be no doubt of my legitimacy?"

"None, whatsoever."

She sank back into the chair and released an extended breath. Apparently, her father hadn't been a complete rapscallion after all. "I shan't pretend I'm not delighted. It does rather wear on one to think— None of that matters now, does it?"

"No indeed. But there's more, my dear Miss Culpepper." His chestnut eyes fairly twinkled with his secret. "I suspected it might be the case, but naturally, I performed due diligence first. I needed to be certain before I approached you. It's most startling, really, but I think you will be pleased."

"Mr. Shipwreck, I cannot imagine what has you so ... exuberant." Brette laughed. "I'm sure it cannot be more staggering than discovering I'm legitimate."

"Indulge me while I refresh your memory of certain relevant facts. I want to make sure you fully appreciate your position." As he spoke, he poked through the folder, withdrawing documents every now and again.

Brette angled her head. "Yes, of course. Please go on."

"Your grandfather was the Duke of Bellinghamshire."

Old Fusty Boots.

"And your father was his second son. His grace quarreled with his eldest son, the heir, and they never reconciled. Being a spiteful codger, the old duke bequeathed his unentailed worldly possessions to the—and I quote here..." He scrutinized the parchment before him. "'...eldest

legitimate, living offspring produced from the loins of my younger sons.'" He glanced up, his mien almost smug. "There are only two surviving grandchildren, Miss Culpepper. You and one other, *younger,* granddaughter."

Heart and stomach floundering clumsily somewhere in the vicinity of her shaky knees, Brette straightened until she perched on the chair's edge.

Good Lord. He doesn't mean...?

Mr. Shipwreck beamed, his smile stretching to his ears, and his eyes crumpling like folded crepes. "You, my dear, are a very, *very* wealthy heiress with properties on three continents, a copper mine, two ships, a silk warehouse— The list goes on at length. Your grandfather might have been miserly, but he possessed a tremendous business sense. Unusual for a peer, truth to tell. Most abhor ties to commerce."

"I..." She shook her head in dazed disbelief. Had he truly declared Brette her grandfather's heir? "I honestly don't know what to say."

So many options had become possible in the blink of an eye. Including marrying Alex. Nothing could be grander.

Half an hour ago, a lowly by-blow, and now an heiress. And not any heiress, but the recognized granddaughter of the Duke of Bellinghamshire.

Her nose tickled, and she sneezed twice. "Excuse me."

"Bless you," Mr. Shipwreck said, his face still wreathed in smiles.

Fishing her hankie from her reticule, she pressed the square to her nostrils and considered her options. Perchance the house in Belgrave Square could be turned into a school. She must inspect the place. And if not, she had funds to purchase an adequate facility. "So what happens now? How do we proceed?"

"There's the uncomfortable business of informing your uncle, the current duke, that the funds and properties held in trust for his seven-year-old daughter, Genevia, are no longer hers." Mr. Shipwreck rubbed his chin. "I can't think he'll take the news well."

"Most unfair, I think." Brette fingered her reticule's strap. Another conundrum brought about by the circumstances of birth. "Couldn't I set aside a trust for her?"

Brette wasn't about to refuse this most welcome and altogether unexpected gift, but denying her cousin a portion seemed beyond selfish.

"That's generous of you, and you are free to do whatever you wish with your monies. I can draft the documents necessary." He paused, giving her a chagrined smile. "If you trust me to do so. Ravensdale, as your guardian, will have to approve, naturally."

Mr. Shipwreck had gone far and beyond to help her determine her heritage. Unconscionable to sack him now. "Of course I trust you, and I hope you'll agree to help me determine a fair settlement for Genevia too. I don't think Heath will have an issue with me bestowing funds on the girl. She's an innocent in this."

Genevia shouldn't be penalized for being born after Brette.

"I'm afraid Bellinghamshire, the younger, is nearly as crusty a curmudgeon as his father, though without the common sense of a parsnip.

The vegetable would probably do a better job of managing Bellinghamshire's monies, truth be told." Mr. Shipwreck grew more solemn, tense even, as he gave his earlobe another tug. "And you should know, he's aware of your existence. Has been for weeks now, apparently. His man of business has been snooping around, asking questions, poking his nose into your affairs."

"Should I be concerned?" For an odd reason, the cocky rider passing the house this morning came to mind. Where, exactly, had she seen the blasted horse before?

Mr. Shipwreck regarded the cracked door and scrunched his forehead. "Let me close the door before we continue."

What would Alex say when he learned of the turnabout in her station? His grandmother?

Brette didn't require or seek the dowager's approval, but now the dame had no grounds for her objections. A wicked smile threatened in anticipation of seeing the Gambwells' reactions when they learned of her good fortune. However, Brette mustn't gloat or be vindictive.

Well, a jot of reveling might be permitted where those tabbies were concerned.

After returning to his seat, Mr. Shipwreck sank heavily onto his chair. "I think caution is sensible, and I wish to speak to Ravensdale on the matter. That's why I'd hoped he'd come with you today."

"Well, perhaps he'll be the one to escort me home, and you'll have the opportunity."

"I do hope that's the case," Mr. Shipwreck murmured while thumbing through more papers in her file. "I don't recall your birthdate, Miss Culpepper. How old are you?"

Sleet lashed the window behind him, a periodic fluffy snowflake in the winter mix.

Treacherous for traffic if ice carpeted the roads. Peters might be delayed, and so might whoever took on the task of ushering her home.

"I'm twenty." And old enough to know her own mind. A notion struck, astonishing and exhilarating, and her breath hitched. She'd inherited enough to open a women's college, and offer her patronage to Alex's ragged school.

Not surprising that she still wanted to help him. Would he view her differently because her lineage had become acceptable? Difficult to say. When Society had deemed her unsuitable, Alex had still wanted to marry her, or at least he'd said he did.

Now—

Good heavens.

She might be sought after by the very elitists who'd given her the cut.

Position and wealth, once again, prevailed over decency and character. Too bad for them.

Her loyalty lay with those kind-hearted enough to include her when her heritage had been doubtful.

"And when will you be one-and-twenty?"

He certainly seemed determined on that account, didn't he? Suddenly alert, she cocked her head. "In July. The seventeenth."

He huffed out a breath, drumming his fingers atop the papers. "I'd hoped it might be sooner."

"Why? What difference does it make when I come of age?"

The room had become uncomfortably warm, and she feared she perspired in a most unladylike fashion. What had Mr. Loomis done? Dumped an entire bucket of coal into the stove? She rose to make her way to a tall window, hoping it might be slighter cooler there.

One hand on the sill, she leaned over and peered outside.

No sign of Peters yet or anyone else to accompany her home either. White already dusted the trees, buildings, and sidewalks. Given the unexpected snowfall, they'd better arrive soon, or the trip home might prove adventuresome.

She sucked in a raggedy breath, an unpleasant jolt to her middle making her stomach go wobbly. An unmarked black coach stood parked beneath a tree on the opposite side of the street—the same one from earlier?—and the horseman she'd seen riding past the house this morning spoke to its occupant.

So did the clerk Mr. Loomis had just sent to Highfield House Place.

Pauly paused, pointing at the brick building housing Mr. Shipwreck's offices, before nodding and accepting a fist-sized bag from someone inside the coach. He promptly tucked it within his coat, and with a guilty look around, ducked his head and strode away.

The weasel.

The horseman remounted, and touching his hat, also left, his horse's hooves kicking up miniature snow mounds. *This is where I've seen him before.* Right here or near Mr. Shipwreck's office almost every time she and Heath paid a visit.

Even squinting, Brette couldn't identify the coach's occupant, but she'd wager her new fortune the dowager reigned within. Pounding her

441

cane and issuing starchy orders, glaring the whole while.

Could she see Brette?

A shadow fell across the coach's window, and her nape hair stood on end. She quickly moved away from the opening, unease tapping a rapid tempo along her spine.

So, the note delivered this morning had probably been bait to lure her here.

Brette wasn't a fribbling fool. She'd not as much as poke her nose outside this building without Heath or Alex by her side. Preferably both. Except, they didn't know she needed an escort, and due to the blackguard clerk's duplicity, they wouldn't soon either.

But Jenkin knew where she'd gone, and when Peters returned, she could send him to the house to get help. No need to work herself into a dither.

"Mr. Shipwreck?"

He peered at her above the top of his eyeglasses.

She swept her hand in the window's general direction. "Your clerk, Pauly, just accepted what I assume was a bribe from someone in a coach across the street. I'm convinced my missive will not be delivered."

Mr. Shipwreck made a disgusted noise in his throat and threw down the papers he'd been reading. Earnestness replaced his former joviality. "I shall return you home safely myself, and I think we now know who planted the false letter to you, don't we?"

She retraced her steps, inexplicably chilled. Anxiety did that to a person. "I suspect there's something you're not telling me."

"Ah... Well..." The most flustered she'd seen him, he huffed out a lengthy breath and rubbed his nose. "You might as well know, Miss Culpepper. You will soon enough, in any event."

For pity's sake. Now what?

"Bellinghamshire's man of business stopped in the day before yesterday and informed me that, over a month ago, the duke petitioned for your guardianship. As your nearest living blood relation, not to mention a ranking duke, he's likely to have the request granted."

Those who sow good intentions eagerly await the fruit of their actions.
~*Appearances and Attitude—The Genteel Lady's Guide to Practical Living*

15

Unable to sit, agitation making her edgy, Brette paced in Mr. Shipwreck's office.

Careful to stay away from the window, she folded her arms and tucked her chin to her chest. She'd removed her outer wrap, and accepted a cup of tea from a most repentant and remorseful Mr. Loomis. When Mr. Shipwreck told him of Pauly's treachery, the secretary had become so distraught, she'd feared him on the brink of an apoplexy.

Mr. Loomis had promptly sent Jacobson out the rear entry, a letter secreted in his pocket, and a coal bucket in his hand. No matter that the coal bin practically overflowed. Mr. Shipwreck had provided Jacobson with funds to hire a hack a block or two away. No one should have to walk to Highfield in this miserable weather.

She puffed out her cheeks and turned to march in the other direction. What a deuced bumblebroth. Just informed she was an heiress, and mere moments later, learning her greedy uncle intended to rip her from her family.

Venturing near the window, she peeked outside. Snow steadily sifted from the sky now.

"The carriage remains there." Probably not the dowager herself, but a hireling. "And mine hasn't returned yet. I cannot imagine what the delay is, unless Peters is having difficulty negotiating the roads because of the snow."

"I'm prepared to leave with you as soon as he arrives." Mr. Shipwreck set his quill aside. "Unless we have word from Highfield before then."

"There's absolutely no way to prevent Bellinghamshire from this quest?" Brette returned to the chair she'd thrown her mantle over.

Mr. Shipwreck slumped into his chair and removed his spectacles. He rummaged in his coat pocket, and after withdrawing a handkerchief, set about polishing the glass.

"As to that, Miss Culpepper, I've been thinking, and I believe there are a couple of options.

First, I could make the argument that removing you from the only family you've known is unnecessary given you will be of age in a few months." He fluttered the cloth. "The courts are bogged down and might consider the case a waste of time. On the other hand, Bellinghamshire's powerful and might call in favors."

His kind always did. "How likely is the court to dismiss the case?"

He pinched the bridge of his nose and wagged his head back and forth. "I'd estimate we have about a fifty percent probability of winning, if you're willing to take the chance. That is, if the petition hasn't been approved already."

Fifty percent? Only one in two? Not odds she favored, by any means.

"What's the other possibility?" Brette ran her fingertips across the cloak's smooth velvet, the fabric strangely soothing, as was the repetitive motion.

"At this time, the inheritance is legally yours, so I could swiftly draft documentation assigning it in its entirety to a trustworthy person of your choice. As your acting guardian, Ravensdale can authorize the transaction. Once you come of age, the person you've selected can transfer everything back to you. Since I believe it's your money Bellinghamshire is after, he mightn't proceed with the guardianship claim."

Fingers still pressed to his nose, he closed his eyes as if deep in thought.

Much more appealing than the first suggestion. Mayhap he could do both?

"Except—" Mr. Shipwreck crumpled his mouth and opened his eyes.

What she saw there didn't encourage her.

Brette's anticipation plummeted off a cliff. "Except what?"

"Bellinghamshire could contest the procedure, though he's not likely to prevail unless he's already been assigned, or is close to being assigned, as your guardian. In which case, the transfer would be null and void."

Rot and bother.

What if the Chancery Court favored the duke?

Well, Brette wouldn't meekly pack her belongings and toddle to wherever the blazes her uncle lived. She'd vanish until her first-and-twentieth birthday. Eight months wasn't overly long.

Heath would help. Leventhorpe and Alex too.

Alex. How could she vanish and put him from her life?

One step at a time. It might not come to that. No sense getting ahead of yourself.

"It seems to me, Mr. Shipwreck, that the most critical thing at this point is discovering precisely how far the guardianship process has progressed." She'd better plan for the worst while hoping for the best.

He tucked several papers into a folder as he nodded. "Indeed. And I shall begin inquiring as soon as I've seen you home. Let's hope Lord Ravensdale is present, and I might have a word with him."

Two knocks announced Mr. Loomis again. He peered around the door. "Miss Culpepper, your coach has arrived."

Finally.

"Thank you, Loomis. I shall accompany Miss Culpepper. If Lord Ravensdale seeks her here, please tell him I've taken her home. And please inform her coachman I need a word with him." He placed his hat upon his head then draped a cloak across his arm before seizing his walking stick.

"Yes, sir." Bobbing his head, the secretary offered another apologetic smile. "Should I keep your intentions from anyone else who might inquire as to either of your whereabouts?"

Brette hadn't a doubt Mr. Loomis would go to his grave before revealing their plan.

"If Lord Wycombe should happen by, he may be apprised as well." Perhaps Alex would be home to receive the note. After tucking her handkerchief into her reticule, Brette swung her cape around her shoulders, secured the frogs, and gathered her other possessions.

Mr. Shipwreck lifted his cane a couple of inches. "It contains a short sword. Can't hurt to be prepared."

Against what, precisely?

A moment later, Mr. Loomis admitted Peters.

Hat in his hands, his attention shifted from Brette to Mr. Shipwreck. "My apologies for my tardiness, miss. After waiting in a lengthy line at the alchemist, a coach accident forced me to take a different route. The roads are getting slick too. I think it wise to depart at once."

"In a moment…Peters, is it?" Mr. Shipwreck raked his gaze over the burly coachman. "Miss Culpepper was followed here. Even now, we believe someone may lie in wait for her in the carriage parked across the street. I'll be riding with her, and I was curious if you carry a firearm."

Peters didn't flinch at the unusual requests. "I noticed the coach too. Thought it odd, sitting there on a day like this. The coachmen look miserable." His mouth tipped up. "And yes, I have a loaded pistol beneath my seat and a knife in my boot. His lordship insists upon it."

Thank goodness, Heath had had the foresight. Nevertheless, apprehension made Brette edgy. "We will flank Miss Culpepper as we exit. I'll have my secretary and clerk escort us as well. Drive directly home, taking the most public route, though it's slower. We want to be seen."

Peters bobbed his head. "A maid is in the carriage too, sir. She's a trifle—Flora upsets easily."

His consideration warmed Brette, and she'd make Heath aware.

"I don't think anyone would dare try anything. Nonetheless, we should be alert." For a solicitor, Mr. Shipwreck seemed uniquely prepared.

Moments later, hood covering her bonnet and surrounded by men, Brette descended the steps. No sooner had she left the building than the carriage across the street's door swung open, and a tall, dignified man emerged.

Not the Dowager Countess Wycombe, and given his first stare of fashion trappings, he wasn't anyone's lackey. He was, however, surprisingly surefooted considering the slushy ground. His elongated strides rapidly swallowed the between them. "Miss Culpepper?"

His drivers followed in his wake; huge chaps easily as strapping and intimidating as Peters. This didn't bode well.

"Don't speak, keep your head lowered, and get into the coach. Pull the shades too." Mr. Shipwreck basically heaved her into the interior a mere second before Peters slammed the door shut.

Mr. Shipwreck and his clerk placed themselves between the approaching man and the coach as she scrambled to yank the shades down.

Before she'd completely lowered the second one, the man grinned and flicked his wrist at them. "No need for this. I'm simply collecting my ward."

Dear God.

Bellinghamshire? Her uncle?

Flora, her eyes dinner-plate round, jerked the lap robes to her chin. Teeth chattering, she whispered, "Miss Brette, what's happening?"

"*Shh*, Flora. I'll explain later. I need to hear what being said outside." Brette pressed her ear near the freezing door. Blast, but the coach was cold within. A veritable ice box.

Peters didn't dare climb into the driver's seat in case Brette needed help staving off the three men, and neither could Mr. Shipwreck enter the carriage for fear of the men snatching her when he did.

She swallowed the bile rising to her throat, truly afraid for the first time in her life. What did her uncle intend to do with her? If the situation hadn't been so bloody frightening, she might've laughed at the absurdity of it.

"And who might you be?" Mr. Shipwreck demanded, defiance in every starchy syllable. He didn't seem the least intimidated by the duke.

"Bellinghamshire." The duke's amiable tone hardened. "And the young woman in this coach is my niece and ward."

Done with pleasantries already?

Flora whimpered.

"*Shh*, it will be all right, Flora." Brette didn't know how.

"Ward? You are gravely mistaken, sir. Lord Ravensdale is her guardian," Mr. Shipwreck said.

Bellinghamshire laughed, a rather pleasant sound for such a vile man. "Not according to the Chancery Court, he isn't. I must insist you relinquish her to me before I have to take unpleasant measures or bring the authorities into it."

Muffled horses' hooves, along with springs squeaking and the whooshing of wheels turning, announced a vehicle's approach. Brette held her breath.

Let it be Heath or Alex.

Almost crying her frustration aloud when it rolled past, she pressed her forehead against the window.

Did Bellinghamshire truly think he could seize her outside her solicitor's office and haul her off, pell-mell? Surely he wasn't dimwitted enough to presume she'd go willingly?

Screeching and clawing and kicking? Yes.

Willingly? Never.

What an arrogant buffoon.

"I should welcome the authorities' intervention," Mr. Shipwreck boldly challenged. *Remember to double his fee.* "So unless you possess a writ proving you are whom you say you are, you will return to your conveyance and allow us to depart in peace." *Brilliant. A well-delivered blow.* "I'm certain you wouldn't want an attempted abduction linked to your name, Your Grace."

Oh, and another full-on facer. Well done you, Mr. Shipwreck.

She'd triple his fee. Indeed, she would.

A second coach's approach rang along the pavement, and before it lumbered to a halt, Heath's welcome, but angry voice rang out. "What goes on here?"

Her relief profound and fighting tears, Brette allowed herself a jubilant smile.

"Bellinghamshire, surprised you're about on a miserable day like this."

A joyous tear did leak from her eye. Dear Alex had come too.

"I thought you preferred the comforts of White's or Brooks's." A steely edge tempered Alex's geniality.

She tried to peek below the shade's folds, but only the thickly falling snowflakes and a row of men's backs met her inspection.

"Or a gaming hell, losing more funds," resonated a third droll voice. Leventhorpe? How was it possible he was here too?

Oh, you just try taking on this trio, Bellinghamshire.

Inhaling a bracing breath, Brette unlatched the door. She thrust it open, accidentally bumping Jacobson's back. He must have ridden back with Heath.

"I beg your pardon."

"Quite all right" His lips quirked, and he presented his hand to help her step down. "Which vehicle will you take, miss?"

"I don't know yet." Intentionally ignoring his grace, she cocked her head. Relation or not, they'd not been introduced. "Shall I ride with you, Ravensdale, or will you and the others join me?"

Everyone swung to face her.

She waved at Alex and Leventhorpe. "So wonderful to see you both."

More than wonderful. Marvelous. As was the flummoxed expression on her uncle's face.

Alex, his hands balled and the wrath of God accenting his angular cheeks, broke into a pleased smile. She'd rather like him to punch her uncle.

"My dear niece, no sense in prolonging the inevitable. Do come along with me and meet your aunt and cousin." Bellinghamshire's mouth swept into an artificial smile, pleating the edges of his blueish-green eyes.

Her eyes.

Except a worldly toughness glinted in his.

He doesn't like me any more than I like him.

Brette leveled him her frostiest glance and angled her head. "Your Grace, do you normally conduct business in the midst of a snowstorm? I have an ill maid within this carriage, and rest assured, before I go anywhere with you, the team pulling this coach will sprout wings and fly."

Heath, Alex, and Leventhorpe chuckled.

"Reminds me of her cousin." A wicked smirk bent Leventhorpe's mouth.

"Her sister too," Heath agreed with an equally rakish grin. "Shall we?" He indicated Brette's carriage.

Something near a growl of fury escaped Bellinghamshire. "I have been awarded her guardianship, Ravensdale. It's merely a matter of receiving the documents from the court."

Heath lifted a shoulder an inch, and made to enter the carriage, Leventhorpe on his heels. "Well, until you have received them, she will remain with me."

Leventhorpe stepped into the coach and winked at Brette as he settled on the opposite seat. "Having yourself an adventure, are you?"

"Indeed. I've had quite the most remarkable morning." Had she ever. She raised the shades, and waved at Jacobson grinning at her from outside. He deserved a handsome tip. "Whatever are you doing in London, my lord?"

Leventhorpe waggled his auburn eyebrows. "Brooke wrote us and hinted you could use reinforcements."

She had?

Heath tossed a steely look over his shoulder as he entered the equipage. "Try to take Brette before you have proof of guardianship, Bellinghamshire, and I shall cut you down where you stand."

*Love is realized and practiced not by those with good intentions,
but by those whose actions and words are honorable and pure.
~Appearances and Attitude—The Genteel Lady's Guide to Practical Living*

16

Something close to a sneer skewed Alex's mouth, and he raised a brow at the duke. His most you-unworthy-dog-go-lick-your-arse brow. Bellinghamshire possessed unsavory secrets he most definitely didn't want shared in the upper salons.

Alex folded his arms, asking softly, "Been to confession recently, Your Grace?"

Bellinghamshire blanched and suddenly found the pavement fascinating, but he didn't answer. He couldn't since Alex had been his rector and knew when the duke had last spilled his contemptuous guts.

Unworthy of Alex, especially given his previous position, but too satisfying to forego. After what Bellinghamshire had meant to do to Brette, his grace would receive no mercy.

A distinguished looking man—must be Shipwreck—a ruddy-cheeked red-headed youth, another fresh-faced youth, and a nervous, twitchy fellow keenly observed the exchange.

Alex pressed his advantage. "Seen Lord Dupresse of late? Heard he's seeking another young bride. What kind of a heartless, self-serving, despicable blackguard would force a woman to marry such a whoremonger?"

"Dupresse is after a wife again? Somebody's bloody desperate." Raven's incredulous question floated from the carriage, made louder by the snow-muffled outdoors.

"True," Leventhorpe acknowledged. "However, I want to know why Hawk thinks the problem critical enough to mention during the worst weather in years and when Bellinghamshire has stupidly threatened to make off with one of our own? One might suppose Hawk knows something more of the situation." The coach bounced lightly. "I shall find out."

Leventhorpe peered past the open doorway, such a look of feigned innocence on his face, Alex suppressed a snort. "I say, Wycombe, don't suppose you know the unfortunate bride's name?"

Silence, as heavy and dense as the falling snow, met his cheeky question.

"Me?" Brette's comprehending gasp made Alex curl his fists. God would forgive him for laying Bellinghamshire out. Surely He would.

Smart chap, Leventhorpe. He'd deduced Bellinghamshire's intent too.

Alex gave a terse nod. "Oh, indeed, I do, and every fire in hell *will* freeze first."

Bellinghamshire's alarmed gaze flew to Alex's as a huge snowflake landed on the duke's nose.

Yes, white definitely tinged the lines bracketing his grace's mouth.

Bellinghamshire pounded the coach's side. "This isn't over, Ravensdale, but I'm not going to argue in public. My solicitor will be in touch."

He stomped to his carriage. Halfway there, he lost his footing and, arms flailing, skidded a few paces before landing on his arse. Cursing, he attempted to stand and fell again.

A feminine giggle rent the air.

Alex recognized the contagious laugh and grinned.

"Don't stand there, idiots. Help me up." His grace's drivers rushed to do his bidding as Alex made to join the others in the coach.

Two seats remained in the cramped conveyance. He could either shove himself onto the same bench as his two over-sized friends, or take the spot beside Brette.

Easy decision.

After quickly brushing snow from his shoulders, Alex climbed inside. As he slid onto the seat beside her, she offered him a sunny smile.

"I'm heartily glad to see you." Her gaze lit on each of the men in turn. "I confess, I was terrified."

"Me too," Flora volunteered. "I was afeared I'd swoon."

She sneezed and, seizing a well-used handkerchief, blew her nose. Brette patted the maid's hand. "It's all right now."

Shipwreck stuck his head into the door's opening. "The weather is too foul to stand here and go into detail, and I need to send my staff home. But suffice it to say, Miss Culpepper received the bulk of her grandfather's estate. He," the solicitor jerked his thumb in the direction of the carriage slowly pulling away from the curb, "doesn't own the clothes on his back. My advice? Find a safe place to hide her away until this is sorted out. Send me a note, and I'll meet you at Highfield Place House to discuss our options. Don't come here again."

With those words, he doffed his hat and made his way to his establishment, shooing his shivering staff before him.

"Hide me away?" Brette pulled a face. "Is that necessary?" Her countenance grew more troubled. "Alex, did you mean me? Has my uncle promised me to a ... a reprobate?"

A kind term for Dupresse.

"Fear not, Brette. It won't come to pass. I promise you." Alex took her hand, despite both Raven and Leventhorpe's raised brows. "Raven, I have an idea." Alex motioned to Leventhorpe. "Would you mind terribly escorting Flora to Highfield? I need to speak with Raven as Brette's guardian."

Too bad propriety forbade him asking Raven to leave too.

Leventhorpe's keen gaze assessed the snuffling, chaffed-nose maid. "Of course. I confess, I'm dying to know how Brette came to be Old Fusty Boot's heir, but I can wait to learn the whole of it."

Moments later, he and Flora, snuggly wrapped in a lap robe, climbed into the other coach and went on their way.

"First, I need to clarify something Shipwreck stated." Raven leaned forward, curiosity lighting his face. "You're the old duke's heir? How?"

"My parents married after all, and because my grandfather quarreled with his firstborn, he rewrote his will. It stipulated that the first legitimate offspring of either of his younger two sons was his heir." She lifted a shoulder an inch. "That's me."

Alex whistled. "I'll bet Bellinghamshire's beyond furious."

"Desperate too, I'd say." Though casually spoken, Brette wasn't as relaxed as she pretended, and her gently curved mouth held no joy. "There's little chance he won't be named my guardian? Even though I'll be one-and-twenty in eight months?"

Raven shook his head, and rubbed his neck. "Bellinghamshire's your uncle. I'm merely your cousin's husband. Unfortunately, the sod has more of a legal claim than I do. That's why I left in such a rush this morning. A friend in the Chancery Court alerted me, and I spent the morning trying to determine how far the duke's claim has proceeded so

I'd know what to do."

Alex crossed his arms and relaxed against the seat. "A husband would have a stronger claim."

"So what's your plan, Hawk? I suspect Bellinghamshire has gotten his way, and I'll shortly receive word Brette's been named his ward." Raven gave her a reassuring smile. "Hell *will* indeed freeze before I permit him to take you, my dear. Your sister would have my hide. If we have to, we'll leave England until you're of age."

Shivering and her teeth chattering—cold or nerves?—Brette hauled a robe onto her lap. "Thank you, Heath, but I fear you'll have no choice, and I can't allow Brooke to travel when she's expecting. Besides, your child should be born in England. I think I need to disappear for a spell. I won't tell anyone where I am until I come of age. The duke will have control of my fortune though."

"I have a better solution." Beneath the robe, Alex gathered her hand in his, and her encouraging smile made his heart trip over itself.

"Truly, Hawk? Now? You cannot wait at least until we reach Highfield?" Raven shook his head, reproach and empathy evident in his kind smile. "You need coaching on the matter, my dear fellow. A gentleman simply doesn't propose three times with an audience. It's most awkward for everyone."

Alex tucked Brette's hand close to his side. "This from a man who proposed *after* he won a woman's virtue in a wager and would've made her his mistress?"

"He has you there, Heath." Brette didn't seem the least perturbed that Alex intended to propose. "But before we go further, there's something I must ask you, Alex."

"Oh, my God." Raven's flabbergasted gaze bounced between them. "You're two of a kind. I should object, I suppose. But honestly, I can't think of one logical reason." He pointed at the blanket lying beside Brette. "Do you want me to cover my head with that robe and provide you a semblance of privacy?"

Could've obligingly ridden in the other coach.

Brette darted him a do-be-quiet glance before swallowing and meeting Alex's eyes. Her beatific mouth curving into a gentle smile, something akin to love glowing from the sea-green depths, she grasped both his hands.

Alex's lungs stalled. For certain she didn't mean to—

"Will you marry me, Alex? As soon as we can get a special

license?"

Brette wanted to marry him. This woman who'd imprinted her smile, her essence on his soul wanted to be his wife. And the brave, daring darling asked him in front of her guardian.

"My dear, I'll be delighted to answer your question when we are alone. I was going to suggest we have a private moment when we get home." He gave Raven a quelling look. "I know you aren't the least romantic, but I am."

"Yes, so I've observed." Sarcasm thicker than molasses dripped from Raven's words.

In fact, Alex had arranged to have sweets and flowers delivered, and in his chambers an elegant ivory velvet box held an exquisite emerald-cut blue-green diamond, the likes of which he'd never before seen. He'd known the moment he spied the ring, rimmed with double rows of white diamonds, it must be Brette's.

The coach had barely skidded to a stop before Alex alighted. The day had grown twilight dark. Difficult to believe the clock had yet to strike one. He handed Brette down. "Will you meet me in the drawing room in thirty minutes?"

She gave him a saucy smile. "That long? How about fifteen? I just need to change into my slippers." With a little wave, she hurried ahead of him into the house.

As Alex and Raven ascended the stoop together, Alex gave Raven a sheepish grin. "I suppose I ought to formally ask for Brette's hand in marriage."

Raven slapped his shoulder as they stomped snow from their boots. "I believe we are way beyond that. If I refuse, I'll have the cousins wishing me ill. You have my blessing. She couldn't be marrying anyone finer. As soon as the weather clears, I'd be happy to acquire the special license. I don't think we dare wait."

"Well, as to that. I may have overstepped the bounds. Once my grandmother told me of Bellinghamshire's plans, I obtained a license before I returned home. A benefit of being a former cleric."

Raven stopped in his tracks. "Your grandmother told you? That's a story I need to hear."

Alex grinned. "She's coming around nicely. Especially since I offered to let her live with Brette and me."

Raven's guffaw echoed off the entry walls and ceiling. "You are a saint, Hawk. A bloody saint."

A half an hour later, having collected the ring from his chamber and carefully displayed the flowers and sweets on the tea table, Alex checked the clock near his head for the sixth or seventh time.

One arm braced against the mantel, he stared into the fire, the flames, almost hypnotic. What delayed Brette?

She'd been the one to suggest fifteen minutes. Had she changed her mind?

Maybe this was too overwhelming, too rushed.

If she regretted her impetuous proposal and didn't come down, he'd forgive her. How could he not? His bruised heart wouldn't soon recover, though, and he closed his eyes, mouthing a silent prayer that something else delayed her. Nevertheless, her happiness mattered above everything, and no matter what the future held, whether their paths intertwined or separated, Brette would forever be branded upon his spirit and heart.

"Alex?"

Slowly, hesitant to face her, to hear what she might say, he raised his head.

A vision of loveliness stood silhouetted in the doorway, and his breathing stalled. She'd changed into a stunning periwinkle gown. A delicate blue rose garland encircled her hair, and dainty earrings hung from her shell-like ears.

"I'm sorry I'm late. I decided to change." After closing the door, she floated further into the room.

Surly a positive sign. No chaperone and a firmly closed door He held his arms wide. "Come here."

She flew into his embrace, where she was meant to be, the sweetest of homecomings. In his arms, for eternity.

He tilted her chin, and she closed her eyes. Their lips met in a kiss penetrating his inner-most being, fusing her soul with his. From the first moment he'd seen her, his spirit had recognized its mate.

Nuzzling her neck, relishing her little passionate sighs and gasps, he teased her. "So, minx, do you want my answer?"

She laughed and pointed at the crimson roses and sweetmeat assortment. "There's my answer, I think."

"No, not entirely." Alex removed the ring from his little finger and folded to one knee.

Holding one of her hands in his, he slipped the diamond onto her finger.

Holding up her hand, she admired the jewel. "It's utterly breathtaking. Thank you."

"Let me finish, darling, else I muck this up and ruin the moment." He drew in a deep breath.

Ought to have rehearsed this part more, but he'd give it a go, nevertheless.

"Brette Anastasia Wiliminia Culpepper, will you grant me a lifetime of overwhelming joy, happiness I don't deserve—yet covet with my whole heart—and agree to take this humble, flawed man who loves you more than he loves his own life as your husband?"

She cupped his cheek, giving him a tender smile. "Are you going poetic on me, Alex? The effects of having been a cleric or a would-be actor?"

"Is it working?" Weren't women supposed to get teary-eyed and say yes straightaway? Not tease and ask cheeky questions?

Brette kneeled before him and, cradling his face, pressed her soft, sweet mouth to his. "I never needed anything but to know you love me as much as I adore you. And that was why you wanted to marry me, not because you felt obligated. I've loved you since you descended from the carriage at Esherton Green, and I couldn't tear my eyes from you. I intended to tell you that last night."

"Ah, and I assumed you invited me to your bed."

"Well, I was, rather, in a roundabout way." Her throaty chuckle, more of a tantalizing purr, had him reconsidering his scruples.

Alex helped her stand then gathered her tempting form into his embrace. Contentment flooded him, warm and secure. He could remain like this for eternity. "Believe me, I've never wanted anything more, except to make you my wife, which I was determined to do before accepting so irresistible an invitation."

Cheeks rosy, Brette murmured, "My intentions went astray."

"You haven't answered my question, darling." He nipped her lower lip. Could a clergyman be persuaded to perform the ceremony this afternoon?

"How's this for an answer?" She stood on her toes, wrapped her slender arms about his neck, and kissed him with such tender reverence that tears stung behind his eyes. "Will that answer do, my dearest love?"

He swallowed and squeezed her tight. "That'll do. Indeed. That'll do."

The most powerful intention is no match for unconditional love.
~*Appearances and Attitude—The Genteel Lady's Guide to Practical Living*

January 1823 High Wycombe

Brette slipped her wrap off, and after tossing it on the armchair beside the window, slid into bed. Even with the hearty fire, a slight chill lingered in the chamber. Alex would have her warm soon enough though.

He promptly hauled her into his strong embrace, and she snuggled against his solid chest, the soft, golden hairs tickling her nose. "*Brrr.* It's snowing again. Our company may be here a while longer than expected."

Dropping a kiss on her nose, he towed the bedcovering over her shoulders. "I'd better keep you warm then, Lady Wycombe, and I enjoy having your family. They get along famously with Grandmama and are most forgiving of her tetchy moments."

"They are, aren't they? We didn't know our grandparents. I think Brooke and Blythe have adopted Grandmama as theirs. I'm sure Blaike and Blaire will too when they meet her. Besides, she's rarely peevish now. Love and acceptance have changed her, softened her ragged edges."

"They have indeed," he murmured into her hair.

They'd transformed her too. The remarkable man lying beside her had carved a niche in her heart and taken up permanent residence there.

"Be warned though, my darling wife. I've detected her eyeing Brooke's belly before turning her matriarch's eye on me. She's expecting an announcement soon."

"In due time." Blythe also increased, and Brette expected she'd soon be in the family way as well. Until then, she coveted this time with Alex. Breathing in his manly scent, she permitted a small upward tilt of her mouth. She wouldn't tire of his smell. Or him. He'd introduced her to passion exceeding her dreams and a love she'd believed beyond her.

He rested his chin atop her head, his breath warming her scalp. "Happy, love?"

"Deliriously so." They'd been married two months, and each day brought her greater joy. "Are you? I don't mean us, but in general? You readily admit you weren't cut from a cleric cloth—"

Alex chuckled, while drawing lazy circles on her bare shoulder, causing shivers of pleasure. "I'll say I wasn't. I'm sure the Lord will have much to say to me on judgement day. Mr. Dalton's a far better fit than I ever was."

"You're too hard on yourself, Alex. You did your best. That's all anyone's able to do, especially when forced into circumstances not of our choosing. But the earldom— You didn't covet a title either."

"I didn't expect to inherit, and I failed to contemplate the enormity of the position." His exploration gravitated lower, and he caressed her hip, pulling her nightgown up until he met bare skin. "In many ways, it's much like being a rector—the care and responsibility and the wellbeing of others fell to me. I can only hope I'm a better earl than my cousin was."

Tracing his bristly jaw with her forefinger, enjoying the whiskers abrading her skin, she kissed his neck. "There's no doubt of that, darling. If he hadn't tupped the footman's sister, gotten her with child, and the poor thing hadn't died during childbirth, her grief-mad brother wouldn't have set the fire. It doesn't excuse his revenge, but I'm sure he felt utterly powerless against a peer."

"I give you my word, I won't abuse my title. I'd much prefer to use the power accompanying the earldom to help the less fortunate. I guess a portion of my former life will always remain with me."

She raised her head and sought his eyes. "I know you won't, Alex. You're not like your cousin or my uncle." A muffled giggle escaped her. "I can't help but laugh when I recall Bellinghamshire's expression when he stalked into the drawing room a week after our ugly encounter. There we were. Me on your lap, and your hand..."

Alex's chest shook with mirth. "A gentleman catching his niece in a compromising position ought to have demanded I marry you instead of victoriously waving court documents and telling you to pack your belongings."

"And when you told him my leaving would ruin our wedding

trip—" Laughter bubbled up her throat, and several seconds passed before she composed herself. "I don't think I've ever observed a grown man more confounded."

"Almost as enjoyable as the Gambwells' reactions in Hyde Park the next day." He kissed her nose. "Most wicked of me, I confess. I'm not sure whether our marriage or your change in status befuddled them more."

"The world is full of kind, decent people, and I refuse to let the others steal my joy ever again." Brette touched his nipple, grinning when he shuddered. She liked this power over him.

"Well said, my love." Alex's exploration grew bolder, and familiar sensations awakened. She'd acquiesce in a bit. She wanted to savor this moment, commit it to memory.

Shifting, Brette rested in the groove between his shoulder and chest and scrutinized the canopy overhead. Dust in the pleats? Years of neglect contributed to High Wycombe's private chambers being in sore need of repair and refurbishing.

At first, Alex had argued against Brette using her inheritance to improve and restore the manor, but when she reminded him she was his helpmate, he'd conceded. He'd also readily agreed to a trust for Genevia; one her parents couldn't borrow a shilling from.

Brette gripped his hairy thigh. "Alex, I nearly forgot. I received a letter from Mr. Shipwreck today. He's found a property he thinks perfect for our charity school." She tilted her head to look at him. "I'd like us to tour it as soon as possible. He doesn't think it will remain available for long."

Alex angled his chin upward before resuming his sensual assault. "When the weather clears again, we can journey to London. Any luck with a location for the women's college?"

She suppressed a gasp when he boldly cupped a breast. He was certainly determined to seduce her tonight. His methods were proving most effective. She could barely gather her thoughts.

What had he asked? Oh, yes. The college.

"Nothing yet. I think I may wait until Blaire and Blaike return and ask what their opinions are. Based on their experiences, they may have useful tips, and between the foundling hospital and the charity school, I'm sure I'll be kept busy."

"Don't forget attending to your wifely duties." He squeezed her bottom and rocked his pelvis into her thigh, his arousal evident.

"*Tsk.* Duties are something one's obliged to do." She palmed his heavy, silken flesh, earning a gasp of pleasure. "This, dear husband, is a morsel of heaven on earth."

The Buccaneer and the Bluestocking

A lady of refinement takes utmost care to consider that every word whispered in confidence 'tis oft' heard repeated many miles away.
~*Scruples and Scandals-The Genteel Lady's Guide to Practical Living*

Port de Lyon, Lyon, France
Early Evening 17 March, 1823

A stuffed-to-its-capacity portmanteau in one hand, and a small sack of food in the other, Blaike inhaled a fortifying breath as she stepped from the rickety coach. A brow raised, half in relief and half in wariness, she surveyed *Port de Lyon's* bustling wharf.

Situated at the intersections of the *Saône* and *Rhône* rivers, the busy harbor hummed with activity. All sorts of vehicles rumbled to and fro, while merchants huffed past, their covered carts containing coveted silks and other treasures.

Vendors enthusiastically hawked their wares alongside street urchins and beggars haranguing passersby for a coin or two. Stevedores and gruff seamen of every nationality called to each other above the din as they loaded and unloaded cargo. Others drunkenly staggered along, leering at or propositioning the few women braving the docks at this hour.

Except for the Culpeppers, a male or a stern-faced chaperone accompanied any other ladies of gentle breeding, distinguishing the respectable females on the wharf from the doxies beginning their work as twilight's mantle descended.

Despite the impropriety and the thorough scolding they'd receive when they reached home, Blaike and Blaire had journeyed to Lyon and would sail to England unchaperoned. They had much explaining to do to their family upon arriving home.

No, rather Madame Beaulieu, proprietress and head mistress of *Les Dames de l'Académie de Grâce,* had much to account for.

The deceptive, conniving witch.

Institute for higher education, indeed.

What utter poppycock and claptrap.

Les Dames de l'Académie de Grâce was nothing but a glorified finishing school. Which, Blaike strongly suspected, doubled as a brothel. Far too many unexplainable comings and goings by men visiting the other house on the property at all hours.

A shudder rippled down her spine that had nothing to do with the brisk March air.

Several laughing or jabbering French sailors in crisp blue and gold uniforms hurried past as her twin Blaire, came to Blaike's side.

Blaike only understood a smattering of their words, but what she did comprehend heated her cheeks.

One debonair officer with a pencil-thin black mustache, winked, while another tossed a pastry scrap to a pair of hungry-looking mongrels.

Teeth bared, they snarled and snapped, each vying for the largest share.

Poor beasts.

She'd experienced hunger; was experiencing it at this moment, as a matter of fact. To stretch their swiftly dwindling funds, she and Blaire had shared their two meager meals a day, and neither had eaten since breaking their fast with tea and toast at dawn. Scant money remained in the reticule hanging from Blaike's wrist; a worry that cramped her stomach worse than lack of food.

Blaire's purse held little more.

The rolls, cheese, and apples Blaike had purchased from the inn this morning would have to suffice until they boarded the ship home. Pray God they sailed soon. If not . . .

A distinguished looking man—a ship's captain from his attire and confident bearing—descended a gangplank and was met by several other finely dressed gentlemen awaiting him on the waterfront. He slashed a casual glance in Blaike's direction, then brazenly pivoted to more fully observe her. A slow smile curved his mouth, crinkling the scar lancing his left cheek as he stared.

He doffed his brown leather Continental hat and inclined his head.

At once, the others turned to see what had captured his attention.

A rotund fellow wearing a gaudy canary-yellow coat boldly withdrew his quizzing glass and put it to his eye.

Ridiculous. As if he could see them any better through the lens that far away.

When the captain, or whomever he was, continued to regard Blaike and Blaire, his mien almost speculative, she angled her back toward him. In her limited experience, men misinterpreted even the most casual of glances as an invitation.

Besides, the last time her nape hair had stood at attention in this manner, she'd been brutally accosted. After tucking the food beneath her arm, she switched her heavy valise to her other hand and pressed her palm to her hollow midriff.

An assortment of noxious smells hung heavily in the air, and Blaike wrinkled her nose before releasing a slow, gusty sigh.

"Lord, it reeks most awfully." Blaire raised a slightly soiled gloved hand to her nose. "What is that stench? Rotting fish and—?"

"I'm not sure, but I agree. It's most disgusting. But at least with the breeze the air is slightly fresher than the fusty interior of the coach." Barely. Blaike arched her spine, stretching the stiff muscles from bum to neck. "I swear, someone let a billy goat live in that conveyance."

"Maybe Brette's grandfather, old Fusty Boots, used it a decade or so ago." Blaire chuckled as she, too, examined the pier. Their cousin's grandsire, the Duke of Bellinghamshire's malodorous feet had been legendary.

Three and a half days they'd rattled about in the stinking, poorly sprung equipage. Why, even now whilst standing, Blaike could yet feel the rhythmic jostling. Flattened from constant wear, the seat provided minimal padding against the jolts and bumps. She'd be surprised if a spot remained on her or Blaire's bodies that didn't sport bruises.

Although . . .

Not all of her welts could be blamed upon the poorly sprung, well-used coach.

She closed her eyes for an agonizing instant, remembering—

"*Zut.*"

The sour-tempered driver swore beneath his breath, and she glanced over her shoulder, wincing when he hauled their small trunk from the boot and dropped it on the ground with the same distaste as a sack of weevil-infested grain.

He'd been miffed since the first day and the vails he'd expected hadn't been forthcoming. As much as Blaike would've liked to have passed him a coin or two, their dire circumstances required her to economize at every opportunity.

"*Odeur putride*," he grumbled.

Indeed. Most putrid.

Wrinkling his nose, he swore again. "*Merde. Le navire esclave est au port.*"

"Did he say a slave ship is in port?" Blaire's gaze flew to the rows of towering masts lining the gloaming sky.

"I shudder to think so." Blaike opened her eyes. Queasiness tensed her stomach even as the vile odor clogged her throat. "God help them."

"But I thought slavery had been abolished in France." After tossing Blaike a distressed look, Blaire scrutinized the ships nearest them as if she sought to see the pathetic wretches confined inside the stout hulls.

"It was, but I remember reading somewhere the ban hasn't fully taken effect yet."

The twins situation paled compared to those desperate souls so brutally torn from their home and everything familiar.

At least she and Blaire more or less knew what their futures held.

Just over a month ago, when the situation at the academy had deteriorated to intolerable, Blaike had secretly written and posted a letter to her sister, Blythe, Marchioness of Leventhorpe. She'd asked her to arrange passage home as hastily as possible and said she would explain the reasons later. Suspecting Madame Beaulieu steamed the wax seals loose and read their correspondences, Blaike had asked Blythe to respond in code.

In her reply, Blythe was to mention a date for a house party and that would be the day they were to sail. Too dangerous to name the ship, but she'd say the arrangements had all been made, or something of that nature.

Though Blaike and Blaire had already planned on leaving later in the spring when the weather improved, a recent incident had compelled their immediate departure.

'Flight' more aptly described their leave-taking.

Blaike didn't know how they'd have managed if it weren't for Blythe's generosity—or rather her husband's—and her assurance their passage had been arranged. She and Blaire were to inquire at *Port de Lyon's* Harbor Master's Office regarding the matter.

"Blaike?" Worry roughened Blaire's soft voice around the edges.

"Yes, dearest?"

"What if the ship we're to sail upon isn't in port yet? We are nearly a fortnight earlier than the date Blythe gave us."

It didn't bear contemplating, for the coach and lodging from Geneva had exhausted the monies they'd managed to secret away at the academy these past wretched months.

She could always try to sell their clothing and few pieces of jewelry, though the gems had been gifts from their guardian, the Earl of Ravensdale. True, their garments were of the finest quality and the latest fashion, but they hadn't many with them. They'd escaped the school in such a rush, that the bulk of their possessions were left behind along with instructions where to ship them.

Honestly, cows were more likely to crow than either she or Blaire were ever to see their belongings again. Madame Beaulieu would claim the lot as her due for some fabricated reason or other. The woman hadn't a virtuous or honest bone in her skeletally thin body.

Offering Blaire a reassuring smile, more forced confidence than actual bravado, Blaike searched for the Port Captain's Office. "All will be well, I'm sure of it. I feel it in my bones. We've come this far, and surely we deserve a little grace after enduring more mishaps than a Greek tragedy—"

"A broken wheel, a fallen tree, a lame horse, and a flooded creek." Blaire held up three fingers, then a fourth, followed shortly by a fifth. "Required to sleep leaning against one another in a common room that second night. Not to mention I'm hungry enough to lick crumbs from a biscuit tin, and our driver has the temperament of a wounded—"

"Bear." They were forever finishing one another's sentences.

"He is most surly, even though we've done our utmost not to inconvenience him." To ease the pinching between her shoulder blades, Blaike rolled her shoulders.

"True." Blaire shook her blond head, the once crisp silk flowers adorning her hat flopping with the motion. She slipped her hand into the crook of Blaike's elbow. "We have each other though," she said, giving her twin a little hug. "I know we'll manage somehow."

"This is all my fault." Blaike pressed her lips together and dragged in another deep breath. "I'm truly sorry, Blaire."

Tears tingled, but she blinked them away. The time for remorse had passed. Wallowing in regret and self-pity wouldn't help now.

Balancing her hat boxes while making a comforting noise in her throat, Blaire slipped her arm around Blaike's waist. "Stuff and nonsense, dear one." She leaned into her sister's side. "And know this,

Blaike. Your secret will always be safe with me. I shall never, *ever* breathe a word. If anyone is to know the whole of it, you will do the telling, not I."

Those dratted, stubborn tears welled again, and Blaike swallowed. Mortification burned to her marrow. "I know. And I trust you. But we aren't the only ones who know what transpired. Should it become public knowledge, our entire family will be—."

"Shamed." Sternness tightened Blaire's pretty features briefly. "Perhaps, but it was not of your doing," she insisted. "I believe, even when dark secrets are exposed, honorable and decent people can rise above the gossip and stigma."

Easier said when you weren't the one nearly despoiled and caught dishabille by Madame Beaulieu. Never mind that Blaike had been the victim of a calculated scheme, and that was why she'd determined never to be manipulated into doing anything against her will again.

Despite her protests of innocence, she'd been judged, tried, and found guilty by the headmistress in mere moments. Compromised beyond redemption, her reputation and good standing utterly tattered, remaining at *Les Dames de l'Académie de Grâce* had been inconceivable.

Much too convenient the headmistress happening upon Blaike in the gardens just then.

Why, the despicable woman had implied Blaike had no recourse other than to become a courtesan. Another reason why Blaike suspected Madame Beaulieu was an entirely other kind of *madam*.

"God forgive me, but I truly loathe Jonathon and Jacqueline Severs," Blaike whispered. "And Madame Beaulieu isn't far behind. They should all face imprisonment."

"Vile, all three to their foul cores." Blaire tapped Blaike's forearm. "But, think on it. We aren't likely to ever lay eyes on the Severs again. They're American, from a banking family, I believe Jacqueline said. And if we do, I'll be the first to cork Jonathon Severs for you. In fact, I think I'll take pugilist lessons. Fencing too." She skewed her mouth sideways. "I suppose I'll have to get Heath's permission, since he's our guardian. That's a bit of a bother."

She struck a pose, her fist poised before her face, and giggled. "Do you think he'll—?"

"Agree? Not likely."

"*Mademoiselles*." Again, the contentious driver harrumphed behind them.

Blaike and Blaire swung to face the peevish man.

"*Capitaine de Port de Sa Majesté.*" He pointed to an official looking building a block down and across the way before towing their trunk to plop it beside them.

He couldn't have stopped the conveyance in front of the building?

Plain spiteful, that.

Surely he didn't expect them to haul the chest themselves? The trunk was far too heavy and cumbersome. Besides, they each already held a portmanteau, and Blaire also carried two hat boxes. Furthermore, with the riff raff scuttling about the docks, they daren't leave the trunk unattended.

"Port Captain? Har-bor Mas-ter?"

Blaike pointed at the building, and Blaire frowned at the trunk. Neither had learned enough French to communicate well during their ill-fated venture.

"*Oui.*" Mouth turned down, their driver summoned a sullen nod.

Blaike mentally calculated her funds again.

Could she spare a coin or two?

Her tense stomach cinched further. She had no choice.

After drawing her reticule off her wrist, and setting their meager food supply upon the chest, she loosened the strap.

"*Pardonnez-moi, mais puis-je vous offrir mon aide?*"

2

Blaike started and glanced up to see the man approaching who'd
been watching her and Blaire earlier. Perhaps late in his fourth
decade or early in his fifth, he bestowed a cavalier's smile upon them as
he sketched a bow.

Three burly sailors accompanied him, each more coarse and
intimidating in appearance than the former.

Making a pretense of returning her reticule to her wrist, she eyed
the trio from beneath her lashes. What she observed didn't reassure her.

The first, an enormous African his bulging muscles straining
against the fabric of his partially unbuttoned shirt, grinned widely,
revealing missing front teeth. The second, perhaps a Turk or Arab given
his soiled cranberry-colored turban, fingered the hilt of a wicked
looking saber belted at his waist. And the third seaman sported a long,
braided beard and numerous tattoos on every exposed inch of flesh,
including his face.

She didn't want to speculate what the rest of the crew was like if
these three were the captain's officers. Never having seen pirates
before, she couldn't be sure, of course, but these rapscallions fit every
depiction she'd ever read.

Right down to the gold hoop in the Turk's ear.

Blaire must have reached the same conclusion, for she edged
minutely closer to Blaike.

A prickly shudder skittered across Blaike's shoulders.

A renewed reminder why young women didn't travel unescorted.

Her nostrils quivered.

A most unsavory—*unbathed*—lot.

Except for their leader.

Flawlessly groomed—*togs of the first stare of fashion* as she'd heard dandies described in London—he oozed charm as well as a faint, musky cologne.

Attractive in an experienced, man-of-the-world manner, he wasn't overly tall. In fact, she and Blaire each stood at least an inch taller. Nonetheless, he still exuded power and self-confidence. The scar lashing his face suited him in a bizarre sort of way.

How had he come by it?

He rather looked like a Barbary Pirate or corsair more than a respectable ship's captain.

A similar thought had sprung to mind the first time she'd seen Captain Oliver Whitehouse.

Truth to tell, she'd had many fanciful thoughts about Captain Whitehouse these past months.

The leader spoke again. *"Est-ce que je peux vous aider avec vos bagages?"*

Not exactly certain what he'd asked, Blaike believed he might've offered to assist with their luggage. "Please pardon me, but I do not speak French fluently."

A delighted smile brightened his face, and he clasped one hand across his waist as he bent into an elegant bow.

"Splendid. You're British, as am I. I was but offering my assistance with your baggage." He gestured to the chest. "Please permit my men carry it to wherever you might need." He glanced, almost too casually given his hand resting on the carved handle of a knife tucked into his waistband. "Have you any other luggage? Perhaps a tardy traveling companion's as well?"

Fishing for information, that.

He'd find his probing wouldn't get satisfied.

Blaike wasn't born yesterday. Pure foolishness to reveal that no fire-breathing dragon such as Mrs. Hobbs, their chaperone on the passage from London, would join them shortly. And the lady's maids who'd accompanied them from London had been sent home within a week of arrival.

Madam Beaulieu didn't condone her pupils being waited upon, most especially when other attendees didn't have abigails.

After withdrawing a few francs from his coat pocket, the captain passed them to the waiting driver.

"*Merci beaucoup.*" The surly bear's demeanor transformed into grateful servitude. He tapped two fingers to his forehead in a smart salute before shutting the coach door and climbing atop the seat. A moment later, the vehicle trundled away.

Exchanging a resigned glance with her twin, Blaike stifled a sigh and forced her lips to bend upward into a grateful smile.

"Thank you for your kindness. We're going just there."

She indicated the Harbor Master's Office.

"Quaco. Demir." The stranger picked up the food sack, then sliced his other hand at two of his gargantuan men, indicating they should lift the trunk.

The African and Easterner did so with pathetic ease.

"Eades, carry the ladies valises."

Definitely a man accustomed to giving orders and having them promptly obeyed.

"Aye, Captain," Eades said in a thick accent Blaike didn't recognize. He extended his dirty, chipped-nail hand for Blaike's portmanteau, his lecherous gaze dropping to her bosoms.

Blaike reluctantly passed him her bag, as did Blaire with even less enthusiasm.

She hugged her hatboxes close to her chest, however. "I'll carry these."

Clutching their food bag in a fist, the stranger extended his elbows. He clearly expected Blaike and Blaire to take either arm.

"Sir, while we do appreciate you and your crew's gallantry, it would, nonetheless, be most unseemly to take your arm when we've not been properly introduced." Blaike slid Blaire a sideways glance.

Something akin to distress flashed in her twin's sapphire eyes.

So, she feels it, too.

Unease flooded Blaike at being obligated to him.

Annoyance cast a fleeting shadow over his face, hardening his craggy features for an instant. Just as swiftly, his peevishness disappeared, and he produced another amiable smile, the warmth not quite reflecting in his glacial pale blue gaze.

Then, at their continued hesitation, he nodded, approval pleating the corners of his eyes. "Most wise to be cautious, especially when you're traveling alone. I am Landon Abraham, captain of the *Black Dove,* and citizen of London when I'm not at sea."

Was it her imagination, or did he have the very slightest of accents?

Was he truly British, then?

For certain, Blaike didn't want him to know no chaperone would accompany them, but neither could she lie outright. At the moment, she wasn't sure her inability to tell a taradiddle without giving herself away was a strength or a curse.

What to do?

Perhaps a fellow female passenger—a married woman—might be persuaded to assume the role if promised payment once they reached London. Yes, indeed that might suffice quite well. It wouldn't exactly be a lie to say they'd meet their companion on the ship. Surely others had booked passage as well. If naught else, they'd be traveling companions for the voyage's duration.

"Our companion and her husband are to meet us aboard the vessel." That clever husband bit just popped into her mind.

Blaike slid Blaire a telling look.

Comprehension dawned, and her twin's eyes rounded.

"Indeed, they will. Our guardian always insists on the most respectable of chaperones." She nodded a trifle too enthusiastically while shifting her hatboxes.

An immense emerald-cut ruby ring glinting on his forefinger, Captain Abraham scratched his jaw. "Excellent. All manner of motley scoundrels roam *Port de Lyon's* wharf. You can never be too cautious, Miss . . .?"

Again, a hint as broad as an old dairy cow's behind.

If Blaike refused an introduction, she'd seem surly and ungrateful. Perhaps, however, revealing her peerage connections would detour any unwanted attention or misplaced notions he might have.

"I am Blaike Culpepper, and this is my sister, Blaire. Our cousin, Brooke, is married to Heath, Earl of Ravensdale. He is also our guardian. Our sister Blythe is wed to Tristan, Marquis of Leventhorpe, and we've another cousin, Brette, who is Alexander, Earl of Wycombe's wife."

Dash it all. That sounded more like an uppity boast than a deterrent.

An unabashed grin tipped the captain's lips. "You've quite a number of unusual names, and all beginning with Bs. Does it ever get confusing?"

"Yes. Often." A common occurrence, and something the Culpeppers had to explain time and again. "Unfortunately, our mothers continued a family tradition wherein the female offspring all receive names beginning with Bs."

Blaire piped up. "But Mama and Aunt Bess took it a step further and exercised what little power women of their generation had by selecting gender-neutral names. Surnames actually. If we'd been males, our given names would've been the same. It's been a bit easier now since there are only two remaining Miss Culpeppers, Blaike and me."

None of this was any of his business.

"Perhaps you're acquainted with one or more of the lords?" A less than subtle reminder about who he was dealing with.

Something more sinister than amusement or inquisitiveness lurked in his gaze as he answered Blaike's question. "Alas, I have never had the privilege of meeting their lordships. Though I do occasionally call upon my . . . um, grandmother . . ." His intense gaze shifted to the right the merest bit, and he made a nonchalant gesture. "The Dowager Duchess of . . . ah, Brantham when I'm in England."

The Duchess of where?

Sounded like a breed of cattle or type of chicken. Plus, he seemed rather hard put to recall his own grandmother's name.

"I would consider it the highest honor to assist two damsels far from our homeland." Captain Abraham delivered another engaging smile while surveying the dock once more.

Whatever was he looking for?

Apparently satisfied, he drew his attention back to Blaike and Blaire. "Please, forgive my boldness, but I've never seen lovelier twins. You resemble angels or goddesses with your splendid hair."

Much, *much* too forward.

Besides, given the five Culpeppers all possessed the same fairy-like shade of hair, they'd heard that pretty praise far too often for it to turn their heads.

His compliment received thin smiles. Nothing more.

Time to thank Captain Abraham and send the tenacious fellow on his way. Something about him set Blaike's teeth on edge. Her nerves, as well. She, too, glanced around, searching for what, she didn't quite know.

Something out of the ordinary.

Or someone to rush to their aid.

No knight was going to come galloping along on his steed and rescue them. No chaperone with a heavy purse, a basket of flakey

French pastries, and tickets for their passage would bustle across the wharf, hailing them. No dashing buccaneer—like the fascinating Captain Whitehouse—would sprint across the dockyard, order the captain to leave off, then escort the twins safely to their ship.

After delivering the luggage to the harbor master's doorway, Captain Abraham's men lounged against the porch posts or railing, awaiting their leader's instructions. They also repeatedly scanned the surrounding area, their postures alert, almost menacing.

It struck Blaike then.

Miscreants all, the seedy lot.

Captain Abraham held the office door open, and jutting his square chin toward the weathered gray benches arranged before the dirty, low windows, wordlessly directed his men to wait there.

To a man they nodded, yet sly grins quirked their mouths as they brazenly trailed their lewd gazes over the twins.

Blaike's nape hairs sprang upward in renewed alarm.

Reluctance hardly described the sensation bombarding her. She didn't want this man interfering in their business. Looping her arm through Blaire's, she summoned her most beguiling smile.

"You needn't waste any more of your valuable time on us, Captain Abraham. I'm sure you've much to attend to."

She extended her hand for the sack containing their food, and he somewhat reluctantly relinquished it. They might have dire need of the pouch's contents.

"We are most grateful for your assistance."

"Yes, thank you." Blaire scarcely bestowed a glance in his direction.

With a dismissive nod, Blaike practically lugged Blaire into the dim office, refusing to look over her shoulder to see if Captain Abraham still stood in the entrance. From the flesh rippling up and down her spine—and across her bum, too—she'd bet on it.

"I feel like spiders are skittering over my behind," Blaire whispered. "He gives me the—"

"Shivers. Me too," Blaike acknowledged as her eyes adjusted to the darker interior. Why hadn't a lamp or a taper been lit, for pity's sake? "Let's hope the harbor master speaks English."

A wiry little fellow with the most elaborately curled and waxed mustache she'd ever seen, opened his eyes and yawned as he unhurriedly angled his booted feet to the floor.

Well, that explained the shadowy office. He'd been napping. Quite deeply too from the befuddled gaze he turned upon them.

After cutting the doorway a swift glance, and tipping his head the slightest bit—at the captain?—he sauntered to the counter.

Heavens.

Up close, the hair topping his upper lip was even more . . . astonishing. Blaike could scarcely wrench her focus from his ghastly whiskers as she placed the food atop the scarred counter. A full six inches or more extended to either side of his thin-lipped mouth, transfixing her in a grotesque way. Like an oddity at Bullock's Museum of Natural Curiosities that repulsed and mesmerized simultaneously.

However did he manage to eat or drink with that . . . *appendage*?

A sudden vision of a dainty china teacup hanging from each ornate curl, followed at once by another image of the thickly waxed strands swaying about like tentacles sprang to mind, and only by sheer force of will did she keep from laughing.

She drew her focus away for a moment to collect herself lest her trembling lips expose her struggle. Lips sucked in and eyelids cast downward, Blaire fussed with her hatbox straps, evidently as overcome with humor as Blaike.

The harbor master rested his forearms atop the scuffed wooden surface, his lips bent into a tolerant smile. Or perhaps insolent better described his curving mouth.

"*Comment puis-je vous aider mesdames?*"

"Yes, please. *Oui, s'il vous plaît.*" Blaire set her hatboxes on the countertop.

That was about the extent of Blaike's French as well.

"Do you speak English? Anglais?" she asked.

"*J'ai bien peur que non.*" Giving a rueful smile, he shook his head. His stiff mustache didn't move a jot.

"Of course he doesn't," Blaike muttered, exhaustion, hunger, and worry rendering her short on patience and politesse. Shouldn't a port captain be multi-lingual?

She met Blaire's fretful gaze.

No help for it.

They would have to impose upon Captain Abraham after all. Blaike half turned toward the door.

"Captain, I fear we must inconvenience you once again."

A prudent woman heeds this truth: a
gssamer fine thread separates listening to gossip and
listening to a secret. Make sure you know the difference.
~Scruples and Scandals-The Genteel Lady's Guide to Practical Living

3

An I-told-you-so, just this side of gloating smile curved Captain Abraham's mouth; he'd already strode halfway across the scratched floor in need of a good sweep.

"What is it you need to inquire of Monsieur Meunier, Miss Culpepper?"

"Please ask him what vessel the Culpeppers' passage to London has been arranged on." Blaike's stomach took the opportunity to announce its dissatisfaction by rumbling loudly.

Blaire sent her a compassionate glance.

However, the captain didn't flinch. Perhaps he hadn't heard or he was playing the gentleman, for which she was grateful. He rattled off her question, and a swift discourse took place between him and the agent.

Monsieur Meunier rifled through a couple of piles of papers on his desk, then the stacks behind the high counter. Every now and again, he posed another question to Captain Abraham before murmuring to himself, shaking his head, and inspecting more files.

His attention frequently slid to Blaike and her sister.

At last, he placed his palms atop the counter, and his expression apologetic, shrugged his thin shoulders. "*Je ne trouve rien sur ton transport.*"

The captain removed his hat and scraped his fingers through his curly dark brown hair, the ruby in his ring, glowing blood red in the dim office. "Are you positive passage was reserved for you, ladies? Meunier cannot find any correspondence or payment confirmation."

Speechless for an instant, Blaike stood on her toes and scrutinized the disorderly mounds on the other side of the counter. "He must be mistaken. Our sister wrote and assured us everything had been arranged."

Sympathy softening the angles of his face, Captain Abraham shook his head. "He's not. If Meunier says there's no passage booked for you, then there's not."

"Blaike, what are we to do? How are we to get home?"

Blaire didn't normally panic, but she knew full well what their circumstances were. It would take weeks for the mail ship to deliver another letter and then bring them a response.

What were they to do in the meanwhile? Where would they live? How would they eat?

Captain Abraham smiled kindly, almost in a fatherly way. Yet, within the depths of his artic eyes, Blaike glimpsed a trace of cunning. Not a man to trust despite his helpful overtures.

"No need to fret, Miss Culpepper. Providence has smiled upon you." He winked and returned his hat to his head. "As it happens, I have room for two passengers on my vessel. You'll have to share a stateroom, of course."

Either they stay stranded in *Port de Lyon* for weeks without sufficient funds or board the *Black Dove* and risk whatever might befall them under the captain's watch.

The choice was akin to asking Blaike to choose between death by fire or by water. Clearly Blaire didn't favor the captain's offer either. True aversion glinted in her troubled gaze.

As frightening as trying to find accommodations and the means to support themselves was, the other consideration cramped Blaike's lungs and dampened her palms in dread. There was something to be said about women's intuition, and hers fairly screamed, *Refuse his offer*.

He pivoted to glance out the dusty window, his shrewd-eyed gaze darting here and there.

Certainly a suspicious sort, wasn't he?

Honest men weren't this paranoid or edgy. More confirmation they should depart his company at once despite their grim situation.

Blaire gave the briefest negative shake of her head before he turned around again.

An elbow resting upon the countertop, the captain raised a calloused finger toward Blaike and her sister as he said something to Monsieur Meunier in what sounded like Spanish. For certain it wasn't

French.

The harbor master fingered his gaudy mustache, his gaze swinging between Blaike and Blaire before he at last gave a slow nod. "*Oui.*"

Didn't they know it was rude to discuss people in another language? And why Spanish and not French? All the more reason to bid the captain *adieu.*

"That's most generous of you, Captain. However, the plain truth is, we haven't funds to purchase tickets. They were to have been prepaid for us."

Monsieur Meunier wouldn't meet her eyes, and she narrowed hers.

Was the scoundrel lying? But why?

And about what, exactly?

It did no good to insist on examining his documents either, since she read French even less skillfully than she spoke the language. That shortcoming had irritated Madame Beaulieu no end.

How she'd railed at the twins, calling them *bête comme les pieds.*

Stupid as one's feet.

Why, because they didn't speak another language and hadn't become fluent in French while in Geneva? There'd been no need to read and speak French at Esherton Green, the dairy farm that had been their home until a few months ago before their cousin, Brooke married Lord Ravensdale.

Captain Abraham lifted a thick shoulder, then bold as brass, chucked Blaike's chin.

She inhaled abruptly and retreated a step.

Monsieur Meunier gave a high-pitched feminine giggle, and she lashed him a chiding glance.

"You are related to three lords, ladies. Naturally, I shall suspend payment until we arrive in London." Captain Abraham extended an arm toward the doorway. "Come, you're tired and given your stomach's growling, hungry, too. Permit me to escort you to my ship. I can even arrange hot baths for you."

The notion of being naked within a mile of him sucked every drop of moisture from Blaike's mouth.

Blaire's also, it seemed, for she swallowed audibly, and pale as alabaster, retrieved her boxes.

Too blasted bad they'd never learned to shoot a gun, for the small unloaded pistol purchased as a gift for Blythe and tucked into one of the hatboxes might've been of some actual use about now. For certain

Blaike would demand lessons once back in England.

Blaire's teasing about fencing and boxing lessons rather appealed too. Women should be permitted ways to defend themselves every bit as much as men.

The thumping of heavy feet announced new arrivals. Blaike grasped the sack of food and cast a disinterested glance toward the entrance. What she saw plummeted her heart to the scruffy floor boards.

Captain Abraham's men had entered, and the expressions on their faces confirmed her burgeoning fears.

His good-natured mien evaporated, sharpening the lean planes of his face as he edged closer, and an ominous shroud of trepidation descended upon her.

"Captain, don't force me to become rude. We've declined your offer." She grasped Blaire's elbow. "Now step aside. We're not boarding your ship."

All pretense of civility gone, he seized Blaike's upper arm in a crushing grip.

"Alas, I must insist otherwise."

Incensed over the news Oliver had just received, he and his wiry second-in-command, Jack Hawkins, strode across the wharf, anger resounding in every click of Oliver's boot heels upon the dock's coarse wood. He needed a dram or two, mayhap an entire bottle of brandy to take the edge off his fury.

This afternoon, two brokers in Lyon had reneged on shipping their cargo with him.

Spineless poltroons.

Oliver hadn't been pleased when the twitchy silk merchant dressed like a damned canary stammered his feeble excuse, all the while mopping his chubby face with his handkerchief and darting fearful glances right and left. But when the winemaker babbled the same contrived reason for breaking their contract after years of satisfactory business association—his blood had boiled.

Someone was set on systematically sabotaging and defaming him. Someone who also kept telling merchants Oliver's name was Oliviero de Casabianca.

True, de Casabianca meant Whitehouse, and *Nonno* had changed their surname to the English equivalent when he and *Mamma* had immigrated to England, over forty years ago now. Oliver assumed his grandfather had done so because he'd wanted to blend into the new country he called home. Nevertheless, Oliver's given name had never been Oliviero, so someone was deliberately spreading that lie.

Someone who'd taken the time to learn of his Italian heritage.

Every sign pointed straight to Landon Abraham, the cockscum.

If Oliver owned a pirate's treasure, he'd bet every last gold coin and glittering gemstone that the *Black Dove*'s captain had been besmirching his reputation and integrity once again. Third port just this past year, and the feeble tale was always the same. This targeting wasn't new. Far from it. Abraham had beleaguered him for years; their mutual hatred had led to an ongoing feud.

Too bad he hadn't succeeded in ending the sod's life those many years ago. God knows, he'd tried. But a small-for-his-age skinny lad had been no match for the strapping sailor who'd set fire to *Nonno's* shipping office, also burning their living quarters above. At the time, Oliver hadn't known Abraham's name, and so the cur evaded punishment for murdering *Nonno*.

At thirteen Oliver had found himself a homeless orphan.

Well, not exactly.

A muscle jumped in his jaw, he clamped his teeth so hard.

He *had* a father. George Theodore Talbot, sixth Viscount Willoughby. Willoughby owned several houses, carriages, dozens of horses, and had three legitimate offspring.

Not willing to venture down that unpleasant, too-often-trod path again, Oliver turned his thoughts to the tale he'd heard more than once since arriving in port last week.

Away on business, Monsieur Seaulieu, a wealthy textile manufacturer, had found his home torched when he returned. It seemed his daughters had rebuffed a ship captain's advances at the theater. The culprit's description matched Abraham, right down to the ruby ring on his forefinger and the scar on his face.

God how Oliver despised the cur, yet he maintained his outward composure. Inside, bitterness and contempt roiled on. He didn't need to hear another lecture on forgiveness from Hawkins at the moment, for he didn't trust himself not to tell his mate what dark abyss he could cram his well-meaning sermon into.

Hawkins didn't deserve that disrespect.

Taking a slow, deliberate breath, Oliver ordered the chaos hammering his ribs to cease.

It ignored him, as it had for years.

How he envied Hawkins's serene disposition. Oliver would never understand why the gentle soul hadn't gone into the ministry rather than taking to the sea.

He'd asked, umpteen times actually, and Hawkins always smiled and said, "God's plans are better than man's."

Whatever the blazes that meant.

Indignation roughened Hawkins's usually gentle voice as he trotted beside Oliver. "The vendors' insinuations are ludicrous, my boy."

He snorted, then spat into the dirt.

Was he actually peeved?

"Accusing you of sympathizing with Napoleon during the war. Because you're half Italian. Pure . . . pure twaddle, I say." Hawkins sounded like a prim and proper dowager or a poised spinster.

"Twaddle? Not codswallop? Balderdash? Fustian rubbish?" Despite the severity of the moment, Oliver suppressed a grin.

No matter how angry or outraged he became, his first mate did not curse. Unlike M'Lady Lottie, the vulgar-mouthed parrot Oliver had inherited last month. What that obnoxious winged termagant squawked made even his ears burn on occasion.

Hawkins's most outrageous expletive—one Oliver had only heard uttered twice in the many years they'd been acquainted—was *bleeding son of a barnacle's bum.*

Other than giving him a gimlet eye, his first mate didn't respond to the jesting. "Not only have the wars been over for years now, you were scarcely out of short pants in 1815." The older man chuckled as he hurried to keep up with Oliver's pace. "I remember well the angry, scrawny whelp who signed on as a cabin boy those many years ago."

Oliver cracked a grin then.

"And I remember well the Bible-quoting sea tar who kept lecturing me on forgiveness and controlling my temper. Oh, and honoring my father, though why you think I should is beyond me." His grin faded into a scowl. "But it still means the cargo hold won't be full, and we both know I need every contract filled to pay the crew and to make payment on the *Sea Gypsy*."

He'd already delayed payment twice. If forced to do so again, he might find himself without a ship to captain.

Then what in hellfire would he do?

"Aye, I know. But the good Lord has a reason for everything." Hawkins fell silent, a sure indication that he was petitioning the almighty on Oliver's behalf.

Right now, he'd take help from any source that offered it. Even the Almighty's, though Oliver wasn't a believer in that sort of thing. He'd seen too much and experienced too much to believe in a loving God.

The devil?

Hell, yes.

In the form of Landon Abraham.

While Oliver had captained the *Sea Gypsy* for four years, he'd contracted to purchase her last year when her owner died and his nephew, Neville Longhurst, had inherited. Truth to tell, for once, fortune had been with Oliver.

"Oliver, do you think Abraham's behind Seaulieu's house and warehouse burning?"

"Aye. I'd wager the *Sea Gypsy* on it. And I pray someone saw him this time, and he finally gets his due. Two servants died in the blaze."

Shops. Houses. Granaries. Ships.

Too many properties mysteriously went up in flames, always when Abraham was known to have been in the vicinity. Yet the *bastare* escaped justice again and again.

Probably after offering someone a sizable bribe to provide him with an alibi. How a person could be utterly corrupt to their marrow, Oliver didn't know. If Abraham ever had any redeeming qualities, he'd long since abandoned them.

Oliver wouldn't be the least surprised to learn the murmurings that Abraham had begun dabbling in smuggling and piracy were true. Smuggling, Oliver well-understood, and even he'd been tempted to accept offers to transport contraband. In the end he'd refused, not willing to risk confiscation of his ship, should he be apprehended.

A hand pressed to his temple, Oliver considered his current options. If he sailed to Bari instead of London, might he obtain additional cargo?

Perhaps, but he had no guarantee he'd be successful, and his clients waiting in England wouldn't be pleased at the delay. He couldn't afford to lose their patronage, too.

He'd rather swab the decks with his bare arse than ask his sire to speak on his behalf to his cronies. Oliver was dogged in his determination to make something of himself without accepting a pence or any form of help from Willoughby, even if the man had offered numerous times.

Offered too late to save *Mamma* or *Nonno*.

Deep in thought, Oliver marched along, glancing up after a few moments to note his whereabouts.

"Ballocks."

He'd been so absorbed in his ruminations, he'd strode past the tavern. As he turned on his heel, something compelled him to slice a fleeting glance toward Meunier's office.

Meunier, the greasy weasel. Another miscreant deserving of retribution.

Wordlessly, Hawkins pivoted too, his lips still moving in silent entreaty to his Lord.

The port master likely knew something of this latest treachery. Swimming from Barbados to London with one's feet tied proved easier than getting that corrupt sod to confess to any underhanded dealings, however. Everyone knew he was easily bribed and often looked the other way at nefarious dealings occurring at *Port de Lyon*.

A wonder he still held his position.

Catching a glimpse of moonlit-spun hair, Oliver stumbled to an abrupt halt.

A woman of honorable character knows full well there are people who gather secrets, swearing to confidentiality, while all the while, they contemplate who they'll tell first. Such are to be avoided lest they contaminate you with their duplicity.
~Scruples and Scandals-The Genteel Lady's Guide to Practical Living

I t couldn't be.

It bloody-well shouldn't be.

The Culpeppers in Lyon?

Oliver squinted, peering into the dingy window's small panes. Another equally blonde head bobbed into view for an instant.

He planted his hands on his hips, his mouth flattened into a grim line.

"Blast, damn, and devil a bit. What the hell are *they* doing here?"

"Who?" Hawkins gazed about confused, then cocked a grisly brow. Pulling his cap from his head, he scratched his bald pate. "You mean Abraham's vermin yonder? It's not the first time we've encountered that plague in port. Best to avoid them, I say. The Good Book tells us not to keep company with fools."

"No." Oliver made a disgusted sound in his throat and shook his head. "That's disturbing enough, but I fear—and I hope to your God I'm wrong—I've just spied Blaike and Blaire Culpepper in Meunier's office."

Hawkins replaced his cap while slowly rotating to face the building square on. "Burn me. That doesn't bode well. For the misses Culpepper, I mean. Think Abraham's in there with 'em?"

"I would stake my life on it. Find at least a dozen of our crew as rapidly as possible and meet me there." Hand resting on his sword hilt, Oliver canted his head in the building's direction. "Webb, Melville, and Grover just went into the *Le Savire et le Cygnet.*"

Hawkins gave a short, jerky nod. "Likely more are inside the ale house, too."

Oliver had meant to join his men in the tavern and drown his ire as he attempted to assess this latest obstacle before they weighed anchor tomorrow. "Send crewmen to ready the *Sea Gypsy* for defense and others to round the men up. We cannot weigh anchor until the tide turns, so we'd best be ready to protect her once the Culpeppers are on board. And Hawkins, say a prayer while you're at it. I have a feeling we're going to need reinforcements."

"Aye, Cap'n. Straightaway." Hitching his trousers at the waist with one hand, and grasping the crude pewter cross dangling from his neck with the other, the elf of a man set off at a brisk pace.

Oliver pivoted toward the harbor master's and, brushing his fingertips across his short beard, contemplated the situation.

Plain idiotic to approach Abraham and his thugs alone, but Blaike didn't know the danger she and her twin were in.

Abraham's alleged association with slave traders in the East put them in great peril. He'd sell the twins on the auction block, and given their unusual height, magnificent blond hair, and exquisite sapphire eyes, they'd bring a king's ransom. Abraham probably had entertained the same idea about Seaulieu's pretty honey-haired daughters.

Devil take it.

Why were the Culpeppers in Lyon?

Weren't they supposed to be at that academy for another year and a half? The last time he'd been in London, neither Ravensdale nor Leventhorpe had mentioned them returning early.

From the corner of his eye he saw a few of his men approaching, their expressions grave.

Hawkins must've apprised them of the urgency.

As long as more of Abraham's mangy crew didn't also show up, things might be settled without a major brawl or the constable intervening. Delaying the *Sea Gypsy's* departure because her crew cooled their tempers in jail meant another direct hit to Oliver's none-too-heavy purse.

If he lost the *Sea Gypsy* . . .

Giving himself a mental shake, he directed his musing to the matter at hand.

"Too much to hope the authorities might arrive and arrest Abraham for setting the fire," Oliver muttered to himself. "Regrettably, I seldom have that kind of good fortune."

"I said unhand me, you . . . you Johnny bum."

Blaike.

Despite the very real danger, his lip twitched at her depiction of a horse's arse.

Most people couldn't tell her and her twin apart, but Oliver had been able to since they first met. Her sister had a small mole by her right eyebrow that Blaike didn't. Blaike's voice was slightly huskier than her twin's, and her eyes fairly sparkled with azure mischief when she was amused.

Which was frequently.

His spirit also recognized another discontented, driven soul, though she hid it well beneath lowered lashes and a skillfully masked expression. A people-pleaser from what he'd observed, she did her utmost to keep from distressing others.

At what cost, though?

"Ouch, you brute." A pained cry filtered through the office's open doorway.

Oliver sprinted across the wharf, half-listening for his men, and half-straining to hear Blaike or her sister. They had some explaining to do, by Jove. However, his first concern was seeing the twins safely aboard the *Sea Gypsy.* No easy task if Abraham and the barbarians he surrounded himself with were determined otherwise.

Slowing his pace, he crept onto the low porch. A board creaked, and he froze mid-step. A swift glance over his shoulder reassured him. Several of his men hurried in his direction.

The crew was the family he'd longed for since his grandfather had been murdered. Loyal and dedicated, each hand on the *Sea Gypsy* would sacrifice their life for another's.

All except for the new cook they'd taken on in Jamaica after McMaster indulged in too much mumbo and stumbled off a pier. He'd hit his head and drowned. Fairnly, his replacement, was a queer one, and he hated M'Lady Lottie as much as the bird despised him.

Oliver slowly drew his sword and peeked around the doorjamb.

Abraham held Blaike's arm in a cruel grip as she wrestled to free herself, defiance shooting from her glorious eyes.

Blaire stood statue still, terror radiating off her.

"You will either walk of your own accord, or you'll be carried, writhing and shrieking," Abraham threatened, shaking her so hard, a few tendrils slipped loose from their pins.

Blaike cried out again, and Blaire lunged forward, pulling on Abraham's forearm. The hatboxes she held tumbled to the floor. "Stop it, you evil lout! You're hurting her."

Exquisite in a rumpled Pomona green and lavender traveling gown, Blaike went rigid, arching away from him. "You—" She veered his men a panicked glance. "They would not dare. Besides, someone would come to our aid."

She trembled so hard, her jaunty little hat shook atop her shimmering hair, yet she stoically attempted to keep her composure.

"I would dare, and no fool would interfere with a concerned father disciplining his run-away daughters, right chaps?" Brow cocked, Abraham laughed, deep and sinister. Eyes glittering with malicious excitement, the whoremonger was relishing their fear.

"Aye, Cap'n. You've been plain heartsick with fear for them," Eades agreed before he and his mates guffawed, pounding each other on the back and shoulders. "Bet they smell good. Ladies always do. I wouldn't mind carrying either wench." His lewd appraisal stripped the twins bare. "Toss her over my shoulder and squeeze her plump arse as I walk."

Oliver's hand grew numb from the stranglehold he had on his sword. He shot a glance over his shoulder. Just a few more moments . . .

"No. If it comes to that, Demir will carry the other twin. I trust him not to molest her." Scowling, Abraham narrowed his eyes to slits and leveled each of his men a murderous glare. "They are to remain untouched. Do you understand? Virgins until we reach Cairo." Nostrils flared, he licked his lips. "They'll bring us a bloody fortune."

"Dear God, no." Blaire staggered backward, banging into the counter and kicking a hatbox. Revulsion drained her face of color as she pressed a hand to her throat, exchanging an horrorstruck glance with Blaike.

"Let me go, bloody blackguard." Blaike renewed her frantic struggles, several more flaxen strands tumbling to her shoulders as she jerked and tugged. "And how can you be so certain we're virgins. We might not be."

Abraham chuckled again.

"If you aren't, then I'll sample your charms myself on the voyage and let my officers share your twin." He leaned nearer, mere inches separating his gloating face and Blaike's white-as-fresh-milk countenance. "And I'll still sell you, though unfortunately, for far less."

She swallowed, and closing her eyes, averted her face.

Deadly rage hummed through Oliver. It pounded in his ears, welled in his chest, and inflamed his blood. He wanted Abraham dead. By his hand.

Throughout it all, Meunier leaned nonchalantly against his desk, arms folded. No surprise that cawker wouldn't help two women in distress. His perverse preferences ran to young boys, often supplied by Abraham.

How many women had he abetted in trafficking, the whoremonger?

"*Naturellement*, I'll receive *mon habituel* fee?" he said.

Blaike gasped, and her eyelids flew open as she swung her infuriated gaze to him. "Spawn of Satan. You do speak English!"

"*Oui*." He shrugged, fingering his atrocity of a mustache. "Anglais, Espanol, and bits of others."

Abraham hauled a resisting Blaike closer, his lust apparent. Only his greed would keep him from despoiling her the instant he had her aboard his ship. "I'll tend to this one myself. I have other ways she can be of use to me on the voyage."

Such scorching fury engulfed Oliver at the crude insinuation, he bit the inside of his cheek to keep from revealing his presence. Daring a last glance behind him, he twisted his mouth into a satisfied smirk.

Pistols, swords, and dirks drawn, his men advanced.

"You'll dance in hell first."

Blaike released a hoarse cry and spun to face the entrance, relief blossoming across her exquisite features.

"Captain Whitehouse! Oh, thank God. I knew Blythe had made arrangements for our passage."

Where had she come by that false notion?

If Blaike had arrived a day later, the *Sea Gypsy* would've already made the Mediterranean.

He wouldn't have been able to save them from a fate too horrific to contemplate.

Oliver, his legs spread-eagle and sword in hand, impaled Abraham with his gaze. How he longed to bury his blade in the libertine over and over. He pointed a finger toward Blaike and Blaire. "Their guardian entrusted me with the Culpeppers care on the voyage here, and I shall see them to London. Unlike you, I'll make damned sure they're returned to their family safely."

Oliver's men clambered onto the porch and into the office.

Metal scraped against metal as Abraham's men drew their weapons. They were outnumbered at least three to one, and though Abraham wasn't one to back down from a fight, he preferred to skulk round under the cover of darkness. A noisy, attention-grabbing ruckus wouldn't serve him well.

"*Tsk, tsk.*" Shaking his head, Oliver jabbed a thumb over his shoulder. "You may want to rethink your impulse, lads. Scabber your blades. Now. Better yet, drop them."

To a man, Abraham's crew shot their captain a questioning gaze.

He gave a tense jerk of his head, and muttering vulgarities, they dropped their knives and swords. The metal clanged loudly as it hit the floor.

Hawkins edged to Oliver's side. "Cap'n, everythin' is as you bid, and I've had the misses' luggage taken to the ship."

He hurried to retrieve Blaire's hatboxes, then passed them to a deckhand.

"Excellent." Adjusting his grip on his sword, Oliver wielded the tip at Abraham. "I believe Miss Culpepper asked you to unhand her."

Abraham did so, hate curling his lip. The motion pleated the scar Oliver had given him that fateful night. "You expect me to believe *you*, uneducated gutter filth with scarcely two coins to rub together and a known by-blow, were entrusted with the Culpeppers' passage here?"

If the cur intended to shame Oliver with his revelations, he fell short of the mark. Everything he said was true and common knowledge.

Blaike stabbed Abraham with a lethal glare before she swept Oliver a pity-filled gaze. The sympathy in her shining eyes cut a gash far deeper and more painful than Abraham's spiteful words.

"Yes, he was, Captain. Because he, unlike you, is a man of integrity, despite the origins of his birth." She took her sister's hand, and they scooted past the lurking hulks. A few feet from Abraham, Blaike whirled around. "Honor and high character can raise a person above their birth and circumstances. Most especially if whatever shadows them wasn't their fault. That is why, Captain Abraham, you will always, *always,* muck about with the lowest," her attention gravitated to his men, "most vile of offensive creatures."

She marched to Oliver, ushering her trembling sister before her. "Captain Whitehouse, if you would be so kind as to escort us to the *Sea Gypsy*. I've quite enough of French hospitality for a lifetime."

White lines framed her mouth, revealing just how much effort it took to retain her composure. Most women facing the prospect of being sold into white slavery, would have dissolved into hysterics.

"Wait outside," he gently ordered, touching her arm.

Lips pursed, she gave a brief nod as she passed.

"Don't let Abraham or his brutes move until we are well away from here," Oliver instructed Hawkins. He gestured to more of his crew, then pointed at Abraham's thugs. "You make sure they don't budge, either. And search them all for other weapons."

"As you say, Cap'n." Hawkins canted his head toward Oliver's men. "Lads, check their boots, while you're at it."

As his mates rushed to further disarm Abraham and his crew, Oliver took the opportunity to corner Meunier. Once he'd sheathed his sword, Oliver grabbed the harbor master by his collar and shoved him so hard against the wall pinned with an assortment of bulletins, two fluttered to the floor.

"You'd be wise to resign your position and disappear into the gutters where your kind belongs, Meunier." Righteous outrage humming through his blood, Oliver tightened his hold. "Because I assure you, when the Culpepper Misses' family learns your part in this debacle, those powerful lords will demand retribution. You won't stand a maggot's chance in a hen yard of escaping unscathed."

Meunier's jaw hung slack, and he quivered like a fledging leaf buffeted by a North Sea gale. His damned mustache still remained morbidly stiff, though.

"God, I hate that revolting thing." Oliver yanked his dagger from its cover, and Meunier released a strangled terrified squeak. Oliver slashed off either side of the offending atrocity, dropping the disgusting waxed strands onto the floor. "Consider that a favor. It made you look like an imbécile."

Eyes closed, a tear dribbling from the corner of one, Meunier sagged against the wall, gasping.

As Oliver returned his blade to its leather case, he grimaced. "Soiled yourself, did you? Be a good chap and light a lamp before attending to that offensiveness."

A few men snickered.

"The sod shite himself?"

"Twiddlepoop."

"Buggering Molly."

"Enough," Oliver snapped. Like hens sensing weaker chickens, the men attacked with barbed rejoinders. He'd meant to scare the hell out of Meunier and teach him a lesson—not subject him to ridicule, even if he deserved it. "Tend to your tasks."

Besides, the Culpeppers were only a few feet away and shouldn't be exposed to such course language.

As Meunier shuffled to do Oliver's bidding, Abraham attempted to follow the twins.

The *click* of Hawkins cocking his blunderbuss drew everyone's gaze.

"Abraham, I'm thinkin' you've not repented of your evil ways nor made your peace with the Good Lord. As much as it would grieve me to send any soul to burn in hell for eternity, if you move another inch, I'll blow a hole in your skull—right between your shifty devil's eyes—and ask The Almighty's forgiveness afterward."

"You don't have the ballocks, you puny little bastard," Abraham sneered, though he stopped sidling toward the entrance. "My men would run you through."

Hawkins raised the pistol, pointing the barrel squarely at Abraham's forehead, and lifted a boney shoulder. "You'd be dead, and I'd be enterin' the pearly gates. Good enough for me. Besides, they'd have to get to me, and I'm thinkin' a lead ball would find a home in each of their ugly faces before they moved a foot. Cannot help but think it'd be an improvement in their ugly appearances."

Hands fisted, his face contorted in frustration, Abraham swiveled to face Oliver. "We will meet again, Whitehouse, and next time, I promise you, I'll not be as amiable."

This is amiable?

Oliver chuckled. "I'll look forward to it."

Dusk had settled on Lyon, and with it, the cold that early spring evenings bring. His stomach growled, reminding him he hadn't eaten since disembarking the *Sea Gypsy* this morning.

He actually looked forward to the journey home now—a vast change from a mere hour ago.

The blonde beauty waiting outside could be credited for that.

More commotion drew Oliver's attention outdoors. Flanked on either side by columns of soldiers, the first two carrying lanterns, an important-looking man and what Oliver presumed was the constable made straight for the Harbor Master's Office.

Well, now. Mayhap Abraham was about to get his comeuppance after all.

Oliver raised a brow and rubbed his beard as he angled Abraham a considering glance. "I'm fairly certain that gentleman is Seaulieu. Wonder what brings him here? He looks to be in a fine fettle, too."

"Hell and damnation," Abraham mumbled, shifting toward the window. "Meunier, is there another way out?"

Meunier had disappeared into a back room.

"*Ah, ah, ah.*" Hawkins clicked his tongue. "I warned you not to move an inch. And keep your hands where I can see them, you scurvy sea-dog. You wouldn't want me to pull the trigger when all you were doin' was satisfyin' an indelicate itch, now would you?"

Oliver bent into a mocking bow. "I'll say my farewells. Far too many soldiers approach to fit comfortably in here. I confess, if I wasn't keen to see the Misses Culpepper to my ship, I'd linger to watch the outcome."

"Sod off, Whitehouse." Abraham spared Oliver a sneering glower before he returned his rapt attention to the window and the advancing soldiers.

"Hawkins," Oliver said, "I'll see you aboard ship."

"Aye, Cap'n." He grinned and sliced a quick glance heavenward. "Looks like the Good Lord heard my prayer 'bout reinforcements."

"Indeed."

Pleased to have bested Abraham this round, Oliver stalked onto the porch. Those of his men not inside the office or on his ship loitered nearby, each alert and ready to jump into action should the need arise. To a man, they watched the soldiers' progression, their weather-browned faces curious.

Blaike and her sister rested on a time-worn bench, arms around one another's waists. Shoulders hunched and gazes wary, weariness blanketed them. He couldn't venture to guess what had brought them to Lyon, but he'd be bound it wasn't anything good.

He might not have a full cargo hold, but he'd have the pleasure of Blaike's company on the voyage home. Not a bad trade-off at all. Actually, it would be a pleasurable hell, having her near once more and never being able to declare himself.

Still, he'd take the treasured gift.

Her soft mouth turned up into a tired, fragile smile at his approach, then suddenly her eyes became huge and terrified, and she lurched to her feet, pointing.

"Oliver! Behind you!"

Eyes often reveal the secrets of one's heart, and an
astute woman will watch to see if they confirm what is spoken.
~Scruples and Scandals-The Genteel Lady's Guide to Practical Living

5

B laike dashed into the captain's shadowy quarters, holding a lantern before her.

"Hairy-lipped trollop!"

Giving a startled yelp, she spun toward the grating voice.

Its salmon-crested head cocked to the side, a white bird sat atop a perch inside a cage. An odd assortment of things hung inside, including silverware tied together, ropes, wood pieces, colorful beads, rings, and a mirror. Beside the cage stood a sturdy perch made from a branch. It, too, had several items dangling from it.

Must be toys.

Why did it surprise her that Oliver had a pet bird?

Was it new, for surely Blaike would've heard its screeching on the previous voyage?

Why couldn't he have a normal pet like her cats, Pudding and Dumpling, or dear toddling half-blind, mostly-deaf old Freddy, their Welsh corgi?"

"Hello luv." The bird flapped its wings, revealing subtle yellow on its underwings.

"Hello to you, too." *Rude little beast.* "Your master's been hurt."

After setting the lantern aside, Blaike untied her bonnet and tossed the dainty hat and her reticule onto an impressive desk covered with charts and an assortment of interesting looking nautical tools, as well as an hourglass, quill, and an unusual bronze ship shaped inkwell.

What were the instruments used for?

A few detailed, excellent sketches of sailing vessels lay upon the desktop as well, and several more adorned the great cabin's walls. Had he drawn them? She was no expert at such things, but even she could recognize immense talent when she saw it.

Her attention drifted back to the curious gadgets.

Mayhap when he recovered, she might ask Oliver to show her how to use them. She'd always been interested in ship's navigation.

On the voyage from London, she hadn't been inside his cabin, and now amid a crisis, she was intrigued about the contents?

Had she known what Geneva held for her, she'd never have set foot on the *Sea Gypsy* last autumn, and Oliver wouldn't be bleeding all over the floor right now.

Twisting her mouth, she eyed the dark stain marring her spencer. Ruined for certain.

"I want out. I want out," the bird demanded.

And have it flying about as Blaike tended Oliver?

Not a chance.

Besides, how did she know it was friendly? That beak looked positively dangerous.

'No, you may not come out right now." Did the creature understand? Didn't birds just mimic words and sounds?

"Curse ye, cockscum."

Good heavens.

Was there ever such a foul-mouthed creature that wasn't human? She sent Oliver a castigating glance. Just where had the beast acquired his or her vocabulary from?

No time for that now.

Oliver had been shot.

He groaned, opened his eyes again for an instant, then the lids fluttered shut once more.

Several times on the way to the ship, he'd done the same, even uttering a low oath more than once. He'd suffered a blow to his head when he collapsed, and that had frightened her as much as the ball to his shoulder.

The wound didn't appear fatal, but then, what did Blaike know of such things?

Swiftly scanning the chamber, she spied a Turkish towel draped over a washstand. She grabbed it, another smaller cloth, and the plain white porcelain basin, then rushed to spread the towel upon the rich maroon, nut brown, and beige counterpane spread atop the bed dominating the stateroom.

"Quickly, put the captain on the bed, and one of you light the lamps in here. It's far too dark to assess his injuries."

"Hell's ballocks and bells," the bird squawked.

Two burly seaman, their faces creased with worry, carefully helped their captain to his bed.

Bobbing up and down, the bird yelled, "Bugger yourself."

"Beg your pardon for that," the younger sailor said, canting his head toward the foul-mouthed fowl, his face flushed red as the scarf tied around his neck.

"What kind of bird is it?" After unfastening her spencer, Blaike slid the jacket off, letting it drop to the floor. She toed it aside. Blood marred her gown across her bosoms as well. At least she didn't have to worry about covering the garment whilst she treated Oliver.

"A Moluccan cockatoo," the older seaman offered as he went about lighting the lamps attached to the walls and the one atop the desk.

"Do you have a surgeon on board, Mister . . .?" Blaike raised her head after checking Oliver's neck for a pulse. It beat sure and strong beneath her fingertips. "Forgive me, but I don't know your names."

"I'm Tom Grover, the quartermaster," the stocky red-head in his fifth decade said. "And this here is Jimmy Webb, our bosun's mate."

The younger, somber-faced fellow didn't look to be much older than Blaike. Yet from his serious expression and even more solemn eyes, she guessed he'd not had an easy time of it.

"Is anyone on the ship medically trained?" Blaike shoved a curl behind her ear.

His face pinched with anxiety, Mr. Webb shook his head. "No, miss. Our other cook used to take care of those things, but Fairnly's new. He ain't never treated our crew yet, and I don't know if he has the know-how McMaster did 'bout medicine."

Goose butt feathers. It just figures.

She pulled Oliver's unlaced crimson shirt farther apart, trying not to stare at the manly display of crisp, black chest hair. She lifted hers and Blaire's reddened handkerchiefs from his wounded right shoulder. After dropping them into the basin, she folded the smaller square and pressed it to his injury.

That much she remembered.

Pressure to stop the bleeding.

She closed her eyes, summoning up every recollection she could of times at Esherton Green when a person or a creature had been injured.

There weren't a whole lot, truth be told.

"Move yer fat arse," the cockatoo shrieked, and Blaike jumped.

"Can one of you possibly take the captain's pet somewhere else?"

"*Umm,* she ain't exactly friendly." Mr. Webb eyed the cage. "There's a larger cage on the poop deck, but Cap'n Whitehouse doesn't like M'Lady Lottie above deck while we weigh or drop anchor."

"Drop anchor 'twixt yer thighs," she squawked, flapping her wings.

"M'Lady?" Blaike arced her brows in disbelief even as heat scorched her cheeks. "With that vulgar vocabulary? Surely you jest."

"McMaster was raised in a whor— Um . . . that is, his mother was a—"

"Cook," Mr. Grover hastily offered. "Mrs. McMaster was one fine *cook.*"

"Aye, yes. A . . . a cook. In a broth—house of ill-repute. McMaster must've learned his extraordinary skills from her," Mr. Webb stammered.

Mr. Grover made a peculiar choking sound and frantically shook his head.

"Cooking, I mean. She taught McMaster how to cook. Not to . . ." Mr. Webb colored redder than Oliver's shirt but forged on. "M'Lady was his as a boy, and now that he's died, she won't eat much for anyone but the cap'n. Grieving, he says. We think she's about twenty years old."

Wonderful. Almost two decades to learn curses, vulgarities, and insults from strumpets and sailors. And whoever heard of a ship's cook also being the medical officer? Was the ability to wield a butcher knife the only qualification to appointment as a ship's medical officer?

"What's yer pleasure?" M'Lady Lottie asked, hanging upside down.

"I suppose that means she must stay." Blaike sighed and shook her head. "Can you at least cover her cage?" She pulled a quilt from the foot of the bed. "Here, use this."

Perhaps the bird would cease her obnoxious chattering.

Mr. Webb hurried to do as bid

"Bloody whoremonger," M'Lady Lottie screamed as the quilt descended, then in a softer, plaintive voice called, "Petey? Petey?"

"That was McMaster's given name," Mr. Grover volunteered, his worried gaze trained on Oliver.

What would happen to M'Lady Lottie if Oliver too—

No. He would be fine. He must.

"I shall need hot water, clean cloths, long strips for a bandages—a cut up sheet will suffice." *What else?* "Salve if you have it, whisky, and..."

"Stop fussing over me," Oliver grumbled.

"Shush, and save your strength." Raising the cloth a fraction, she bent over him and examined the wound again.

A vague aroma wafted upward from his bronzed skin. Fresh, yet slightly musky, too. Maybe even a hint of cinnamon, cloves, and coffee. Most tantalizing.

Did he go shirtless when at sea? The notion caused an interesting quiver in her belly.

And utterly ridiculous that she'd notice at a time like this.

Glancing upward, her attention caught on the beard covering his olive-toned jaw. He was the only man she knew who sported facial hair, and she found it quite suave, as she did his dark coloring.

Was his beard soft or scratchy?

Enough ogling the unconscious man. For pity's sake, Blaike Regina Lillian Culpepper.

"Petey?" Pitiful and heartbroken this time. After a bit of shuffling around and feather ruffling, M'Lady Lottie fell silent.

Blaike scrutinized Oliver's injury again. Not really a hole, but more of a long furrow.

Did he need stitches?

Should they send for a surgeon? A physician?

How was she to know?

She'd never doctored anyone before. Blythe had always tended the sick and wounded.

If a physician were summoned, might that delay the ship's departure? Somehow she knew that would infuriate Oliver. It was worth the risk if doing so saved his life, however.

Did Blaike have the stomach to suture the wound?

Gads.

She swallowed, her attention drawn to his striking face.

Yes, if she must.

Her disgruntled empty tummy took the opportunity to churn sickeningly and momentary light-headedness engulfed her. Taking measured breaths, she willed the dizziness to go away. It didn't help that she was so famished, her navel gnawed at her backbone.

She glanced at the sailors, then blew out a sigh. "At least fetch the other supplies, Mr. Grover, at once, if you please. Your captain bled quite a lot on the way to the ship."

Not to mention the blood he'd lost while transferring him below deck, as their stained clothing testified.

Blaire had nearly swooned at the sight of so much blood: one of the few differences between the twins. Blaike possessed a stronger constitution, and unlike Blaire, didn't suffer from *mal de mer* either.

Poor Blaire.

If this was like the first crossing, Blaire would spend the first three days curled into a miserable ball in her berth, yet she hadn't said one word of protest about the return voyage by sea. Prior to leaving the academy, they'd discussed traveling by land most of the way home, but Blythe hadn't known that.

"Aye, miss. We'll get what you need." Mr. Grover slanted another troubled glance at his captain.

"Can you also look in on my sister, and if possible, see that she has a bite to eat?" Hopefully, he'd change his clothing first, else he might be picking Blaire off of her stateroom floor.

"Of course, Miss. I'll ask for tea as well," Mr. Webb offered.

Blaike rolled up her sleeves, then attempted to pin her drooping hair. "Tell her I'll be along as quickly as I can. She doesn't handle blood well, else she'd also help." A smile tugged her mouth upward. "Better to let her have a lie down rather than risk her swooning and getting knocked in the head, too."

They'd barely reached the door when a sharp rap preceded Hawkins rushing into the cabin as if chased by the devil himself. He pulled up short upon seeing Mr. Grover and Mr. Webb.

"What are you still doin' here?" A note of fear crept into Mr. Hawkins's voice and the look he hurled Oliver bordered on panic.

His countenance grave, Mr. Webb rubbed his furrowed forehead. "We just now got the cap'n to his chamber, sir."

Given the profuse, under-their-breath swearing coming from all three men, it'd been no easy task.

"And we're about to fetch medical supplies for Miss Culpepper to tend him," he said.

"Off with you then, and no dallyin'." Hawkins swept his cap from his head and then stuffed it into his waistband.

"Aye, sir," chorused Grover and Webb as they hurried from the captain's quarters.

"For the love of God, stop blathering and be gone." Oliver was not a compliant patient.

M'Lady Lottie stirred. She made soft, throaty noises and ruffled her feathers, but hurled no ear-burning phrases.

"How is he?" Hawkins asked without preamble, giving the quilt atop the birdcage an inquisitive glance.

Eyes closed, Oliver mumbled, "I'm fine."

Blaike exchanged a knowing glance with Mr. Hawkins and lifted a shoulder.

"I'm honestly not sure. I don't know if the captain needs his wound sewn. I've no experience with serious injuries. He hit his head when he fell, but it's not bleeding. He woke almost immediately, but other than cursing a bit, hasn't said much. He does have quite a bump though, near a scar along his hairline. I think those are his only injuries."

"I'm capable of explaining my own condition, Miss Culpepper."

"Don't be so crotchety to the lass," Hawkins admonished as he rushed to his master's bed. *Tsking* and *tutting*, he examined Oliver's head and then the gash.

"Leave off, Hawkins." Oliver flinched and turned his head away.

"Good thing you're such a stubborn, hard-headed fool. Just a nasty lump that'll give you a whale of a headache. Your shoulder is barely scratched, thanks to Miss Culpepper's warnin'."

That was a scratch?

She offered a tremulous smile. "I wasn't quick enough. Monsieur Meunier still managed to shoot Captain Whitehouse."

"Just a glancin' blow. Hardly a nick at all," Hawkins assured her, though worry creased his brow and pulled his silver-whiskered jaw downward.

Who was he trying to reassure?

Blaike or himself?

Oliver groaned again, and his thick-lashed eyelids fluttered open. Pain had darkened his eyes to coal-black, and he shut his lids again. He swallowed audibly, his Adam's apple bobbing up and down the strong column of his thick throat, then he licked his lips.

Blaike glanced around for something to wet his mouth.

"Do you have anything in your cabin to drink?" she asked.

"Brandy. Bottom left desk drawer," he managed, his voice gruff. Wincing, he raised his left hand and touched the side of his head, whispering through his strong, white teeth, "Ho-ly hell."

"Ho-ly hell," M'Lady Lottie repeated in a raucous sing-song voice. "Ho-ly hell. Holy hell. Hoolee—"

"M'Lady Lottie, hush," Oliver ordered, squinting at the cage. "Go to sleep."

In response, the parrot screeched, "Lift yer skirts."

"Charming." Blaike couldn't have prevented her blush or her brows from climbing up her forehead if forbidden figgy pudding—she adored figgy pudding—for life.

"Need to teach her new phrases, my boy. Scriptures, poetry, nursery rhymes," Hawkins advised, his pointed ears glowing tulip red. He bustled to the desk and momentarily retrieved a bottle and three small tumblers. He raised a glass. "Miss Culpepper?"

"Thank you, no." The few instances when she'd sampled anything stronger than wine or ratafia, she'd found the flavor much too bold.

Oliver attempted to sit up, but she gently yet firmly, pressed him back into the pillows. "You're injured, and until we know how badly, you cannot be moving around."

Dark brows pulled together in a fierce scowl, he reminded her of a surly boy denied his way.

"I cannot be lazing about. I have a ship to captain, and we sail on the tide." Voice stronger than a moment ago, Oliver raised his head again. His dull eyes and the stark angles of his face exposed the discomfort he strove to mask with curt bravado. "Hawkins, my brandy, if you please."

"Aye, Cap'n." A grin twitching his mouth, Mr. Hawkins dutifully brought Oliver his spirits.

Face pale as the pillows cradling his dark head, Oliver pulled his handsome mouth into a taut line and scooted into a sitting position, his movements slow and precise.

"You really shouldn't, Oliver. You'll bleed all over your bed." Blaike rushed to prop pillows behind him as he accepted the brandy from his mate, then tossed it back in one gulp.

"More." He extended the glass, his belly gurgling loud and long.

"Most assuredly not. Especially since I gather from your rumbling stomach, you're hungry, too." Blaike took the tumbler, pointedly ignoring the sudden irritated slashing together of his brows once more. "I know you're in pain, but head injuries can be serious. We must make sure you aren't concussed. Now please, do lie back."

Oliver sighed but complied. Turning a sharp eye on Mr. Hawkins, he asked, "Is everyone aboard? The cargos are loaded, and she's ready to weigh anchor? Are guards stationed as a precaution?"

"Aye, Cap'n, to all." Mr. Hawkins nodded and finished his brandy as well. "I'll go up top and oversee the final preparations. I'll also request a tray for you." He opened the door, and after stepping through the entrance, poked his head back in for a second. "Grover's comin' with the supplies you asked for, Miss Culpepper."

"Oliver, stay put." Blaike pointed her forefinger, giving him her starchiest do-not-test-me look.

Other than closing his eyes and grimacing, he didn't respond.

Most assuredly not a good-natured patient.

With an appreciative smile, she accepted the basket from Mr. Grover. "Thank you."

"I also brought you a medicine chest and a book I found about doctoring that you might find useful." He set both on the desk.

Still not sure how to best treat Oliver, she mentally cataloged the items in the basket. "How is my sister?"

"She's settling into your stateroom, Miss. I've asked that a tray be taken to her, as well." Mr. Grover kept peering past Blaike, worry scrunching his rugged features. He slanted his gaze toward Oliver. "Has he awoken yet?"

"Yes, I have." Material shifted and crackled with Oliver's strained movements, and Blaike whirled to confront him. Slightly hunched, he sat on the edge of the bed, his face wan and a wide palm pressed to the cloth covering his wound.

"Don't you dare stand up, Oliver Whitehouse!" Her voice rang shriller than she'd intended, but ashen and unstable as he was, she feared he'd topple onto the planking.

"I think you're forgetting who gives the orders on this vessel, Miss Culpepper."

Some claim those who keep secrets are wise,
but 'tis far more prudent to have no secrets worth keeping,
much less confidences one dreads having revealed.
~Scruples and Scandals-The Genteel Lady's Guide to Practical Living

6

"There's little chance of that, you codpated buffoon," Blaike retorted.

Going all stubborn and bullish now, was Oliver?

Did he think to intimidate her?

Compared to Madame Beaulieu, he was nothing but a scratching, hissing kitten.

One of his raven brows vaulted ceilingward as he gingerly lifted the reddened square and examined his wound. He gave a contemptuous snort. "I've seen worse flea bites."

Bent on being uncooperative, *hmm*?

Upon spying a small brown bottle in the basket, she tilted her mouth upward into a tiny half-smile.

Laudanum.

Lovely, lovely laudanum.

That changed things a mite, indeed it did. She had just the means to keep him in his surprisingly big bed if he wanted to act the obstinate boor.

"This ship needs a captain, as you yourself reminded me not five minutes ago." She rummaged in the basket a bit more.

Tweezers. Scissors. Needles.

She shuddered the merest bit as trepidation scampered across her shoulders.

Let's hope it doesn't come to that.

"If you injure yourself further, how are we to depart?" Giving him an acrid gaze, she looped the basket onto her arm and marched to the bed.

His expression bordered on exasperated as he snapped, "My crew is perfectly capable of sailing the *Sea Gypsy*."

Ah, good to know. Just in case the laudanum was required after all. To subdue a certain mulish captain.

"I don't doubt that in the least. Remember, I've voyaged with you before." And had covertly watched him like the smitten school girl she was the entire voyage. Head tilted and mouth pursed, Blaike cupped a hip with one hand.

She sent Mr. Grover a sidelong glance. "Is he usually this cantankerous when indisposed?"

"No, Miss. He's always this belligerent." Mr. Grover chuckled, his sage green eyes lighting with humor.

"Stow it, Grover," Oliver practically growled.

Mr. Grover, his eyes twinkling, winked at Blaike. "I should think he'd spare you some leeway since you threw yourself atop him to protect him after he'd been shot."

He'd seen that, had he?

She could feel Oliver's intense scrutiny, drat Mr. Grover.

Blaike busied herself with the medicines to hide the flush sweeping her face.

Oliver turned an annoyed gaze to his man. "It's just a flesh wound. Get yourself topside and help Hawkins. I don't need another nursemaid hovering over me blathering nonsense. Keep a sharp eye out for any sign of trouble."

After delivering a two-fingered salute, Mr. Grover took his leave, still grinning.

He must've concluded the same thing Blaike had.

Anyone as pigheaded and sour-tempered as Oliver wasn't going to cock up his toes any time soon.

She plopped the basket beside his black leather clad thighs.

"I for one don't wish to tempt Fate any further. We're fortunate Abraham and Meunier were detained by the authorities, but I'd rather not linger in port." She lifted the cloths for bandages, then set them aside.

"They were?" That news brought a bit of color to Oliver's pale cheeks, and he straightened. "'Bout time."

A rolled bandage in one hand, she nodded.

"Yes, and those three fierce buffoons with him, too. I hate to think what would've happened if they hadn't already been unarmed. As it was, it took four men to subdue each of them. I'm quite certain one soldier had a broken arm and another a shattered nose before the kerfuffle was over."

"Most likely Abraham will bribe his way out, if not within hours, then days." Disgust riddled Oliver's voice, and his expression turned rather fierce. He slapped his left knee. "Blast, but I loathe corrupt officials and those in influential positions abusing their power."

He searched her face, his anger replaced by concern. "I truly regret that you and your sister endured any of this."

Blaike set the bandage aside, still shaken by the recollection of the violence she'd witnessed but an hour ago. More so by the gun pointed at Oliver's head. If he hadn't ducked and hit Meunier's hand when he spun around . . .

"Did you really protect me?" Voice husky, it almost seemed like he was asking something more. "Is that why your gown is stained with blood? You're not injured?"

"Yes, to the first two questions, and no to the latter."

Instinct.

That was all it had been.

She'd have done the same for anyone.

Wouldn't she have?

As she'd shielded Oliver, trying to stop the bleeding, she had looked on in renewed terror as Abraham and his crew fought the soldiers and Oliver's men. Never had she witnessed such ferocity and savagery.

"One of your hands tackled Meunier as he tried to run from the fray. I think his name is Melville. He showed great restraint, given Meunier had just attempted to murder you. I believe there are others in your crew who would've killed him without a qualm."

She'd rather have liked to club the port master upside his pasty head.

"I deserved to be shot."

"I beg your pardon?"

Tweezers in hand, Blaike blinked in disbelief.

"Why would you say such a ludicrous thing? Of course you didn't. You, Oliver, rescued us from a fate so utterly vile, I can scarce think on it without trembling. He would've let Blaire and I be sold into slavery. I have little compassion for the worm of a man."

"Yes, he's a maggot. A contemptuous blot on humanity. But I humiliated him." Oliver starred across the stateroom, his jaw tense. "I know too well what it's like to be belittled. I should've handled it differently."

Blaike didn't know what to say.

She didn't agree in the least, but suspected something more than his threatening Meunier was at work here.

Holding his right arm against his torso, he sighed and closed his eyes, the lashes dark fans upon his high cheekbones.

"I'm no better than Abraham."

"Now that's absolute rubbish. You'd never have sold my sister and me, would you have?"

Icy fear zipped from her neck to her waist when he didn't respond. She touched his face. "Oliver?"

He opened those incredibly dark eyes, and for an instant, she was lost in their depths—a connection she couldn't put words to holding her fast and quickening her pulse.

It had been thus since they'd first met.

Did he feel it too?

"Blaike." He grazed his fingertips along her jaw, his voice velvety and deep. "Why are you in Lyon?"

The warmth that held her entranced evaporated, replaced by shame and disquiet. She couldn't tell him. Couldn't bear to see either pity or accusation in his eyes because of her stupidity.

"Come, Oliver. We must see your shirt off you before the blood dries any more than it already has. Lift your good arm, and I think I can manage to work it down your other. The shirt is beyond saving, I fear."

Not a minute passed before she regretted her decision. If she thought it was hard to be this close to him, touching him with his blood-soaked shirt, seeing him shirtless, all manly bulges and sculpted muscles . . .

If she were the sort to swoon, she'd feel faint, for certain. Only, the feelings cavorting inside her assuredly didn't make her feel weak. No, tingly and excited and eager to see more of him. To trail her fingers over those same fascinating contours.

Mayhap hunger had her a trifle addled.

Except she'd felt these curious, disturbing, and wholly delicious sensations before.

Blaike had ignored the stirrings he'd roused when they met that night she was introduced to London society, and she'd danced with him: a quivery, jelly-kneed twit. She'd overlooked the peculiar flutters the many times he'd come across her path at assemblies and gatherings. Disregarded the flushes and pattering pulse at Bristledale Court where he was a house guest of her brother-in-law, and her dashed pulse had ran amuck whenever she saw him. Resolutely smothered every nuance of attraction on the voyage to France those many months ago, knowing full well nothing could come of her school-girl infatuation.

But now . . .?

Those suppressed feelings burst forth, much like a shaken bottle of Champagne, once uncorked. And there wasn't a blasted way in all of Christendom to harness them, much less force them back into quiet submission.

Glancing at the umber liquid in the bottle atop his desk, she cleared her throat. Maybe a tot of brandy was a good idea after all.

No, she needed steady hands and a mind not befuddled by spirits.

A distraction.

That was what they both needed.

Something mundane and harmless.

"Did you draw all of these sketches?" Arcing her hand, Blaike indicated the detailed illustrations displayed about the great cabin. "If so, you're incredibly talented."

She chattered on, not giving him a chance to answer, while studiously avoiding looking into his eyes. For when she did, she forgot what she was about, forgot all else except how much she wanted to kiss him.

"I have no skill for either drawing or painting. In fact, I'm abysmal at both." Which Madame Beaulieu pointed out with annoying regularity. "Have you ever considered turning your interests to shipbuilding?"

"Yes, I drew them. But no, I've never given it serious consideration. My grandfather taught me the skill before he died. He was a shipbuilder in Italy, but when his wife died, he moved my mother to England. I've always assumed he'd been presented an opportunity too good to refuse." Oliver made a waving motion. "I've many more rolled up and stored in that chest at the foot of my bed."

"How fascinating." She brushed the back of her hand over her forehead, and stared across the cabin, racking her memory. "I cannot remember her name, dash it all. But I do recall a discussion over supper one evening about an acquaintance of Heath's—a shipping heiress."

Blaike squinted her eyes, searching her memory. "Lady somebody. She lives in Scotland, I believe. If you ever decide to pursue designing vessels or need additional suppliers, she might be a good person to contact."

Listen to her, nattering on like a lonely tabby.

Or a nervous woman much too attracted to a man she shouldn't be.

"You didn't answer my question about why you and your sister are not at school." Oliver grasped a curl she'd missed pinning back into place and gave it a slight yank.

"And I'm not going to. Now, lie back so I can tend to your injury."

How hard could it be to clean and bandage the wound?

Instead of laying down, Oliver grasped her chin between his thumb and forefinger, and tenderly turned her face upward.

"Are you in some sort of trouble, Blaike?"

The more respectable or powerful a person is, the more
certain you may be that they have secrets they don't wish exposed.
~*Scruples and Scandals-The Genteel Lady's Guide to Practical Living*

"**Y**ou are. I can see it in your eyes and in the way you hold
yourself, *cara*."

Oliver endeavored to disregard the cannon thunder in his head and
the fire poker tormenting his shoulder. Good thing he was left-handed,
else his recovery would be even more of a nuisance.

Winged brows drawn taut, Blaike searched his face, hers a bevy of
clashing emotions.

Mindful he'd breached decorum by touching her so intimately, he
lowered his hand to his lap. He had few close friends, and he didn't
need Ravensdale or Leventhorpe calling him out for overstepping the
bounds.

Though for her, it might be worth the blasted risk.

The contour of Blaike's satiny skin pulsed in Oliver's palm, and he
balled his fist as much to preserve the sensation as to prevent himself
from caressing the petal softness again. Or embracing her with his
uninjured arm and soothing the tension from her shoulders and worry
from her usually smooth forehead.

A faint fragrance, floral soap and the merest hint of vanilla,
surrounded her.

Fresh and light, yet subtly tempting. It both aroused and soothed at
once.

Much like her.

Skepticism or perhaps leeriness hovered around the fringes of her
striking eyes as they roved his face. Those eyes that previously had
been so vibrant and teeming with keen intelligence.

Abraham might've caused some of the distrust, but Oliver
recognized a damaged soul.

Didn't he face one in the looking glass every day?

He coiled his hand tighter to keep from brushing her arm in a comforting gesture. If he had the right, he'd do so for the rest of his life, but their stations were too far apart to even consider something so beyond the pale.

So utterly wonderful.

"Is there anything I can do to help?"

"No."

Curt. Final.

She didn't attempt to offer an explanation.

Whatever had occurred had caused her to retreat into herself, and anger at whoever or whatever had made her suspicious, kicked angrily behind his ribs.

Oliver wasn't quite ready to quit the field just yet

She'd been so excited about continuing her education, and something had happened to change that as well as to steal her *joie de vivre*. The joy of life that used to put the rosy hue on her high cheeks, the radiant glow on her face, and the blue-violet glimmer in her eyes had faded into distrust. And he'd be bound, a degree of chagrin lingered there, too.

"May I presume the academy proved a disappointment?"

He leaned against the pillows and crossed his ankles, silently cursing the pain and weakness that forced him to do so.

Blaike's expression grew shuttered, snuffing out the vulnerability she'd exposed, and she dropped her focus to the whisky bottle in one hand and the cloth in her other.

"Let's just say *Les Dames de l'Académie de Grâce* wasn't at all what Blaire and I had anticipated. We're well rid of the place and a few of the people there, too."

He made an affirming sound in his throat.

Much more to that story he'd vow, but it was hers to tell in her own time.

Finished sanitizing her hands with the whisky, she'd wiped each instrument down with the spirit too, then laid them on a clean cloth atop the small storage chest turned bedside table.

"I heard you say you've never dressed a wound. You don't' have to do this." Oliver flicked his fingers toward his shoulder. "I can easily have one of the men tend me."

Hurt and confusion flitted across her features before she shrugged.

"If you'd prefer—"

"No, I do not prefer, *cara.*"

He almost caught her hand in his before he stopped himself. Not only wasn't it wise, to do so would betray the secret he'd guarded these many months. Besides her hands were sterile; at least as much as they could be in this environment. "I just don't want you to feel pressed into doing something you don't want to."

Her eyes narrowed for the briefest moment, and something akin to anger glinted there.

"I've vowed never to let that happen again, so you are safe in that regard, Oliver. But you are correct. I've never doctored a wound before. I shall understand if you want someone with more knowledge to treat you. Except, I've been given to believe your new cook has no experience treating anyone aboard ship either. Perhaps Mr. Hawkins? He seems most capable."

Though her speech was strong, and she met his gaze head-on, he detected more susceptibility beneath her admission. Perhaps he even detected a reluctance to leave him to another's care?

Oliver's manly pride swelled at the notion, no matter how misplaced.

Not that he blamed her in her hesitancy to leave him in Fairnly's incapable hands. The cook was an unfriendly, unbathed cawker, and within a week he'd alienated almost every crew member with his superior attitude. Given a choice, he'd be Oliver's last pick for a nursemaid. Fairnly was superstitious, as well, and Oliver would be bound, he hadn't been pleased to learn two women now traveled with them.

"Fairnly was hired for his cooking skills and naught else."

And only until Oliver could replace him. It had either been Fairnly or no cook until they reached London. As capable and loyal as Oliver's crew were, even they wouldn't have taken kindly to a diet of hardtack for a month or more.

"If you're certain . . .?"

Was that a pleased smile playing around the edges of her pink mouth?

"I'd far prefer your presence to his. You smell much nicer. He reeks of sour ale, garlic and onions, and it's not only because he's the cook. I think there's something foul in the bag he wears around his neck." After winking, Oliver closed his eyes and folded his hands across his abdomen. "I shan't move or even flinch until you're done."

Cloth in hand, she dabbed at his shoulder, and he nearly choked on his swiftly indrawn breath. From the hell-fired burning, he'd vow whisky dampened the piece she applied to his flesh.

"Well, you'll have to move. Else I shan't be able to wrap the bandage around your back, unless someone helps me," she teased lightly.

He'd gargle freshly-cast bullets before uttering a sound of distress, even if the very devil himself stabbed Oliver's shoulder unmercifully this moment.

"Oliver?"

"*Hmm?*" He couldn't manage much more without gasping or cursing.

"Thank you for coming to our aid. You wouldn't be hurt if you'd not been so chivalrous. I realized on the way to the *Sea Gypsy* that you weren't asked to provide passage for us to London, else I presume Lieutenant Drake would've been with you. I had assumed—" She gently daubed at his shoulder. "Well, never mind."

He cracked an eye open, his imbecilic heart leaping within his chest at the breathtaking smile she bestowed on him.

To be able to claim a woman such as her for a life-time.

Now there was fanciful thinking.

Sisters-in-law to marquises and wards of earls did not marry uneducated bastards with empty coffers. Men who called the sea their home and hadn't elsewhere but their ships to lay their heads except for the generosity of his friends on occasion.

Not exactly truth, that. Willoughby had often issued an invitation, as had Oliver's half-brother and sisters. Of course he'd refused, but he also knew deep inside, his rejection of his father would've saddened *Mamma.*

He shut his eyes again, lest he betray himself further. Truth to tell, he was exhausted, and wanted nothing more than to sleep for four and twenty hours.

Ballocks to that.

He wanted Blaike more, but that wasn't ever going to happen.

Catching up on his sleep would have to wait until the *Sea Gypsy* made the Mediterranean Sea. Not much respite to be had, however, before she sailed into the Bay of Biscay, and then they'd best pray for favorable weather. Many a ship had foundered during a tempest in those unpredictable waters.

"Have you any news from home?" Blaike glanced upward, melancholy shadowing her face. "I've missed everyone horribly. Brooke's baby boy arrived the second week of February. I cannot wait to see little Leopold. Have you seen him? Blythe is due in May, and Brette a few months later, I believe."

Fertile bunch those Culpeppers.

What joy it would be to see Blaike's belly round as Oliver's child grew within her. Such fantasies were for fools.

"I haven't had the pleasure of meeting the future Earl of Ravensdale yet. Drake's resigned his commission. Familial obligations." He could've bitten off his tongue for revealing that.

Why couldn't he have blathered something trivial: Gunter's had a new ice flavor or that the king had packed on another stone?

She paused in her preparations, giving him a wide-eyed look. "Oh, I hope nothing unfortunate has occurred."

"His family is landed gentry, and his older brother was shot dead— a hunting accident." Or so everyone was being told. Drake wasn't convinced. "He left behind an . . . ah . . ."

Damned awkward. Should've kept his mouth shut.

Oliver ought not to have mentioned Drake's situation, devil it. Especially since Drake had cast his eye on Blaire months ago, and she'd obviously returned his regard.

Blaike held up a wicked-looking needle, and Oliver broke out into a cold sweat.

She set the miniature spear aside. "We won't be needing that, I don't think."

Thank God.

In the last few hours, he'd called upon God more than he had in his entire life.

"Did he leave behind a wife? Children?" Sympathy creased the edges of her eyes. "So tragic when death strikes someone so young."

"No, a betrothed in a . . . delicate condition." No need for her to tell him his cheeks glowed.

Why did discussing pregnancy turn even the most stalwart of men into stammering milksops?

"Oh, dear. That's most unfortunate. Whatever will she do?" Blaike hadn't judged harshly, as most would a woman in that situation, but instead had shown compassion.

Should he tell her?

She might as well know, so she could tell Blaire, since it was possible Drake would've made a decision by the time they reached London. The next time any of them saw him, he might well be married.

"The last I heard, Drake—*ever the noble chap*—was considering, albeit reluctantly, taking his brother's place. That way the child, if a son, could claim his rightful inheritance."

Blaike's face fell, and she dropped her gaze to the floor, but not before he saw the devastation for her twin in her eyes. "That is very benevolent of him."

"He's a true gentleman, to be sure."

Drake was considering marrying to protect the reputation and lineage of a child that wasn't his, while Oliver's own titled father had never once offered *Mamma* marriage. Bitterness Oliver had striven to dispel for years coiled 'round his belly.

Not for himself; he didn't want anything from Willoughby.

But his mother had loved him until she drew her last breath. Even as a small child he knew she adored Willoughby. Dangerous to love like that. It warped common sense and reason.

Shut up, he ordered his morose thoughts.

Ruminating on the past only tainted the future. Instead, he concentrated on the alluring woman in his quarters. Much more pleasurable and certainly not likely to be repeated on another voyage.

Blaike resumed puttering about, talking to herself every now and again.

He ticked his mouth upward.

What a delight she was.

M'Lady Lottie must've finally gone to sleep. He cringed to think how Blaike would react if she heard the bird's most flamboyant phrases. It might be a good idea to teach Lottie some new, less unsavory quotes, as Hawkins had advised.

"Here, Oliver."

Dragging his eyelids upward, he found Blaike hovering over him, her small bosoms, stained with his blood, dangerously close to his face.

What had he done to deserve this torment?

Hawkins would, no doubt, have an opinion as to that.

With determination that would've made a monk proud, Oliver averted his avid attention. He forced his gaze to stay above her chin.

Blaike held a tumbler filled with a generous portion of brandy. "I've decided you should have something for the pain while I tend you. I'm sure it will still hurt, but perhaps a little less."

Anything to numb his raging senses.

He gulped the strong spirit down, and the next glass too. He welcomed the burning in his belly, and even more the languid warmth spreading through his veins.

No. What he welcomed more than anything was Blaike's sweet touch upon his naked flesh.

"I'm in your capable hands, *cara mio.*"

"*Cara mio?*" She gave him a perplexed look. "Is that Italian? What does it mean?"

"It is. My mother and grandfather spoke Italian at home, and naturally, I learned to as well." Oliver didn't answer the second question since he had no right to call her by any endearment. He raised her hand to his mouth and kissed the knuckles, sanitation be hanged. "I trust you."

*A proper lady is at no time honor-bound to keep a
depraved secret nor compelled to reveal a joyous one.
~Scruples and Scandals-The Genteel Lady's Guide to Practical Living*

8

Hours later, Blaike pressed the back of her hand against Oliver's cool forehead.

He didn't feel hot, but what if he developed a fever?

She hadn't considered that possibility. Keeping the wound sterile had been her chief concern. Other than to wash him down with cool water, she had no idea how to treat a fever.

Heat skated up her cheeks at the notion of bathing his nakedness, and she pressed her hands to her face as she spun away from him.

Her gaze fell on the volume Mr. Grover had brought up with the medical chest.

Surely the book mentioned how to treat fevers.

Her panic subsided, and as she studied one of Oliver's drawings, she finished eating the dried plum she'd been nibbling.

Mr. Hawkins had brought up a tray hours earlier.

Simple fair: Bread, cheese, cold meat, fruit, and tea.

She'd enjoyed every bite, until she remembered Oliver's growling stomach before she dosed him with brandy. The laudanum hadn't been necessary, but now she fretted that maybe she shouldn't have allowed him to sleep until they knew for certain he hadn't been concussed.

Thrashing about in his agitation, he mumbled in his sleep again.

Something about Abraham.

A history existed between those two, she'd vow. Something ugly from the extreme animosity they held for each other.

Yawning, she glanced around Oliver's quarters again.

Only one lamp remained lit on the desk.

When she'd returned from changing her gown and looking in on Blaire, fast asleep in her berth, she found Mr. Hawkins had put the lights out. He'd also tucked Oliver beneath the bedclothes after removing his boots, straightened the cabin, and removed the bloody cloths and clothing.

A true gem, was Mr. Hawkins.

She'd wager not every first mate tended to his captain as if he were his son.

M'Lady Lottie occasionally made little chirping noises, but hadn't screamed anymore blush-worthy expressions.

Arching her back, Blaike stretched her arms overhead. Lord, she was exhausted.

The ship's gentle, rhythmic rocking revealed they'd left *Port de Lyon*.

She'd scarcely paid attention to the shouting and other noises above deck as the crew prepared to weigh anchor. Her entire focus had centered on treating Oliver's wound. It wasn't as deep as she'd first feared, and surely a man as young and strong *and virile*, as he would make a quick recovery.

When another large strand of hair slipped loose from its pins, she blew out a frustrated sigh. Might as well unpin the whole mass then.

Using the looking glass attached to Oliver's washstand, Blaike removed the pins. She tried running her fingers through the length, but encountered several snarls. Upon spying his hairbrush, she boldly snatched it up, then returned to her chair positioned beside his bed.

His black, slightly wavy locks sharply contrasted with the white pillow. The ribbon tying his hair had gone missing on the way to the ship. She rather liked his shoulder length mane. It fit the dashing, pirate image she'd first formed about him.

A romantic at heart, she'd secretly harbored girlish fancies since meeting him at her very first *le beau monde* gathering.

Oliver would fall passionately in love with her and whisk her away on his ship, she fantasized. They'd sail around the world, visiting exotic places, happy as grigs. And when the children came along—three, no make that four—he'd gladly forfeit his carefree life. They'd settle on a cozy farm in the country; perhaps raise sheep or dairy cattle.

Yes, he'd be the buccaneer turned gentleman farmer.

That was before she'd seen his drawings though. He'd never be content planting corn or herding sheep.

She skewed her mouth into a slight pout.

That wasn't the life she craved either—except for that part about sailing from port to port. She'd perish from tedium on a farm, but neither did living an idle life in London, flitting from once social assembly to another, appeal.

Why Blaike was so discontent, she didn't know.

If the world were a fair place, and women weren't considered inferior to men, she'd attend university. Become a scholar or a barrister or a politician. Maybe even a physician or a ship's navigator. Now those careers sounded exciting, and she'd be able to use her intellect, mayhap learn several other languages, too.

Although, vernaculars didn't seem her strong-suit.

Of course, children would be lovely, but she wanted more from life than darning socks, baking pastries, endless needlework, and wiping adorable turned-up noses.

This dissatisfaction had grown since she left Esherton Green. At times such frustration overwhelmed her, she wanted to rail at the injustice. To do so would be futile; she and Blaire had already been given more opportunity than most women.

As Blaike watched the even rise and fall of Oliver's chest, she ran the brush through her hair. She'd always found the action soothing, and soon, drowsiness engulfed her. Oh, to be in her comfortable, sparse bedroom at Esherton, tucked beneath her worn quilt. Life at Esherton hadn't been easy, but it had been safe.

Sedate. Predictable.

And boring as aged, snoozing cats.

She closed her eyes, and allowed her head to droop to her chest. Sleep beckoned, but she feared leaving Oliver, and other than Hawkins, commanding the ship at present, she didn't trust anyone else to watch him.

"Blaike."

She jerked her head up. "Yes, Oliver?"

He slept on, but she touched his brow again just to be sure it wasn't hot.

What agitated him so that even after drinking nearly three full tumblers of brandy on an empty stomach, he muttered in his sleep?

If he hadn't intervened on her and Blaire's behalf, he wouldn't be injured.

A shudder rippled down her spine, and she swallowed.

Thank heavens he'd come along, or at this moment, instead of anticipating a joyful homecoming, she and her twin would be sailing to a horrific fate. Blaike would've thrown herself into the ocean before enduring a lifetime as a sex slave.

Utter nonsense his vowing he deserved to be shot. Meunier was the one who'd earned a hole in his shoulder. Oliver judged himself too harshly.

Yawning again, she wistfully eyed the big bed while setting the hairbrush on the night table anchored to the floor.

Did she dare?

Why not?

There was plenty of room. No one would know, save she.

Fully dressed, except for her half-boots, of course, she'd rest beside Oliver, and if he stirred, she'd be right there. No one could suggest anything untoward had occurred. How could it possibly anyway, when he was injured? For certain his crew would be grateful that their captain was so well cared for.

True, she shouldn't be in his quarters unchaperoned, but neither should she and Blaire have traveled from Geneva without a companion.

Once Blaike had settled herself comfortably—beneath the coverlet, yet atop the other bedding—she closed her eyes. Taking care not to bump Oliver or wake him as he softly snored, she relaxed into the pillows with a long sigh.

Her mind turned to the worry that had plagued her for days now.

"How am I going to explain why we left Geneva?"

"Why did you?"

Oliver's whispered question almost had Blaike tumbling off the bed. She turned her head to study him, his dear face mere inches from hers.

He was awake now and not talking in his sleep.

"Oh, Oliver, I didn't mean to waken you." She touched his chest, almost yanking her hand away as little sparks of sensation where she'd encountered crisp hair skittered all the way up her arm. "Do you hurt? There's laudanum—"

"No. The pain is bearable." After staring at her hand for a long moment, he entwined his fingers with hers, then cast the cage a fleeting glance. Her skin was so pale beside his tanned flesh. "If we keep our voices down, M'Lady mightn't awake yet."

"And squawk something else embarrassing?" Blaike whispered.

"Exactly. What time is it?" He shifted to look out a window. "We're underway?"

She lifted a shoulder. "I'm not certain of the time. Early morning I should think, and yes, we've been underway for a while. I'm sorry I woke you." She apologized again.

"You didn't. I habitually awake and rise early." Oliver glanced around his cabin before his scrutiny came to rest upon her. He gave her fingers a little squeeze. The gesture comforting and natural.

"What has you so tormented, Blaike?"

Perhaps it was exhaustion; or shock from the terrifying encounter with Captain Abraham; or relief that Oliver hadn't slipped into unconsciousness; or simply the need to tell someone what she'd stuffed into a dark, remote niche and feared to utter, but tears leaked from her eyes.

The hot drop trailed over her cheeks, slowly at first, then ever more swiftly.

She turned her face away and tried to extract her hand.

Rather than releasing her, Oliver pulled her nearer, urging her to lay her head in the crook of his uninjured arm.

"Come, *dolcezza*. I still have one good shoulder you can cry on."

His voice had the merest slur. The effects of the liquor or sleepiness? Pray not his head injury.

The temptation proved too great.

With a ragged sob, she yielded. One arm wrapping around his waist, she folded into his side and pressed her face into his strong, wonderful smelling flesh.

"*Cara mia*," he murmured into her hair. "Sometimes the telling of secrets sets one free."

She shook her head. "Not in my case. I'm afraid I'm ruined, Oliver."

He stiffened for an instant.

Shocked by her admission?

Then how could she tell him the whole sordid account?

He pressed his mouth to the top of her head and ran his strong fingers through her hair. The caress soothed as well as stimulated. A dangerous combination.

"I cannot fathom such a thing. Tell me what has happened, and we'll contrive a solution."

Blaike couldn't bear to look at him. To see the disgust or accusation in his eyes. With her face still tucked into the corner of his shoulder, she whispered, "I was foolish and gullible."

The words came forth, one painful utterance at a time. While he simply nodded or made comforting sounds, the awful story spilled from her lips.

"I suspected something sinister was afoot, almost since we arrived at *Les Dames de l'Académie de Grâce*. But everyone was so closed-mouthed. Afraid to speak their suspicions. Far too many gentleman were invited to dine with us, to join us for musicals, to play cards or charades, or to attend dances at the academy for my peace of mind. Often male guests would disappear half-way through the evening, sometimes reappearing, but usually not."

"You think the school is a front for something else?"

Even his breath warming her scalp brought succor to her harrowed soul.

"I'm convinced it is. There were women there, in another house, who never attended lessons. Supposedly, they were former students who'd accepted offers of employment from Madame Beaulieu. Seamstresses, milliners, lace-makers, that sort of thing. We were told they did so because their schooling had ended, and they didn't want to go home. Or else their tuitions hadn't been paid, and Madame demanded compensation."

Blaike rubbed at her wet cheeks, then took the edge of the sheet and dried her face before dabbing Oliver's damp shoulder.

"I'm sorry. I've soaked you." She turned onto her side, and after sweeping her hair out of the way, pulled a pillow beneath her head.

He grasped a handful of her hair and brought it to his face. He closed his eyes and brushed his cheek. "I adore your hair. I've never seen any lovelier. Moonbeams and stars and silver and fairy sparkles and all sorts of wondrous things must've been used to create the color."

"Fairy sparkles, *hmm*? I rather like that, I think."

Quite the romantic, wasn't he? Another lovely thing about her swashbuckler.

His hair, on the other hand, was midnight black. So dark that it appeared almost blue in some light. Tilting her head upward, she asked, "Are you sure I'm not causing your other shoulder pain?"

Oliver's mouth tipped into a tender smile. Dark stubble shadowed his neck and cheeks above and below his tidy beard.

She found the bristles quite enticing.

"I'm fine, and a few tears aren't likely to harm me. I'm made neither of salt nor sugar, so it's unlikely I'll melt." He chuckled, that wondrous deep rumble, and moved his hand to her back, brushing his fingertips up and down her spine. "About your concerns at the academy. Not exactly forthright of the headmistress, but I don't know that she did anything illegal, *cara*."

"That's what I thought at first, as well. Until a pattern emerged. A girl would attend supper when we had male guests. However, the next day, we'd be told she'd departed or chosen to enter Madame Beaulieu's service." Blaike idly plucked at his coverlet, replaying those final days at the academy in her head.

"Then, a certain gentleman, Jonathon Severs, started paying marked attention to me. The headmistress kept pairing us at dinner, for the entertainment, and so on." Mouth turned down, she scrunched her nose in remembered disgust. "He was much too forward, making vulgar insinuations, touching me, and trying to get me alone. Blaire and I cried off attending functions, but if we didn't put in an appearance, we weren't fed. If it hadn't been for my sister's constant presence, I know not what might have happened."

"I thought you'd both lost weight. So this Madame Beaulieu basically used extortion to force you to cooperate with her matchmaking?" Though Oliver continued to gently caress her shoulders and back, rage tinged his mild inquiry.

"Yes. When we still resisted, she fabricated some codswollop about our tuition being tardy. I knew that to be a bald-faced lie. Heath paid the entire two years' room, board, and tuition in advance. He made sure Blaire and I knew that when he gave us pocket money for fripperies or fallalls. It's that money we'd hid away and used to hire the coach and pay for the inns when we fled the academy."

"But why did you have to flee? Couldn't you have written a letter home?"

"We—I—did. And Blythe responded that she'd made passage arrangements. That's why I first thought that you . . ." She cast him a swift glance, only discerning concern and interest in his ebony gaze.

"Anyway, the night we fled, I was foolhardy. I followed one of the new girls and a gentleman who'd often been Madame Beaulieu's guest out into the garden courtyard. I should've waited for Blaire to return from the necessary, but I was afraid for Maria. She was only fifteen.

The evening was too cold for a walk in the gardens, but a pathway led to the other house, and I feared that's where he meant to take her. I should've known it was a trap when Jacqueline Severs made a point of telling me Maria had been escorted outside."

Oliver stilled his caresses for a moment. "Another Severs? Related to Jonathon, I presume?"

Blaike nodded, drawing in a shaky breath.

"His sister, and every bit as evil as her brother. There's something distinctly off, truly queer, about those two." Even now, recalling what transpired next turned her skin to ice, made her flesh crawl, and she felt on the verge of casting up her simple dinner.

She shivered, and Oliver nudged her closer to his strong warmth.

"What happened?"

"I'd no sooner left the veranda, than Jonathon was upon me. Groping and pawing, tearing my gown."

Eyes pinched closed, she relived the terror.

"With one hand clamped over my mouth, he tried to drag me behind a row of shrubberies, but we Culpeppers are no small misses, except for Brette, that is. I fought him, but he managed to throw me to the ground. He—"

At the memory, she trembled head to toe.

"He climbed on top of me, and . . ."

A decorous lady holds fast and buries any secrets that can harm innocents, but readily share secrets which bring joy and happiness.
~Scruples and Scandals-The Genteel Lady's Guide to Practical Living

9

Blaike shuddered, once again experiencing the revulsion and terror. Oliver hugged her tightly to his chest and whispered fiercely, "I'll kill the cur if I ever come across him. I swear, I shall."

"I thought he was going to ravish me. I wanted to die."

"He . . . didn't?"

Did relief weight his question?

"Almost, but just before—"

She had to stop for a moment and take a calming breath.

Every time she thought of that night, she re-experienced the awfulness.

"His sister, Blaire, and Madame Beaulieu interrupted. "I don't know whether it was by chance or by design, but to everyone, it looked as though I'd been compromised. I fear if Blaire hadn't been there also, those other two might have let him finish."

Would've cheered him on, the depraved pair.

"I still feel so soiled."

"Blaike," Oliver nudged her chin upward until she met his tender gaze in the dimness. The lone lamp's weak glow added an almost romantic aura to the great cabin. "You were the victim of what I'm quite confident is an ongoing scheme to despoil women and force them into prostitution. You were only trying to help Maria."

"I was, and it makes me ill that I don't know what became of her. If indeed she was even outside that evening." She stared at the overhead beams. "We should've left the academy and alerted the authorities as soon as we suspected something afoul was taking place. But everyone at home was so proud of us. And such a vile accusation needed absolute proof. We didn't trust Madame Beaulieu not to concoct some plausible excuse either."

He folded her into his embrace once more.

Nothing before had ever felt as effortless or right.

Oliver might not be of noble birth or be able to list prestigious universities he attended, but he was an honorable, decent man. She'd take that over the other characteristics in a heartbeat.

He spoke into her hair. "You'll have to tell your family, *bella*. Madame Beaulieu mustn't be allowed to continue."

"I know." And she would, as soon as they reached London. Oliver was right. Madame Beaulieu must be stopped. A wonder her duplicity had gone undetected this long. How many innocent girls had met their ruin at the academy?

M'Lady Lottie ruffled her feathers, making a throaty, purring sound, and Blaike held her breath lest the bird start her shattering screaming. After a moment, when the cockatoo remained quiet, she relaxed.

Oliver shifted slightly, his firm thigh bumping hers and causing a fascinating jolt to streak up her leg.

"I'm curious." He smothered a yawn. "How is it this Miss Severs escaped the same destiny as the others?"

Blaike pondered his question for several long moments.

Yes, just how had Jacqueline escaped that fate?

"I suspect she and her brother must've been co-collaborators with Madame Beaulieu." A yawn forced its way past her lips as well, and overcome with drowsiness, she burrowed deeper into his sculpted side.

"Might I ask you a question, too, Oliver?"

He moved his head a touch, making a drowsy, affirmative noise.

Did she dare?

It wasn't her business, and she didn't want him to think she was poking her nose into something that concerned only him. That was exactly what she was doing, though.

"I suspect there's deep animosity between you and Captain Abraham that goes beyond what he wanted to do with Blythe and I."

He went rigid.

"*Cara mia*, that's a statement, not a question."

Eyes remaining shut, Oliver ran his fingertips the length of her arm from shoulder to elbow, then back again. He cracked an eyelid, and gave her an undecipherable look, then sighed, his reluctance tangible.

The ship's gentle swaying had lulled Blaike half-asleep.

"Never mind. I shouldn't have asked." She settled a jot deeper into her pillow. How easy it would be to slumber here. "You need to rest in any event."

"I don't mind telling you. The tale's ugly, however."

Oliver paused for such an extended moment, she believed he'd changed his mind.

Finally, he exhaled a long, troubled breath.

"When I was thirteen, I came home one evening from delivering a letter to a ship's captain for my *nonno*—my grandfather. I discovered him dead beside his desk, a wicked ivory-handled dagger protruding from his chest."

Blaike couldn't prevent her distressed half-cry, half gasp.

Why had she asked? Snooped into Oliver's personal affairs?

He needed to recover, not have old emotions and trauma stirred once more. Particularly those caused by the spawn of Satan now locked in Lyon's jail.

"A man—Abraham—was tearing the place apart." Oliver stared overhead, as if seeing the horrific scene again. "The contents of the shelves and desk drawers were strewn all over the floor, and he'd even yanked drawings and signs from the walls. I thought him a burglar. Determined to kill him for murdering *Nonno*, I jumped on his back. Using the scrimshaw knife my grandfather had gifted me at Christmastide, I slashed his face."

So that was how the cur acquired his scar.

"I'm so sorry, Oliver. It must've been horrible and tragic for you, and I overstepped when I asked." She pressed her flattened hand to his chest, his strong heartbeat pulsing against her palm. "Please, you needn't tell me anymore. I see how painful it is for you."

He tightened his fingers on her arm for a second. "I haven't talked to anyone about that night."

Her heart gave a queer skip.

Was he doing so now because he felt as safe and comfortable with her as she did with him?

"I was a skinny, undersized waif, and he shook me off like a week-old kitten attacking a boarhound. When I landed, I hit my head on the corner of the desk," Oliver pointed at his L-shaped hairline scar, "and was knocked senseless."

"Dear God," she breathed, stricken by Abraham's evilness.

"You'll think I'm dicked in the nob, Blaike, but I swear I was roused by my mother calling my name, over and over."

"I don't think that's fanciful at all, Oliver. There's much in this world that cannot be explained."

A rough sound, part grunt, part confirmation, echoed in the back of his throat. "Flames were already climbing the front walls when I came to. I'm convinced Abraham knocked the lamp over deliberately. Fires always follow in his wake."

Jaw slack, she jerked her head up. "He meant to kill you too, the fiend!"

"Apparently." He sounded more resigned than weary or angry.

"But why, Oliver? What does he have against you? Or your grandfather?"

A few strands of his surprisingly silky hair tickled her nose, and she brushed them away. Then balled her hand against the temptation to press her lips to the pulse ticking in his corded neck.

A swell lifted the ship, and she rolled a smidgeon closer to him. She didn't bother scooting away.

"That, *cara*, is something I've asked myself for half my life now. And I'm no closer to an answer than I was that night. Unless he truly was a thief and after the contents of the desk's hidden drawer, though there wasn't a whole lot there. I managed to collect *Mamma*'s jewelry—just emerald and diamond embedded hair combs and a matching pendant, ring, and earrings. I was always fascinated with them as a child."

He gazed into the distance as if seeing another time and place. "She was so beautiful wearing them. Right before she died, she said I should gift the parure set to my wife."

"How did she die?" It was brazen of Blaike to ask. "I lost my parents in a carriage accident."

"Childbirth. Another son. He only lived a few hours. My sire—Viscount Willoughby—insisted on paying for the burial costs."

"Oh."

Bitterness deepened Oliver's voice when he mentioned his father, and Blaike wasn't about to poke that wound, too.

The subject was understandably difficult for him.

He cleared his throat. "Before escaping out the back door, I also grabbed a few of *Nonno*'s drawings as well as the rest of the secret drawer's contents. There wasn't much. Only a leather-bound packet containing documents and letters written in Italian and a small bag of coins."

Tears blurred Blaike's vision. Oliver truly might've died.

No wonder he despised Captain Abraham.

"That money is what I used to survive until I convinced a captain to hire me on as a cabin boy, even though I was really too old for the position. On this very ship, as a matter of fact. I keep the jewelry, packet, and the drawings in a secret compartment in my chest's false bottom." He flicked a calloused finger toward the end of the bed where the trunk sat and, yawning, shifted his legs again.

"Do you know what the documents are?" If his grandfather kept them hidden with money and gems, might they be valuable or important?

"No. I don't read Italian, and moreover, a sailor doesn't have coin enough to spare to hire a reputable fellow to translate them. So I've never had them interpreted."

"Had I been you, my curiosity would've nearly killed me, not knowing what they said." She'd never been altogether patient with puzzles or riddles.

He twisted his mouth up on one side. "I figured if they were truly important, *Nonno* would've told me about them. I've only even glanced at them once or twice. They still smell of smoke and the memories of that night—"

She rushed to change the subject. "So it was just you and your grandfather then?"

Here they lay, chatting in hushed tones like intimate friends—*or lovers*—as if it hadn't been months since they'd last seen or spoken to each other. It seemed like yesterday they'd last spoke, so comfortable and contented was Blaike.

"Yes. My mother died when I was seven."

"I cannot conceive how hard that was for you." He must've been such a lonely child. "My sisters and I, our cousins too, lost our parents, but we had one another. I imagine you were very close to your grandfather then."

"Practically inseparable, except for the almost three years that I attended Eton. That was Willoughby's inflexible demand."

Ah, so that's why he disdained the man.

Oliver rubbed his nose, his mouth twisted into a cynical line. "I'm sure a few pockets were heavily lined for granting him the favor. I wasn't well received, being younger than the average chap in attendance and a by-blow to boot. Even children look down their well-bred noses at those born on the wrong side of the blanket."

Cruising over the waves, the ship echoed with creaks and the whoosh of the ship's bow meeting the ocean. Blaike found the subtle sounds relaxing, though an occasional bang from above or a resounding grate interrupted her reverie.

"It wasn't any fault of yours, Oliver. And look what you've accomplished." She waggled her fingers in the air to indicate the *Sea Gypsy*. "Quite remarkable, I'd say, for someone so young."

"I'll be eight and twenty in a few days, *cara*. I did meet Drake at Eton. We became fast friends at once."

A wicked chuckle shook his broad chest and quirked his mouth into that rapscallion grin she found so irresistible.

"I cannot count the number of instances he came to my defense," Oliver said. "Even planting a few good facers on my behalf. The last time, he broke Chatterley's squat nose, and Drake was sent down for good." Rubbing between his eyebrows, he exhaled a deep breath. "So, I ran away. Home to *Nonno.*"

"And your father, the viscount? How did he take the news?"

Blaike's cousin, Brooke, had explained Oliver's circumstances when they'd first met him, and he'd proven himself an exemplary gentleman. She'd done so to remind the girls not to judge someone because of their birth or station in life.

Sternness sharpened his face. "He arrived at *Nonno's* office in his fancy coach, the Willoughby gold and blue coat of arms gleaming proud and bold against the glossy black paint. Every bit the nobleman accustomed to having his way, he ordered me back to school."

Oliver affected a lofty air and voice raised disdainfully, announced in a pretentious accent, "'The men in our family have always attended Eton until they go to university. I expect the same of you, young Oliver. Most especially since your instructors tell me you have an extraordinary talent for recall.'"

He shut his eyes once more, his derisive snort loud in the still cabin. "As if he had any right to tell me what to do."

Actually, the viscount could be admired for acknowledging his illegitimate son and sponsoring his education. But now wasn't the time to tell Oliver that, nor had she the right. Blaike had no idea how she'd feel if she'd been the illegitimate offspring of a noble. "But you didn't go?"

"I told him to bugger himself, for which *Nonno* made me apologize, and then he agreed to allow me to visit Willoughby thrice a year for a fortnight each time." Chin jutted, he squinted his eyes, appearing very much the intractable child. "*That* punishment far exceeded my offense."

"It seems to me your father wanted a relationship with you. Perhaps wanted to make amends for . . ."

Oliver speared her a sharp look.

Now she'd waded into it, bringing up that indelicacy. She cleared her throat. "What were they like? Your visits, I mean?"

"Willoughby was always thoughtful and kind, as were my half-brother and sisters. I cannot fault any of them in that regard." He scratched his nose as the call of a lone gull sounded. "Even now, I often receive invitations to one affair or another they are hosting. I never attend."

Someday she'd ask him why, but not today.

His last three words ended that thread of conversation as succinctly as if he'd said, "Mind your own business."

"What did he mean by your talent?" Pulling the coverlet over her shoulder, she also closed her eyes.

"I can see something once and remember it with great precision and detail." The revelation seemed more pained than proud.

It didn't take someone terribly astute to recognize the subject bothered Oliver. Though he'd answered her initial question, he'd raised numerous more. That discussion would have to take place later. He could scarcely keep his eyes open.

"Shut yer mouth." M'Lady Lottie muttered crankily. "Blasted dillberry maker."

"Oh dear. We've roused your cross bird." Blaike held her breath, hoping Lottie would go back to sleep. After a handful of minutes, when the cockatoo didn't say anything more, she relaxed.

Oliver had closed his eyes again, pain pinching the corners of his strong mouth.

Her hatred for Abraham rivaled that of hers for Jonathon Severs. Appalled and a mite frightened at the fury engulfing her, she pursed her lips. "I'd say you have good reason to despise Abraham. I hope he never gets out of jail." She raised up a few inches, and searched Oliver's wan face. Her curiosity demanded satisfaction.

"Why didn't he get punished for what he did?"

Oliver's eyes remained closed as he answered, fatigue etched in every word. "Years later when I learned his identity, I tried to have charges brought against him. Too much time had passed. And besides, the authorities said it was my word against his."

If he'd been a powerful lord, with coin to toss in their direction, they'd have acted, she'd be bound. "What do you think he was after?"

The edges of his eyes creased as he considered her question. "I honestly have no idea."

He fell silent, likely lost in disagreeable memories.

That'd teach her to pry in the future. Nevertheless, she'd learned much about this fascinating man, none of which shocked or dismayed her. If anything, what she'd discovered made her admire him more. He'd overcome much.

With a resigned little huff, she pressed two fingers just over the bridge of her nose.

"I really should go, Oliver. I've delayed far too long. This is most inappropriate."

He'd keep this breech of decorum to himself, she didn't doubt. Oliver wasn't the type to toss confidences of this nature about. And she'd be bound, he'd tuck away for safekeeping what she revealed about Madame Beaulieu and the Severs until she was ready to tell all.

Still, her limbs weighted with fatigue and uncustomary serenity, she made no effort to rise.

"Oliver?" she mumbled against the marble wall of his chest.

Deep, even breathing revealed he'd fallen asleep once more.

Good. He'd find respite from those dreadful recollections.

Blaike ought to leave, but she hadn't been this content in a long while. Sighing, she snuggled closer, inhaling the scent that was uniquely him. She'd indulge a short while longer, for this opportunity surely wouldn't be repeated.

"*Ti amo*, Blaike," he mumbled. "I love you."

How many treasures have been lost or lives
ruined from a careless slip of the tongue? A secret worth
keeping is a secret worth guarding, whether yours or another's.
~Scruples and Scandals-The Genteel Lady's Guide to Practical Living

10

"Grab yer ankles, wench."

Oliver bolted upright, and agony exploded in his shoulder and head.

"Holy God," he gasped, pressing his good hand to the pigeon egg-sized lump near his temple. He didn't know which was worse: his gut-wrenching hangover or the skull-cracking pain stabbing his noggin.

"Lord help me," he groaned, though it sounded more like a strangled croak than a prayer.

Would Hawkins chastise him for using the Lord's name in vain or praise him for a pathetic attempt at supplication?

M'Lady Lottie screeched loud enough to crack the beams again.

Only respect for McMaster kept Oliver from selling the annoying creature to the first street peddler who made an offer. That, and he knew Lottie would die from a broken heart. He couldn't be that cruel, despite her being a major inconvenience.

Her cage rattled violently. "Twattling peg-puff!"

"Lottie! Shut up."

He lowered his legs over the edge of the bed, his mind still sleep-befuddled.

"Shut yer trap. Shut yer trap." Furious flapping ensued, then angry banging. "I want out."

"Give me a minute." Having a bird her size careening about his quarters wasn't ideal, but when he took her topside, she loved to perch either on the poop deck's taffrail or the crow's nest. After climbing the rigging, she'd screech foul expletives and sexual innuendos, much to the crew's amusement.

Just then, his memory came crashing back, as forcefully as the cannon fire exploding in his head.

Blaike.

He tensed, then cautiously looked behind him.

No gorgeous, blue-eyed vixen lay there. He almost picked up the pillow and sniffed it to see if it smelled of vanilla to make sure she'd ever lain beside him.

Maybe he'd dreamed she'd been cradled in his arms when he fell asleep again.

He hadn't imagined her torrid tale of why she'd fled Geneva.

Anger, fierce and scorching sluiced through him. Severs better hope he never encountered Oliver. Or Ravensdale or Leventhorpe for that matter. All three possessed black tempers when it came to protecting their own.

Except Blaike wasn't Oliver's to protect.

Didn't matter.

In his heart she was and always would be.

He'd teach Severs a lesson he wouldn't soon forget.

"Ol-eeve? Ol-eeve?"

More irritated clanging resounded from within the cage. "Move yer arse."

"It's Ol-i-ver. And I am moving my arse, as you so crudely put it."

He quirked his mouth upward on one side. Now he was carrying on conversations with temperamental birds? M'Lady Lottie had started using his name, too. Well, her version of it. Perchance, that meant she was adjusting to McMaster's death.

Oliver squinted out the small wooden-framed panes.

The sun wasn't too terribly high, so he hadn't slept the day away. So much for seeing the *Sea Gypsy* on her way, however. Nonetheless, he'd spoken the truth when he'd said his crew was capable of sailing the ship without him. He couldn't ask for more reliable or skilled men, with one exception.

Fairnly.

Maybe Oliver would hire a cabin boy to look after M'Lady Lottie. He had to hire a surgeon anyway. A lad would like that assignment. He would've when he first took to sea. London had plenty of unfortunate lads who would leap at the chance to have a place to rest their head each night and a full belly, to boot.

Yes, that might be the answer to the bird he'd inherited and didn't have the heart to get rid of. He knew what it was like to have the only person who loved you die and leave you alone, homeless, and dependent on others.

With extreme caution, so as to not aggravate his pulsating shoulder or risk dislodging his head from his neck, he shuffled to M'Lady Lottie's cage. Once he'd pulled the quilt off, he unlatched the door, and she flew out.

After circling the stateroom thrice, she landed on her perch and proceeded to groom herself. One foot in the air, reminding him of some the less decorous things she'd witnessed in her former life, she trained her burgundy-brown eyes on him. "Go outside?"

"Yes, when I've dressed." He'd forego his shave today. His hammering head couldn't even take Hawkins's gentle razor strokes.

Resting his hands on either side of the mahogany washstand, Oliver examined his shoulder in the looking glass. A neat bandage wrapped across his chest and around his back. Blaike had done remarkably well for her first attempt, and pride as well as appreciation blossomed behind his breastbone.

No hysteria, fainting, or weeping. Just cool composure, even though she hadn't known what she was doing. She was one strong woman, and by far, one of the most intelligent he'd ever met.

After splashing his face with water and brushing what tasted like burnt peat from his teeth, he tossed a towel over his unharmed shoulder and reached for his hairbrush. Only it wasn't in its usual place. Slowly scrutinizing his quarters, his gaze came to rest on his night table.

Breaking into a wide grin, he retrieved it.

Wasn't this interesting?

Amongst the boar bristles lay several silky, white strands. Blaike had used his brush. Such an intimate, domesticated thing to do. He couldn't erase his much-too-pleased grin.

"Outside!" M'Lady Lottie shrieked.

Would he ever become accustomed to her screams?

Oliver finished dressing, not without muttering several curses and getting his sore arm stuck for a minute. Now he understood why men had valets. With some care, he added a vest, a belt at his waist, but gave up trying to tie his hair back. Lastly, he drew on his boots, again uttering several colorful phrases that made M'Lady Lottie's language seem almost chaste.

Giving a short whistle, he held out his uninjured arm, and at once, she swept from her perch and landed on his forearm where he secured a strap to her ankle, lest she try to fly away. With clipped wings, she wouldn't get far, but he still fretted that she might end up in the ocean.

"Let's go, M'lady. I have a mind to see how my crew and passengers fare."

More on point, a particular captivating passenger.

He grabbed his hat from its hook beside the door and crammed it on his head as he made his way along the narrow passageway.

Once topside, he took a moment to survey his ship before seeing to feeding the cockatoo. In vivid blue and unexpectedly smooth waters, the *Sea Gypsy* flew along, the wind filling her sails, and leaving *Port de Lyon*, far behind them.

Excellent.

That placed them that much farther out of Abraham's reach. He'd seek the revenge he vowed, and Oliver must get the Culpeppers to London without delay. The day was soon coming that either he or Abraham would not walk away from an encounter with one another.

On deck, Oliver inhaled the tangy sea air, bearing the merest hint of salt and fish, deep into his lungs.

His crew oiled the masts, repaired rigging or sails, or went about the dozens of other tasks required of a clipper. Men nodded, waving or calling hello as he passed. To a man, they appeared relieved to see him up and about.

"Good to see you, Cap'n." Hawkins trotted across the deck, three deep furrows ridging his forehead. "How are you feelin'?"

"Like I've been run over by a frigate and hungry as a hog. Although too much brandy last night has my stomach a mite wobbly."

He glanced at the sails, noted the bright sky strewn with a few feathery clouds, then satisfied all was at it should be, ran a hand down M'Lady Lottie's chest.

"Lottie luv," she chirruped before scampering up his arm and cuddling close to his good shoulder.

To his credit, Hawkins kept a straight face. "Your Miss Culpepper is yonder."

He pointed to the poop deck.

Blaike, enshrouded in a hooded emerald cloak, chatted gaily with Melville. He appeared to be showing her how to knot two pieces of rope. Whatever men had not become smitten on the first voyage would likely fall under her spell this crossing. Then, she'd have the entire lot wrapped around her dainty little finger.

"She's not my Miss Culpepper." Though Oliver did like the sound of it.

Still, it wouldn't do for the hands to get the wrong impression. As much as he wished it otherwise, there could never be anything between him and Blaike. For her sake. It wouldn't do for any sort of speculative tattle to start either. Seldom could inaccurate gossip or secrets ever be fully snuffed.

"As you say, Cap'n." His voice quivering with suppressed humor, Hawkins yanked his bright orange and red knitted cap lower over his elfin ears. "She hasn't broken her fast, either. Should I bring a tray up? I think she'd enjoy eatin' in the open. The weather's most pleasant, and you could share a picnic—"

"A picnic?" Just what was his first mate about? Oliver cocked a brow, and M'Lady took the opportunity to nip his ear. "Ouch, you she-devil. What was that for?"

"Her way of givin' you a kiss." Hawkins chuckled while pulling his earlobe. "She used to groom McMaster's hair and even peck his lips."

Oliver drew the line there. Not the least bit sanitary.

Besides, he didn't trust the cantankerous bird not to pierce his lip or gouge an eye. He gently moved her back to his forearm. McMaster had been much too lenient with the cockatoo, giving her time and attention Oliver, as captain, simply couldn't spare.

Maybe what she needed was a mate.

And have *two* of the noisy, demanding beasts on board?

Oliver would have to think long and hard on that.

His attention strayed to Blaike again.

She nodded and deftly twisted the ropes into what appeared to be a rolling hitch, though he couldn't be certain from this distance.

"Where's Miss Blaire?"

"The poor lass ails from seasickness." Hawkins waved his rough hand toward the fairly calm water. "I hate to think how she'll suffer if the weather turns petulant."

It likely would. If not in the Mediterranean, then almost certainly in The Bay of Biscay.

Hawkins shifted his feet and scratched his neck whilst sending Blaike a speculative glance. "About that picnic—"

"Fine." Oliver conceded, happy to seize any excuse to spend time with Blaike. "Have simple fare prepared. Bread, porridge, boiled eggs, tea for Miss Culpepper and my usual spiced coffee should suffice."

He didn't think he could get anything else down, despite his empty stomach's gurgles and growls.

The fresh, albeit chilly wind, did much to clear his head, though did nothing for the constant thrum in his shoulder. Oliver made his way to the poop deck, mindful not to jostle his wound. "Good morning."

Blaike whipped around, and a becoming pink tinged her high cheekbones. "Good morning. How did you sleep?" A slight crease pulling her fair brows together, she dropped her gaze to his shoulder. "Did the bandages cause you any discomfort? You're not feverish or bleeding?"

"No fever or bleeding, and I slept well, which is why I'm so late rising."

No, he was late rising because he drank too much and a certain blonde siren had made herself comfortable in his bed, luring him back to slumber.

He couldn't recall the last time he'd yielded to the temptation to fall back to sleep. It just showed how much Blaike affected him. He'd best watch himself, or he'd find his well-laid plans tumbling bow over stern.

"Hawkins tells me you haven't broken your fast either, so he suggested we share a tray here. The weather may not hold, and when it turns, it won't be safe for you to come above." Why was Oliver rambling on, making excuses? Just ask her if she wanted to eat with him.

"I've only been up for a short while myself." The merest smudge of purplish-blue half circles shadowed her lower lashes. She pulled her cloak tighter, and smiled at M'Lady Lottie. "Poor Blaire finally drifted to sleep, and I didn't dare eat in our cabin for fear she'd smell the food and begin retching again. I hoped to have ginger tea prepared for her. If you have any on board, that is."

A breeze wafted by, teasing the curls over her forehead.

"I honestly haven't the slightest idea whether we do or not, but I can have Hawkins ask Fairnly."

Melville chuckled when he saw the cockatoo still trying to cuddle Oliver. "Looks like she's taken to you, sir."

"Might I pet her?" Blaike turned an inquisitive gaze to Oliver. "She's lovely, isn't she? Sort of peach tinted all over."

"Except for her language," he agreed. "Which, I believe you've already heard."

"Yes. She has a most *colorful* repertoire." Blaike chuckled, a pleasant melodious sound.

"She needs to get to know you before she'll accept your touch." Oliver withdrew a piece of apple from M'Lady Lottie's cage. "Give her this."

M'Lady Lottie sidestepped down his arm, eager for the treat.

Blaike offered the fruit to the cockatoo, and M'Lady Lottie grasped it in her claws. "Tit over arse, she goes."

Rather than become offended, Blaike burst out laughing. "I had no idea a bird could learn so many words and phrases."

"You haven't heard her worst yet, I'm afraid." Oliver removed the strap from the cockatoo's foot, then set her on her perch, but left the door open.

"Won't she fly away?"

"No, her wings are clipped. But she'll climb every rope on this ship, given the chance. She's become stuck twice, too. I've had to rescue her, since she terrifies the rest of the crew."

M'Lady Lottie made a sound suspiciously like a person passing wind, followed by a loud burp. She bobbed her head as if proud of her achievements.

"Her talents are quite . . . erm . . . diverse, it seems." Blaike couldn't decide if she was more amused or appalled.

"Indeed." A boyish slant to his firm mouth, Oliver scratched his chin, then smoothed his beard. "Melville, can you find something to use as a makeshift table and seats for us?"

"Aye. Will crates do?"

Blaike nodded. "Yes, that would be perfect."

Another thing to admire about her.

Nothing pretentious or pompous about any of the Culpeppers, but Blaike seemed to genuinely not care about the niceties many of her station expected. Few ladies with her connections would be content to sit atop a turned over crate and dine with rough sailors milling about.

In short order, Melville had assembled their improvised dining area. M'Lady Lottie crawled up the outside of her cage after enjoying an assortment of treats, and Hawkins appeared with their tray.

He gave them a toothy smile and set their food on the box serving as their table. "Miss. Cap'n."

"Thank you." Oliver gave the lumpy porridge the once over with a dubious gaze. "Would you mind asking Fairnly if there's any ginger to make tea? It might help with Miss Blaire's *mal de mer*."

"Aye. Straightaway." Still grinning, and looking entirely too pleased with himself, he wandered away, whistling what Oliver knew to be a favored hymn.

After gracefully sinking onto a crate, Blaike draped a serviette on her lap.

"I was wondering if you'd teach me how to use those interesting instruments I saw on your desk?"

Gifted is the lady who knows what secrets to hold
fast in her heart and which mysteries are better off revealed.
~Scruples and Scandals-The Genteel Lady's Guide to Practical Living

11

Oliver went rigid.
Teach her?

M'Lady Lottie scampered down the side of her cage. "Cheeky wench," she said, erecting her coral-toned crest.

Showing off for Blaike, was she? Or jealous mayhap?

Blaike rotated to observe her.

"She almost seems to respond, doesn't she, Oliver?"

Did she realize she had addressed him by his given name again?

Yes, he was an intimate friend of her guardian and brother-in-law, but protocol should be observed. Nonetheless he found it incongruously pleasing that there was another area that she didn't regard as necessary. She was truly an original woman. Diamonds of the first water, her guardian had called the Culpeppers. But Blaike was more than an exquisite beauty. She possessed a brilliant mind, keen wit, and a charming sense of humor.

But then he already knew that about her.

Just one of the many reasons she intrigued and fascinated him. How was it possible to love someone so intensely, more with each passing day? Bewitched and besotted. That was what he'd become. And a hopeless, romantic fool.

Blaike, her head tilted at the adorable inquisitive angle that was hers alone, still waited for his response.

"Sometimes, I think she does understand and answers me. Or maybe she reacts to inflections in voices or certain words cue her responses. McMaster oft' boasted how intelligent she is, and he swore she conversed with him." Oliver swallowed a spoonful of gloppy, barely tepid porridge and shuddered.

Yes, seeking Fairnly's replacement took precedence when the *Sea Gypsy* docked in London.

Loathe to waste the food, he lifted another spoonful to his mouth. His stomach reacted rather violently to the globby mass.

Mayhap he should forgo breaking his fast until his belly had decided it wasn't going to toss the unappetizing contents onto the decking. Instead, Oliver poured himself a cup of coffee.

"Would you like to try a taste of my coffee?" He angled the pot toward her cup. "It's *caffè d'u parrinu*. An Italian specialty made with Arabic coffee flavored with cinnamon and cloves. I confess, I drink far too much of the brew."

He'd personally taught Fairnly how to make the beverage. Poorly prepared food was one thing, but improperly prepared coffee bordered on sacrilegious.

"It sounds heavenly. I'd love to try a cup." She gave him a coquettish smile. "That must be why you smell like spices."

He didn't dare ask how she'd come by that knowledge.

After pouring a cup and passing it to her, he lifted his cup to his nose. Inhaling the soothing aroma, he took a savory swallow. Every time he smelled *caffè d'u parrinu*, the scent hurtled him back to his earliest memories of *Mamma and Nonno* sitting at the kitchen table, chatting in Italian, drinking the steaming beverage, and eating pizzelle, Oliver's favorite pastry.

"*Mmm.*" Raising her cup to her nose, Blaike too sniffed. "It smells wonderful." After taking a sip she sighed in pleasure. "It's amazing. Such rich flavor, but not too strong. I'd like to try it with milk sometime."

"Alas, we've no cows below deck, else I'd rush to accommodate you." Oliver glanced about, and assured that no one would overhear him, leaned forward. "Did I dream it, or did I fall asleep with you beside me?"

Blaike fixed her attention on his face as fresh color rose on her ivory cheeks. Her gaze meshed with his for an extended, poignant moment.

Around them, the usual din of shipboard life continued, yet it seemed as if it was just the two of them, in this special time and place reserved for them alone. For this brief glimpse into each other's soul.

She fidgeted with her serviette before she too peered 'round.

No need to tell him she knew full well her reputation would suffer further if it became known she'd shared his bed, no matter how innocently.

Making a pretense of reaching for a boiled egg, she whispered, "I stayed until I was certain you were all right. But as you must know, I had to leave before I was discovered."

"Tuppence fer a tup," M'Lady Lottie announced in her sing-song voice.

Oliver's and Blaike's gazes locked again, but in amused shock this time.

"That's a first." He offered an apologetic upward hitch of his lips. "I'm rather leery of what else she might say."

Blaike covered her mouth and giggled. "I know I shouldn't laugh, for she's truly awful, and I don't want to encourage her, but I suppose she's to be admired for her intelligence and aptitude."

"You used my hairbrush."

Oliver hadn't meant to blurt it out like that. Like an accusation.

"I . . ." A gust whipped by, almost pulling the hood from Blaike's head. She snatched at it, just managing to keep her hair covered, then shivered. Skewing her lips sideways, she gave him an adorable, contrite smile. "I did. Forgive me, please. I know it was intrusive of me."

"I don't mind." He took another sip of the strong coffee to help wash down the lingering taste of porridge. "Whatever I have is yours to use."

"That's most generous of you." The mischievous twinkle that so often used to sparkle in her gaze appeared. "So, will you teach me?"

Her face radiated excitement. Such eagerness glowed in her eyes and her cheeks made rosy from the stiff breeze.

He should say no to such flummery.

A man with a jot of common sense—and not a glutton for punishment—would have done.

Instructing Blaike in the intricacies of mapping and navigation meant spending intimate time with her, smelling her delicious essence, inadvertently touching her.

If Oliver possessed an iota of sense he'd deny her request.

He didn't have the time, he could argue.

It wouldn't be proper, he might contend.

But I want to.

And honestly, he was flattered that she'd showed an interest.

"I shall, but only when I have no other duties that need my

attention."

She gave a delighted little clap and squeal. "Thank you!"

When she looked at him like that, there wasn't anything he wouldn't do for her.

God save him from himself.

Aye, and save him from sapphire-eyed goddesses smelling of vanilla.

Four afternoons later, Blaike and Blaire stood near the poop deck's rail, watching the crew prepare for a celebration.

Oliver's birthday was today, and in preparation for tonight's festivities, a few sailors had brought treasured musical instruments on deck. They included two fiddles, a tabor pipe, a pan flute, and a little guitar unlike anything Blaike had ever seen before.

A barrel of rum had been rolled out for the occasion, and Oliver had ordered extra rations for each sailor as well. She secretly hoped there might also be dancing, and that he'd request a waltz from her.

She'd wanted to do something special for him, since he'd basically saved the twins' lives, though he repeatedly denied doing so when she and her sister thanked him again. However, there was no practical way to bake any sort of a special treat.

Just as well, for Fairnly gave her the shivers. His lazy eye didn't bother her in the least, but the peculiar leather pouch covered in illegible scribbles and hanging from a leather strip about his neck made her skin pucker.

Oliver was right too.

If the man had seen the inside of a bath tub in the past month, she'd lop her hair off. More than a little unsettling to have someone so malodorous preparing their food.

Turning her face into the wind, her twin sighed. "I'm so glad to be out of our stuffy cabin. I pray the weather holds for another week."

Oliver had said they'd entered the Bay of Biscay and should expect the conditions to turn heavy soon, but Blaike hadn't the heart to tell Blaire. Today was her twin's first day above deck. Still pale, and certainly thinner, she didn't need to know her constitution would be tested again. And soon.

"Pretty bubbies," M'Lady Lottie said.

When that didn't earn anything more than a raised brow from either twin, the cockatoo flapped her wings and screamed, "Hopper-arsed whore."

A few sailors chuckled or commented on her latest coarse adage.

Hard to believe they hadn't heard them all before.

Blaire grinned at the cockatoo, now dangling upside down in her cage and playing with a bell. "She certainly is entertaining. Do you think someone actually taught her to say those awful things, or did she learn by overhearing them?"

"I have no idea, but it's not that easy to get her to say new things. I'm trying to teach her a few less unsavory phrases." So far, the effort had proved futile, even when tempting her with cooked beans, which Oliver said were a favorite treat. "She turns her back on me when I try to get her to say, 'Pretty bird.' Instead, she squawks, 'Lady—'"

"Bird." Blaire chuckled while grasping her raspberry colored cloak closed where it gaped slightly at her neck. "I'm fairly certain that's another term for a lightskirt."

"Well, considering where she spent the first several years of her life, I'm not the least surprised."

"Odd that, don't you think? Do you suppose she was a gift from a . . . patron?" Blaire placed a raisin on her gloved palm, then extended it toward the precocious bird. "Me-ow. Me-ow."

"Meow? You want her to meow?" Blaike laughed. "Perchance we can teach her to moo, baa, and oink as well."

Blaire rolled a shoulder. "Any utterance would be an improvement over her current sculduddery." She pushed her hand farther into the cage. "Me-ow. Me-ow."

M'Lady Lottie cocked her head, snatched the raisin with her beak, then swiftly swallowed the fruit.

"You didn't even try to say meow." Blaire leveled the bird a perturbed look.

"Mort. Prime mort. Moooort!" the cockatoo screamed.

"Definitely not a meow," Blaike giggled. "So far I've heard her say trollop, whore, lady bird, and mort." She pushed a strand of hair back beneath her hood. "I blush to think what other terms for ladies of the evening she may suddenly squawk."

They weren't supposed to know about such women. Nevertheless, anyone who'd spent any time in Town attending fashionable assemblies had heard whispers about *those* creatures.

Light skirts, Demimondaines. Lady birds. Bit o' muslins. *Chêre-amies.* Cyprians. Courtesans.

My, the *haut ton* certainly had a number of names for the unfortunate women. Perhaps because for all of the upper ten thousands' pretense of propriety, immorality ran rampant among their prestigious, often hypocritical ranks.

How many of those soiled doves had been reduced to that low status through no fault of their own?

Seeking Oliver's familiar form, Blaike scanned the ship's deck. She'd found herself doing that often these past days. Also found herself recalling over and over those final, startling words he'd uttered in his sleep.

Blaike. I love you.

Could it be true?

For a moment, her pulse thrilled at the notion then stuttered to its regular rhythm. If he felt that way, he definitely knew how to hide it.

Never a flirt, and certainly not wanting to appear fast, she'd attempted to subtly let him know she had warm feelings for him, too.

Perhaps not love. Yet.

But definitely something bubbled behind her chest every time he turned those black as molasses eyes on her. Most assuredly the feeling was worth exploring further.

She turned her face toward the billowing sails. There was something majestic and invigorating about being on the open sea. A freedom lacking on land. Which was odd, because a ship more closely confined her.

Oliver said if the winds held, they'd make port early. The news didn't excite her as much as it did her twin. The ocean's swells lifted and lowered the ship, the motion soothing and exhilarating. Blaire wouldn't likely agree with that assessment either.

Trying not to be too obvious, Blaike swept her gaze across the ship once more.

Where was he?

Not a hint in his mannerism or speech suggested he held her in any special regard. Except for that first night when he'd been half-foxed. Even during her two navigation lessons, he'd been as polite and formal as a hired tutor. He'd made sure they were in full view of his crew as he showed her how to use the sextant and never even as much as touched her unless necessary.

In fact, since that first night, he seemed to avoid being alone with her.

Even when she changed his bandage, Hawkins or Webb puttered around the cabin. She might not be an expert at ship hierarchy, but she was fairly certain the first mate and the bosun didn't generally feed birds, clean their cages, make beds, or conduct other trifling duties such as polishing their captain's boots.

The expected invitation to dine with him had not manifested either.

Confound it.

Confound him.

Blaike didn't quite know whether to be miffed or admire him for his diligence in protecting her reputation. Or . . . the unwelcome thought barged into her speculations. Mayhap he wasn't as fascinated with her as she was with him?

Then why would he say something that provocative as he slept?

The unconscious mind was a marvelous thing. It revealed what a person refused to acknowledge when they were awake.

At least that was her unproven theory.

Blaike found herself almost desperate to be alone with Oliver. To recapture that magic of the first night. To encourage his interest. To hear him whisper those lovely, magical words again.

Beyond that, she hadn't considered. For certain, she wasn't about to divulge what he'd muttered in his sleep.

Perhaps he might declare himself before they reached England.

Slow down.

One step at a time.

But time ran short. They'd reach London within a week.

Scrutinizing the decks once more, she saw him disappearing through the companionway.

"Blaire, it's time to change Captain Whitehouse's bandages. Would you like to stay here, since you've been cooped up below for so long?" Touching her sister's shoulder, Blaike smiled. "I know such things make you a bit queasy. I can ask Mr. Hawkins or one of the other officers to keep a watchful eye on you if you are uncomfortable being alone. However, the sailors have been nothing but respectful and helpful to me."

Leaning on the railing, her sister closed her eyes. "I'd rather stay here, if you don't mind. I'm not fond of enclosed spaces, and the odors lingering below make my stomach a bit tetchy. Besides," she angled her head to peer at M'Lady Lottie. "I'm determined to teach her to say something."

Blaike squeezed her sister's fingertips. "I shan't be above fifteen minutes."

Unless she could tempt Oliver to kiss her.

Oh, now there was a delicious notion.

Precisely how did one go about such things?

Even when motives are pure and good-intentioned, divulging a secret is akin to opening Pandora's box. All manner of complications may arise so judiciously consider the consequences before opening your mouth.
~Scruples and Scandals-The Genteel Lady's Guide to Practical Living

12

Oliver winced as he slid a palm inside his shirt collar.

Sure enough. His fingertips came away damp and red-tinted.

Confound it.

Served him right for pushing himself too hard too soon. If Blaike had seen him acting the rigging monkey to rescue M'Lady Lottie before the twins came up top today, she'd ring him a peal, to be sure.

After making quick work of removing his coat and vest, he shucked his shirt. He seldom wore neckcloths at sea. No society hoity toities aboard the *Sea Gypsy* to look down their noses at him in condemnation for forgoing fashion for common sense.

Truth to tell, he only had two neckcloths in decent condition, and those he saved for times when a cravat was required.

Even the coat he donned this morning was for the benefit of the Culpeppers. He usually just captained the ship wearing a shirt, trousers, and boots.

Bright scarlet stained the cloth affixed to his shoulder, and he wrinkled his forehead in frustration as he rummaged through the basket of bandages.

How hard could it be to replace the scrap?

He scowled.

Cutting the bindings circling his ribs and back he could manage, but wrapping new ones might prove tricky.

Hawkins should be along any moment to discuss tonight's activities. Care needed to be taken that none of the men overindulged, and monitoring the crew fell to the first mate. Especially since the clouds on the horizon portended what could become a nasty squall.

Oliver had plotted a course that should keep them ahead of the tempest; if the wind held, that was. But at sea, as he'd learned a long time ago, nothing was guaranteed. Far wiser to always assume the worst and take precautions.

Hawkins would advise divine entreaties, but prayer without a plan seemed foolish.

Oliver glared at the linens binding him. His first mate could be pressed into lending a hand with the bandage, though he was as worthless as Oliver with this sort of thing.

Scissors in hand he stood before his washstand. He tilted the mirror to better see his wound and had just slipped one blade under the strips below his arm when a knock rattled his stateroom door.

"Come."

As usual, Hawkins's timing was impeccable. What would he do without the man?

Neck bent to see his handiwork, Oliver clamped his teeth against the shooting pain and edged the blades farther under the bands.

"Just what do you think you're doing?"

Blaike.

He started and jabbed the blade into his ribs.

"Ouch, blast it! I nearly impaled myself." Withdrawing the scissors, he sent her a frustrated scowl. "What are *you* doing?"

"Your dressing should've been changed hours ago." Her lovely eyes grew round as groats as she raked him with her reproachful gaze, then they narrowed to accusatory slits. "Oh, Oliver. You're bleeding again. What have you been doing?"

She hurried to him, unclasping her cloak as she flew across his quarters. After draping her wrap over his desk chair, she pushed her sleeves to her elbows.

"How did this happen? Your wound has been healing so well." She pulled her mouth taut. "At least I thought it was. Perhaps I should've sutured it after all. Or cauterized it. That book," she pointed to the thick, russet leather volume on the corner of his desk, "recommends doing so to stop bleeding."

Doubt shadowed the gaze she lifted to meet his.

"The fault isn't yours, Blaike. It's mine. A captain's duties are often rigorous."

And he'd have to be on his deathbed to permit a fire-heated blade to sear his flesh.

549

She needn't know he'd climbed the rat lines earlier to rescue an enraged bird screaming, "Bums and bubbies" and "fusty luggs," as the *Sea Gypsy's* crew hooted and guffawed below.

At least M'Lady Lottie provided a welcome distraction for the men.

"It's a good thing I followed you." Pointing to the bed, she took the scissors from him, her gaze lingering a trifle overly-long on his hairy chest. "Sit down, please."

Oliver obeyed, leaning back on his hands, and tracking her graceful movements. He'd never tire of that. Or hearing her voice. Or her laughter.

Acutely conscious of his nakedness, for an instant, he considered how he might partially cover himself. He pitched the notion aside almost immediately.

Blaike wouldn't be able to tend to her ministrations if he did.

She'd seen his chest numerous times over the past few days, but there'd always been someone else present to make the situation more respectable. And less torturous for the carnal cravings he must deny. Far too tempting to have her touching him when, with every pore, every nerve, he longed to take her in his arms and kiss her luscious lips until they both gasped.

In fact, he'd like to kiss every part of her, starting with her bowed mouth and ending with her dainty toes, worshipping every curve in between.

Concentrate on something else.

Not the sweet essence wafting from her pearly skin.

"Do you want a dram of brandy or whisky first?" Blaike asked, bending over him. "We'll call it an early beginning to your birthday celebration."

She gave him a playful smile, that familiar mischievous light glinting in her arresting blue eyes.

Was she flirting?

If only he had the right to encourage her. To declare himself. To utter the words tapping at the back of his teeth.

"Oliver? Do you want a drink?"

The question tore him from his reverie.

"No," he managed while slanting his head to better smell her hair.

Sunlight and blossoms. And Blaike.

If he lived to be a one-hundred year old curmudgeon, he'd never forget her scent. Or the feeling of contentment and completion it roused in him. They were embedded upon his memory, entrenched in his emotions, for all time.

"I never partake when I know the crew will imbibe." A wise captain didn't indulge when his crew celebrated, particularly with a storm bearing down upon them. As it was, he'd have to limit their festivities. They'd not grumble overly much, for the men also knew the dangers of underestimating the fickle weather or the equally capricious ocean.

"The bleeding has stopped, but I want to sterilize the wound again." Her pretty face pinched in concentration, she gingerly snipped the bands from beneath both of his arms. "It will burn something fierce, I'm afraid."

Definitely don't think of the tempting handfuls mere inches away and pressing against her simple blue gown.

A gown that allowed the slightest alluring view of the satiny mounds the bodice caressed.

Damned lucky fabric.

He groaned, and not from the slight tugging of his shoulder as she drew the strips away.

"I'm sorry." One long-fingered hand resting on his good shoulder, she glanced up, her eyes brimming with sympathy. "Am I hurting you?"

Yes. His manhood twitched an answer.

His aching heart pinged in agreement. *Aye*.

"I'm fine. Just hurry and rewrap it. I have things to do." His response came out much terser than he'd intended.

Blaike quickly lowered her lashes, surprisingly dark given her pale hair and brows, but not before he saw the hurt and disappointment his sharp retort caused.

After cleansing the gouge, she laid a fresh square on it, and with practiced ease, rewrapped his shoulder. Dismay radiated from her, silent yet potent, as she worked.

"Forgive me, *cara*." Though he knew he shouldn't, he caressed her satiny cheek. "I'm angry at myself, not you."

Angry that he couldn't control his feelings toward her, physical or emotional.

Angry that they lived in such an unjust world that he would never be able to declare himself.

Angry that she could never be his.

Angry that he'd have to hurt this wondrous woman. That he'd have to watch the affection glistening in her glorious eyes fade, then die when they reached London, and he delivered her to her family without a backward glance or a word of farewell.

Lest on that day, she see his desolation and realize the colossal untruth he professed when he told her she meant nothing to him.

Blaike slowly lifted her lashes, and what shined in the depths of her eyes caused Oliver's heart to stop for an instant, then resume beating with the force of a winded racehorse.

She wanted him, too.

God curse him for a fool, but he wrapped his other arm around her trim waist, ignoring the angry stab of pain it caused his injury. He drew her, unresisting, between his thighs, then ever so gradually, slid his hand over the nape of her neck and urged her nearer so that their mouths touched.

Flames burst behind his eyelids and passion streaked through him as wild and uncontrolled as if someone had touched a spark to black powder, igniting a firestorm.

Blaike made a throaty, hungry noise and edged nearer, her thigh bumping his length and sending his lust spiraling ever higher.

What he'd meant as a tender brush of lips to comfort and reassure her, a swift stolen taste of her honeyed mouth, exploded into desire so strong, his head spun.

Palms splayed, he held her, his tongue teasing her plump lower lip until her mouth parted.

Her hand on his shoulder flexed then clenched. Snaking the fingers of her other hand into his hair, she angled her head to permit him deeper access.

No timid, shy miss here, but a woman who gave as much as she took.

Inexperienced and a trifle clumsy at first, she learned the art of kissing with prodigious aptitude.

"Oliver," she moaned, arching into him.

Never had hearing his name sounded so seductive.

Kicking his chiding conscience, as well as his once noble intentions overboard, he clasped Blaike to his chest and lay back on the bed, taking her with him.

The ropes supporting the mattress squeaked as their weight jarred the bed.

"Your shoulder," she gasped, settling atop him.

"Will be fine," he murmured against her mouth, while daring to squeeze the luscious mounds of her behind. "*Ti adoro.*"

He did adore her.

She sank into his chest, their legs and tongues entangling.

The pain in his shoulder paled in comparison to the burning passion for the woman in his arms.

He'd regret this.

Aye, but he'd also treasure this precious encounter for the remainder of his days.

How often had he imagined kissing her sweet mouth? Those dewy, pink lips? Wondered what it would be like to hold her svelte form in his arms? To have her melt into him with a woman's desire as she did now?

'Twas more profound and soul shattering than he'd dreamed.

He'd known to yield to this mad urge was foolhardy and reckless. Knew deep in the recesses of his spirit, he'd never be satisfied or content with mere kissing. Recognized on a primitive level that no other female would ever make him feel this way. That he'd never want another woman with such desperate intensity after her.

He loved her.

Sei la mia anima gemella.

Blaike *was* his soulmate. He'd guessed it from the beginning but had denied the probability.

"*Mmm,* you smell good. Like your coffee. Spicy and," she sniffed his neck, "maybe a hint of cedar too. Very manly."

God help him.

She framed his face with her hands, raining hot, moist kisses over his face and jaw. Rubbing her satiny cheek against his, she released a soft sigh. "I adore your beard."

Was that sultry siren's voice his Blaike's?

She ran her long fingers down his torso, then spread them through the hair on his chest, gently tugging.

The sensation had him on the cusp of spilling into his trousers.

"I've wanted to do this since I first saw you shirtless."

His muscles quivered and jumped in eager response to her exploration.

"And I've wanted to kiss you since I first laid eyes on you," Oliver confessed.

Stupid to reveal that. It hinted at something that could never be.

"And you waited this long?" The smile curving her mouth held more than delight. It revealed a woman's promise. "I'm not sure if I'm flattered or peeved."

He was a selfish arse, for he reveled in the knowledge despite the impropriety.

She feathered her hand down the narrow track of hair that disappeared into his waistband, then boldly looking him in the eye, slipped her fingers beneath the fabric.

Her smile—sexy, wanton, and willing—almost had him tearing open his trousers' falls, hoisting her skirts, and seizing the bliss coupling with her would bring them both.

Instead, Oliver grabbed her hand.

"Blaike, Stop. You don't know what you're doing."

"Of course I do." A suggestive half-smile tipping her mouth, she arched a brow. "Have you forgotten, I was raised on a dairy farm? I know full well what happens between the sexes. The act doesn't frighten me, though I believe males mount from behind don't they?"

Such a matter of fact question. She wasn't the least bit embarrassed or shy. Just curious, adorably naïve, and brazen.

Face crumpled in puzzlement, she eyed his groin. "I need to be on my hands and knees, don't I?"

Yes, by Poseidon.

On her knees. Her back. Her incredibly long legs about his waist. Straddling him. Over his desk. Sitting. Standing . . .

With her firm, alabaster breasts pressed to his chest, practically spilling from her bodice, Oliver was pressed almost beyond control to resist her innocent invitation.

Except a woman like Blaike expected marriage.

Deserved marriage.

Her family would demand a union if he selfishly took what she so generously offered. If Ravensdale or Leventhorpe didn't have him keelhauled, drawn and quartered, or challenge him to a duel. Blaike merited more than a hurried tumble or the modest, often difficult, life of a sailor's wife. For if Oliver couldn't convince Longhurst to accept a partial payment, the *Sea Gypsy*—*home for almost fifteen years*—was lost to him.

He had friends and family who would lend him funds. As much as he required, truth be known.

No.

If he succeeded in extracting himself from the gutter he'd been born into, he'd do so on his own. No one else would be able to take any measure of credit.

That was why Oliver had never planned on marrying. He must be faithful to the sea, for she'd given him his start. He'd never contemplated anything else. Didn't know how to do anything else. The sea had always been, would always be his future.

Not the aroused vixen in his bed, as much as Oliver might wish it otherwise.

If naught else, he was a pragmatic man. Life's realities had taught him not to put store or hope in things unseen. In what-ifs and maybes. Which, as much as it troubled Hawkins, was why Oliver couldn't share his first-mate's faith in an all-knowing deity.

Besides, Blaike's sister and cousins had all married well. Made brilliant matches, truth to tell. Each married to a lord of the realm.

She could, too, someday.

If he stayed away.

Her fascination would fade in time. She'd recognize her infatuation for what it was: confused gratitude brought about because he'd plucked her from Abraham's clutches.

What driveling rot, his cynical conscience scoffed.

Blast it all. At times, Oliver truly detested his integrity.

Still, he must refuse that which he wanted most. That which would make Blaike his until death separated them. That which might assure his happiness, but at the expense of hers.

Closing his eyes and clamping his jaw, he clutched her exploring hands.

"*Dolcezza,* sweetheart, we must stop before we're discovered. I shan't have you compromised because of me." He sat up, gritting his teeth against the agony now stabbing his shoulder. "I thought you were Hawkins when I bid you enter. He's expected any moment."

Her eyes widened as chagrin tightened her features.

"Why didn't you say so earlier? We might have been interrupted."

Blaike jumped from the bed.

Adjusting her clothing, she rushed to the washstand where she smoothed her hair, darting confused glances at Oliver in the looking glass. She mightn't be experienced in passion, but she'd recognized his desire.

Silent since she'd leaped from his bed, she tidied the medicine basket, then gathered the soiled cloths and dropped them in the washstand basin.

Just as silent, he donned a fresh shirt, then shrugged into his coat.

Noisy footsteps, more like stomping, echoed outside Oliver's quarters, along with a warbling whistle. That, too, seemed rather loud and contrived. A couple of times, someone bumped the passageway bulkhead—hard—then hollered a cheerful greeting. Either the fellow was half-soused already or deliberately making his presence known.

Hawkins.

Subtle as a hippopotamus in a ballroom.

Blaike didn't seem to notice. She'd moved to his desk and picked up the volume he'd been reading. Or at least tried to read. He found *Gulliver's Travels* more vexing than entertaining.

Perchance, the recurring thoughts of Blaike interrupting his reading might be more to blame than the novel.

"You and your sister are welcome to any of the books in my library." Not extensive to be sure, nonetheless, the built in bookshelf below the windows held two-score volumes. "I have decks of cards and a chess board, too."

"Oh, thank you. I'm sure she'll be as eager as I am to accept your offer."

Her enthusiasm didn't reflect in her eyes. She'd rather he gave her more lessons in navigation and astronomy, he'd be bound.

Oliver despised the uncertainty he read in Blaike's posture and expression. And damn his eyes, he couldn't, didn't dare, reassure her.

His love *must* remain a secret.

Theirs wasn't a misunderstanding that a simple conversation would solve. Perhaps in gothic tales, true love endured whilst the characters lived in poverty, content with nothing more than their lover's company. But such was fanciful fluff. Ridiculed and shunned, hungry, cold, and perhaps even ill. Those as well as other hardships would chink away at love until nothing remained but disillusionment and resentment.

Call him a coward, but he couldn't bear to have Blaike gaze at him with disenchantment, scorn, or bitterness.

Three sharp raps preceded Hawkins calling, "Cap'n? I need a moment."

Oliver finished securing his hair, for to leave it down would surely raise his mate's suspicion. Not a gossip by any means, Hawkins was more apt to lecture Oliver on moral failings if he suspected anything had occurred.

"Come."

At once the door swung open, and the first mate shuffled inside, nodding a greeting. "Miss. Sir."

Oliver didn't miss the swift, assessing glance Hawkins sent Blaike. He could expect a sermon later. He'd stake his reputation on it.

"I'll join my sister." Blaike swung her cloak about her shoulders. "I've left Blaire alone far longer than I anticipated. Oliver, do try to refrain from opening your wound again." She glanced out the window, furrows creasing her forehead as she secured the frogs at her throat. "Those clouds don't look friendly."

"I think if we stay our course, we'll run ahead of the storm." Oliver couldn't be positive, naturally. He tentatively flexed his shoulder, hating the stiffness that limited his movements.

"What was it you needed, Hawkins?"

"A sail's been sighted a fair distance off."

Not unusual by any means.

However, what Hawkins *wasn't* saying sent alarm tingling the length of Oliver's spine.

He cut Blaike a troubled glance. "Why don't you go topside and see how your sister fares?"

His men wouldn't conceive of touching either woman, but Blaire didn't know that, this being her first day topside.

"Not until you tell me why Mr. Hawkins's face looks like a goose's back end." Blaike folded her arms. A Mother Superior's acrid glance held less starch or challenge.

Too smart, his Blaike.

Jaw unhinged at her comparison, Hawkins swung a desperate glance to Oliver.

Rubbing his temple, Oliver shrugged. "She'll know soon enough. Give over. What has you wearing such a Friday face?"

"She's pacing us, and she's not flying any colors, Cap'n."

When deciding whether to disclose a secret, a far-sighted woman
considers who might most benefit and who will be most harmed.
~Scruples and Scandals-The Genteel Lady's Guide to Practical Living

13

Friend or foe?

Blaike peered at the horizon, striving to catch a glimpse of the ship
Hawkins said was out there, somewhere off the *Sea Gypsy's* starboard
side. Though she trusted Oliver completely, trepidation nevertheless
padded across her shoulders.

If friendly, why hadn't the vessel struck her colors?

Maybe ships only did so under certain circumstances.

What type of vessel pursued them?

A pirate ship?

Captain Abraham?

Could the *Sea Gypsy* outrun her if need be?

She was a sleek clipper, but could a larger ship overtake her?
Blaike's knowledge of mariner protocol wouldn't fill an infant's shoe.

At the helm, Oliver conversed in low tones with Mr. Grover, Mr.
Hawkins, and a couple of other officers. None appeared particularly
harrowed or concerned. No doubt, these situations were common
enough and seasoned seamen took the occurrences in their stride.

She wasn't altogether sure she ever could.

Swinging her attention the port side, she pinched her lips together.

Sullen charcoal-colored clouds billowed low over the rolling,
white-capped waves. Possible danger lurked on either side of the
grayish-green waters as night enshrouded the vessel.

Even the air smelled and felt different: a sweet, pungent scent that
tickled her nostrils and heightened her awareness whilst making her
prickly all over.

Oliver had directed the helmsmen to stay the course, right between
the two potential threats. He'd even ordered the galley stove

extinguished, and at this moment, the crew was stowing away or lashing down anything that might be tossed about in rough seas.

Or in a battle?

The *Sea Gypsy* had but one gun deck as well as a chase gun on the bow and stern. She wasn't designed for lengthy fighting.

Cold sweat dampened Blaike's underarms, and a peculiar metallic taste filled her mouth. She'd been afraid before, had been terrified when Captain Abraham said he intended to sell her into sexual slavery. But she'd never tasted this kind of fear. Nor smelled it before either, yet she kept catching whiffs of an unsettling, acerbic aroma.

"Blaike, why has Captain Whitehouse cancelled tonight's celebration? And why is the crew scurrying about like squirrels preparing for winter?"

Blaire touched Blaike's forearm, two neat rows wrinkling her forehead.

What to say to not worry her further?

Might as well tell her the whole truth. Intelligent as she was, she'd soon figure it out for herself.

"A storm brews, and another ship's sails were sighted earlier. We don't know if the vessel is friendly." Blaike summoned a cheery smile, which quickly slid into a compassionate curve of her mouth at her twin's distraught sound.

"I confess, I'm not made for seafaring." Features strained, Blaire hunched deeper into her cloak. "I rather dislike everything about it."

No doubt the prospect of angry, roiling seas caused her distress, making Blaike all the more grateful she didn't suffer from seasickness. She'd seen the havoc the condition wreaked upon her twin and worried for her health.

"Don't fret, dearest. Oliver says he thinks we'll stay ahead of the storm, but he's taking precautions just in case."

"Doodle sack."

The wind carried M'Lady Lottie's latest crudity to where Blaike stood, one hand resting on the smooth rail.

Locked in her cage, she voiced her annoyance at being confined.

Would Oliver secure her below until the threats had passed?

"Blaike! Look." Her voice thick with dread, Blaire shook Blaike's shoulder.

Twisting to look where her twin pointed, Blaike's lungs constricted as her heart seemed to swell to twice its normal size behind her breastbone.

The ship she'd strained to see had emerged from twilight's nebulous glow, a large black silhouette on the seascape.

How had she gained on them so quickly?

Why would she if she meant the *Sea Gypsy* no harm?

What if the occupants needed help, though?

Wouldn't they have given a distress signal then?

A fat raindrop splattered onto her nose as she threw a glance over her shoulder.

Oliver, his strong legs spread, held a brass spyglass to his eye, as did Mr. Hawkins, both directed at the looming vessel. Even from where she stood, the grim line of his mouth and the harsh planes of his face were visible.

If her stomach hadn't already been a gnarled knot of anxiety, it would've turned to stone.

Her worry wasn't for herself.

As captain, Oliver was at greatest risk if an unfriendly vessel overtook and boarded them.

The eyeglass still held in place, he said something to his first mate, and with a sharp nod, Mr. Hawkins sprinted into action.

"All hands on deck," he bellowed. For such a small man, he possessed an impressive shout.

Foe then.

Fright's sharp claws scraped along Blaike's nerves.

The *Sea Gypsy* swung to port, facing into the gale.

"Oh, this isn't good, is it?" Blaire grasped Blaike's hand. "I may cast up my accounts right here."

"Take deep breaths, and try to stay calm. Look at the horizon" Sound advice if a potential enemy's ship didn't hover there. Even Blaike's robust constitution wobbled a mite. "I trust Oliver. He knows what he's about."

She did trust him, but sailing directly into a tempest meant that tactic was less dangerous than engaging the ship swooping down upon them.

Cold, heavy pellets fell faster from the sky, even as the wind tore Blaike's hood off.

"Misses, you'll need to go below now."

Mr. Grover touched his hat, his countenance taut with tension.

"Cap'n's orders. And there'll be no hot meals served until further notice. Someone will deliver hardtack, water, dried apples, and cheese to your quarters when they're able. The Cap'n also doesn't want any unnecessary lamps burning. Once you're in your cabin, you must remain inside until advised otherwise. The passageways won't be lit, and with the ship bobbing about, it'd be dangerous not to stay put. "

Bobbing? This was dashed more than bobbing.

"We understand." Blaike cast a fretful glance toward the wicked clouds.

They'd be stuck in the ship's bowels with no light and roiling on the mountainous waves.

For how long? Hours? Days?

Blaike looped arms with Blaire, now as pale as the sheets billowing from the masts above.

"I vow, after this, I'm never setting foot on a ship again." A hand pressed to her throat, Blaire swallowed.

Sailors scrambled up the rigging and rat lines, hollering to one another. Howling wind and crashing waves muted their call. Brave and daring at any time, in this weather, their actions were positively heroic. Likely an absolute necessity, too.

"At once, if you please, Misses."

Probably a dozen things requiring his attention, Mr. Grover hurried away.

Even as Blaike and her sister cautiously made their way across the deck, the wind whipped into a frenzy, lashing her face with icy, bean-sized drops. The raw force of nature was something to behold. At once glorious and terrifying. Candescent purplish-white lightening branches rent the distant sky, followed by muffled explosions of thunder.

"A moment, please." Striding to the companionway, M'Lady Lottie clinging to his hand, Oliver addressed them both, but looked at Blaike. "Can I impose upon you to take her to my quarters, and put her in her cage? She has food and water enough to last a couple of days. I don't know when I'll be able to get below again."

Extending her arm, Blaike nodded. "Of course."

"Bedded and buggered," the cockatoo said, except she lacked her usual ornery attitude.

"Are we actually sailing into that?" Blaike tilted her head at the ominous mass as he transferred the disgruntled bird to her.

"No." The wind had torn his hair free, and it hung in saturated tendrils to his shoulders. "That would be suicide. I'm using the squall's perimeter as a shield. Night will be fully upon us within the hour. I intend to use them both to mask us from the other vessel, which I'm sure you've seen."

"Do you know who the other ship is?" She accepted the cockatoo, surprised at how heavy the bird was.

He nodded, shoving a hank of hair from his eyes.

"I do, and we don't wish to encounter them. Which is why I've chosen this course. The *Sea Gypsy's* cargo will act as a ballast, and I'm veering her into an area with the shallowest waves and lowest winds. I've also given the order to periodically dump a gallon or two of oil to calm the waves for us. Not too much though, else the other ship will spot us or benefit from the oil."

Blaike couldn't form the words burning on the tip of her tongue. Perchance, she didn't really want to know what he so obviously withheld.

Just who was pursuing them?

Maybe the gallivanting around the high seas with Oliver wasn't such a cheery prospect after all. There was something to be said for boring and safe.

And solid, unmoving land.

Without pirates or other scallywags.

"Blaike, I'm not feeling at all well. If you don't mind, I'll go to our cabin straightaway and lie down."

If Blaire felt this miserable already, Blaike dreaded what the next few hours would bring. Her twin truly might very well never sail again. Even Blaike's tummy protested the merest bit at the ship's increased churning.

"Yes, go along, dear. I'll be there just a soon as I've dealt with M'Lady Lottie."

Summoning a weak, closed-mouth smile, Blaire descended the ladder.

Blaike touched Oliver's wound, then searched his eyes. "You will be careful, won't you? Promise me? I'll fret until I see you safe again."

Bold of her, but what if something happened to him?

She wanted him to know she cared, even if now wasn't the time to declare her affection.

Angling his back, partially sheltering her from the furious elements, and likely the crew's regard as well, he grazed her cheek with his rough thumb.

THE BUCCANEER AND THE BLUESTOCKING

"I promise. But you must make me the same promise, *cara. Sei tutto per me.*"

The ship heeled violently to starboard, and he stumbled into her.

M'Lady Lottie screeched her outrage, digging her claws into Blaike's fingers. "Bawdy baskets."

Blaike didn't even want to guess what bawdy baskets were.

For certain, something that would turn her cheeks pink.

"I must go. Get below, *cara.*"

Oliver kissed her forehead, the act so endearing and natural, she couldn't object.

Had no inclination to.

She clutched his soggy shirtfront with her free hand.

"Wait, Oliver. What does it mean? What you just said to me in Italian?"

He winked, a roguish twinkle in his eye and looking every bit the rakish pirate she'd likened him to be those many months ago. "That's my secret."

"Oliver. That's not—"

The *Sea Gypsy* crested another gigantic wave, hurtling them into the companionway.

Pain ratcheted from shoulder to hip, and she gasped. Still, he wasn't getting off so easily. Clutching his sodden shirt, she shook it.

"What does it mean, you stubborn man?"

"Cap'n!" Such urgency filled Hawkins' voice, her blood congealed in her veins.

"It means, you are everything to me, *amore mia.*" After casting a grim look behind him, Oliver gave her a firm push. "Go. Now. I cannot have you distracting me, and if you're up here, I shan't be able to concentrate on anything but your safety. Pray we survive the next few hours and lose the other vessel."

What fool would try to overtake a ship on the cusp of a gale?

Over his shoulder, the outline of sails obstructed the angry horizon.

That one, whoever the lunatic captain might be.

Stifling another gasp, Blaike clambered down the ladder, no easy feat, wearing long skirts and with a frightened bird bobbing and swaying.

And swearing.

Thrice, M'Lady Lottie's wings battered her face.

A single lamp hanging near the ladder lit the passageway. How soon before it was extinguished?

Minutes likely.

She must hurry, not at all certain she could find her way to her cabin in a pitch black passageway.

"Lottie scared. Hurry. Hurry." Her agitation growing, M'Lady Lottie chattered non-stop. "Hurry. Dunnock doxy. Bushel bubby. I'm scared. Petey? Hell's bells. Limp as lace."

"*Shh*, Lottie. I cannot think with you blathering."

Had Blaire made it to their cabin all right?

She'd looked positively green around her mouth, and panic had glinted in her eyes. Probably afraid she was about to cast her crumpets in view of all. Mayhap another slop bucket would be a good idea. But where to get one amidst this chaos?

If they'd been permitted light, Blaike would borrow the medical journal and research how to treat seasickness other than ginger tea. Though Fairnly had prepared several cups a day for her sister, the brew didn't help appease her nausea.

Why she was so afflicted, yet Blaike barely so didn't make any sense at all. They were so similar—identical—in almost every other way.

"Petey? Ol-eeve? Lottie afraid."

Poor Lottie. She wanted her owner to comfort her.

"I know, Lottie. It's all right. I'll take care of you."

Holding the terrified bird close to her midriff, Blaike ran a soothing hand down the cockatoo's back.

As Blaike jostled down the ever increasing dimmer passageway to Oliver's quarters, bouncing from bulkhead to bulkhead as she trundled along, M'Lady Lottie tottered on her fingers. Amazing the sheer strength of the bird's feet.

She bustled into the great cabin. Mindful of the rows of windows and what Mr. Grover had said about lighting lamps, she left the door open. The dim passageway light barely sufficed to illuminate the chamber.

Nonetheless, Blaike had been inside so many times, she easily made her way to M'Lady Lottie's cage, only banging her shin once on the trunk usually situated at the foot of Oliver's bed.

She squinted round the cabin. Most furnishings were fixed to the deck, but those that weren't had shifted. Like the chest, now in the middle of the cabin, as well as any unsecured items from atop his desk.

"There you are." She rested her hand against the wooded dowel, and the cockatoo shimmied onto her perch. "I know you don't like your cage, but it's for your own safety."

"Randy rantallion," the bird muttered peevishly as Blaike latched the door.

"I'm positive I don't want to know what that is."

Shaking her head, she shivered, soaked to the skin. She didn't relish trying to change into a dry gown and chemise in the dark.

"From your lively discourses, Lottie, I'm beginning to presume women of low virtue also have tetchy dispositions."

A monstrous wave battered the sturdy vessel, rattling the windows and banging the door shut. Blaike stumbled sideways, crashing into the washstand. A moment later, the ship pitched hard to port, and she was thrown to the deck. Her right knee, hip, and shoulder collided with the unforgiving wood, and she yelped as piercing pain speared her.

M'Lady screamed in alarm, flying around her cage in terror. "Hell's bells. Devil's at the door."

An occasional shout could be heard above the furor and the vessel's anguished creaks and groans as the gale pummeled the ship.

A book skidded across the floor and *thunked* into the bulkhead.

This was the squall's fringe?

The *Sea Gypsy* bobbled about like an acorn below a waterwheel.

Blaike rolled over, and breathing heavily, assessed her injuries. Cautious and tentative, she flexed and stretched. Nothing appeared broken, but her knee and shoulder ached something awful. If these were the shallowest waves, she never wanted to experience anything worse.

That notion of sailing round the world could bugger itself.

Pray God Blaire had wedged herself in her berth. She was likely terrified.

All the more reason why Blaike must get to her twin.

Eyes squeezed shut, and jaw clenched against an unladylike oath, she sat up. With a groan, she shoved to her feet, then hands held before her, shuffled toward where she thought the door ought to be.

The *Sea Gypsy* rolled again, diving into a trough between the towering walls of water.

The abrupt motion launched Blaike forward into the trunk. She cried out as her knees connected with the unyielding chest, and again as she toppled to the side, smashing her head against the bed.

'Tis a simple, but profound secret, and one a charitable
woman heeds: Everything worth doing, is what is done for
others without regard or expectation of recompense.
~Scruples and Scandals-The Genteel Lady's Guide to Practical Living

Two days later, the first metallic traces of dawn feathered the sky as Oliver trained his spyglass across the gold, copper, and bronze seascape. No more worrying about being sent arse over chin into the fitful ocean now that the wind had abated to a peevish breeze.

The worrisome Bay of Biscay lay behind them and England ahead.

A modicum of tension eased from his shoulders, and he rubbed his nape. His gamble, the riskiest and with the highest stakes he'd ever wagered, had paid off.

With a practiced eye, he scrutinized the ocean one final time.

Not a sign anywhere of the *Black Dove.*

Despite being a motley lot, he wouldn't wish the *Black Dove's* hands to a watery grave—except for Abraham.

That assling deserved to rot in Davy Jones's Locker.

Oliver couldn't summon a jot of forgiveness for him.

Nevertheless, if the *Black Dove* had sustained damage enough to keep them well away from the *Sea Gypsy,* he, too, might offer a prayer of thanksgiving as Hawkins had repeatedly these past few hours.

One had to admire his first mate's faith, even if he didn't understand it.

On either side of Oliver, Hawkins and Grover also perused the ocean with their spyglasses. The sun edged higher on the horizon, spreading her warmth and vibrant hues over the mild swells.

"No sign of another sail, Cap'n, nor a suspicious cloud overhead." Hawkins grinned before angling his gaze skyward and silently acknowledging his God. Again. "I know it ain't right, and I'll have to repent, but I sincerely hope that bleedin' son of a barnacle's bum met his maker. If so, hell's fires are burnin' hotter, for certain."

Oliver and Grover exchanged amused glances.

Make that thrice Hawkins had sworn in front of Oliver.

They closed their spyglasses, the sounds of the brass cylinders sliding shut a satisfying reminder they'd survived the nerve-racking ordeal.

Only just.

"Well done you, sir." Grover shook Oliver's hand. "I confess, yesterday I had my doubts we'd escape that witch's squall. Made me wish I had Hawkins's strong faith, it did."

"With a lesser crew, we wouldn't have done. I commend you all," Oliver said.

He would've like to have offered his men a bonus, but given the cargo holds had room to spare, he didn't dare make such a generous offer. He might just ask Ravensdale a question or two about that shipping heiress. Perhaps she had need of another clipper to transport her goods.

Nonetheless, pride squared his shoulders the merest bit.

Not only had they evaded Abraham, they'd make England day after tomorrow, days ahead of schedule.

Bitter-sweet, that.

Only one more sunrise with Blaike.

A morning months ago at Leventhorpe's country house, sprang to mind. Oliver had suggested she ought to see a sunrise from the deck of a ship.

Even then, she'd enchanted him.

Still, he must let her go. He must.

Grateful that Blaike had obeyed him, he'd neither seen nor heard from her since ordering the twins below. M'Lady Lottie had been curiously silent as well.

The storm and the threat from another vessel served as vivid reminders why he couldn't ask Blaike to remain aboard the *Sea Gypsy*. Last night, missing her horribly though she was safe within the bowels of his ship, he'd entertained that ludicrous notion for all of thirty seconds before reality clobbered him.

Actually, it had been a bucket hurtling across the deck, and plowing into his shoulder blade that brought home the truth.

With painful and undeniable clarity.

Water and oil didn't mix.

Residents of Mayfair's mansions and Whitechapel's slums didn't hobnob together.

Pockets-to-let commoners didn't consort with the gently bred. Such were life's inarguable facts.

The queer pull behind his ribs twitched again, as it did each time he faced that undisputable truth.

For a time that first night, he fretted he'd miscalculated and ventured too near the squall, and the *Sea Gypsy* and all aboard her might be lost. Nevertheless, setting any course that would've permitted Abraham the opportunity to overtake them had been inconceivable. Better the twins should drown than endure what he intended for them.

Bloody exhausted—the only crew member to not have caught a few moments of rest—Oliver yawned, wide and gusty. He needed sleep before he dozed off whilst standing and toppled into the sea.

"Hawkins, you're in command. I'm to bed for a few hours, but I'd like a bath first. Also, have one of the men inform the Culpeppers that they may leave their cabin. In fact, order them baths, as well. We've water enough for certain now, and I'm sure they'd enjoy the luxury."

He clapped his first mate's boney shoulder.

"Fairnly is to outdo himself today. I want hot food for everyone, and lots of it. Simple fare is fine. Salt-pork, beans, potatoes. The men have earned a reward, so they're to have an extra ration of rum as well. If he balks, tell him he hasn't had to earn his way these past two days. Allow him to choose a couple of men to assist him. And please send someone below to bring M'Lady Lottie up. She won't let me sleep a wink if she remains in my quarters."

"Aye. I'll see to it all." A grin still etched upon his weathered face, Hawkins swaggered away whistling his usual hymn, only pausing in his warbling to give orders to a couple of sailors.

Oliver would have liked to personally see how Blaike had fared, but he hadn't asked for a bath because he longed for a hot soak. He stank of sweat and sea. Fear too, if he were wholly honest with himself. Mayhap he'd check on her after he'd washed.

Just to make sure she was all right.

To see if she *and* her sister needed anything.

Then he could relax and close his gritty, leaden eyes.

Yawning again, he strode to the companionway, taking time to thank and compliment his men as he went. Truly, they'd performed magnificently, and he couldn't be prouder.

He'd already shrugged out of his stiff coat and was unbuckling his belt when he made his quarters.

Lottie's mutters and titters carried to him in the passageway. She'd kick up a dust when she saw him, for certain.

Bracing himself for her loud welcome, he stepped across the threshold and was brought up short.

Blaike sat at his desk, reading a book, the cockatoo perched behind her on the chair's back. A lock of Blaike's unbound hair clenched in her foot, Lottie plucked at the shimmering strand with her beak.

The bird spied him and shrieked, "Ol-eeve! Hello Luv." She swayed back and forth, back and forth, cooing, "Luv Ol-eeve. Missed Ol-eeve."

He couldn't help but chuckle at her exuberant greeting. "Hello, Lottie. How are you?"

"How are you?" she mimicked. "Tired as a trull."

There was the Lottie he'd expected.

"Hello, Blaike."

Nowhere near the words Oliver wanted to say.

I was terrified for you.

I feared the ship was lost, and I'd never see or speak to you again.

I wish life was fair, and I dared to offer for you.

I love you. Senza di te non sono niente.

Without you I am nothing

"Hello, Oliver."

Blaike slowly stood and offered him an almost shy smile. Attired in a serviceable slate gray gown, she'd never appeared lovelier to his hungry gaze.

"I came to feed Lottie. I felt so sorry for her, I let her out for a few minutes again. I hope you don't mind. I'm still trying to teach her new words, too. She's nearly got pretty bird."

She pushed her hair behind her shoulders, and the brilliant mass tumbled to her firm derriere.

Mamma's combs would look stunning in her hair.

As Blaike moved across the cabin, the rising sun's rays burst in, illuminating her countenance—horribly swollen and bruised on the right side.

"My God, *cara mia*. What happened to your face?" Oliver dumped his possessions on his chest as he rushed to her.

For once, Lottie didn't offer a raunchy response. Rather, she flew to his bed and proceeded to parade up and down the counterpane, chattering away in cockatoo.

"I tripped over your trunk that first night. Actually, I was thrown and struck the foot of your bed." Blaike gingerly touched her head. "The cut isn't very big, but I cannot put my hair up. It hurts to twist and pin it."

"Purdy birrr-dy. Purdy birrr-dy," Lottie muttered, testing the new words. "Lottie purdy birrr-dy."

"*Mia cara,* I'm so sorry.

Despite reeking like a London beggar, Oliver pulled her into his embrace, cradling her as if she were the frailest of flowers. Her hair, a shiny curtain, trailed over his arms. Floral and vanilla essences wafted upward from the long tresses.

A whorl of emotion constricted his throat, and he had to swallow twice to dislodge the lump.

Blaike might've been killed. Or lain in his cabin injured and suffering these past two days, and no one would've known, save her sister. And the twin was too ill to move, let alone venture to his quarters.

Guilt and remorse burrowed through him, leaving him raw.

"I should've seen you safely to your cabin. Should never have asked you to take Lottie below."

Tilting her head, Blaike peered into his eyes. "Nonsense. You were needed above. It was an accident. Unexpected things happen, Oliver. No one is to blame. How are we to enjoy life if we constantly worry about misfortunes besetting us? We all have good days and bad days, mishaps and blessings."

She was right, of course.

It wasn't humanly possible to control every circumstance, to completely protect those he loved. Yet more than ever he was compelled to admit the *Sea Gypsy* wasn't the place for her, as much as he wished it otherwise. He acknowledged full-on the risks a life at sea portended, and he'd not expose her to that peril.

Blaike belonged safely on shore, the lady of a grand estate, her every whim anticipated and met.

He gently separated the hair just to the right of her forehead. "The laceration isn't very big or deep, but you do have a sizable knot where you hit your head. Do you have a headache? I think we've powders somewhere. Maybe in the medicine chest."

Her shoulders quivered, and he firmed his embrace. She'd endured so much, been so brave and strong. A good cry might do her good.

The shaking grew stronger, and then she giggled.

Out loud and wholly delighted.

Oliver stiffened.

Blaike was laughing, not weeping?

M'Lady Lottie also giggled, sounding very much—alarmingly so—like Blaike, then proceeded to yell, "Time to shite" before flying back to her cage and doing just that.

Mortified, he shut his eyes.

That confounded cockatoo would be the death of him. How old had McMaster said those blasted birds live to? Thirty or more years?

What was Oliver to do with her for another decade?

Blaike laughed harder, fingers pressed to her middle in glee. "That bird is utterly awful."

Would she never cease to surprise him?

Where was the hysteria and self-pity most women would've displayed? The accusations and blame? The affront at Lottie's vulgar vocabulary? Instead, Blaike laughed, her beautiful bruised face glowing with humor.

"I'm sorry. But I'm imagining our homecoming. Both of us with lumps on our heads, my face." She swept her hand in the air. "Your shoulder." Her mirth subsided, and with a silly smile yet bending her mouth, she said, "We're quite the pair, aren't we? And lud. If you dare bring M'Lady Lottie ashore . . ."

Finding Blaike's humor contagious, he chuckled before carefully kissing the bridge of her upturned nose.

Another fit of giggles overcame her. "I can only imagine the reactions. The censuring looks and slack jaws. The whispers and swishing fans. The theatric swooning."

He well could too, and that was why the cockatoo would never be introduced to Polite Society. Any society.

"I'd quite like to witness that, truth to tell." She wiped the tears of laughter from the corner of her eyes.

"I agree, we are quite a pair." How complete his life would be if only they could be life-long mates, too. With concerted effort, he forced his mind to another less melancholy topic. "You'll be happy to know, that other than a few bruises and abrasions, no one suffered any major injuries."

"I'm so glad. I fretted, wondering how everyone had fared. However, I knew I'd be a distraction and possibly put you or the others in danger if I disregarded your orders and went above deck." She slid a glance at Lottie preening her underwing. "That's why I came to see Lottie often. She helped occupy the time and my vivid imagination didn't run away quite so frequently."

He leaned away, and cupping her delicate shoulders, sought her eyes. "How is your sister?"

Toying with his shirt front, Blaike sighed.

Chagrin assailed him when she touched his soiled clothing. A homeless vagabond reeked less, but Blaike's nostrils hadn't so much as quivered.

"My sister's glad the ship has stopped trying to dump her from her berth every two minutes. Nonetheless, she vows she's never setting foot on a vessel bigger than a row boat for the remainder of her life."

Blaike pushed her hair behind her ear, revealing the slim column of her swan-like neck.

"She discovered, much to her relief, that although ginger tea didn't help with her *mal de mer*, hardtack did. I gave her mine as well since the biscuit worked such wonders. She's still asleep. Has been for hours now. Once the ship settled into a regular rhythm again, she was out like a snuffed candle."

A noise in the passageway reminded him they'd soon be interrupted. "I expect my bath or else a man to take M'Lady up top at any moment."

"Of course. I'll leave you then." She stepped away, her long hair swishing slightly with her movements.

At once Oliver longed to gather her back into his arms, but a whiff of stale sweat assailed him. Best wait until he'd donned fresh clothing.

"I ordered baths for you and your sister, too. Why don't you use my water since she's asleep, and I can bathe above?"

"You don't have to do that, Oliver. I'll wait." She touched his bearded jaw. "You're exhausted. I know you haven't slept. I'll come back in a few hours. We'll dine together, and you can teach me more about astronomy."

She leaned into him and whispered naughtily, "Or anatomy."

Cheeky, adorable wench.

"Wanton wagtail." Lottie flapped her wings, then sidestepped along her perch, head cocked.

"Lottie," Blaike scolded over her shoulder. "Say something nice."

"Luv-ly Lottie," the cockatoo promptly responded.

Oliver clasped Blaike's hand to his face, then turned the palm upward and kissed the tender flesh there.

"Il mio cuore è solo tua."

Fully above the horizon now, the sun's radiance burst into the chamber, and through the shimmering glass, a rainbow shone in the distance. The light and the colorful arc seemed somehow symbolic.

A sign.

Even after that horrendous storm, when he feared all might be lost, the blazing orb ascended to its usual place in the heavens.

Her expression at once playful and serious, Blaike clasped his hands in hers. "You did it again. Said something to me in Italian. It sounded very much like an endearment. Was it?"

Anticipation tinged her words.

Despite his best efforts not to encourage her affections, he'd failed. That such a woman cared for him humbled and exhilarated. Made him wish he had other options besides a lifetime at sea.

Tilting his head, not so very far because she was almost as tall as he, Oliver kissed her crown, pouring forth all the reverence he held for her in the swift, light touch of his lips.

"I said, *cara*, my heart is yours."

The gold flecks in her sapphire eyes glittered with unspoken emotion.

"And you love me."

A statement, not a question. Straightforward as always.

"Aye, I do."

Achingly, crushingly so.

Curse him for seven kinds of fool. The words he'd said in his head, in his heart, hundreds of times whispered forth. Three syllables that could change the course of his life forever.

"And you want to marry me."

God, was there ever a woman like her?

Hadn't he just vowed to do what was best for Blaike, to let her go?

"I do. More than I can express with mortal words."

The door rattled, announcing either his much anticipated bathwater, or the poor fellow who drew the short straw and was obligated to see M'Lady Lottie above deck.

Bestowing a beatific smile upon him, Blaike clasped her hands before her.

"Oliver. What are you waiting for? Ask me to marry you."

If only he could.

Even bruised and swollen, she was the most exquisite creature he'd ever seen.

"I . . ." How could he devastate her? This most precious treasure?

Brows drawn taut, she cocked her head and drew near him again.

"Is it because I haven't told you I love you, too?"

She laid her palm on his lapel.

"You must know I do, of course. So very, wonderfully much. And for such a long time." She gave a tinkling, self-conscious laugh, and dropped her gaze to the floor for a second. "I have, I think, since I first saw you striding across that ballroom looking very much like a dashing buccaneer. You rescued me that night, too."

Standing on her toes, she brushed her mouth against his, and electricity jolted to his bone's marrow.

It took every bit of self-control and dogged determination not to enfold her in his embrace, tie his chivalry and noble intentions to the ship's anchor, then toss them to the bottom of the Atlantic's depths for all time.

"My answer would be yes. As soon as feasible." Her eyes lit up impossibly more, her exuberant smile exposing her neat white teeth. "Can you marry us? I'm not sure if that's permitted, but wouldn't it be a marvelous surprise for my family?"

Loathing himself for what he was about to do—what he must do— even though carving his heart from his chest with a dagger would hurt less, Oliver grasped her upper arms. With all the tenderness he could husband, he set her from him.

"I'm not asking you to marry me, Blaike."

He firmed his hands briefly, conveying his earnestness.

"Not now. Not ever."

Shock mixed with utter anguish ravished her features.

"But why?" she managed, devastation now causing the glistening in her eyes that a mere instant ago had held such joy. "I know you love me. I've seen the way you look at me, and you said so in your sleep. And I love you. Utterly and profoundly."

He'd said so in his sleep?

Bugger it. No wonder she'd been so buoyant. So confident.

Unable to look into her stricken gaze a moment longer, lest his noble intentions desert him, Oliver presented his back. For if he didn't, if Blaike vowed she loved him once more, his resolve would crumble like a termite infested log.

She touched his arm.

"Please. Oliver."

His whispered name forced past Blaike's tight lips, conveyed her life-altering torment and disbelief.

"Don't do this. Don't reject my love."

"Gentry and common bastards do not wed, Blaike. You live in a fantasy world if you think they do."

He did this for her sake. She'd understand someday. Eventually, when her emotions had calmed, reason would reign. And, in time, her heart would heal.

The pulverized organ that somehow managed to continue beating in his chest never would.

Hands fisted, spine rigid with suppressed emotion, he tucked his chin to his chest.

"Until we reach England tomorrow, Blaike, we should avoid each other."

Only an utter fool breathes the slightest hint of a
secret to a gossip. For confidences like wild creatures,
caught and caged, escape the instant the door is opened.
~Scruples and Scandals-The Genteel Lady's Guide to Practical Living

15

Just over two weeks later, Blaike sat, ankles crossed, in the drawing
room's window seat at Highfield Place House. Freddy, his soulful
eyes observing her every move, rested his hoary snout on one of her
thighs. An unopened book lay upon the other.

She fiddled with the edges of the novel's pages and puffed out her
cheeks, releasing a long breath.

In recent days, she sighed far too often. It must be a symptom of
the blue devils. How long did recovery from a mangled heart take?

No. The real question was how long before she stopped loving
Oliver?

Pain lanced behind her breastbone once again, and she whispered
lest anyone overhear and ask more prying questions, "I'll never stop.
Ever."

Truth to tell, it sounded more like she made vow.

Freddy, ancient and decrepit now, perked his ears up and wiggled
his bobbed tail as he licked her hand. Curled together on the navy
brocade settee as they were wont to do, the equally aged cats, Pudding
and Dumpling slumbered on.

Bending over, she rubbed Freddy's chest, his favorite petting spot.

"I missed you too, my sweet friend. I feared we might lose you
before I returned home."

Life without the pudgy little dear would never be the same.

Wonder of wonders, she even missed M'Lady Lottie's raucous
screeches.

Straightening, Blaike uncrossed her ankles and patted Freddy's
thick back. "As soon as Blythe and Brette arrive, we'll go walkies.

How's that? Even baby Leopold is permitted to go today, the weather is so mild. Doesn't that sound like fun?"

Not really.

Little stirred her interest lately, much less a walk in which she painted a false smile upon her face and pretended all was right with the bleak world.

Only in the past couple of days had the discoloration on her face faded to almost nothing, and she felt confident enough to venture out now. Although if she looked closely, there was the slightest greenish-yellow tinge on her cheekbone. A fine dusting of rice powder concealed the mark, else she'd not have agreed to the outing or having to explain yet again how she came by the injury.

After their walk today, the women had an appointment for the final fittings of their new gowns to be worn at this Friday's welcome home ball.

Blaike would've preferred to dispense with the folderol, including tonight's supper party, but the others wouldn't hear of it. Besides, her twin was so excited at the prospect of seeing everyone again, Blaike couldn't be the cross patch and ruin her fun.

Blaire's enthusiasm might have something to do with an expectation she'd see Lieutenant Drake. Blaike hadn't told her of his change in status after all. Not only did she not want to crush her twin, she didn't know exactly what his position was, and she refused to spread speculation. Blaire would know soon enough in any event.

Nothing remained secret for long in the *haut ton's* elite parlors or assemblies.

At least Blaike wouldn't have to worry about encountering Oliver and suffering that painful awkwardness. Once the family had learned of his role in rescuing the twins in *Port de Lyon* and again his masterful feat eluding the other vessel at sea, they lauded him a hero.

So far, and much to Blaike's relief—and consternation, bother it all—he hadn't accepted any of the many invitations sent his way and remained conspicuously absent

He'd not even seen her off the *Sea Gypsy*.

That had hurt awfully, his not bidding her farewell, and even gentle Blaire had commented on his lack of consideration.

A contrite, rather flustered, Mr. Hawkins had conveyed Captain Whitehouse's apologies.

Bitter tears stung, and she shut her eyes.

Simple everyday things—eating, speaking, *breathing*—took her full concentration. Her mind, the rebellious, undisciplined thing, continually turned to Oliver.

And the same question resounded over and over, the clamor never ceasing and even waking her each night after she'd finally fallen into a tormented sleep.

Why?

Even though she suspected he had acted out of a ridiculous honorable notion, she'd humbled herself and written him a letter asking him—pleading with him—to reconsider.

He hadn't replied.

A fresh wave of humiliation engulfed her. Nevertheless, she'd had to try.

Then, at dinner last week, Heath had mentioned Oliver intended to sail for the Caribbean soon, and implausibly, Blaike's heart fractured further. He truly meant to go on with his life, as if what had transpired between them had never occurred—meant nothing to him.

"There you are, dearest."

A sunny smile arcing her mouth, Blaire glided into the room, whilst tying her bonnet's lilac colored ribbons. The double ruffles of her elegant black embroidered lavender walking dress rustled with her movement. She'd regained a small amount of weight and healthy color once more brightened her cheeks.

Unlike Blaike, she glowed with happiness and couldn't disembark the *Sea Gypsy* swiftly enough.

Blaike's twin angled her head, disquiet crinkling the outer edges of her face.

"I'm worried about you, Blaike." After nudging Freddy aside, she sank onto the window seat's mulberry hued cushion. "I know you pine for Captain Whitehouse."

Blaike pulled her attention from the fashionably dressed passersby and searched her sister's compassionate countenance. No sense denying it. Her twin knew her too well. She lifted a shoulder.

"It will pass. These foolish things always do, don't they?"

It must. For a lifetime of this agony proved too awful to contemplate.

"*Hmm*, you cannot convince me of that," Blaire denied. "I may have been sick as death most of that horrendous crossing, but I do know you didn't return to our cabin until the early morning hours that first night. And I've seen how you look at the captain when you think no one is watching."

She squeezed Blaike's fingers. "He did the same, you know. Couldn't keep his gaze off you. I thought for certain . . ."

A sad, dismayed laugh escaped Blaike.

"As did I." She swept her hand across her forehead, almost as if she could wipe the memories from her mind. "He said he loved me. And in the next breath, he said he'd never ask me to marry him. 'Not now. Not ever.' His very words."

"Oh, Blaike, darling." Blaire rapidly blinked, her eyes shimmering with sympathy. "I'd like to plant him a facer for hurting you, the *roué*."

That was one French word Blaike understood well.

Emotion strangled her for a long moment, and she almost crumbled under the pain rending her soul. "I just don't understand why he rebuffed me when I know he loves me, and he knows I love him."

"Nor do I." The lines of her mouth ribbon thin, Blaire too gazed out the beveled window, the diamond-paned leaded glass windows above showering them both in miniature rainbows.

Freddy settled more snuggly against Blaike, his tubby body shuddering with a contented groan. His light snoring and the clock *tick-tocking* atop the fireplace's Italian Bardiglio marble mantel filled the pregnant silence.

Laughter resounded in the hallway, and in a jiffy, the others bustled into the room, Brooke carrying her wee son. "Are we ready?"

She peered at Blaike and Blaire expectantly.

Blaike nodded. "Yes, I just have to put on my redingote and bonnet."

"Jenkin." Brooke addressed the butler. "Should his lordship return home early, please inform him we've gone for a stroll. Also, I forgot to mention, Mrs. Tremblay and her assistants are expected later for our fittings. Please show them to the floral salon when they arrive. Have Cook prepare light refreshments as well. Five fittings can be rather tedious."

In a trice, Blaike had donned her outer garments, and the entourage, complete with Nurse pushing Leopold's pram, made for the park. The sunshine and the other foursome's excited chatter did help to ease Blaike's doldrums. The women had always been close, and she'd missed her sister and cousins terribly those awful months in Geneva.

That complete story had yet to be revealed, though Brooke and

Heath had been apprised of Blaike's suspicions regarding Madame Beaulieu, as had Blythe and Leventhorpe.

At once, Heath had penned a letter to the ambassador.

Blaike couldn't bring herself to share the rest of the sordid tale quite yet.

Maybe she never would. What need was there?

Blaire would go to her grave with the knowledge.

If Blaike had actually been despoiled, and not just set upon, the risk of a child might've necessitated the telling. But by the grace of God, she'd been spared that degradation.

The sun warming their backs, Brooke and Brette strode arm in arm, each holding a parasol. Brooke held Freddy's lead as well, whilst Blaike and Blaire flanked a very pregnant Blythe. They too, carried unopened parasols. Across the way, the flush of pink and white cherry tree blossoms were visible near Kensington Park's entrance.

Red squirrels darted across the plush lawns, pausing on their haunches every little bit, their tiny black noses twitching as they searched for predators.

As Blaike and the others strolled along, several of *le beau monde's* denizens warmly welcomed the twins home, while others, curiosity burning in their probing gazes, remarked on the premature return.

Blaike's and her twin's rehearsed response remained the same.

They'd missed their family far more than anticipated and with the birth of their new cousin, had opted to return home earlier than planned.

Those who looked upon them kindly accepted the explanation, and society's strictures silenced those inclined to prying.

Brooke glanced behind her, her cheeks glowing from the fresh air.

"I forgot to mention. Our numbers for supper tonight are slightly increased. Heath ran into an old friend of his at White's yesterday. Viscount Sethwick and his wife will join us along with Captain Whitehouse. The Viscountess owns quite an extensive shipping enterprise, and Heath wants to introduce her to the captain. He thinks it will be mutually beneficial." She turned her mouth up into a tolerant smile. "I did scold him for bringing a business element into our celebration of your return, but as Captain Whitehouse is a particular friend and we owe him such a debt of gratitude, I knew you wouldn't mind too terribly much."

Mind?

Was Brooke out of hers?

Of course Blaike minded.

She nearly gargled her tongue to mask her shock. Then the dread blanketing her.

Oliver at dinner.

No. no.

She just couldn't.

Not yet.

Not sit at the table with him and blather nonsensical twaddle, as if he hadn't torn her heart from her chest and tossed it upon the wharf for gulls to feast upon.

Blaire leaned forward, catching Blaike's attention. The question in her wide eyes fairly shouted, *What are you going to do*?

Fingertips pressed to her forehead, Blaike muttered to herself, rather more peevishly than she'd intended, "I do believe a megrim to rival Jupiter's has come upon me." Never mind that she'd never had a megrim in her life until this very moment. "I shall be forced to take to my bed at once, likely for days."

At least a week, until the *Sea Gypsy* weighed anchor for warmer shores, carrying Blaike's love and heart with the vessel.

Blythe gave her a gimlet eye, then bent near and whispered for her ears alone.

"I hope you're not expecting one of us to clobber you with a hammer to alleviate your headache, as Jupiter requested. If I recall my Roman mythology correctly, it killed him. Besides, dear one, your head isn't what's aching. Your heart is."

Blaike shot her an astounded look. Was she so transparent?

Who else knew?

Brooke? Brette?

Likely, they all did.

Her focus shifted to their backs.

Was dinner someone's misplaced attempt at matchmaking?

She leveled a severe glance at Brette, notorious for her meddling in that department.

No, Heath couldn't know what had transpired between Blaike and Oliver. A coincidence was what this was, and she grudgingly admitted a beneficial one for Oliver. She'd mentioned Lady Sethwick to him herself.

Well, not by name, but by reputation.

She couldn't begrudge him the opportunity. But by Jove, she could be absent from dinner. She had all afternoon to contrive a believable excuse.

A sprained ankle was not out of the question.

Leopold cooed and giggled, and at once his doting aunties surrounded his pram, admiring the handsome babe with his mother's vibrant, almost violet eyes. The future Lord Leventhorpe would be a favorite of the ladies, to be sure.

"Best be careful, Brooke. We may spoil him." Brette chuckled as Leopold waved his little fists. Her regard sank to Blythe's swollen belly, and she half-winked. "That goes for your little one, too."

"You're a fine one to talk. In a few months, we'll have three darlings to simper over." Blaire motioned to Brette's less noticeable mound.

Brooke gave her son a doting smile and caressed his plump cheek. "A child can never have too much love, I don't think."

So caught up were they with the infant, they didn't pay attention to passersby. On such a lovely day, one expected crowded foot paths, to encounter acquaintances, perhaps extend an invitation to call or come for tea, or even witness a scandalous *tête-à-tête*.

Blaire's muffled gasp had four more pairs of eyes swooping to where she stared. She quickly schooled her dismayed features and turned her attention elsewhere, but not before Blaike saw the confusion in her eyes.

Lieutenant Drake strolled away from them on a pathway across the greens, an elderly dame attired in black from her bonnet to her parasol on one arm and an attractive brunette in a superb jonquil walking gown on his other.

The woman Oliver had mentioned? And in public together, too.

Blast, now Blaike might—no would—have to explain to her twin.

Biting her lower lip, Blaire observed the lieutenant's progress from the corner of her eye.

He glanced their direction briefly, then saying something to his older companion, guided her down another pathway.

Had he glimpsed them, and that was why he'd steered his companions in the other direction?

Even as she formed the thought, he angled his head just the merest bit, cutting the Culpeppers another sideways look. Actually, his focus was riveted on one particular pale-faced Culpepper.

"Well, isn't this a pleasant surprise?"

An insightful lady knows well that secrets,
much like surprises, though favored by some,
are abhorred by others. Neither is right nor wrong.
~Scruples and Scandals-The Genteel Lady's Guide to Practical Living

16

N o. Not this too.
He couldn't be here.

Jonathon Severs just couldn't.

Not on top of everything else.

Nausea and fear battled for supremacy within Blaike's bell.

Blaire's dismayed gaze collided with hers

Mustering every jot of self-control she had, Blaike turned a bland gaze to him. Dressed like a popinjay, his coat a shade this side of fuchsia and trimmed in Pomona green, he rather resembled a parrot, right down to his hooked nose.

Dread trotted a spiky path down her spine.

His leering gaze widened in appreciation as he took in Blaike's sister and cousins. "I don't believe you ever mentioned there were five of you, Miss Culpepper. Quite exceptional, I must say."

To a woman they responded with expressions frostier than a January dawn in Geneva.

His sister, wearing a smug smile, clung to her brother's arm, her manner more possessive than sisterly.

"Hello Blaire. Blaike. What a coincidence. We just arrived in London three days ago. Our elder sister, Anne, is to wed Lord Desmond in a fortnight." She angled her chin in a superior fashion. "He's an earl, you know. I doubt you've met him. Lord Desmond only travels in the highest circles."

Blaike had never mentioned her peerage connections to the pretentious twit. Titles weren't important to her, but she longed to rattle them off just to see Jacqueline's flummoxed expression.

When Blaike didn't return the Severs's greeting, Brooke slid her a puzzled glance. Savvy and possessing a keen intellect, she'd swiftly deduce something was as off as cream left in the sun for a week.

Brooke angled her head, appearing every bit the regal peeress. "May I ask how you are acquainted that you address my cousins so informally?"

Blaike didn't wait for an answer.

Spine rigid, she looped her arm through Blaire's, and wordlessly, they pivoted and strode in the other direction.

Never before in her life had she cut someone. But so help her God, the urge to beat Severs and his snotty sister to a pulp with her parasol so overwhelmed Blaike, her rage frightened her. She hadn't thought herself capable of such fury or of wishing someone bodily harm.

"Oh, Blaike," Blaire whispered, nearly running to keep up with Blaike's brisk pace. "What are we to do? Why are they here? Did you notice Jacqueline's snide—?"

"Snarl?"

For wasn't that how rabid animals behaved before they attacked? Blaike curled her lip in contempt. "How could I miss it? You can bet our sweet Freddy the others did as well."

"I'm sure of it." Blaire exhaled loudly. "What a deuced conundrum."

So much for keeping the surreptitious matter in Geneva quiet.

Dragging in a shaky breath, Blaike pursed her lips.

"I'll have to tell all. Then hope to God Raven, or Leventhorpe—or both—can threaten that bounder to such an extent, Jonathon will be forced to leave London. He doesn't dare even hint what he attempted. But his sister . . ."

Blaike's stomach flipped over like the time she'd eaten tainted fish and had been violently ill.

"She'll twist the truth. The tattle she contrives could cause damage to our family's standing." She squeezed her parasol handle so tight, it was a wonder it didn't snap under the strain. "I'm sure Heath and Tristan will think of a plausible—"

"Excuse. Yes, yes, of course they will. They're all powerful lords with many influential friends." Blaire dared a swift half-glance over her shoulder. "Those social climbing mushrooms don't know what they're up against."

She lifted her head and slid a covert glance toward where they'd last seen the lieutenant.

He'd disappeared from view.

Sadness deepened the contours of Blaire's pale countenance, and Blaike clamped her jaw because her beloved twin also faced heartbreak.

"Girls. Wait for us," Brooke called, as she and the others scurried to catch up.

Hardly girls anymore.

Blaike slowed, then stopped before turning with a forced upward bend of her mouth.

Probably looked more like a grimace than a smile. Even after several weeks, she wasn't ready to reveal the ugliness to the rest of her family. Odd since she'd had no qualms telling Oliver about the incident.

Honestly, though the ordeal had been traumatic and she could scarcely stand to look upon Jonathon Servers, she fretted more about *le beau monde's* reaction and how it would affect the others. Women and their families had been ostracized for less, even if the scandal weren't of their making or was no fault of theirs. Yet clandestine assignations were not unusual for married women.

She couldn't help but be galled by the hypocrisy.

Despite her intent to ignore them, her attention gravitated to the Severs. Arm in arm, they strolled in the other direction, their heads close together and apparently in an earnest conversation.

Plotting no doubt, the fiends.

Well, she'd not cow or hide in disgrace. She was the victim, and far past time women began to stand up against such assaults on their person instead of retreating in shame.

Again the notion of learning some sort of self-defense poked its head up. The idea didn't seem as farfetched as it once might have.

Radiant in a white embroidered muslin gown and breathless from her hurried walk, Blythe pressed a palm to her distended belly. She glanced downward and chuckled. "Someone didn't like Mama rushing about. I swear this babe is playing leap frog in there."

Brette touched Blaike's arm and angled her parasol's tip at the retreating Severs. "Whatever was that all about? I've never known you to be so abrupt."

A nicely worded way of saying rude.

Nurse was almost upon them with Leopold, his cheerful gurgles earning him an affectionate smile from the middling-aged woman.

Freddy, tongue lolling and eyes mere slits as he enjoyed the sunshine, sat inside the pram as well. Too much for the old boy to toddle to and from Highfield.

"Indeed," agreed Brooke, her gaze shifting between Blaike and her twin. "Though I expect you have good reason for abandoning your manners."

"I think it best we save that conversation for home." Blaike met each of their concerned gazes in turn as her twin made a sympathetic sound of agreement. "It's an unsavory tale and one I don't relish the telling of."

"Very well." Countenance contemplative, Brooke touched her chin with two fingers. "I don't usually form an opinion upon first meeting someone, but for those two I'll make an exception. That Miss Severs had the audacity to demand to know who we were. Must be an American custom, for I believe, given their accents, that's where they hail from."

Two laughing boys in deep blue and gray striped skeleton suits ran by in pursuit of a yapping Cocker Spaniel, dragging his lead.

"Jolly, come back here," called the elder boy.

They careened too near the pram, and Freddy barked, a weak, near-sighted warning.

Behind the lads, and holding a slightly older girl's hand, what had to be their frenzied governess scurried after the scamps.

"Masters Jesse and Travess. Stop chasing that wretched beast this instant!" Offering an apologetic smile, she bustled past the women while complaining to her other charge. "Miss Brianna, I do not know why they must always be into mischief. Frogs in the parlor yesterday, and a snake in the larder the day before."

The peach-clad girl shook her head, causing her neat russet ringlets to bounce.

"Why? Because they're boys, Miss Snowdrop, and all boys are made of snips and snails and puppy dog tails. Remember the poem?"

"And when they're young men they're made of sighs, and leers and crocodile tears. Add lies to that, too," the disgruntled governess huffed.

Even Blaike had to smile at the child's matter-of-fact explanation.

Brooke, however was having none of it. She bent low and kissed Leopold's pudgy cheek. "Not a bit of it, my love. Snails indeed. Boys can be sugar and spice too."

Yes, cinnamon and cloves in particular.

Blaike could almost smell Oliver's scent, feel his lips sinking onto hers and his tongue plundering her mouth.

A much more somber troupe climbed Highfield Place House's stoop a quarter hour later than had departed.

No sooner had they reached the top step than the door swung open to a rather frazzled Jenkin.

"My lady, his lordship, as well as Lords Leventhorpe and Wycombe just arrived with Captain Whitehouse. And a *bird*."

Such disdain riddled his voice and puckered his face, at another time Blaike might've been amused.

Instead, she sucked in a great gulp of air and balked at the entrance so suddenly, Brette and Blythe plowed into her.

Oliver here? With M'Lady Lottie?

How could she bear to see him and not make a complete cake of herself?

"Sluice yer gob," came a familiar screech. "Blast and damn."

"Good heavens." Blythe peered around, seeking the culprit. "Who or what is that?"

"M'Lady Lottie," Blaike and Blaire said in unison.

So confounded did the others appear, Blaike offered by way of an explanation, "She's a salmon-crested cockatoo that spent several years in a—*erm*—house of ill-repute."

"This ought to be most entertaining." Blythe chuckled, while looking about for the bird again.

What had possessed Oliver to bring Lottie to Highfield?

Blaike wasn't noddy enough to believe he'd toted the bird along for a visit.

Still in a dither, the typically unflappable Jenkin rattled on as he closed the door, moisture actually beading his forehead and upper lip.

A first, that.

"That *creature* has stationed itself in a hanging pot in the solarium." Radiating disapproval, he elevated his chin and cinched his mouth.

"Jenkin?" Blaike said. "Where might we find the gentlemen?"

She wasn't about to specify one particular swarthy-skinned sea captain.

"In a bedchamber, Miss. There's been a fire on the captain's ship. The physician has been sent for."

A scrupulous woman knows that much like diseases wastes
the body, secrets oft' tarnish the soul as do the scandals they cause.
~*Scruples and Scandals-The Genteel Lady's Guide to Practical Living*

Once Oliver's coughing fit ceased, he shrugged off Ravensdale and Leventhorpe's helping hands and collapsed onto the bed.

"I cannot think Lady Ravensdale will be pleased to have this fine counterpane stained with soot and smelling of burnt timber, canvas, and the Thames."

"My lady won't consider it for an instant," Ravensdale claimed and gave a slight shudder. "Lest you forget, she operated a dairy farm for years. Trust me, my friend, when I tell you that stench is not something easily forgotten. And we are all grateful beyond words for what you did for the twins. We are indebted to you, Oliver. A ruined bedcover is naught."

Rather than answer, Oliver grunted, momentarily overcome with angst.

The Sea Gypsy.

What would his crew do now?

They were good men, decent men, and they needed employment. For certain, a few might find positions on other vessels, but what about Hawkins? He wasn't a young man anymore.

At least Longhurst had insured the *Sea Gypsy*. He'd not fuss overly much at the ship's loss.

Why should he?

He never wanted any part of her except for Oliver's payments, and now Longhurst could collect the insurance, too.

For a flash, devastation rendered Oliver mute and immobile.

Now what did his future entail?

Hire on as a hand once more?

How could he when he'd captained his own ship these past years?

All was truly lost to him. Every hope and dream. Every ambition and goal. Gone up in orange flames.

After facing that dismal prospect, he forced his thoughts elsewhere, dredging up a speck of gratitude for what had been avoided. No hands had died, except Fairnly. No cargo yet loaded. His almost-paid-for ship had been anchored away from the docks, thus preventing a catastrophe beyond measure.

Three things to be grateful for.

Focus on those for now.

Time to fret about the other later. When his head didn't ache like a Lochaber Axe had been laid to his nape.

"Where's M'Lady Lottie?"

Raising his head a couple of inches, he peered about the finely appointed chamber.

"I take it you mean that evil-tempered, winged demon with a spear for a beak?" Leventhorpe scratched the bridge of his nose, then examined the crimson-stained handkerchief wrapped around his hand, covering the bite he received whilst helping haul Oliver onto the dock. "I think Jenkin chased her into the solarium. I've never seen the man so flustered. He actually bolted after her, flapping his arms and yelling. She called him a pimp whiskin."

Raising a brow, Wycombe grinned. "Somehow, I don't think our staid Jenkin appreciated being compared to a pimp. Wherever did she learn such language?"

"In a bordello," Oliver replied. "And Lottie was protecting me, Leventhorpe. That's why she bit you."

Why did that embarrass him?

His lesser station and lighter pockets had never caused him chagrin with these men, but a crazed bird from a whorehouse attacking those same friends did?

Devil a bit, his ravaged throat felt as if he'd swallowed glass shards. He eyed Leventhorpe's hand. "You probably ought to have that looked at. I have no idea how serious a bird bite can be."

"Sound advice, I think. The physician is expected shortly, in any event." Ravensdale leaned a shoulder against the bedpost, his intense scrutiny belaying his casual mien. "As is my wife, according to Jenkin."

Which meant Blaike would be here soon as well.

Oliver had counted himself fortunate that when they'd arrived the women hadn't been at home. He fully intended to depart just as soon as he could stand without the room spinning like a toy boat caught in a maelstrom. He'd not wanted to come here at all and protested loudly and strenuously against doing so.

Despite his objections, like fussy old tabbies, Raven, Leventhorpe, and Wycombe had bustled him into a carriage and made straight for Highfield Place House. They hadn't heeded his complaints, probably wrongly assuming manly pride motivated his reluctance.

They were wrong.

He'd refused each invitation thus far to spare Blaike more sorrow.

Why Ravensdale had insisted on inviting him here when he'd have preferred to meet at Lady Sethwick's London office he couldn't fathom. He still hadn't come to terms with dining here tonight. Not that he'd be able to now, dressed only in a stained and torn lawn shirt, equally abused trousers and barefoot, to boot.

He couldn't even care for M'Lady Lottie now, much less a wife. What would become of the peevish cockatoo?

In a matter of hours, he'd been reduced to nothing.

More confirmation he'd made the right decision regarding Blaike, though he'd lived in a haze since seeing her disembark the *Sea Gypsy*. Careful to remain in the shadows, concealing his presence amongst the wharf's many buildings, he'd not been able to resist one final glimpse of her.

Pivoting in a slow circle, she'd surveyed the docks, and his heart had ripped asunder.

Not a doubt she searched for him.

And he hadn't a qualm that she loved him either, which made letting her go all that much more unbearable.

In obvious disappointment, her pretty mouth had turned down and her shoulders drooped the merest bit.

Impotent frustration had overwhelmed him, and he'd slammed his fist into the building's rough siding. He flexed his hand, his nearly healed cut and bruised knuckles a potent reminder of the folly of loving her and taking his rage out on unyielding wood.

Daring to peek at his friends from slitted eyes, he tensed at the pity edging each of their faces. Likely they knew full well everything he owned, save the clothing on his back, his mother's jewels hastily stuffed into a coin bag and tied with the string still hanging from his neck, and the bird raising a ruckus below were all he had to his name now.

There yet remained the small hope that Lady Sethwick might actually consider the clipper drawings he'd had sent round, or perhaps even have need of a ship's captain. That might've been discussed tonight, too.

That opportunity had gone up in flames as surely as the *Sea Gypsy* had.

Despair, second only to losing his beloved Blaike encompassed Oliver, and for a moment moisture stung his eyes.

"Whitehouse?" A tinge of alarm leeched into Leventhorpe's voice, and he poked Oliver's shoulder.

"I'm not incapacitated, nor do I need a physician or anyone fussing over me." Unless it was his sweet Blaike. He'd gladly accept her ministrations. Except he'd broken her heart, and now she most likely loathed him.

Particularly since he hadn't answered her letter.

He'd started to.

More times than he could count as the wadded foolscap littering his quarters could attest before they burned to cinders today. Yet every missive turned into a moonstruck swain's pathetic and not the least bit lyrical proclamation of devotion and adoration.

Ravensdale snorted his disapproval. "Nonetheless, you'll permit Dr. Barclay to examine you."

"Bloody blueblood, giving orders as usual," Oliver rasped, his voice hoarse as much from shouting as inhaling smoke. And swallowing a barrel full of river water as Lottie ranted her outrage whilst clawing his back.

"I don't suppose I need to remind you, that blue blood also runs in your veins." No real censure weighted Ravensdale's words.

An elbow across his gritty eyes, Oliver swallowed against the stinging of his raw throat and the cramping in his lungs. His shoulder complained no small amount as well. "I just breathed a bit of smoky air. I'll be fine."

"Old chap, that was more than a bit of smoke. Your ship lit up like someone torched a fireworks factory." Leventhorpe's dry retort earned him a glare beneath Oliver's crooked elbow.

"Probably because someone placed explosives on her."

By someone Oliver meant Fairnly, the turncoat.

It seems after the *Black Dove* limped into port last week, Abraham had bribed the blackguard. Only, the reckless idiot had blown his hand off and practically disemboweled himself. As he lay dying, he'd confessed all to Oliver.

Hawkins and Grover also witnessed the admission before Oliver realized the futility of fighting the spreading flames and ordered them over the Sea Gypsy's side. Surely with their testimony Abraham would see a noose now, or at the very least, the inside of a prison cell for a long while.

Raven's short chuckle relieved a jot of the tension in the bedchamber. "Queerest thing I've ever seen. You swimming toward the wharf with that obscenity screaming bird bobbing on your back. Drew quite a crowd."

"Do shut up, Ravensdale." Oliver needn't be reminded of the hooting and guffawing onlookers.

"Thank God you're all right, Whitehouse. I confess, I initially feared the worst. Pure luck we were on our way to Stapleton Shipping and saw the fire." This from Wycombe, a former rector.

Oliver ought to introduce him to Hawkins. They'd get along famously.

Where was Hawkins anyway?

He'd made it to shore, hadn't he?

Sudden fear stabbed behind Oliver's ribs. "Did anyone see my first mate, Jack Hawkins?"

To a man they shook their heads.

"No, I'm afraid not." Wycombe swept Oliver a compassionate gaze. "We rushed to help you while others assisted your crew. I'm sure he's fine, however."

Ravensdale scraped a hand through his hair. "I'll send a missive to the harbor master and make an inquiry, if that relieves your mind."

"I'd appreciate it." If something had happened to Hawkins . . .

"Oliver?"

Blaike swept into the room, her lovely face taut with worry, and her bonnet clutched in one hand. She barely spared the other men a glance.

"My lords." In her typical, no-regard-for-what-is-customary-fashion, she bustled to the bed. After tossing her hat near his feet, she laid a hand on his good shoulder and bent over him.

"There was a fire? Aboard your ship? Is Abraham responsible, that snake? Are you hurt? Was anyone injured?" She threw a frustrated glance to the doorway. "Where is the doctor?"

Before he could answer, Miss Culpepper and Ladies Ravensdale,

Leventhorpe, and Wycombe glided into the chamber, each still wearing their bonnets.

Hound's teeth. From their expressions, you'd think he'd died or was horribly maimed.

"Heath, what can we do to help the captain?" Lady Ravensdale asked, her tone fraught with worry.

Not a captain any longer. That truth shredded Oliver's already ragged soul further.

"Jenkin," said her ladyship, "send a footman to fetch one of his lordship's nightshirts, please."

The butler was here, too? Yes, just inside the doorway there.

Why not sell tickets and invite the whole of London? Oliver could well use the proceeds to keep out of the poor house.

Lady Ravensdale removed her bonnet and gloves, then passed them to the butler. "Also request wash water, and I think perhaps tepid tea with honey to soothe Captain Whitehouse's throat. Oh, and please send a note to Mrs. Tremblay asking her to come an hour later."

Jenkin accepted the other ladies' bonnets and gloves as well. "At once, your ladyship. I believe I heard the front knocker. I'll have Dr. Barclay escorted up straightaway and a footman bring a nightshirt."

"You wear a nightshirt, Raven?" Wycombe chuckled, low and teasing. "Cannot for the life of me picture that."

"*Shh*, darling." Lady Wycombe scooted to her husband's side. "It's not nice to poke fun at Heath just because you don't wear one."

Unused to being the center of so many concerned glances, so much pity, or such warm regard, Oliver rather wished he could climb beneath the bed. He closed his eyes lest any of his friends see the sudden moisture that blurred his vision.

"Blaike," Lady Leventhorpe said, "is the poor captain unconscious?"

"I am not, your ladyship." Stifling a groan, he sat up. "And I'm not injured either, so there's no need for fussing or nightshirts. I'll take my leave momentarily."

Where he'd go, shoeless and without a groat, he hadn't determined yet.

"The devil you will." Raven's grim countenance brooked no arguing. "I'll not hear any more of that gibberish. You'll reside here for the foreseeable future."

Oliver would see about that.

"Oliver, be careful." Blaike grabbed the pillows, and as she had aboard the *Sea Gypsy,* tucked them behind him. "There, now lean back." A smile ticked her mouth up on one side. "This is getting to be a habit, me taking care of you."

Aware of the multiple pairs of eyes trained on their every move, he swallowed, then cleared his throat.

Finally, more for something to distract them from his pathetic state, and their avid glances swinging between him and Blaike, he lifted the gems from around his neck. He took Blaike's hand and placed the pouch atop her palm.

"These were my mother's. I'd be honored if you'd accept them."

Too bold by far and assuredly beyond the mark.

Women didn't accept gifts from men unless they were from a family member or their betrothed. He could never sell the set though; even if it meant he'd face debtor's prison. And there was no one else he'd rather have the jewels. Besides, on London's streets, he'd likely be robbed of the emeralds in a trice. Far, far better Blaike have them than take the risk of his mother's most prized possession being hawked.

Attention riveted on the exchange between him and Blaike, no one made a sound.

Fair brow puckered, she loosened the cinched leather closure, and then dumped the contents on the bed.

From the bedside window, soft late morning sunlight illuminated the brilliant green and white stones.

"Her gems?" She picked up a comb and ran her pointer finger across the bright jewels. A shrewd look entered her startling blue eyes before she narrowed them, pinning him to the fluffy pillows. "You told me she meant these for your wife."

Blaike didn't think . . .?

No. No. She couldn't.

Not after what he'd said aboard the *Sea Gypsy.* He'd been perfectly clear. Brutally clear.

One of the women in the chamber made an odd sound.

He couldn't be sure which, since he'd lost the ability to drag his gaze from Blaike. As he tried to figure out what she was about, and how to gently unravel this new bumblebroth, a satisfied yet challenging smile curved her dewy mouth.

From below, voices echoed in the entry, and a bird's chirrup carried through the window pane.

"Not the most romantic proposal, to be sure." She slipped the ring on one finger, then another. "I fear it's a trifle big."

It dawned on him then.

She knew exactly what she was about, the minx.

He'd carelessly opened the door, and she'd snatched the opportunity like a starving urchin clutches a dropped half loaf.

"Blaike . . .?"

She wouldn't dare go that far. Wouldn't twist his words and his intentions. Wouldn't exploit his oversight and trap him.

Would that be so very awful?

"Then again, you don't generally do things the conventional way, do you, Oliver?" She shook her head, her pearl earrings swaying with the motion. "That's one of the things I most love about you. You do the unexpected."

She was one to talk.

"Truth there," Raven, or it might've been Leventhorpe, muttered, his voice so brimming with amusement, Oliver bit his tongue to keep from telling him to sod off.

This wasn't funny.

Actually, had it been someone else, he'd have been highly entertained as well.

He searched Blaike's guileless face. She'd admitted to loving him in front of everyone. No hint of bashfulness or uncertainty flushed her cheeks or shadowed her expressive eyes.

"I rather prefer being unorthodox myself. It's so freeing." She grasped his hand and held her other up, admiring the ring's oval setting.

The glance she lowered to Oliver held such love and adoration, it awed him.

Humbled him.

Frightened the hell out of him.

"I accept. How soon do you want to wed? As soon as the banns have been read?"

*A woman of noble character knows that secrets and lies go
hand in hand, and our greatest secrets are the lies we tell ourselves.
~Scruples and Scandals-The Genteel Lady's Guide to Practical Living*

18

And there it was.

Everyone started jabbering at once, but the buzzing in Oliver's ears muffled their exact words. He thought he heard exclamations to the effect of, "Silliness, acting rashly, unbecoming behavior, isn't done, unscrupulous and scandalous."

Blaike remained stoic, her pert chin angled in defiance. "Thank you for your concern, but this is a conversation between Oliver and me. I assure you, it's not the first time we've discussed marriage."

It almost sounded conceivable, perhaps even respectable, the way she said it.

Disapproval pulling the planes of his face taut, Raven's reproachful gaze took in each of the other men in the room, one by one. "Why I should be surprised you didn't approach me first, Whitehouse, when neither Leventhorpe nor Wycombe bothered to either, I cannot fathom. Yet I am."

Blaike still held Oliver's hand, only now she clung to him, as if she needed his support and strength. Yes, she had acted imprudently and impulsively, and God help him for a smitten fool, he loved her all the more for her courage to seize what he'd been too afraid to pursue.

The bed squeaked slightly as he adjusted his position.

Never would he humiliate her by publically denouncing her impetuous, and perhaps, slightly fool-hardy decision. Didn't he also know what it was to love so desperately?

"Where is he? In there?" demanded an imperious, but distinctly refined voice, followed by the rhythmic thumping of a walking stick banging upon a wooden panel in the corridor.

Blaike withdrew her hand from Oliver's, and also removed the ring and placed it with the other gems but didn't budge from her station beside his bed.

"I say, where *is* my son?"

Willoughby.

Bloody maggoty hell.

Could this day get any worse?

How had he learned of Oliver's mishap?

Hawkins, the interfering busybody.

Likely he feared Oliver had nowhere to go and no one to turn to, so he'd rounded up anyone and everyone the first mate thought might help.

That was where he'd disappeared to the moment he'd made the wharf. Good thing the *Sea Gypsy* likely lay at the bottom of the River Thames, for Jack Hawkins no longer held the first mate position.

"Father, if you'd permit the majordomo, he'd direct you."

Lionel Talbot, Oliver's half-brother also?

Oliver cut Blaike a sideways glance.

Jaw sagging, she gaped at the doorway before she tore her attention away. "Oliver? Is that your family?"

He gave a terse nod and clamped his teeth as a feminine voice joined the others.

"Yes, Papa. You mustn't be so impatient."

Which sister, Vivian or Sylvia?

"Sylvia is right. You'll only upset Oliver further, Papa. Isn't that so, Doctor?"

Of course the other sister was here, too.

The whole deuced family. Had they brought their spouses and broods of offspring?

"As I haven't examined the patient yet, I cannot make that determination. Mr. Drake, you might be in a better position to answer Miss Talbot's question since you claim a close friendship with the captain." More than a hint of annoyance weighted the good doctor's tone.

Oliver did groan then.

Drake too?

What in God's name had Hawkins told them?

That he lay dying?

Blaike sank to the mattress, concern pleating the corner of her eyes. "Are you in pain?"

Oliver spared her a haggard glance. "Aye, agony, but it's not physical."

"I presume that open door is my son's chamber?"

Arrogant sot, claiming his fatherly prerogative.

"Captain Whitehouse's chamber is just here. If you'd lower your walking stick and permit Dr. Barclay to pass? " Jenkin's request was dry as ash and just as acerbic.

When Oliver had Hawkins alone . . .

Six more people crowded into the already overly full bedchamber.

Make that seven.

The footman arrived with a folded nightshirt, which Oliver had no intention of donning whilst still breathing. However, unlike the other intruders, once the servant had delivered the garment, he beat a hasty retreat.

"Sir, a missive arrived for you a short while ago." Jenkin passed Oliver the note.

Hawkins's familiar scrawl lashed the neatly folded paper. Best read it later when Oliver's curses wouldn't offend the ladies. He handed it to Blaike. "Would you put that on the bedside table for me, please?"

"Of course."

Oliver exchanged nods with his sire, brother, and Drake who immediately sought Blaire, but only offered her the merest cant of his head in greeting.

Rather than respond in kind, she remained bland-faced and turned her regard back to Oliver.

Blaike must've told her twin about Drake's change in circumstances.

Oliver's sisters each swooped in to kiss his cheek, as if he were a most treasured brother.

"I'm so relieved you aren't seriously hurt." Sylvia gave him a watery smile, and the most peculiar sensation rattled around the vicinity of his ribs.

"Drake, might I ask why you are here?" Oliver had guessed the truth of it, but wanted confirmation.

"Hawkins sent word. It sounded serious." Drake didn't seem the least apologetic for intruding. He pulled a crumpled scrap from his pocket. "Actually, the note was brief. *Explosion SG. All lost in fire.*

Captain gravely injured. At Ravensdale's."

First time Oliver had ever known Hawkins to stretch the truth.

"Is it true then, Oliver?" Worry lined Sylvia's pale face as her gaze skittered over him, from head to holey-stockinged toes. "You're hurt?"

"I was injured in *Port de Lyon*. Shot, if you must know." Oliver wasn't about to tell them Blaike had cared for him.

He swept his family a cool glance. Why couldn't he accept their warm regard? Why must he always keep them at arm's length?

Mamma. That was why.

"Hawkins notified all of you as well?" Oliver asked.

"No, just Father." Vivian's attention gravitated to Blaike sitting beside Oliver for the third time. "Did you forget? Our families have tea together on Mondays."

How cozy.

Her cheeks pinkened, and she shot Oliver an abashed look. "You've been invited numerous times too, Oliver."

He had. And never responded to a single invitation.

Wasn't he the churlish sod?

After greetings had been exchanged, Dr. Barclay took charge. "I need to examine my patient, if you please."

He looked pointedly at the door.

"Doctor, Lord Leventhorpe should have his hand examined as well." Blaike had noticed, Leventhorpe's injury, had she?

Dr. Barclay glanced to where she pointed. As he puttered in his bag he asked, "What happened, my lord?"

Leventhorpe glowered at his makeshift bandage. "A cranky cockatoo wanted a taste of me."

That elevated Dr. Barclay's grizzled brows several inches. "A cockatoo, you say? Don't believe I've ever treated a bird's bite before. I'll tend you when I've finished with Captain Whitehouse."

"Why don't we all go through to the drawing room, and I'll have a light repast prepared?" Lady Ravensdale held her arm out, indicating the others should go before her.

Everyone but Blaike, her twin, and Willoughby filed out.

"Blaike? Aren't you coming?" Her sister, one hand resting on the door jamb, paused at the entrance.

Blaike reluctantly stood, then brushed Oliver's hair off his forehead. "Yes. I'll come back when the doctor says I might." She faced Willoughby and dipped into a half curtsy. "I look forward to conversing with you below, my lord."

Willoughby inclined his gray streaked head. "And I you."

"We'll speak later, Captain," she said, skirting the bed.

Back to propriety was she?

Because of Willoughby's presence?

With an unreadable final glance at Oliver, she accepted her twin's arm, and they departed.

"That young woman is in love with you." Willoughby, still hovering at the foot of the bed, leaned on his elaborate walking stick.

"I know, but—"

Before Oliver could finish, Willoughby's attention sank to the gems scattered beside Oliver's thigh, and he inhaled a ragged breath. He came round the side of the bed. His haughty countenance softening, he lifted the necklace.

"I gave these to your mother the first time I proposed."

Though there are no bars or locked doors, a long kept secret
can still imprison one. Consider carefully the cost of freedom.
~Scruples and Scandals-The Genteel Lady's Guide to Practical Living

19

Oliver didn't seem perturbed.

Half listening to what Mr. Maddox sitting to her left said, Blaike observed Oliver from beneath her lashes.

My, but he looked so different.

Wearing borrowed evening clothing, his beautiful midnight hair shorn and beard shaved, he appeared every bit the proper English gentleman. Relaxed and amiable, a ready smile upon his firm mouth, his infamous glower hadn't put in an appearance the entire evening.

Earlier, when he'd entered the drawing room with his new fashionably short hair and clean-shaven face, the others' compliments had muffled her stifled gasp. She'd thought him striking before, had adored his long hair and beard, but now?

Well, he quite took her breath away.

In the most feminine, fluttery manner.

Blaike glanced across the table for the umpteenth time.

His tanned cheeks contrasted with his well-defined, slightly paler jaw.

Ninny, stop staring.

Her gullible heart pattered faster, as it had whenever her eyes met his tonight.

Thank goodness, Dr. Barclay had declared him none-the-worse from escaping the fire aboard the *Sea Gypsy,* but had prescribed an abundance of fresh air to cleanse Oliver's lungs. Such a thing wasn't to be had in London, for Town's skies were notoriously sooty.

Much to her astonishment, the good doctor had praised Blaike's care of Oliver's shoulder. Nonetheless, he expressed the merest concern that infection might set in after the dip in the less than pristine Thames.

Promising to return in a couple of days, the doctor left instructions about what signs to look for, and he was to be sent for at once should any symptoms occur.

Dropping her focus to the roast partridge on her plate, Blaike wadded her napkin as remembered panic stalled her breath for a moment. Such terror had gripped her when Jenkin had said there was a fire. Even now with Oliver sitting but feet away from her, hale and hearty, her stomach remained woozy. How he'd managed that swim with his shoulder not completely healed, she couldn't comprehend.

Sensing his perusal once more, she lifted her head.

He sent her a dazzling smile, so intense, she quivered from neck to knee. From the confident arcing of his black brow, he knew how he affected her.

This genial demeanor was good, wasn't it?

There'd been no opportunity for them to talk, but surely he wouldn't be this affable if he remained vexed with her. Truth to tell, for a man who'd just lost his ship, he didn't appear wholly devastated.

Quite the opposite, in fact.

She couldn't put her finger on exactly what, but there was something different in his comportment aside from the drastic change in his appearance. Whatever had transpired between Oliver and his father had transformed them both.

While they'd waited for Dr. Barclay to finish examining Oliver, no one had mentioned that awkwardness of Blaike's peculiar potential betrothal. How could they, with guests present?

That was the one unfortunate rub in all of this.

Mr. Drake—strange to not call him lieutenant any longer—had been most reserved in his attentions to Blaire. Truthfully, other than the cursory hello, he'd not spoken to her, yet his gaze continually followed her 'round the room.

To her twin's credit, Blaire acted the composed woman of refinement, chatting and smiling with their visitors, and not once did she turn soulful eyes to him.

Blaike knew full well the supreme effort that façade had cost her sister.

She hadn't completely escaped repercussions for her wild impulse in Oliver's chamber, however. After the guests had departed, and as the women excused themselves to go to their fittings, Heath had taken her aside. He'd asked to see Blaike in his study tomorrow morning. At ten o'clock sharp. Likely to chastise her unseemly, impetuous, and shameful behavior.

A smile pulled her mouth upward.

Dear Heath. He'd had no idea what he'd taken on when he married Brooke and was appointed the other four Culpeppers' guardian. He'd done remarkably well for a man with no sisters.

She supposed it would be the perfect time to tell him about the Severs, too.

Along the length of the table, the guests laughed and chatted, their conversations mixing with clinking china and silverware. And every now and again, a raucous, muffled call filtered into the dining room from a disgruntled M'Lady Lottie, sequestered in the solarium.

Somehow, someone had managed to procure a good-sized cage, and Blaike had helped gather items for the bird to play with as well as food for the cockatoo.

She'd spent several minutes soothing the frazzled creature, and couldn't contain her jubilant smile when Lottie obediently toddled onto her perch repeating, "Purdy bird, purdy bird. Purdy, purdy, birdy, bird."

A mortified gasp replaced her upturned lips when, a moment later, M'Lady Lottie turned to Heath, fanned her salmon crest, and said in a woman's coy voice, "Shag fer a shillin', guv."

His eyebrows had vaulted toward his thick hairline before he replied through his laughter, "Alas, my wife won't permit it. But thank you for the kind offer."

"Raven. For shame." He'd received a sharp rap on his arm from Brooke for his tasteless humor.

Oliver turned to address something Lady Sethwick said.

That appeared to be going splendidly, and Blaike had the absurd childish desire to clap her hands in delight at his good fortune. For certain, he deserved some grace. Fate hadn't been altogether kind to him.

He nodded at whatever her ladyship said, and a shock of hair fell over his forehead, just above his scar.

Canting her head, Blaike considered him.

No denying his cropped hair became him. Why had he decided to have the rest lopped off, and his beard too?

A small stab of alarm had her squeezing the wine goblet's stem.

Had that to do with his father, too?

Was it possible, Oliver had fashioned a plan about his future so swiftly?

Did it include her?

She took a sip of wine, as another hot flush engulfed her at her gumption in his chamber. Of course she'd known he wasn't proposing, and she was fully aware she'd backed him into a corner, so to speak. Naturally, she had no intention of forcing herself on him. But if misplaced honor and pride were what prevented him from asking for her hand, then she'd fight for Oliver.

Fight for their love.

Make him fight for it, too. If that was what he wanted as much as she did.

Didn't he realize not everyone was fortunate enough to find the one who made their heart and soul whole?

Nothing to do if Oliver truly wouldn't marry her.

She'd not humiliate herself any further.

In fact, Blaike very well might accept the Sethwicks' generous offer to visit Craiglocky Castle. Anytime, they'd said. She'd never been inside a medieval keep before, let alone stayed in one. It might prove just the distraction she needed.

If Oliver couldn't be persuaded to see reason.

To let love guide him and trust what came after.

Dinner dragged on for hours, it seemed, as did the men's brandy and the ladies' tea afterward. At long last, everyone gathered in the drawing room.

Blythe made straight for the mahogany pianoforte and Lady Sethwick joined her. In a moment, their expert playing filled the room.

Near the fireplace, Oliver chatted with Lord Sethwick and Heath. He ran a finger over the marble mantel and said something to Heath. After Heath responded, Oliver smiled and gave a brief bow, then headed in Blaike's direction.

The moment was at hand. He meant to discuss her impulsive act, sure as feathers stuck to warm tar.

Her palms dampened, and she swallowed.

He didn't appear the least bit angry, but she was still nervous as a goose the week before Christmastide.

Her future might be decided within the next few minutes.

Well, her future with Oliver. At least she'd know, one way or the other.

She stubbornly disregarded the maddening little voice that

reminded her he'd already had his say aboard the *Sea Gypsy.*

He bowed before her chair, his gaze holding a silent message. Good or bad, she couldn't discern. Neither could she decide if she preferred this refined man or the unpolished captain who'd first stolen her heart.

"Ravensdale has said I might take a turn about the solarium with you since it's begun to rain, and I cannot take the stroll I'd anticipated."

My, he sounded every bit the polished gentlemen. Where had her swaggering buccaneer gone? He'd anticipated a stroll with her, had he?

Blaike rose, acutely aware every eye in the room had turned to them. More than one pair of lips turned upward knowingly. She'd got herself into this conundrum, and she'd have to deal with the consequences.

"I'm sure M'Lady Lottie will be happy to see you. She said pretty bird today."

"Yes, and a great number of other less polite things as well," Leventhorpe offered dryly as he stood beside his wife, turning the music pages.

"Shall we?" Oliver extended his elbow.

The solarium lay along the corridor on the opposite side of the house. More nervous than she could ever recall being with him, Blaike searched for something to break the strained silence.

"Why did you cut your hair and shave your beard?"

Oliver ran a hand over his smooth jaw, and offered a lopsided smile. "I thought I might make a better impression on Lady Sethwick if I didn't look like an ill-kempt marauder."

"No such thing," Blaike denied. "Your long hair was lovely."

They'd reached the solarium, and he opened the door.

Candles burned in several sconces on the walls, and the sweet perfume of Brooke's prized gardenias tinged the humid air. Lottie's new cage had been placed beneath a pair of potted ficuses, and some large leafed plants formed a half circle behind the cage.

"Hello, Lottie."

Immediately upon spying Oliver, she launched into her usual dancing and bobbing as Blaike covertly twisted the key in the keyhole.

"Ol-eeve. Ol-leeve."

"I don't think she's ever going to pronounce your name correctly."

Blaike unlatched Lottie's cage, and at once the cockatoo soared through the airy room, weaving and dipping before landing on a hanging pot. Truth to tell, the greenhouse would make an ideal over-sized birdcage for her and even slightly resembled her native habitat.

Oliver remained silent, his ebony gaze never leaving Blaike.

Uncomfortable under his intense scrutiny and uncertain why he hadn't yet broached the subject that was at the forefront of both their minds, she made her way to the wicker sofa with it's coral, yellow, and sage floral cushion. After tossing a matching pillow aside and settling on the seat, she plucked a couple of dead blossoms from the salmon colored begonia atop the matching wicker table.

The silence dragged on, until her nerves became taut and her stomach wobbly, and she feared her dinner might reappear. Oh, how she dreaded hearing what Oliver in his pity or compassion couldn't bring himself to say.

Fine then.

She'd spare them both the prolonged discomfit.

Better to have it done and over.

"Oliver, I apologize for placing you in such an uncomfortable position earlier. That was unfair of me and manipulative as well. You made yourself absolutely clear that day in your quarters. I . . ." How could she tell him that she'd hoped—prayed—he'd changed his mind? Wanted to beg him to give their love a chance.

I shan't cry.

Head slanted, she focused on Lottie preening her feathers rather than his beloved features. Her heart would shatter, loudly and in as many pieces as dropped crystal, if she had to witness the relief in his expression when she told him what she must.

Closing her eyes briefly, she inhaled a fortifying breath. She wasn't a whiny, weak-kneed miss. She'd take responsibility.

"Of course I shan't hold you to that ridiculousness. Neither will I ask you to be the one to tell my family. After all, you heard their reactions in your chamber. They won't be the least surprised."

Why didn't he say something?

Gritting her jaw against the pulsing ache in her throat, she commanded the moisture in her eyes to go.

I. Shall. Not. Cry.

He'd wandered to one of the gardenia bushes, and now held one of the fragile blooms in his sun-browned hand. "You've changed your mind then?"

A lady of discernment bears in mind that just because
someone reveals a secret, it doesn't mean they're telling the truth.
~Scruples and Scandals-The Genteel Lady's Guide to Practical Living

20

"**N**o. I assumed . . ."

Blaike wet her lower lip, and brows scrunched, peered at him. Finally, she managed, "I don't know what to say to make things right, Oliver."

A traitorous tear fell onto her hands folded in her lap.

The drops would ruin the fine satin.

This pale cerulean and ivory gown, with its delicate blue roses embroidered at the hem, cuffs and neckline had been selected because it made her eyes appear bluer and her skin creamier. She'd chosen it to impress him. Had wanted to be pretty for him.

"I love you. I tried to stop, because I know you said you would never ask me to marry you. But, God help me, I swear I cannot."

Head tucked to her chest, she whispered the last words, and in that moment knew them to be true. She would never, could never, cease loving Oliver. Some women were meant to love a single man. It seemed she was one of them.

"*Amore mia*, I don't want you to."

Then Oliver was beside her, gathering her into that wonderfully strong embrace she yearned for and remembered so well.

His unique manly essence combined with soap, and the brandy he'd imbibed after dinner drifted to her nostrils. Eyes closed, she breathed him in, this man who'd become such a vital part of her life. She'd do anything for them to be together. Even toss her scruples aside and risk scandal, so great was her love.

Oliver spoke into her hair. "I've regretted those words every second since I stupidly, cruelly uttered them. Please tell me you can forgive me."

"Of course I forgive you." Blaike smiled and touched his cheek. "I forgave you as soon as you said them. When you love someone, forgiveness comes easily."

A door slammed shut somewhere in the house, and laughter carried down the corridor. Either Lady Sethwick or Blythe continued playing the pianoforte.

He grasped her hand and brought it to his lips, giving each knuckle a reverent kiss.

"Tonight, *cara*, I finally saw reason. With humility and the full knowledge of how very blessed I am to have your love, I implore you to marry me."

At once her vision blurred, and she struggled to speak. "Truly, Oliver?"

"Aye, truly, *bella, Ti adoro*."

"What made you change your mind?" Threading her hand through his hair, enjoying the thick, silky strands sliding between her fingers, she said, "I'm positive it wasn't my rash behavior in your chamber. No one makes Captain Oliver Whitehouse do something he doesn't want to."

Holding her tighter, he laughed, a warm self-deprecating sound.

"Actually, my father revealed long held secrets to me, and now I understand so much." He kissed her damp cheeks, then her mouth for a splendid, far too short moment. "He'd asked my mother to marry him, several times truth to tell, but she refused."

Blaike stiffened and angled to stare into his tender gaze, not at all sure she'd heard him correctly. "Why would she do that? You told me she adored him."

A violent gust of wind pelted rain against the glass.

Startled, Lottie flapped her wings. "Hooligans. Bolt the door."

Secure within Oliver's embrace, Blaike snuggled closer. Let the storm vent her wrath. Nothing could disturb her contentment.

"She did love my father. But *Mamma* felt unworthy, and claimed commoners and aristocrats shouldn't marry."

That sounded far too familiar.

Oliver had said that exact thing.

"According to my father, *Mamma* vowed those unions caused untold difficulties and heartache. She believed if they married, it would bring shame upon Father's dynasty, and she feared it would eventually taint their love."

Did he realize he'd been referring to Willoughby as his father since this morning?

Brushing his smooth jaw with her fingertips, Blaike shook her head, confused.

"Balderdash. She must've endured shame and ridicule bearing a child out of wedlock. Look how it affected you? Didn't she consider that?"

Oliver leaned back, drawing her with him until she practically lay beneath him. "She did, and yet she still wouldn't marry my father or even let him set her up in a house. You see . . ."

He paused to kiss her collarbone, then trailed his tongue across the quivering flesh to her shoulder.

Such bliss infused Blaike, it was all she could do to keep her thoughts straight and not forget all and ravish him.

"Go on," she managed, hardly recognizing her own passion-laden voice.

"I'd much rather kiss you, and give you that anatomy lesson you requested." Oliver's husky tone suggested he was as overcome as she. "Except I fear we might be interrupted. That might prove a mite awkward."

"We won't be disturbed." She waggled her brows, a naughty smile tugging her mouth sideways. "I locked the door."

"Why you sly wench you." He tickled her ribs, and she giggled.

Who was this playful devil?

"You can give me a lengthy lesson afterward. In fact, I insist upon it." Perhaps—hopefully—a whole lot more than kissing might occur. Well, not too much more. For certain, someone would be along soon to ensure propriety wasn't breached.

She nudged Oliver in the ribs. "What is this secret the viscount told you?"

"Father confessed he didn't know everything either. Only what *Mamma* had shared after the last time she refused his suit. It seems my grandmother—my *nonna*—was the youngest and favorite daughter of an Italian nobleman, Francesco Rossini. She fell in love with *Nonno*, a humble shipbuilder, and eloped when my great-grandfather forbade them to see each other. Her father disowned her—never spoke to her again."

"How cruel. It must've broken her heart."

Blaike shifted, and the wicker creaked. Surrounded by windows on three sides, the solarium still held the day's heat, despite the cranky weather outside.

"I think it did. But my great-grandmother wrote letter after letter, trying to persuade *Nonna* to return home. Without her husband. Or her child of sin. *Nonna* was Catholic, but *Nonno* wasn't, and so her mother condemned their child too."

"I don't believe I like your great-grandmother at all."

"Nor I. According to my father, my great-grandmother blamed my *nonna* for everything from her father's ill-health and losing his sight, to her married sister running off with her lover, and her brother's sons drowning and leaving no male heirs."

"That's awful. She sounds like a spiteful, bitter woman." What kind of a person did that to their child?

"She only stopped when *Nonna* died. By her own hand. My *mamma* found her. That's when *Nonno* moved to England and changed his name from de Casabianca to Whitehouse so the Rossinis couldn't find them. After a few years they did though. Another sister wrote *Mamma* once in a while, usually to announce a death or a marriage in the family."

"Oliver, do you think those are the letters?" Blaike's eyes rounded in distress. "Oh, no. Did they burn, too? Now you'll never know—"

He placed two fingers on her lips. "*Shh*, don't fret, *cara*. I took your advice and had the entire packet, the letters and the documents, translated."

Exhaling a great puff of air, she relaxed once more. "I'm so relieved. And I confess, terribly curious."

"I wish *Mamma* hadn't been so afraid. Today, after Father told me what she'd done, I realized I was following in her footsteps. Forsaking the one I adore for fear of society's strictures and what might happen."

Blaike sighed, and draped an arm about Oliver's brawny shoulders. "It's not for us to judge your mother for her decisions. Unless someone has been in the same circumstances, experienced the same trauma, they haven't any right to say what should or should not be done. Even then, they shouldn't."

"Now you sound like Hawkins." Oliver shook his head, his lips quirked in exasperation. "You know that note he sent?"

She nodded. "Yes."

"He apologized for overstepping the bounds, but said I was too pig-headed to accept help from those who care about me. So he'd taken matters into his own hands. He also said he'd call on me when he returned from visiting his daughter in Deal." A rueful smile tipped Oliver's mouth. "I didn't even know he had a daughter."

"What will he do for work now?"

"Lady Sethwick assures me she can find him a position, but I've half a mind to make him our butler. If you're in agreement."

One of Blaike's winged brows twitched. "Our butler? We don't have a house."

More on point, what would Oliver do now?

He pushed her gown off one shoulder, and as he nibbled his way to her neck, slid one hand up her thigh. "*Ti desidero.*"

Good heavens.

Forget the reading of the banns.

That took much, much too long.

She'd demand they be wed by special license.

He caressed a particularly sensitive spot on her hip, and she all but dissolved into a mass of desire.

Tomorrow.

Yes. They must be wed tomorrow.

He edged her bodice lower.

"Pretty bubbies," M'Lady Lottie cried.

Blaike and Oliver both burst out laughing, and he left off his explorations.

"When we are married, she'll not be anywhere near our bedchamber. In fact, I'm searching for a mate for her. Maybe that will keep her occupied." He sat up, then smoothed his hair. "We should get back and announce our official betrothal. I'm certain curiosity has them conjuring all sorts of interesting scenarios."

Biting back a disappointed sigh, Blaike also set about straightening her clothing. Everyone probably knew what was transpiring in the solarium. Nevertheless, Blaike needn't broadcast her indiscretion by returning to the drawing room rumpled.

As it always did, her curiosity demanded satisfaction, and she asked the question that had been tickling her tongue all evening.

"Oliver, has her ladyship offered you a position as well?"

Blaike stood and shook out her skirts, and after smoothing the satin with her hands, checked the pearls at her neck to make sure the clasp was in place at her nape.

"She has. Lady Sethwick quite likes my drawings and would like to commission me to oversee the building of a new clipper straightaway. However, I begged her indulgence until I settled a few matters."

"Come here, *amore mia*." He opened his arms wide.

Blaike willingly stepped into his embrace once more. Her head resting on the firm expanse of his chest, her curves melding with his rigid lines, she fit there as if they were two halves of the same mold.

"How do you feel about a honeymoon in Italy, *cara*?"

Did he jest?

She arched away from him.

No. He appeared perfectly serious.

"Italy? Whyever would you go there?"

"Because, *amore*, I learned this very afternoon that amongst those documents you so wisely persuaded me to have translated, is a deed to a marble quarry and what looks—at least on paper—to be an extensive estate in Naples. It seems great-grandpapa didn't completely disinherit his adored daughter, after all."

Ah, that's why he'd been asking Heath about the fireplace. It was made of Italian marble. "Of course we should go. If that's what you wish."

"So much time has passed, the deeds might not be valid anymore. I know nothing of such matters. Naturally, I'll need to consult with a solicitor, here as well as in Italy." He lifted her chin, searching her eyes. The merest trace of vulnerability fringed the corners of his dear face. "You should know you are marrying a man who at this moment, owns nothing but an annoying cockatoo. All I have to offer you is my love, and I do so unreservedly."

"That's all I require, Oliver. I've never cared about possessions."

She wrapped her arms about his waist and hugged him tight. He was her everything. It would be enough to fall asleep with him at her side and wake to the same in the morn.

"Where you go, I go, Oliver. On a ship. In an apartment above your office. A hovel in the Himalayas or a mansion in Rome. All that matters is that we are together."

His head inched lower until his lips were but a hair's breadth away from hers.

"Blaike, *Il mio cuore è solo tua.*"

"My heart is yours too, Oliver."

Tilting her head and cupping his nape, she sealed her vow with a passionate kiss.

Fortunate is the woman who knows this secret:
for love to grow, she must risk giving it away, so it may dwell
and flourish in the heart of the only person she trusts to keep it safe.
~Scruples and Scandals-The Genteel Lady's Guide to Practical Living

Naples, Italy
4 August, 1823

The entry's gold leaf grandfather clock peeled midnight as Oliver took the marble stairs two at a time.

His bride waited above, probably fast asleep given the late hour.

As he had since they'd arrived nearly two months ago, he marveled at the ostentatious mansion's architecture. It was quite the grandest, *gaudiest,* house he'd ever seen.

He and Blaike had gaped like country bumpkins upon crossing the threshold that first day. It hadn't taken them more than five minutes to decide this wasn't the place for them. Hence, Villa de Rossini had discreetly been put up for sale for a price that boggled but, which Signore Parodi, his solicitor, had insisted was quite fair.

The profitable quarry in Carrara Valley, Oliver opted to keep.

Pauper poor mere weeks ago, now he possessed wealth beyond anything he'd ever conceived. He and Blaike could have a home wherever they liked—France, Italy, even America—but she preferred to live near her family.

Wonder of wonders, he wanted to be near his, too.

Passing beneath his ancestors' gilded portraits, he paused at his great-grandsire, Francesco de Rossini's likeness.

Not a doubt who Abraham—not his real name—had descended from.

No, Lanzo Abramo Rossini possessed the same sly, close-set eyes and slightly sneering upper lip as his grandfather.

As vile as a dried horse turd in his mouth, the knowledge that Oliver was cousin to the knave who now called Newgate home stuck in his craw. Likely Abraham would remain imprisoned the rest of his days, unless his sentence was commuted to deportation to Australia instead.

Untying his neckcloth, Oliver continued down the corridor and yawned. He'd been up at dawn three days in a row.

The day Abraham torched *Nonno's* office, he'd been after the deeds to Villa de Rossini and the marble quarry.

His mother, the grand aunt who'd trotted off to England with her lover, had learned of the documents when her father died, and she'd returned home in disgrace for his funeral. She thought her bastard son was more entitled to the properties than *Mamma*. Or Oliver, another bastard and the only other remaining male in the family line.

Abraham had wrongly assumed the documents had been destroyed in the fire he set and never attempted to steal them again. He'd turned his festering disappointment into tormenting Oliver at every given opportunity.

Outside his chamber, Oliver paused, enjoying the peacefulness.

No screeching cockatoos.

M'Lady Lottie and her mate of six weeks, Michelangelo, were no doubt snuggled together on their perch in the conservatory. Neither would be pleased to leave their lush home, but another just as grand would be found for them in England.

Thirty servants staffed this great house. Yet the only sounds disturbing the tranquility were the whisper of a mild breeze caressing the sheer panels covering open windows as well as crickets' and cicadas' songs filtering from the balconies on this side of the manor.

Before Oliver lowered the latch, he also said a quiet prayer of thanks for the entrancing woman beyond the door.

Seems Hawkins's faith had at long last borne fruit.

The angry bitter man Oliver had once been had been replaced by one who daily gave thanks for the many undeserved blessings bestowed upon him.

Quietly opening his bedchamber door, his heart swelled behind his breastbone. He'd never tire of seeing that vision.

Blaike, her wondrous hair spilling over her shoulders, wearing nothing but a sleeveless nightgown, lying in their bed, waiting for him.

She gave him a drowsy smile and held her arms open in invitation. "You're later than I thought you'd be, darling."

After an embrace and a hungry kiss that promised more, he divested himself of his boots.

"That's because, *cara mia,* Signore Parodi found a buyer for this monstrosity. A duke, no less. He wishes to take possession before the end of August, if you're in agreement."

"I'd like that. I haven't hardly seen Blythe's darling Effie yet, and Brette is due any day."

"I'm done in, I tell you. Tomorrow, I refuse to rise before seven." In a few quick movements, Oliver divested himself of the rest of his clothing.

Blaike's welcoming smile turned seductive as she perused his naked form. His wife wasn't the least inhibited, and in fact, after finding a naughty book from the seventeenth century in the library, had made several creative suggestions regarding their love play.

"I think," she said, trailing her fingertips along the bottle green satin sheet, "I shall take up painting. Just so I can have a nude likeness of you to peek at whenever I please."

Smothering another yawn, he edged between the sheets. The other bedcoverings had been turned back to the foot of the bed due to the room's summer heat.

"*Bella,* I've seen your attempts at drawing, and I fear I'd resemble a troll. You'll just have to be satisfied with seeing me in the flesh."

"*Hmph,* if you weren't so dashed attractive, I'd be offended. But then again, you make a valid point. I possess abysmal artistic abilities."

Blaike came willingly into his arms, laying her shiny head upon his shoulder and placing a smooth-as-satin milky white leg upon his hair-covered thigh. The emerald and diamond ring, now sized to fit her ring finger, sparkled in the candlelight.

Drawing lazy circles on his chest, she kissed his shoulder,

"I had a most interesting letter from Blythe today. The Severs have been chased back to America in disgrace by their brother-in-law, Lord Desmond. Seems they were found in a compromising situation." She swirled his chest hair with her forefinger even as he caressed a velvety buttock. "With each other, no less."

"Never say so." Oliver couldn't keep the shock from his voice.

Sailors saw and heard many things that would appall respectable society, but even he hadn't encountered that particular perversion.

"Good riddance, I say, even if Ravensdale and the others essentially had already banished them to *le Beau Monde's* outermost fringes because of what they did to you."

"Oliver?" Blaike raised up on her elbow, the white waterfall of her hair billowing onto his torso.

"Yes, *amore?*" Hand on her trim waist, he edged her higher until she lay upon him, their legs tangled beneath the mussed sheet. His manhood's gradually swelling suggested that perhaps he wasn't so very tired after all.

Her mouth a mere inch from his, she flicked her pink tongue out to lick her lower lip.

"I read an interesting passage in *The Ladies' Delight* this evening that I should very much like to attempt." She gave him a wide-eyed look, seductress and innocent combined. "If you aren't too tired, darling, that is."

"*Cuore mio*, my heart, I shall never be too tired, as long as I have breath in my lungs and blood flowing through my veins to show you how much I love you."

The Lieutenant and the Lady

Sensible ladies of quality refrain from believing all they see and hear; for flour looks like chalk and the mockingbird's song is often an imitation.
~Prudence and Propriety— The Genteel Lady's Guide to Practical Living

Temple of the Muses Book Store, London, England
Late April, 1823

B last and damn. The ugly rumors were true, then.

Something fragile splintered in Blaire Culpepper's heart. Lurking behind the dusty bookcase, she plopped her frilly parasol on the closest shelf. She grasped the edge, arms extended and head bowed, and braced herself. Sucking in a ragged breath, she fought the scorching pain radiating behind her breastbone.

She bit her lower lip hard to still its quivering.

Stiff upper lip, she admonished herself severely. *No tears. Absolutely none.*

Until this very moment, she'd not believed the unsavory tattle. Refused to consider Julian had become a fickle *roué* in her absence.

When they'd returned from Geneva and her twin Blaike had taken her aside and revealed Lieutenant Julian Drake's change in status, Blaire kept hoping—praying—the *on dit* wasn't true. *He wasn't like that...Wasn't a scapegrace or a rapscallion.* Even when she'd seen him strolling in Hyde Park with the beauty now at his side, she'd believed there must be another explanation.

She'd been wrong. So bloody wrong.

Only a few feet away, as dashing and handsome as ever, he stood—all gorgeous six feet two inches of him—with Daphne Trudeau clinging to his arm.

Why, Julian? Why?

A heartbroken, inarticulate sound escaped Blaire.

The matron perusing the nearby books slanted her a worried

glance.

"Are you quite all right?" The distinguished woman took a step nearer, peering upward at Blaire in marked concern. "You're as pale as chalk. It's Miss Blaire Culpepper, isn't it? I'm Lady Pipperly. We met at Almack's some months ago. Do you need to sit down? You're not going to swoon, are you?"

Was Lady Pipperly afraid she'd be crushed given Blaire's unusually tall stature?

Eyes misty, despite her admonishment of no tears, Blaire shook her head and seized the book closest to her curled fingers' stranglehold on the shelf.

"No, nothing of the sort. I'm fine, my lady. I'm simply excited to finally find a copy of…"

She blinked to clear the hot moisture from her eyes then skimmed the book's title.

The Crimes of Love by the Marquis de Sade.

Good heavens.

Her ladyship slapped a gloved hand to her ample chest, her papery cheeks flaming bright red. Condemnation turned her tightly pursed mouth downward.

"Not at all the sort of book a young woman of *good* breeding should consider." Nose elevated and face pinched, she made a disapproving sound in her throat. "I must say, I'm appalled your guardian would permit you to read such immoral drivel."

She could scarce bring herself to glance at the tome Blaire clutched to her chest.

Blaire's guardian, Heath, the Earl of Ravensdale—Raven to his friends—would not approve. Nor would her sisters or her cousins. Only fast or unconventional ladies dared read the notoriously wicked book, no matter how curious they might be about the contents. Prudent misses observed propriety, else they found themselves banished to the countryside.

Honestly, at the moment, Blaire wouldn't mind the chastisement. Banishment would be a blessing. At Culpepper Park, she wouldn't run the risk of encountering Julian at every turn. At every miserable assembly, musicale, theater excursion, rout, or ball. Always, with the utterly charming Miss Trudeau in tow.

Her heart still thumping an irregular rhythm, Blaire slid a sideways glimpse over the top of the neat row of books beside her. Only his broad back was visible between the narrow shelves. A back and shoulders she knew to be deliciously solid and well-muscled from having danced with him on several occasions.

"I wonder…" Shrewdness replaced Lady Pipperly's censure. "Lord Ravensdale isn't aware of your preference in reading material, is he?"

Blaire had no doubt Heath would after today, even if the accusation wasn't the truth.

She eyed the black volume with its ornate spine.

Still…

"Should we…?" After a swift, furtive glance about, she edged nearer to the matron. "Should *we* take a peek inside and see if there are any illustrations?"

A phony smile plastered on her lips, Blaire schooled her features into deceptive innocence. Amazing how she could have an inane conversation with this busybody whilst each beat of her mangled heart reminded her of Julian's treachery. And her own naive gullibility.

Eyes enormous and unblinking, her ladyship opened and closed her mouth before spluttering, "P…p…ardon?"

Blaire gave her a conspiratorial wink, shifting her eyes back and forth in a guilty manner. If the chinwag wanted something to gossip about… Well, in Blaire's current disgruntled mood, she was happy to oblige.

"Drawings," she whispered naughtily. "I'll be bound, they're quite something." She flipped the top cover open just to hear Lady Pipperly's outraged gasp again. "Do you suppose there are any nudes?"

"Utterly scandalous!" With a shake of her white head that sent the silk flowers adorning her bonnet to convulsing, Lady Pipperly hastened away, muttering, "What impudence. How does the chit ever hope to snare a husband? I shall inform Lord Pipperly and Ravensdale at once."

I don't intend to snare anyone, Lady Pipperly. Nor do I give a ragman's scorn what your ignoble spouse thinks.

If memory served, his lordship had been making merry and groping unsuspecting misses' buttocks that evening at Almack's. He'd received a stinging pinch from Blaire's cousin Brooke, the Countess of Ravensdale, before she'd herded her charges from the assembly room.

A wayward impulse ticked Blaire's mouth upward an inch, and she ran her gloved fingers over the book's gold engraved cover. In a perverse sort of way, it seemed appropriate that she'd inadvertently picked this wicked book from amongst the hundreds she might've selected.

Crimes of love, indeed.

Not the sort of misconducts she might've imagined, she'd be bound. Such as pistols at dawn, romantic *tête-à-têtes* in curtained alcoves, or forbidden dalliances beneath the stars. Or... Her attention gravitated to the narrow opening above the books and the man just beyond. Leading a woman along and then tossing her aside without an explanation.

Amid a swell of justified anger, with a flip of her fingers, she snapped the cover closed.

She removed another leather-bound volume from the chest-high shelf. She set it aside as she surreptitiously observed Julian from her hiding place.

Since when had she become a skulking coward?

Even without his scarlet uniform, his striking, virile looks commanded attention, particularly of the feminine nature. Though a scar marred his left cheek, more than one lady in the bookstore regarded him appreciatively; some from beneath half-lowered lashes, others with bold gazes and inviting smiles.

Heaven forbid she wore the same calf-eyed expression as those ninnies.

At once, she arranged her features into composed indifference, but her crushing grip on the edge of the shelf revealed her strain to anyone looking closely.

And then there was Miss Trudeau. Attired in black from the jaunty, lace-edged bonnet atop her burnished curls to her dainty feet peeking from beneath the first-stare-of-fashion redingote, his companion radiated elegance and refinement.

What Blaire suspected might be jealousy gave her a couple of sharp pokes in the vicinity near her heart.

The prudent thing to do—what Blaire ought to have done immediately upon spying him and the exquisite brunette hanging from his arm—was to collect her maid and exit the busy store as discretely as possible. Before Lieutenant Drake noticed her and politeness forced them to acknowledge each other. He was a particular friend of her guardian after all, and she couldn't very well give him the cut.

She'd prefer to be spared the awkwardness of a politesse conversation with him.

And with the inarguably lovely Miss Daphne Trudeau.

But just this once, Blaire rebelled at doing the sensible thing, even if it meant saving herself further distress and possible humiliation. Her dashed curiosity about the woman who'd so easily replaced her glued her bold, new, ebony-and-scarlet floral half-boots to the floor.

That and her inability to haul her attention from Julian's beloved face.

She still loved the scoundrel. She'd believed he'd felt the same for her.

You're being unfair, Blaire Grace Eleanor Culpepper.

She was. She wouldn't lie, even to herself.

Lieutenant Drake had never declared himself. *Not lieutenant anymore. He resigned his commission and is a gentleman of considerable standing now.* To her knowledge, he'd never approached Heath to ask if he might call upon her or pay his addresses. At no time had he ever said anything directly about returning her regard or expressing an interest in courting her.

Had Blaire imagined everything?

Were her feelings truly completely unrequited?

A blistering wave of chagrin washed over her, and she squeezed her eyes shut. No. She had not imagined it. She hadn't.

Whenever in her company, his treacle brown eyes beneath slanting brows had tipped upward at the corners, something warm and inviting in their depths. His almost shy smile grew ever wider, and when bowing over her hand, he'd held it a trifle longer than proper. When they'd danced, he'd not taken his compelling gaze from her, and a time or two or three, his strong hand had caressed her spine the tiniest bit. Those involuntary hints she hadn't manufactured, and she treasured the memory of each.

Why, even her sisters Blaike and Blythe had commented on his obvious interest.

Blaire wouldn't have thought Julian the sort to place importance on titles or position, and disappointment flattened her lips into a firm line. Quite apparently, she didn't know him nearly as well as she'd supposed.

Miss Trudeau laughed, a light musical tinkling—*why couldn't she bray like a belligerent donkey?*—at something the older woman accompanying her had remarked. Resembling the beauty a great deal, the petite lady, also attired entirely in black, addressed Julian, and he gave a short—almost terse—nod.

It seemed he'd inherited more than the estate and holdings when his brother died. From what Blaire observed, he did indeed court his deceased brother's betrothed. That had to set a record for gaucheness. Alfred Drake had been buried scarcely two months ago.

With such a recent death in the family, galivanting around London wasn't done. She couldn't help but suspect Miss Trudeau or her mother the instigator, although Blaire didn't know them well enough to form such a mean opinion.

Momentary remorse pricked her conscience, and she stiffened. Was she becoming a jealous shrew? It was bad enough to be discarded with the same ease as coffee grounds, but to become a harpy over the insult?

By George, that she refused to do.

Spying upon the happy couple however, wasn't beneath her?

Bah!

Stooping lower, she tilted her head at an awkward angle to better watch Julian and Miss Trudeau. Hopefully no one observed her antics. Likely, that uncouthness would be reported to Heath as well.

Blaire's dashed height proved a nuisance even in this, and no doubt her curiosity would result in a cricked neck. She pulled her mouth to one side, considering the handsome pair.

Daphne Trudeau didn't resemble a woman in mourning or a heartbroken betrothed either. From the sunny, *devoted* smiles she bestowed upon Julian, one would think she hadn't a care in the world. And that they were an affectionate couple.

Perhaps she hadn't loved her betrothed and their joining had been a union of convenience or a business arrangement. Such agreements weren't uncommon.

Wasn't she related to a duke?

His niece?

Blaire recalled hearing that tidbit somewhere since she and Blaike had returned from Geneva. The gossip rags fairly brimmed with speculation about Julian and Miss Trudeau and suggested a formal announcement could be expected very soon.

Another maelstrom of emotion welled in Blaire's chest, and she had to swallow twice to dislodge the lump constricting her throat. Learning another had engaged Julian's affections during her six-month absence had come as a shock.

She'd thought—hoped—he harbored more than mere fondness for her, and during those horrid months away at school, she'd indulged in silly school-girl notions that once she was back on English soil...

Never mind, she ordered her capering thoughts. *What's done is done*.

His chiseled chin on full display, his wavy toast-brown hair slightly mussed beneath his hat, Julian's bored gaze roved the bookstore. He periodically tapped his fingertips against his long, black-clad thigh.

Impatient?

Annoyed?

She'd never known him to be either, but she obviously hadn't known him as well as she'd presumed, had she?

Blaire squinted. Did fine lines of strain bracket his mouth? Was that a muscle flexing in his jaw? If he was a man besotted, she was the Queen of Egypt.

She well knew smitten men. Hadn't she witnessed her sisters' and cousins' courtships? Hadn't she watched their beaux' transformations into doting swains?

Odd disappointment swept her that Julian should care about titles and position. It also stung that she should be the only one of the five Culpeppers to miss the mark on love. Her arrow had gone wide, to be certain.

Enough lurking behind bookshelves as if she'd something to be ashamed of. She had entertained warm feelings for a good-looking man who didn't return them.

So what?

Loving someone who didn't love you wasn't a crime.

A derisive chuckle escaped her as her focus fell on the outrageous novel. She was tempted to buy it, if only for a distraction from her doldrums.

She wasn't so bold. *More's the pity*.

Shaking her head in self-reproach, Blaire shoved the books back into their slots, determined to find her maid Flora and depart at once. She still had gloves to collect for Brooke and yarn to purchase for the blanket she was knitting for the babe Blythe expected soon.

Truth to tell, a distraction of some sort might be just the thing.

A noble cause, perchance?

But what?

Blaire tapped her chin with her forefinger, considering her options. She didn't enjoy the typical charities ladies of refinement participated in. Surely, there was something to pique her interest, to keep her mind off Julian's betrayal.

Ah, well. She released a soundless sigh.

Something would come to her.

Another cleansing breath steadied Blaire's unruly pulse and calmed her uneasy musings. Brow crumpled in reflection, and adjusting her bonnet to make sure it sat straight upon her head after her contortions to spy upon him, she pivoted toward the end of the aisle and pulled up short.

God help her. There stood the very objects of her musings.

Julian. And Miss Trudeau.

Dash it all to ribbons. Blaire had delayed too long to make her escape.

She snatched the wicked book from the shelf once more, lest he think she fled because of him. Her pride refused to let her bolt.

His eyes—a shade somewhere between pecan and coffee with milk—brightened, the way they always had when encountering her. They softened, the edges crinkling endearingly. As if on cue, his well-formed mouth swept into that familiar jovial, slightly seductive, upward arc that made her tingly and melty to her suddenly freezing toes.

He'd removed his hat, and a shock of almond-brown hair had tumbled onto his high forehead.

"Hello, Miss Culpepper."

She honed in on his deep voice, unusually melodious for a man.

Why couldn't he have greeted her impersonally? As if they were mere casual acquaintances? Or ignored her altogether?

He gave a ghost of a bow, his attention straying to the books behind her before dropping to the volume she crushed in her grip. "I'm surprised to see you here, considering the vast library at Highfield Place House."

"Lieutenant." She bobbled a shallow curtsy then quickly hooked her parasol over her wrist. She held the unsavory book to her chest, making certain the title faced her. "I'm shopping for a birthday gift."

Partially true.

Heath's birthday was next month. But she'd been desperate to escape her family's pitying sad-eyed looks and had practically dragged Flora from the house, promising to run errands for the others while she was out and about.

It was trying enough grappling with her own heart ache and disappointment without her family unknowingly feeding the fire of disenchantment with each sympathetic glance, grave sigh, or encouraging word.

"Julian, Mama beckons us." Miss Trudeau pressed her other hand to his upper arm possessively. "You know how demanding she is. We'd best not dawdle and test her patience."

She flashed him a coquette's smile, but every ounce of warmth left her big, pansy-brown eyes when her attention swung to Blaire.

A light crease pulling her brows together, Blaire glanced back and forth between them.

If Miss Trudeau and her mother were this problematic before the vows were exchanged, Julian could expect a difficult time. The army officer she knew and adored wouldn't have acquiesced to being ordered about so easily.

Why the drastic change?

He spared Miss Trudeau a rather taciturn look. "In a moment."

Most peculiar.

"We haven't time to chat with your...ah... *acquaintance*," Miss Trudeau insisted, just shy of impoliteness while tugging quite forcefully on his forearm.

Blaire's temper heated at the way Miss Trudeau uttered acquaintance, as if Blaire were an undesirable, a courtesan or demimonde.

"Forgive me my manners, ladies. I forgot you haven't been introduced." Julian quirked his mouth into a boyish half-smile, apparently prepared to endure his future mother-in-law's wrath by delaying his departure further. "Miss Daphne Trudeau, may I introduce Blaire Culpepper, ward of the Earl of Ravensdale and sister-in-law to the Marquis of Leventhorpe? Miss Culpepper, Miss Trudeau."

Blaire's stomach sank in a queer manner. Had he deliberately hinted at her connections while failing to mention Miss Trudeau's? Why? Did he try to protect Blaire or was he boasting about his connections?

"Miss Trudeau." Blaire tilted her head a fraction and forced her stiff lips upward. She refused to claim meeting the woman was a pleasure, no matter how delightful Miss Trudeau was. Or given the past several long moments, wasn't.

Miss Trudeau tittered, putting a fine-boned hand to her mouth.

"Goodness me, you are a long meg, aren't you? I'd heard of the towering Culpeppers but thought the descriptions were exaggerations. I see now I was wrong." She leaned a trifle closer. "Do you use lemon to lighten your hair to that shade?" She patted the shiny, russet curls framing her face. The annoying perfect things bounced right back into place. "I could never be so daring as you. I'd be terrified my hair would fall out and I'd be bald as an egg. Besides, so many women of loose virtue are blonde…"

Baring her claws already? *Hmm*, and they'd just met. Very interesting and not a little peculiar. Was Miss Trudeau uncertain of Julian's interest or commitment?

She peered at Blaire's hairline intently. Did Miss Trudeau think to spy a receding hairline? Perhaps she tried to determine if Blaire wore a wig.

"Daphne, all of the Culpeppers have been blessed with such unusual light hair." Though gentle and tolerant, firmness tinged Julian's words. His hungry gaze slowly roamed Blaire's face, almost as if he couldn't help himself.

She recognized something of herself in his ravenous look.

Unfair she screamed inwardly. Don't look at me like that. Like you still care.

Miss Trudeau noticed his rapt attention too, and had her flashing eyes been a blade, Blaire would lie disemboweled.

What game did Julian play?

One she wanted no part of.

He'd made his choice, and it wasn't her. Why would she pine for a man who so easily replaced her once she was out of his sight, anyway?

She gave herself a mental shake. Enough.

"Excuse me, please. I'm already late." My, she sounded perfectly composed. A tribute to acting skills she didn't know she possessed until this very minute.

Blaire dipped her chin and, summoning her tattered dignity, swept toward Flora, hovering at the end of the bookcase. She wasn't really late, but she'd grasped the first excuse that sprang to mind.

Poor dear. She was probably uncertain if she should interrupt.

"Come, Flora. I'll make my purchase, and we can be on our way. We've two more errands, and I promised we'd be home in time for tea. Brooke is expecting callers." The latter was for the benefit of Miss Trudeau, lest she think she succeeded in scaring Blaire away.

She took Flora's elbow and steered the servant toward the counter, whilst also steadying the maid's uneven gait. She didn't need to look behind her to know two pairs of eyes tunneled into her back—one remorseful and the other lethal.

Nothing quite as disquieting as being despised on sight.

"Yes, miss." Flora fell into step beside Blaire. A short while later, blessedly without encountering Julian again, they'd gained the street.

Blaire welcomed the bracing coolness against her burning cheeks.

"I helped ice the dainties for today's tea," Flora abruptly announced, pride warming her plain features as she limped along.

Blaire patted the maid's shoulder. "That was very well done of you. I shall look forward to sampling them that much more."

A bit of the tension knotting the muscles in Blaire's neck eased, and she tipped her head to study the sky, contemplating whether to walk or take the carriage. A few pewter-tinged clouds obscured the blue, but the earlier threat of rain had blown by.

They'd walk, then. Slowly, so Flora could keep up. The fresh air might help clear Blaire's tumbling thoughts and would delay their arrival home. She couldn't prevent one last glance toward the Temple of the Muses. As she did, Julian, his hat once more upon his wavy hair, stepped over the threshold.

Alone. How had he managed to escape Miss Trudeau's clutches?

His compassionate gaze swept Flora before coming to rest on Blaire. "Miss Culpepper, might I have a moment?"

Blaire's heart gave a floppy, eager judder.

Silly, stupid, gullible thing.

Hadn't she experienced enough pain?

Flora's intense interest didn't go unnoticed either. The maid might be a bit of a slow stop, but she'd discerned the undercurrent radiating between Blaire and Julian.

"I don't think that would be wise." Blaire shook her head, denying his request. "And a public street mightn't be the best place for such a conversation, in any event." Not to explain why he'd thrown her over. She couldn't be positive there wouldn't be temper or tears on her part.

She hated admitting that weakness, even to herself.

"If you truly wish to speak with me," she pointed out, "you're welcome to call at Highfield Place House."

Of course, he knew that already.

Was he uncertain of his welcome, and had he been waiting for an invitation, given he courted another?

Would Heath allow the visit?

He'd become awfully protective of his wards since marrying

Brooke. More than likely Heath would permit it, since Julian was a good friend and he'd already called once since Blaire's return. Not to see her but rather, Captain Oliver Whitehouse, now Blaike's betrothed.

Vexation crept along Blaire's shoulders as she recalled the uncomfortable reunion that day.

Why had she told Julian to call?

It could only lead to more heartache. But didn't he deserve the opportunity to explain himself? *To what purpose?* Blister it. Her emotions and thoughts swung back and forth like a clock's pendulum. She couldn't make up her bloody, dratted mind about anything these days, especially about what her future held.

That must become her primary focus. Not mooning over a man practically betrothed to another. Steely resolve straightened her spine. Yes, that was precisely what she'd do. Set her own course, and devil take anyone attempting to dissuade her.

"I shall call at the earliest opportunity." His keen gaze warm and apologetic, Julian inclined his head just as the shop door swung open, and Miss Trudeau and her mother sailed forth.

"My, my, Miss Culpepper." Frost in January was several degrees warmer than Miss Trudeau's wintery countenance. "You do seem intent on commandeering my intended's attention. Do I truly have to warn you away from him?"

A lady of substance neither resorts to weeping to
have her way nor puts her faith in other women who do.
~*Prudence and Propriety— The Genteel Lady's Guide to Practical Living*

2

Julian flexed his jaw against denouncing Daphne's false declaration right then and there, as well as chastising her for her inexcusable rudeness. He hadn't proposed. *Yet.* In fact, he hadn't broached the subject of marriage, despite Daphne and her mother's constant, overt hints that they expected and welcomed his suit.

Daphne's presumptiveness rankled, raising his ire. He hadn't missed the jealous glint in her eye or her malice when he'd introduced Blaire either.

Blaire's berry-toned redingote cast a becoming pinkish shadow on her fair skin, as did the cerise colored ribbon tied below her pert chin. Rubies set in silver filigree dangled from her dainty ears, and she shifted the book she'd purchased higher in her arms as she stared at them.

Better to remove Daphne than permit her to draw Blaire's blood with her increasingly tart tongue. Of them all, Blaire was the most egregiously used, the most deserving of compassion and an explanation.

"Good day, Miss Culpepper."

Tipping his hat, reluctance in each step, he permitted Daphne to all but drag him in the other direction. He felt very much like a naughty dog on a short lead.

Normally he'd quash her overstepping, but Joan Trudeau's starchy, unforgiving, narrowed-eyed regard revealed she disapproved of his conversing with Blaire. He couldn't risk Joan raising a public breeze, for he wouldn't put it past her to direct her displeasure toward Blaire for all to hear.

Darling Blaire didn't deserve that.

On more than one occasion, he'd had the unfortunate experience of witnessing one of Joan's dust-ups. She might be diminutive in form, but Daphne's domineering mother possessed a formidable disposition.

Unlike her foul-tempered parent, Daphne didn't typically shout and rail when angry. These past weeks, he'd learned Joan was just this side of an obstinate child when thwarted. She held no compunction about openly voicing her displeasure, much to his irritation.

No, beautiful, cossetted Daphne complained, wept, and pouted, wallowing in self-pity.

For hours.

Or days.

In the many months he'd known Blaire, he'd never once seen her resort to anger or tears when disappointed. He'd lost track of the number of times Daphne had done so since Alfred's death, and he was already heartily sick of it.

While Alfred might have considered Daphne an excellent choice for the future mistress of Montclere, Julian couldn't pretend the same conviction. He found women prone to weeping at trifling things beyond tedious—no doubt as a result of having been raised by one.

Dinah Drake was still wont to resort to waterworks more frequently than the most tolerant of men could abide. Though Julian loved his mother and pitied her plight, at seven-and-twenty, his patience with her constant black moods had long since grown thin.

An heiress in her own right, Julian couldn't recall a time when his mother had been happy. Seven years older than Father and afflicted with a crippled foot as a result of a break when she was a toddler, when she wasn't crying or refusing to leave her bed, she moped about Montclere, disheveled and muttering beneath her breath.

She also imbibed far too liberally in sherry and laudanum. At times, weeks would pass without him seeing her.

And the arguments she and Father had...

God above. No child should hear the vile, hateful things his parents spewed at each other. Early on, he'd learned to crawl into his older half-brother Alfred's bed, and they'd hide their heads beneath the blankets. Their three younger sisters professed to do the same.

He supposed Mother had a right to be angry at the lot fate had dealt her. Though pretty enough, with her maimed foot, no man would wed her until Father came along and charmed her. She'd often complained how he—a handsome widower—had tricked her, playing the doting swain until they married and he'd assumed control of her monies.

Father vowed he'd more than done right by siring four children on her.

"Julian, I should like an ice from Gunter's."

He tightened his jaw, just short of gritting his teeth. With each passing day, Daphne became more demanding. Almost three years Blaire's senior, at nearly three-and-twenty, Daphne's childlike behavior chafed worse than riding bare-back naked. Enduring her was one thing, but her mother was another matter entirely. He'd have to suffer both if he made her his bride.

Only he had no intention of permitting Joan to live at Montclere. He'd buy her a comfortable cottage on the other side of England. Daphne could fuss and object all she liked, but no power on earth would convince him to allow her mother to live with them. Neither woman had an inkling he was on to their plot and intended to dash it to shards.

If he wed Daphne.

How could he when he loved another? Loved Blaire so much that upon seeing her today, he'd almost swept her into his arms and declared himself right there.

He couldn't, of course.

Family honor insisted he wed Daphne and soon. After all, she carried Alfred's child. But Julian's heart and mind rebelled at the notion. He'd be consigning himself to a lifetime of misery, he had no doubt.

Two soldiers walked past, smart and neat in their uniforms. He recognized neither. He missed the military. He missed Blaire far more.

Like a tippler craving his whisky, Julian couldn't resist another look and glanced over his shoulder.

Countenance bland, she hid her bewilderment magnificently, but those beautiful eyes—a color somewhere between violet and sapphire blue—condemned him for a faithless lout. With each forlorn blink, she drove a dagger deeper into his heart.

He longed to shake Daphne's hand lose and bolt back to Blaire, to explain everything. To finally declare himself and beg forgiveness for causing the hurt shimmering in her eyes.

He couldn't, no matter the ache in his heart.

Or hers.

Leastways, not with Daphne and her mother in tow.

Besides, no amount of explaining would change the circumstances he found himself embroiled in, and he couldn't reveal Daphne's delicate condition. Not without ruining her and indirectly causing hardship for the innocent babe she carried.

Fiend seize his honor.

Devil take Alfred for dying so young.

Averting her face, Blaire presented her back, as effectively shutting Julian out as if she'd slammed and bolted a door in his face.

He deserved her scorn and rejection.

I'm sorry, my darling Blaire.

He'd call at Highfield Place House and try to explain the conundrum he found himself in without revealing the more intimate details. He hadn't quite figured out how. The wisest course of action would be to avoid Blaire until he made his bloody decision.

Time was short. Too short.

Daphne professed to be three months along already. Miraculous she wasn't showing, but today's fashions did much to hide any hint of a swollen belly.

He could delay the marriage a fortnight, mayhap a month at most. *If* he did wed Daphne, there'd be tattle, chin wagging, and whispers when the child arrived a few months after the union.

Bloody impossible choice.

He was a man of duty and integrity, and his family's standing was paramount. Generations of Drakes' incessant drinking had tainted the once noble name.

Julian meant to see it restored.

However, he never wanted or coveted Montclere. Alfred had been welcome to the estate, though it infuriated Mother that her stepson should inherit what her monies had essentially built.

That was one reason Julian had chosen to buy a commission in the army. It was a decent profession that had kept him away from his father's unreasonable demands and his mother's incessant whining for years.

Julian would like to think he was noble and self-sacrificing, but the truth was, he'd never have considered taking Daphne as his wife if it weren't for the babe.

Stifling a frustrated sigh, he dragged his attention to the woman on his arm.

Sable curls peeked from beneath an elegant bonnet, the silhouette of her pert nose and bowed lips a perfect complement to her ivory skin.

No one could deny his brother's betrothed was a diamond of the first water.

Well, she had been Alfred's intended before he'd gone deer stalking, drunk as a sailor, and been tossed headlong from his mount. *Stupid fool. Drinking and hunting.*

Julian clenched his jaw and pinched his mouth into a steely line, still unable—*and unwilling*—to commit to the most obvious and practical course of action

He'd hinted to his chums, Captain Oliver Whitehouse and Raven— that was, the Earl of Ravensdale—that he was considering nuptials with Daphne in his brother's stead. Alfred's progeny wouldn't suffer the disgrace of illegitimacy, and if the child were a boy, he'd also gain his rightful inheritance.

The babe shouldn't be made to suffer because of his or her parents' poor choices.

But nuptials with Daphne meant giving up Blaire forever. Now, when Julian finally possessed a social standing worthy of courting her.

He closed his eyes for a heartbeat, agony sharp and raw twisting in the organ, rendering him breathless.

I love Blaire.

He had loved her from afar for months and never thought he'd be able to declare himself. A lieutenant in His Majesty's army was hardly a match for a gentle woman, ward to an earl, and sister-in-law to a marquis. Toward that end, as a humble soldier with little to offer her, he'd deliberately refrained from encouraging her, though he couldn't deny the wonder in her gorgeous blue eyes or the faint flush upon her ivory cheeks when circumstances brought them together.

Those times, he'd looked his fill, committing to memory every detail of her cherished face, the lilt of her voice, her contagious laugh, even the turn of her wrist when she fanned herself. Nothing about Blaire was trivial or unimportant.

When the news of Alfred's death had reached him, after the initial gut-wrenching grief, the tiniest spark of hope had ignited. Julian had inherited Montclere and all that went with the estate. He'd become landed gentry, a gentleman of considerable worth, and almost Blaire's social equal.

Fate or God had gifted him an opportunity he'd never dreamed of.

Before Daphne revealed she was pregnant, he'd even entertained the notion of approaching Ravensdale with an offer for Blaire's hand before Alfred's mourning period ended. Not that Julian wanted to wait to wed, but social strictures ought to be observed. How ironic he now contemplated dismissing propriety to prevent Daphne's shame from becoming public knowledge.

She chatted animatedly with her mother as they meandered along the pavements. She was everything a lady of breeding should be: beautiful, cultured, educated, and trained to the position her entire life.

What she wasn't was moral.

But then, who was he to judge her?

Or Alfred, either?

For God's sake. Couples frequently shared a bed prior to the exchanging of vows. Daphne and Alfred could never have anticipated he'd die a scarce week before their wedding, leaving her with child and on the verge of ruin.

If Julian didn't marry her, the *haute ton* would persecute Daphne, niece to the pockets-to-let Duke of Montbaard or not. Joan's only other hope was to pawn her daughter off on an aged degenerate who wouldn't mind claiming the babe in exchange for a young, beautiful wife.

Daphne didn't possess a large dowry—or any dowry for that matter.

Only a centuries-old noble name and considerable influence, which were things Alfred and Mother valued more than Daphne's attractive outward trappings it seemed. The lure of the Drakes' wealth must've enticed Daphne—and her ambitious mother—to consider landed gentry for a match.

At the corner, Julian turned and cast a sidelong glance in time to see a tawny colored, hairy flash dart out in front of Blaire and Flora.

The maid stumbled, and Blaire lurched to steady her as another pup plowed into them. Both women tumbled to the pavement.

Nearly at his carriage, Julian signaled to the coachman. "Please see the ladies home, Hayes."

"Yes, sir." Hayes leaped from his seat.

Daphne balked, a pout marring her features.

"Julian, whatever are you doing? I thought we were going to Gunter's." She cast a glance down the lane and gave a dismissive wave of her hand. "You needn't trouble yourself with them."

"Indeed," her mother agreed, mouth pursed and face creased with irritation. "Others are already rushing to their aid, the clumsy dolts. I think in her *delicate* condition, our dear Daphne ought to be the focus of your concern."

Scorn hardened Julian's face, and he barely swallowed a sharp retort.

"Miss Culpepper is the ward of my good friend and the sister-in-law to another. I cannot ignore her plight." He pried Daphne's fingers off his forearm. For someone so petite, she possessed an unexpectedly tenacious grip. "Hayes will see you safely home or to whatever other destination you desire."

"Julian…" Daphne's lower lip quivered, and her eyes glistened. *Let the watering commence.* "You mean to abandon us for…*her*?"

"The matter is not open for discussion," he ground out.

Angrier than he ought to be by her manipulation, he spun away then dashed down the street.

Blaire needed him.

By the time he arrived at her side, she and her maid had regained their feet, thanks to a kindly passerby. Other than lop-sided bonnets and soiled gloves, neither appeared the worse for wear. Or so he thought until Blaire turned her head, her porcelain face flushed pink. Her cheek bore a scrape, and another red mark marred her temple.

The two mongrel pups that had tripped them cowered together in a nearby doorway, trapped by a trio of taunting youths. One poked at the dogs with a stick, and when one puppy yipped in pain and terror, the miscreants erupted into gales of laughter.

"Stop that, you little devils!" Fire in her eyes and chin tucked at a determined angle, Blaire stalked toward them, wielding her parasol like a short sword. Julian hadn't a doubt she'd wallop the boys if needed. "Get away from them, you bullies. Shame on you for picking on those unfortunate creatures."

The lads rounded on her, defiant sneers contorting their faces.

Until their focus shifted to Julian directly behind her, brandishing his walking stick. Respect laced with a good dose of fear transformed their countenances. He motioned them away with a curt swipe of his cane then pulled his brows together into a severe crease.

"Be gone, riffraff. Before my temper is roused."

As one, the trio bolted away.

"*Shh.* They cannot hurt you anymore," Blaire crooned, gingerly resting her left arm against her torso as she edged nearer to the quivering puppies. "Poor dears."

"Blaire, is your arm hurt too?" Julian asked.

Perhaps she had other injuries and was too proud to admit it.

She sliced Julian a brief, guarded look. "I wrenched it when I fell. I'm sure it's nothing." She squatted and placed her parasol on the ground before extending her hand, back upward. "It's all right. Come here. You needn't be afraid. I shan't hurt you."

Heads down, the dogs huddled together.

Flora limped close and shook her head. A few more loose strands escaped her coiffure. "Poor little wretches. They look starved."

The rigid outline of their ribs poked through their mangy coats, and when the dogs raised their timid, haunted eyes to Blaire's and one gave a pitiful whine, Julian made an impulsive decision.

He fished a coin from his pocket. "Flora, purchase two meat pies from the vendor there." To make sure she understood, he pointed to the nearby hawker.

Perusing the lane, Julian spied Ravensdale's coach. With a sharp wave, he caught the coachman's attention and at once, the chap slapped the reins and directed the team in their direction.

Crouched onto his ankles, Julian, too, coaxed the frightened dogs. "You're safe now. We won't hurt you."

Blaire shook her head, and the thin line of her pretty mouth lengthened in displeasure. "I just cannot grasp wanton cruelty."

From the odd inflection in her voice, he'd be bound tears clogged her throat.

"Why, Julian?" She raised her luminous, bewildered eyes to his, her ivory cheek already starting to bruise. "What need is there to be so hateful, especially to defenseless animals?"

Did she realize she'd used his Christian name?

Upset, her emotions running high, likely not. As compassionate and kind-hearted as Blaire was, she couldn't fathom the evil which compelled others to maliciousness. He touched her elbow, wishing he had the right to hug her to his chest and soothe the distress from her face.

"The world is an unjust place, I fear, Blaire."

Don't I know that all too well?

A muffled noise alerted him to Flora's labored approach.

Tongue poking between her teeth as she concentrated on putting one foot in front of the other, the maid returned with the pies, balancing one in each hand.

He accepted the first pastry and handed the other to Blaire.

Between them, they enticed the puppies closer. After a hesitant sniff, the dogs gulped down the treats and gave a tentative wag of their bushy tails.

From their long snouts and downward pointing floppy ears, they appeared to be part border collie. Each sported a white strip down the center of their foreheads. He scooped the pair into his arms, and his heart all but melted when one licked his chin.

His valet would have an apoplectic fit when he saw the hair on Julian's new coat.

"Sir, may I assist you?" Ravensdale's coachman asked.

What was his name again?

"Please." Julian handed off the pups, one to the coachman and one to Flora. "Put them in the barouche."

Fond of dogs himself, Ravensdale wouldn't complain about hair in his conveyance.

Julian hoped.

Blaire had retrieved her parasol and risen to her full height. The white lines framing her mouth revealed what she was too proud to say. She *was* hurt and worse than she let on.

Admiration weighted with a good dose of concern tightened his chest. His brave darling. In the same situation, Daphne would be a helpless, sniveling watering pot.

It wasn't fair to keep comparing the women, yet he couldn't help notice their vast differences, including coloring and build. Blaire: tall, willowy, and fair. Daphne: petite, curvy, and dark of hair and eyes. Blaire: sweet-tempered, kind, intelligent, and independent. Daphne: petulant, child-like, grasping, and seemingly incapable of forming a thought without her mother's approval.

"I'm seeing you home." Julian's tone allowed no argument.

Blaire gifted him a wan smile. "That's not necessary."

"It is," he insisted. "Because not only am I concerned about you, if Raven won't agree to allow you the dogs, I'll give them a home at Montclere."

Freddy, the Culpeppers' aged corgi, mightn't be keen about new companions either. More importantly, Julian needed to know Blaire's condition, and his sense of chivalry demanded it as well. Only a self-absorbed sot would bundle a hurt woman into a carriage and send her on her way. In love with her, he could no more desert her than he could lop off his own hand.

Her features softened, and her grateful smile sent his pulse capering. How could the upward turn of a pretty mouth rattle him? He, a hardened soldier who'd looked his enemy in the eye and had killed in the line of duty more than once?

It wasn't just any woman's mouth, but the precious lady dearest to his heart.

Without preamble, Julian cupped her good elbow and assisted her into the carriage.

Flora followed and, after plopping beside her mistress, fidgeted with her cape. The servant worried her lower lip.

"Are you hurt bad, Miss Blaire?"

Blaire shook her head. "I'm sure it's just a bruise, Flora."

The ugly red streak marring the perfection of her cheek oozed droplets of blood. Julian fished his handkerchief from his pocket and extended the cloth. "Your cheek is bleeding a bit. Just here."

To indicate where she bled, he touched his face, wishing they were alone and he could dab the scrape.

Surprised appreciation rounded Blaire's eyes. She accepted the square and carefully pressed it against her skin, wincing slightly as she patted her cheek.

Sitting on their haunches, the puppies occupied the opposite seat.

"Scoot over chaps." He gave them an affectionate, tolerant glance. "And do not for an instant think this is going to become a habit. Most especially inside the house." He shook a finger at them, and they peered at him with adoration. "No dogs on the furniture."

Mother might collapse in hysterics if Julian traipsed in with the pups, but by thunder, he now owned Montclere. If he wanted dogs, he'd have dogs. *That* he had control over.

Their tails thumped the seat, and Blaire's mouth tipped up again as she wadded the cloth and handed it to Flora. "Please see that Lieutenant Drake's handkerchief is laundered."

"Yes, Miss Blaire." The cloth disappeared into the folds of the maid's cloak.

Julian nudged the dogs aside before tapping the roof, and the carriage rocked into motion.

Blaire closed her eyes and leaned against the plush squabs, cradling her injured arm with her other hand. "Thank you, Lieutenant, but isn't your intended going to be miffed with you for deserting her?"

Her eyelids drifted open, and their gazes meshed across the

carriage.

Flora, hunched into a corner, appeared to have fallen asleep already.

He scratched the dogs behind their ears, earning ecstatic doggy grins in return.

Blaire's attention drifted to the mongrels and then met his again. She asked so much more with her wary glance.

"Miss Trudeau is not my intended, Blaire."

Wise is the woman who understands trusting
too much is risky, but she also knows not trusting
enough can be torturous, steal one's joy, and turn the soul bitter.
~Prudence and Propriety— The Genteel Lady's Guide to Practical Living

3

Blaire nodded at Jenkin as she swept into Highfield Place House.
Flora and Julian trailed right behind her, each bearing a dirty
puppy. Over her shoulder, she eyed their progress. Flora's pup lay
content, gazing at her with adoration whilst Julian's licked and nipped,
wiggling the whole while as it tried to play with him.

"Hold still, you little devil. My chin is not your chew toy." Julian's
upward turned mouth belied his grumbling as he ran his hand down the
pup's spine.

"Jenkin, please have a footman feed these poor darlings and then
bathe them. Once that's done, the dogs may be brought to my chamber."
She gave the butler an apologetic smile. "I shall need his lordship's
permission to keep them, naturally."

Jenkin's lips edged up the tiniest jot at the corners. Pets always
meant more work for the staff, but beneath his austere exterior, he was
as soft and sweet as warm custard. More than once she'd caught him
passing Freddy a tasty treat.

Besides, the puppies might prove just the distraction Blaire needed.

At home, anyway.

She simply must find a worthwhile task to occupy her time now
that there'd be no more education abroad. The days of the five
Culpepper misses doing everything together had passed as well. All
except Blaike were married, and Oliver Whitehouse had proposed
recently. If Blaire's twin was anything like the other Culpeppers, she'd
soon be with child too.

Melancholy gripped her, as she weighed her options. For an
unmarried gentlewoman, there weren't a whole lot that held much

appeal.

"Of course, Miss Blaire. I'm sure Cook can muster up a hearty meal for them." With the subtlest gesture, Jenkin summoned two footmen.

The young men toted the squirming pups below stairs, their polished shoes echoing on the equally shiny floor.

Julian brushed at the multitude of hairs adhered to his coat. They proceeded to cling to his gloves. With a resigned sigh, he handed Jenkin his hat and, after removing the offending, hair-covered gloves, passed them to the butler as well.

"Please also inform his lordship and her ladyship that Miss Culpepper is injured and requires a doctor's attention at once, Jenkin."

Blaire stiffened at Julian's forwardness then winced when pain radiated from wrist to elbow. That was the soldier in him coming through. He was a man used to issuing orders and having them obeyed without question.

Well, he wasn't doing so on her behalf.

"I am not so incapacitated that I'm not capable of making that decision, Jul—er, Lieutenant Drake." She turned to the maid, who patiently waited for instructions. "Flora, please help with the puppies, and watch that they don't cause too much mischief in my chamber. See if the housekeeper has an old coverlet that might be used for their bed. I think the nook between the wardrobe and the window will do nicely. But first deliver these there."

Blaire passed the notorious naughty book wrapped in innocent brown paper as well as her gloves, parasol, and bonnet to the docile servant. Thank goodness Flora couldn't read, not that she'd open the package without permission anyway.

"Yes, miss." Flora hobbled after the footmen.

The butler looked expectantly at Blaire's redingote. "Miss?"

Before Blaire admitted in front of Julian that she wasn't capable of unfastening the outer garment one-handed, she'd chew marbles. Nothing for it. It would have to remain until her abigail could help her.

"I'm still quite cold, Jenkins," she said by way of explanation for keeping the outwear.

"Shall I send for a physician, Miss Culpepper?" Worry lined the kindly butler's face. "Neither Lord nor Lady Ravensdale are at home. However, I expect them shortly."

"Blaire, trust me in this." Concern darkened Julian's eyes to a rich russet "I am a soldier,"—*not anymore*—"and do know something of injuries. I cannot, in good conscience, leave you without assuring you aren't seriously hurt. If your arm is broken, it will need to be set at once."

She feared he might be right, dash her bloody rotten luck. Her forearm burned like a hot poker stabbed to the bone's marrow. Flora's limp had seemed more pronounced when she walked away too, and it couldn't hurt to have the maid examined, if only to make sure she hadn't other injuries.

Fine, then. Blaire might as well cut two roses with one snip. She and Julian could have the conversation he'd requested while awaiting the physician.

"Very well. Send for Dr. Barclay," she conceded with a dip of her head. "We'll await his arrival in the drawing room."

She'd taken one step when her stomach growled, and she swallowed against a surge of nausea. Feeling peculiar—not quite faint, but distinctly muddled—she pivoted. Though the thought of eating made her want to cast up her accounts, sipping a cup of tea might soothe her tummy and bolster her constitution.

"Please ask Cook to prepare tea and a small repast as well."

An icy wave swept her, and she shivered, automatically reaching to rub her arms until her injured limb protested with an unholy stab of pain. *Mother of God.* Stifling an involuntary groan, she averted her face to prevent the men from seeing her distress.

A couple of minutes later, she and Julian stood in the stylish but comfortably furnished drawing room, the door left open for propriety's sake.

Freddy raised his gray muzzle, his opaque eyes searching blindly as he gave a muffled woof.

"It's just me, sweet boy."

Blaire let him sniff her hand, and after a lick to her thumb, with a satisfied groan, he lowered his head and resumed his nap on the royal-blue brocade armchair. She rubbed his soft head. They mightn't have the precious dear much longer.

The thought was unbearable. He'd been part of the family for over fifteen years, since her parents died and she and her sisters came to live with Brooke and Brette.

"Blaire, permit me to assist you from your coat." Julian flashed a charming, sympathetic smile.

Why must he be so blasted genial? Far better if he treated her abominably, for then she might learn to hate him. But this solicitous man proved impossible to resist.

A combination of annoyance and mortification swept her. Botheration. he'd seen past her attempt to hide her discomfort. "I hardly think that's appropriate, Lieutenant. Neither do I believe Heath will approve."

"But he's not home, and for the doctor to examine you properly, you'll have to remove it in any event."

Right again. Why must he be so pragmatic?

She couldn't object again without sounding churlish or childish. Truth be known, although a minute ago she'd been freezing, with the annoyingly cheerful fire crackling away in the hearth, most indelicate moisture dampened her forehead and underarms.

A silent sigh lifted her chest.

"All right, Julian."

In this she must concede or continue to wear the coat and risk sweating and smelling like a race horse. Then she could sit. For in the last long moments, the room had begun spiraling and dipping in the oddest fashion, and her ears rang as if full of water.

Was this what swooning felt like? She'd never fainted, but surely this must be what the unnerving sensation was.

Julian stepped nearer and took one hand. "You've grown pale. Are you quite alright?"

"I'm fine." She wasn't. She dropped her gaze, but not before noticing the fine, dark stubble covering his jaw or his wonderful scent filling her nostrils.

Why must he smell so confounded...manly?

Julian already oozed masculinity. He needn't smell splendidly of soap, leather, and some aroma she didn't recognize but which suited him perfectly. And which made her all the more aware of him as a desirable man.

Like she needed anything else to jolt her acutely tuned senses. It had been thus between them—well, at least for her—since she met him at her first ball in London.

His new togs, looking as they'd been tailored straight from the latest fashion plate, became him. He wore all black from his Hessians to his superbly fitting coat. Only his grey and silver striped waistcoat and his cravat, crisp, white, and tied in a simple knot, interrupted the severity of his attire. All bespoke reserved quality.

His bent finger brushed her chin, and she sucked in a startled half breath.

"Pardon," he breathed, a husky timbre mellowing his deep voice as he lowered his head to better see the confounded frog closures.

Whoever invented this method of closing a garment must've been a mean-spirited or prudish nun or monk and hell-bent on frustrating the wearer too.

She started and gasped when Julian continued loosening the fastenings from their moorings and his journey took him past her breasts. A streak of sensation zipped from where he'd bumped her to lodge in the pit of her stomach.

Zounds.

What had she been thinking?

What had *he* been thinking?

His expression remained impassive, as if the intimate contact didn't faze him and as if unfastening women's garments was an everyday occurrence.

That ugly twinge of jealousy prodded her again, shrill and unkind and persistant.

Maybe not every day, but a soldier—a man of his caliber—knew a thing or two about the feminine form, she'd bet her delightful new boots.

She crinkled her nose into a slight scowl. Had he performed the same gentlemanly service for Miss Trudeau?

"There, all finished." A hint of huskiness turned his voice raspy, and a fine sheen of moisture beaded his upper lip. Perchance he wasn't as unaffected as he appeared.

She shifted her focus to the fire. Or mayhap after coming in from the brisk outdoors, the room's heat took a toll on him as well.

"Let's slip it off your good arm first," he suggested. "And then your injured one. Hold your right arm out."

Blaire complied, yet she couldn't prevent the small yelp of pain when agony rippled from wrist to elbow as he eased the garment from her.

"I'm sorry." Julian draped the coat over the back of the settee. "You are pale as a freshly laundered cravat. Sit down before you faint."

"I do not faint," she denied. However, there was a first time for everything.

Increasingly light-headed, she sank onto the nearest cushion, mindful not to jostle her arm. She slid her eyes shut and rested her head against the settee's back. The carved mahogany made an uncomfortable pillow, but she felt so wretched, she didn't dare move.

"Here, Blaire. Lift your head."

One eye cracked—to open both was too great an effort—she raised her head enough for him to slip a tasseled pillow beneath her head and neck.

"Better?"

Tenderness tempered his smile and brought tears to her eyes.

"Yes." She squeezed both lids tight. She would not cry in front of him.

"Good, good," he murmured.

The thought that had niggled the entire carriage ride home slipped from her mouth.

"You said Miss Trudeau is not your intended, Julian. Surely you are aware that there is chit-chat to the contrary."

Against her will, she peeked at him through half-shut eyes. To say a dark cloud descended on his countenance didn't begin to describe the hardening of his contoured features or the storm flashing in his eyes.

"I thought you were above listening to gossip."

How dare he accuse her? *He* was the one who had the explaining to do. *She* was the one Miss Trudeau had very deliberately warned away from her intended.

"It's not gossip when you've spoken to those closest to me and admitted you've entertained the idea," she retorted, suddenly cross with him. "And it's not chatter, Lieutenant, when in their concern for me, they made me aware so that I mightn't make a complete dithering fool of myself." Done with her scold, she clamped her lips together. She'd said too much already.

A satisfied, almost triumphant grin replaced his stormy countenance as he lowered himself beside her. He cupped the hand of her uninjured arm. "Why exactly, would you make a dithering fool of yourself?"

Oh, the odious man. He knew.

One starchy brow raised high, she turned a gimlet eye on him, silently warning him to leave off.

More the fool he for continuing to peer at her expectantly, a hint of mischief and something suspiciously like affection in his eyes. He'd no right to lead her on when he was parading about London with another on his arm—a woman he couldn't deny he entertained the notion of a union with.

"This isn't about me," Blaire pointed out, her tone dry and reproachful. She tore her focus from the dark honey of his suntanned hand with its fine dusting of dark hair.

Withdrawing her hand, she refused to meet his disarming gaze. Instead, she pressed her fingertips to her throbbing and, yes, swollen arm. She flinched and bit the inside of her cheek against another wave of pain.

Probably broken, then. Most inconvenient with two rascally pups bounding about upstairs soon. Julian had best say whatever was on his mind. With each passing moment, she felt ever more horrid, and she longed to lie down. Good thing Jenkin had sent for the doctor.

And where was the deuced tea, for pity's sake?

Did they have to send to China for it?

She wasn't above venturing to the kitchen and preparing the brew herself. Lord knew she'd done it often enough at Esherton Green before Brooke married Heath, and he'd hauled the Culpeppers to London.

Esherton Green...

A surge of homesickness engulfed Blaire. Maybe that was her solution—to leave London and go home. She tucked the idea into a niche in the back of her mind to explore later.

"What is it you wanted to discuss with me, Lieutenant?" She attempted to sound disinterested. As if her heart didn't ache anew in his presence, and as if she felt nothing more for him than she would for any casual acquaintance.

He didn't answer straightaway. His attention remained focused on the oversized painting, encased in a grossly ornate frame, of Heath's medieval ancestor astride a powerful black steed.

She took the opportunity to study the straight blade of Julian's nose, his rugged jaw, and the neatly trimmed sideburns framing his face. How had he come by the still pinkish scar on his cheek?

Her tummy flopped to think he'd been injured in a battle. She shouldn't care for him, shouldn't care what happened to him. But as she learned from watching her sisters' and cousins' romances bloom, the heart had a will of its own and oft disregarded logic and reason.

Her rebellious heart had determined she should love Julian and no other for all time, even though he couldn't be hers.

His chest rose and fell in an almost soothing, steady rhythm. At last, after exhaling a long breath, he faced her. He didn't speak at first, just examined every inch of her face. Such tenderness radiated in the depth of his eyes, she was helpless to break eye contact.

This was foolish and couldn't end well. She was positive, yet she didn't look away.

Voice low and hushed, he said, "As you are aware, I'm sure, Miss Trudeau was my late brother's betrothed. They were to have wed the week after Alfred's death."

Blaire nodded. He hadn't revealed anything new.

Indecision battled in his nut-brown eyes before he ran a palm over his face. "I believe I can trust your discretion, for in order to make you understand, I must reveal sensitive details." He screwed his mouth tight, a warrior's ferocity stealing over his features for a moment.

Eyes narrowed, she tried to read his expression. Did he look so fierce because of what he had to say, or because he wanted to make sure she would keep his confidence?

"Of course, unless it involves danger to you or someone else." That was the only time she'd reveal a confidence. "I cannot keep an oath of silence if that is the case."

"Not danger exactly," Julian denied. "Though two people could suffer greatly. Miss Trudeau carries my brother's child, and if the babe is a boy, he is the rightful heir to Montclere."

Every ounce of air left Blaire's lungs.

Julian needn't tell her that her jaw sagged worse than worn-out stockings.

Already fighting waves of dizziness, she grasped the settee cushion to steady herself.

Her mind raced back to the book store, to Daphne's winsome smiles and flirtatious glances. How could a woman carrying another man's child behave so? Didn't she mourn Alfred Drake at all? While Blaire could empathize with Miss Trudeau's difficulty, Julian sacrificing himself for the child's sake seemed extreme.

Besides, how did he know she told the truth?

She wouldn't be the first young woman to use devious means to snare a man in the parson's mousetrap. Why, Blythe had saved the Marquis of Leventhorpe, now her husband, from just such a wily wench.

This is different. Miss Trudeau had been betrothed. She has no reason to lie.

Revealing something so disgraceful to Julian must mean she spoke the truth. She risked much by sharing such a shameful secret. She was probably quite desperate, and the smallest twinge of pity for her plight pinged against Blaire's ribs.

Wait...

He'd said Miss Trudeau *wasn't* his intended.

More confused than ever, Blaire shook her head and promptly regretted the movement when her noggin objected with a sickening stab.

Forget the tea. She truly did need to lie down. Mustering her self-possession, she pressed two fingertips between her eyes in an effort to clear the fuzzy sensation filling her head.

"I fail to understand why you feel the need to confide something so personal to me, Lieutenant." His chivalry came as no surprise, but she couldn't honestly say she appreciated the gallantry. Admitting she wasn't as benevolent as she'd believed herself to be came at a cost to her self-respect. "That's between you and Miss Trudeau, and I cannot think she'd be pleased to know you confided in me."

She pulled a pillow onto her lap and, cringing, laid her injured arm atop its welcoming softness.

Much better.

"She wasn't exactly genial to me earlier," Blaire said, grateful for his sturdy shoulder to lean into, even if doing so was just this side of wicked. Then again, she didn't imagine the waves of dizziness assailing her just now.

He took her hand once more, tracing his callused thumb over her knuckles. "I told you because I don't *want* to marry Daphne."

He raised his hooded eyes framed by lush sable lashes, and what Blaire saw there, bold, undeniable, and wonderous in its transparency, sent an electric thrill jolting to her toes.

And hope. Wondrous, ridiculous, pitiful hope.

"I want to marry you, Blaire, and no other."

A virtuous woman is well-served if she recalls it is naïve
to trust everyone but prudent to trust those of noble character.
~Prudence and Propriety— The Genteel Lady's Guide to Practical Living

4

Scarcely a blink later, Blaire slumped against Julian, her head rolling forward.

He caught her around the shoulders before she tumbled onto the floor. Alarm thrummed through him as he cradled her in his arms, searching her wan face. Had she sustained more than mere scrapes when her head hit the pavement?

Freddy lifted his muzzle and sniffed the air before jumping off the armchair and toddling over to stand on his hind legs and nudge Blaire, whining.

Uncanny how the dog knew something was wrong.

Supporting her limp form, Julian shot a vexed glance to the doorway and then to the portico mantle clock. How could only ten minutes have passed since they entered the room?

Where was the bloody physician? Mayhap he hadn't been in his office or there'd been another emergency. Should he have Jenkin send for another?

"Blaire?" Blaike Culpepper plowed in, followed by the Earl of Ravensdale; his wife, Brooke, cousin to the twins; and Captain Oliver Whitehouse, Julian's closest friend.

All still wore their outer garments.

Bloody perfect timing.

A guilty flush crept up Julian's neck, and his neckcloth tightened perceptibly.

"Jenkin said he's sent for Dr. Barclay because you're hurt—" Miss Culpepper gave a distressed cry upon spying her insensate sister and dashed to her twin. She knelt beside the settee, giving Freddy a comforting pat atop his head. "*Shh.*"

She reached for Blaire's hand, but Julian stopped her with a brisk shake of his head.

"Careful, Miss Culpepper" he cautioned. "I believe her arm may be broken."

"Whatever has happened, Lieutenant?" A trace of accusation made Lady Ravensdale's clipped words crisp as she untied her bonnet before placing it and her gloves on the rosewood end table.

Miss Blaike took a moment from fussing over her sister to remove hers as well and then passed them to her cousin.

All the while, Julian held Blaire. Not that he minded, but the impropriety couldn't be ignored.

Her ladyship eyed his arms encircling Blaire before arching an accusing golden eyebrow. "Well, Lieutenant Drake? We're waiting."

Distinctly starchier.

He hadn't done a single ungentlemanly thing, and yet he felt disapproval radiating from her. Because he embraced Blaire or because of his involvement with Daphne? Had he been relegated to the rank of rogue or rakehell now?

Julian inclined his head in acknowledgment of her question and returned his attention to Blaire's pale face. "She's swooned. At least I hope that's all it is. As you can see from her face, she suffered a fall. I pray she's not concussed. Can you clear this settee of pillows? I'll lay her here."

Lady Ravensdale and Blaike made swift work of doing as he requested. Once Julian had laid Blaire upon the couch, he stood staring down at her and raked a hand through his hair. "I'm concerned she hasn't regained consciousness yet."

Not more than a couple of minutes had passed, but every second inched along painfully slow.

Jenkin entered bearing a salver. "Sir, Dr. Barclay has sent a response." His grizzled brows snapped together when his attention fell on Blaire. "Does Miss Blaire require smelling salts, my lady?"

Her ladyship considered Blaire, still insensate "Yes, please."

Ravensdale broke the seal, swiftly reading the contents. He held the paper up and gave it a slight shake. "The doctor will be along as soon as he's able. He's tending another patient at present."

Whitehouse and Ravensdale had divested themselves of their greatcoats while the women fretted over Blaire. Jenkin collected the garments, and after draping them over his forearm said, "A tea tray has been prepared. Should I bring it now or would you prefer I wait, my lady?"

Blaire moaned, rolling her head from side to side.

"Later would be best, I think." Anxiety rendering her pale, Lady Ravensdale leaned over the back of the sofa and brushed a lock of hair off Blaire's forehead. "Also, Jenkin, please send notes 'round to Ladies Livingston and Klepper expressing my sincerest regret that I must cancel my invitation to tea due to a family emergency."

"Yes, my lady." Jenkin slanted his head in acquiescence.

Her troubled gaze sank to Blaire once more. "Do send a footman for my smelling salts at once too."

"I think something a mite stronger than tea is in order. Brandy for all, Jenkin." Raven joined his wife behind the settee and, after tucking her to his side, pressed a short, comforting kiss to her temple.

"At once." Tossing his dignity aside, the majordomo all but ran from the room, his coat tails flapping like dual black flags on his ample behind.

"How did you come to be here, Drake?" Raven cocked his head, his expression a mixture of curiosity and confusion. "Am I mistaken, or did I overhear you proposing to Blaire?"

Blaike inhaled sharply. Her brow knitted in bewilderment, she exchanged a telling look with Whitehouse. He gave an almost imperceptible shake of his head, and she dropped her fretful gaze back to her twin.

Devil a bit and bloody damned hell.

See where Julian's impulsiveness and desperation to reassure Blaire had landed him? He choked off a more vulgar oath. How was he to explain himself? He'd sound like an arse no matter what he said.

He hadn't exactly proposed, just tried to convey to Blaire how much she meant to him before she fainted. As if his situation wasn't complicated enough, now he was obliged to explain to her family he hadn't been asking her to marry him, only declaring who he'd prefer to marry.

His head and logic insisted on one woman, but his heart and love wouldn't release another.

He was an utter knave. A bounder and a cad.

If Julian revealed his conundrum Raven might very well demand pistols at dawn or ban him from ever speaking to Blaire again. The latter caused him more angst than the former.

"Seems none of us has gone about seeking your approval before proposing, Ravensdale, but at least your tenure as guardian is nearly over and you can put that worry behind you." Whitehouse chuckled and winked at Blaike, saving Julian from an immediate answer.

Blaike pinkened, her eyes brimming with adoration.

Envy grappled with joy for her and Oliver's happiness. They had what Julian most coveted and, in his current situation, feared he'd never have.

Blaire's eyelashes fluttered, and smoothing her twin's hair away from her face as she stirred again, Blaike asked, "Shouldn't we carry her upstairs?"

"No, you should not," Blaire said, her voice the merest thread of a whisper. "I've heard every word since Jenkin entered with the note from Dr. Barclay."

She slowly lifted her eyelids, but for all of her bravado, the pain shimmering there stole Julian's breath. He needn't be a seer to know what he saw was more than physical pain, and it was directed at him. The bitter taste of self-loathing filled his mouth.

She'd heard Raven's question and was aware Julian had failed to answer.

From the severe angle of Raven's brows and his probing stare, he'd also noticed—and wasn't happy about Julian's lack of confirmation.

For an instant before Blaire swooned, a spark of hope had lit her beautiful eyes. Only a churl fanned the ember into a flame without giving her a legitimate reason to believe there could be more between them.

He wouldn't do that.

She made to sit up, and Blaike and Lady Ravensdale hastened to assist her.

"I wish you'd wait for the doctor to arrive, Blaire." Blaike sank onto the settee. Freddy had managed to haul his portly behind onto the cushion and lay with both paws atop Blaire's thighs. "Does your arm hurt horribly? The lieutenant said he thought it might be broken."

Features taut, Blaire pushed several loose strands of flaxen hair off her face. "He may be correct. I shan't deny it hurts something fierce, as does my head."

Julian didn't miss her deliberate avoidance of looking his way.

She motioned weakly to her sister and cousin. "Brooke, Blaike, would you please help me upstairs?"

Julian stepped forward. "With Raven's permission, I'll carry you."

"If anyone carries her, it will be me." Flintiness tinged Ravensdale's voice, giving Julian pause.

"My legs assuredly are not broken, gentlemen. I shall not suffer further indignity by being hauled to my chamber like an infant. Tumbling onto the street in full view of the *ton* succeeded in bruising my pride quite enough, thank you." Admirably poised, her movements deliberate, she rose.

Her sister and cousin hovered on either side of her, ready to assist but allowing her the self-respect she desired.

Freddy jumped to the floor as well.

She finally met Julian's eyes, and a cannon ball to his gut would've done less damage and hurt far less. Her resigned, wounded gaze, absent of accusation or anger eviscerated him.

"As we've had the discussion you were so keen to have, Lieutenant, I shall bid you… *good-bye.*"

The last whispered word was more than a farewell until they met again. In his very bones he knew it for what it was. A permanent leave-taking.

Blaire had made her decision, saving him from having to make the unbearable choice.

No! No!

Julian fisted his hands and clamped his teeth so tightly they might crack from the pressure.

It couldn't end between them like this. By God, he refused to let it. Her, ravaged by hurt and humiliation, and he, frustrated beyond reason for the lot which fate or providence or God had dealt him.

You've lost her. And he couldn't breathe. Couldn't think past that awful, mind-crippling truth. To hell with prudence and propriety. Blast his damnable honor. Throwing caution in the face of desperation, he extended a hand.

"Blaire, please…"

For a long, interminable moment, absolute silence reigned in the room as everyone swung astounded glances to him.

Everyone except his sweet Blaire.

Her steps measured, shoulders unyielding, and spine straight, she labored toward the doorway, Freddy snuffling at her heels.

"Have Jenkin send the doctor straight up when he arrives," Lady Ravensdale said to no one in particular. "Thank goodness we didn't require the smelling salts after all."

Julian couldn't drag his focus from the opening until their footsteps faded into silence. Cupping his nape, he spun to the fireplace, lest Whitehouse or Ravensdale see the devastation that must surely haunt his face.

Julian would sacrifice his life for Britain without hesitation. For Whitehouse and Raven too. And most especially for Blaire. But the cost of marrying a woman he didn't love for the sake of his brother's innocent child... That would take every ounce of resolve Julian possessed.

"Whitehouse, would you excuse us, please?" The earlier anger in Raven's tone had been replaced by something which sounded suspiciously like pity.

"Of course." A trace of empathy colored his voice too. "Drake, I'll call upon you this evening. We can chat then."

Julian might well be too bloody drunk to chat.

Few people understood him better than Whitehouse. They'd been friends since Eton, but Julian couldn't discuss this intimate matter with him.

He managed a stiff nod, his attention trained on the crackling fire. Silence filled the room for several long, discomfiting minutes.

"So, are you going to explain yourself, Drake? How you happened to be holding my unconscious ward in your arms? How did you know she had taken a fall?"

Resting his forearm on the mantle, Julian cut Raven—now sitting in an armchair—a wary look. He didn't appear angry, and he was perfectly within his right as Blaire's guardian to question Julian. As briefly as possible, he explained all except seeing Blaire at the bookstore and his declaration about whom he wanted to marry.

An ankle crossed over his knee and an arm draped across the back of the armchair, Ravensdale regarded him thoughtfully. Deceptively and dangerously calm to Julian's soldier's eye.

"Then, I owe you my thanks for seeing to Blaire and Flora's wellbeing." He rocked his Hessian-clad boot up and down. "Nonetheless, you still didn't answer my earlier question. Did you or did you not propose to Blaire? Because the woman I saw leaving this room was not a happy bride-to-be."

Remorse kicked Julian hard in the ribs. He might as well come clean. It benefited no one not to.

"I did not propose, per se." Disgust burned the back of Julian's throat. "I told her she was the woman I *wanted* to marry." If he were free to choose. Circumstances had cheated him of the choice.

Raven's foot stilled, and an inscrutable expression descended on his features. "Forgive me for being obtuse, but is there a difference? Why, devil take it, would you say that to Blaire if you didn't intend to ask for her hand?"

A log fell into the coals, sending embers spiraling up the chimney behind the ornate screen.

"Fiend seize it, Raven." Smacking his closed hand against the mantel, Julian shook his head. "What I want to do and what my bloody duty requires me to do are two very different things. I was a soldier for nine years. I well know the difference."

Jenkin entered with the brandy. "Shall I pour, sir?"

"No, thank you." Ravensdale flicked his fingers. "Has the doctor arrived?"

"Not yet. I'll inform you the moment he does." On silent feet, the butler retreated once more.

Crystal clinked, followed by the unmistakable sound of liquid being poured into a glass. A moment later, Raven nudged Julian's arm.

"Here, Drake. You look like you could use a dram or two."

Or three. Or an entire bottle.

He wouldn't though. No matter how angry or upset, he didn't get soused.

His grandfather, father, and brother had been drunken sots. He despised drunkenness, and becoming good and foxed would only bring a temporary reprieve to an impossible situation. Nonetheless, Julian tossed back a generous gulp, welcoming the burning path to his stomach.

"Now, tell me why you told Blaire you wanted to marry her and no other. And do be careful of your answer, Drake, for I'd hate to have to challenge you to an affair of honor," Raven said, only half jesting as he scratched his nose.

"There's no need for dramatics, Raven."

Julian took another sip before sitting at the piano and running a hand over the keys. He hadn't played in a very long time. "If I were free to marry any woman, I wouldn't hesitate to ask you for Blaire's hand." He glanced up, a deprecative closed-mouth grin skewing his lips upward on one side. "I love her. Have for months."

One knee cocked, Ravensdale remained standing, his head angled and gaze intense.

"Don't you think that was cruel? Especially to a woman you profess to love? To tell her that you want to marry her and then leave her dangling? Are you or are you not going to marry Daphne Trudeau? You've been seen galivanting all about London with her on your arm."

He gave a derisive snort. "Not exactly galivanting."

More like being dragged hither and yon—always with the babe being used to manipulate him. When had his ballocks shriveled? When had he relinquished his self-respect? A man could go mad, facing the decision Julian was being forced to make.

Ravensdale wasn't done lecturing. "Poor taste if you ask me, old chap—your brother newly buried and all. The rumor mill is fairly buzzing with conjecture, and just this morning, Brooke informed me the gossip rags have linked your names."

No surprise there. Joan Trudeau had made it her mission to drop intimations at every turn.

Ravensdale raised his forefinger from his glass and pointed it at Julian. "You are playing both women along, and for all of your professions of doing the honorable thing, your actions smack of cowardice. Make a bloody decision."

Each word was delivered like a pugilist's practiced blow—further damaging Julian's bruised conscience and magnifying his guilt. Ravensdale was absolutely right. Julian had been acting the poltroon, and for a soldier, there was no greater shame. He deserved his friend's disdain.

Blaire's too.

Even Daphne's.

Ravensdale slammed his brandy glass atop the marble mantel, at last giving full vent to his fuming ire. "And until you do, Drake, you are not to so much as glance at Blaire. And I'm bloody serious. When I took on the Culpeppers' guardianship, I did so promising to protect them. You cannot continue to toy with her emotions and not be on the receiving end of my wrath."

Julian gave a terse nod.

"You're right. I've behaved abominably." All because he couldn't forswear Alfred's child, he'd have to renounce his love for Blaire. Which was the greater sin in God's eyes? He knew full well which he'd regret until he drew his last breath.

Blaire. Sweet, beautiful, Blaire.

"I beg your pardon, Raven, and Blaire's as well. Please, do tell her that for me."

Since he wouldn't be afforded the opportunity to do so himself. Unless he wrote her a letter. But how could he pen the words that would shred both of their hearts?

Julian finished his brandy then carefully set the glass atop the piano before standing. "If you aren't able to keep the two pups Blaire rescued from the streets, I'd like to have them."

That launched Ravensdale's brows skyward.

"Pups? As in more than one?" He directed his focus to the ceiling where the unmistakable sound of scampering four-legged creatures carried below. "So that's what that commotion is. All we need is more animals underfoot."

"As I said, I'd be happy to give them a home at my estate." Julian very well may have lost a friend today as well as the woman he'd always love. "I can see myself out."

Unless he could extract himself from this bumblebroth, he wouldn't be back.

Four things are impossible to mend: broken promises, trust, faith, and hearts. Content is the woman who avoids such calamity.
~Prudence and Propriety— The Genteel Lady's Guide to Practical Living

5

Ten days later, her heart heavy and mind numb, Blaire leaned forward and peered out the coach's soiled window. The headache from her mild concussion had subsided days ago and, unless she jerked or bumped her head, had been reduced to nothing more than a mild irritation.

Four days of bone-rattling travel, along with her inability to sleep, had left her exhausted and irritable. More maddening was her incapacity to decide upon a course of action now that she and Julian were finished. Ended before they'd begun, actually.

Knowing he'd wed that sable-haired beauty seared her heart as if a molten blade speared the organ. Then was twisted round and round. The forces driving her from London—a broken heart, humiliation, devastation, and desperation—would fade in time. *Hopefully.* If God were merciful.

She must resolve to set her own course, especially when she turned one-and-twenty in just over a year. If only she could prove Daphne Trudeau a lying imposter as Blythe had been able to do with the chit determined to trap the Marquis of Leventhorpe into marriage.

Blaire possessed no qualifications for employment other than becoming a governess or a finishing school teacher. She slowly straightened, mulling the not-so-preposterous idea over. Perhaps not a perfect solution, but certainly one worth considering. Mayhap a governess to a prestigious family in America. Or Italy. *Or Timbuktu.* Anywhere where she'd never encounter Julian and his wife.

A sigh, sad and pathetic even to her ears, whispered past her lips, and she turned her gaze to the outdoors once more.

Nothing but pristine English countryside in varying shades of green met her scrutiny as far as she could see. In the lush meadow beyond, a goshawk perched on an aspen branch, scouring the field below for its next meal. In the distance, a few ominous charcoal-tinted clouds, stacked high and portending more rain, dotted the horizon.

The puff of air she forced out through her nose bespoke her frustration. All they needed was more unfavorable weather to further slow their progress. Twice this morning, the coach had become stuck. A coachman and the two outriders accompanying her to Culpepper Park had been obliged to lean their shoulders into the equipage while Flora and Blaire waited a bit farther along the muddy road.

Blaire's departure from London had been so abrupt there hadn't been time to notify Culpepper Park's staff. It wasn't uncommon to arrive at a country home without prior notice. Aristocrats and gentry did so all the time. Nevertheless, she couldn't help but feel a trifle guilty at the lack of consideration.

The coach slid sideways again, and her stomach tumbled over itself. She couldn't recall a more miserable journey, emotionally and weather-wise. Well, the voyage from Port de Lyon had exceeded this one for physical discomfort. Lord above, she never intended to set foot on a boat again. A shudder rippled from shoulder to shoulder and down her back. She'd never been so ill in her life. That experience was forever etched in her memory.

What about your possible plans to become a governess for a family on another continent?

She made a sour face. Bloody hell. There was that confounded consideration, but what was suffering *mal de mer* compared to facing Julian and his wife?

Her destination still days away, she longed for a hot bath and her own bed. She wasn't sure what her stay at Culpepper Park would bring. She'd never been away from her twin before, and this was the first time she'd live alone except for the small staff residing there.

On the opposite seat, tucked into the corner and snoring softly, Flora dozed. The maid had slept most of the trip, which wasn't uncommon for her. She was still too thin, partially because she forgot to eat half the time. Save for a few bruises, she'd suffered no injuries from her fall.

A nudge to Blaire's thigh drew her attention, and her first genuine amusement of the day tipped her lips.

Zeus was dreaming.

He and Apollo—the names of the rascally pups she and Julian had rescued—lay curled in a heap of multi-colored fur, gangly legs, and oversized paws on the seat beside her, snoozing away as well.

Thank goodness the pair slept.

When awake, the rambunctious imps tumbled about growling, nipping, playing, and in general, making the cramped carriage ride strained.

Running her fingers down Apollo's spine, she managed another small smile. Culpepper Park was the best place for these energetic chaps. She looked forward to the pups meeting Clio and Thalia, Lord Leventhorpe's collies, one day soon.

Highfield Place House had been in a constant state of upheaval since their arrival, and more than one piece of furniture now bore teeth marks from their gnawing. Freddy had never been such a naughty rapscallion.

Her injured arm rested in a sling, not broken, but badly sprained and equally as severely bruised. That it wasn't broken came as a tremendous relief, for there was no way Heath or Brooke would've permitted her to travel, let alone stay at the house with only Flora as a chaperone.

It wasn't until she'd actually used her hand to hold her teacup that they'd finally agreed to her request. They'd never know what effort it had taken to keep her pain masked. Nonetheless, she had every intention of obeying the doctor's orders and resting her arm for the next few weeks.

Paws twitching whilst he made cute puppy noises, Zeus dreamed on. Blaire idly ran her ungloved fingers through both dogs' coats.

I am not running away.

You are. At least be honest about it.

Yes, she was. But she needed time to herself without concerned family hovering about until she decided on the next step in her life. That very well might be escaping to another continent, but it was her decision to make.

The coach's rhythmic swaying lulled her into a drowsy state, and she, too, slid her eyelids closed. As usual, Julian's face drifted into her mind's eye. Sleep was a blessing, and she welcomed its oblivion. While awake, no matter how firmly she scolded and vowed to do otherwise, her mind strayed to him, much like a river runs downhill to the sea. The waterway had no more control over its path than she did over her wayward musings.

The cracks fracturing her heart ached anew each time she thought of him. When she'd all but begged Brooke to allow her to leave London, it was fear of running into Julian again that made her so frantic to flee town.

Self-respect, as much as pride, motivated her to depart with all due haste. For Blaire wasn't altogether certain—even if Julian were married—she wouldn't make a fool of herself over him. She might even entertain unsavory notions if that was the only way they could be together. That ugly truth, acknowledging her lack of character and her sinful contemplations, brought no small amount of self-castigation.

Her family would be horrified and disgraced if she were to act so rashly. Not that Julian had ever hinted at anything so shameful. No, she allowed, *she* might be the one given to such rashness.

When and how had she become so wicked?

And that was why she'd fled. Why she seriously contemplated leaving England altogether.

Truth be known, daily seeing her sisters' and cousins' blatant happiness scraped as sharply as thorns, and she bled on the inside, raw and red from the deep gouges.

She wasn't vexed—she didn't begrudge them their joy. But neither did she wish to be a depressing presence in their midst. Though she refused to dwell on her doldrums, more than once against her will, her eyes had filled with tears, and she'd swallowed past the constriction blocking her throat.

Love was awful.

Such a brilliant, beautiful torment.

With deliberate intent, she filled her lungs and turned her musings to the scenery outside. A glimpse beyond the window revealed the wind had kicked up a notch, and tree branches dipped and undulated in the breeze as the tall grasses swayed in a matching cadence.

She squinted at the depressing sky. Would the impending weather hold off until they reached the inn? Eyeing the muddy toes of her boots and the few dried brown splatters on the hem of her black-striped, slate carriage gown, she hoped so.

Except for one short trip when Culpepper Park was still under construction, she hadn't been back to her childhood home. Well, the park wasn't her childhood home. Esherton Green, the adjacent property owned by her cousin Sheridan Gainsborough, had been. No one had seen or heard from Sheridan since Heath had sought guardianship of the Culpeppers and paid the bounder to disappear a year ago.

Good riddance of bad rubbish.

If only Blaire were a man, she knew exactly what she'd do. If she were a gentleman of means, that was. She'd always wanted to visit Scotland. And then America. Then Rome—perhaps even the Caribbean Islands. But such a life was forbidden to an unmarried, underaged woman with only a maid as a chaperone. It just wasn't done.

Maybe... *Maybe...*

She'd cut her hair, dress as a man, and go to university to study law or medicine or something else women weren't permitted to do. Things that men decided the female sex wasn't capable of.

Lips stretched tight, she suppressed a sound just short of a frustrated growl.

It was so blasted unfair; even simpering bacon-brained oafs were afforded opportunities women weren't simply because of their gender. Having been raised on a farm, she was quite aware of the anatomical differences between males and females, and from what she'd observed, that...*appendage*... differentiating the sexes, didn't do a thing for males' intellect or their common sense either.

In fact, quite often their manhood rather seemed to be in the way.

A gust of wind slammed into the coach, rocking it from side to side, stirring Flora from her nap.

"What was that?" she asked sleepily. "Has a storm come upon us?" She gripped the side of the coach and leaned forward to stare out the window.

Caught up in her ruminations, Blaire hadn't noticed the growing gloom. Even as the realization crossed her mind, a torrent of rain descended from the leaden-gray skies, and thunder complained loudly in the distance. A brilliant flash of lightning divided the horizon over the wildly cavorting trees.

She didn't like the looks of this. Not at all. How much farther to the inn? What if a tree blew down upon the road or the coach? What if the road became impassable?

Originally, she'd thought Heath too protective when he'd insisted on the outriders, but she'd become ever increasingly grateful for their presence.

The wind—an angry tempest now—battered the coach, pummeling it incessantly. Shades of gray had replaced the landscape's former cheerful greens. The temperature had dropped in the coach as well, and she rubbed her arm with her good hand. She'd forgone a lap robe, and the warm stone provided this morning by the inn they'd stayed at last night had long since grown cold.

She'd only traveled this road a few times. On each occasion this particular stretch where the road hugged a smallish mountain tested her nerves to their utmost. A high embankment girded the track on one side, and a steep drop-off paralleled the other.

Two things frightened the wits out of Blaire—sailing, because she suffered so horridly from malaise, and heights. Dragging her attention from the terrifying spectacle to her right, Blaire summoned a smile to calm Flora.

The maid tortured the ends of her shawl and, her eyes round as guineas, wet her lips. She whispered, "I be scared."

"Nature's power is something to behold, isn't it, Flora?" Blaire attempted to cast a positive spin on the dramatics unfolding outside.

Fully awake now, the pups knocked against each other as they tried to remain on the seat. Zeus whined, attempting to crawl onto Blaire's lap.

"No, Zeus. I'm sorry love, you cannot. Your brother would want to as well, and I'm not supposed to jostle my arm at present."

The vehicle shuddered against the unrelenting battering, and a sudden jerk had Blaire holding her breath and digging her fingers into the seat.

Lord, please protect us.

Horses whinnied, and men's hoarse shouts sent her heart diving to her half boots as she sat up straight, her spine rigid in alarm. The next moment, the coach came to an abrupt halt, banging her sore arm into the carriage side and nearly catapulting her onto the floor.

"Ouch." Sucking in a haggard breath, she grabbed her arm and scooted backward onto the plush seat again.

Zeus had toppled onto the floor with a surprised yelp. He turned soulful eyes onto her.

"Come here." Blaire patted the cushion. "You're all right."

Were they?

"Miss Blaire...?" The maid's voice quaked as she huddled farther into the corner of the coach.

A couple of seconds later, the coach dipped as at least one driver descended from his seat.

"Flora, stay inside. Try to keep the puppies calm." Blaire cast a quick look out the window, but could see nothing out of the ordinary. "I'll be right back as soon as I find out what's happening."

She opened the door and barely stifled a gasp. A scarce four feet lay between the coach's wheels and the plunging precipice. Thankfully, they'd already passed the steepest cliffs, but even a tumble off the road here could be deadly.

A succession of shots boomed, their eerie echoes carried by the howling wind. Blaire started, her heart hurtling to her throat as she slapped a hand over her mouth.

God above!

Were they under attack by highwaymen? Before she could step from the vehicle, Nelson—Heath's coachman and her temporary body-guard—approached.

"Miss Culpepper, we've come upon a coaching accident. I've sent O'Bradi and the outriders to investigate." He turned his collar against the cold and damp. "They had to shoot all but one of the other team's horses."

"Unfortunate beasts." Sadness tightened her throat at their horrid fate. *One just never knew what might befall one, did they?* "What of the occupants?"

"We don't know yet." Nelson pulled his cap down on his head, hunching further into his collar against the bitter wind. "I think it best if you stay here until we know how badly injured the passengers might be."

Blaire stood taller, peering over the door and down the road. What appeared to be a coachman from the other vehicle lay sprawled partially off the road. In the eerie gloom, between the shrubberies and trees jutting up from the cliffside, she detected a slowly rotating carriage wheel.

Her flesh raised from waist to neck, and she shuddered. The travelers might be terribly injured. What if she hadn't come along?

"I shall come with you, Nelson." Already gathering her skirts in one hand, she allowed him to assist her from the conveyance. "If there's a female aboard, it may comfort her to have another woman nearby."

She turned and looked inside the coach. "Flora?"

The maid stopped petting the dogs, who were taking turns trying to mouth her hand, and turned worried eyes in Blaire's direction. "Yes, Miss Blaire?"

"I'm going to check on the passengers of the other vehicle. I want you to remain here. Do you understand?" As Blaire spoke, she slipped her arm from the sling then pulled the cloth over her head, gritting her teeth against a twinge of pain.

They might need the strip for bandages.

Giving a shallow nod, Flora swallowed audibly, something just short of terror glinting in her eyes. "I shan't move."

"Good. I couldn't bear if it if something were to happen to you." Blaire squeezed the frightened maid's hand before shutting the door. Taking a bracing breath, she faced the road just as her outriders guided a weeping woman up the hillside.

The furious wind continued wreaking havoc, howling and whistling through the trees and ripping at Blaire's bonnet. After a moment, she untied the ribbons and then, reopening the coach door, tossed the hat onto the seat. At once the maddening gale attacked her hair with the vengeance of a jealous wife. It mattered little. She could function better without the brim and ribbons flapping about, slapping her face.

Hurrying forward, she tried to remember anything that she had been taught by her older sister regarding tending injuries. Nursing wasn't Blaire's area of expertise; it was Blythe's.

The thick mud sucking at her boots, she tromped her way toward the wrecked vehicle. As she neared, what must've been a groom from the destroyed conveyance helped another woman up the slippery incline.

The ladies wept, clinging to one another as they peered at what was left of the coach.

Shoving saturated tendrils off her face, Blaire trudged onward, each step making a sickening squishing noise. She squinted into the wind.

Something about the women...

A flash of icy cold swept her from neck to waist, and sliding to a wobbly stop, she slapped a hand to her mouth, muffling her dismayed cry.

Daphne Trudeau and her mother.

Did that mean...? Was Julian in the coach too?

Dear God, no!

"Julian." His name escaped past Blaire's trembling lips.

No. No. No.

What the devil were they doing here? Why weren't they safely in

London, strutting about like a happily betrothed couple? Heath had said nothing of Julian leaving town as well. If he'd known, Heath had chosen to keep it hidden from Blaire, likely to protect her.

Hiking her skirts to her knees, she tried to run. The merciless muck sucking at her boots refused to let her. Panting from exertion as well as panic, she slogged forward.

"Miss Trudeau? Mrs. Trudeau?"

The women swung to her, jaws sagging, obviously every bit as astounded to see her as she was to see them.

Her lower lip clamped between her teeth, Blaire frantically searched the plundered coach. The two outriders and a coachman struggled to lift another person—*a tall, muscularly built man*—from the vehicle.

"Julian," she breathed through trembling lips, her hands pressed to her middle.

Oh, Julian, my dearest love.

God, please don't let him be hurt badly. I can stand him marrying another, but I cannot bear him dying.

Her attention fixated on the limp form the trio struggled to carry up the hillside, a movement caught the corner of her eye as Nelson approached.

Blaire veered him a hasty glance. "Please escort the ladies to my coach. If they've any injuries, we can try to tend them there." Every drop of moisture had left her mouth from fear for Julian, and she wet her lips. "How much farther to the inn?"

Nelson scratched his chin and screwed his mouth up. "Under normal circumstances, not more than an hour, I'd say, miss. But with this wretched weather and the condition of the road..." He circled his hand in the air. "I cannot be sure."

"Very well." She gave a short nod, redirecting her scrutiny to the still crying women. "Ladies, please allow Nelson to assist you to my coach."

"Julian...?" Miss Trudeau managed between her loud snuffles.

"They're bringing him up the hill even now. But it won't do any good for you to stand here becoming further saturated and putting yourselves at risk for lung fever." Blaire swiftly scanned the women, seeing no obvious signs of severe wounds. Although rumpled, with tears in their garments, as well as a scratch or two on their faces, they didn't appear badly hurt. "Are either of you injured?"

"Of course we're injured, Miss Culpepper! Are you blind?" Mrs. Trudeau huffed indignantly, scowling at Blaire as if she were a halfwit. She made a curt gesture toward the disabled vehicle. "Our coach just tumbled down a ravine. I'm bruised from neck to toe, and I may have cracked a tooth." She wrapped a protective arm around Daphne's slumped and shaking shoulders. "I dare say, we're lucky to be alive."

"You are, indeed," Blaire agreed.

Pray God Julian was alive too.

He must be. He simply must be. The appalling way they'd parted...

Her, bitter and unforgiving; him, broken and pleading.

A tear leaked from her eye, and she hastily knuckled it away lest the Trudeaus notice.

She'd heard him call her name, recognized the entreaty in his hoarse voice. But anger, hurt, and utter mortification had hardened her heart. At first, she'd believed Julian meant to propose. Then the irrefutable, ugly realization that he wasn't going to shattered what little hope she'd retained. He might *want* to marry her, but he would marry Daphne Trudeau instead.

His deuced, bloody, damnable honor decreed it.

A queer pain twinged her heart, and more tears welled in her eyes. She blinked them away and pointed to her equipage. "I suggest you make use of my coach to seek shelter from this abysmal weather."

"Mama, we should be grateful Miss Culpepper came along when she did, else we'd be stranded, and Julian..." Daphne's daring earned her a practiced, acerbic glower from her mother.

"*Hmph.*" Jutting her chin to a haughty angle, Mrs. Trudeau peered at the coach. "What about our belongings?" she demanded, her ingratitude galling. "It's quite apparent you haven't room for our luggage."

Blaire perused the assorted trunks and other luggage scattered near the demolished conveyance. A few had burst open, their contents spilling forth like a freshly gutted animal. Had those all been secured on top of the coach rather than loaded in a wagon? No wonder the vehicle had toppled over in this powerful wind. What could Julian have been thinking?

Perchance he hadn't been able to think straight either. That notion—however right or wrong—wrought a bizarre mixture of satisfaction and remorse in her.

"Once we reach the inn, a wagon can be sent back to collect your possessions." Arm outstretched, Blaire indicated her coach again. If she were a nice person, she'd warn them about the puppies. A mischievous smile almost bent her mouth. Gads, how would the Trudeaus react when they realized they'd be sharing the conveyance with the dogs?

Miss Trudeau grasped her mother's arm and managed between the continual flow of tears, "Come, Mama. Miss Culpepper is right. I shan't want you to catch your death of cold standing in this rain."

Mrs. Trudeau finally nodded, her scraggly hair liberally dosed with gray clinging to her neck and shoulders. "Yes, and we should tend to your health as well, my dear."

She gave Blaire what could only be described as a crafty look. Surely she didn't suspect Blaire knew about Daphne's pregnancy.

"Nelson…?" Blaire lifted her good arm toward the conveyance. "If you would, please."

Elbows entwined, the women proceeded the coachman, the whole while the wind blew Mrs. Trudeau's bitter complaints and Daphne's copious weeping back to Blaire.

She remained cemented to the spot, unable to look away from Julian, limp and unmoving.

Pray God, there was a physician available near the inn. As the men gained the road, she rushed forward, trying to determine how seriously hurt he might be.

Other than a nasty gash on his forehead, it was impossible to tell.

Blaire bit her lip again to keep from crying out her anguish. Dissolving into a fit of emotions would benefit no one, and from what she'd observed so far, the Trudeaus were useless in a crisis.

"Miss, we best see the gentleman to your coach and hurry to the Tankard and Anchor. He doesn't look good," O'Bradi advised. "You know these people?"

She gave a mental shake.

"I do." She glanced around and then indicated Julian's coachman sitting on the ground. "Help him into the coach as well, and the rest of you will either have to sit with the driver or ride double with the outriders." The one surviving horse from Julian's team would need to be tied to the rear of the coach as well. "Move along now. There's no time to waste. Lieutenant Drake requires a physician at once."

Failure to regain consciousness after a blow to the head was very serious.

What if he never woke up?

Stop it. Another hysterical woman is the last thing Julian needs right now.

Closing her eyes, she struggled for composure. She must keep her wits about her when she entered the coach, especially if she were to endure the Trudeaus' trying company. That alone was tiresome enough, but not knowing the extent of Julian's injuries would test her mettle until they reached their lodgings.

A few tense moments later saw him settled in the coach, still insensate.

Flora and the Trudeau women occupied one seat. Julian sandwiched between Blaire and the pale-as-paste servant sat on the other, whilst Zeus and Apollo made a general nuisance of themselves nibbling everyone's shoes.

"Stop that, wretched creatures," Mrs. Trudeau snapped, giving both dogs hard shoves in their ribs with her toe.

Flora gasped and turned accusing eyes on her.

Julian groaned softly, drawing every feminine eye in the coach.

The coach's progress was slow, not only due to the foul weather and miry roads but the additional weight in the vehicle. Blaire nearly chewed her lower lip raw fretting for Julian. She kept her sling pressed to the ugly gash at the back of his head, and the bleeding seemed to have stopped.

Why hadn't he woken yet?

Worry-induced nausea coiled in her stomach.

"Miss Culpepper," Mrs. Trudeau's grating voice interrupted the weighty silence. "Rather peculiar you being right behind us, I must say. Some might suggest you're so desperate to snare the lieutenant for yourself that you followed us from London."

Blaire lifted a brow high, stifling the curt retort springing to her lips. How could the woman be so hateful even in these circumstances? And raising a private issue in front of servants was far outside the bounds.

"I assure you, I wasn't." It vexed to have to defend herself against the false accusation.

Daphne might've resorted to those measures, but Blaire was above such shenanigans. Coming upon Julian's coach was a coincidence, pure and simple. Or an act of providence, not that she generally believed in that sort of thing.

Clearly, from the mocking smirk Mrs. Trudeau sent her, she didn't believe Blaire.

"I'm on my way to my familial home near Acton in Cheshire." Was Julian's estate near Culpepper Park? Hounds' gnashing teeth. She'd never considered that.

She worked her gaze over Daphne's and her mother's faces. Something was as off as week-old porridge with those two. Leaning forward, one finger on her chin, she regarded them thoughtfully. "What are *you* doing away from London?"

Daphne gave a little trilling laugh, touching her hand to her throat. Her eyes shifted side to side, and she looked everywhere but at Blaire. She gave Julian a cautious glance.

"Why, we're off to Montclere to wed, of course."

A woman of virtue holds this truth dear:
When you wonder if you can trust someone, if you
are honest with yourself, you already know you cannot.
~Prudence and Propriety— The Genteel Lady's Guide to Practical Living

6

Tankard and Anchor Inn
Cheshire, England

Blaire paced outside Julian's chamber at the Tankard and Anchor Inn. The physician had arrived a half-hour ago and remained closeted inside. Four doors down, Daphne and her mother occupied another humble room.

The younger Trudeau was none too happy about having to share, but the proprietor only had three chambers available, and Blaire and Flora weren't sleeping in the common room just so the Trudeau women might each have their own.

Arms folded and chin tucked to her chest, Blaire pivoted and made the return trip down the poorly lit corridor. A single window at the far end, tucked high into the eave's arches, filtered a smattering of shadowy light.

Her half boots rapped softly on the well-worn wooden floor with each tense step. She'd asked the physician to examine the injured coachman as well. It couldn't hurt to have him assess Daphne either, particularly given her delicate condition. Daphne hadn't complained about any pains, but Blaire was positive Julian would want to ensure his niece's or nephew's well-being.

She rotated her stiff neck in a slow circle. The past two hours had been nothing short of harrowing. The carriage had inched along the soggy road, and the whole while Julian slouched, unconscious beside her. Mrs. Trudeau's barbed stare and Daphne's theatric little huffs every few minutes had worn on Blaire's nerves.

The only bright spot had been Apollo and Zeus. After the kick to their ribs, the darlings took one look at Mrs. Trudeau's cantankerous countenance and had scuttled behind Blaire's legs. Zeus's snout poked out from behind her right leg and Apollo's, her left.

Blaire had always believed dogs were good at determining a person's character. The pups' behavior proved it.

Filling her lungs, she directed her attention overhead then blew her breath out in a whoosh. A few cobwebs hung from the crude rafters, but she couldn't complain about the simple but relatively clean lodgings.

The staff were friendly and eager to please, and a wonderful aroma wafted upward from below, teasing her nostrils. Her stomach grumbled, reminding her she hadn't eaten anything but a half piece of toast for breakfast this morning.

She'd sent Flora to make sure their room had clean linens and to make arrangements for a bath later. Afterward, she'd given the maid permission to take a nap with the puppies.

Blaire's mind came 'round to the thought that had tormented her since she'd settled beside Julian in her carriage. He'd wasted little time departing London to exchange vows with Daphne. She shouldn't have expected anything else. After all, Daphne's pregnancy would be apparent soon, no doubt.

Blaire shook her head in self-disgust. She shouldn't be shocked or hurt. He'd been forthright from the beginning. *"I want to marry you, Blaire, and no other."* She'd cling to that profession for the rest of her life.

In some odd way, his admission that she was his preferred choice helped her accept the situation a mite easier. It was probably best that he hadn't said he loved her, for if he had, she might've hurled her scruples in the face of morality and propriety and...

Well, she wasn't quite sure what she'd have done.

Still, she could—would—go on if he wed another. He didn't do so out of love for Daphne, but out of duty.

But if Julian died...

Turning to make the reverse journey once more, she tamped down the morose thought.

He will be all right.

He must be.

Idly rubbing her sore arm, she wandered down the passageway, leaving little crumbles of dried mud with each step. How she wished her sisters and cousins were here right now. They'd always been the biggest support for each other during trying times. But this was something Blaire must deal with by herself, especially if she wanted to convince her family she was capable of managing her own life.

Joan Trudeau poked her head around the doorframe, her coiffeur restored to its normal tight bun.

"Has the doctor said anything yet about Lieutenant Drake, Miss Culpepper?"

"No." Blaire shook her head. "He hasn't come out yet."

As the words left her mouth, the slightly lopsided chamber door opened with a protesting squeak.

Dr. Durnham—a dapper little fellow with a neatly trimmed bright red beard, wiry eyebrows, and even wilder hair poking every which way—peeked upward at her over his spectacles. Shorter than she by a good eight inches, mischief twinkled in his date-brown eyes.

With his green paisley waistcoat, he very much reminded her of a cheery leprechaun.

"How is Lieutenant Drake?" Tense with expectation, her interlaced fingers clenched so tightly the tips of her fingers grew numb. Blaire awaited his response.

Shoving his spectacles up his thin nose, a genial smile bent his mouth and pleated the corners of his eyes. "He's regained consciousness, I am happy to say, but the blow to his forehead was severe."

Daphne's head popped out her doorway too. Likely, she'd heard the doctor's voice. "Miss Culpepper?"

"The lieutenant has awoken," Blaire said. She'd like to have learned his condition before they intruded.

"My darling Julian is awake?" Daphne flew down the corridor, her mother right on her heels.

Did the woman never let her daughter do anything without her?

Eyes glistening—*must she weep about everything, for pity's sake?*—Daphne clutched the physician's arm. "Please, Dr. Durnham. How is my betrothed?"

Exactly how soon had Julian proposed after seeing Blaire home the day of her tumble?

The long and short of it was he'd not wasted much time. The knowledge shouldn't sting, but it did.

Extracting his arm, the doctor gave her a kindly smile, though a jot of censure snuffed the jollity in his eyes. "As I was telling Miss Culpepper, he has regained his senses."

Joan Trudeau's lips bowed in what Blaire supposed was meant to be a smile, although given her perpetual frown, it looked more like her stomach pained her. Badly.

"Thank goodness for that." She nodded and clasped her hands at her waist. "I feared my dear Daphne would tragically lose another betrothed."

Blaire fixed her teeth, not only against the urge to tell Joan this wasn't about her *dear Daphne*, but also against the pain her words caused.

"Yes, Lieutenant Drake is awake," Dr. Durnham said. "But…"

"But what?" Daphne's lower lip trembled, a sure sign she was about to become a fountain once more.

How could Julian bear her incessant weeping? Blaire covertly eyed Daphne's tummy.

Maybe she was being unfair. Didn't pregnancy make women more emotional? She couldn't recall Brooke, Blythe, or Brette succumbing to tears, but none of the Culpeppers had ever been one to cry at the drop of a pin.

Joan leaned in, her pointed nose practically poking the startled doctor in the face.

He took a step backward, his grizzled brows forming a vee.

"Are you saying all is not well with my future son-in-law? Does he have internal injuries or broken bones? What's wrong with him?" Eyes brimming with suspicion, her jaw sagged. "Is he…Is he *addled*? Has the blow to his head rendered him a senseless simpleton?"

The horrified glance she sent Daphne said much.

Dr. Durnham's countenance hardened, and something akin to impatience or annoyance flickered in his eyes and leaked into his tone. "I dare say his intellect is intact, though he's suffering from a nasty concussion—"

Daphne gasped and clapped a hand over her mouth. "Oh, my poor Julian."

"You say his faculties are intact?" Joan persisted. She had the audacity to twirl a finger near her temple. "He's not dim-witted or queer in the head, is he?"

What if he was? Would that keep her pregnant daughter from marrying him?

"I cannot be one hundred percent certain. Head injuries take time to heal. Especially if there's been damage or bruising to the brain." The doctor straightened his waistcoat then glanced at the women in turn. "What has me most concerned is Lieutenant Drake's amnesia."

"Oh no," Blaire breathed, the merest wisp of a sound.

"*Amnesia?*" Daphne covered her eyes with her hands for a moment. She wore no engagement ring, but that wasn't uncommon. "Does he remember anything, Doctor? *Anything* at all?"

Lips pressed flat, Blaire leaned away the merest bit. Why did Daphne's question seem more cunning than concerned?

"He doesn't know who he is and, so far, has no other memories, though he may recognize you when he sees you. It's doubtful, however. The good news is that most often amnesia is short-lived. As he heals from the concussion and the swelling in his brain subsides, and because he's otherwise a hale and hearty young man, I expect him to fully recover."

"What am I to do, Mama? What if he doesn't ever remember me? How can we be married?" Daphne collapsed onto her mother and dissolved into another fit of weeping.

'Twould be to his benefit not to remember her in Blaire's estimation. *And yours too* whispered a begrudging little voice.

"Hush, Daphne. All will be well. Haven't I always taken care of you? This is a minor setback." Joan *tutted* and *tsked* as she patted her daughter's back.

Not so minor if Julian didn't regain his memory in a timely fashion.

Dr. Durnham's countenance grew a bit sterner as he buttoned his coat. "I also recommend Lieutenant Drake be kept as calm as possible and not subjected to intense emotional displays. He won't understand why you're upset." He looked pointedly to Daphne's chamber. "Perhaps you should retire to your room until you have composed yourself, Miss Trudeau? I'll look in on you in a few moments."

"Yes, yes. That's what we shall do." Joan towed her sniffling daughter away, all the while professing everything would be all right.

His keen focus swung to Blaire. "I suggest the lieutenant remain here and not be moved for at least a fortnight. I don't even want him to leave his bed for a week, but I'll be bound a strapping fellow like that will rebel after a few days."

He was right.

Julian wouldn't like being confined to bed.

"The brain is a fragile thing, Miss Culpepper." He regarded her for an extended, thoughtful moment. "I've only seen it once in my career, but there have been instances of amnesia where something unpleasant has occurred and the patient doesn't want to remember their past. It's too painful. You wouldn't happen to know if there is anything that Lieutenant Drake wouldn't want to remember, would you?"

Should Blaire tell him? Could Julian's reluctance to marry Daphne truly factor into his amnesia? Yes, the doctor should know. It might determine the course of Julian's treatment. She flicked a glance to his chamber then to Daphne's closed door, making certain she wouldn't be overheard.

"His brother died recently, and he's not wedding Miss Trudeau willingly."

"*Hmm*, that might be enough. What we must do is convince him he has something to look forward to. Give him a reason to want to remember." His expression contemplative, Dr. Durnham straightened his cuffs then buttoned his coat. "I shall check in on him each afternoon. If something arises in the meantime, have one of the stable lads or a servant fetch me at once. Particularly if he loses consciousness or there's bleeding from his nose or ears."

"Yes, of course. I agree. He shouldn't be moved."

She'd write home and explain the situation. There was no need to notify the staff at Culpepper Park since they weren't aware she was coming. Likely, her entire family would descend on the inn within a week's time—as much out of concern for the lieutenant as to ensure propriety. The males would, at least—all bravado and outraged masculine pride.

Such a journey would prove more difficult for her sisters and cousins.

Brooke's two-month-old son made traveling risky, and Blythe's baby was due next month. Brette might manage the trip since her babe wasn't expected until late August or early September. But Blaike, on the other hand, would undoubtedly be on the next coach out of town.

Mayhap Blaire would delay her letter to Brooke a day or two or…six.

What about Julian's family? Were they expecting him? Wouldn't they be worried at his delay? Should she send them a letter? Would Julian want her to? Drat it all, she didn't know.

Maybe she could find out from Daphne if they'd alerted Julian's family to their arrival.

Yes, that's what she'd try to do.

Dr. Durnham gave her an assessing look. "How, might I ask, are you acquainted with the lieutenant?"

She couldn't very well admit he was the man she adored and thought to marry. Not with his betrothed a few feet away.

"He's a good friend of my family's and my guardian's."

True enough.

She cupped her sore arm, holding it close to her waist. She'd overdone it these past couple of hours, and the niggling ache that had begun in the coach had become a full-blown throb. As soon as she'd seen Julian, she would don another sling and take a dose of headache powders too.

"Well, I'd much prefer you were in charge," Dr. Durnham said.

Me too.

He inclined his head toward Daphne's room. "Miss Trudeau is flighty and prone to emotional outbursts. I've gathered her mother is far too starchy and stern to make a good nurse either. You though…" A benevolent smile warmed his plain features. "I believe you have a sensible head on your shoulders, and you appear far stronger than either of the Trudeaus. Could I impose upon you to oversee the lieutenant's care in my absence?"

Wouldn't that send Daphne and her mother into a fine fettle? All the more reason to accept.

"I have little nursing experience," Blaire admitted. "But my guardian had a concussion once, and recently, my sister's betrothed was involved in an explosion. I assisted with their convalescences. I'm confident I can manage if you tell me what I need to do. My maid can help too."

Flora liked to feel useful, and bringing fresh water, towels, or whatever else Blaire might need would keep her busy. Blaire would see if there were a few tasks she could do around the inn as well.

"I mainly need him monitored to make sure he doesn't pass out again or try to do too much too soon." Dr. Durnham's forehead pleated like an unopened fan. "He may feel dizzy, unbalanced, and nauseous, which may require you to steady him. Vomiting is not uncommon, nor is difficulty concentrating."

"Is the lieutenant also aware of these symptoms, so he doesn't become alarmed?" Blaire asked.

"Yes, I've told him, but you may need to remind him. He may also have blurred vision or slurred speech, though I detected neither. And he'll have a headache to rival Zeus's after his daughter Athena was born fully armored from his forehead." He chuckled gleefully at his own joke. "I need to know if he worsens immediately. As I said before, I'd prefer he stayed abed for the next week at least."

Unlikely unless Blaire tied Julian to the mattress.

He rubbed his jaw. "I don't suppose he has a valet, does he?"

Did he? Blaire had no idea. "I don't believe he was traveling with one, but I'm sure I can impose upon one of the menservants to assist with his more delicate requirements."

"Excellent." Dr. Durnham's focus dropped to her arm. "You've been favoring that limb. I wasn't aware you were also involved in the accident."

"I wasn't. I took a tumble a few days ago." She lifted her arm slightly. "It's not broken, merely sprained."

She didn't mention how badly for fear he'd change his mind.

"Ah, sprains are often more painful than a break." Another frown wrinkled his forehead and tipped his mustached mouth downward. "Perhaps I shouldn't impose upon you. I suppose if they must, the Trudeaus—"

"No. I'll do it. My family would expect and want me to." Would they under the circumstances? She smiled to soften her words. "I'm ever so much better, and when I wear my sling, I barely notice the pain. I promise to use good judgement and not overtire my arm."

He frowned at the cracked doorway, clearly unconvinced. "Let's give it a try for a day or two and then see where things stand, all right?"

"Of course. Doctor, I'd like for you to tell the Trudeaus you've asked me to look after Lieutenant Drake. I don't believe the news would be well-received coming from me, nor would they believe me." They weren't likely to have a full-on conniption fit or fly into a high dudgeon in the doctor's presence either.

"As you wish, Miss Culpepper. As the lieutenant's physician, I shall insist they abide by my preference."

Blaire's attention drifted to Daphne's doorway.

Should she?

"I think it would be wise for you to examine Miss Trudeau as well." She glanced up and down the corridor then quietly said, "She is with child."

THE LIEUTENANT AND THE LADY

Bushy eyebrows wriggling, he smoothed his mustache. "Well, now. That explains much. Indeed, it does."

Blaire brushed the back of her hand against her forehead. "Please don't mistake my revealing the confidence as gossip. I am concerned for the child's welfare, and quite naturally, Miss Trudeau doesn't want her condition to become public knowledge. The coach was quite mangled, and given the lieutenant's concussion, I fear Miss Trudeau might've been jostled about violently as well."

"I agree, and I'll keep your confidence." He gave her a rather dashing wink. "I'd have discovered her condition during my examination in any event. How far along is she? Do you know?"

Blaire shrugged and rubbed her arm. She'd not have him believing Julian was the father. "More than two months. Her betrothed—the lieutenant's brother—died two months ago. That's why Lieutenant Drake is marrying her."

Given his eyebrows scampering up his forehead, the widening of his friendly hazel eyes behind his spectacles, and the momentary slackening of his jaw, Blaire had flummoxed the good doctor.

"Well, I'm not certain I've ever encountered a situation like this." He thrust his jaw out and sucked his cheeks in. "Awfully noble of the lieutenant, I must say."

Yes, bloody, wonderfully noble.

Daphne, now composed and as lovely as ever, exited her chamber along with her mother. "I should like to see Julian now, Doctor."

She completely ignored Blaire.

"Momentarily." He cut Blaire a conspiratorial glance. She did like him. He was no fool. "I've asked Miss Culpepper to oversee Lieutenant Drake's care when I am not here."

"But...I'm his affianced." Daphne jutted her chin out mulishly. "*I* should care for him."

"Indeed, good sir. We don't require *her* help." Joan's snide, thin-lipped smile reminded Blaire very much of a viper's.

"Miss Culpepper has experience tending concussion patients. Have you?" Dr. Durnham asked.

Her lower lip sticking out in a belligerent manner, Daphne shook her head. "No, but—"

He turned to Joan. "And you, madam?"

"No, I haven't either," she scoffed, flapping her hand

contemptuously. "But that's beside the point. We—"

"No, madam. It is precisely the point." Dr. Durnham drew himself up, his flinty-eyed glare staring her down. "A concussion of this nature is very serious. I must insist on the more experienced of you ladies monitoring my patient. I shan't jeopardize the lieutenant's health to satisfy petty envy or misplaced pride."

The last was said with such fervor, his brown eyes bulged behind his spectacles.

For once, Daphne and her mother were rendered speechless.

"Have I made myself clear? Because I can prohibit either of you seeing him at all." He wavered his pointer finger between them.

Sounding as if she'd swallowed glass shards, Daphne managed, "Yes, Doctor."

Her mother's set jaw and flattened lips revealed she barely controlled her tongue and temper.

"May I see Julian now?" Daphne asked, spearing Blaire a frosty glance.

He nodded and stepped aside. "Please keep your visit short. Not more than fifteen minutes. As I said earlier, he'll likely not remember you and trying to might cause him strain and stress that won't be good for his recovery. No crying either, or I shall have to forbid you from seeing him."

Well done, Doctor.

Daphne gave a weak smile before disappearing into Julian's chamber, her constant shadow right behind her.

A moment later, Julian's beloved baritone resounded, sounding much stronger than Blaire had anticipated.

The doctor took Blaire's elbow and steered her a few steps away from Julian's doorway. Voice lowered for her ears only, Dr. Durnham said, "Your concern for Miss Trudeau is commendable, Miss Culpepper. I quite agree with you. She should be examined. It's not my position to judge others but to care for my patients' health. I'll attend her as soon as she leaves his chamber. Meanwhile, I'll look in on the injured coachman and ask for a tray to be brought up for the lieutenant."

Satchel in hand, he strode down the corridor to the stairway leading to the servants' quarters.

Blaire closed her eyes and leaned against the coarse wall. As horrible as it was, part of her wished Julian would never remember Daphne. That was utterly selfish and beneath her.

What kind of life would that be for him?

He'd made his choice, and who was she to condemn him for wanting what was best for the innocent child?

Dredging up her composure, wishing she had armor to don as well as a shield and sword to protect herself against the Trudeaus' attacks, she, too, entered Julian's chamber.

A bandage encircled his head, and he lay propped against the pillows, wan but not fragile. Daphne stood on one side of the bed holding his hand while her mother hovered—much like a cranky crow—on the other.

Bewilderment lined Julian's face as his attention gravitated from Daphne to Joan, and he licked his lips before withdrawing his hand from Daphne's. Her distressed doe-eyed gaze speared to her mother, and Joan gave an almost indiscernible shake of her head.

As Blaire made her way to the foot of his bed, Julian's warm caramel eyes met hers, and she swore a flicker of recognition glowed before disappearing. A minute smile curved his mouth, and her heart leapt.

She hadn't a doubt he'd recognized *her,* albeit it had been for less than a blink.

"I'm sure you'll remember me soon, darling." Daphne gave Julian one of her sunny smiles. "Our wedding was to be next week."

Really, Daphne. He cannot recall who you are, but why should that stop him from trotting down the aisle with a complete stranger?

Not a doubt existed that she, most probably with the help of her intrusive mother, had decided the wedding must take place as planned, whether Julian remembered her or not.

Did they fret about his memory taking weeks or even months to return and that, in the meanwhile, Daphne's stomach would grow ever larger?

She was in a bit of a pickle—well, a deuced huge pickle—and Blaire struggled to husband more charitable feelings for her. Not with much success. Perhaps if she'd been kinder to Blaire and less manipulative with Julian compassion might've softened Blaire's heart toward her.

Daphne formed a slight moue with her mouth. "Naturally, Julian, we can delay our wedding…. If you wish to."

He cast her a look so incredulous, Blaire bit the inside of her cheek to keep from bursting forth with an unfettered laugh.

"I'm sure you understand that regaining my memory is my priority at the moment." Heavy censure dripped from his clipped words.

A trifle paler, Daphne lowered her lashes and gave a slight nod, but not before Blaire saw a flash of resentment spark in her eyes.

Ah, Daphne wasn't as biddable as she play-acted.

Julian's regard gravitated back to Blaire and remained there, heating her blood.

"Perhaps you should consider sending a letter to Julian's family, apprising them of the accident and the postponement of the joyous union." It took every bit of Blaire's self-control to pretend indifference.

Daphne flashed her a contemptuous glance and raised a hand to her brow, paler than she'd been a few moments ago. "That's not necessary. Our departure from London was…*um*…sudden. No one expects us."

Sudden? *Hmm.* Why would that be?

"Oh, so no wedding plans have actually been made yet?" Blaire's kept her face impassive, silently congratulating herself for catching them in another colossal lie. With those two it was nearly impossible to sift fact from fiction.

"She didn't say that." From across the bed, Joan's hostile glare pinned Blaire to the wall.

Daphne wavered the slightest bit then sank onto the edge of the bed. "Forgive me, Julian. I'm feeling a bit unsteady."

The look he leveled her wasn't exactly sympathetic or welcoming.

Those nasty little sharp claws tiptoed across Blaire's shoulders again. Was Daphne truly unwell, or was it an excuse to sit beside him? Never before had Blaire had such churlish thoughts. Jealousy was an ugly, ugly beast.

A moment later, a maid entered bearing a tray. She bobbed a half curtsy. "I'm Ellie. Doctor said Lieutenant Drake should try to eat somethin'."

"I'm feeling rather famished myself." Joan hungrily eyed the fragrant stew and thick slices of brown bread.

"Yes, ma'am. He'd like to know if you prefer to dine in the

common room, or if you'll take a tray too?" The servant's perusal included Blaire.

"A tray will suffice," Joan sniffed loftily. "We cannot risk endangering ourselves or our reputations by dining with common riffraff. Although I fail to see why the doctor has concerned himself with where we eat."

"I'll take a tray as well if it's not an inconvenience, Ellie." Blaire offered an encouraging smile. "My maid can fetch mine, however. Would you send her up to me, please, when you see her?"

"Yes, miss." She returned Blaire's smile before leveling the Trudeaus a bland expression.

"Was there something else?" Joan asked impatiently.

Blaire bristled at her condescending tone. One could learn a lot about a person's character by observing the way they treated servants and animals.

Ellie didn't flinch under Joan's arrogant stare. "My mother would like to know if you'd like—"

With an inarticulate cry, Daphne crumpled onto Julian.

He stiffened and pulled his hands out from beneath her, eyeing her slumped form like one would a moldy potato.

"Daphne?" Joan rushed around to the other side of the bed and began patting her daughter's face. "Wake up, my darling."

Even Blaire grew alarmed.

Dr. Durnham stepped through the entrance, followed by Flora. "Ah, it appears I've returned just in time. It seems I have another patient to tend." He sent Blaire a telling look. "Let's assist Miss Trudeau to her chamber, shall we?"

Five nights later, Julian awoke suddenly. From the stillness surrounding him and the faint silvery glow peeking through the shuttered windows, dawn must be near. He stretched his legs on the lumpy mattress and winced as soreness speared him from ankle to collarbone.

Confound it, he felt as if he'd been keelhauled.

He yawned widely then stilled.

I know my name.

His name was Julian.

Well, at least he remembered his first name.

Julian. Julian. Julian.

Julian…what?

He closed his eyes, straining to remember.

Bloody hell!

Naturally, he'd been told he was Lieutenant Julian Drake, formerly of His Majesty's army, but except for his name, he couldn't remember anything.

Couldn't remember who he was. Where he was from. Who the women were who visited his chamber every day…

Not even the one who'd so theatrically fainted atop him.

Nothing. His mind was a blank slate.

Except, there was something familiar about Blaire Culpepper. Something that resonated deep inside him, in the depths of his being. He couldn't explain the connection, but it was an accord, a unity that went beyond knowing who either of them was.

Twisting his mouth into a wry grin, he brushed his hand across his eyes. Was he a poetic sort? Given his current rambling musings, he must be.

He touched his forehead, careful not to disturb the bandage. First probing the raised bump there, he then ran his fingers along the cloth until he found the tender spot at the back. The headache that had plagued him since first awakening five days ago had subsided to a dull throb.

Dr. Durnham explained Julian had been in a serious carriage accident. That he was, in fact, lucky to be alive.

Miss Culpepper had confessed that the carriage was a splintered shamble and all but one of the horses had been so badly injured they'd needed putting down.

Amazingly, neither of the women in the carriage had been seriously hurt. Everyone had worried that wasn't the case when Miss Trudeau fainted, but after being carried to her chamber and examined, she'd admitted her nerves had overcome her.

Julian would vow Miss Culpepper didn't collapse in a fit of vapors when overwrought. Her shy little maid either.

The doctor vowed Julian could regain his memory in a few days, or a few weeks, or a few months... Nothing like being precise, blast it.

There was also a slim chance he'd never regain all of his prior memory.

He pounded the sheet in frustration and shoved into a sitting position. Today, come hell or high water, he meant to rise from this infernal bed. The nausea had finally passed, and his head didn't threaten to topple from his shoulders with the merest movement. His stiff, underused muscles demanded he move.

He flexed his arms and legs before fingering his ribs and torso. He was a fit man, accustomed to physical activity. In the muted light, he held his hands out and, squinting, tried to examine them. He pressed the pads of his fingers together, the now familiar calluses rubbing against one another.

Who the devil am I?

The women had told him of course, but the man they described seemed like a stranger.

The petite, coquettish young lady, Daphne Trudeau, claimed they were betrothed and were to wed in just a few days. Shouldn't he feel something for her? If she were the woman he loved and asked to be his wife, wouldn't his spirit feel a connection with hers?

Even if he couldn't remember her?

He couldn't deny she was an attractive little bundle, but she stirred nothing more than mild curiosity. If he were completely candid, her wide-eyed coyness bored him.

Her mother, on the other hand, was a fright. She'd spent the past five days reciting memory after memory. Telling him who his family was. Reciting in mind-numbing detail how Daphne and he had met. Describing what their future together would be.

Blister and blast. It all rang of windbaggery.

He mightn't know much beyond who they said he was, but Julian could detect a liar when he heard one. Miss Trudeau might not be telling tarradiddles about everything, but she wasn't being completely forthright either.

Even her little fainting episode had been fabricated, he'd vow. He couldn't say how he knew. He just did, and the same instinct that told him she play-acted warned him not to trust her.

Resting his head against the headboard, he closed his eyes and summoned the face of Blaire Culpepper.

At once, peace enveloped him.

She was a wonder.

Why couldn't she be his betrothed?

Intelligent, quick of wit, and an excellent conversationalist with a ready smile and a delightful sense of humor. Now there was a woman he could see himself with for the rest of his life. His old self was a bloody idiot if he'd had the chance to court Blaire and had instead proposed to Daphne.

Hours later, quiet rustling and soft humming stirred Julian from his slumber.

He cracked an eye open then grinned upon spying Blaire setting out his breakfast. Today she wore a simple cream-colored gown trimmed in lavender and green. Once again, a feeling of contentment settled on him. As if this was the most normal thing in the world, for her to prepare his breakfast.

The shutters had been thrown wide and the window opened a fraction to let in the refreshing spring air. Outside, birds chirped and called to one another, and somewhere nearby cattle lowed, and sheep baaed. Boisterous male voices carried to him, and a stab of envy speared his ribs.

Those people knew who they were. Their lives hadn't suddenly ground to a halt.

"Good morning, Miss Culpepper."

He maneuvered into a sitting position. Scraping his hair off his forehead, being careful not to touch the painful bump there, he crossed his ankles beneath the bedcoverings.

She glanced up from arranging the table, and a radiant smile blossomed across her face.

"Good morning to you too, Lieutenant." She tilted her head in the endearing way he'd come to know. "Feeling more yourself today?"

"I am. I remembered my name."

Her pups' ears perked up the minute they heard him speak, and the dogs promptly scrambled onto the bed. He ruffled the soft fur atop their dappled heads and indulged in watching Blaire putter about.

"You shouldn't let them on the bed. They'll think they're always allowed such privileges, and I fear they are going to be much larger dogs than I first thought." She stood back and admired her handiwork then adjusted a glass. She waved her hand at the dogs. "You helped me rescue them, but I don't suppose you remember that."

A flash of a bookstore whisked through his mind. Then, in rapid succession, the faces of a trio of sneering youths, a confused maid holding meat pies, and an argument with Daphne. He'd had more of these instances the past two days, which he hoped meant his memory was beginning to return.

He'd not said anything to anyone yet, not even Dr. Durnham.

A peculiar sense of foreboding made him wary. Mayhap that was his soldier's instinct.

"Your breakfast is ready." She shooed her playful pups off the bed. "Stay down, boys. Lieutenant Drake doesn't need the two of you bouncing about whilst he is recovering."

Yes, he reminded himself again. He was Lieutenant Julian Drake. Formerly of His Majesty's army and now landed gentry, a gentleman farmer, and owner of Montclere. His father had died, as had his elder brother in an accident of some sort, but his mother and sisters were alive.

"I thought you might be tired of staying abed, and yesterday I asked Dr. Durnham if you mightn't eat your breakfast at the table this morning." She flicked her fingers towards the sausages and eggs.

Julian sniffed, and his stomach growled. "I'm famished."

"It's no wonder. You mostly slept the first couple of days, not eating enough to keep an ant alive."

She pointed to a lumpy pile topped by a folded towel. "I've also asked for a bath to be prepared for you, and we found your shaving supplies, tooth powder, and your hairbrush. The doctor says we can remove your bandage today, and you can wash your hair as long as you don't soak your head in the tub. I've also asked that your linens be changed."

Honestly, the bath held more appeal than breakfast. Julian smelled, plain and simple. He grinned and ran a hand over his bristly jaw. "You, Miss Culpepper, are a godsend."

She planted her hands on her narrow hips and cocked her head again. "But you must take care when washing your hair not to disturb your wounds overly much."

"Yes, ma'am." He gave her a smart salute.

"I'm being terribly bossy, aren't I?" She gave a self-conscious chuckle. "I apologize. That's what comes from being the youngest and finally having an opportunity to tell someone else what to do. Well, Blaike and I are the youngest. I'm actually a couple of minutes older."

"Your twin, right?"

He pulled back the bedcoverings and swung his legs over the edge of the mattress.

"What do you think you're doing?" Blaire scurried to the bed. "You may be feeling much improved, but I have my orders. And Dr. Durnham made it clear you are not to go gadding about on your own."

He hid his amusement behind his hand. Protective, wasn't she? He liked that about her. A tide of contentment washed over him. In fact, he liked a great deal about Blaire Culpepper.

He angled his head to look up at her and winked, checking another grin when a charming shade of pink colored her cheeks.

"Well then, if you would permit me the use of your shoulder, I believe I can manage perfectly well." Despicable of him to use his invalid state to touch her, but she had offered her assistance.

"Can you stand on your own?" Blaire bent near and braced an arm beneath his.

Her scent, fresh and womanly, wafted to his nostrils before momentary embarrassment assailed him. He reeked of sweat and unwashed body. If she noticed, she hid it well.

She was surprisingly strong. Her tongue peeking from the corner of her mouth and her adorable chin set at a determined angle, she leveraged him upward.

He swayed a mite before adjusting to being on his feet for the first time in days.

She peered up at Julian, her features taut with concern.

For him.

Heat, like warmed almond oil, started behind his breastbone and flowed outward to his ribs and torso. They were so close he could see the silvery shards in her eyes and a couple of adorable freckles on her equally adorable nose. She was tall, but not too tall. The crown of her head reached his chin, and he had the sudden urge to pull her near to see if her rounded form fit as neatly against him as he suspected it might.

He wanted to kiss her. To touch his lips to her bowed mouth and run his tongue along the sweet seam.

She'd gone perfectly still, and when she flicked her small tongue across her lower lip, awareness slammed into him with the force of a battering ram.

Her sapphire eyes glinted with longing. She wanted to kiss him too.

Seeming to come to her senses, she gave a self-conscious little laugh and dropping her gaze, adjusted her grip around his back.

"Let's see you to the table, Lieutenant, shall we?"

Dear God, yes.

Before he made a complete clodpate of himself.

As she poured tea and he placed his serviette in his lap, he scrutinized the simple chamber. The book she'd been reading to him sat on the nightstand, and a shawl lay draped across the nearby armchair.

Julian furrowed his forehead. Had she been sleeping in the chair? She took her nursing duties seriously, didn't she? He took a bite of egg and, as he chewed, considered her. He quite enjoyed looking at Blaire Culpepper.

"Miss Culpepper, as grateful as I am to be rid of these clothes"— for he'd been in the same pantaloons and lawn shirt since the mishap— "I don't see anything for me to change into."

She'd wandered to the window but turned her head, her mouth tipped upward. "Oh, I sent my men back to salvage as much of your luggage and the Trudeaus' as they were able. They'll bring a fresh set of clothing with your bathwater."

"What would I have done without you?"

Her smile slipped, and unmistakable sadness shadowed her pretty face. Leaning a slim shoulder against the wall, she fiddled with the wide lavender ribbon beneath her breasts and turned her attention outdoors once more.

Julian studied her from beneath half-closed eyelids as he ate. Yes, she was familiar. Very familiar. An undisputable diamond of the first water. But it wasn't just her exquisite exterior that he found so mesmerizing. It was her. Blaire. She was utterly enchanting.

And he'd said something to dismay her.

Perhaps it was time for a little test, though why he felt the need to do so baffled.

"Blaire?" He jiggled his fork toward the armchair. "Have you been sleeping in here?"

He was gratified to see another becoming flush color her face.

She met his bold appraisal unflinchingly. "Yes, I have, for part of the night at least. I feared leaving you unattended. But you mustn't say anything to anyone. My reputation would be in tatters."

Hooking an arm over the back of his chair, he ran a finger over the handle of his knife. "Why would you take such a risk?"

She dropped her attention to the floor then lifted a shoulder. "The doctor couldn't be here, and I know those suffering from concussions shouldn't be left alone."

Was that all?

This woman, who claimed he was a friend of her guardian—a guardian he couldn't recall—risked ruination by staying at his side for part of each night. He couldn't imagine his supposed betrothed making the same sacrifice, though she and her mother spent many tedious hours with him during the day. More than once he'd feigned exhaustion and the need for rest to be spared their dull company.

Truthfully, Blaire oughtn't to be in his chamber right now either. He mightn't have his personal memories, but he still knew societal expectations.

He bit into a piece of toast and nodded. "Yes, that's true. Men have been known to never wake up. I knew a captain a few years ago who that happened to."

Her gaze flew to his, and she gave a delicate half gasp. "You've remembered something."

Slowly, he set the toast down.

"I did. But just a fleeting glimpse. It's as if everything is right here." He pointed to his head. "And with the slightest shift, all will come flooding back to me. Like a curtain pulled aside, and I can see everything clearly. But, blast it." He banged his fist upon his thigh. "It's beyond frustrating to be unable to recall my past at will."

She hurried to the table then crouched beside him, placing her hand atop his. Her long fingers clasped his sun-browned hand, pale ivory against bronze.

"You will remember, Julian. I don't doubt it for an instant."

With the knuckles of his other hand, he brushed her delicate jaw line. "But my beautiful Blaire, will I like what I remember?"

Her features closed as surely as if she snapped a book shut. She rose to her full height. "That, I cannot say. When that time comes, you'll have to decide. Now if you'll excuse me, I'll check what's delaying your bath water."

Ominous premonition raised his nape hairs, much like when he'd faced danger on the battlefield.

Another brief recollection.

They were coming more frequently.

"Blaire, there's something I'm not going to like remembering, isn't there?"

Palm on the door handle, her back to him, she paused.

Ever so slowly, she faced him, a concert of emotions flitting across her features. She opened her mouth then pressed her lips together, hesitation warring with compassion in her vibrant eyes.

Yes, there was something. And he definitely wasn't going to like it. Still, he'd rather know now.

"You can tell me, Blaire. I'm going to learn of it sooner or later. And I'd prefer to hear it from you rather than anyone else or even as a startling, unpleasant recollection."

How had he come to trust her in such a short amount of time? Her attentiveness and care of him might explain it in part. What was her motivation for taking on the burden? Could she truly be that kindhearted? Or was she compelled by something else?

"Blaire?" He extended his hand, fingers spread and palm upward. "Tell me, please."

Clearly in an agony of indecision, she closed her eyes, her golden-tipped lashes fanning across her high cheekbones. At last, she shook her head and met his eyes, regret and sorrow within hers.

"No. Dr. Durnham said you're not to be overly stressed or upset. When you regain your memory is soon enough for you to know. I shan't risk you relapsing."

Something more than just diligent, conscientious nursing went on here. Why, he could almost believe... Almost convince himself she cared for him. A great deal, given her hesitation to upset him or cause a relapse.

He stood and gripped the table for support, expecting a rush of dizziness, but when the room failed to tilt and spin, he approached her. Putting a crooked finger beneath her chin, he nudged it upward until her gaze met his. He nearly gasped at the pain he saw shimmering in the depths of those gorgeous eyes.

"Why is it I'm betrothed to Miss Trudeau, but even without my memory, my heart tells me you are the woman I should love?"

If a woman means to conquer the unknown, she
must trust. And trusting herself in a world dominate
by men and societal strictures is the very essence of valor.
~Prudence and Propriety— The Genteel Lady's Guide to Practical Living

Blaire practically ran the length of the corridor, desperate to reach her chamber before tears overcame her. The last thing she expected to hear from Julian when he could scarce remember anything was that he thought he should love her.

Her, not Daphne.

His mind couldn't remember their love but his heart did.

Fate was beyond cruel.

She rushed into her room, pausing only long enough for Zeus and Apollo to trot in behind her. Thank God Flora wasn't here. Cramming a fist to her mouth, Blaire shut and bolted the door then sank to the floor, unable to hold back her sobs any longer.

The pups shoved their noses into her face, whining and licking her as dogs do when they're worried about their owner.

"I know, boys. I know."

She buried her face in her hands, at last giving way to the sorrow shredding her heart. Oh, how she wanted to tell Julian the truth, but genuine fear that the shock might do him harm kept her mute.

And a ridiculous, misplaced sense of justice and fair play.

To reveal the truth when he couldn't recall the reasons for his decision smacked of manipulation. How easy it would be to put a slant upon her words, to influence him. To turn him against Daphne. She'd seen enough subtle coercion by Daphne and her mother with no regard to Julian's mental state that she refused to cast the same die.

She was better than that.

She must be better than that.

Julian would remember, and once he did, only he could decide if he was making the right decision in marrying Daphne.

"Oh, Julian," she whispered, "I love you too. I have for so very long."

Even as an awkward seventeen-year-old new to London, that first night when he'd strode across the ballroom, his crimson uniform jacket the perfect complement to his dark coloring, she'd been smitten.

At first, she'd assumed it a school-girl infatuation, but each time she saw him, her fascination grew. Her love for him those long, horrid months in Geneva helped her endure.

After several moments, she collected herself enough to rise from the floor and crawl onto the bed, hugging a pillow to her middle. She hadn't the energy to scold the puppies for clambering onto the mattress and cuddling beside her.

The innkeeper wouldn't be pleased to find dog hair on the bedding. She must remember to leave an extra coin or two for his trouble.

These past days had been a gift, and she didn't begrudge a single moment spent caring for Julian. She'd never be able to do so again, and she treasured each memory.

Daphne and her mother continued to seethe and complain at every opportunity about Blaire attending him. After the first two days, Blaire usually made an excuse to escape the room when they put in their appearances. For if she'd stayed, she didn't know if she could've kept her mouth shut and not refute the tripe they fed him.

Neither had an ounce of shame or a conscience either. They knew *she knew* they fabricated poppycock. Nonetheless, they continued blathering twaddle.

How Julian had fallen madly in love with Daphne when he'd met her and begged her not to honor the customary mourning period. How Daphne had only been conceding to her uncle's wishes when she agreed to wed Alfred. How much she adored Julian and couldn't wait to be his wife. Oh, and how she and Joan had already been conferring with him regarding the refurbishing and upgrading of Montclere.

Balderdash and rubbish.

With a ragged sigh, Blaire opened her eyes.

Well, at least Daphne's health hadn't suffered from the mishap. The morning after her theatrical swooning episode, Blaire asked Dr. Durnham about the babe.

He'd hesitated before saying, "I assure you, Miss Culpepper, Miss Trudeau is in fine health. You'll understand if I cannot ethically divulge more."

So why had she fainted? Were the vapors an affliction of some pregnant women?

The quaint but well-used writing desk situated beneath the only window in the chamber beckoned. Far past time Blaire wrote Brooke and Heath and told them she hadn't made it to Culpepper Park yet. She'd not share details other than that Julian had been in an accident, had a concussion, and the doctor had asked her to help care for him.

Her own concussion troubled her not at all anymore, thank goodness.

Swiping at her face, she sat up. "Boys, I need to pen a letter home."

They answered by rolling onto their backs, paws waggling in the air: a blatant invitation for her to rub their tummies. She indulged them for a minute, grateful for their company.

Julian improved daily, and it was unfair not to inform her family where she was. The only balm to her conscience was that the staff at Culpepper Park hadn't known she was coming. Unless they received a letter addressed to her, they'd be none the wiser and no one would have been fretting.

Head wooly from her cry, she shuffled to the washstand feeling like a hundred-year-old woman. After splashing cool water on her face, she patted it dry, then grimaced at the pitiful woman staring back at her, red rimmed eyes and all. It would only take a few moments to compose a letter explaining the situation and promising she'd continue on to Culpepper Park shortly.

Just as soon as Julian departed for Montclere.

She'd not forfeit one minute of his company before forced to. Some might deem her pathetic and desperate, pining after a man betrothed to another, but her love couldn't be shut off like a keg of ale's tap or snuffed out like a taper candle.

Hot and fierce anger burned behind her breast toward Daphne, the charlatan.

Blaire knew full well she was being uncharitable, but too often the kindhearted and compassionate fared worse than selfish twits like Daphne.

For days Blaire had struggled to subdue the ire riddling her. She'd attempted to reason with herself, and even tried summoning sympathy for Daphne's position. But the more she became acquainted with Daphne and Joan, the more Blaire was convinced they exploited

Julian's sense of decency and used guilt to bend him to their selfish wills.

Two short knocks on her door sent the pups to barking and her heart to racing. Botheration. She set the quill down, the letter only half finished. Had someone heard her crying? Please not Daphne or her termagant of a mother. She couldn't take their nastiness right now.

Mayhap it was Dr. Durnham. Yesterday, he'd said he would stop by the inn this morning, and she'd forgotten to tell Julian.

Thrice more, sharp raps rang out.

Oh goodness, could it be Flora knocking, worried because she couldn't enter their chamber? This morning, Blaire had asked her to launder her undergarments.

"Just a moment, please."

She dashed to the mirror above the washstand, pleased to see no telltale signs of her emotional outburst remained. She smoothed her hair and, after pinning a serene expression on her face, opened the door.

One shoulder braced against the doorframe and his ankles crossed, Julian stood there, as sexy as sin, blast him. He'd shaved, and a few damp curls over his ears defied his neatly brushed hair. His cologne wafted to her. Despite herself, she inhaled deeply, her nostrils flaring.

Must he smell so utterly scrumptious?

With a great deal of effort, she collected her rambling thoughts and met his avid gaze.

"Whatever can you be thinking, Julian?"

Blaire quickly took his measure, making sure he wasn't about to topple onto his beautiful face. He seemed robust enough. Truthfully, he radiated virile masculinity, and her traitorous femininity rushed to notice.

"Dr. Durnham was most clear," she reminded him, not firmly as she'd intended, but breathlessly. "You're not supposed to be gadding about just yet. It's only been five days since you were concussed."

Julian straightened and gave her a naughty wink, and of course her pulse skipped a delicious beat. Did he know the remarkable effect he had on her?

"You are incorrigible Julian Drake."

"So my mother reminds me on a regular basis." He leaned in, his mouth but an inch from her ear. So close in fact, his breath warmed her skin, tantalizing and exciting. "While I trust the good doctor's medical opinion, my dear, I swear, if I'm not permitted fresh air, I'll go mad."

She supposed suggesting he thrust his head out the window wouldn't suffice.

He flashed one of his rakish smiles that always made her tummy go wobbly and extended his elbow. "Take a walk with me. Please, Blaire. You've been cooped up inside as well, caring for me."

The offer tempted her something awful. Four days of sunshine had dried any evidence of the storm, and spring blossomed full-on outside. She'd forgotten how much she missed living in the country these past months. Heath abhorred country life and much preferred London, so the Culpeppers rarely ventured from civilization, as he called it.

A small crease across his nose pulled Julian's brows together. "You're a trifle pale yourself."

"I'm perfectly fine."

A doubtful dark brown brow skewed upward, and he searched the room behind her as if seeking a clue. "Are you sure?"

She wasn't certain whether to be flattered or chagrined that he'd noticed. So much for hiding her bout of tears.

One of the pups bumped against her leg, and she grabbed the doorjamb to steady herself. "Truly, Julian. I was just writing to Brooke."

He leaned nearer, and the scents of soap and a crisp cologne surrounded her. Concern darkening his eyes to deep molasses, he touched her cheek with his rough forefinger.

God help her, she yearned to throw her arms about his waist and hug him with all her might.

"Have you been crying, Blaire?"

She turned her face away, taking two steps backward. How could he know?

"I shall take a short stroll with you because, I confess, I feel confined myself. But you must promise me, the instant you feel the least unwell or weak, you will tell me." She dared to meet his eyes and was slightly taken aback at his bemused expression.

The wretch. Did he laugh at her concern? Did he think she fussed over him too much?

"Promise me, Julian."

"I promise." Pressing a palm to his chest, he bowed his head in a dramatic fashion. *Drat the charming scamp.* He gestured before them and clasped her hand, tucking it into his elbow. "Shall we?"

"I need my bonnet—"

"What goes on here?" Ascending the last riser, Joan lurched to a halt and stabbed Blaire an accusing look. "I'm very pleased to see you out of bed, Lieutenant, but unless I'm mistaken, it appears as if you're going somewhere with Miss Culpepper."

Her acerbic tone clearly indicated he should do no such thing.

"As you can see, Mrs. Trudeau, I'm feeling much improved, and I've asked Miss Culpepper to take a stroll with me. The spring weather is not to be missed."

He didn't temper his words with a smile, but eyed her taciturnly with a challenge in his eyes.

"Miss Culpepper is your nursemaid, nothing more. That duty should've fallen to Daphne and me. I still don't understand why that elf-of-a-doctor ever thought otherwise." Accusation tainted her words and the steely stare she directed toward Blaire. "I'm sure my dear Daphne will walk with you if you were to ask." Joan sidestepped, extending her arm toward her room. "She's in our chamber...ah...resting."

Probably still abed since the clock had yet to chime ten.

She clearly believed he'd concede simply because she suggested it, never mind how discourteous her actions were to Blaire.

"But I didn't ask her," Julian said, not a hint of apology in his manner.

Blaire very much liked this Julian. Indeed, she did. She might've allowed a smile—just the tiniest, bittiest one—to arch her lips as satisfaction sidled in her veins.

Joan's mouth worked, opening and closing rapidly, reminding Blaire of the bass Uncle Thomas used to catch. Eyes narrowed to hostile slits, the irises barely visible, she pointed her finger at Blaire.

"I know exactly what you're up to, young lady," she fairly hissed, "and it shan't work."

"I'm not up to anything."

Unlike her and her sly daughter.

"I'm simply taking a walk with a family friend, Mrs. Trudeau. I'll remind you that you do not have the right to dictate who my friends are, nor what I do."

Speaking her mind at last felt wonderful.

Lifting her nose high, Joan endeavored to look down the long appendage at Blaire. Considering she stood several inches shorter, her attempt proved comical.

"Daphne and I are perfectly able to see to the lieutenant's needs now, Miss Culpepper. There is no reason for you to linger any longer. Does your family even know where you are?"

A trio of well-placed jabs which Blaire deflected with a bland expression.

"Since Dr. Durnham specifically asked me to oversee Lieutenant Drake's care, I'll leave when he tells me my services are no longer needed."

Blaire's defiance rendered the harpy speechless.

Without donning her bonnet, Blaire stepped from her room and presented her back to the horrid woman. She glanced at her dogs.

"Shall I leave the boys here, Lieutenant?"

"No, let's bring the chaps along." Julian bent and scratched each of the dogs' heads. "They're probably as eager to enjoy the day as we are."

The resounding slamming of a door farther along emphasized Joan's displeasure.

As Blaire descended the stairs, he asked, "Where did you say you found them?"

He flicked his fingers toward the two dogs cavorting along behind them.

Cocking her head, she stepped aside so the pups could push their way past her. "You helped me rescue them from bullies near the Temple of the Muses."

"Did I?" He ran a finger down his nose. "I've always liked dogs, but my mother isn't fond of them."

Blaire pressed her fingertips into his strong arm. "You've remembered something else. That's wonderful."

"Yes." He squinted the merest bit. "They're fleeting nuances that flit through my mind. No more than shadowy images and thoughts. They're right there teasing me, and the moment I reach out to grasp them, they evaporate."

He scrutinized the common room.

No one paid them any mind except the innkeeper, who gave a polite nod as he wiped a table.

"Remarkably," Julian said, "when I try to remember, I cannot, but whilst I'm attending to other things, little flickers come back to me."

"I expect it will happen more and more often now. You must tell Dr. Durnham when he comes today." She pressed his arm again to gain his attention. Certainly not because she enjoyed feeling his solid muscles flex beneath her fingertips. "Oh, I almost forgot, Julian. The doctor has a commitment this afternoon, so he'll be here this morning sometime."

"Very good."

Julian led her through the front entrance, and at once the puppies bounded off to greet another dog and explore the outdoors.

Blaire shaded her eyes.

She really ought to have put on her bonnet. Her fair skin was prone to freckles and sunburn. But Joan vexed her so, she couldn't wait another instant to be away from the contentious woman.

Lord help Julian with that shrew as a mother-in-law.

The sobering thought dampened Blaire's spirits, and it took supreme effort to keep her pleasant expression.

"I remembered a few more things after you left my chamber, Blaire. I know my horse's name, and I remember Oliver Whitehouse."

"Captain Whitehouse is betrothed to my twin." Joy welled within her, and she gave him a brilliant smile. "I'm so glad your recall is improving quickly. In no time your full memory will have returned."

And then he'd know why he'd asked Daphne to be his wife and not Blaire.

Liars will exploit the trust of the innocent and honorable,
and a clever woman knows not to trust words but actions.
~*Prudence and Propriety— The Genteel Lady's Guide to Practical Living*

9

Having reluctantly left Blaire in the courtyard when Dr. Durnham arrived to exam him, Julian now followed the doctor's finger with his eyes. Back and forth, up and down as the physician directed.

"Good, good," Dr. Durnham murmured. "How's your headache today, Lieutenant?"

"Much improved. It's become more of an annoyance than real pain," Julian said.

The doctor probed the knot on Julian's forehead before moving around to examine the bigger bump at the back. "And your memory?"

"Increasingly better." he hid a wince when the doctor pressed a trifle too hard. "I'm having frequent glimpses of past memories and am increasingly able to recall simple facts."

The doctor leaned around him, interest crinkling his eyes. "Such as?"

"My horse's name, that I have three sisters, who some of my friends are…a few hazy memories of military assignments."

What he hadn't remembered yet, and what vexed him to no end, was the lack of recall about Blaire. He felt certain she was more than a family friend as she claimed.

And she had been crying this morning.

He recognized the signs: spikey lashes, slightly reddened nose and swollen eyes. After all, he had younger sisters, and his mother was wont to weep for no reason other than Cook served marmalade rather than strawberry preserves at breakfast. She also complained incessantly about the unfairness of a woman's lot in life.

Ah, another glimmer.

And then there was Daphne Trudeau. He couldn't count the number of times she'd become tearful in his presence.

Blaire wasn't that sort of woman.

No, in fact, he doubted she ever let anyone know when she cried. She'd done her utmost to convince him she hadn't been weeping. A couple of spikey lashes and a dried tear on her cheek gave her away.

What worried him most was that he might have been the cause of her sorrow.

He kicked himself to Kent and back for speaking out of turn. Ballocks. He should never have given reign to his tongue and made that comment about loving her. Most especially he shouldn't have when he was betrothed to Daphne.

Would the Julian with intact memories have been so tactless or daring? *No.* Gut instinct told him the other Julian wouldn't have. That Julian was discreet and cautious. Self-disciplined and controlled.

He mightn't be able to remember much of his former life, but he intuitively knew that his honor was paramount. A gentleman of integrity did not tell a woman he felt something for her when he was promised to another.

"Well," Dr. Durnham said, pulling his earlobe. "You've recuperated swifter than I'd anticipated. Other than your memory's not fully restored, there's no reason you cannot continue your travels as long as you're cautious. I'd prefer you used a private coach rather than a rented conveyance, if possible. Better springs mean less jarring for you." He screwed his mouth tight and gave Julian a severe look. "No heavy exertion and, most especially, no shaking or vibrating movements to your head in your eagerness to reach home."

But that was the crux of it.

Julian didn't want to continue on to Montclere, which was where Daphne and her mother vowed they were bound. For his wedding, which was supposed to take place in two days' time, according to the women.

Everything in him mutinied at the notion.

By God, he wasn't going to marry a woman he couldn't remember. If that meant postponing the wedding indefinitely, then he would.

"What would you recommend, Doctor?"

Dr. Durnham sucked his lips in, considering Julian.

"What's your instinct saying to you?"

Julian spun the ring on the little finger of his left hand around and around.

"In all honesty, I feel lost. In limbo. On the one hand, I wonder if returning home would jar my memory, and on the other, recollections have steadily been sifting back to me here. Perhaps I should continue to convalesce here a while longer, though I confess, I cannot abide being confined to a bed for another week."

"No need for that." The doctor chuckled and snapped his bag shut. "What you say has merit, but it's been less than a week. Your brain has not healed entirely, by any means. Why don't you give it a couple more days and then make a decision?"

Nodding thoughtfully, Julian rubbed an eyebrow. "All right. Who knows? I may wake up tomorrow morning with my memory fully intact."

"I'd be delighted if that were the case." At the door, Dr. Durnham paused and turned halfway toward him. "Still, I'd advise against straining to remember. As I said, your brain is still healing. You need to be prepared to be patient, Lieutenant. Nevertheless, I'm very pleased with your progress so far, and I'm confident you'll eventually have complete recall."

Julian stood and flexed his spine. The need to do something physical, to exert himself, almost overwhelmed.

"Doctor, am I permitted to ride horseback?"

The doctor shook his head, regret softening his elfin features. "No. Not yet. You cannot do anything to jostle your brain, just yet. I'm sorry."

"So, I'm reduced to strolling about the courtyard like an old tabby. Might as well take up knitting or tatting." Julian didn't make an attempt to conceal his frustration.

"All in good time, my dear fellow. All in good time. And don't knock knitting. I find it quite relaxing." Joviality danced in Dr. Durnham's eyes. "Why don't you see if Miss Culpepper or perhaps the innkeeper has a book you might read? But make sure you have sufficient lighting and don't overdo it and strain your eyes either." He opened the door, his mouth skewed to the side in apology. "I'll see you tomorrow afternoon."

Julian slanted his head and blew out a long breath. He didn't need his memory to tell him he didn't like being idle or that he preferred physical activity.

Perhaps Blaire had a deck of playing cards, and they could wile an hour or two away together. Or mayhap the proprietor possessed a chessboard.

Or a piano. Did Julian play? Would Blaire know? In fact, that was just what he'd do. Seek Blaire and ask her preference on how to spend the afternoon. In her company, time flew by.

He opened the door, nearly plowing into Mrs. Trudeau. Had she been eavesdropping, her ear pressed to the panel, while the doctor was inside? Nothing would surprise him about the tetchy woman.

Flora turned down the corridor holding a stack of linens. After offering Julian a shy dip of her head, she disappeared inside the chamber she shared with Blaire.

"Did you need something, Mrs. Trudeau?"

"Please, call me Joan."

When he didn't respond, she fluttered a hand near her throat. "Daphne and I thought perhaps you'd enjoy taking tea in a private parlor this afternoon, seeing that you're up and about now." Her bent mouth was nothing short of calculating, and the hairs on his nape snapped straight up in warning. "Mayhap a game of Whist or Loo to pass the time as well?"

An idea formed, a wicked idea that he held no remorse for entertaining. "A game of whist." It required four players, while Loo could be played with fewer. Jolly good. Another memory. "Why, that sounds...delightful." He loathed the game, but if Blaire partnered him... "I'll ask Miss Culpepper if she'd like to join us as well."

"But... But..."

Joan's stammering revealed much. What had she against Blaire? Animosity fairly radiated from the cantankerous woman.

"Pardon me." Julian stepped forward, forcing her to retreat. He closed his door behind him then turned the key in the lock before dropping it in his jacket pocket. "Is that a problem? I cannot think that you would exclude Miss Culpepper after her kindness to me, as well as relieving you and Daphne of the burden of my care."

"Of course we must appreciate Miss Culpepper's...ah...lending a hand at the doctor's insistence. She'd not have inconvenienced herself otherwise, I'm certain."

She still refused to acknowledge the obvious. Neither Dr. Durnham nor Julian wanted anyone other than Blaire tending him.

"But surely you must understand how unseemly it appears when you spend time with her, rather than your betrothed." Joan folded her hands before her, her expression expectant. A peeved glimmer shone in her pupils, and once again, he searched the vast empty corridors of his memory for a logical reason—*any reason*—for why he'd choose to marry Daphne.

He didn't love her. Of that he had no doubt.

Her nose practically twitching from curiosity, Joan boldly pried, "What did the doctor say today?"

Julian started down the passageway, forcing her to keep pace with him. "I continue to recover."

"And will we be departing for Montclere soon?" So tense her features might crack from the strain, she bent her mouth upward.

Is that supposed to be a smile? Children will run in terror if she turns that hideous expression on them.

"Have you given any more thought to the wedding date, Lieutenant?"

Enough.

Rage, scorching and swift, throttled up his chest and heated his blood. Drawing to a halt, his jaw clenched so tight his teeth might crack, he faced her.

"Joan, until I have fully recovered my memory, there won't be a wedding. There won't be any discussion of a wedding either. I'm not about to exchange vows with a woman I cannot recollect." His uncustomary rudeness might be blamed on his condition. Or his simple dislike of the termagant. Slanting her a flinty look, he probed, "Is that understood?"

A storm descended onto her countenance, and she stepped closer, fury spewing from her slitted eyes. "It's that Culpepper chit, isn't it? She's been talking against my dear Daphne. Oh, I should've known. She's always been jealous of Daphne. That's why her family sent her away from London. She wouldn't listen to reason—wouldn't let go of her obsession with you." Smug satisfaction pursed her mouth. "There was a terrible scandal associated with her return from Geneva, you know."

Another tide of ire sluiced him. Leave it to the sly hag to try to tarnish Blaire's reputation.

"It's interesting, don't you think, that I've not seen Miss Culpepper display any untoward behavior? I cannot say the same of your *dear Daphne.*"

An unfettered, decidedly sarcastic grin swept his mouth upward.

Oh, yes. This Julian is quite refreshing.

A lovely chap.

Too bad this version of me cannot remain when my memory returns.

She poked his chest—hard—all restraint flown in her fit of temper. "I shan't have it, I tell you. I shan't! You're not spending any more time with the devious chit. Not a minute more. Do you hear me?"

Did he hear her? By God, half the bloody countryside could hear her shrieking.

"Daphne's cried herself to sleep every night since we've been here, and in her delicate condition…" She slapped a hand over her mouth, her eyes wide and appalled.

Julian jerked his head up, his blood turning to ice in his veins. "*Condition?*"

"Oh dear, I wasn't supposed to say anything just yet. Daphne will be most unhappy with me." False remorse vied with triumph in Joan's eyes. "But soon it will be obvious to all. She did swoon the other day, you know."

Dread, icy and merciless sank her talons into his shoulders. Despair trumpeted a fanfare in his blood. "Are you saying Daphne is with child?" He could scarcely form the words. "*My child?*"

"Yes." She lifted her chin in self-important defiance and no small amount of victory as well.

Hellfire.

No one need tell Julian every ounce of blood drained from his face. It pooled in his boots, and he braced his hand against the nearby wall to steady himself. The notion of bedding Daphne didn't appeal any more than mounting a dockside whore.

Had he been intoxicated?

Was he a drunkard?

Not likely. He hadn't craved spirits during his convalescence.

"That's why, Lieutenant Drake, it's imperative that the ceremony takes place soon. I'm sure you'd have remembered in due time."

Joan's attempt to reassure him as she cut a guilty glance up and down the passageway failed miserably. She'd no more unintentionally revealed the confidence than he'd ever have boxed naked at Gentleman Jack's Boxing Salon.

"But what happens if your memory doesn't return for months? Does Daphne have to bear the shame of your sexual congress alone?" She firmed her thin mouth. "I pray you are too much a man of honor to allow that."

Fiend seize honor.

Everything in Julian protested her claim. Shackling himself to a woman who set his teeth on edge now—when he couldn't remember a single detail about her, never mind when his memory returned—was beyond him.

He couldn't have impregnated Daphne. He couldn't have. Not the smallest spark of desire warmed his veins for her. Yet, his very being burned with longing for Blaire.

Eyes closed, Julian forced the bitter words past his lips. "How far along is she?"

Hell. Hell. Bloody Goddamned hell.

"About six weeks," Joan murmured, her false demureness making his teeth ache. "That's why we were going to Montclere. To protect her from London's rabid tattlemongers."

He flashed hot then cold then hot again, nausea roiling in his gut.

It's not true. It cannot be true.

My God, just what kind of a rotter was he? If Daphne was six weeks gone, he'd straddled her scarcely a fortnight after his brother had been buried.

What kind of woman was she to bury her betrothed and bed his brother within days? Bile, hot and bitter, burned the back of his throat as self-loathing pummeled his ribs.

A thought struck, and he jerked his head up, pinning Joan with an unwavering stare. "Has she been examined by the physician, to make sure there were no ill effects from the carriage mishap?"

She bobbed her head. Too eagerly? Too pleased with herself?

"Yes. Yes," she hastily assured him. "That day she swooned. Everything is perfectly fine, thank God."

Trapped.

Ensnared.

With no way out. For Julian would never abandon his child.

The urge to hit something, anything, consumed him as the walls closed in, sucking the air from his lungs and slowing the blood in his veins.

He must make his way outside.

Must be away from the Trudeaus and even Blaire until he could breathe again. Until reason returned and he could bring the frustration-borne wrath sluicing unchecked through every pore under control.

"Excuse me, please." He sketched a brief bow.

"Yes, of course. But…" Joan wasn't ready to give up the field quite yet. Her tenacity might be admired in another. She lifted her head, another of her unnerving closed-mouth smiles dividing her face. "Shall I tell Daphne we can expect to see you for tea, then?"

With Blaire?

Would that be fair?

Giving a curt nod, Julian spun on his heel. As he strode down the passageway, each thump of his Hessians resounded like a death knoll.

If providence dictated his future was with Daphne and that terror of her mother, he prayed to God he never regained his memory.

Keep company with those whose trust has been earned and be wary
of those demanding your trust without earning it through their
behaviors.
~Prudence and Propriety— The Genteel Lady's Guide to Practical Living

10

Holding the rose Julian had plucked from an early blooming bush in the courtyard, and happier than she had any right to be, Blaire hummed as she wandered into the Tankard and Anchor.

Unfettered by responsibility and duty, the Julian she'd walked with until Dr. Durnham arrived a short while ago proved irresistible. She might very well be setting herself up for more heartbreak, but as she determined to do from the moment the doctor had asked her to care for Julian, she would treasure each and every moment spent with him.

The innkeeper had graciously allowed her to put Zeus and Apollo in a pen behind the inn with his two beagles. When she'd left the pups, the foursome romped about like old friends, and she'd enjoyed a relaxing half hour in a cozy, overgrown arbor, basking in the knowledge that Julian cared for her.

Waiting until after Mr. Atkins finished pouring a dram for two elderly gentlemen, she approached him.

He turned his cheerful countenance upon her.

"I wanted to thank you again, Mr. Atkins, for allowing my dogs the use of your kennel." The rascally pair weren't meant to be indoors all the time. Far too energetic and into mischief.

Had Freddy ever been so rambunctious?

Mr. Atkins chuckled, revealing a missing front tooth. "Aye, yer very welcome, lass. My missus just put the kettle on. Can I interest ye in a cup of tea? It's her own brew. She made seedcake this mornin' too."

"That sounds heavenly."

Since Julian had been injured, time to herself had been scarce, much less a chance to relax and enjoy a cup. There really wasn't any pressing need for Blaire to stay on at the inn and care for him now. The worst danger had passed, yet she had no intention of asking Flora to pack their belongings and instruct the coachmen to prepare to depart.

Blaire angled her head in greeting to Heath's men engaged in a lively game of dice. Hopefully, they weren't gambling away their wages.

"I'll have my missus brin' it to ye in there." Mr. Atkins tipped his head toward the two private parlors situated off the main room. He scrutinized his patrons then winked. "Best not to have ye eatin' out here alone, I think."

"Have you seen my maid?" The servant couldn't be left on her own too long, else she'd become confused and even frightened at times.

He chuckled as he threw a towel across his shoulder. "Aye. She's been entertainin' my youngest on the porch out back. Never saw the lassie take to a stranger so before. Mrs. Atkins is grateful no' to have the imp underfoot or pullin' at her skirts, I can tell ye." He shot a glance to the kitchen. "Do ye need her?"

"No. I just wanted to make sure she wasn't in the way." Holding the velvety, pale pink petals to her nose, Blaire sniffed the rose again.

A little rush of satisfaction zipped up her spine. Wouldn't Daphne have a conniption if she learned Julian had given Blaire a flower? She intended to press it between the pages of her Bible as soon as she returned to her chamber. A romantic keepsake—likely the only she'd ever have—from the man she'd given her heart to.

Even if he'd never know it was his.

Still lost in her musings, Blaire wandered down the short passage leading to the parlors then hesitated.

Which one had Mr. Atkins wanted her to use?

Did it matter?

"But, Dr. Durnham… Surely you understand my difficult position. I would make it worth your while. I have money—" Daphne's almost frantic whisper filtered into the corridor.

Blaire swung her attention to the closest door, open an inch. Biting her lip in indecision, she cast a furtive glance behind her then edged nearer, turning her head to better hear their conversation.

She'd been reduced to eavesdropping.

Badly done of you, Blaire Culpepper.

Yet she made no effort to move away.

"Miss Trudeau, what you're asking of me is unethical." Thick censure laced the doctor's equally quiet voice. "I cannot pretend that you're with child and also lead others to believe that falsehood. Most especially for coin. I presume your fit of the vapors the other day, for which I found no cause, was part of your ploy as well?"

Blaire slapped a palm to her gaping mouth, barely smothering her astounded cry.

Daphne *wasn't* expecting?

Oh, God. Oh, God. Julian was free.

"But I swear I was. I... I lost the babe and was afraid to tell Julian." Sniffing and an indelicate blowing of her nose commenced. "He wanted his child so desperately, you see," she snuffled between theatrical sobs.

His child?

The room spun in a sickening manner, and black spots flickered before Blaire's eyes. She put an unsteady hand to her brow.

"We're marrying anyway. What does it matter if he finds out I lost the child afterward? We'll have more children."

Why, the conniving wretch. Every muscle tense with her wrath, Blaire balled her fists against the urge to pull every hair from Daphne's head after boxing her ears. A dozen times.

"Your affianced doesn't seem the unreasonable sort to me," Dr. Durnham said. "Even though his memory hasn't fully returned, I suggest you present him with the truth. Something of this nature shouldn't be concealed."

Daphne isn't with child.

Giddiness swiftly followed by dismay swept Blaire.

But she still intends to entrap Julian.

Was she ever really pregnant? Had it all been a contrived lie, carried out by Daphne and her fishwife of a mother? Such outrage battered Blaire that she couldn't breathe. A vice squeezed her lungs, refusing to let her inhale more than short puffs of air.

"Yes, Doctor. You're right. But, please, I beg of you, please." Daphne's voice quaked. "Don't say anything to Julian just yet. I'll tell him myself."

Blaire just bet she would.

After vows were exchanged, or when Zeus and Apollo performed ballet in Covent Garden.

"I keep my patients' confidences, Miss Trudeau. However, if the lieutenant asks me directly, I shall be obliged to tell him the truth. I suggest you not delay."

Footsteps echoed, and holding her breath, Blaire scampered into the other parlor, leaving the door partially opened. She peeked through the crack, behaving and feeling very much like a criminal.

Dr. Durnham stepped into the corridor. "Good day, Miss Trudeau."

Daphne didn't reply. Or at least, Blaire couldn't hear it if she did.

The doctor heaved a hefty sigh, shaking his head as he took his leave.

Head bowed, a hand pressed to her mouth and the other her stomach, Blaire ordered her thoughts to cease clanging about. Should she find Julian and tell him what she'd learned straightaway? The doctor had told Daphne she should. Still, Blaire worried what the shock would do to him.

The unmistakable sound of porcelain or crockery breaking in the opposite parlor yanked her from her reverie.

"Damn little troll, telling me what to do," Daphne sneered in the other room. "If that quack thinks he can keep me from marrying Julian, he's dead wrong. I've worked too hard to quit now."

Blaire jerked upright, scarcely believing her ears. The other parlor door flew wide open, slamming against the paneling, and she pressed flat against the wall as Daphne stomped past.

"I'm done living like a pauper. I mean to be mistress of Montclere, one way or another, as Alfred Drake learned when he tried to toss me aside. Dr. Durnham best take care lest an accident like the one that befell Alfred doesn't happen to him too."

Blaire remained motionless for several moments. Actually, she wasn't sure how long she stood there trying to process what she just heard.

If Daphne killed Alfred for calling off their wedding, would she dispense with Julian after they were married as well? Was that her intent all along? Blaire's heart nearly stopped in her chest then began beating so painfully hard she hunched over, pressing both hands to her breastbone.

And what role did Joan Trudeau play in all of this? Were both women murderers?

The worst fear Blaire had ever experienced turned her ice cold. Even greater terror than when Captain Abraham tried to abduct her and Blaike in Port de Lyon to sell them into sexual slavery.

She must warn Julian. But what would the shock do to his

recovery, and would he believe her? Still, she couldn't let him think he was betrothed to that witch and that she carried his child. She squeezed her eyes shut against her clamoring thoughts. *Dear God. Keep Julian safe from that monster.*

Toward that end, she retraced her steps into the common room. She must dispatch a letter at once. Catching Nelson's eye, she angled her head to indicate she wished to speak with him.

He excused himself from the dice game and, buttoning his coat, strode to her. "Yes, Miss Culpepper?"

"I need to speak with you privately please, Nelson."

Blaire cast a quick glance over the other men as she led him to a parlor. Once inside, she closed the door and indicated that he should follow her to the farthest corner of the room.

"Miss Culpepper, is something wrong?" Concern lined his forehead.

She took a step near. "How trustworthy are Julian's servants?"

"I cannot say for certain, miss. They seem decent enough chaps, and Hayes has been very concerned about Lieutenant Drake since we arrived." He glanced to the closed door then back to her. "Is something afoot?"

Blaire nodded and began pacing back and forth. "I fear so. I've overheard a conversation that gives me cause to believe Lieutenant Drake's life may be in danger. I want O'Bradi to deliver an urgent letter for me."

His craggy features sinking into deep furrows, Nelson searched her face. "All right, Miss Culpepper. I've never known you to overreact. If you say the lieutenant's life may be in danger, then I suggest we also post a guard outside his room."

Blaire shook her head. "I already considered that, but it will alert the people I suspect that we're on to their scheme. Besides, I don't think Lieutenant Drake would stand for it."

"We can be discreet. Patrons have left since we arrived. I'll see if there's another room available near the lieutenant's. I can also make sure he's watched, whether downstairs or outside." He pushed his hat back farther on his head before venturing, "Forgive my impudence, but has this something to do with Miss Trudeau?"

Blaire couldn't suppress her surprised expression. "Why would you ask that?"

"Because Hayes has hinted that Alfred Drake's death mightn't have

715

been an accident." He skewed his mouth sideways. "He's none too fond of Miss Trudeau or her mother either."

Dread and alarm made Blaire shiver as she nodded. "I basically just heard as much from Miss Trudeau's own mouth."

"How soon do you wish O'Bradi to leave?" Features taut, Nelson glanced to the door again.

"As soon as I finish my letter. I'm hoping he can reach London in four days." Blaire folded her arms and resumed pacing.

His expression grave, he blew out a long breath. "What about your safety, miss? You've been entrusted to my care until we reach Culpepper Park. I cannot allow you to put yourself in danger."

That thought had crossed Blaire's mind as well.

If Daphne had any inkling Blaire had overheard her essentially admitting to having something to do with Alfred's death... Another chill skittered down her spine at the thought, and she shuddered to think what could happen.

She stood before the fire, warming her hands and collecting her bearings.

It had become imperative that Julian regain his memory immediately. Even if that meant she had to share their history, her love for him—anything to jolt his mind into remembering everything.

Lips pressed tight, she crossed to the window. How fast could O'Bradi make the journey? Was four days unreasonable?

Her breath caught. Julian strode toward the Tankard and Anchor.

Where had he been? She absolutely must see him before Daphne did.

Marking his progress, she sliced Nelson a swift glance. "The lieutenant is returning to the inn just now. Would you please tell him I wish to speak with him at once? Make it clear the matter is urgent, and no one else is to know. I'll meet him at the dog kennel behind the inn. Then, I'll finish my letter when I'm done speaking with him. Have O'Bradi prepare to depart within the hour."

Nelson's attention speared to the window.

"If it eases your mind at all, Lord Ravensdale insisted that everyone who accompanied you be armed." He patted the slight bulge at his waist. "We'll keep the lieutenant safe until his lordship arrives." He turned to go then swung back around. "Do you think you should notify the magistrate?"

"Yes, I'll write him as well." She glanced out the window once more. Julian had almost made the courtyard.

"You will be careful, won't you?" Nelson asked. "Lord Ravensdale will have my neck if you're harmed."

"I give you my word. I shan't be reckless." She made a shooing motion. "Now hurry before Lieutenant Drake comes inside."

Blaire waited a few anxious moments after he left before exiting the parlor. A doorway lay at the far end of the corridor, and she prayed it was the same one she'd seen when she'd put the pups in the kennel earlier. Tamping down her panic, she hurried along, trying to find the right words to say to Julian.

"Miss Culpepper, whatever are you doing?"

Joan Trudeau.

Blaire groaned inwardly and swore a vile oath in her mind.

Another few feet and she would've made good her escape. Alarm scraping across her shoulders, she slowly pivoted. Where had Joan come from? Had she been across the passageway? Eavesdropping? Had she seen Nelson leave?

Pinning a neutral expression on her face, Blaire motioned toward the narrow door.

"I'm retrieving my dogs from the kennel." An impulse seized her, certain to send the woman on her way. "Would you care to help me? I'd be ever so grateful. The two can be quite a handful for one person." Blaire rolled her eyes and pinched her nose. "They rolled in cow dung."

Joan grimaced as if she'd asked her to pick up fresh manure bare-handed.

Shaking her head, Joan retreated a couple of paces, one palm held out before her as if she warded off demons. "Mercy, no. I cannot think why the proprietor permits them inside at all. I'd never allow filthy animals in my home."

"Lieutenant Drake likes dogs. In fact, if I hadn't been able to keep Zeus and Apollo, he intended to take them to Montclere." Awful of her to goad Joan, but honestly, Blaire had had enough of being bullied.

Joan's entire mien changed.

At once sheer vehemence lined her face, and she stalked forward, jutting her finger at Blaire. "You need to be on your way. Lieutenant Drake has recovered sufficiently. Your services are no longer required."

Thought she could dismiss Blaire like a common servant, did she? Blaire notched her chin upward. "I'll leave when I'm bloody good and ready and not one minute before. And I'm not ready. Not by any means."

Air whistled from between Joan's pursed lips. She fairly shook from rage. "I'm warning you, you impudent chit. Leave Lieutenant Drake alone."

Planting her hands on her hips, Blaire stared her down. "Or what?"

Above all, listen to your instincts,
and deal cautiously with those who claim to be
trustworthy. A truthful person doesn't boast about their honesty.
~*Prudence and Propriety— The Genteel Lady's Guide to Practical Living*

11

Julian reached over the enclosure in an attempt to quiet Zeus and Apollo's excited yips and whines. The pups clawed at the fencing, hopping up and down and licking his hands. The two beagles in the pen pushed their snouts into his palms, eager for attention too.

"Calm down, chaps." He glanced around. "Where's your mistress? I thought she was supposed to be out here."

Several yards beyond the dog kennel, clucking chickens pecked the ground, hunting for insects. A larger enclosure containing ducks and geese paralleled the chicken run, and behind that lay a meadow where goats and sheep milled about. A chicken squawked, announcing she'd laid an egg.

He'd been nothing short of astounded when Nelson approached him and quietly asked Julian to accompany him to the stables. Astonishment had turned to concern after Nelson confided Blaire wished to meet Julian behind the establishment and, Nelson emphasized, they should do so secretly.

Julian's angry tramping along the well-traveled lane this past hour failed to bring him closer to accepting that Daphne carried his child. Sitting upon a fallen log and hurling stones with all of his might at a nearby tree hadn't succeeded either.

Reciting every curse word he knew—there were a considerable number, some quite inventive—hadn't made a jot of difference.

Only a cad of the worst sort deserted a woman he'd impregnated. Even if Julian had no memory of a relationship with Daphne, he couldn't abandon her and the child.

A commotion at the back of the lodgings drew his attention.

Speaking to someone inside, Blaire slipped out the doorway.

"Your threats mean nothing to me. You can toss your cousin, the Duke of Montbaard's name around all you wish. Don't forget my guardian and a cousin-in-law are earls and my brother-in-law is a marquis, all of whom have powerful peerage connections."

She stepped over the threshold, shutting the door with a distinct thump behind her.

Closing her eyes, drawn and pale, she put a hand to her forehead. She sucked in a long, rasping breath as she leaned against the weatherworn panel.

"She's evil. Just evil. Vile to her very core. They both are."

The Trudeaus?

Her pups' barking increased to a frenzied pitch upon spying her, and in a few long strides, Julian crossed the grassy patch to the porch.

"Blaire?"

Her eyes flew open at his approach, and chagrin pinkened her cheeks.

"What's happened?" Julian waved toward the door, and she followed the movement with a vexed look. "Nelson said it was urgent that you speak with me, and I couldn't help overhear your exchange. Who were you speaking to?"

He'd bet his honor it had been one of the Trudeau shrews.

Rather than answer him, two neat lines wrinkled her forehead. Her expression pensive, she perused the area and then motioned in the direction of a lean-to filled with stacked wood.

"Yes, I must speak with you, Julian. And it's important that we're not overheard."

Tense lines framed her mouth, her pretty lips pulled into a flat ribbon as she continually scanned the area.

Acute warning tightened his spine. His soldier's intuition flared into full alert, and he carefully scrutinized the back of the inn for danger signs.

"Come." He held out his hand.

Without hesitation, she placed her palm in his, and he didn't let go as he led her to the woodshed. She gripped his hand tightly, and he studied her profile as she walked beside him. In all the days she had cared for him, he'd never seen her this distressed.

"Let me calm the dogs before someone comes to check why they're barking so." She paused at the kennel. Bending over, she patted her dogs' heads. "Give me a few minutes, boys. Then I'll let you out. I promise."

The beagles enjoyed a rub behind their ears as well.

Julian allowed her a moment with the dogs before guiding her to the shed. "Something has you distraught, and I would know what it is."

Once inside the outbuilding and out of the lodging house's direct view, she withdrew her hand. Running her tongue over her lower lip, she crossed her arms, clearly uneasy about what she wanted to say.

"Julian, I need to tell you something, most of which may be difficult for you to hear or understand because of your lack of memory." Her voice quivered the merest bit. She mustered her composure and plowed onward. "But you must be made aware, even if it upsets you."

He stepped nearer and drew her into his arms, tucking her into his chest and whispering in her ear. "*Shh*, sweet Blaire. It cannot be so very bad, can it?"

She smelled of sunshine and flowers and...Blaire. He kissed the top of her head, the action so natural he might've done it a thousand times. He could stand like this forever, this precious woman enfolded in his embrace, breathing in unison, the world forgotten.

"Julian. You must listen," she murmured into his chest, even as she wrapped her arms about his waist. "I fear your life may depend upon it."

He edged her chin upward. What he saw shimmering in her eyes, beyond the worry and the fear, deeper in their arresting purple-blue depths, made his heart swell. The quickening in his veins played testimony, a confirmation that she felt something for him too.

He'd not been wrong about her.

Something glorious sparked between them.

He dipped his head lower, then ever lower still, brushing the sweetness of her satiny mouth with his. He had no recollection of ever kissing anyone as wondrous nor had any remembrance of the last time he'd lain with a woman.

This touch was as exciting and frightening as if he'd never kissed a woman before.

Truth be told, since he'd no memory of ever doing so, this was his first kiss, and with a woman his soul recognized as his other half.

Desire, hot and uncontrollable, tunneled through his veins, a tidal wave of want and need.

She sighed against his mouth and parted her lips, allowing him access to the honeyed cavern within. Wrapping her arms around his neck, she arched into him, returning his kiss with a fervor that matched his own. Several delicious moments passed as he explored her mouth and breathed in her essence. His very spirit demanded he make her his, even as his conscience berated him for being a selfish, opportunistic cawker.

Someone whistling off-key neared the building, and he froze. He pulled Blaire farther into the woodshed's deep shadows, one finger to his lips, cautioning her to keep quiet.

Her eyes wide, she nodded and pressed into him.

He didn't want to contemplate the consequences of being found in a compromising position, particularly with his pregnant betrothed inside the inn. That sobering thought cooled his ardor and renewed his annoyance.

A few tense moments later, the whistling faded, and they were alone again.

"He's gone," he whispered in her ear. "Tell me what has you so worried and why we must meet clandestinely like this?"

Blaire cut him an upward glance through her surprisingly dark eyelashes before looking away. He hadn't missed the uncertainty in her eyes.

"You're being deceived by Miss Trudeau and possibly her mother as well. Daphne isn't pregnant with your brother's child."

"No," he agreed, hesitant to say more. But for Blaire to trust him, he must always be honest with her. "She's pregnant with...mine."

He braced himself for her response. Her condemnation and scorn. Perhaps even her hatred.

Blaire chuckled, a lighthearted, contagious burble. "So, they fed you that drivel as well? They've no shame. None whatsoever."

He expected a great many reactions, but laughter wasn't among them. That was another thing about Blaire Culpepper that fascinated him. Just when he thought he knew her well, she surprised him.

"How do *you* know it's untrue?" He pounded a nearby piece of wood, at last giving vent to his frustration. "Devil it, *I* don't even know if it's a lie. I do know, however, that I can scarcely abide being in the room with her and cannot imagine that I've asked her to be my wife, let alone..."

He stopped himself just short of being indelicate. A man simply didn't discuss bedding another with the woman he adored above all else.

"You didn't ask her willingly, if that's any consolation. You were being gallant, since you believed she carried your brother's child."

"My brother's seed, you say?" Disgust snapped the heels of his relief. What game did the Trudeaus play? If it hadn't been for Blaire, he very well might've fallen for their scheme too.

Her lips swept upward, tenderness glowing in her eyes as she touched the scar on his cheek. "Someday, I want to know how you came by that."

"I was attacked by a surly sailor." The memory sprang to mind as vivid as if it had happened yesterday.

Why couldn't he remember a thing about Blaire or Daphne?

"I'll vow you were being chivalrous, weren't you?" How could she jest at a time like this?

"Actually, yes." He wasn't going to tell her the sod tried to force himself on a doxie. He regarded her through half-closed eyes. "You haven't told me how you're certain their story is pure claptrap."

"I know it's utter balderdash because today I overheard her trying to bribe Dr. Durnham. She wanted him to continue to allow you to believe she's expecting." Blaire pulled a face. "She's not pregnant. Personally, I suspect she mightn't have ever been with child."

Julian's scowl turned murderous. "Does her mother know this? Because she told me not more than an hour ago that Daphne was six weeks along."

"Yes, well, Daphne and her mother seem to be full of twaddle and tripe. You confided in my guardian, Lord Ravensdale, and a couple of your closest friends that you were considering marrying Daphne. Only because she carried your brother's child." She brushed a piece of bark from her sleeve while surveying the yard. "You also told me just over a week ago your reason for doing so. If the child was a male, he would receive his rightful inheritance."

"Quite the self-sacrificing, noble chap, aren't I?" Had he really been willing to go to such an extreme? He couldn't be certain he admired such a fellow.

"I heard Daphne claim she lost your child and was afraid to tell you, Julian."

"And do you believe her?"

Maybe Daphne hadn't told her mother she'd miscarried. That was possible. But had the child been his brother's or his?

A fragile arc bent Blaire's peach-tinted mouth, and she gave one short shake of her head.

Lord, he adored the color of her hair—would love to see the silvery white tendrils down, billowing around her shoulders and to run his fingers through its silky length.

"No. I don't believe her. And do you want to know why, Julian?" Blaire put her palm on his chest, just over his heart. Her sapphire eyes searched his, a message in their depths. "Before I left London, you told me that you want to marry me and no other."

He barely suppressed his whoop of joy.

"I knew it. I knew there was something between us." He gathered her into his embrace once more, hugging her tightly, and she giggled. "I vow, Blaire, this entire matter will be settled before we leave the Tankard and Anchor. Daphne and her mother's scheme will be exposed." He kissed her forehead for a long moment. "I can never thank you enough for preventing me from making a horrendous mistake."

"Honestly Julian, Daphne has told so many lies, I cannot sift fact from fiction most of the time when it comes to her. There's more you should know." She touched his arm, compassion softening her voice. "I overheard her say that Dr. Durnham best take care lest a mishap like Alfred's doesn't happen to him."

Julian stiffened and, taking a step backward, searched her face. "That sounds an awful lot like she had something to do with my brother's death."

"It does, and Hayes, he's your coachman, has suspicions regarding Alfred's death too."

He looked beyond her at the myriad of dusty spiderwebs dangling from the rafters. "Well, the plot thickens, doesn't it?"

"Julian...?"

He cupped Blaire's cheek, running his thumb back and forth across the silky flesh. "Yes, my love?"

She gifted him with a smile so radiant, it humbled him that this magnificent woman should love him. He'd forgo remembering his past if his future included her.

"Daphne said that nothing would prevent her from marrying you." She clutched his arm in her earnestness. "I fear if you tell her you're not going to, she'll try to do you harm too."

He lifted his timepiece from his pocket and, squinting in the dim light, flicked open the cover. With a satisfied sigh, he snapped it shut and returned it to his pocket.

"Joan Trudeau insisted I join her and Daphne for tea and a game of cards today. I should very much like you to accompany me. This matter will be settled once and for all."

Uncertainty flickered across Blaire's face.

"Are you sure that's wise, Julian? If she had anything to do with your brother's accident, she was cunning enough to not arouse suspicion. I think we're better off pretending that we don't know anything at this point. The doctor said if you ask him directly whether she is with child, he wouldn't hide the truth."

"Well then, that's just what I'll do. Tomorrow, when he comes to check on me, I'll make sure Daphne and her mother are present."

"I'm sending one of my men to London," Blaire said, "with a missive for Ravensdale asking him, Leavenworth, Captain Whitehouse, and Wycombe to come here straightaway." She shuddered and rubbed her hands up and down her arms. "After my earlier conversation with Joan, I believe it's not beyond her or Daphne to attempt mischief with me as well."

Julian snarled, "Just let them try."

"Raven can be here in a week if the outrider rides hard." She leaned into his embrace. "We've dealt with the Trudeaus thus far, I say we play along until Ravensdale and the others arrive. You can ask the doctor about her condition then."

Julian cocked his head, considering her suggestion. "That might put them off their guard, thinking they've won me over." He kissed her temple, the hair satiny beneath his lips. "I'd much prefer we leave now."

"I doubt she'll ever be convicted of your brother's murder, then." Blaire linked her fingers with his. "If she did kill him or was involved, don't you want to know the truth?"

"Yes, Blaire, I do, but not at the risk of harm befalling you. I don't need my memory to know that nothing is as important to me as you are." He placed her hand on his chest. "Do you feel my heart beating?"

"Yes." Love blooming across her face, she flattened her palm. "Yes. I feel it."

"My heart knew I loved you, even when my mind couldn't remember." He brushed her mouth with his again.

The dogs renewed their barking frenzy, warning of someone's

approach.

"Shut up, you stupid mongrels," Joan hissed at the dogs. "Where is that meddling chit? I know she's meeting with Drake somewhere. No one knows where either of them is."

A woman's intuition is no insignificant thing. Nurture and trust it.
For unlike friends and lovers, intuition is never fickle.
~Prudence and Propriety— The Genteel Lady's Guide to Practical Living

The next week passed relatively uneventfully—boring as plain porridge, to be honest.

After waiting for Joan to stomp back into the house the other day, Julian had finally agreed it was best he play along with her and Daphne's demands. Toward that end, he met with the women daily for tea and a card game or two and had even consented to afternoon strolls.

She couldn't prevent the twinge of envy that the Trudeaus enjoyed his company, but she was convinced this tack she and Julian had decided upon was the wisest course.

The Trudeaus must believe Blaire had given up and that Julian had conceded to marry Daphne. Still, the triumphant smirks and disdainful glances Daphne and Joan leveled Blaire whenever they encountered one another galled to no end.

For the umpteenth time, Blaire scoured the lane in anticipation of Ravensdale's arrival. Her excuses for why she yet remained now that Julian no longer needed her care wore paper thin.

First, she'd claimed Flora was unwell, and the poor maid had been required to stay in their room for three days. Then Blaire vowed one of the horses was colicky, and Heath absolutely wouldn't permit another team to draw his coach. The latest contrived excuse was that a coach axel had been damaged from the weight of the extra passengers, and the coachman had only just discovered it needed repairing while he made preparations for them to depart.

Blaire had repented much for telling the tarradiddles.

Dr. Durnham had declared Julian fit for travel, and she feared he couldn't delay his departure much longer. Each day after tea, Julian pretended exhaustion and retired to his chamber for a long nap. His memory continued to return. Sometimes, he said, the flashes were mere wispy glimpses, and other times, entire episodes tumbled into his mind bright and clear as if they'd happened the day before.

Even now, Julian was ensconced in the parlor, and to keep her mind occupied, she'd taken Zeus and Apollo for a walk. It rankled, scraping her patience and goodwill. An unfortunate pebble was the recipient of her petulance as she kicked it across the road.

Flora trailed behind, picking a flower every now and again.

Spring had displayed her full majesty the past couple of days. Birds flew here and there, their melodious songs filling the air. Red squirrels scampered across branches, and in the sundrenched meadows on either side of the rambling lane, calves and lambs frolicked about.

Not quite as chilly as yesterday, Blaire raised her bonneted head to the sun for a brief moment, enjoying the rays upon her face. She didn't dare do so for very long, for certainly freckles would sprout upon her nose.

She'd always been an early riser. Living on a dairy farm, the Culpeppers hadn't the luxury of staying abed until midmorning or later. Mornings continued to be her favorite time of day, so it wasn't any great bother to meet with Julian each morn in his chamber for a half-hour. They planned their strategy for the day and generally avoided one another otherwise.

Daphne and her mother would have no reason to be suspicious, which lessened the likelihood of any harm coming to either Blaire or Julian.

She also met Nelson in the stable daily after breaking her fast, and he assured her that neither her outriders nor Hayes had noticed any irregular behaviors from the Trudeaus. Well, nothing outside of their usual peculiar actions.

No doubt they thought they had Julian good and snared and had dismissed Blaire as a troublesome nuisance, unworthy of any further regard.

As Blaire wandered along, she considered what the next few days and weeks might bring.

Things had taken a wonderful, unexpected turn. As she'd traveled from London, she'd believed her life wouldn't include Julian. But now...

Now that Daphne wasn't with child, he wasn't compelled to protect the babe, and although he'd vowed he loved Blaire, he'd still made no mention of marriage.

Until he was fully his old self again, the point was moot.

Unlike Daphne, Blaire wouldn't consider marrying him until he'd regained as much of his memory as was possible.

Dr. Durnham maintained that with the vast gains Julian had made thus far, his memory would be fully restored in short order. Blaire had her own private beliefs as to why he might've lost his memory.

If the doctor was right and Julian couldn't face a lifetime with Daphne—*or her mother*—mightn't he subconsciously have suppressed his memory so he wouldn't have to wed her?

Blaire smiled, the kind of upward sweep of her lips a woman content with life enjoyed when she could give free reign to her love and knew she was loved wholeheartedly in return.

The dogs bolted off in pursuit of a rabbit, and she hurried through the knee-high grass after them. "Boys. Come here." Skirts raised in a most indelicate fashion, she ran after them. "Zeus! Apollo! Come back here this instant."

"Can I help, Miss Blaire?" Flora called from behind her. With her lame foot, there wasn't much the maid could do to catch the naughty rascals.

Breathing hard, Blaire stopped her pursuit. Chasing the pups was futile. "No." She tucked her parasol under one arm. "They'll come back."

Glancing around to make sure no one else was about, she put her fingers in her mouth and released a piercing whistle. She hadn't whistled since living at Esherton Green. Prim and proper ladies didn't make such vulgar noises.

The pups stopped in their tracks, heads cocked. Circling around, their ears erect and tongues lolling, they looked to her.

Flora clapped in delight. "Brilliant, miss."

The puppies trotted back, and as they did, Blaire bent and picked a handful of wildflowers beside the road. They'd make a nice gift for Mrs. Atkins. No breeze stirred today, unlike the blustery tempest that had ushered them to the Tankard and Anchor Inn.

Such an odd name for the lodgings. There wasn't a major waterway in any direction for miles. Julian confided Mr. Atkins had been a man of the sea before marrying. Perhaps that's why the place bore the unusual name.

As she and Flora stepped back onto the road, four horsemen

approached, followed by a coach-and-four. Catching Flora's arm, Blaire yanked her off the track then squatted to grab the dogs by the scruff of their necks. Her sprained arm barely ached anymore.

"Stay, boys. Stay," Blaire ordered.

The sun blinding her, she glanced up, squinting as the lead rider cantered to a stop.

"Blaire?"

Relief suffused her, and she released her dogs. "Heath, thank God, you're finally here."

He dismounted and gestured for the others to do the same. Her brother-in-law Tristan, the Marquis of Leventhorpe; her cousin-in-law Alexander, the Earl of Wycombe; and Captain Whitehouse promptly slid from their saddles as well.

Gratitude filled her heart that they came on such short notice. Blaire pointed to the conveyance. "Who's in the coach?"

No sooner had the words left her mouth than the door flew open, and Blaike jumped to the ground before the coachman had a chance to lower the steps.

"Blaire," she cried, waving. Blaike ran to her, and they hugged, talking and laughing all at once.

As they separated, Blaire dabbed the corners of her eyes and glanced over Blaike's shoulder. Brooke—carrying Leopold—a very pregnant Blythe, and Brette had descended from the equipage as well.

"All of them?" Blaire turned an astonished glance to Blaike then to Heath.

He replied with a sardonic twist of his mouth. "Blaire, did you honestly think there was any chance your sisters and cousins would remain in London when you asked for our help?" He swept his black-gloved hand toward the other men. "Especially given the possibility you were in danger?"

"Of course we wouldn't," Blaike huffed, giving him an indignant look.

"Blythe wouldn't have it, as she told me in no uncertain terms." Tristan eyed his wife's distended belly as she made her way to him. "Let's hope my heir doesn't decide to put in an early appearance."

Wycombe chuckled, his gold hair glinting in the sunlight. "Brette was no better. She vowed if we didn't permit them to come along, they'd make the journey on their own."

That sounded like the Culpepper Misses. Well, the former

Culpeppers.

"See what you have to look forward to, Whitehouse?" Heath's smirk belied his sarcasm.

Captain Whitehouse removed his hat and ran his forearm across his forehead. "I didn't even attempt to dissuade Blaike. You forget. I spent weeks at sea with the twins. I, too, know how close they are."

Blaike bestowed a loving smile upon him. "And you were perfectly wonderful, Oliver."

By that time, the other women had reached Blaire, and another round of hugs ensued.

A moment later, the coachman set Freddy on the ground. He barked a weak greeting and waddled after the women. Practically blind, arthritic, and impossibly fatter than a week ago, he patiently tolerated Zeus's and Apollo's exuberant hellos.

"Now, Blaire, tell us what the devil is going on. Your missive raised more questions than it gave answers." Heath speared a swift glance to the inn, just visible at the top of the knoll. "How long have you been here?"

"Flora, please take the dogs back to the inn for me." Blaire couldn't risk the maid overhearing. "And add these flowers to your bouquet for Mrs. Atkins."

"Yes, miss." The maid accepted the blooms then bent to pet Freddy. Gathering the dogs' leads in one hand, she slowly trundled back to the inn.

"I've been here several days." So much had changed since leaving London. "Since Lieutenant Drake's coach accident, actually. Dr. Durnham, he's the physician treating the lieutenant, asked me if I would stay and tend to his care. I couldn't say no."

"Blaire, your reputation..." Brooke sliced Heath a worried glance.

"Flora has shared a room with me, and the Trudeaus have done their utmost to make sure the lieutenant and I are never together." Her family needn't know about the times she had been alone with him.

Blaire regarded the inn too. She'd prefer Daphne and her mother didn't see her family until Blaire had a chance to apprise them of everything. Unfortunately, the arrival of four horsemen and a carriage wouldn't likely go unnoticed. She could only hope they were still at tea or had returned to their chambers.

Enough guests came and went that perhaps they wouldn't notice new arrivals.

Four more silver-blonde women? Not bloody likely.

Blaike squeezed Blaire's hand. "Whatever has happened? I've been worried sick. Heath said she's not with child after all? And that she might've had something to do with Alfred Drake's death?"

"Yes." Blaire shooed a fly away from her face. "That's all true, but I don't think this is the best place to discuss it. Besides, you must be tired and hungry."

"She has a point. Considering my arse is aching from days of pounding in the saddle and I'm parched dryer than the Sahara." This from Leventhorpe, never one to mince his words.

"My dear, I can appreciate your discomfort." Blythe arched a reproachful curved eyebrow, fanning her fingers over her rounded belly.

Tristan gave her a contrite look. "More reason to make haste and see you settled comfortably, my dear."

Fifteen minutes later everyone relaxed in one of the private parlors. The ladies sipped tea while the men enjoyed a tankard of porter. When Brette confessed they hadn't eaten since before dawn, Mr. Atkins had hurried off to have a meal prepared.

They awaited Julian's arrival as well.

Neither he nor the Trudeaus had been in the common room when Blaire and her family entered. However, it wouldn't take long for someone as shrewd as those sly women to put two and two together and realize something was afoot.

Now, though, Blaire needn't fear for her or Julian's safety.

Nelson stood guard outside the door, ensuring Daphne and her mother couldn't eavesdrop on the conversation inside. As briefly as possible, she'd revealed all she knew.

Everything except Julian's vow of love. That could come later, but for now she wanted to savor the secret.

"I've asked Dr. Durnham and Magistrate Oakley be shown here directly." She'd not met with the official yet. In her letter, she'd begged him not to alert the Trudeaus by coming to the inn and poking around. There was time enough for that later, and as long as they believed she wasn't a threat anymore, they'd leave her alone. Instead, she'd encouraged the magistrate to start his investigation at Montclere.

His terse reply had been loaded with questions and recriminations. However, he'd honored her request and not sought her out at the lodging house.

For if he had done so, Daphne surely...

Blaire put a halt to her dark musings. No need to fret about that any longer. Her family had arrived, and no harm could come to Julian now. Taking a sip of the fragrant tea—it truly was a masterful blend—she wandered to the window.

What did Daphne hope to accomplish with her charade? Why was she so desperate to become the mistress of Montclere? Perhaps she'd always been evil. Perhaps her mother had encouraged that side of her.

The woman was queer in the attic, to be sure.

If Blaire remembered correctly, Julian had confessed to Heath that he believed his brother had died after a hunting misfortune. Tattle had it he'd been foxed and thrown from his mount. There'd been no inquiry at that time. However, given what Blaire had written the magistrate, one had been initiated.

Just wait until Daphne learned that.

The door opened, and Julian entered. He wore a midnight-blue wool tailcoat today, the color a perfect complement to his dark hair.

At once, their gazes collided across the room. She didn't care who noticed or whether they approved. She refused to hide or deny her love for him any longer.

She'd learned how Heath had sent Julian from Highfield that day. Although her family meant to protect her and she appreciated their concern, equipped with the knowledge that Julian loved her, she'd become emboldened.

Once Daphne had been dealt with, Blaire believed with all of her heart his memory would return full on.

Standing just inside the door, he looked from person to person, uncertainty etched across his handsome features. Brows pulled into a severe vee, his keen regard searching, he studied each face in turn. He'd lost weight. The sharp planes of his face and more pronounced cheekbones made him appear more ruthless, but not any less attractive.

Blaire handed her teacup to Blaike, who'd come to her side when he entered, and hurried to link her arm in the crook of his elbow and offer her reassurance.

How awful it must be to see close friends and not recognize them.

Face drawn and eyes shut, he put a hand to his forehead, mumbling, "Blaire, I need to sit down."

"Heath," Blaire said. "Julian's not well." He wavered the merest bit, and she put an arm around his back to steady him.

In a trice, Heath and Whitehouse strode to either side of Julian and guided him to the nearest chair, which Brette vacated for him.

He sank onto the cushion, and Zeus and Apollo promptly tried to clamber onto his lap.

"Those two think they're lap dogs." Tristan's dry observation earned him a couple of mouth twitches from the others.

"Not now," Blaire said, shooing them aside and kneeling beside the chair.

Taking Julian's hand between hers, she studied him. "Are you all right? Does your head hurt? Dr. Durnham should be here shortly."

Had it been too much of a shock seeing his friends all at once? Blaire hadn't thought to consult the doctor about that possibility.

One elbow on his knee, he cradled his forehead in his palm.

"What can we do?" Heath place a hand on Julian's shoulder.

His chest expanding from a deep gulp of air, Julian sat back in the chair and squinted up at Heath. "I'm fine, Ravensdale, but what are you," he flicked his fingers at the others, "and everyone else doing here?"

He remembers.

He looked around again, clearly bewildered. "And where, exactly, might I ask is *here*?"

Being trusted is more desirable than being loved. For you can
have trust without love, but you cannot have love without trust.
~*Prudence and Propriety— The Genteel Lady's Guide to Practical Living*

13

Julian's head pounded bloody awful, worse than battle drums being played against his skull. The last thing he remembered clearly was the coach slanted at a precarious angle and Daphne and her mother screaming hysterically before they plummeted down the embankment.

He scanned the room's occupants once more, his regard settling lastly on Blaire hovering near his left knee.

At once, peace filled him. God, how he loved this woman.

"You've remembered everything." Shock or joy or perhaps both widened her eyes.

"Not everything. Why I am here is murky. It feels like I've been dreaming and just awoke." He raised his eyes, flabbergasted to see encouragement in his friends' gazes and compassion on the women's faces.

Obviously, they knew something he didn't.

"Julian, don't you remember anything of the past several days?" Blaire touched his knee, evidently unmindful of her guardian's disapproving frown.

"I thought it was all a dream," he said again, giving a confused shake of his head and touching his temple. "Everything is hazy. Unclear."

"You had a carriage accident and suffered a severe concussion. You temporarily lost your memory and have been at the Tankard and Anchor Inn since." She sat back on her heels, her lower lip caught between her teeth.

Sorrow filled her expressive eyes. "I'd say from your befuddled countenance you've recalled everything. Except for what transpired since your accident. Am I right?"

"I remember little of being here at all, Blaire."

Disappointment shadowing her face, her eyes grew luminous, and he was at a loss as to why.

"Why are *you* here?" he asked in an attempt to shift everyone's attention away from him.

"My coach came upon yours after the crash," Blaire said. "At the behest of the doctor treating you, I've cared for—"

Outraged feminine protests sounded outside the door, followed by a low-toned, masculine voice.

She swung her head toward the entrance, her features pinched taut with apprehension.

Julian winced inwardly. He'd know that shrewish voice anywhere: Joan Trudeau. Too bad he hadn't forgotten her or the reason they'd been on their way to Montclere.

"I don't care what Lord Ravensdale's instructions are, you impudent cur." The distinct sound of a foot stomping echoed through the door. "My daughter's betrothed is inside that room. I insist you allow us in."

Grimacing, Julian gave a curt nod to Wycombe, and at once the earl strode to the door. His mouth twisting wryly, he pressed the handle, and Nelson stepped aside.

Joan and Daphne barged into the parlor, coming to an abrupt halt upon spying the occupants. Wariness replaced Joan's outraged expression.

"What's the meaning of this?" she demanded, once again eschewing protocol and manners.

Married to Daphne, this was what he could expect for the rest of his life.

Brooke, holding Leopold and swaying back and forth, turned an icy stare upon her. "I don't believe you are owed an explanation, and demanding one is certainly beyond the pale."

Daphne pulled herself erect and, in a pompous manner very much like her mother's, jutted her chin upward. "Everything pertaining to my betrothed is my business, Lady Ravensdale."

Rising, Julian swept Daphne and Joan a cold glance. "I understand that we've been here for a number of days." His focus dropped to Daphne's stomach for a fraction before meeting her watery eyes. Tears already? "I trust you weren't injured in the crash?"

Daphne slapped both hands over her mouth, droplets immediately trailing from the corner of her eyes. "Julian. You've regained your memory."

"Thank God," Joan grumbled. "Now we can be away from this horrible, vermin-infested place." Her attention slid to Blaire, the insult clearly directed at her. "And you and Daphne can be married at once."

"Enough." Hands fisted, angrier than Julian had ever seen her, Blaire glared right back at the Trudeaus. "Enough of this codswallop. Enough of these two despicable women's lies." She cut them a brusque gesture with her hand. "Daphne is no more pregnant than I am."

A lethal inflection lowering his voice, Ravensdale said, "My ward had bloody better not be with child."

Blaire turned on him, her fury wildly beautiful. "Don't be an utter arse, Heath. Of course I'm not. You do Julian a disservice by suggesting something so dishonorable."

She defended him. And she'd said arse to Raven. A joyful grin threatened to tip Julian's mouth.

"But that deceptive woman," she pointed to Daphne, "is not expecting."

Every muscle in Julian's body rigid, he faced Blaire full on. "Why would you say that, Blaire?"

She grabbed his hand. "Julian, remember. It wasn't a dream. Please remember what I told you days ago. I overheard her telling Dr. Durnham she wasn't with child."

Daphne released an outraged cry, and her mother rushed forward, hands clawed, as if to attack Blaire.

"You lying trollop," Joan snarled, spraying spittle in her rage.

Julian stepped between Blaire and Joan. Just let her lay a hand on Blaire and he'd completely forget he was a gentleman. "Tread carefully, madam, for my patience has long since been spent."

"You see the drastic measures she'll go to in order to prevent Julian from wedding Daphne?" Joan cried. She flung a wild look at the others. "From doing the right thing by her?"

Blaire's family regarded Joan with the same warmth they would have adders in their beds. From the stony stares directed at her and Daphne, they believed Blaire.

God help him, how Julian wanted to as well.

Lady Wycombe, one hand caressing her tummy, glanced between Julian and Blaire then swept a contemptuous look to Daphne. "Were you ever even *enceinte*?"

Daphne buried her hands in her face.

"How can you humiliate me like this, Julian?" she wailed. She could be commended for her acting ability, if not her decency. "How could you tell everyone about my unfortunate circumstances? You have no honor."

Honor was a peculiar thing, Julian had discovered of late. What one person deemed decent, another might consider contemptible and the reverse as well.

"Perhaps we should leave and permit them a bit of privacy." Always the voice of reason, Lady Ravensdale gave a pointed look toward the still open door. "I'm sure we're providing quite a spectacle."

A jot too late to worry about that now.

"By all means, close the door." Julian canted his head toward the entrance. "As for your leaving? I'd rather you stayed."

After exchanging looks, his friends nodded.

He breathed out a long breath and dropped his hand to his side.

"I regret embarrassing you, Daphne, but they," he swept a hand around the room," are as dear to me as my own family." Dearer, truth to tell. "And Blaire is the woman I love. Who I shall always love."

Another round of startled sounds echoed throughout the parlor.

Blaire's eyes softened, and perhaps—just perhaps—a glint of moisture shimmered there as well. While her show of feminine emotion warmed his heart, Daphne's continued blubbering merely irritated.

After a quick rap on the door, the coachman poked his head in. "I beg your pardon, but Dr. Durnham and Magistrate Oakley are here. You asked they be shown in at once."

Three men entered, each attired in somber black except for their neckcloths.

Which was the doctor?

Ah, the perky chap with the satchel, no doubt. Yes, he did seem vaguely familiar.

Wycombe perched on the arm of the chair his wife had settled into. "This ought to prove entertaining."

"*Shh*, darling," Lady Wycombe scolded with an affectionate pat on his thigh.

"Why…Why is the magistrate here?" Daphne's eyes, huge and panic-filled, sought her mother's.

The diminutive chap with fiery red hair approached.

At once Julian felt at ease.

Dr. Durnham gave a satisfied nod. "Brilliant. Your memory's returned, Lieutenant." A flicker of concern pleated his face. "But…?"

"I'm afraid Julian cannot remember the time he's been here as clearly as we'd like, Doctor." Blaire's disappointment was tangible; worse was Julian's guilt for disappointing her.

"*Hmm*. I've read that can happen, although it's rare. Far more common to permanently lose short-term memory. We've still much to learn about amnesia." He peered up at Julian. "Seems you exchanged a fortnight's memories for a lifetime's. Not a bad deal, in my estimation."

Blaire placed her hand on Julian's forearm, and he glanced down. If he could spend the rest of his life with this woman—the keeper of his heart for eternity—and not Daphne, what a gift that would be.

"Julian." Blaire pressed her fingertips into his arm. "Ask the doctor if Daphne is with child. You'll know for certain then."

Julian studied the entreaty in her eyes. He had no reason to doubt Blaire, and every cause to distrust Daphne. Cupping his nape, he firmed his mouth. "Doctor…?"

"No. No, Julian. Don't ask him. I… I…" Daphne ran to Julian and grabbed his other arm. "She's right. I…"

Casting a frantic look to Dr. Durnham, she received a bland look in reply. She'd get no help from that quarter.

"I did tell the doctor that I'd lost your child." Voice quavering, tears dripped from her eyes. "But…I was so afraid to tell you," she finished in a pathetic whisper.

Her mother jumped into the fray, bobbing her head and licking her lips. "Yes. Yes, that's true."

"You will not succeed in trapping him into marriage." An Amazon's mien about her, Blaire cast a scathing glance to the Trudeaus.

Julian could almost see her in armor, her long legs muscled and tan, a gold helmet gleaming upon her head and sword and shield in hand. And she fought for him. For him.

Skewing Blaire a hate-filled glare, Joan wrapped her arm around her daughter's shoulders. "You may not remember, or perhaps you're choosing not to, Lieutenant Drake, but we had a discussion days ago. I told you then Daphne was six weeks along with your child."

A chorus of outraged gasps and low angry male rumblings filled the room.

"Enough," Julian all but snarled, past the point of caring about civility. He jerked his arm loose from Daphne's death grip. "You dare claim I fathered a child on you too? That's a colossal crock of sh—"

Teeth and hands clenched, he spun away, fighting for control. He'd never struck a woman, but so help him God, he was perilously close to doing so. Putting two fingers to his temple, he rubbed them in a circular motion. "I may not remember everything that happened this past week, but I can unequivocally say that I did not father a child on you, Daphne."

Her face reddened, and she twisted her handkerchief in her hands. "Julian, can we have this conversation in private, please?"

"No, we cannot. I want witnesses." How had Alfred ever become involved with this devious woman? "Up until the carriage accident, you swore you carried Alfred's child. And now you claim I impregnated you?"

Daphne bit her lip then opened her mouth. No sound came out.

Her mother on the other hand, growled like a rabid dog.

The magistrate and the other stern-faced fellow had wandered to a corner of the parlor. He folded his arms, and ankles crossed, leaned against the windowsill. Given his steely countenance, the magistrate bore more unwelcome news.

The other chap seemed engrossed in the scenery beyond the window, but from his years as a soldier, Julian recognized a man on high alert.

Dr. Durnham sighed then righted his spectacles. He shook his head. "I advised you to tell the Lieutenant the truth, Miss Trudeau. If you don't do it now, I shall."

"Do shut up, Doctor, you noxious little troll." Fluttering her hand as she would at a fly upon seedcake, Joan had dispensed with all semblance of decorum.

"Momentarily, my dear lady. Momentarily." Facing Julian, the doctor seized his coat's lapels and rocked back onto his heels. "In my professional opinion, Lieutenant, it's highly doubtful Miss Trudeau has ever been pregnant." Dr. Durnham casually took in Joan's livid countenance then delivered the *coup de gras.* "Ever."

The breath whooshed from Julian's lungs. Simultaneous jubilance and disbelief jockeyed for control.

"Pardon?"

He wasn't certain which of the former Culpeppers spoke his thought aloud, except it wasn't Blaire.

Daphne gasped and stumbled backward, plowing into her mother. "You cannot know that."

"You are correct," the doctor agreed, not the least ruffled. "I cannot for certain, which is why I said it's doubtful. Not impossible. I can however, unequivocally vow you are not with child now nor appear to have suffered a miscarriage in recent months."

Blaire exchanged a flabbergasted glance with her twin, and Whitehouse whistled between his teeth.

"Didn't see that coming," Leventhorpe murmured.

Magistrate Oakley straightened. "Now that that's out of the way…"

Just what was their business here?

"Constable Martin." He signaled to the other man. "Place these women under arrest. For murder."

Everyone seeks to be loved, but a wise woman
insists on trust as well, for the best evidence of trust is love.
~*Prudence and Propriety— The Genteel Lady's Guide to Practical Living*

W hat had Magistrate Oakley discovered so quickly?
Blaire had written him but a week ago. She couldn't imagine
what evidence could be so damning he'd arrest both women without
preamble.

"Murder?" Thorough confusion puckering her face, Blythe touched
Tristan's arm. "You didn't mention anything about a murder."

He took her hand in his. "I didn't want you to fret, sweet."

"Murder?" Brooke repeated, fanning her face with her hand. "Oh,
dear me."

Leopold wiggled and fussed, and she adjusted him in her arms,
cooing softly.

"Martin." Magistrate Oakley speared a speaking glance to Daphne.

At once, the constable strode across the room to assist. He seized
her by her upper arm, amidst her shrieks of outrage.

"Unhand me, you filthy cur," she screeched as she tried to punch
him.

The magistrate did the same with Joan, who succeeded in
walloping him on the side of the head before he constrained her hands
behind her back.

"You've no proof," Joan spat. "Nothing to tie us to Alfred's murder.
It was Dinah Drake's doing. She hated Alfred."

"Mother! Be quiet." Daphne's scathing glower failed to temper her
mother's struggles.

"You wouldn't be under arrest if I didn't have conclusive proof,
madam." He grimaced when her heel connected with his shin. For such
a small woman, she was remarkably tenacious. "I didn't mention whose
murder you were being detained for, either."

That gave her pause for all of two seconds before she redoubled her efforts. "Contemptible arse. Putting your hands on me. Noble blood runs in my veins. My cousin the Duke of Montbaard will hear of this affront."

Apollo and Zeus circled the struggling women, growling low in their throats.

"Come." Blaire snapped her fingers. Tails between their legs and ears lowered, they skulked to her.

Doing a commendable job of restraining the thrashing and kicking woman, Magistrate Oakley canted his head toward Julian. "I shall need to speak with you at your earliest convenience. There are unfortunate details you need to be made aware of."

Details? Blaire would hazard to guess, from the official's grim expression, these details involved Julian's mother.

"Is this evening convenient?" Oakley dropped his attention to the struggling woman he restrained.

One hand on his hip and the other at his nape, his face strained, Julian gave a barely perceptible nod. "Yes. You can expect me before six."

Blaire slipped her hand into his. He'd been through so much. Learning foul play had factored into his brother's death must be unbearable. Particularly if his mother was involved as Joan implied.

He gave Blaire's fingers a little squeeze, his attention still trained on the furious, cursing women.

His long legs eating up the distance, Leventhorpe hurried to open the door. As soon as he did, two more men stepped inside to aid the lawmen.

"I think—" Captain Whitehouse placed Blaike's hand on his arm and angled them toward the door, "—now would be a good time to leave Drake and Miss Blaire alone. I'm sure they've much to discuss."

Heath scratched beneath his nose and, after leveling Julian a long look, at last gave a grudging nod. "Yes, let's allow them a few moments' privacy."

"Would you mind terribly taking Zeus and Apollo with you?" Blaire adored the pups, but now wasn't the time for their antics. She pointed to the door. "Go boys. Flora can watch them in my chamber."

After giving her confused looks, they yielded to the coachman's coaxing. The biscuit he pulled from his pocket and broke in half didn't hurt either.

Blaire's sisters and cousins, accompanied by the men who'd captured their hearts, filed from the parlor. Brette and Alex, carrying Freddy, brought up the rear.

As the coachman leaned in to grasp the door handle, Julian signaled to him. "Would you please remain at your station for a bit longer? I don't wish to be interrupted."

The man's curious gaze swung between Julian and Blaire before his eyes widened with understanding, and he gave a minuscule nod.

Blaire wandered to the window, excited and nervous to be alone with Julian now that he remembered who he was.

In the square, the constable and magistrate struggled to deposit the still thrashing Trudeaus into the waiting coach. At least he hadn't bundled them off in a prison wagon. He'd allow them that small degree of dignity.

Not quite sure what she felt at the moment aside from relief, Blaire swallowed. She couldn't muster sympathy or pity for either of the Trudeaus. But neither could she rejoice they'd been caught, for their futures were dismal at best.

If convicted of Alfred's murder, in all probability, they'd hang.

That sobering thought cast a depressing mantle over her newfound joy. Had Julian's mother truly played a role in his brother's death?

A moment later, Julian clasped Blaire's shoulder and gently turned her to face him. He brushed his knuckles along one cheek, the most tender expression in his eyes.

How long she'd waited to see that look directed at her.

Expression somber, Julian considered the coach, as the magistrate climbed inside and shut the door.

"I cannot fathom I actually had contemplated wedding Daphne. I tried to convince myself that honor and duty drove me. And perhaps they did to a degree, but I see clearly now that I was beyond stupid and foolish for disregarding your precious love."

Blaire covered his hand caressing her cheek and, eyes shut, leaned in to his calloused palm. "I also tried to convince myself you were being noble and self-sacrificing. And I know you only considered marrying her for the babe's sake. But I confess, I was angry, despite your altruistic intentions. And I was jealous. So awfully jealous that I didn't much like myself."

"You had every reason to be, my darling." He enclosed her in his embrace, and it was the sweetest homecoming she'd ever experienced.

"I wronged you greatly."

"Would you still have married her if she was pregnant?"

A rueful smile quirked his mouth.

"No. In fact, the reason we left London was because I'd finally realized I wasn't martyr material and had told Daphne I wouldn't take Alfred's place. Being a loving uncle and providing for the child was the most I could offer. I was taking them to Joan's cousin when the coach overturned." Self-depreciation hardened his face. "If I'd stood firm and insisted their possessions be sent along afterward, the vehicle wouldn't have been top-heavy and blown over in the storm."

Well, that answered that question.

He must've been truly desperate to sever ties with Daphne.

"Once I'd deposited them safely, I meant to travel straight back to London and ask for your hand."

Burying her nose in his chest, Blaire inhaled deeply, savoring the scent that was Julian. She relished the strength of the sculpted planes of his chest beneath her cheek and the sinewy arms encircling her. She wrapped her arms about his waist and clasped her hands together. She never wanted this moment to end. This moment they were finally able to declare their love for each other.

He kissed the crown of her head. "Did I forget anything of import this past week?"

"Well, if you consider our first kiss something of import, then yes, you did." She slanted her neck, giving him a coy look.

His eyes lit with desire, even as his attention dove to her mouth. "We kissed? Our first kiss? And I have no memory of it?"

"You also called me your love." She fiddled with the folds of his cravat.

He hugged her so tightly she giggled.

"Julian, you're crushing me."

He relaxed his hold a fraction. "While I'm infinitely grateful to have regained my memory, I'd say providence is most unfair, not allowing me to remember our first kiss."

"Well…" Blaire raised up on her toes, looping her hands about his neck and drawing him near. "I'd say you're a very lucky man."

He shied a skeptical brow upward.

"My darling, we will have another first kiss," she said. "How many couples can claim such a privilege?"

She swept her lips across his, and he needed no further invitation to plunder her mouth. One hand splayed between her shoulder blades and the other at her waist, he urged her nearer, ravaging her mouth with a hunger that thrilled and excited.

She met each stroke and parry of his velvety tongue with her own and slid one hand into his silky hair, clutching the tendrils as he leaned her backward, kissing her jaw, her chin, her neck, and even nibbling her ear.

He lifted his mouth an inch from hers and whispered, "How does that first kiss compare to the other?"

She recognized the longing glinting in his eyes, for surely hers mirrored the same yearning.

"Oh, I do believe this one was immeasurably better." She traced his angular jaw with her gaze then reached up and did the same with her finger. "I love you, Julian."

He stood upright, drawing her with him. One of her hands raised to his mouth, he pressed his lips against the knuckles. "And I..." He kissed her hand again. "Love." Then kissed her forehead. "You, my darling."

He emphasized the last with a firm, sweet kiss to her mouth.

At some point during their embrace, the coach containing the Trudeaus had left the courtyard, and the quiet of the country settled upon the Tankard and Anchor once more. Contentment Blaire had only dreamed of welled in her heart, and she lowered her eyelids against the mist blurring her vision.

Goodness. She'd become as weepy as Daphne.

Julian raised her palm to his mouth, holding it there for a long moment. Raw pain and regret glinted in his eyes, deepened to umber from emotion.

"Can you forgive me, Blaire? For almost making a mistake that surely would've assured us both a life of unhappiness? For not putting our love first and not fighting for us. For not doing more to investigate my brother's death, and for taking Daphne at her word. Can you learn to trust me again?"

"Oh, Julian, love holds no record of wrongs, and of course I trust you. Love without trust is meaningless. Besides, you couldn't have known Daphne and her mother were such charlatans."

No one could've guessed how vile they turned out to be.

"You were grieving for your brother and worried for his child," Blaire said. "That *was* noble and decent. And perhaps when you've spoken with the magistrate, you'll have a better understanding of what transpired. Although, I must confess, I cannot fathom minds capable of scheming the way they did."

He captured her lips again, not the ravaging hunger from before, but a gentle, apologetic onslaught on her senses.

To convey the love overflowing from every pore, she returned his kiss, still afraid that something would happen to ruin this happiness. From his ragged breathing and strained features, the same desire hummed through his veins. If it wasn't for the servant just outside the door and a suspicion her family loitered in the hallway, she'd suggest she and Julian make use of one of the settees.

My, I've become positively wicked.

"Was our second kiss to your satisfaction, my darling?" Primal male gratification rumbled in Julian's voice.

She swatted his back. "Conceited beast. Fishing for compliments. You know full well I enjoyed every moment of it." Yet, trying to catch her breath and bring her cavorting pulse under control, she laughed. "Still, I think we should practice a bit more."

"In good time, my darling." Julian dropped to one knee, both of her hands clasped in his.

"Julian. You don't need to do this."

"I don't deserve you. I don't deserve your forgiveness, but if you consent to be my wife, Blaire, I swear by all that is holy that every minute of every hour of every day I shall strive to make you happy. Marry me. Please. And let's not have a long engagement. I want us to wed as soon as possible."

He pressed her fingertips in his earnestness, as she urged him to his feet.

The reverent kiss he placed on her forehead broke the tenuous grip on her emotions. Tears leaked from the corner of her eye as she nodded.

"Of course. I'll marry you, Julian. It's what I've wanted for so very long. And I agree. Let's not wait."

He wiped her tears with his thumbs, his own eyes suspiciously moist.

"Thank you, Blaire. Thank you. I'm a man blessed above all others. I'll have to go through the formality of asking Ravensdale for your hand, but I cannot think he'll refuse."

"Trust me, darling. Brooke won't let him."

Male laughter echoed in the corridor before fading away along with the tramping of heavy boots.

"What do you think of a double wedding, Julian? I've no doubt Blaike would be thrilled at the idea. We could marry at Culpepper Park or Montclere. I have no preference. The latter would certainly be more convenient for your family. Why, we can even have Alex perform the ceremony."

"I cannot think of anything more perfect," Julian agreed. "I'd actually prefer to wed at Culpepper Park. I haven't many fond memories of Montclere."

"Then, Culpepper Park it is."

A grin lit his face, reminding her of the Julian of old. "Do you know when I first knew that I loved you?"

He gathered her near once more, and she savored his solid arms embracing her.

She shook her head, "No, tell me."

"It was at Bristledale Court. That morning when Brette was so upset because she thought for certain she was being banished for her matchmaking antics. You and Blaike flew to her side to comfort her. I knew in that instant that no other woman would do for me."

Blaire tilted her head, more dratted tears blurring her vision.

Lud. She *had* become worse than Daphne. If this was what love did to a person, she didn't mind it all that much.

"It took you that long? I loved you far sooner. It was that evening Tristan fell off the piano stool whilst turning the music pages for Blythe. You laughed, and in that instant, I was lost—completely enamored."

"You fell in love with my laugh, minx?"

Blaire gave him a teasing glance through her lashes. "Well, the rest of you is not objectionable either. Now, kiss me again."

And he did.

When you are vulnerable to love, you give
another the power to break your heart whilst trusting they
never will. Choose wisely then, whom you give your heart to.
~*Prudence and Propriety— The Genteel Lady's Guide to Practical Living*

Culpepper Park.
25 December 1823

B laire smiled into her cup of hot mulled wine as Leopold giggled and crawled across Zeus, lying on his back. Not to be outdone, Apollo flopped over as well, allowing the toddler to scramble atop him too.

The dogs, infinitely patient and gentle, adored Leopold— handsome, sturdy little chap—as much as he loved them.

One arm about Blaire's shoulders, Julian ran a finger up and down her arm, just below the sleeve of her ruby red gown. She leaned into him, offering a contented sigh.

He lowered his head a fraction, whispering in her ear. "Happy, my love?"

"Immeasurably." Beyond what she could've dreamed.

This was their first Christmas together, the first time the five former Culpepper misses, their husbands, and their children had gathered to celebrate the holiday at Culpepper Park.

Blaire hoped it became a tradition.

Greenery, red and gold ribbons, and an assortment of other decorations bedecked every common room in the house. Even the dogs wore gay ribbons around their necks.

Comfortable in adjacent chairs facing the ornate carved oak fireplace, with a huge Yule log snapping and crackling behind the screen, Brooke and Heath presided over the gathering.

The tapers from the two beribboned candelabras reflected in the mantel's built-in mirror cast a cheerful glow over the room.

Heath gathered Brooke's hand in his, and their fingers entwined rested them atop the chair arm. That was one of the things that Blaire appreciated most about the men who had married her sisters and cousins and Julian as well: None thought it unmanly to demonstrate their affection.

On the opposite settee, Blythe cradled Effie on her lap. With her mother's vibrant sapphire eyes and her father's auburn hair, she already showed signs of the beauty she would become. That little cherub's early arrival, a mere two days after Blaire had departed the Tankard and Anchor Inn, had delayed Blaire's and Blaike's wedding for a couple of weeks.

The double wedding had taken place right here at Culpepper Park, on a sunny morning the first of June.

Tristan chucked his daughter's chin, sending her into a fit of giggles, which caused Brette's baby, three-month-old Henry, to erupt into laughter as well.

Leopold crawled to his cousins and, his tongue poking out, hauled himself up on his Uncle Alex's knee. A spot of drool trailing down his chin, the toddler joined in the merriment.

The cousins were already fond of each other, and Blaire prayed they'd be as close as she and her cousins had been.

Of its own accord, her attention gravitated to the chair brought from Esherton Green specifically for Freddy. It had been his favorite to nap in since puppyhood.

Tonight, as it had since October, it sat empty.

For a moment, sadness weighted her heart. After fifteen and a half years, dear, sweet Freddy had left their world. Blaire still mourned his passing, as did the rest of the family.

Heath, forever grumbling about dogs being underfoot ever since that long-ago day when Freddy had peed on his boot, had promptly gone out and acquired two more Welsh corgi puppies. Those little scamps, with their needle-like teeth, were in the kitchen, snuggled in their bed asleep for the night.

Oliver emptied his cup and, after placing it on the side table, said, "Drake, I thought you mentioned your sisters might join us for the holiday."

Another wave of sorrow, for an entirely different reason, engulfed Blaire.

A shadow passed over Julian's face, and she curled her fingers around his.

"Sadly, they're still struggling with our mother's death," he said softly, the pain in his voice revealing he did as well.

No one ever discussed Dinah Drake's suicide. She'd been gone for months—since the day after Magistrate Oakley arrested the Trudeaus, but disgrace and grief kept his sisters cloistered near their husbands and homes.

According to the magistrate, Julian's mother had conspired with the Trudeaus to eliminate Alfred. She'd been livid that the fortune she brought to her marriage would go to her stepson and not her son.

The impoverished Trudeaus—foisted off on one relative after another like unwanted riffraff—couldn't resist the lure of wealth Dinah promised for helping dispose of Alfred. She and Joan had been childhood friends. When Joan and her daughter had come to live with a distant cousin whose estate bordered Montclere, the women had become reacquainted and hatched the dastardly plan to dispose of Alfred.

Dinah had heavily drugged his brandy flask before he set out alone to stalk deer. He frequently hunted game in December and January and often went alone, rarely returning with a stag.

The henchman Joan and Daphne hired had followed him. When Alfred tumbled from his horse, insensate, the killer had finished him off, making it appear like an accident. That craven had long since fled the area, and of those responsible for Alfred's death, he alone escaped justice.

Entrapping Julian hadn't been part of the scheme, and Daphne's threat to harm him had compelled Dinah to confess to her part in Alfred's death. She'd never anticipated the extremes the Trudeaus would go to in order to see Julian and Daphne married, nor had she considered they might dispose of Julian to control his wealth.

Despite the happiness of the day, a shiver stole down Blaire's spine. She hadn't a doubt Daphne would've killed Julian eventually.

Blaike, sitting on Blaire's other side, leaned nearer and whispered, "Do you think it's time?"

"I do." Her surprise would assuredly lift Julian's spirits.

Blaire placed her cup on the tea table, laden with beautifully decorated Christmas biscuits, pastries, cakes, and other dainties. The staff at Culpepper Park had gone beyond themselves to make the family's first Christmas here one that would forever live in their memories.

Grabbing her twin's hand, Blaire stood.

Together, hands still clasped, they stood with their backs to the fire.

"Blaike and I have a surprise we've been—"

"—waiting to share with you," Blaike finished.

At Julian's confused glance, Blaire curved her mouth into a secretive smile.

He thrust his chin at Oliver—a silent question in his eyes.

Oliver hitched his shoulder, shaking his head. "Don't look at me. I haven't a clue what is going on either."

Eight curious stares rested on Blaire and her twin as she and Blaike exchanged a private look.

"Oh." Brette clapped a hand over her mouth. "I know."

Blythe's and Brooke's gazes tangled, and they, too, erupted into beaming smiles.

Heath shook his head, asking no one in particular, "How do they do that?"

"I have no idea." A finger on his chin, Alex also shook his head. "But I'll tell you, it takes some accommodating."

Julian ran a hand over Apollo's head, now lying on the seat Blaire had vacated. "I cannot tell you how many times they've finished one another's sentences or said the same thing simultaneously."

Tristan, just this side of smug, slung an ankle over his knee. "Come on chaps. You're more astute than that. I've figured it out."

"This is our first Christmas at Culpepper Park, and with so much to be thankful for, Blaike and I have saved a surprise for you." Blaire squeezed her sister's hand, the signal they'd agreed upon.

In unison, they said, "We're expecting."

Julian and Oliver lurched to their feet amid cries of delight.

Giving her a tender kiss, Julian scooped Blaire into his arms. "Darling, why didn't you tell me?"

"We wanted it to be a surprise for everyone."

He laid his hand atop hers, resting on the shimmering silk covering her still flat belly.

The others clapped and cheered their approval.

Zeus and Apollo barked theirs.

"This calls for a celebration." Heath rose and, grinning as if he'd just been told he was to be a father again—which he was—tugged the bell pull.

A beaming Flanders entered. "Yes, sir?"

No doubt he'd heard the good news, for like any majordomo worth his salt, he generally lingered nearby.

"Flanders, we have more reason to celebrate tonight besides the birth of our Savior. Mrs. Drake and Mrs. Whitehouse have joyous news. Please bring champagne and glasses for all."

A former soldier himself, Flanders pulled his waistcoat down and clicked his heels together. "May I offer my congratulations, Mr. and Mrs. Whitehouse and Lieutenant and Mrs. Drake?"

"Thank you, Flanders," Heath said as the others joined in with their congratulations.

Who would've thought that the risqué wager between Heath and Brooke so many months ago would've brought their family so much happiness? Oh, how the five Culpepper misses had mourned leaving Esherton Green, especially for the city, but if they hadn't, none save Brooke would've found the loves of their lives either.

Blaire too had resented the disruption and feared her uncertain future, but the blessings that had resulted were beyond anything she could've imagined. And next June, she and Blaike would be mothers.

Flanders arrived bearing the champagne, followed by a footman with a tray of crystal flutes. Once he'd poured the champagne, Flanders cleared his voice. "Your Lordship, if I may?"

Heath dipped his head.

"On behalf of the staff and myself, Happy Christmas." He managed to keep a straight face as Zeus seized a flap of his tailcoat, tugging and jerking amidst playful growls. "We hope..." With a rather commendable flip of his wrist, he wrested the abused fabric free. "You enjoy many more at Culpepper Park."

Zeus flopped onto his haunches, a strip of tailcoat dangling from his mouth.

"Zeus. Naughty boy," Blaire scolded.

He dropped the cloth and lay flat, his paws covering his eyes. A chorus of laughter erupted.

Once the servants had departed, Flanders—resembling a wounded penguin—and Heath had passed champagne to the adults, they stood in a circle.

He raised his glass, his attention sweeping the assembled. "To family, whether by blood or by choice."

"To friends for life." Tristan lifted his glass as well.

Brette kissed Henry's chubby cheek. "To untold blessings."

"And health and long life." Blythe touched her bent forefinger to the corner of one eye.

Oliver snaked an arm around Blaike's waist and tucked her to his side. "To courage."

"To forgiveness," Alex murmured, still very much a vicar-turned-earl at heart.

Julian canted his head. "To trust."

"And Faith," Brooke said.

Blaike nodded, her smile wobbly. "And hope."

Blaire tucked her free hand into the crook of Julian's elbow. "To the greatest of all. Love."

The Honorable Rogues™

A Kiss for a Rogue
A Bride for a Rogue
A Rogue's Scandalous Wish
To Capture a Rogue's Heart
The Rogue and the Wallflower
A Rose for a Rogue

Castle Brides Series

The Viscount's Vow
Highlander's Hope
The Earl's Enticement
Heart of a Highlander (*prequel to Highlander's Hope*)

The Blue Rose Regency Romances:
The Culpepper Misses Series

The Earl and the Spinster
The Marquis and the Vixen
The Lord and the Wallflower
The Buccaneer and the Bluestocking
The Lieutenant and the Lady

Highland Highland Heather Romancing a Scot Series

Triumph and Treasure
Virtue and Valor
Heartbreak and Honor
Scandal's Splendor
Passion and Plunder
Seductive Surrender
A Yuletide Highlander

Wicked Earls' Club

Earl of Wainthorpe
Earl of Scarborough

Seductive Scoundrel's Series
A Diamond for a Duke
Earl of Wainthorpe
Only a Duke Would Dare
A December with a Duke
What Would a Duke Do?
Earl of Scarborough
Wooed by a Wicked Duke
Duchess of His Heart
Coming soon in the series!
Never Dance with a Duke
To Lure a Duke's Lady
Loved by a Devilish Duke
Wedding her Christmas Duke
When a Duke Loves a Lass
How to Win A Duke's Heart
To Love an Irredeemable Duke

Heart of a Scot
To Love a Highland Laird
To Redeem a Highland Rogue
To Seduce a Highland Scoundrel
Coming soon in the series!
To Woo a Highland Warrior
To Enchant a Highland Earl
To Defy a Highland Duke
To Marry a Highland Marauder
To Bargain with a Highland Buccaneer

Boxed Sets
Lords in Love
To Love a Reckless Lord
The Honorable Rogues™ Books 1-3
The Honorable Rogues™ Books 4-6
Seductive Scoundrels Series Books 1-3
The Blue Rose Regency Romances-
The Culpepper Misses Series 1-5

About the Author

USA Today Bestselling, award-winning author COLLETTE CAMERON® scribbles Scottish and Regency historicals featuring dashing rogues and scoundrels and the intrepid damsels who re-form them. Blessed with an overactive and witty muse that won't stop whispering new romantic romps in her ear, she's lived in Oregon her entire life, though she dreams of living in Scotland part-time. A self-confessed Cadbury chocoholic, you'll always find a dash of inspiration and a pinch of humor in her sweet-to-spicy timeless romances®.

Explore **Collette's worlds** at

www.collettecameron.com!

Join her **VIP Reader Club** and **FREE newsletter**. Giggles

guaranteed!

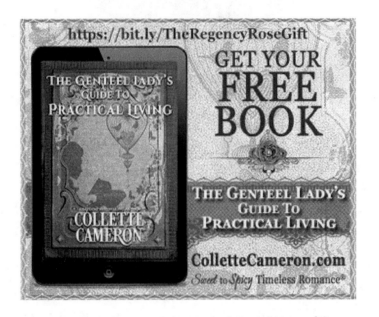

FREE BOOK: Join Collette's The Regency Rose® VIP Reader Club to get updates on book releases, cover reveals, contests and giveaways she reserves exclusively for email and newsletter followers. Also, any deals, sales, or special promotions are offered to club members first. She will not share your name or email, nor will she spam you.

http://bit.ly/TheRegencyRoseGift

Follow Collette on BookBub

https://www.bookbub.com/authors/collette-cameron

Brookfield Rehab
Left at light past
highscool - 2 blocks
Battleground

9 781950 387335